Brothers Nicholas Williams and Anthony Williams are the authors behind this compelling and absorbing thriller. Both have their roots as leaders in the music industry and each has travelled the world extensively.

Creativity is at the heart of their lives. As musicians and songwriters, they wrote and produced two UK chart hits in 2021, and in 2023, Nicholas released the *Bellum Sanctum* soundtrack.

To Pamela and Gareth Williams, our wonderful parents

Nicholas Anthony

BELLUM SANCTUM

AUSTIN MACAULEY PUBLISHERS™

LONDON ★ CAMBRIDGE ★ NEW YORK ★ SHARJAH

A CIP catalogue record for this title is available from the British Library.

ISBN 9781035824571 (Paperback)
ISBN 9781035824588 (Hardback)
ISBN 9781035824595 (ePub e-book)

www.austinmacauley.com

First Published 2024
Austin Macauley Publishers Ltd®
1 Canada Square
Canary Wharf
London
E14 5AA

Table of Contents

Preface

Clouds and darkness are round about him: righteousness and judgment are the habitation of his throne. A fire goeth before him, and burneth up his enemies round about. His lightnings enlightened the world: the earth saw, and trembled.
Psalms 97

Chapter 1
The Fire Lookout

Var, Southern France, Present Day

Daniel's hill—or so he thought of it—rose neatly above the surrounding forests, just a few miles back from the Mediterranean. From his lookout post above the Provençal countryside, he could see as far as the Italian Alps and down to the busy port of Cannes. Across the sea, even the mountains of Corsica would sometimes emerge, appearing like a mirage on the horizon.

Dr Daniel Bayford was enjoying his early retirement in these warmer climes. After a long career as a British government scientist—a career that ultimately drove him into notable, and often celebrated, eco-activism—he now loved his part-time job as a forest fire lookout, spending his free time theorising and writing.

His newfound outdoor life had provided other benefits too. Now fit and tanned, his rugged good looks meant he would often catch the eye of stylish ladies in Cannes. More often than not, Daniel was oblivious and did not respond to the admiring gazes. Even so, he had managed a brief fling with the highly-strung village artist. This did not end well as Daniel criticised her paintings a little too much. Finally, she threw his clothes from her bedroom window, generating much glee amongst the villagers. Although this incident was well in the past, it seemed no one would ever forget it—much to Daniel's annoyance.

Nearly wine o'clock, Daniel thought, as his old Citroën van rattled its way back down the hill and bounced him off his seat.

God! Julie again! Daniel was annoyed but reluctantly reached for his mobile.

'Hi, Julie.'

'Hi, Daniel. How are you? Can we come down and see you soon?' Ignoring the lack of response, Julie probed deeper: 'Have you a new woman yet?'

Julie was an old friend of the family and had the irritating tendency to mother him. Not only that, she caused him to recall the break-up with his previous partner.

'Let me call you back, I'm driving,' was Daniel's blunt response, as he pulled up outside his villa. He just wanted a quiet evening at his barbeque with a glass of wine.

On Sunday mornings, Daniel would join the men in the café for a simple breakfast, invariably washed down with local wine. The topics of conversation would switch between wild boar hunting and women, not forgetting very rude discussions about the baker's wife. Their merriment was only interrupted by groups of old men in lycra, sweating heavily after cycling the arduous route up to *Tanneron*.

In moments of boredom, Daniel would survey the austere prison perched high above the town of Grasse. He would wonder how the inmates coped with their incarceration; in such contrast to the freedom of those admiring the *Mimosa* in the valleys below. This springtime sea of yellow would soon fade and parch, only adding to Daniel's unease.

As temperatures rose in the summer, the *Mistral* winds would be drawn from central France, causing the locals to shake their heads in consternation. A lightning strike or a solitary pyromaniac could easily ignite the undergrowth. The *Mistral* would then drive a wall of flames, consuming homes and the tinder-dry forest.

That August evening, the sky went dark and the air was still. Except for the cicadas clicking in a shrill chorus, there was hardly a sound. Between the black clouds, shafts of sunlight lit up the hillside, and for a while, all seemed tranquil.

After three years of working the hot summer months, he knew what would happen next: the wind would suddenly pick up. It would not be a wind like the *Mistral* but downdrafts from the towering cumulonimbus expanding relentlessly towards the edge of the atmosphere.

Below the lookout tower, a hut housed Daniel's equipment—remnants of his scientific days. An untidy array of meteorological instruments and his favourite: a hand-driven Van der Graaf generator. Daniel would amuse his visitors by cranking the handle and producing miniature lightning shows and then explaining the power of thunderstorms.

The radio link with the fire department chattered incessantly, but Daniel was not listening; he was staring through the window at the heavy black clouds that now seemed to touch the mountains. The hairs on the back of his neck were standing up. Daniel was not sure whether this was the static electricity building or his childish excitement. Suddenly, just as he expected, the gloomy air was filled with flashes of lightning.

'Daniel, are you there? Over.'

It was the lookout calling from the *Massif de Tanneron*, just a few miles to the west.

Daniel grabbed the microphone and acknowledged his presence. 'Yes, Pascal, I'm here. Over.'

'Can you see the smoke?' his colleague asked.

Sure enough, as Daniel turned to the north, he saw the grey pall. Wiping his face, he did not know if it was smoke, or the sweat of his brow making his eyes sting.

In time with the pulsating din of cicadas, came an even louder, low-frequency sound. Three helicopters, laden with water, rose past Daniel on their heroic mission to extinguish the fire. As they disappeared in a swarm down to the *Lac Saint Cassien*, they momentarily reminded him of mechanical beasts from a science fiction movie.

That next morning, Daniel would not be driving up his lovely green hill. Instead, he would be tasked to find the cause of the fire. The acrid smell of the smouldering forest was overpowering. That day in August, even the rising sun was unwelcome, only adding to Daniel's discomfort and burning his cheeks. In this desolate landscape, nothing was left alive, just black charcoal stumps and dirty white cinders blowing in his face.

Near the source of the fire, Daniel noticed a small mound lying in a pool of ash. As he approached, he knew that this small heap had once been a living creature. Daniel pulled the hunting knife from his belt and slowly forced it through the crusty black layer and into the soft flesh below. He repeated the action, somehow relishing the resistance of the hard crust and the strangely satisfying feeling of his knife breaking through. Daniel was salivating as he ripped off his rucksack and grabbed the paper package within. After several more cuts, he crudely placed a slice of the wild boar onto some bread and forced it into his mouth.

Daniel enjoyed his unexpected breakfast and thought how much better it would have been if it had been washed down with a good red wine. As he threw the knife to the ground, an extraordinary thing happened. Just like the Van der

Graaf generator, there was a spark. Not just the spark from a knife striking stone, but a pulse of energy that dazzled and crackled like a tiny bolt of lightning.

As Daniel kicked about in the ash, his eye was caught by a small rock glinting in the sunlight. Although small enough to fit in his palm, it felt much heavier than he expected. Without a second thought, he brushed it down and popped it into his rucksack.

Back at the tower, Daniel confirmed to the fire department that the fire had, as suspected, been caused by a lightning strike. *Funny*, he thought, *this is not the first time this has happened on the hillside.*

Almost daily someone would drive the dusty track that snaked up to the shabby hut, for Daniel was a charming and interesting character. They would all love to sit there, admiring the views and listening to his stories.

'*Bonjour, Oncle!*' Daniel's bright-eyed young niece beamed at him and ran to see the view. Daniel's French sister-in-law, Sophie, smiled kindly.
'*Ça va*, Daniel?'

After a short pause, Daniel responded. '*Oui, ça va, Sophie.*'

'That was quite a fire. So, it was an act of God, not some pyromaniac then?' enquired Sophie.

'Yes, it was a lightning strike from the heavens. God was taking revenge on you wicked French people!' Daniel teased them with a grin.

His niece Brigitte looked perplexed. 'Why is God so angry with us, Uncle?'

'Well,' replied Daniel, 'he's not *really* angry. Not now. I was just joking, but many years ago, people did wicked things. Over the mountains in Italy, there is a church in Turin called *Monte dei Cappuccini*. When French soldiers attacked the town three hundred people hid in the church, but the soldiers broke in and massacred them all.'

'That's so awful. Was God angry with the soldiers?' quizzed Brigitte.

'Yes, He certainly was.' Daniel was excited now. 'You see, the captain struck the holy box with his sword to open its lid. Can you guess what happened?' Brigitte shook her head. 'The box burst open and a bolt of lightning shot out, striking the captain dead. This became known as the miracle of *Santa Maria del Monte.*'

'Your machine makes lightning like that, doesn't it, uncle?'

'Yes, it certainly does,' beamed Daniel.

Chapter 2
The Call to Arms

Clermont, The Kingdom of France, 27 November 1095

Henri spent his life toiling in the fields for his master and always prayed for enough food to feed his family. Every evening, they would kneel together and despite their dismal existence, would thank God for the little they had.

Looming high over the fields to the west of Clermont, conical hills of ancient lava, long since overgrown with forest, pierced the low-lying mist. Henri was busy gathering wood when he heard the sound of hooves. He looked up to see Guillaume, his master's son, approaching him on horseback. The black stallion stamped impatiently and snorted plumes of breath into the cold air. Guillaume struggled with the reins and then, clutching his hat, looked down at Henri. 'Henri, do you not know? My father has summoned us to the town.'

'Why, my Lord?' replied Henri, casting an eye over Guillaume's fine, warm clothes.

'The Pope himself will address the clerics now already gathered. Your master commands that you attend.' As Guillaume turned his horse and rode away, he called back, 'All the townsfolk will be there. So, forget the wood and be on your way.'

But the Clermont winters were cold, so ignoring the order, Henri began pulling the little wooden cart back to his dingy dwelling, where he joined his wife and two children huddled around the fire, eating bread and soup.

After a few minutes, he stood up and announced, 'Come, my dear Isabella, bring the children. Today we will see the Pope in Clermont.'

'Really? He is *here*? Today? What will he speak of?'

'He will forgive us our sins. He will bless us all.'

'But what about the sheep? Master said you have to move them today.'

'It's fine. Master sent Guillaume to fetch me, so we must go now. Seeing the Pope will be a great occasion.'

As they trudged their way into town, Isabella shivered and reached for Henri's hand. He steadied her and tried to remove the clods of mud gathering on her skirt.

'He talks with God, doesn't he?' his daughter asked.

Henri thought for a moment. 'He is very powerful and we must hear what he has to say.'

Isabella stared back. 'But will he ask God to bring us more food? Will he ask Our Lord to stop the storms that are destroying our crops?'

Henri did not reply. but instead pointed out the others joining them on their way. Everyone in Clermont knew the Pope was coming and by now hundreds had assembled in the nearby field. As Henri's family craned their necks to see the arriving wagons, they were jostled by a group of soldiers causing them to slip in the mud.

'Come close,' Henri said, trying to reassure his now distraught children.

The excitement rose further as a group of priests moved forward towards Pope Urban II. and his brightly-clad entourage. The groups of ragged peasants, their clothes steaming in the dank air, pushed, and shoved to get a better view. Ahead of them, were soldiers on horseback weaving through the crowd, attempting to create some order around those in religious finery.

'Where is the Pope?' asked Isabella. 'I can't see.'

Just as Henri pointed to one of the wagons, the Pope cast his hand in a demand for silence. A hush fell across the expectant throng; even the horses calmed.

'Your brethren in the Holy Land urgently need your help. They have lost many battles and their land has been occupied. The Turks and Arabs have already conquered Romania, and have now reached the shores of the Mediterranean. I beseech you in the name of the Lord to bring aid to our fellow Christians. Spread the word, you all must help rid that vile race from the lands of our brethren. *Our Holy Land. Our war cry is DEUS LE VOLT!'*

By now, the crowd was animated; louder and louder their voices chanted the war cry of the First Crusade: '*Deus le volt! Deus le volt! DEUS LE VOLT!'*

'God wills it! God wills it! GOD WILLS IT!'

The Pope cast his hand again. Silence descended once more.

'Today, every man who pledges his allegiance to God and this great crusade, will be cleansed of their sins. Every man who joins us will escape punishment for their crimes. May those against us be struck down by God, for they are doomed to purgatory and eternal damnation. You must join us. Come forward now, and pronounce a solemn vow. Each man will be blessed and will become a true warrior of the church. God wills it!'

The Bishop of Adhemar climbed onto the wagon and, with a cross raised above his head, joined in the call to arms.

'Brave men, come forward and pronounce your vows!'

Isabella turned to Henri and tugged at his sleeve. 'Please don't go,' she pleaded.

Henri held his weeping wife. 'God wills it, but I will ask our master to keep you and our children safe. I will return, for our foes will surely be struck down by God.'

Chapter 3
The House of the Gods

La Gran Sabana, Venezuela, Present Day

The Toyota 4x4 powered its way up the tree-lined track. Its driver, an auburn-haired thirty-something, seemed more intent on the car's radio controls than the rough and tortuous route ahead.

All around, spectacular plateaux rose like giant fortresses of rock from *La Gran Sabana*—a vast and ancient landscape of grassland, scrub, rivers, waterfalls, and jungle at the borders of southeast Venezuela. Loud bursts of static from the radio were being matched by flashes of lightning and deafening rumbles of thunder. Towering over the plateaux was an enormous cumulonimbus cloud.

'Hey! Kara! You won't get a reception out here…Shit!'

Her passenger, a clean-cut all-American student, replete with a checked lumberjack shirt, was taking over control of the car's radio when the impact with a deep pothole bounced them skyward.

Dr Kara Williams was unfazed. 'Tod. The static. Listen to the static!' She threw him a quick smile. 'And look! We're practically underneath it.'

Kara flicked on the headlamps. The storm was blotting out the last of the late afternoon light. Rain then pelted the windscreen without warning.

'Damn it!'

'Looking for these?' Tod leant over to activate the wipers. 'The wipers are on the stick, Kara, and the brake's the big guy under your feet. Look, do you mind slowing down a little here? I mean, what's the panic?'

'The panic, Tod, is…WOW! Nice!' Lightning sliced the air just metres from the car. 'The panic is that this is the best storm we've had since Lake Maracaibo. So, we can't afford to miss it.'

As they ascended, the track had all but disappeared, trees now gave way to low shrubs, and the vehicle emerged into the open. After a steep final manoeuvre, they reached the top of the plateau with the full majestic power of the storm all around them.

Up ahead, were a pick-up truck, two more 4x4s, six large, army-style tents, and, set apart from the main encampment, a large metallic structure with a tall pole mounted above it. One of Kara's team had appeared at the entrance of one of the tents and spotted the approaching vehicle. Lightning pulsed within the clouds overhead, illuminating the torrential rain and the entire mountaintop. Pools of manmade light provided some relief against the growing gloom.

'Yo, Kaz! Tod!'

'Oh, God! That's all I need,' Kara muttered to Tod, as they stooped under a shared umbrella. Running towards them, a clipboard held above his head, was a small, long-haired, bearded man. Kara had been forced, she felt, to recruit students she did not know into her team. Professor Steel, her mentor and project leader, had said it would help grease the wheels when it came to gaining support from the Venezuelan government. So, here was her token 'local' student, Mario Fernandez. In fact, Fernandez had been invaluable. He was just a little too ebullient for most of the team.

'Not a good idea, guys. I mean, umbrella in a storm? Santa Maria! And there's me thinking you're so clever.'

'If I was clever, Mario, I'd be sitting in a nice cosy room by an open fire, preparing a lecture on Planck's constant. But I'm not. So, I'm here instead. Getting wet. With you. And please, where did you get this Kaz from?'

'Er. *Si*. Sorry, Doc. I set up THEIS over there. We have all systems go.'

About fifty metres from the main laboratory tent stood The High Energy Inductor System—nicknamed THEIS. It was Kara's masterpiece. The main body of the device was around five metres tall and three metres along each of its four steel sides. Projecting from its top was a ten-metre lightning conductor that tapered to a point. A series of cables ran from THEIS to four satellite-like dishes positioned on the ground about ten metres away. More cables ran back to the main tent.

As Mario led the way, Kara muttered to Tod. 'Can we get rid of this guy? Send him back to Caracas? He's way too intense.'

'I...sorry. What was that?'

'To the tents, Mario!' Kara said smiling. Tod stifled a laugh.

'What about satellite data?' Tod asked Mario.

'LIS and MTG both indicated early signs of intense activity in the infra-red. Looks like a good one.'

'We don't need satellites to tell us that,' said Kara, as Mario led the way to a large open-sided tent. Inside, were three men and a woman, all in their mid-twenties to early thirties, stationed at computers and an array of flight-cased scientific instruments.

One of the team threw Kara a towel. She was standing on one of the rubberised platforms dotted around the rest of the tent's interior. 'Thanks,' she said, as she rubbed her shoulder-length hair dry. 'Are we set?'

'We're set,' one of the team announced.

The inside of the tent's roof was being lit up almost constantly as nearby lightning ripped through the air. The accompanying cracks and booms were almost instantaneous. None of the scientists flinched. They had all experienced storms of this magnitude many times before—and worse. A few months earlier they had been taking measurements on a boat anchored in the middle of *Lago de Maracaibo*, a lake known as the lightning capital of the world, and for good reason. It lies in a unique location. Cold mountain air from the Andes descends and combines with the moist, warm air over the lake, resulting in thousands of lightning strikes almost every night. Up here, high over *La Gran Sabana*, they felt relatively safe.

'Beany?'

Beany, a petite thirty-one-year-old with a short pixie, bleached blonde haircut, began reading out a series of measurements from her computer screen. '3 dot 4 4, 18 7, 8 dot 8 1.'

'Perfect! Let's do it!' Kara called out and sat down at her computer.

Beany continued, '3 dot 6 9, 18 9, 9 dot 3 0.'

Kara called out, 'Activate in 3, 2, 1!'

Mario hit the Return key on his keyboard. THEIS, previously a dull, inert-looking structure, was suddenly bathed in a translucent blue light that moved like a veil caught in a gentle breeze. The entire team donned ear protectors. One or two put on goggles; the rest focussed on their laptops. The air seemed to fizz expectantly.

When the hairs on her arms sprang up, Kara knew. She closed her eyes.

A fraction of a second later, a blinding, vertical bolt of lightning exploded in front of the scientists sending out a shock wave that blew back their hair and the canvas of the tent and rocked the tent lights hanging from the ceiling. The cracking sound, starting in the highest of frequencies, descending rapidly into a thunderous sub-frequency boom and registering more than 170 decibels, came almost instantaneously afterwards. It was as though the sky itself had been ripped in two.

Seconds later it was all over. Darkness returned almost as violently.

THEIS appeared untouched, lit faintly by the diminishing twilight—now a slither of light in the west. The lights that hung inside the tent were still swaying. The after-rumble rolled away over the plateaux. More lightning pulsed high in the cloud above and in the distance.

'Welcome to the *tepui*, everyone,' Mario Fernandez said.

'The what?' asked Tod.

'It's what the Venezuelans call these plateaux,' said Kara. 'It means The House of the Gods.'

The storm continued well into the night.

Chapter 4
The Siege

Antioch, Syria, May 1098

More than two years had passed since Henri left France, joining the thousands of fellow Crusaders on their long march eastwards. Arriving on those distant shores, Henri had met a small group of fellow Frenchmen and stuck close to them. Progress had been slow and violent; the campaigning gruelling and bloody. But the small band of inexperienced warriors did their best to look out for one another.

But the loose and often short-lived friendships were of little comfort to the peasant farmer from Clermont. Every night, he would thank God for saving him and pray that the Lord would guard over them.

Henri laid back and stared at the stars. *I could desert*, he thought, *and all this will soon be just a terrible dream… But how can I desert my friends?* For the first time, the endless fighting, the disease, the lack of food, the heat and the cold, and most of all their heavy losses, caused Henri to question his faith. And the unfamiliar lands made him yearn yet again for his family and his peaceful life tending sheep. *At least the stars above me are the same*, he thought.

The following morning, Henri stood amongst hundreds of fellow soldiers before the massive citadel of Antioch. He stared in disbelief at the dozens of towers and great walls. 'This is truly a great fortress,' he said. 'How can we take it?'

'We have been besieging them for many months,' one of his comrades replied.

'But this could take many more months. How much more must we fight for these lands?'

Their captain began addressing them: 'Unless there is a miracle, be prepared to die. The Turks are fierce fighters.'

'But the Pope said God would strike them down,' Henri called out.

'Good Christian, God willing, you, all of you, will return home one day but we *must* take Antioch. Then we will continue our quest into the heart of the Holy Land and win Jerusalem.'

June 1098

Well beyond the walls of Antioch, mounted knights, followed by men-at-arms and thousands of common foot soldiers, entered the Crusader encampment, their gonfalons fluttering high above their heads.

One of the knights steered his mighty destrier away from the line of soldiers and galloped towards a tent, where he dismounted. Dust, kicked up by his horse, swirled and eddied around him. From the tent, the Norman knight, Prince Bohemund of Taranto, leader of the Crusade emerged.

'Good news, my Lord,' said the knight, bowing. 'The razzia was a success. We have at least three weeks of food for men, horses, and oxen.'

Bohemund surveyed the returning throng. He nodded slowly but looked grim. 'Losses?' he asked.

'No more than twenty men, Sire. They must have been weak and sick when we left but did not want to bring dishonour to their names.'

The knight's squire had now joined his master along with several foot soldiers. Being near Bohemund, one of their great leaders, was something they all wanted to experience—a story they could share and embellish when they returned home from this, the greatest of holy quests.

Seeing he had an audience, Bohemund raised his voice, 'Good Christian men, one and all. We pray for the souls of those who gave their lives.' *The men before me look exhausted*, he thought. *They need encouragement, now more than ever.* 'You have done well. This is a test of our resolve, of our mettle, of our faith. God *is* with us. In His name, we *will* be victorious. DEUS LE VOLT!'

'DEUS LE VOLT!' they all cried, raising their weapons.

Bohemund entered his tent and slumped in his chair. He was tired, hungry, and in bad mood.

'A drink, my Lord?' His squire was standing by his side.

'The only drink that can quench my thirst is the sweet taste of Turkish blood on my lips and tongue.'

Their attention was drawn to the tent entrance, where voices could be heard. After peering outside, the squire returned to Bohemund's side. 'There is a man from the city who wishes your audience, my Lord.'

'Ah, yes. This I must hear. BRING HIM IN!' he bellowed.

A man was bustled in by two guards and thrown at Bohemund's feet.

'This is the Armenian of whom we spoke, My Lord,' announced one of the guards.

Bohemund ran a hand over his beard and looked down at the prostrate man. 'Look at me!'

The Armenian looked up. 'My Lord,' he blurted.

'Why,' began Bohemund, 'should I trust a traitor?'

The Armenian lowered his head. 'My Lord, I am no traitor.'

'LOOK AT ME WHEN YOU ADDRESS ME!' roared Bohemund. 'I want to see your eyes when you speak.'

The Armenian duly obeyed. 'I am no traitor. I am a Christian, like you. And I have good reason to help. My wife and daughter…,' the man's voice quivered. 'My wife and daughter were raped by those you wish to defeat.' He breathed heavily, gathering what strength he could. 'I seek revenge, my Lord. Pure and simple.'

Bohemund looked into the man's eyes. 'What is your name?' Even in his dishevelled state, Bohemund was a frightening figure.

'Firouz, my Lord,' he replied, bowing his head to avoid the gaze of his inquisitor.

Bohemund grabbed his sword and began walking in a circle around the cowering Firouz.

'Pure and simple, you say,' said the knight. 'And yet, I was told that you *simply* wished for money. So, did you lie about that, or are you lying to me now? Hmm? Which is it, Armenian?' Bohemund began swiping his sword through the air in long, slow arcs.

Firouz could neither speak nor move. His eyes darting this way and that.

'Speak!'

'M-m-my Lord,' he stuttered. 'What I said and what I say to you now, my Lord, is true. I wish to flee this city with my family and require enough provisions for our long journey. No more.'

'Money *and* freedom. You ask a lot. Has it occurred to you how many more will suffer by your treachery? My men are desperate. I'm sure the first thing they'll do when we breach the city walls, and after we slaughter the vermin heathens, will be to satisfy our pent-up lust for the women and girls. Of course, we'll be interested only in the young, pretty ones. The rest will be meat for dogs and rats.' He looked at the two guards and smiled. The two guards sneered and laughed.

'My Lord if you will permit me.'

Bohemund stopped brandishing his sword, stabbed it into the floor, and stood, legs akimbo. 'Why are you so afraid, Firouz? Aren't you a commander like me?'

Firouz raised himself slowly off the floor. 'I am only the commander of one gate, not a great leader of men like you.'

'Ah, yes. The gate commander. Our way into the city.'

'Yes.'

'Why should I trust you?' Bohemund asked again.

The Armenian thought hard. He was facing a mighty warrior, one who despised weakness. He stared into Bohemund's eyes, swelled his chest with a deep breath, and threw back his shoulders. 'I swear by Almighty God,' he said looking to heaven with hands clasped, 'and by the lives of my wife and daughter.'

For what seemed to the Armenian like minutes, Bohemund stared back. A gust of wind flapped the walls of the tent. Outside, the noises of the camp rose and fell. The eyes of the squire and guards darted between the two commanders.

The warlord finally broke the silence. 'Show me!' he said, pointing to a table where a model of the city had been constructed. Firouz's shoulders dropped with relief.

'This is impressive,' Firouz said, as he studied the walls and towers. 'And very accurate. Here, this is my gate on the western wall. And this is the Tower of the Two Sisters. Arrive under the cover of darkness in the early hours. I will watch out for you and lower a ladder from the tower.'

And so, the plan was laid.

Two nights later, Bohemund led more than five hundred of his best fighters to the city walls. Lying in wait, Bohemund scanned the darkened ramparts. Sure enough, a ladder soon appeared from a window high above in one of the towers. Bohemund was the first to make a move and, after looking up, the first to begin the risky ascent. His men followed close behind. If Firouz was lying and had laid a trap, Bohemund would exact his revenge on anyone in his way.

Bohemund climbed slowly, carefully, quietly, and was now only a few steps from the window. He signalled to the men immediately below him to remain quiet then climbed the last few steps, careful not to make a sound. He stopped just below the window's edge and listened, then quickly hauled himself inside and withdrew his sword. Holding it with both hands, he scanned the dim room he now found himself in, swishing the sword as he did so. It was empty.

There was no sign of resistance. Firouz had been true to his word and had dismissed the sentries under his command. Bohemund and his men descended the stairs that Firouz had advised them to take. When they emerged into the street, their presence was detected. A group of three Turkish soldiers stood open-mouthed as the knights issued from the doorway in droves. Two of the knights rushed them, one wielding his sword, the other an axe. The first Turk took a hit from the sword, which buried itself deep into his side. The man screamed and collapsed in a pool of blood, writhing on the ground. Meanwhile, the second Turk's head had been sliced half off by the blow of the axe. The third Turk, no more than seventeen years of age, frozen to the spot, was now pleading for his life.

'Sorry, I don't understand you,' said the knight with the sword, as he plunged it into the young man's groin and yanked it upwards, spilling his guts.

The screams shattered the night-time stillness. Turks emerged from everywhere. The Crusaders stabbed, hacked, and slashed their way through them with ease. Blood poured and squirted from the countless wounds they inflicted on the terrified defenders. This was a blood lust. The Crusaders now saw an end in sight and they wanted it more than anything else.

'SOUND THE WAR HORNS!' Bohemund commanded.

A large force of Turks had mustered by the Bridge Gate, but they were no match for the brutal, marauding Crusaders, who slaughtered every last one in minutes. The gates were flung open.

Back at the Crusader's camp, the horns had reached the ears of the thousands waiting. They were now charging towards the city's gates. The horses' hooves thundered—the dust in the dim light rose like a cloud. More horns sounded. Men bearing lances, spikes, and poles festooned with gonfalons ran with all their might, screaming the war cry: *DEUS LE VOLT!* GOD WILLS IT!

The city was theirs.

With the moans of the dying resounding in his ears, a priest was wandering through the aftermath. Amongst the cries, he heard a faint call: '*Aide-moi…Aide moi…!*' Moving closer, he could see an injured foot soldier lying in a pool of blood amongst the dead. The wounded soldier repeated his words and waved a small crucifix at the priest.

'Bless you, my son. What are your injuries?'

Before the soldier could reply, the priest beckoned to some nearby soldiers. 'Come quickly! He is one of us and badly injured.'

Dripping water over the soldier's parched lips, the priest leant closer. 'What is your name my brave warrior?'

'I am Henri from Clermont.'

'You have fought well Henri and God will save you. We will take you from this place. Do you have family?'

Henri whispered. 'Isabella is my dear wife and we have two children.'

The priest reassured Henri. 'I pledge that I will ask that you may be returned to France. For you can send word of God's great victory in Antioch.'

As Henri drifted into delirium, images of his family sprang into his mind and for the first time in many, many months, he was happy.

The following day, Raymond D'Aguilers, a slight, timid-looking man entered Count Raymond's quarters, where a group of knights had assembled. 'My Lord?'

'We wish to hear your account of our glorious day.'

'Of course, my Lord, my Lords.' And so, the priest and chronicler raised the scroll he was holding and began: '*Piles of heads, hands, and feet were to be seen in the streets of the city. It was necessary to pick one's way over the bodies of men and horses. Indeed, it was a just and splendid judgement of God that this place should be filled with the blood of the unbelievers, since it had suffered so long from their blasphemies. The city was filled with corpses and blood.*'

'INDEED, IT WAS!' one of the knights boomed. 'I can still smell their blood.'

'And I can still taste it!' said another knight, clapping his comrade on the back.

'You did well, my friend. A fine use of the sword!'

'My Lord,' a priest interjected. 'There is a brave soldier recovering from his wounds and his family awaits him. I seek your permission to send him home.'

Count Raymond was jubilant. 'This man is surely a great Crusader. Send him home! He can spread the word of our triumph.'

The room soon erupted with accounts of the battle, laughter, and cheer. This was a great day.

'Huzzah! Glory to God! Death to the unbelievers!' cried the count.

'GLORY TO GOD! DEATH TO THE UNBELIEVERS!' they all roared.

Chapter 5
Day of Destruction

Syria, 10 Years Ago

Bakr al-Ahdal had only ever missed one olive harvest, the last one. It was now over a year since he had returned to his family home and he was glad to see the little village come into view.

Night was falling as the boys playing football in the street turned and stared at Bakr's unfamiliar car. He waved to them, but they had already turned away to resume their unruly game. After a few more metres, Bakr turned the battered Toyota up the rough track to his home. As the car hit each bump, the beam of the headlamps oscillated up and down, briefly illuminating the front of his family home.

Even before the ancient wooden door was fully open, his two sisters scrambled through the gap to embrace him, overjoyed at his return.

His mother waited inside the doorway. 'We are so happy to see you Bakr. Look, the others are here and we have prepared a meal. You must be very hungry.'

'Yes, I am.' Bakr smiled as he hugged his tearful mother.

As he closed the door behind him Bakr felt comforted by the familiarity of its great weight and the smoothness of the wood. For centuries, this ancient door had protected his family from the burning heat of day and the cold desert nights.

Most days, just before the sun rose, the deck of the US carrier in the Red Sea was quiet; this day, it was alive with the sound of boots clattering across the metal deck, and stern announcements resonating from the speakers around the ship.

Lined up on deck was a Reaper drone, a grey, sinister, windowless aircraft laden with two missiles. Surrounded by screens the remote pilot adjusted the controls and remembered he was once a gamer on PlayStation. 'Affirmative. Target acquired. Launching now.'

In an instant, he launched the eerie machine on its inevitable mission to mercilessly seek out new victims.

That same morning Bakr's mother and sisters stood happily outside the house, watching the small group of men heading down the dusty, desert track.

His younger sister, Ani, called to them jokingly, 'Make sure Bakr does his fair share of the work today!'

Bakr glanced back smiling, and waved. That morning he laughed and exchanged stories with his friends and cousins as they made their way to the olive groves.

As a boy, he had resented the labour. But now as a young man, the memory of those cool mornings and the friendship in shared work returned and made him realise how happy he had been. The prospect of a simple lunch under the trees now seemed appealing. Even the tired trudge home at the end of the day would make Bakr feel good, completing a simple but mentally rewarding hard day at work with his comrades.

Soon they were at the top of the nearby hill and the first rays of the sun were warming their bodies. Yet Bakr could sense something: a low thunderous sound that was all around him, resonating on the valley walls.

He jumped in fear as the ominous rumble became a deafening roar as if a supersonic express train had passed inches over his head. The shock wave from the exploding missile threw him breathless along the rocky ground, the sharp stones ripping at his flesh.

After a few seconds, Bakr raised himself slowly to his knees, and turned instinctively towards the village. A cloud of dust now partially obscured the view and he could see a silent wave of brown dirt, rolling like the Californian surf towards him.

A gentle breeze began to clear the dust over the village and with a simultaneous surge of adrenaline, Bakr and the others began running, holding up their arms and calling out the names of their loved ones. As they reached the village they separated in a desperate race, each to their own home.

Bakr's head was pounding and his ankles buckling as he stumbled over the rocks strewn across the short track to his home. He felt distant and strangely removed as he saw the solid old door, rising through the dust like a massive tombstone in a wilderness of broken timbers and rubble.

Now only framed by the remaining pieces of wood and stone into which it was first mounted centuries ago, Bakr clambered past the door on his knees. He scratched frantically at the rubble, ignoring the cuts on his hand and the dust that was now sticking to his blood. Bakr finally gripped Ani's hand but it was cold and lifeless. As he wiped the dust from her peaceful face, he ran his fingers through her soft black hair. At that moment Bakr broke down and wept uncontrollably. The finality of that day now engulfed him as he struggled to lay Ani alongside her sister and mother.

Chapter 6
The Holy Lance and Rain of Fire

Antioch, Syria, 14 June 1098

It was early evening. A knight walked purposefully through the hot, narrow, and grim alleyways of the great citadel. Behind him, following less assuredly was his servant.

'Keep up, man!' the knight hissed.

The servant was struggling to match his master's pace. As they threaded their way through the labyrinthine streets, unseen figures in doorways called out for food. The voices were as feeble as the owners that uttered them. Yet more desperate citizens stepped out in front of the knight, hands cupped and raised, begging for help and the tiniest morsel of food. The soldier simply pushed them aside. A growing band of silent children was following in the wake of the two men. The children had learned that quiet persistence would often pay.

'They won't listen to me. Please, master,' the servant pleaded, as he staggered after the knight.

The knight stopped and turned sharply to address his servant. 'You serve me well, Peter. You're a good man. And yes, I am mystified as to why God chose you. But He moves in mysterious ways, that's for sure. So, come! Have faith! We *must* share your news.'

The entrance to the Crusader headquarters was guarded. The knight stepped forward. 'Make way!' he announced. 'We have important news for their Lordships.'

The two guards seemed unimpressed. They looked at the knight and his servant. 'And who are you?'

'I am William, Lord of Cunhlat. This is my servant.'

Beckoning the visitors forward, one of the guards led them inside towards a room lit with flambeaux and candles. 'My Lords, a knight and his servant have important news, and request your audience.'

Raymond, Count of Toulouse—one of the initial leaders of the First Crusade—turned to face the new arrivals. Behind him was Bishop Adhemar of *Puy-en-Velay*—the representative of Pope Urban II in the Holy Land. He was seated at a candlelit table, a single plate of food scraps before him, which he seemed to be inspecting. The knight and servant knelt. The bishop signalled for the soldier to rise and talk.

'My servant, Peter Bartholomew,' began the knight, 'has had a great vision. I beg you to hear him.'

The bishop waved his hand dismissively as he spoke, 'How can the vision of a *servant* concern our great cause?' he scoffed.

'Please, My Lord,' replied the knight, 'grant him the chance to speak, as I have known him many years, and know he would not say an untrue word.'

'Oh, so we are to embrace the endorsement of a low-ranking soldier...'

'I am William, Lord of Cunhlat...' the knight began defensively, annoyed at the bishop's words.

But Count Raymond interrupted, 'Welcome, William, Lord of Cunhlat. We thank you for your services in our great cause.' The count then turned to the bishop and continued, 'My great army wishes good news. Visions are from God, so let this man have his say.'

The bishop frowned and resumed his meal.

Lord William turned to Peter, who rose slowly and raised his head to speak. 'My Lords, over the last three months I have received visions from Saint Andrew. Each time he told me that the Holy Lance, the very spear that pierced Our Lord Jesus at the cross, lies buried in the cathedral here in Antioch. I believe it to be a great omen. I beg my Lords, search for the Holy Lance.'

The bishop frowned again and shook his head in disbelief.

'I, too, have heard of this,' the count exclaimed. 'Only today, James the Priest, swore he had the same vision. He called it the Spear of Destiny. My Lord Bishop, James' reputation is most excellent.' The bishop nodded slowly—he seemed to concede. The count continued, 'We should search for this great relic. It will then be our talisman of power, and with it, we can hold the world in our hands. This will be *our* Spear of Destiny.'

A few days later, on the night of June 14th, Christian guards were patrolling the citadel battlements. In the sky, an intensely bright light suddenly caught their eyes. Their immediate thought was that they were under attack from fiery projectiles hurled from Muslim trebuchets.

'SOUND THE ALARM! WE'RE UNDER ATTACK!'

The soldiers ran to their battle stations to make ready for the onslaught.

'No, wait!' another guard said. 'That's fire from heaven!'

The men's cries subsided, as they marvelled at the trail of fire as it shot across the sky. The fiery streak then split apart into multiple streams. Most headed straight into the Turkish camp outside the city walls; another single trail streaked into the square below.

On hearing the alarm, Count Raymond.

'Look my Lord!' One of the guards called down from the battlement, pointing to the ground.

There in front of the count laid a brilliantly glowing stone. As he moved towards it, he could feel its radiating heat.

Turkish Encampment, Outside Antioch, Syria, 14 June 1098

Inside their camp, the Turkish soldiers were diving to the ground in fear. The night sky was pouring down fiery rocks. All around were hot glowing stones.

Captain Ersoy rushed to the opening of his tent, and stood, trying to take in the scene. He looked up. *The Christians are bombarding us!* he thought. He was about to step out when one of the projectiles smashed the ground close to his feet. The captain fell back. More of the fiery missiles pounded the earth with loud hisses. The captain stumbled forward from the meagre cover of his tent and looked at the projectile that had nearly hit him. *A stone, a stone glowing hot, but a small stone*, he thought. He looked up again. The trajectory of the missiles confused him. They were entering the encampment from behind, not from the city and the besieged Christians.

When the bombardment ceased, the Turkish soldiers emerged cautiously. They continued to look skyward, fearful that the fiery shower was unfinished.

The Turkish captain surveyed the scene. Out of curiosity, he kicked one of the tiny pieces of rock. It hardly moved. For such a small stone it felt as if it were a hundred times bigger. He ran to the next, it was still glowing and smouldering. The captain stood and stared, transfixed by the depth of colour and beauty of these wondrous stones.

'This is a sign. An omen,' someone called out.

The captain swung around to see who had spoken. A man with a long beard, dressed in elaborate, damask robes of pure silk and a plain *keffiyeh* stood before him.

'Ah, the sage of Damascus,' the captain said. 'I grant that your predictions have been accurate, so speak.'

Some of the Turkish soldiers had gathered around to listen. Still glancing upwards, they pressed forward, eager to hear what the sage had to say.

'It is a good omen. These...,' the old man said slowly, pointing to the stones, 'are fallen stars from heaven.' He raised his eyes and arms to the sky then turned to his listeners. 'I have had a vision of this. Not so long ago, I had a dream of golden lights falling from the sky. Allah then whispered in my ear: *"Behold! This is the power of God. Use it well, use it wisely."*'

'Old man,' the captain said, 'these are just rocks. Hot and heavy, and quite beautiful, but rocks nonetheless. What power? What more can you reveal from your vision?'

'Alas, nothing more. Except, I have the feeling that *I* must guard them. Perhaps Allah will bless me with another vision.'

This was enough for Captain Ersoy. He called to his men, 'Quickly! Each man must mark a stone that glows. Stay with your stone and we will gather them.'

A rumble of thunder distracted the captain. He looked up. High above, storm clouds were gathering.

More than two hundred and sixty men stood and waited, watching the light disappear on the stones that were scattered like stars across the dusty landscape. The captain commanded the men to each gather a stone and bring it to a waiting wagon, where they were placed carefully into jars.

The first soldier looked down. The stone by his feet seemed alive with light. Tentatively he reached down and gripped it. It was cool enough to the touch, but the dancing light within its facets captivated him. As he lifted it from the earth his fascination turned to surprise; the stone was so heavy.

The captain knew in his heart that the old sage was right: that the stones were special and needed to be kept. *Besides, who am I to question the word of Allah?* he thought. *Maybe the sage will have another vision, a vision that will reveal the power of these fallen stars and the power of God.*

Chapter 7
The Researcher

British Virgin Islands, Caribbean Sea, 14 Years Ago

Prince Al-Musan's mega yacht, *Marid*, gleaming white under the tropical sun, dominated the many boats in Coral Bay.

The prince was reading an old, leather-bound tome on board in his office. He had placed bookmarks and was jumping from one page to another. Several equally old books were scattered in front of him across the antique desk. He would then consult an ancient map, a series of historic documents, and a map of the stars displayed across three computer screens, before writing short, rapid notes.

This was his pastime, his passion.

As the only son of a Syrian textile company owner, he had inherited what many considered a small fortune. The company had been producing cotton and silks for generations. But from his early twenties, Al-Musan had doubts about the company's viability. After returning from his education in England, his confidence had grown, and what started as debates with his father about the direction the company should take soon turned into heated arguments.

'What do you know of the textiles? What do you know of our family's business? Nothing!' his father had once shouted.

'Father, I'm telling you. China will destroy this company.' Al-Musan had replied as calmly as possible.

'Listen to me! I have spent my life supporting this family and this business. A business, I do not need to remind you, that has been in our family for centuries! You owe it to your forefathers. Do you have no respect for them? For me?'

Al-Musan bowed his head. He was proud of his DPhil in Medieval History and hoped it would win him respect. But his father was unyielding. What the outspoken son said next, though, changed everything. 'Our forefathers were wise. I have every respect for them. They were smart enough to see the fortunes that could be made in cotton and silk. But that was then. THIS IS NOW!'

There was no reply. His father's face had turned ashen. Beads of sweat had sprung across his forehead; his breathing laboured. He threw a hand across his chest and closed his eyes, his face a portrait of pain.

'Father?'

When his father passed two days later, Al-Musan cried uncontrollably.

It was the last day he would show that kind of raw, visceral reaction, but not that level of emotion.

Al-Musan had matured overnight. As the sole heir, he had been thrust into a world of responsibility.

Over the next twenty years, Al-Musan invested wisely. From millions he made billions and created some of the world's most successful businesses; many of them household names. His public persona presented a good-looking, enviable, philanthropic, playboy billionaire, always seen at the must-see event, with an arm around a new, unknown beauty, although the tabloids and chatter amongst the glitterati pointed at his inability to retain a girlfriend for more than a day. Some columnists commented on his promiscuous lifestyle with envy; others deplored him for his extravagance and alleged misogyny. The more serious commentators eyed him with suspicion—too good to be true, they would say. He must be hiding something. No one, however, could deny his generosity.

Insights into the real Prince Al-Musan, now in his forties, remained elusive. Those close to him were deeply loyal. They practically shared his lifestyle and were paid handsomely. The fact that they could tell the world that behind the gushing public persona the prince was a control freak, an obsessive, and a sociopath, never entered their minds; theirs was a job worth holding onto.

Besides, there was a lot more to the prince, and they knew it all too well. Events in those succeeding years had moulded an altogether different man from the one his father had known.

Al-Musan was smart. Very smart. His business empire was extensive, and the prince was as well known for his success as he was for his flamboyant lifestyle. Politicians, large corporations, film stars, musicians, and the well-healed all loved to be associated with him. And yet, few were aware that he had achieved a doctorate from Oxford University, no less.

It was during his time amongst the dreaming spires that he overheard a group of students refer to him as *that rich Syrian prince.* It had been a balmy summer evening. He had pulled up outside one of the popular watering holes in his open-top Lamborghini. *Prince Al-Musan*, he thought, smiling. *I like that. I like that a lot!* He recalled one of the many quarrels he had had with his father and the talk of their forefathers. Al-Musan decided to start digging into that family history. The genealogical trail eventually faded, but there was enough to support the notion of a distant regal connection. More to the point, there was nothing to disprove it.

It was not until his second year that he began dating Jane. She was not the envy of her girlfriends, though. *He's handsome, yes. But, well, you know, too mysterious and exotic*, was what one had said. She dismissed their criticisms, putting them down to jealousy and subtle racism. When she relayed what Al-Musan had later confessed to her—*The rumours are true, Jane, I am a prince*—her friends' qualms and misgivings multiplied. Two months later, she ended the relationship. But Al-Musan did not mind. He had lost his virginity and was now known as Prince Al-Musan. Adopting the self-imposed title helped propel his business empire to dizzying heights of success.

Now, in one of his rare private moments away from commerce, he was continuing to pursue that passion for research. It was a rare treat, but one he pursued with the same vigour and purpose as his business.

The prince's private aide, Hassan, knocked gently on the open door of the office. 'Sir, your guests have arrived.'

'Good. Bring them to the upper aft deck in five minutes.'

The prince, bare-footed, strode confidently onto the deck. The first of his visitors was a native British Virgin Islander man in his fifties, well-built, and beaming from ear to ear. The second was a white woman of around forty years of age in a floral dress, smiling politely.

'Welcome aboard the *Marid*,' Al-Musan said in his impeccable English, his arms out wide in a welcoming gesture. The prince was all charm and warmth.

'Your Highness,' began the man, 'on behalf of the island's inhabitants and, of course, our project, we would like to thank you for your kind generosity. We are truly grateful. I would like…'

The prince seemed bemused by the man's nervousness and formality. 'Please, before we start, may I offer you some refreshments?' Without waiting for an answer, the prince beckoned one of the crew.

'Thank you.' The guests said in unison.

'Now,' said the prince, 'you were saying before I rudely interrupted you?'

Sensing her colleague had said all he could, the woman spoke next. 'Indeed,' she said, 'protecting this environment and its bio-diversity is not only important to these islands but the whole world. I'm sure you agree, Your Highness.'

'Yes, I do. You know, I often wonder if my generosity is borne from a sense of guilt. Many would see this,' he said, indicating the craft on which they stood, 'as excessive, and that people like me are consuming the world's resources faster than anyone. But I am very much aware that wealth and success are nothing if, in the pursuit of those goals, one ignores the consequences. I have already implemented a series of strict sustainability policies across all my businesses. You may have seen a great deal of media coverage on this.'

'Yes,' the male guest piped up. 'I read articles only last month in the Financial Times and Wall Street Journal.'

'And what did you think?' the prince pressed the man.

'Your comments came across as totally genuine and earnest, which I now know from our experience with Your Highness are utterly true.'

'Yes, a rare example of good reporting, replied the prince. 'There are plenty of articles about me based on nothing but tittle-tattle. So, it's good to know that the media can report the truth. And I mean every word of what I say. After all, we need to think of our children and their children.'

'Fine words, Your Highness. Do you have children?' said the woman.

'Yes, I have a small boy. I would like more, but I'm much too busy saving the world,' the prince replied laughing. 'I just hope my small contribution here will help.'

'It's beyond our wildest expectations,' said the man.

'And your support for the abolition of the mega yacht marina proposal will send the right message to others. For that we cannot thank you enough, Your Highness,' the woman added confidently, but inwardly grappling with the apparent contradictive nature of the prince's donation.

'It is my pleasure. I feel better knowing that I am not responsible for damaging this paradise any more than necessary.'

As the prince walked them to the yacht's helipad and the waiting helicopter, the woman asked, 'Would Your Highness mind if we have a quick photo for the press?'

'Of course. Hassan!' The prince's aide quickly appeared. 'Please take our guests to the stateroom. No wait, take them on a tour of the boat first. I shall join you shortly.'

The aide handed the prince a tablet PC, and led the guests off. 'The *Marid,*' he began 'is one of the largest yachts in the world with a crew of sixty-five…'

The prince strolled back to the upper aft deck, studying the tablet PC. His face had changed from one of beaming effusiveness to brooding severity. One of his other men approached.

'Yes?' the prince enquired without looking up.

'Sir, your London contact is ready.'

'Good. Give him the new account details and the names of the four men who will join him,' the prince said, handing the tablet over.

'Yes, sir.'

'We set sail for Arsuz this afternoon. Tell the captain.'

'Sir.' The crewman headed inside.

Prince Al-Musan turned and looked out at the yachts that sat serenely on the inviting waters. It was just after midday and the threat of afternoon rain was in the air. A rumble of thunder made the prince turn his gaze to the southeast. Beyond the delicate white clouds hanging like islands of candyfloss on a deep blue ocean, a massive cumulonimbus dominated the horizon. He watched, waiting for a flash of distant lightning, and was soon rewarded. After running a hand over his trimmed beard, he headed inside.

Later that afternoon, the *Marid* was weighing anchor, its chain rumbling and clanking its way into the chain locker within the hull. The prince's guests had disembarked two hours earlier, happy with their photos and ecstatic with the prince's donation. Neither they nor anyone else on the islands had given a second thought to the boat's name, inscribed in gold above the anchor. Mentioned in traditional tales, *Marid* in Arabic has several meanings: one is *rebellious*; others include *demon* and *powerful devil*.

North London, UK

On a cool, grey early evening more than four thousand miles away, in a room in the rear of a small clothes shop, Bakr al-Ahdal sat alone at a table, reading a message on his phone. There was a bank account number and four names: Mohammed, Abdul, Jamal, and Bekkali. He knew the first name was Mohammed Faasil. The others were probably assumed names. Either way, his plan had been approved. It was time for action. *Finally*, he thought.

Chapter 8
The Spear of Destiny

Antioch, Syria, June 1098

In the Crusader headquarters deep in the heart of the Antioch citadel, Count Raymond strode purposefully towards the door of his chambers. He was followed by Bishop Adhemar.

'This is folly,' the bishop argued. 'How can you believe the words of a simple servant?'

The count stopped and turned. 'You may doubt the words of a servant. But do you doubt the words of James the Priest? A servant of God?'

'Listen to me! Your men are tired. Perhaps this was no vision of God, but a hallucination brought about by starvation. What if this comes to nought? What if you find nothing but soil and dirt?'

'Losing your faith, Bishop?' the count replied.

The bishop's face dropped. 'How dare you suggest such a thing! I am the chosen representative of His Holiness the Pope. Don't you forget that!'

Count Raymond ignored him and stepped out into a small courtyard, where his men had been ordered to gather.

'The stone that fell at my feet was a great omen from God!' the count began, as he surveyed his weary troops. 'Visions have ordained that a wonderous and priceless treasure awaits us. A treasure that will fulfil our great destiny.' The count sensed that he had already raised their spirits. 'Today, we will enter the cathedral of Antioch and search for the very spear that pierced Our Saviour, Jesus Christ, on the cross. Today, we will find the Holy Lance!' A huge cheer rose from the ranks. 'TODAY!' the count said raising his voice, 'WE WILL FIND THE SPEAR OF DESTINY!'

The roars of approval continued.

Count Raymond was the first to enter the gloom of the cathedral. The odours of ancient stone and wood filled his nostrils, as he knelt and whispered a supplication before crossing himself and rising. His men and the knight's servant, Peter Bartholomew, followed with similar reverence. The count held up a hand to his men and then nodded to Peter, who walked slowly down the nave alone. He stopped halfway and looked around. Then, quickening his pace, he headed for the high altar.

'THERE!' the servant called out, pointing down.

The flagstones behind the altar were soon lifted, exposing an array of scurrying insects. The damp soil below was soft and came up easily as they attacked it with their tools. Taking turns, Peter and the soldiers dug for hours.

As the light began to fade, Count Raymond could hear the men still hard at work. Their muffled voices and the striking of tools echoed off the cathedral walls. The count wished that he shared their belief and determination. But now he doubted his previous elation and decided to leave.

Unknown to the count, Peter the servant, assisted by the soldiers and even the chronicler, Raymond D'Aguilers, had been working frantically. They had created a hole several feet deep. One of the soldiers climbed out. D'Aguilers looked down at the bare earth and shook his head. He, too, was now having doubts.

Peter jumped in and began his third shift.

He had been digging again for several minutes when his blade hit something hard. He stopped and crossed himself, muttering a few words of prayer, before continuing his excavation with renewed fervour. He dropped his tool and scratched at the soil with his bare hands.

He suddenly stopped; his face still pointing down into the small pit. 'I have found it. I have found the Holy Lance,' he said under his breath. Finally, he looked up and cried out, 'I HAVE FOUND THE SPEAR OF DESTINY!'

***

News of the miracle discovery spread fast, and the effect on morale was equally miraculous.

Prince Bohemund assembled the other Crusader leaders. in the main hall of the headquarters.

'We prayed and we prayed,' Bohemund began. 'Many were giving up hope of salvation from this torment and unending siege. Many *have* given up and deserted our great cause. Their faith has been broken and they will suffer in Hell for their sins and their treachery.' A banging of swords on the floor indicated agreement amongst the warlords encircling the hall. The prince went on, 'But those of us with an inner strength and *true* faith continued to pray. And God sent us not one, but two signs. First, a stone from heaven, the likes of which no one has ever seen before fell at the very feet of Count Raymond here.' Everyone turned and smiled at the count, who acknowledged with a modest smile and a raised hand. 'And then came a second sign, a vision seen by a simple servant. Surely, this was a true test of our faith.' Those present once more stomped their swords repeatedly against the stone floor. Bohemund continued, 'We believed in this servant and we were rewarded.'

Bohemund strode across the hall towards a large white banner emblazoned with the red Crusader cross. He gripped the cloth and turned towards his audience. 'THIS,' he bellowed, 'IS OUR TALISMAN. THIS IS OUR SPEAR OF DESTINY!' With that, Bohemund yanked at the cloth away to reveal a metal standard topped with the true relic—the spear that had pierced Jesus on the cross.

The effect of seeing the talismanic standard stunned those present into silence and awe, for mounted at the spear's head was the stone from heaven, shimmering with light. It was as though God was making his presence visible. Some of the warlords were so moved, tears welled in their eyes. It was a divine moment, and the events leading to the spear's discovery were seen as miracles. All those present that day would never forget their first sight of the Spear of Destiny and, God willing, would recount the experience for many years to come. They felt blessed and it brought joy and hope to their hearts. Their reverie, though, was broken when Bohemund's booming voice filled the hall once more, 'TOMORROW, WITH THE SPEAR OF DESTINY HELD HIGH IN FRONT OF OUR RANKS, WE WILL ATTACK THE HEATHENS. WE WILL BREAK THIS SIEGE. WE WILL BE VICTORIOUS! GOD WILLS IT!'

Brandishing their swords high above their heads, the warlords repeated the war cry: 'GOD WILLS IT! GOD WILLS IT! GOD WILLS IT!'

Chapter 9
Daniel's Hut

Tanneron, Southern France

'*S'il vous plait*!' implored Brigitte, emphasising each word. She was standing in front of her uncle's desk in the villa.

'English, Brigitte. You should practice your English. It's the international language.'

Brigitte scowled. 'Please can we go to the hut? You promised.'

'I'll make us a small picnic first,' Daniel smiled.

With the hut in sight, Brigitte let go of her uncle's hand and ran the last few metres to the door.

It was late morning on Daniel's hill and the heat was already intense. The cicadas were deafening. *They're like an audible thermometer*, Daniel mused; *the hotter it gets, the louder they become.* A soft breeze wafted two small trees either side of the hut, the shadows dancing over the roof, providing some relief from the summer sun.

'*Un moment, ma petite, les clés.*'

'English, uncle! You said we must speak in English.'

Daniel laughed and handed over a bunch of keys, now a ritual for them. At that moment, memories of Brigitte's mother, his sister, flooded back. His poor little sister. He missed so much, even though nine years had passed since her untimely death during riots in London.

At the hut, the little girl had no problem unlocking the padlock. She ran in and flicked on the main light. Daniel entered the relative coolness of the hut and put down the small knapsack he had been carrying. 'It's hot Brigitte; would you like a drink now?'

'No, thank you, uncle.'

Her smile reminded him so much of his sister.

The hut was a chaotic den of scientific instruments, screens, books, globes, charts, and magazines, some of it scattered over a bench, the rest balanced precariously on a series of shelves and a battered filing cabinet. There was hardly an inch to spare.

Brigitte had gone straight to the main working area—a bench—and placed her finger over the switch of an Anglepoise lamp. 'Uncle, the light!'

Daniel smiled and turned off the main light.

'And now, ladies and gentleman…,' Brigitte began.

'Gentle*men*. Plural, Brigitte,' Daniel corrected.

'Er hem, and now ladies and gentlemen, the incredible, the amazing, Electric Lady!'

Brigitte flicked on the lamp. Two silver orbs, one large, one small, seemed to jump into existence, hovering just above the girl's face like metallic planets floating in the infinite void of space. This was Brigitte's prize: a Van der Graaf generator. Brigitte stroked the larger of the two shiny spheres. Her uncle had made the contraption himself. Rather than a motor, there was a handle for turning the vertical belt that built up the charge in the larger sphere. Brigitte now began turning this handle with both hands, faster and faster, her little face, lit by the lamp, showing the initial exertion required to get the machine up to speed. The whirring cogs got louder. Daniel had designed the gearing such that, once going, the task of turning the handle would get easier.

'That should do, Brigitte.'

Brigitte knew the machine intimately. Continuing the motion with her left hand, she released her other hand and slowly raised it to the larger sphere. Her hair sprang up vertically. They both laughed.

'The incredible, the amazing, electric woman!' Brigitte shouted above the noise.

She began cranking the handle with both hands again, but this time removed her right hand to operate a lever that controlled the movement of the smaller sphere. The gap between the two orbs closed causing a spark to jump across with a loud crackle.

Daniel had left Brigitte to amaze her imaginary audience. He opened a small metal case, which he had placed on the end of the bench. Inside, nestled in layers of soft cloth, was the blue stone he had found. He looked around and spotted what he was looking for—his microscope.

With the device now in front of him, he gently placed the gem under the microscope and peered into the eyepiece. He selected a different lens and adjusted the focus. '*Mon Dieu!*' he whispered, adjusting the focus again. Brigitte continued with her noisy Electric Lady show. 'My god!' Daniel said again a lot louder, almost laughing. 'Brigitte! Look at this!' He was staring into the microscope and beckoning her excitedly.

Brigitte stopped turning the handle and walked over to her uncle's side. 'What is it, uncle?'

Daniel stood aside to let his niece have a look. The gem was alive. It was alive with tiny filaments of light; static-like charges sizzling all over its surface.

'*Ah, c'est beau!*' Brigitte breathed in.

She looked up and the two of them stared at each other, cautious smiles on both their faces. Brigitte then returned to gaze at this new wonder.

'Brigitte, please turn off the lamp.'

Reluctantly, the girl did what she was told. After all, her uncle was full of surprises. Perhaps he had one more. Daniel took his turn again at the microscope as the room darkened once more. 'This is incredible, Brigitte. The stone…it must have somehow attracted the electricity from the Van der Graaf.'

'Can I see again, please, please?' Brigitte was pushing her uncle out of the way.

Daniel groped his way in the gloom to the generator and began cranking the handle. 'Tell me what happens, Brigitte.'

The girl was silent for a while. 'It's getting, er, more bright, uncle.'

'Brighter? Yes?'

'Yes, I think so, brighter.'

'Let me try to build the charge,' Daniel said, as he wound the handle. The activity around the stone and, it seemed, deep within it, grew in intensity. The fine, fiery tendrils were more numerous and more complex, creating what looked like a miniature atmosphere of electrical chaos. Some of the electrical filaments shot outwards away from the stone. Brigitte recoiled slightly each time this happened.

'What can you see now, Brigitte?'

'It is very busy. It is like a small storm, yes, a light storm.' Daniel continued to crank the handle.

'Uncle, now it is …AYE!'

Brigitte jumped backwards, one of her arms instinctively across her face. A large arc had leapt at least two metres from the large sphere straight at the gemstone. Brigitte fell backwards, crashing hard into the filing cabinet.

'Brigitte!' Daniel had released the handle and turned on the desk lamp. He quickly discharged the Van Der Graaf with the smaller sphere, worried that another discharge could cause further injury or a fire. Fire was always uppermost in Daniel's mind.

'Brigitte, are you OK?' He reached down to his niece and put one of his arms around her back to support her.

Brigitte winced as she straightened. 'I'm OK, I think. But my eye…'

Concern swept across Daniel's face. *Of course*, he thought, *she was looking at the magnified stone when the spark hit it. That can be as dangerous as looking at the sun through a telescope.* He examined her face and eye. Reassuringly, he said, 'It should pass. Keep your eye closed for a while.'

Brigitte then cried and her uncle gave her a hug. It was a hug for his long-lost sister, too.

Chapter 10
The Mount of Infidels and
the First Guardian

Turkish Encampment, Outside Antioch, 15 June 1098

By dawn, the wagon was loaded and ready. Two mules had been tethered to it. Captain Ersoy had selected three of his men and had them dress in simple robes. He looked towards his tent and beckoned to the sage. The old man, dressed in similar robes, approached slowly, using his staff as support. He looked up at the captain.

Ersoy placed his hands on the sage's frail shoulders. 'Today, you and these men are monks. If you encounter any Christians, tell them you are returning to your monastery in *Gâvur Dağ*—the Mount of Infidels—for food. Allah has appointed you as the guardian of these stones.' The sage nodded and the captain lowered his arms. To his men, he said, 'You are on a mission for God himself. The sage is your guide. Treat him well and keep him safe. You will travel with him to the chosen place and leave him there. Return here when your mission is complete. You are dressed as monks because monks provide the Christians with provisions, so it's in their interest to give you a safe passage. Go slowly and carefully. The weight of the stones is great. There are empty jars on top of those containing the stones in case you are stopped and inspected. They will let you pass. Make sure they do!'

The soldiers all nodded. The sage threw his staff into the wagon and held out a hand.

'Help him up!' barked the captain.

Two of the soldiers hoisted the old man onto the front of the wagon. The sage then pointed ahead and the party of bogus monks set off with the precious cargo.

The wagon trundled and bumped its way along the flat stony road that led north from Antioch along the Orontes River valley. They passed the Christian encampment without incident.

The old sage sat upright, eyes shut, a hand on each knee. In the rear of the wagon, the two soldiers leant forward with frowns on their faces.

The great citadel, with its tens of thousands of besieged inhabitants, was behind them, and the sight of four monks on a rickety wagon laden with jars drew little attention. Ahead and to their left rose the mountains and their destination.

The driver of the wagon turned to the sage. 'How far, old man?'

'We will reach the mountain pass by sundown. We rest there. On the morrow, we will reach the secret cave by mid-morning.'

Black Mountain, Syria, 16 June 1098

'Keep the stones in the jars. We will need to make several trips,' the sage instructed, pointing up the rock-strewn slope that loomed above them.

They had stopped by a river, deep within the mountains. One of the soldiers was leading the mules to the water.

'I saw a monastery,' said one of the other soldiers. 'We should be quick. If we are approached by real monks, that may lead to trouble.'

'For that reason, we should not pray during daylight. We are doing Allah's work, so He will forgive us,' the sage said.

Soon, each soldier was loading several jars into his own sack. It was already hot as the men laboured under an unbroken, deep blue sky.

'These are heavy! This will take more than a few trips,' said one of them.

'Stop complaining!' the other soldier said. 'Better here than that hell-hole of a camp.'

'Allah will reward you for your efforts, too. I can also manage a few jars,' the old man said and led the way up the slope.

The climb was difficult, but the sage knew the easiest route. After half an hour, the first load of jars had been secreted deep inside the cave, in a space hidden from view.

With the occasional help from the sage, it took the men at least ten ascents to deposit and conceal all the jars.

It was early evening. The sage sat alone at the back of the cave. A small lamp flickered next to him. From the nearest sack, he removed a jar, took out the stone it contained, and held it to the light. 'What power do you hold?' he whispered. A rumble of distant thunder made him look up briefly. His eyes then returned to the stone. As he turned it, he thought he saw it glimmer from within. The sage looked at it more closely. *A trick of the light*, he thought, and returned the stone to its jar. He stood up and laid the sack with the others—out of sight.

Night fell and a canopy of stars lit the sky and mountains. The two mules stood motionless by the river. The soldiers were exhausted and lay asleep on their blankets beside the wagon.

Above them, on the slope opposite the cave, stood the sage. Ahead of him, dominating the sky was a star. *Or was it two?* he thought. He had never seen such a bright star. Surely, it was another sign. Little did the sage know, but he was using Jupiter and Uranus as his guide, heavenly bodies that moved across the field of stars on their solar orbits. That night, the two planets were almost in conjunction. The sage held out both arms and pointed at the dazzling object then lowered them to where he knew the cave was situated. He then slowly moved his arms apart, still pointing. His right arm stopped when it aligned with a nearby monastery. He moved his gaze to his left arm, which had moved in the opposite direction at the same rate. His left index finger was pointing towards a mountain with three peaks. Satisfied, the old man lowered his arms.

The landscape lit up as lightning pulsed and danced above the storm clouds that had gathered to the south; the accompanying thunder rumbling soon after, rolling away into the distance.

The sage's voice echoed across the valley: 'ALLAH BE PRAISED! MOUNTAINS OF HOLY LIGHT!' His thoughts returned to the stone and its mysterious glimmer.

In the deserted cave, a strange glow emanated from one of the jars lying on its side.

Chapter 11
The Florentine Book Collector

Florence, 1536

The sky to the east looked threatening, and yet the mid-afternoon August heat was unrelenting if not intensifying.

Lorenzo Cellini scurried across the *Piazza della Signoria*, dodging other Florentines. Sensing the coming rain, everyone was in an equal rush.

He stopped briefly, tucked the book he was carrying under his left armpit, unbuttoned his shirt halfway, and inserted the book, pressing it close to his stomach. The first spots of rain darkened the dusty paving. Then the heavens opened. Loud calls echoed off the walls. Shutters and doors banged shut. Lorenzo's hat and shirt were soaked through in seconds. His dark brown hair clung around his neck and shoulders. He stooped as he ran, trying his best to protect the book. Two young women, arms linked, trotted past, laughing.

Lorenzo needed shelter. He spotted a large villa with a series of *marcapiano*—decorative cornices that protruded from the building—and, Lorenzo was relieved to see, a roof that nearly overhung the entire, narrow street. The villa's doorway was slightly recessed. It was here that he took shelter and looked up. The sky was a muddy brown. The tops of the buildings were still illuminated by the late summer sun. Rivulets of water ran down the roof tiles and walls, and along the street. As quickly as the rain had come, the street emptied. Lorenzo inspected the book. It was still dry. He decided to wait.

Ten minutes later, he threw open the single door to his house and stumbled in. The rain had stopped, leaving the streets cleaner but the air muggy. The city was now bathed in the sun's dying rays. The sky immediately above, though, was dark and brooding. Enormous clouds folded and churned high into the sky— a raging palette of black, greys, and white, fringed with orange.

After throwing down his hat and quickly changing his clothes, Lorenzo picked up the book and headed across the principal room of his modest dwelling—a dim space packed floor to ceiling with tomes, scrolls, and manuscripts. Illuminated by a single window, he began viewing its content through a crude lens.

A nearby church struck the hour. The bell was accompanied by a roll of thunder that started low but concluded in a crescendo that travelled over Lorenzo's house.

Inside, the air remained constant, providing relief from the hot summer months and not unreasonable comfort the rest of the year. For the sake of his collection, Lorenzo knew that a stable atmosphere would keep any dampness at bay and be better for the preservation of his extensive investment. His modest income, however, limited his ability to control his precious space. He only lit his fire when the cold seemed to creep its way through the stone walls and chill his bones, and would only open the window when the stifling heat made the same unwelcome invasion, sapping his energy and causing him to drop to sleep over his work. For the rest of the time, the book collector would add layers of clothing, often sitting at his table wearing a coat, which he also used as an extra blanket on his bed.

Lorenzo would often take a long sniff of the air when he returned home. For many years he enjoyed the mustiness exuded by the collection. Now his nose could no longer detect it; only visitors would frown on entry to his home. Lorenzo knew why, he assumed, but was unaware that the odours of old velum and leather were often overpowered by those of unwashed laundry, stale food, and the bookkeeper's lack of personal hygiene.

For one locked up in his repository for days on end, obsessed with the acquisition and safe-keeping of written works—one of the world's first book dealers, bibliophiles, and avid readers—Lorenzo Cellini was surprisingly tanned. And yet his lean body, hollow cheeks, and unkempt appearance indicated a man that lacked, or avoided, the comforts of a family home, a caring wife, and regular meals, all of which added ten or more years to his present forty-one.

It was close to midnight before the book collector snuffed out the candles and lanterns, and retired to bed. As he lay there, his eyes open, he wondered how far away the storm was. The thunder sounded distant and less frequent. As Lorenzo waited for the next rumble, his eyes closed and he fell asleep.

Chapter 12
Test ADND-8-46.03

Underground Laboratory, Alaska, USA, Present Day

On the ultra-high-definition display was a blurry dark shape. Dr Jeffrey Scott adjusted the controls of the powerful stereo microscope. Part of the object sprang into sharp focus. He carefully moved the slide on which the object had been placed. Details of the object were slowly revealed: the main body had a uniformly smooth matt surface coloured dark grey. Four short arms projected from each corner of the body, each supporting an upward-facing propeller. It was a nano-drone. Scott and his team had been working on it for six years. He quickly selected the strongest magnification. A close-up of the body's surface filled the screen. Far from being smooth, the surface was in fact made up of rows of what, Scott secretly thought, looked like thousands of identical tombstones. How prescient that thought was; how cannily appropriate. The object under scrutiny was fabricated from the latest carbon fibre. He zoomed back out and turned to his team. 'Are we ready?' One of his team nodded. 'Are we recording?' A thumb went up from another of the scientists hidden behind a bank of computer screens. Scott placed a headset on his head. 'OK,' he said. 'This is test ADND-8-46.03. And activate!'

Scott was joined by Dr David Dimitriou. They both looked at the microscope screen. All four of the drone's propellers seemed to go from stationary to maximum velocity instantly. The two scientists looked at each other and smiled. 'Still looks good, Jeff.'

'It certainly does,' Scott replied. 'Are we capturing all the telemetry?'

Dimitriou returned to his computer. 'Yep. Velocity on all motors is good. Temperature stable.'

'Fuel?'

'On track. We're coming up to one minute…and…mark. As expected, that will give our little bird forty minutes fly time. More than enough,' Dimitriou reported, as he quickly typed.

'OK,' Scott continued, 'keep it running until it runs out of juice. We need to be *absolutely* sure we don't experience any failures. Don't forget, we need better than 99.8% success. Even these relatively small amounts of *Donarium* could compromise the nano-mechanics.'

Three hours later, test ADND-8-46.03 was recorded as another 100% success in the long line of parallel tests that made up the multi-billion-dollar project. For the nano-drone phase, the team would now move to exterior testing.

Dimitriou carefully removed the glass slide from the microscope and held it above him, allowing the ceiling lights to shine through. He rotated the slide slowly. 'Wow! Still blows me away,' he whispered.

It was as though nothing more than a small fly had landed in the middle of the glass.

Chapter 13
Guardians

Northeast of Damascus, Early September 1542

Abu Abdallah was Fowaz's favourite student. The two of them, boy and man, had been in deep study since first light. No drink, no food, no break.

Fowaz had prepared for this lesson like any other he had held over the last thirty-seven years. The small, white, stucco-walled room, in which they both sat, had been cleared of all distractions, save the intricately woven rug that provided nominal comfort for the teacher and his student. Minimal, too, was the afternoon light—dusty sunbeams, defined by and thus mimicking across the floor, the single, exquisitely carved window.

Fowaz continued the incantations in his low, mesmeric voice; his words occasionally echoed by Abu Abdallah, who tried his best to adopt the manly voice he so desperately wanted.

Abu's eyes were tight shut. He was oblivious to time, of the random voices outside, the roll of distant thunder, and the ache in his crossed legs.

Fowaz stopped the incantations and smiled. *Abu Abdallah is an excellent student*, he thought. *So much more dedicated than his father. Abu is special. Perhaps now is the time.*

'Abu. I want you to follow me. I have something to show you.'

'But my mother…'

'Don't worry, I have spoken to her. Come, we must go right now.'

Years earlier, Fowaz had told Abu Abdallah that their citadel was as old as the rocks on which it was perched. The houses had lain on flat ground for generations. God, Fowaz had said, found the people to be good and wanted them closer to him. So, he shaped the mountains with his bare hands and placed the houses amongst them.

After nearly an hour of walking and climbing, the teacher and the boy stood side by side on a spur of rock, the citadel far below on the opposite mountainside. In front of them, the jagged foothills stretched out like crumpled paper under the setting sun. Beyond the hills, over the desert, a spectacular electric storm almost as wide as the horizon was creating another of nature's pyrotechnic masterpieces.

Abu Abdallah watched the distant storm. A warm breeze ruffled his hair. 'Why have you brought me to this place?'

'I have...' Fowaz checked himself, annoyed that he had responded so quickly. *This boy. He has a way with him. I cannot reprimand his insolent questioning. I cannot ask him to conclude with "master," or "please, master Fowaz," for this is not insolence*, he thought, *but the talk of natural authority. One to take on a great responsibility.* '...This way,' Fowaz continued. The teacher, indicating the way with his arm outstretched, waited for Abu to pass. He then cast a furtive glance in the direction from which they had come.

The master and his student made their way toward, what seemed to Abu, an impassable rock face.

'There! There! The cave, Abu. The cave.'

Abu glanced back at his teacher, his brow furrowed, then turned back to stare at the rock face. 'Where, master?'

Ah, Fowaz thought, *master, is it now?* He gave a brief smile. 'There, to your left.'

Abu had to stop and peer ahead, squinting, unsure if he was looking at a shadow or a cave. He glanced back at Fowaz once more. Fowaz simply goaded his student on with raised eyebrows and a series of rapid nods.

Abu turned, stooped, and proceeded slowly over the threshold and into the dark, followed by his teacher. A few more paces and he had entered a cool, grey, hollow world. A shiver ran through him, in part from the sudden chill and, he knew, from his growing excitement. He had sensed that he had been chosen for something. That none of the other students was present had not eluded him either; only he and the venerable Fowaz were here.

The outside light had all but lost its influence after just a few steps.

Fowaz whispered, 'Wait!' He produced a small candle lamp and a flint from his robe. 'Hold this!' he said, as he proffered the lamp. Abu's eyes were searching the gloomy surroundings. A spark brought his gaze back to the lamp. Fowaz looked up from the flame to Abu. 'I have brought you to a special place, Abu. A place held secret for generations. A place, which only you and I now know, and which you must never share until it is your time to stand where I stand now.' He turned and raised the lamp before him. 'Climb here. When you reach that ledge, lean over and take hold of what you find,' Fowaz instructed quietly.

A steep but not unassailable mound of rocks led up towards the cave ceiling. A quick survey was all Abu needed before he began the easy ascent.

'Can you see it? Can you feel it?' Fowaz whispered.

Abu was now unsure. What was lying behind the rock? A snake? A nest of scorpions? Abu's breaths were short and rapid. 'Yes, master, I can see many broken jars and some wooden boxes.' Abu's shoulders dropped in relief.

'Bring down the nearest box! Slowly. Carefully, it will be heavy.'

Abu was clutching a small, simple wooden box under his arm as he began his descent, tripping and sliding on the loose rocks and debris. When he reached Fowaz, he held the box out, his arms now trembling under the weight.

Fowaz reached into his robe and produced a small, elaborate key. He offered the key to the box's keyhole and turned. There was a faint click. 'Open it,' he whispered.

A distant rumble of thunder could be heard, muffled, and yet amplified by the cave's reflective interior. Abu, now staring with some consternation at his master, slowly raised the lid.

Abu's mouth and eyes widened in awe and relief. A translucent blue gem was revealed. A blue like the blue you could see in the eyes of some of the babies and children of the citadel before age turned them brown.

'Behold, Abu. A sacred stone.'

'It is so beautiful, master, so blue,' Abu breathed. 'There were other boxes. Do they also contain stones like this?'

'There are two hundred and sixty-three, to be precise, Abu,' Fowaz whispered.

'Wonderful.' Abu looked up into his master's eyes and smiled.

'Wonderful, indeed, Abu. They came from the heavens and rained down like burning hail on the Turkish camp at the time the infidels laid siege to the city of Antioch. For many years they were kept in a cave near that great citadel, a place very similar to this. But when the power of the stones was realised, they were brought here—a safer, more remote hiding place.' Fowaz watched his student return his gaze to the stone, waiting for him to ask more.

Abu's smile turned to a frown. 'Power? Do you mean wealth?'

'They could easily be mistaken for fabulous jewels, a king's fortune, that's true. But they hold an even greater value.'

Abu's words were slow. 'But why…why here? Why have they been kept in this cave, and not in a safe place in our village, master?'

'Ah, Abu. That is a very good question. Let me show you.'

Fowaz raised the small stone in both hands. Without a word, he walked back to the cave entrance, calling back, 'Come!'

Outside, the sun was a dim orange disc, its brilliance dulled by heat and dust. The opposite horizon was now almost black with a thundercloud, topped with tints of the fading sun. Arcs of lightning momentarily connected the ground with the base of the mighty cloud.

'"God cups the lightning in his hands and commands it strike where he pleases. He is angry and I fear the thunder in his voice." Words of a prophet, long ago, Abu.' Fowaz was looking at the distant storm. A small blue spark crackled in the air near him. He placed the stone on a rock a few metres from the cave entrance and stepped back. 'Let us stand over there, Abu.'

More sparks and now short, blue-white arcs crisscrossed the air near the stone.

'Can you feel a change, Abu?'

'The air, it, it feels different, master.' Abu was transfixed by the display around the stone. He had never seen anything like it.

The arcing intensified. Abu stepped back against the rock face. His and Fowaz's hair began to stand on end.

'I am afraid, Master Fowaz. What is happening?'

Suddenly, a large crackling arc zigzagged in the air over the stone for several seconds. Abu stared at the stone. What seemed like miniature lightning had formed within it. He looked at the storm, thinking that the stone was acting as a mirror. But no, there was no lightning in the distance at that time. He returned his gaze to the spectacle before him. Now several large arcs were dancing around the stone. Abu cowered; his hands raised slightly, ready to cover his face. He was unaware that Fowaz was standing tall; his eyes closed, his arms outstretched, mumbling some quiet incantation, as the magic continued around the stone.

A deep rumbling sound caused Abu to look back at the storm with growing alarm. A small yelp left his mouth. The noise built rapidly. Suddenly, the entire area was filled with fine, blue-white filaments, a complex web of light, ever-changing. A new high-pitched, fizzing, crackling sound added to the now tremulously deep rumble. Fowaz's incantations were now more urgent. And from the storm across the desert came a thunderbolt of light, which, in the blink of an eye, had jerked and leapt from the valley floor up the mountain into the small, incandescent blue stone. The lightning flashed its intensity into Abu's eyes, its jagged body and forks imprinted on his retinas, its blinding route etched into memory, its massive energy charging the air with God-like power. The stone glowed fleetingly with the brilliance of a supernova. Abu tumbled to the ground crying out in pain.

Then all was dark and deathly quiet, but for Abu Abdullah's frantic breathing.

Chapter 14
Manuscripts

Florence, 1542

'And how did you say these came into your possession?' the book dealer, Lorenzo Cellini, enquired in his soft, slow voice, not looking up from the manuscripts.

From the shadows, Snr. Giovanni Foscari, a sturdy, middle-aged, and well-dressed merchant stepped forward. 'In France, during my recent travels. A priest was selling a handful of works. It was in the market square of an unremarkable town. I forget which. Auri… something.'

'The church is always desperate for money,' muttered the collector. 'Aurillac?'

'I'm sorry?'

'The town. Was it Aurillac, perhaps?'

'Yes, I think it was.' The merchant looked surprised. 'Do you know it?'

'Hmm?' uttered the collector, briefly looking up at his guest. 'Er no. I have visited many places during my travels, of course. How else do you think I amassed this?' He raised his right hand and waved. The merchant took in the ceiling-high collection of books, scrolls, and parchments. 'Naturally, I welcome visitors like you who save me the trouble of packing my bags by bearing written works of any kind. The knowledge therein is…' Cellini hesitated, his finger tracing the outline of what he thought may be a star constellation drawn to the side of the text.

'Priceless?' the merchant suggested.

'No, interesting. Sometimes fascinating. And should be guarded for posterity.'

'Indeed, then such works carry a good price, no?' Foscari prompted.

'Well, *Signore*, that depends. There are very few with the wisdom to realise the importance of recording facts and events; fewer still with the requisite education *and* means to commit them to the written word. But what some consider important is worthless to others.' His finger continued down the manuscript. *This is a fine document*, he thought, *written by someone with particular attention to detail.* His finger had stopped at what was clearly a map— a land with a sea to its west. 'There is also the matter of quality,' he continued without looking up. 'Those works that are painstakingly drawn up by scribes over many months, those with detailed and beautifully crafted text, illuminated script, and rich colours; such works have an aesthetic value regardless of subject matter. The *really* important and very best works are those on law, land ownership and maps, matters of state, and the entire bible.'

'Which makes you a wealthy and powerful man.'

The collector looked up, slid back his chair, and sprang to his feet. He gave the appearance of someone who had been insulted but continued in his gentle tone. 'No, those finer works are for the privileged few—the church, the rich, and the powerful. Sir, my humble surroundings reflect my worldly wealth. But I see from your fine attire that you are a successful trader in…?'

'Alum.'

'Ah, alum! Of course. I can see that trading in that commodity is more lucrative than mine is in books. My collection is more interesting than profitable. Truly valuable works are held by those in power. I am but a humble collector and guardian of what remains, or at least a portion of it. Besides, I do not count my wealth in florins or gold ducats, *Signore*. My wealth, my pleasure…' Cellini looked around the room, smiling, '…my pleasure is in knowing that all this will be here when I'm long gone from this world.

Foscari watched Cellini move amongst his collection. 'But you do trade in these books?' the merchant asked.

'Yes, that's true. I eke out a modest living through the sale of, how should I say, these less important works. So, yes, I am willing to offer you payment for this manuscript. As to its value, I will need to study the contents further. Call on me in three days and we will conclude our business. Do you have any knowledge of the manuscript contents?' As he spoke, Cellini was scanning a collection of scrolls on one of the many shelves.

'No. I was told by the priest that they were written by…,' Foscari produced a letter from within his silk-brocaded *giornea*, '…the historian, Raymond

D'Aguilers. The priest gave me this provenance. It's in French, too, of course.' He held the letter aloft.

'Please, on the table.' Cellini had turned to his guest briefly before renewing his search. Foscari placed the letter alongside the manuscripts. 'I also collect maps. Did I mention that?' the collector continued, carefully pulling out a series of scrolls.

Cellini rolled out the first scroll. 'There. France. And here, if I recall, is your unremarkable town.'

Foscari leant over the map, almost tracing the journey he would have taken. 'Yes, that's it, Aurillac. You are an impressive man, *Signore* Cellini. I would say your talents are wasted.'

'Not at all. We live in a wonderful city in extraordinary times. You see, *Signore*, I regard knowledge as more valuable than any financial gain I may make from using the knowledge itself.'

'They say that knowledge *is* power,' said the merchant with a wry smile.

'And in the wrong hands that could mean trouble. I have no intention of using the knowledge in this room for malevolent purposes. My interests are principally academic—for the benefit of all. I simply wish to earn enough to fulfil my meagre requirements. Worry not, *Signore*, I will give you a fair price.'

The collector sat down, placed the visitor's texts in front of him, raised the viewing glass, and resumed his study.

'Do you have an idea of their true value?' Foscari asked.

Cellini looked up. 'Well, *you* have an idea, as you purchased them from the priest. Wanting to know their *true* value makes me suspect that you got them at a good price.'

Foscari laughed. 'You would make a good alum merchant, *Signore* Cellini.'

'Well, I *am* a merchant of books.'

'Yes, of course. So do you have a rough price for me?'

'As I said, I need more time. So, I cannot give you an estimation. I can give you an idea of what we have here. Having read the first few lines and based on the place names and diagrams, I am sure this is an account of a battle or siege in the Holy Lands. Based on the material, the style, and the fact that it is an account written in French, almost certainly one that took place during the time of the Crusades.'

'That would be three or more centuries ago. That must increase its value, surely?'

'Historical accounts of wars fought long ago hold no real value. Those were primitive times. On a military level, we have come a long way. My initial assessment is that it is more a curio than a useful or indeed valuable document. But I will study it further for a more thorough evaluation.

'Very well,' Foscari said. 'I will see you in three days.' The collector did not reply. The visitor then added slowly, 'And...I'll see myself out.'

'Hmm? Oh yes, if you wouldn't mind.'

Lighting a candle against the growing gloom, the book dealer listened as the door opened, briefly letting in the sounds of the street. When he heard it close, he took the second, smaller scroll and opened it up then slid the candle closer. Asia Minor was written across the map. Picking up his lens, he surveyed various coastlines. He unfurled the manuscript and surveyed the map diagram once more, this time with the lens. The map was devoid of place names. Cellini thought this strange. 'I have a puzzle to solve,' he muttered. The only details were of mountains running parallel to a coastline, a single building, a river, and a town with many towers. One of the mountains was higher than the rest and had three peaks. But Cellini gave this no special importance and considered it merely an artistic embellishment. He turned his attention to the town. His lens magnified the drawing. 'Yes, a fortress city,' he said out loud. Back over the map, he focussed his attention on Syria, moving the lens inland from the coast. The lens magnified the city of Antioch. He compared its position with the map on Foscari's document, the line of the river, and the position of the mountains. *Yes, this had to be it*, he thought.

'Bravo, Lorenzo! I knew it was in Syria.'

With that, Lorenzo Cellini rolled up the maps. Once again, he moved his lens over the drawing of the stars: a single large one dominated the cluster. Not recognising the star formation, he wanted to dismiss it but wondered why it was there. *And*, he thought, *what was the building in those mountains?* The book collector scanned the accompanying text. His French was good enough to make a quick translation. He decided to write down some of the words and phrases:

Gardien du destin—guardian of destiny
Le sage de Damas—the sage of Damascus
Commander des Turques—captain of the Turks
Montagnes de Sainte Lumiere—Mountains of Holy Light
Pierres du Ciel—stones from Heaven

The Florentine book collector looked at the words he had written. He then wrote: *Religious omen?*

Cellini sat for several minutes contemplating his latest procurement. 'A historic curio,' he announced finally to the room, 'well executed and in fine condition.'

Satisfied, he poured himself wine. Cellini had already decided upon his price, a potential buyer, and his potential profit.

Chapter 15
Sotheby's

West London, UK, 6 Years Ago

'Lot number 16, a collection of manuscripts on vellum, written in gothic bookhand; rubric and paraphs in red and gold, with diagrams, central France, 11th century, by the chronicler Raymond D'Aguilers on the siege of Antioch.'

The auctioneer, Sara Alcott, turned to where an apron-wearing member of staff had placed the lot. Above the manuscript, a large screen displayed a series of close-up images of the work.

'Do I hear 50,000 Pounds? 50...60...70. I have a bid of 70,000 Pounds.'

As she scanned the room, the auctioneer's smiles of encouragement appeared to be helping. Her charm and pleasant demeanour were in stark contrast to the staid, sombre-looking collectors seated before her.

'80...90. The bid stands at 90,000. Do I hear 100,000 for this fine and very rare, first-hand chronicle from the time of the Crusades?'

After the initial flurry, the bidding had slowed. The auctioneer then announced: 'I have a new online bid. 100,000. 100,000 Pounds is the new bid. Do I hear 110?'

She made a note and surveyed the room with her winning smile. 'The bid stands at 100,000. Going once...twice...sold for 100,000 Pounds. Thank you,' she concluded and made a further note. 'We come now to lot number 17, an Illuminated Book of Hours manuscript on vellum with exquisite borders of flowers and birds in gold, blue, yellow, and green. I have an opening bid of 20,000 Pounds...'

Aboard mega yacht, Marid, the Ionian Sea off Greece

Prince Al-Musan was typing into a laptop. A second large screen at the end of the cabin displayed lot no.16. His aide stood by his side; hands folded in front.

'Yes!' the prince declared and closed the laptop.

'Congratulations, Your Highness.'

'I have advised Sotheby's that you will collect the manuscripts in person, Hassan,' said the prince. 'Take the helicopter to Corfu today. My plane awaits you there. Notify me immediately you return from London.'

'Of course, Your Highness.'

Chapter 16
Eurostar

Paris, France, Present Day

Ahmed Hashim fought his way onto the Paris Metro at Place Saint Michel. He could not help wondering at the fantastic array of people all around him. Luckily, he spotted a flip-down seat next to the Metro carriage door. He stepped carefully past the four dogs laying across the floor. Two big Alsatians, one Rottweiler, and another big white dog snoring and dribbling. For the first time, Ahmed felt intimidated. Each of the dog handlers was dressed in black with combat boots and *Securité* sewn into their uniforms. The smell of old boots drifted about in the warm air of the train. He was unsure if this was the handlers or their dogs. Funnily, their uniforms did not match, but they each had a badge sewn in with *Maître Chien* and a vicious dog profile. Their shaven heads and badges reminded him of the brutal CRS he had seen beating fellow Arabs in the Parisian streets. Ahmed settled down. One of them opened their jacket and out of the lining peered a tiny white puppy. The shaven youth was not a man but a boyish girl, she looked up and said, '*Il a que un mois.*'

'*Il est mignon,*' Ahmed replied smiling.

The girl's male colleague simply glared at Ahmed. There was real malice in his look. One of the dogs stirred, about to stand up. The handler jerked his lead sharply. '*Asseoir!*' he grunted in a deep voice then resumed his stare.

Ahmed's command of French was excellent. So too, was his ability to control his emotions. Born and raised in the UK, his Algerian father met his French mother in Paris, while both studying at the Sorbonne. When they both won places at Cambridge, they moved in together and married a year later. Their only son was born two years later. Ahmed's childhood had been loving and stable. But as a teenager, he never felt settled. It was irrational, but he felt foreign in his own country. When he abandoned his promising education to fight instead with "his brothers" in Syria, he never returned to his homeland. Indeed, he probably never could. He had been blacklisted by the UK government. His parents did their best to win the authorities over, appearing on several TV news interviews as the respectable academics they were. In all those very public appearances, his mother and father had tears in their eyes.

"Château d'Eau," came an announcement over the Metro PA.

Only two more stops, he thought. He looked out of the window at the station sign. *What a great cryptic crossword clue*: "Stop in Paris for feline taking note in double the water." *Château d'Eau. I should write crosswords for the Daily Telegraph.*' he mused.

The Eurostar departed the Gare du Nord on time. Ahmed was enjoying his first-class window seat and the attention from the waiter. One hour earlier it would have been a different story; even first class would have been packed out.

During breakfast, Ahmed's constant attention to the passing countryside had not remained unnoticed. So, when he reached into his bag, the man across the aisle raised his glasses and peered over. The small device in Ahmed's hand looked like a large phone but was displaying something different.

The outside was now a blur, but Ahmed would repeatedly look out of the window and tap the device. This curious and repetitive behaviour had lulled Ahmed's observer into a doze. Only when a train from the Channel Tunnel flashed past, did the man wake up to see Ahmed scribble a note and pack the device back into his bag.

Chapter 17
Down Street Cell

London, UK, Present Day

Bakr al-Ahdal had been waiting a long time to start his mission. After all the inactivity and lack of equipment, at least now he had the men he needed. His cell was ready but there had been no instructions or communication for months. Seven months earlier, a man unknown to Bakr had transferred him money and told him the names of the four men who would join him. When Bakr had enquired what he should do after this, he was told sternly to wait and do nothing. But Bakr was impatient. He already had his crude and terrible plan.

Three of those four men were now gathered around Bakr in the dingy room behind the clothes shop in North London. It was 10 am on a dark and rainy Sunday. The low scudding cloud combined with the dirty windows gave the impression of night-time; the only illumination being the dusty fluorescent tube.

'Where is Mohammed?' Bakr demanded.

Jamal looked at the other two and answered, 'He says he didn't want to drive, so can we pick him up?'

'PICK HIM UP?' Bakr roared.

'He has a new car and doesn't want to leave it here.'

Bakr shook his head with disbelief. 'THIS is *not* a picnic trip!'

'He also said it would be unwise,' Jamal continued, 'because of CCTV.'

Bakr knew that Mohammed was right. London was now the most monitored city in the world. Every major route was surveyed twenty-four hours a day. It was almost impossible to go anywhere without being recorded. Every vehicle entering the city was automatically scanned, the ANPR system linking the registration plate to each owner. Theoretically, any suspect vehicle could be spotted, but Bakr did not know how quick the police reaction would be. Still,

Bakr had decided not to take any chances. Mohammed's excuse was the very reason why he had devised a simple system to cover their trail.

'So, where do we pick him up?' Bakr was still fuming.

'He said here,' Jamal said passing over a small scrap of paper.

'Where is this?'

Jamal was on his phone. 'It's near Baker Street station. Mohammed is getting the underground there.'

Bakr snatched the phone from Jamal and stared at the screen. He hit the direction button. This seemed to calm him. The pickup point was not too much of a deviation.

'OK,' Bakr said, 'we go now. We collect Mohammed, then stop to change the plates. I have found a good location near Kings Cross.'

He began passing out the contents of the black plastic bags that had been stacked in the corner. First, he tossed some grubby high-visibility jackets on the floor and then handed each man a dark, oily overall. 'Look, my brothers, there are the boots; you should be able to find a pair to fit you. Hurry! I want to be there by midday. Here, Abdul, take these for Mohammed.'

Abdul quizzed Bakr, 'Why do we have to change the plates again?'

Neither Abdul, Jamal nor Bekkali, had ever been to England before and would be lost without him. Bakr enjoyed the stature he gained from his local knowledge.

'Although we have fake plates on the van, we need to keep the police from following our trail. Once we have the new set on, this will break the link to North London. Also, these plates are the same as an identical London Transport van, so it will not be suspicious.'

Within minutes, the men were throwing their hi-vis jackets in the back of the Ford Transit. Abdul clambered in first. Bekkali, a tall, athletic-looking man, slid a toolbox into the rear, climbed in, and slammed the back doors shut. Bakr stood by the gate and beckoned to Jamal to drive the van out into the litter-strewn street.

They spotted Mohammed easily enough. He had chosen a quiet back street near Baker Street station. Mohammed joined Abdul and Bekkali in the rear of the van, shook their hands then began putting on his overalls and boots. Soon they were on Marylebone Road heading past Regents Park.

Bakr turned to Mohammed. 'When I say we meet *together*, I mean we *meet together*. Don't do that kind of thing again!'

Mohammed had not expected such a welcome and looked at Abdul and Bekkali. They simply stared back. 'I'm sorry,' he blurted. 'I won't let you down.'

Eighteen minutes later, Jamal backed the van against the wall in the deserted street. Young Abdul scrabbled over the big flexible pipes strewn in the back of the van and opened the rear doors. Within seconds he had ripped the old number plate from the Velcro holding it in place and replaced it with the new one. Next, he ran around the front and, quickly checking the street, swapped the front plate in the same manner.

Bakr was nervous, 'Quick, all of you, put on the hats, jackets, and gloves, it will look better. Jamal, move over! I will drive now.'

Soon they were passing Marble Arch and heading south on Park Lane. Bakr knew this area well, but the others were fascinated. Young Abdul called from the back of the van, 'There's a police car coming!'

Bakr had already heard the siren and could now see the flashing blue lights in his mirror. He relaxed when the dark blue unmarked car passed them in the bus lane. At Hyde Park Corner, Bakr turned onto Piccadilly. After a few metres, he took a left turn and slowed.

'This is it.' Bakr exclaimed, pointing at the entrance to Down Street. The ruby-red bricked building, which was once a tube station, was obvious. Part of the façade had been converted into a newsagent since the station's closure, but to the left was a wooden door, which still provided access to the ghostly station.

Bakr had discovered the abandoned tube station by accident, just the previous month. Walking by, he could not fail to recognise what it was. After quick research on the internet, Bakr confirmed that it was possible to descend into the system and that the old station lay almost exactly halfway between Green Park and Hyde Park Corner. Winston Churchill and his Cabinet even used the station as a safe conference centre during the Blitz.

Ventilation of London Underground's vast single-track tube tunnel network has largely been achieved by the piston effect of trains moving the air. This still provides a basis for achieving a considerable level of air movement within the network, as, without this, travel would be unbearable. Bakr understood this well and knew it would be a key element of his plan.

Bakr's men wasted no time erecting the red and white pedestrian barriers. The newsagent was closed and Bakr had previously established that there were no CCTV cameras in the immediate vicinity. Everything looked ordinary, and the occasional pedestrians passing by, hardly cast a glance in their direction.

Mohammed lifted the heavy-duty power drill to the wooden door and within twenty seconds had broken the lock. The moment the door was opened, Mohammed was nearly blown off his feet with the force of the draft from the trains down below.

Bakr raised a smile, 'This is perfect! Quick hurry, get the piping.'

Mohammed, Bekkali, and the others calmly gathered the lengths of corrugated piping that, once connected, would descend over one hundred and twenty metres into the depths of the abandoned station.

Bakr walked down a narrow flight of steps and arrived at the top of the original spiral staircase. There were over one hundred steps down through the twenty-one-metre shaft. He continued down a passageway. The loud noise of passing trains felt alien to him; unlike a normal tube station, with the sound of screeching brakes, the trains were simply hurtling past on the tracks down below at full speed.

Bakr continued over the sealed bridge that spanned the Piccadilly Line and shone his torch down a short staircase to the old platform. Apart from a dozen or so grills and a locked door, the platform was completely bricked up. As the next train thundered by, Bakr choked on the dust that was forced through the open grills by the pressure wave. As the noise of the train subsided, Bakr was aware that the pressure effect was being reversed. The grills whistled with the sound of the air being sucked back down the abandoned lift shafts and rushing out into the tunnel. He turned and sprinted back up the stairs to the sealed bridge. As he turned the corner, he could see the beams from the torches of Mohammed, Bekkali, and Abdul gyrating as they wrestled with the cumbersome piping. 'How much more is left?' shouted Bakr.

'Only two more lengths!' replied Mohammed.

Bakr knew this would not reach the old platform so he ran up to join them. Together they rushed to connect the last two sections, taking them to the middle of the bridge. Bakr's heart started pumping; he knew he had miscalculated the length of piping needed. They had already been inside the abandoned station for too long and at any time someone may become suspicious.

Mohammed and Abdul were now just staring at the end of the pipe. Bakr knew he had to act decisively but was perturbed by the wall around the bridge and its appearance of strength. Still, there was no choice, he thought, but to break through the smooth old tiles and the layer of bricks that separated them from the track below.

'Abdul, run and get a hammer and chisel, quickly! Make sure you bring the heavy hammer as well and the power drill,' commanded Bakr. 'It's OK Mohammed,' he continued. 'We will smash through the tiles and remove some bricks as soon as Abdul returns. I am sure there will only be two or three layers.'

Bakr was reassured to have Mohammed. At over six feet tall and weighing well over one hundred kilos, Mohammed could cope with this minor obstacle easily.

With great force, Mohammed smashed the hammer into the tiles but with virtually no effect, apart from a few splinters, which fell to the ground.

'Wait, take the smaller hammer, and use the chisel. We must remain calm,' said Bakr in a reassuring manner.

It took Mohammed ten minutes of toil to remove the tiles from a small section. By now sweat was running from his brow. Even though it was March, the tube system was warm and humid.

Bakr pushed Mohammed aside and, taking the large power drill, began drilling through the exposed and crumbling brickwork. He was right: after thirty seconds he felt the drill piece break through the final layer. After drilling another twenty holes Bakr stepped aside, leaving Mohammed to carefully remove the bricks and place them on the ground.

As they peered through the hole into the gloom, they heard the growing rush of an approaching train. Air then suddenly blasted through the hole, blowing brick and cement dust into their eyes. Ten seconds later the train had rumbled under their feet, and again the process was reversed: the train now sucking the air behind it and causing a ghostly whistle in the lifts and grills.

Bakr took the pipe and forced it into the small opening they had made. As an added precaution he stacked the loose bricks around the pipe, holding it firmly in place.

When they eventually emerged on the quiet street, Jamal had long since cut a neat hole at the bottom of the door and had glued the circular section back in place. He pointed to his handiwork. 'Look Bakr, the hole is ready. If you push it gently, the glue will break.'

Bakr pulled the door closed and then with a single blow from the hammer sealed it shut with a nail. Looking at the others he announced in a quiet tone, 'Brothers, we have a long night ahead and this will be the hardest part. Our preparations are made, so I know we will succeed. But this is just the beginning and you must remain calm. Now we will rest, as we start again at 4.00 a.m.'

Chapter 18
The Mountains of Holy Light

Nur Mountains, NW of Antakya, Turkey, Present Day

Eight minutes after leaving the helipad on the *Marid*, the ACH145 helicopter was now speeding low over the mountains of Southern Turkey, north of the Syrian border.

'We're approaching the coordinates, Your Highness,' reported the pilot.

Prince Al-Musan, upfront in the co-pilot seat, hollered over his headset, 'Look for the river, and land us there.'

'Roger, Your Highness,' the pilot replied.

The prince turned to address those seated in the rear. He had bought the helicopter with the maximum seat configuration. All seven of the rear seats were occupied by crew from his yacht.

'Soon you will understand the importance of this mission. One day, you will tell your grandchildren "I was with Prince Al-Musan in the Nur Mountains." In Turkey, the mountains are called the Nur Daglari. Nur Daglari means Mountains of Holy Light. You would not believe how appropriate that name is.' The prince removed his sunglasses and looked forward. This was the culmination of years of his research. There! That's our destination. Mount Amanus.' He continued with undisguised enthusiasm. 'Mount Amanus has had many names. In the Middle Ages, writers called it the Black Mountain. With so many Christian monasteries and hermits in these parts, the Turks called it the Mount of Infidels. We call it Jabal al-Lukkam. What we seek lies there, hidden by a wise man disguised as a monk during the siege of Antioch over nine hundred years ago.'

The helicopter, heading towards the rising sun, then slowed and banked to the left. Everyone on board turned their heads to look. The mountains were peppered with rocks and sparse vegetation with no obvious place to land.

'I can see our landing site, Your Highness. The dried-up river. Just as you said.'

The helicopter came to rest on a wide, pebble-strewn area, its rotors still running; all but the pilot disembarked. Two aluminium flight cases and several rucksacks were removed and stacked on the beach. The prince raised a hand to the pilot, who ascended and flew off back to the yacht.

The prince took out a radio. 'Papa Zero Two this is Papa Zero One. Comms check. Do you read? Over.'

'Roger, Papa Zero One, loud and clear. Will rendezvous with you as planned. Papa Zero Two out.'

'Roger and out.'

The prince's men stood ready for instructions.

The prince took out a tablet PC and studied the screen's contents for a few seconds and looked up. 'Up there! You two, come with me. Bring that flight case. The rest of you stay here. We'll be back soon.'

The prince pointed towards a steep slope and led the way. The sun had risen over a mountain to their right, and so had the temperature. The three men covered the ground steadily, stepping around the scrub as they climbed. The prince strode ahead, eager to reach his goal. Everything he had discovered, the historical texts, the diagrams, the myths, they all pointed to this location. *I must be right*, he thought.

The prince reached a level area and looked back down. The two men were not far behind. The others were sitting on the pebbles by the river.

'Binoculars,' the prince commanded, holding out his hand. The prince peered through them, scanning the mountain on the opposite side of the valley. *Nothing. Maybe I need to go higher*, he thought and continued.

Fifty metres further up the prince spotted a large, flat rock. His pulse quickened. This looked more likely. The place all those years ago where the old sage had stopped to help others locate the hiding place. It was the only large rock he could see. When he reached the slab, the prince viewed the mountain opposite once again. He did not need the binoculars this time. There it was: the monastery, albeit a ruin. And yet, there it was, almost one thousand years later. He looked again, this time to the left. And there, hidden from view lower down the slope but visible now, was the mountain with the three peaks.

'Yes! Allah is great!'

The two men of his forward team had again caught up. Neither had any idea why they were halfway up a mountain in Turkey. On the tablet PC, the prince loaded a map of the night sky. Rotating on the spot, he raised the tablet, before settling on a position.

'This,' he said, 'is the night sky in this location around sunset on June 16th, 1098, two days after the siege of Antioch had ended. Jupiter and Uranus were in conjunction and the brightest objects in the sky. Right…there,' he said, pointing ahead. 'I have the three coordinates!'

The men continued to look utterly mystified. They had never seen the prince so animated; so excited. Little did they know, but the prince's research had become his quest. And his quest had become an obsession.

'"*Betwixt the monastery and the middle peak and below the double star*",' the prince quoted under his breath.

During his research, a new volume by the French chronicler, Raymond D'Aguilers, famous for his accounts of the First Crusade, had come to light. It was a chance discovery, and it had been the turning point for Al-Musan. Articles reporting the find hinted at some of its tantalising content: not just accounts of the siege of Antioch, but the mention of a strange event—*Pluie de feu*—rain of fire. The words had jumped out of the page, for these were the words of the myth that had first inspired and more recently consumed Al-Musan. *Here*, Al-Musan had thought, *could be the answers.*

When it was authenticated by experts of the highest authority, it was immediately auctioned, and Al-Musan knew he must have it.

He remembered rebuking himself for not travelling to London himself. *Bidding online—what was I thinking? That was risky and foolish.* And when the manuscripts were his, he wondered why he had despatched and entrusted Hassan to collect them. Instead, he had to wait for his aide to return. It seemed like an eternity.

Pouring through the text all night, he had almost given up hope. But then read the words which, recorded by D'Aguilers, were those of a lowly Turkish soldier. The man described how he and two of his fellow soldiers had provided escort for *Le sage de Damas*—the Sage of Damascus—deep into the mountains, where they helped to secure *Pierres du Ciel*—stones from Heaven. As for the exact location, the soldier had been sworn to secrecy. But the offer of more Byzantine gold coins had swayed him.

Al-Musan's heart had leapt. He had then turned the page. And there, to his utter delight, was a map, what looked like stars, and the words: *Entre le monastère et le pic moyen et sous l'étoile double.*

'Hold this exactly like this,' the prince instructed one of his men. The man dutifully held the tablet aloft at a slight angle, facing out across the valley. The prince positioned himself behind the man and then held out his arms, his right arm pointing to the remains of the monastery, his left to the middle peak of the distant mountain. Drawing his arms together slowly they met in line with the planets on the display. He then lowered his arms down the mountainside opposite. *This is how the old man would have done it*, he supposed. He knew it was an unnecessary gesture since he had the exact location of the two planets, and the hiding would lie directly below. But his vantage point on the mountain was unique. Only here could one see both the monastery and the mountain with three distinct peaks. Still, he derived pleasure in repeating what the sage must have done all those years ago. He regarded it as a form of reverence, an unspoken acknowledgement; one, he believed, that would bring him luck.

The prince swung round. 'Open that one,' he ordered, pointing at the flight case. The prince bent down and took out a theodolite and tripod. He lined it up along the line he had drawn with his arms and peered through the telescopic eyepiece, moving the theodolite slowly up and down.

To one of the men with him, he said, 'I've set the theodolite on the vertical line I'll be following with the rest of the team. You need to tell me if we stray from that line. Just tilt it up and down like this.' The man nodded as the prince handed him a radio. 'We're on channel 2, ok? My handle is Papa. Yours can be Delta. I'll let you know when your job here is done and you can join us.'

Back on the river bank, the prince set off with the rest of the team, this time up the opposite slope. It was steeper and more treacherous.

'Papa, this is Delta, come in. Over.'

'Papa here, go ahead. Over.'

'10 metres to your right. Over.'

The team shifted their angle of ascent.

After twenty minutes of slow, arduous climbing the prince stopped and looked up. There was a sheer rockface. 'Get ready. We may need the ropes.' He then wondered how the old man and soldiers had made it, carrying what they carried. 'No, wait! There must be an easier route. Stay here!' The prince set off further to his right. 'Delta come in. Over.'

'Go ahead Papa. Over.'

'Using your binoculars, can you see an easy way up?'

Delta located the prince easily enough and scanned the slope.

'It's difficult to tell, Your Highness.'

The prince returned to another of the team. 'You, open the flight case.'

Inside the second of the two flight cases was a drone which the prince quickly removed and set into action. The four propellers whirred into life, the motors buzzing like angry wasps. The prince then deftly guided it up and rotated the drone so that its camera pointed at the slope above them. Looking at the screen, he steered the craft up ten metres and across in both directions. He repeated the manoeuvre several times, making methodical sweeps of the steep, rocky slope. On one pass the prince halted the drone. It hovered perfectly about thirty metres to the right of them. He panned the camera to the left and zoomed in. 'There,' he murmured. On the screen, he could make out a dark slit in the rockface. He skilfully repositioned the drone across to the left while simultaneously panning the camera to the right. He could now see his target from directly in front. The slit had disappeared. 'This is it. It must be,' he said, louder this time. 'A cave visible only from the side.'

Ten minutes later the prince and his team had reached a narrow ledge. There was no doubt now. There was the cave.

The prince was the first to slip through. It took a moment for him to adjust to the gloom. The cave floor was relatively flat with a smooth surface peppered with fine rocks. He shone a powerful torch around. *Nothing*, the prince thought. *But this must be the right place.* He took a few steps further in. His men entered and scanned the interior with their torchlights.

'Your Highness, up there!'

The prince turned to see where his man was pointing. 'Yes, I see.' Shining the light upwards, he could see that the slope stopped, separated, it seemed, from the roof of the cave. He clambered up. Yes, there was a hidden area behind the top of the slope. He laid down flat and shone the torch to reveal a sunken space, no bigger than an average room. He scanned the entire area, the torch flitting this way and that. But for a few rocks, it was empty. Nothing was there.

'No. This cannot be. No! NO! NO!'

The prince's cries echoed off the walls of the cave, and he buried his face into his outstretched arm.

Outside, perched on a rock a few metres above the cave, and almost invisible thanks to the small, camouflaged case that contained it, a lens pointed down at the cave entrance. A red light on the rear of the camera had been on since the arrival of the prince and his men. The motion sensor camera was transmitting.

Chapter 19
Thermobaric

North London, UK

In the dimly lit London flat, with its shabby net curtains flapping in the breeze, Bakr and Jamal were sipping tea.

'So, what's the idea?' enquired Jamal.

Bakr leant forward. 'You know what a thermobaric weapon is, Jamal?'

'Yes, the Russians used them in Syria and Ukraine—it's what they call FOAB—the father of all bombs.'

Bakr's expression became stern but showed signs of excitement. 'We will have a really big one…You will see.'

East London, UK

Bakr had surveyed the routes the tankers took from the fuel depot east of London and had now planned the ambush point precisely. This would be the riskiest part of the mission, especially as they were to repeat the same tactic three times.

In the gloom of that Monday morning, the five men approached the deserted junction. Bakr suddenly felt very exposed. Their white Transit van was virtually the only vehicle about. Any police vehicle would surely take an interest in them. Still, Bakr took consolation in the firepower they had and realised they could shoot their way out if necessary.

Crossing through the traffic lights, Bakr drove the van another two hundred metres before pulling into a small parking area. Turning the van back to face the road, Bakr turned off the lights and the engine. He had a clear view five hundred metres to the right, past the drab and decrepit offices lining the street.

Within minutes, their first target could be seen on the slight curve in the distance. Due to the narrowness of the road and the various parked vehicles, the petrol tankers from the depot would be travelling at less than 30 mph. Bakr turned on the engine, nodded to his men in the rear of the van, and pulled slowly out into the street, turning back towards the traffic lights. By now the tanker was closing on the van, but Bakr continued to drive slowly towards the green traffic lights. The tanker's airbrakes hissed as if they were annoyed. Finally, some fifty metres from the junction, the lights turned red and Bakr slowed to a stop. At the same time, Mohammed slid open the side door. All four gunmen jumped out and ran to both sides of the lorry's cab. In a single movement Mohammed jumped up the step pulling open the driver's door and without hesitation blasted the astonished man with his shotgun. In a well-rehearsed manoeuvre, Mohammed then reached for his pistol and at point blank shot the mortally wounded man in his head.

Dragging the dead man from his seat Mohammed lifted him across his shoulder, allowing Jamal to take his place. Within a few seconds, the dead body was in the back of the van and the grim cortege was crossing the lights that had now turned back to green. Jamal watched the white van as it turned right across the junction, disappearing from his sight, before commencing his pre-planned route.

Once again, they waited. But this time they had barely parked before the next tanker appeared. In the back, Abdul was wrapping the corpse in black bin liners and sealing the grisly package with ducting tape. Bakr pulled the van out in front of the second tanker and in the same way crawled slowly towards the green lights. This time the lights were not going to change, so he shouted to the men, 'Open the door, get ready!'

Bakr jammed on the brakes as he approached the defiantly green lights. He could hear the lorry moaning as it came to a sudden halt a few feet behind. The men poured from the van, and once again Mohammed mounted the truck step. But the door would not open. Without hesitation he raised the shotgun and fired through the window, hitting the driver full in the head. This time there would be no need for the pistol. In minutes, Bekkali was driving the second tanker on its way to London, with more than 10,000 litres of petrol in tow.

By the time the third petrol tanker rounded the curve, Bakr, Mohammed, and Abdul had become members of a deadly production line. As Mohammed dumped the third body in the back of the van, Abdul jumped in, too. Then, without even waiting for Mohammed to climb in the tanker, Bakr sped off in the van causing Abdul to fall backwards over the bodies.

Abdul laid the wrapped bodies against the back doors and then checked inside the eight heavy tea chests tied against the inside of the van. The explosives inside them would obliterate the van and its contents from the face of the earth. For good measure, it would also add to the mayhem of that day.

Central London

Jamal was the first to arrive in Piccadilly. He turned the tanker into Down Street, pulled up adjacent to the old station, and jumped out. The area was deserted; the shops would not open for hours. Jamal quickly lifted the pipe from the side of the tanker and proceeded towards the wooden door. Just as he had prepared it, the wooden section fell away easily and he was able to reach through and grab the end of the pipe put in place the previous afternoon. The connection was relatively easy. After checking the connection to the outlets on the tanker, he quickly and deftly climbed on top and opened the first valve. Satisfied that the first fuel compartment was now emptying, he descended the small ladder and went back to the cab. Inside he reached over for the paper rolls, printed boldly with words: HEATING OIL.

By now the petrol was spewing from the pipe onto the quiet eastbound track of the Piccadilly Line. Nearly ten thousand litres had spread onto the tracks by the time Jamal turned his tanker back onto Piccadilly.

Bekkali arrived next and felt nervous. He had not seen any sign of Jamal and everything seemed too quiet. Nevertheless, he jumped swiftly from the cab and over to the wooden door. As agreed, Jamal had replaced the panel and had blocked the pipe on the other side to prevent blowback. This gave Bekkali confidence and he returned to the tanker and proceeded with making the delivery. Just like Jamal, Bekkali took care to apply the HEATING OIL stickers.

With the final tanker, Mohammed was facing the biggest risk and he knew that time was against him, with twenty thousand litres of petrol now evaporating in the tunnel. At any minute the first train would be rushing through and beginning distribution of the inflammable vapour. Bakr had already admitted that he could not predict the outcome, although he understood that effectively they were turning part of the London Underground into a thermobaric bomb. For a moment the savagery of their plan disturbed Mohammed and he tried to imagine what would happen.

Nervously, he connected the pipe from his tanker and on top, he could feel the rush of fuel vibrating beneath him as it began its journey. By the time he was ready to empty the last compartment of the tanker, the street was becoming busy and Mohammed was overwhelmed with panic—no one who knew the area could fail to be suspicious. A passing man stared and Mohammed froze for a second. If he opened the last valve the plan was complete. Mohammed clambered along the tanker and hastily opened the last valve. As he descended, the man looked at Mohammed. 'What the hell are you doing?'

As Mohammed's feet touched the ground, there was the unmistakable smell of petroleum in the air. Despite all the precautions, small amounts had been leaching from the pipes and as the first train passed down below, petrol vapour was being forced back up the shafts.

Mohammed ignored the man and started to walk away. In an instant, his instincts told him to run, and run he did. Mohammed had always been strong and he knew that if he ran he would survive. After a few minutes, he arrived in Grosvenor Square and finally slowed to a walk.

The man in Down Street was certain. For fifteen years he had walked the same route. But this day his suspicions were aroused. For the first time in his life, he dialled 999. 'Hello, police, please…Hello, yes, my name is Foster…I'm in Down Street…No, not Downing Street, Down Street off Piccadilly. There's a petrol tanker here…there's something wrong!'

The police were sensitive these days and no time was wasted despatching a car to investigate. Within minutes, a police car was speeding into Down Street.

Down below, the trains were already thundering along the eastbound line, like massive pistons, pushing and pulling the explosive gas through to Green Park. By now the ventilation shafts up to Down Street Station were acting like valves, releasing the surplus petrol and air mixture each time a train ran through.

As the police officers jumped from the car, the strong odour of petrol was unmistakable. The officers walked briskly towards the petrol tanker and the gesticulating man.

'Can you smell it? It's not heating oil! The guy unloading it, he's run away!'

The sergeant looked confused as he spotted the pipe disappearing through the hole in the wooden door next to the newsagents. Pushing against the sealed door he looked at the man, 'What's behind here, sir?'

The well-dressed man pointed with his umbrella, 'This is the old Down Street tube station. He's put petrol down there! Can't you smell it?'

The young PC managed to kick open the door, releasing a new wave of fumes and the last few litres of fuel, which spewed onto the pavement, contaminating their boots and trousers.

Deep below them, a disaster was brewing. With every train, the petrol fumes mixed with oxygen spread further and by now the passengers at Green Park were clasping their mouths and noses. Bakr had no idea how terrible his plan was. He did know that petroleum had a flashpoint below 21 degrees, well below normal room temperature. He also knew that the London Underground, even in March, was significantly warmer than this and that the evaporation rate would be very high.

Over the passing minutes, the suction effect of successive trains had dragged the fumes further along the eastbound tunnel, reaching as far as the crowded platform at Piccadilly Circus and further to Tottenham Court Road. The network of tunnels connecting the Piccadilly Line to the Bakerloo Line was becoming infected, too. This invisible vapour was seeking out every crevice and spreading like a deadly fog, preparing the thousands of beings in this human anthill for vaporisation.

Even now, as he stared into the void of the stairway that led to the abandoned platforms, the police sergeant failed to understand what was happening. By now he had the taste of petrol in his mouth and was feeling slightly giddy from inhaling the acrid vapour. Another passing train forced a new blast of fumes through the open doorway.

The sergeant desperately tried to recall his training for this situation. *First, eliminate all sources of ignition and then ventilate the area*, he remembered. With this sudden realisation, he grabbed at his radio.

'For God's sake, stop the trains! Shut off the power!'

Just as the emergency room operator got the message, a tube train began pulling out of Green Park station. Inside the train were people from all walks of life, each with their own particular mission. The little wheels screeched and occasionally there was a bright spark caused by intermittent electrical contact on the rail. Like a fairground ghost train, the fully laden carriages squeaked and groaned, part of a giant procession of mechanical caterpillars, worming their way underneath the city.

Ignition was inevitable. The explosion accelerated, spreading through the labyrinth of tunnels leading to dozens more stations. Pumped along by the moving trains, the petrol vapour had penetrated the nooks and crannies along the tracks. Almost like a small tactical nuclear weapon, the fireball was at over 2,500 Celsius, racing through the tunnels at blinding speed.

Two young women had just emerged from the busy Covent Garden Station and were visibly excited by the prospect of their day out. Their happy chatter was soon interrupted when the blonde exclaimed, 'My God, can you hear that…?'

The two women and the mass of people around were all frozen in astonishment at the sound of rolling thunder. A few of the crowd looked up at the buildings and skyward, but most were simply transfixed. None had any idea that the deep rumble was a fireball and pressure wave, rocketing along the tunnels.

For a moment the other woman had paused…she could not think. Let's go!' she then snapped.

Instinctively, they began walking away through the static group of people around them. It seemed the crowd had now morphed into actual 'living statue' entertainers—just like the ones to be seen everywhere in Covent Garden.

Seconds later they were mowed down as a tremendous pressure wave spurted out debris and super-heated vapour up from the tube—the station entrance now indistinguishable from the mouth of some mythical monster.

The original ignition point was at Green Park station. In seconds the roaring blast wave had fanned out. Spurting from entrances, ventilation shafts, and manhole covers along the network of lines.

Down below, in the spider's web of tunnels, the effect of the fireball was terrible. Those not killed by the blast or incinerated would fall victim to the rarefaction of the atmosphere. Thermobaric devices create a vacuum that sucks in all the oxygen, rupturing the lungs.

By now more than five hundred trains were travelling the underground with thousands of people in the entire network. Almost everyone above ground in central London could hear and feel the deep rumble of the event. Politicians in the Commons Chamber at Westminster were momentarily silenced, some jumping up from their benches in alarm. Pedestrians and shoppers froze. No one had experienced anything like it. Not knowing if it was the start of something worse made it all the more terrifying.

Many began to realise that something dreadful was happening. Some unseen and unknown horror.

Chapter 20
Overtime

SO15, Counter Terrorism, Metropolitan Police, London, UK

It was 1.37 a.m. Detective Inspector Steven Jubb was sitting at his desk, his face illuminated by three computer screens. He had called it a night at around 11 p.m., and had started to drive home, but had then rung his wife to say that he had been called back in. He had not. But he knew he could get away with it. Claire was used to it.

Steve had only been with SO15, the specialist counter-terrorism branch of London's Metropolitan Police, for eight months, and had been called in on numerous occasions. *Claire, you don't want to know the kind of shit that's going on every day*, he had said to her just one day into his new job. *We've got about half a dozen real threats and about a hundred and fifty active suspects up and down the country.*

Claire guessed he would be up to his neck in it, especially when something as big as the recent attack had taken place. 'Yeh, of course, honey. What time will you be back?'

Steve knew that her question was just part of the drill. She did not expect a real answer. His work would always be shrouded in secrecy.

Jubb was one of the many SO15 officers tasked with tracking down the terrorists behind the tube attack. None of it followed the usual pattern. It was devastating...ingenious. The entire team was convinced that it would be looking for brand-new suspects. The extreme right had been ruled out; so, too, the growing number of environmental activist groups. The assumption at this stage—and it was a big one—was that the perpetrators had to be jihadists.

Jubb's boss had sent him and eighteen others home, leaving around twelve of the team to work through the night. But he simply could not resist the excitement—the thrill of the chase. *This is the best bloody job in the world*, he thought.

Jubb made a series of mouse clicks, sighed, looked at the wall clock, and leant back in the chair. He was living off adrenalin, caffeine, an e-cigarette, and a pack of chocolate digestives. He took a drag from his fake cigarette and picked up his phone. 'Sir, what have we got on those tankers?… Yeh, I know… Claire's fine about it… Well, I just… Great, I'll see you in a min.'

DCI John Mason was the senior officer on duty that night. He was in the main operations rooms with four of the team, Simon Cummings, Troy Taylor, Jenny McKenzie, and Bill Jacobs.

'Here he is. Alright, Steve? You creeping up to headmaster again?' Cummings teased.

Jubb smirked.

'Steve, I'll give you thirty minutes on this then you're getting some shut-eye,' said Mason. 'Dyer's expecting you back on at 8.'

'Sorry, sir.'

'Anyway, why the tankers? We've got nothing to go on. One of them ended up on the roof of the apartments opposite. No prints and no DNA except for the known tanker drivers, and they're all dead. The other two tankers were blown to kingdom come on the Edgware Road.'

'Well, they travelled the furthest, so there must be a ton of CCTV.'

'There is and we've trawled it all—from the oil depot and through town,' said Taylor. 'The A1090, the 1306, the A13. I know all the bloody roads by name. Zilch.'

'What about the oil depot itself? Do they have cameras?' asked Jubb.

Taylor frowned and swung around to his PC. 'Let me check who's on that.'

'Steve, I'd be surprised if "Ahmed" and any of his *Middle Eastender* mates had overlooked anything that obvious,' said Mason.

Middle Eastenders, as the team flippantly liked to refer to them, applied to home-grown terrorists and was a play on the name of the long-running TV soap opera. It seemed particularly apt on this occasion, given that the tankers were hijacked just east of London.

Mason continued, 'We're assuming the van we found contained the three charred bodies of the tanker drivers. It's not every day a Transit van lights up the sky and wakes up half of Thurrock. I refuse to call these guys pro, but they're bloody cautious.'

'Matty and Jake visited the oil depot two days ago,' Taylor said, staring at his screen. 'Er, names of drivers, reg plates, times of departure, destinations…shit, 10,000 litres of fuel each. Nope, I can't see anything about CCTV. Oh, security gate guy saw all three out. He says they simply drove off. Nothing out of the ordinary.'

'Steve, I appreciate your enthusiasm. But this isn't helping,' said Mason. 'We're jumping around here on a whim of yours. There's structure to what we're doing. You've got square eyes. I think you need to get that sleep. In fact, I'm ordering you to.'

'Yeh, you're right, sir.'

Mason *was* right. Jubb suddenly felt tired and headed straight for one of the dedicated, windowless lounges, to kip down and get a reasonable shut-eye.

As Jubb lay in the semi-darkness his mind ran over the sequence of events. They had no more witnesses. A passer-by had called the police. The sergeant had raised the alarm. The operator only heard him blurt out: *For god's sake, stop the trains!* before the police officer along with his colleague fell victim to the conflagration. There were remnants of piping that had been laid from the old station entrance. They must have been laid before the tankers arrived, allowing the terrorists to quickly connect up each tanker in turn and deposit its contents.

They had CCTV from Park Lane of various vans entering Down Street the day before. One had false plates, so it was pretty clear that this was the fake workmen's van. Members of the public had seen workers outside the station the day before the attack but took no real notice. But that made sense; they were just workers with piping. On the day of the attack, there were three tankers. Two had been driven off and blown up; the third—what was left of it—had been left at the scene. Presumably, the terrorists would have known, or at least hoped, it would have been destroyed, so had not bothered to drive it off.

Jubb pondered for a moment. *They hadn't bothered to drive it off. So…did the second tanker wait to take the third driver…or…did the third driver take off on foot? If the first tanker had already gone, that would mean two tankers in a tiny street in the heart of London. That would look suspicious. If he was the last one there, maybe he was spooked…spooked by the passer-by.*

Jubb sat bolt upright. 'Shit! What if the last guy simply ran off?'

It was 4.14 a.m. Steve Jubb was back at his desk. He had been pouring over CCTV from the streets surrounding Down Street. Fortunately, there were relatively few pedestrians in this part of Mayfair. When, suddenly, there he was: a man running full pelt. An Arabic-looking man at that. He checked the time from the camera: 17 minutes before the explosion. Judd's heart raced. 17 minutes before? *Why not*, Judd thought. *He's left the tanker, the petrol is still pouring into the station, the fumes would take some time to spread down the line…then a spark and boom!* 'Yes! You bastard. I've got you now, matey,' Judd murmured and clenched his fist.

He pulled up a map on his second monitor. The footage only showed the man running away from the camera on Curzon Street then turning sharp right.

'Now, where are you going? South Audley Street.'

Jubb pulled up a series of CCTV and webcam options. After a few minutes, he had his man back on the screen. The image was perfect. The man was walking now. Jubb was smiling and picking up the phone. 'Dave, it's Steve. Yeh, this is your early morning call. Listen, I've got a little video work for you. I'm sending you the link right now.'

Jubb hung up and stared at the screen then at the clock. It was now 4.32 a.m. He could not think of sleep now, but he knew he should. *Dave won't need too long*, he thought. *I'll grab an hour's kip.*

Back in his sleeping bag, Jubb felt wide awake. But four minutes later, he was in a deep, exhausted slumber.

Chapter 21
Grey Days

MI6, SIS Building, Central London, UK

Outside was another dull day.

Sir George Bradbury looked out from his seventh-floor window and surveyed the early morning traffic as it slipped past under the colourless March sky; the buildings opposite were gleaming with cool silvers, whites, and greys. The entire scene was almost entirely monochrome.

Bradbury's mobile rang. He looked at the screen, took one deep breath, and answered, 'Prime Minister.'

'Good morning, George.'

'Yes, good morning, sir.'

'I've just been speaking with Janet. She's been on the blower with Edgerton over at 5. Seems this could be international. What's your take?'

'Well, with all due respect, sir, that's MI5's way of saying they had no previous intelligence of such an attack. So, yes, it could be international, or a mix of foreign and home-grown terrorists. As you know, there's been precious little to go on. We are aware of several active cells across Europe that could coordinate something like this. But it would be a first. I'm planning more meetings with the French, Germans, Dutch, and Americans. But, and I'm sorry to have to say this, we really could do with more data.'

'You're right, George. SO15 are still trawling CCTV. GCHQ are doing their bit. I hope to God someone finds something and bloody soon. So, it's all "hands

on deck" with this one. Find who did this. Find them quickly. Use whatever means you must, but just do it.'

The call ended and Bradbury looked once more at the grey scene below. He knew he was facing the most demanding task of his life. An order from the PM himself came as no real surprise; after all, Bradbury was the head of the UK's foreign intelligence service, and to find who was behind the vicious and deadly attack did indeed mean all "hands on deck". *Find who did this. Find them quickly. Use whatever means you must, but just do it. Shit! This was it. How long had he aspired to be in this position—head of MI6? You have the top job because you're brilliant. But now you really are on your own. In the hot seat. The buck stops with you, old chap.*

The reality, he knew, was slightly different. The real pressure would be on MI5, CTC, and the plethora of partner agencies tasked with detecting and disrupting terrorist activities across the United Kingdom. Bradbury's task would be to coordinate with his overseas counterparts. But right now, he knew that the starting point was little more than a blank page.

He also knew that the drab weather affected his mood. It always did, as it prompted one dreadfully sad memory.

For the twelve-year-old George Bradbury, born and raised in leafy Surrey, his diplomat father's posting to Kenya was his first feeling of instability in his young years. His mother tried to console him, saying that he would look back and see the move as a positive in his life. But Bradbury was angry and had run to his room, throwing himself on his bed where he bawled his eyes out.

She was right, of course. Mothers most usually are. Arriving in East Africa soon turned into an adventure. He quickly made new friends in the close-knit English community with its small church that he, his parents and, it seemed, the entire population of the small town attended. Their home was a massive, rambling, colonial house, complete with manicured lawns and large established trees. It was a piece of England, except tended by gardeners and cleaned by servants. He rose to become the star pupil at his well-funded and innovative school.

George Bradbury had not only been happy in that foreign land; he was now relishing it.

The move, though, was soon to tear his life apart in more ways than one.

It was on a long-awaited school trip to Tanzania when George had been taken to one side. His headmaster's expression that fateful Sunday was one the young Bradbury would never forget. His town church, the place he loved to enter for its sanctity and calm, had been the target of a terror attack.

His parents had not survived.

George Bradbury's world had been ripped apart in a second.

Four days later he was met at Heathrow by his aunt and uncle, and an unwelcoming grey sky.

Chapter 22
The Journalist

Daniel's Villa, Tanneron, Southern France

'You have a nice place, Doctor.'

Isabelle Deboeuf stood on the veranda of Daniel Bayford's villa, looking out over the rolling hills. Somewhere amongst the mimosa, pine, and olive trees, unseen cicadas made their presence known with their loud, incessant chirping. She breathed in the mix of herbal scents of the warm, early spring air. Paris and her office at *Le Figaro* felt like a million miles away, she thought, as she turned and smiled at Daniel.

'I like the quiet. Well, at least the lack of human noise,' he said, as a nearby cicada added to the bug cacophony.

'Where was the fire?' The young journalist asked, taking out a notepad and pen from her satchel.

'Behind us. Just north of here. I can show you on a map...' Daniel pulled out his mobile and soon had their environs displayed in satellite mode. 'From here to here and across this valley here.'

'Wow, that's a big area. And this was August last year, right?'

'Yes.'

'You've been a fire watch for many years, yes?'

'Yes, this will be my fourth year. But it's not a pastime. It's part-time seasonal work. There are three of us that share the responsibility. The rest of the time, I do academic work.' Daniel did not want to come across as an eccentric; not if the theory that he wanted to share was to be given any credence.

'Indeed. You are a doctor of er...meteorology,' she began, looking at her notes.

'Yes. Us Brits are obsessed with the weather.'

'How appropriate. I take it that global warming has contributed to the increase in fires here?'

'Well, fires are a common occurrence in these parts and have been for decades, if not centuries.'

'You're not a climate change sceptic, are you, Doctor?'

Daniel was about to reply when a male voice behind him made him look up. A slim, bearded man of around thirty years had concluded his phone call and was looking at Daniel. '*Bonjour, ça va?*' he asked cheerfully.

'Ah, this is Romain, my photographer,' Deboeuf said.

'*Bonjour,*' Daniel said, nodding at the new arrival somewhat disapprovingly; disappointed that his interview with the rather pretty young lady was now less intimate.

'Are you OK if I…?' Romain finished his question by holding up one of his cameras.

'Sure.'

'Sorry, I should have told you,' Deboeuf said, sensing Daniel's irritation at the rude interruption. 'Where was I?' she continued, as the photographer began taking shots of Daniel.

'Climate change.'

'Yes, thank you.'

'No, I'm no sceptic.'

'I understand you worked for the British government before retiring here.'

Daniel paused, taking in the journalist's dark, shoulder-length hair and brown eyes. 'As a scientist, yes.' He wondered how deep the journalist had delved into his past.

'As I mentioned when I called you, we're running a series of articles on climate change and its effects on France. Was climate change part of your brief for the British government?'

'No, that was not on the agenda back then. And please don't confuse meteorology with climatology. Put simply, one is short-term, the other long-term.'

Deboeuf looked up from her notes. 'Of course. So, what did governments want with meteorologists back then…twenty-five years ago?'

Probing question, Daniel thought. 'Oh, boring stuff really. Likelihood of floods, heavy snow, and ice. That kind of thing. Look, I know your brief is about climate change, so why did you agree to see me?'

95

'I'm curious, Doctor.'

'Please, call me Daniel. I don't feel like a doctor of science these days. Not here.'

Romain was checking his camera. Satisfied, he pointed, as if to indicate his intention to take some shots of the surroundings. Daniel nodded and Romain set off along the veranda.

'But you are well qualified,' she said. 'And your story sounded interesting.'

'Well, I hope your bosses at Le Figaro agree.'

'Enough to put me and Romain on a flight to Nice to see you.'

'True,' Daniel nodded his approval. 'I'm sorry, I'm being rude. I promised to get you a drink.'

'No problem. Coffee and water would be great.'

Deboeuf followed Daniel into the kitchen and perched herself on the large table in the centre of the room. Daniel could not fail to notice her hitching her skirt slightly, and found it quite erotic. *Wow! French women,* he thought, *there's something about them.*

She was looking up. Above her, a large selection of pans and cooking utensils hung from an old wooden rack. 'I see you like cooking.'

Daniel looked away suddenly when Deboeuf returned her gaze. *Shit! Had she seen him looking at her legs?* he wondered. *Probably! What a jerk!* 'I love food,' he said. 'One of the reasons I moved to France. I'm still learning, though. You're welcome to stay for lunch. I don't have much in, but I'll try not to embarrass myself—or the English nation. Any allergies or dislikes?'

'*Non! J'aime n'importe quoi.* I'm sorry, anything is good, thank you, Daniel.

'If you'd prefer to speak French, that's fine by me. We English are so lazy, and I need to improve.'

'No, it is I who needs to improve. Your French is excellent. I saw that interview you had with the local TV station.'

'There you go,' Daniel said, placing coffee and water next to her. 'Now, let me show you why I think you'll not regret coming all this way. Please,' he said, offering up a chair.

Daniel placed a laptop in front of the journalist.

'My lab is small and stuffy and a bit of a trek from here, so I made this video.' He pressed play.

Daniel had provided a live commentary. Deboeuf watched and listened intently.

"*So, here we have the meteorite.*"

What Deboeuf could make out was not what she had expected. This was no brightly lit, tidy, and sterile laboratory but a small, dim room—cluttered with scientific paraphernalia, books, and papers. The image though was dominated by the two spheres of Daniel's Van Der Graaf generator, which sat on a table in the middle of the room; in the foreground, held in mid-air by a clamp, was the meteorite. The image zoomed in on the rock, long enough for the viewer to take in its gleaming azure blue. The image then zoomed out and Daniel appeared on screen walking towards the table beyond.

"*And here, a Van de Graaf generator. It's an old manual one, as you can see.*"

The video showed Daniel hand-winding the device. A whirring, light, gear-cranking sound could be heard getting faster and faster.

"*And now, we create a spark.*"

Deboeuf expected to see a short spark between the two spheres, but instead, the meteorite in the lower half of the screen flashed intensely, the spark making a sharp, loud crack, causing the journalist to recoil slightly.

'Wow!' she exclaimed.

The commentary continued. "*As you can see, the spark did not jump between the spheres like everyone familiar with this apparatus would expect. Instead, it jumped more than two metres to the meteorite!*"

The journalist looked up at Daniel.

'Wait, it gets better,' he said nodding towards the screen.

In the video, Daniel could be seen walking back towards the camera. The image zoomed in again on the meteorite. The auto-focus settled quickly—the stone now filling the screen. Deboeuf squinted. Small fine filaments of light could be seen dancing within the stone.

"*A most fascinating phenomenon, I think you'd agree,*" Daniel's commentary announced in a quiet yet dramatic voice.

Deboeuf watched, clearly fascinated. 'Quite beautiful and *very* strange,' she said finally after the video had ended. 'How long did it last?'

'Typically, eight minutes. But I have no idea if the energy dissipates, or if it's retained and simply invisible. Mademoiselle, this is beyond our current science.'

The journalist sat staring at Daniel. 'It certainly is. This is…amazing.'

'You see. If the stone can do this with a small spark, could it do the same with lightning?'

'And cause a fire.'

'Yes, but that's not the important thing. This could be a new mineral, a new element. Who knows what it may help us do.'

'A brand-new discovery.'

'I think you people call it a world first.'

'Daniel, show me this lab of yours. I need to see this first-hand. And show me where you found the stone.'

Daniel looked down at Deboeuf's shoes. She followed his gaze. 'They'll do,' he said.

Chapter 23
The Lost World

Central Venezuela

The open truck bearing its load of ranch hands bumped and rattled its way to some unseen destination. The men on board sat hunched on the slatted benches, their heads nodding in unison as the truck dipped a wheel into another pothole puddle. To the right of the vehicle and parallel to the muddy track was the majestic *Orinoco*—South America's second-longest river. Easily outrunning the truck, the river glided past on its seemingly eternal, two-thousand-two-hundred-kilometre adventure.

From nowhere the black helicopter roared close over the truck, startling its occupants; the thumping beat of the Piasecki's blades had been masked by the *Orinoco's* rumble until the machine was practically above them. The helicopter swooped low, briefly following the course of the river, before banking confidently up and away to the right, the sunlight glinting momentarily across its underbelly, as it turned towards the distant highlands.

Richard Ordway gripped the strap by his seat and peered out of his window at the mighty waterway, just before the pilot lurched the aircraft onto its new course. Ordway had travelled all too many times in this style, but he still managed to raise his eyebrows at the pilot's stomach-churning manoeuvres.

He grabbed a headset and, cupping one of the earpieces to his ear, barked into the microphone: 'How much further?'

'About 100 clicks, sir,' the US Navy pilot replied. 'You can see the start of the Guiana Highlands up ahead.'

Ordway spotted the dramatic plateaux rising like a scene from *The Lost World*. His lips formed a faint smile, as he gazed at the landscape rushing below. He grabbed the pilot's map and began tracing their route. The *Orinoco* was the clearest feature. Ordway ran his finger upstream from their current location, back hundreds of kilometres up into the Guiana Highlands, back to the point where, early in the *Orinoco*'s life, part of its flow splits along the *Casiquiare* to help feed the *Rio Negro* and the mighty *Amazon* herself. He then ran his finger forward, downstream, following the greater part of the *Orinoco*, northbound along two hundred and fifty kilometres of Columbian border, then north and eastwards where the river skirts the *Gran Sabana* massif at their point of crossing—the river now the confident adult—to where the *Gran Sabana* meets the flat *Orinoco* plains, and finally to its slowing maturity and ultimate death in the Atlantic.

The weather was fine, and the Piasecki chopper had settled once again on a straight and even course. Ordway put down the map and picked up his unfinished coffee. His mind began darting from one thought to another. *Where was he on his river of life? The confident adult?* He was certainly no spring chicken, but he kept himself in shape. *Yes, I'm not slowing*, he reasoned. *I'm still active. I still feel young. I have purpose. I have goals. It's strange*, he thought, *but everyone has his own, unique river.*

He then pondered whether the Arab fundamentalists he had once chased in his eighteen years of CIA service converge in some unifying stream of martyrdom. There was something enticing about following and even dying for a cause. Sharing a common belief and a precise moment of death. It would, after all, be less lonely. Wouldn't it?

He thought about his ex-wife—the woman he'd failed. They had shared a long stretch of water and now those waters had diverged. His move from the CIA to the Department of Defence was the final straw. Still, what a jerk she'd ended up with. *Bet he's never flown in a helicopter across Venezuela.* The smile returned to his lips.

The pilot glanced at the map. Ahead of them, *La Gran Sabana*—the oldest landform on the continent—a gigantic slab of rock covering nearly half of Venezuela. Its cliffs, rising abruptly from the plains, were simply breath-taking.

'Eight hundred metres straight up,' the pilot hollered. And, as if to emphasise the dramatic change in the terrain and the fast-approaching walls of rock, the helicopter started its sharp ascent. The craft soon thundered up over the cliff top and into another world.

A series of plateaux rose above the ancient, green highland. Clouds clung to the sides of the bluffs, at what seemed the perfect height to emphasise the sheer majesty of these tablelands. The sun, still quite low in the sky was now stronger. The horizon in front of them, however, was black. Lightning dissected the sky.

Ordway grabbed the headset again. 'Ever seen *The Lost World*?' he enquired; his southern drawl now quite noticeable. 'When they find a bunch of dinosaurs on a plateau?'

'Can't say I have, sir,' the pilot replied.

'How about you, professor?'

'I'm sorry, what did you say?' Professor Arthur Steel, the only other passenger, looked up from his files and papers towards Ordway.

'I'm talking about the original version, now,' Ordway continued. 'Saw it when I was a kid. Scared the crap out of me.'

'The original was by Conan Doyle, wasn't it Mr. Ordway? Before film was invented.' The professor had been surprised to discover that Ordway would be hitching a lift from Caracas. Steel knew little about Ordway. He had spoken with him on a few occasions but had assumed he was a government suit sitting behind a desk in Washington. He seemed to be holding the purse strings. *Well, if first impressions count*, thought Steel, *I don't like this guy.*

The professor then wondered what Ordway's real involvement was. Was he a government man, or was he more? If he was government, which department? Ordway had been circumspect in all their communications. Steel was happy for it to remain that way; the least they knew of each other the better.

'My God,' Ordway muttered. 'It sure looks prehistoric down there, don't it? A place inhabited by ignorant heathens.'

'Ah now, it's interesting you should say that. Much of the geology below is made up of Precambrian rock, probably half the age of this earth, so more than 2.5 billion years old.'

'Awesome, professor.'

'And nearly all Venezuelans are Roman Catholic, Mr Ordway. Hardly what you call heathen.'

'Even down there?' Ordway asked, looking out the window at the untouched, tropical landscape of trees, rock, and countless streams and rivers.

'Hardly anyone lives this side of the *Orinoco*.'

'I can see why.'

Rain then suddenly pelted the windshield.

Chapter 24
The Embankment

Central London, 11:19 a.m.

It was just over a week since the attack, but the government, police authorities, and all relevant parties involved in the capital's infrastructure had agreed to reopen the Underground network. London had to keep moving. The UK would not yield to terrorism. Extensive security checks had been made. Underground train drivers and staff were put on shorter shifts for their physical and mental well-being. Despite the efforts and increased presence of the police, there was a distinct drop in commuter numbers.

While many of the lines and stations had been unscathed, platforms, passenger tunnels, and escalators had been scrubbed and disinfected. The aim was to freshen up the many miles of passageways and, of course, erase any reminders of the horrific attack. But for many more weeks, the acrid smell still lingered within the Underground train tunnels themselves. It was as though a new pandemic had struck; nearly all passengers wore face masks or would cover their mouths and nose as trains approached the platform. The irony of those tube trains once again acting as pistons, this time pushing a blast of noxious air before them, was not lost on the subterranean commuters.

SO15 team leader, DCI David Pearson, burst out of his office into the main operations room. 'We've got him. He's just exited Embankment tube.'

A radio operative pressed a call button on his console. 'Delta units. Suspect seen exiting Embankment tube station. Repeat, Embankment tube station. Stand by.'

'The bloody nerve,' Pearson murmured. 'Using the Underground, a week after blowing half of it up.' He looked at the massive bank of monitors. 'We need a drone. Get Andover on the line.' And get me feeds from the Embankment area and half a mile in every direction.'

'Sir, you're through.'

'*Colonel Fisher.*'

'Colonel, Dave Pearson, SO15. We need eyes. We're sending coordinates now.'

'*Roger. We're deploying now. Should be there in 7 minutes. You chaps will have control in a mo.*'

'Thank you, Colonel.'

Following the tube attack, the UK security forces were in even closer cooperation. SO15 now had control of one of the army's latest ultra-high-resolution surveillance drones.

Claire Yates, one of the operators called over. 'We're online, sir.' Her screen was showing video of the Berkshire countryside as the drone sped its way to central London.

'Hey Claire, has my wife put the washing out?' one of the team asked jokingly. The men in the room chuckled. Claire looked up from her video screen and raised her eyebrows in mock disdain.

No more than half a mile from Embankment tube station, the two-man SO15 Delta 7 team had pulled over for a coffee break when Control reported the sighting. They had been tasked to patrol the area around Buckingham Palace. A second attack was highly possible. SO15 units had been positioned at key points across the city. Armed police patrolled the key visitor attractions and transport hubs. Additional police officers, having been transferred in from smaller towns across the country, provided a noticeable presence on the pavements in the West End and City. The regular Metropolitan Police had ramped up their beat policing and vehicle patrols, too. The effect was both reassuring and alarming in equal measure.

'Shit, that's us. Go, Phil!'

DS Phil Evans fired up the black, unmarked Jaguar.

'You're gonna have to reverse up, mate,' said his co-driver, DI Rob Villiers. 'It'll be quicker.'

'That's exactly what I was planning to do. Kind of.' He selected gear and with the way clear pulled out, did a one-eighty on the one-way part of Birdcage Walk and headed off at speed. They both knew that this was one of the quietest parts of London in terms of traffic, but luck was not on their side: a black cab was heading straight for them. 'For fuck's sake!' They had not yet switched on the blue lights or siren. The road was wide enough, but the black cab was forced to swerve.

Vehicles slowed and made way for them, but the traffic was building. The traffic lights before Great George Street were red. Phil switched on the siren. Pedestrians crossing the junction jumped back out of harm's way, as Phil carefully negotiated the junction before accelerating.

'Delta 7 entering Bridge Street. There in two minutes,' Rob reported.

'Roger Delta 7. We've deployed a drone, but try and get a visual.'

'Roger that.'

'Christ, that must be the new guy,' Phil said off-air. *'Try and get a visual.* Der, yeh, OK.'

A flurry of messages from SO15 Control and the teams out on patrol came over the radio. Since the attack, all security forces were on the highest alert; ready to pounce at a moment's notice.

'Delta 2 to Golden Jubilee Bridge.'
'Roger, Control.'
'Delta 4 to Control. We're in Parliament Square.'
'Delta 4, South Bank. London Eye pier.'
'Roger, Control. There in 2.'

'This could be it, Phil. Go as slow as you can, and keep your eyes peeled.'

The Jaguar killed the lights and siren as it turned left and entered the flow of traffic along Victoria Embankment. The SO15 officers began scoping the pedestrians.

Mohammed had already exited Embankment tube station. A newspaper advertising board by the entrance displayed the alarming headline: LONDON THREAT LEVEL: CRITICAL. The newspaper vendor, a craggy-faced, white man in his mid-seventies scowled at Mohammad and mumbled under his breath, 'Yeh, probably one of your lot.'

Oblivious of the vendor's racist incrimination, Mohammad stopped momentarily to get his bearings then crossed the road and headed off down the

Embankment towards Westminster Bridge. Up ahead, a coach load of elderly Swedish tourists had started to spill out onto the pavement.

Back in the Jag, Phil and Rob had been scanning the constant stream of pedestrians up and down and on both sides of the busy thoroughfare, as it gently arced following the bend of the Thames.

'He could be heading in any direction,' Rob muttered. He clicked on his radio, 'Delta 7 to Control. Anything from the drone?'

'Negative, Delta 7.'

'What about CCTV?'

'We're still checking.'

Rob cursed under his breath. They were only a few hundred metres from Hungerford Bridge and the Embankment tube station, and there were too many people. 'Pull in behind that coach. He could be walking here right now. We'll give it five minutes then drive back the other way.'

Phil pulled in. Four more tourist coaches were parked on the opposite carriageway. The tree-lined pavement beyond was dotted mostly with sightseers and day-trippers. Delta 7 sat and observed.

'There!' Phil suddenly said.

Rob followed Phil's eyes and soon spotted their target amongst the group of Swedes, now amassed and blocking the broad walkway. Mohammed frowned and pushed his way through them. One old gentleman raised his hand at him after Mohammed had caused the man's wife to stagger forward.

Rob, camera in hand, fired off about twenty zoom shots. Phil then adjusted his side mirror. 'You got him still?' he asked.

'Yep, but I'll lose him in a second behind those other coaches.'

Rob then quickly reviewed the shots on the camera's display. He stopped on frame 5 and zoomed in then compared to the image on the car's computer screen. 'That's him. Let's go. Delta 7 to Control, we have a visual. Victoria Embankment, riverside, heading south towards Big Ben. Pursuing on foot. Over.'

'Roger, Delta 7. You have Delta 4 on the London Eye pier. Delta 2 on Golden Jubilee Bridge. ARVs and more teams are on the way.'

Dave Pearson in the Control room activated his talk button, 'Deploy all surveillance measures. Observe only. Do not apprehend.'

'Yes, sir,' Rob acknowledged.

The men checked their weapons and put on what looked like normal spectacles.

'Phil, you hang back. I'll make sure we don't lose the fucker.' He and Phil then activated the built-in HD cameras in their glasses. 'Control, you getting this?'

'Roger. Have A/V from both of you.'

Back at Control, screens displayed high-definition live feeds from Rob's and Phil's glasses.

As Rob and Phil left the car, Phil mumbled, 'Zoom OK?'

Phil's image back in the control room zoomed in to a shapely young lady walking away from him. It zoomed in again to her backside.

Dave Pearson interjected again, 'Thank you for the demonstration, Philip. Where's our bloody target?'

'We have him, sir. No problem.' Rob quickly picked out Mohammed, who had now appeared from behind the last of the tourist coaches. Rob started pacing down the esplanade. He was about sixty metres behind Mohammed. His video feed had Mohammed filling most of the screen.

'Control to Delta 4. Anything?'

Delta 4 was positioned on the London Eye pier. One of the two-man team was posing as a tourist. His video feed was on another display back at Control. It showed Embankment wall and the tree-lined esplanade, and Mohammed walking from right to left. *'We see the target. A couple and a few individuals are walking towards him. Not much else. Over.'*

'Delta 2 here. Can't see much from this angle. We're heading further out across the bridge.'

Delta 2 was north of the other teams on the southernmost of the two Golden Jubilee Bridges. Today, most pedestrians were making their way from the nearby Charing Cross railway station to the London Eye and other attractions on the South Bank. The plain-clothed SO15 officers headed in the same direction. Soon, they would have a wider view of Victoria Embankment. Even when they stopped and took out binoculars and cameras with powerful zoom lenses, they blended in well; they looked like any other sightseer.

Phil slowed, his mobile was up against his ear. Rob continued down Victoria Embankment and was now past the last of the coaches. He was now forty metres behind their target.

Mohammed looked out across the grey-brown waters of the Thames at the London Eye then looked ahead. There, he thought, that's where Bakr will be. He stopped at a bench and for the first time looked back.

Phil was quick and had stopped, too, leaning casually on the wall, looking out at the river, and making slight gestures with his free hand as though having a meaningful conversation on his mobile. 'Control, give me Rob's feed,' Phil instructed. The video operator back at Control dragged Rob's image onto a smaller image 'Got it, thanks.' An image popped up in Phil's vision as though suspended in the air in front of his eyes. He could even make out Rob's breathing. Phil was now sharing Rob's eyes and ears.

Rob strode on purposefully as though enjoying the walk, gazing now and then across to the London Eye.

The couple that Delta 4 had spotted were now walking right past Mohammed. He glanced at them, turned towards the road then sat on the bench.

Mohammed's mind was jumping back and forth, first to the events of the previous week, which now seemed like a dream; then to his family, and then to the meeting he was about to have with Bakr—a man who inspired him, but who was also tearing him apart. When he first met Bakr, his overriding emotion was excitement. *Finally*, he remembered thinking, *I, Mohammed Faasil, have a purpose in life.*

But now he felt he lacked that determination. Now he wished that his motivation was as great as Bakr's, a man who had seen his entire family wiped from the face of the earth. Bakr was also from another country. That must make it so much easier. The UK was Mohammed's country through and through, born and raised in Hounslow. He had an OK job and had finally scraped enough money together to get his dream car: a Subaru Impreza, even if it was at the expense of living in a damp, two-roomed bedsit.

His thoughts then turned to his family. He had walked out of the family home two years previously, just two weeks after his 18th birthday, and had never returned. They had just finished breakfast when the conversation switched once again to Mohammed. His brother had asked what Mohammed's plans were, now that he had failed to get into Sixth Form. Mohammed was unprepared for an answer. *Indeed, what were his plans?* His father, who had scolded Mohammed for being lazy ever since Mohammed could remember, stood up to leave the table and announced to his mother and brother: *It seems there is no hope for Mohammed. All brawn and no brains.* And then to Mohammed: *When will you sort out your life, Mohammed? Look at your brother. He will be a manager soon. I...* But his voice trailed off and he left the room shaking his head. Mohammed's mother put a hand on her son's arm. *It's alright, Mohammed. Now, help me tidy up.* Mohammed pointed at his brother and bellowed: *WHY DOESN'T HE EVER HELP YOU TIDY UP?* and stormed out of the house.

Mohammed turned round to see if he could see Bakr. He had an overpowering urge to throw himself on the ground and pray. There was no sign of him. *What have I done?* Mohammed thought. *I have no family now. They will disown me.* He looked up and down the walkway—*just ordinary people going about their normal lives. Allah, please help me. Tell me I am right,* he thought.

It was then that he realised that he and Bakr were not dissimilar: he had no family either. Not really. He now shared the same level of despair, the same level of vindication. He was lost, and Bakr had given him direction.

His thoughts turned again to the present and wondered why Bakr wanted to meet. He did not feel nervous about the bombing. *Bakr will be happy with our...success.* Their audacious plan had worked. They were invincible. *Success,* he thought. *My first success!*

Rob was now about twenty metres from Mohammed and closing. He took out his mobile and began thumbing the screen. To any casual observer, this was someone texting. Rob, though, was activating the phone's video. 'Hello, mate. How are you?' Rob began a pretend conversation. 'Yeh, I'm good, thanks. So, how was the holiday?... Nice.'

Hovering high over the noisy Victoria Embankment Road, the drone was now streaming a grandstand view of the operation. As soon as the target had taken a seat, Dave Pearson started watching the images intently. He guessed this was a rendezvous point. 'There!' he said. 'Who's that?'

The radio operator was quick to relay the development: 'Delta 7. Someone is crossing the road and heading straight for our target.'

Phil pulled away from the wall and turned to face the road, leaning one elbow on the wall, his other hand holding his mobile to his ear. He stole a glance to his left and spotted the newcomer. He saw that his colleague was now just five metres from the bench.

Mohammed sensed that someone was walking up to the bench and turned. Bakr was three paces away. Mohammed nodded slightly. Bakr simply sat down to the right of him, his eyes on Rob, who was now about to walk right past them. Rob's conversation with his mate was in full flow, it seemed; his voice not betraying the fact that his heart was in his mouth. '...well, she would say that, wouldn't she... No, not really, I'm up to my neck in it...' The irony of his comment was intended, of course. *I should have been an actor*, Rob thought. 'How was the movie?' This was code for Control.

'Lower the angle slightly,' Control said. *'That's good. Hold it there.'*

As Rob passed the bench, Bakr raised his hand slightly to silence Mohammed, whom he knew was about to blurt out something. Bakr looked to his left and saw Phil propped up against the wall.

Pearson was leaning over a computer screen. The man at the computer had freeze-framed a clear image from Rob's video of the two men on the bench. Pearson and the computer operator were both comparing Mohammed's face with the earlier St Audley Street CCTV still. 'Same guy. Looks as dodgy as hell,' Pearson mumbled. 'So, who's his little bum chum?' Pearson stood up straight, grimacing slightly. He rotated his head, loosening the muscles in his neck then rubbed his face vigorously. 'OK. Good work everyone. We have our target and a new suspect. You know what to do. Get on with it!'

Chapter 25
The Experiment

La Gran Sabana, SE Venezuela

The Venezuelan student, Mario Fernandez, and his US colleague, Beany, were the first to hear the unmistakable thwap of helicopter blades. The two scientists were eating breakfast at a table, enjoying the view of the distant cloud-topped plateaux and the vast green landscape over a thousand metres below. They looked at one another. Beany stopped chewing.

'Did you hear that?' she said, mouth still full of cereal bar.

'*Si*. Maybe a tourist trip.'

They resumed their repast, thinking that the aircraft must have been miles away. When the sound returned a hundred times louder, both Beany and Mario nearly choked. The black Piasecki helicopter rose—it seemed from nowhere—just twenty metres in front of them.

'HOLY CRAP!' Beany spluttered.

Mario just sat with his mouth open, staring at the menacing-looking machine.

The helicopter was hovering, pointing directly at them. It then pitched forward and flew right over their heads, its downdraught scattering their cups and plates off the table, and practically blowing the young scientists off their chairs.

Beany threw the rest of her cereal bar onto the table. 'I'm gonna give them a piece of my mind,' she said angrily and strode off towards the helicopter, which was now coming to rest beyond the tents.

The rest of the team had emerged and stood viewing the unexpected arrival. The Piasecki kept its engine running.

Mario came up alongside Beany. 'That's military. Maybe we're in trouble with my government,' he hollered over the noise.

Beany pointed towards the front of the helicopter. Mario looked and made a quick frown. A small US flag was visible below the side window. At that moment, the door opened and two men stepped out.

'It's the professor,' Beany said smiling.

'Who's the other guy?'

Beany shook her head.

The door closed and the helicopter rose slowly and turned. After a short hover, it pitched forward and accelerated back towards the young scientists. Beany could see the pilot. She raised her middle finger at him before the aircraft passed over their heads and away.

The professor and the stranger entered one of the tents.

'I guess we'll find out,' replied Beany.

Late in the afternoon, Kara was standing over one of her team seated at his laptop. 'The forecast is still holding,' he said, pointing to a satellite image.'

'Good. What sort of time?'

'Eight, maybe nine tonight. The centre of the storm should pass within five kilometres.'

'That's close enough,' Kara said. 'It looks big enough, too. Show me the MTG data.'

A time-lapse infrared animation appeared on his screen showing the storm clouds from space. Patches of blue, green, yellow, orange, and red raced across the screen, the deeper red indicating the most intense lightning activity. The animation then repeated.

'That's lightning only twenty kilometres north of here. Looks like Professor Steel timed his visit to perfection.'

'Let's hope so.' Kara looked at her watch. She felt anxious. *Whom had Arthur brought with him? And why had he and the stranger disappeared immediately after their arrival without even a hello?*

It was now 20:12. The team had assembled in the main tent and were busy with their duties. Two of the scientists were coming back through the large tent opening, having checked the status of THEIS. Rain had just started. So, too, had the first rumbles of thunder.

Kara was typing rapidly on her laptop.

Standing on one side of the tent, away from the makeshift laboratory, was Richard Ordway, dressed in light chinos and a black, leather bomber jacket that accentuated the hint of red in his short-cropped hair and designer stubble. Kara ignored him. The stranger had not had the decency to introduce himself, so why should she return the compliment? However, his presence was distracting her. She stopped what she was doing, stood up, and walked over to him.

'I'm Kara Williams. And you are?' Kara felt aggressive but found herself transfixed by Ordway's eyes and ineffable smile. He was attractive, she thought, but in a strange way.

'Don't bite, Kara.'

She turned towards the source of the deep voice to see the familiar lean figure of Professor Arthur Steel, lighting a cigar under the far, dark end of the tent. Taking a single puff of the Havana, he stepped into the light. His black skin was lined, his temple hair greying, and his eyes twinkled in the light of the dim electric lamps hanging from the tent's roof.

'Arthur. I wasn't expecting to see you up here. I thought you were still stateside.'

Kara was delighted to see him despite his mysterious absence since his arrival.

'And I wasn't expecting to be here, Kara. How's it all going?'

'I, er…' Kara stole a glance at Ordway. 'We are, well, we're about to run a test right now. Aren't we guys?'

'Yeh. Yeh, that's right. Hello Professor,' Mario said, having turned away from a bank of computers. The rest of the team raised their hands to the professor.

Kara looked suspiciously at Ordway.

'Kara, everyone, this is Richard Ordway,' Steel said.

Tod walked over and extended a tentative hand, but quickly disguised the intended handshake when he saw that Ordway had kept his hands inside his jacket. Kara was nodding, anticipating a response from Ordway. Getting none, she said:

'Well, if you'll excuse me, I have things to be getting on with.'

'I'm sorry, Mr Ordway. Dr Williams is just a little excited here,' Tod said smiling. He then started ushering Ordway towards a platform. 'Please, you should step onto this—it's your insulation from three hundred million volts.'

Ordway suddenly looked less bemused.

'Kara, Mr Ordway has just flown in from Washington. Perhaps you'd like to explain what's happening?' Arthur ended his question with a smile. If there was one person she could trust, it was her old professor, Arthur Steel.

Kara's shoulders visibly lowered. 'Yeh right. OK. Well…' she said, now standing by her computer.

'From the top, please, Kara,' Steel proposed.

'Sure,' Kara smiled at Ordway. *Scary eyes, but he has something about him*, she thought. *Act natural. Be feminine. Don't be a geek!* 'Well what we're essentially doing here is er…' Kara looked for and got assurance from Arthur to continue, '…well, basically…'

'You can talk freely,' Steel said, puffing on his cigar.

'Well, we're tracking storm activities in this region using LIS—Lightning Imaging Sensor. It's a sensor in geostationary orbit that maps all lightning activities in the electrosphere across the tropics, day and night, right down to individual storms like this one. There's a new one we use now on the International Space Station. For extra data, we also uplink to NASA's OTD—or Optical Transient Detector. Now that's a way cool device. Then there's the brand new MTG, which gives us infra-red data.' Kara started to move down a line of equipment and stopped at a display of a satellite image. She turned back to her class. Kara checked herself in mid-flow. *You're doing it again*, she told herself. *You're being a girl nerd, Kara*. She decided to drop the techno babble: 'Once we decide that the storm is sufficiently… big enough, we'll get on-site and rig this little lot up ASAP.'

'We can do the whole damn lot in 40 minutes.' Mario made a sweep with his hand. All eyes quickly returned to Kara.

'You're official storm chasers, then?' Ordway smiled, pleased with his quip.

'Yeh.' Kara snorted 'Kinda.' *God, he speaks*, she thought. She was annoyed with herself that the scientist in her and her enthusiasm for the subject were limiting her discretion and, she felt, her femininity. 'Over there is THEIS.' Kara let her words hang in the air. She was disappointed when Arthur did not take the lead. Her finger was pointing through a wide gap in the tent towards the beating heart of the experiment positioned fifty metres from them. 'The High Energy Inductor System,' she continued. 'THEIS, which, because some see it as tampering with higher powers, acts of God and all that, very quickly became THEISM.'

'A belief in God,' Ordway added. 'I like that.

'Etymologically speaking,' Steel said, 'Theis is derived from the German name Matthias and before that the apostle Matthaeus or Matthew. A name very popular amongst medieval Christians, as it means gift of God. *Mattath* is the Hebrew for gift.'

Kara looked at the professor. Were there no bounds to his knowledge? she thought.

But T, H, E, I, S. Couldn't that be read as THE IS?

'I'm not with you,' Kara said.

'I, S? The Islamic State?'

'Oh, that thought never occurred to me. Luckily, we opted for a single-word acronym. Anyway, our gear has been around way before the Islamic State.'

'Dr Williams is being modest,' Steel interjected. 'She had drafted her first design proposal when she was an undergraduate.'

'Actually, it's more accurately a High Energy Tracker, Inductor and Accumulator System,' Tod said. 'We didn't think that would invite any acronyms or nicknames until someone came up with HETI'S ASS.' A snigger went around the team.

'So, we stuck with THEIS, as opposed to I-S!' Kara continued. 'The name has a certain…'

'Mythical ring to it?' Ordway suggested, smiling.

'Anthropomorphic quality was what I had in mind, Mr Ordway.'

'Does it work?' Ordway was suddenly icy.

Kara swallowed hard. 'I joined the project eighteen months ago and it's constantly being…' she thought better of saying tweaked, '…enhanced. Charge differentials between cloud and ground, intra and inter-cloud, and between cloud and air, are being tracked by this device. The higher the negative and positive charge differential, the more likely there will be a strike. It kind of picks out a nice juicy charge and delivers it right to us. We're effectively using nature to create lightning when and where we want it, and we're getting a better than seventy-three per cent predictive strike accuracy. The good news is the accumulator side of things. Holding on to that enormous energy is something we can do. That's the other device over there.'

'A typical lightning strike generates around 1 billion joules, Mr Ordway,' Arthur butted in, 'Trying to harness the power of lightning is very hit and miss, as I'm sure you can appreciate, there are…'

'A joule. Remind me,' Ordway quizzed.

'That's joule, J-O-U-L-E,' Kara clarified.

'One newton-meter' Tod offered, mainly to impress.

'Yes, I am aware of what a joule is,' Ordway said with a forced smile. 'But in this context?'

Steel interjected. 'One joule per second is equivalent to one watt of energy. So, a typical lightning strike has the same energy needed to light twenty-five million forty-watt light bulbs for one second. There's a lot of energy up there and we'd like to harness it. Many attempts have been made and many failures. With this…,' the professor raised his hand and pointed to the equipment, '…and thanks to Dr Williams and her team here, we are essentially there.'

Kara buoyed up by the professor's praise continued. 'What we need is a way of drawing that energy with certainty and consistency. Capturing it is what we have achieved. Of course, there are a hundred factors we've discovered that could improve…'

'It doesn't work then, does it.' Ordway's abruptness cut her short.

Kara's stomach dropped. Fear, anger, and frustration swept through her. She felt like a child caught out by a grown-up. Kara recalled something she would inwardly recite in such situations. It always helped her. "*You know that they know that you know you're wrong.*" *I can't bullshit this guy*, she thought. The importance of how she should reply sent Kara's heart racing. *Who is this man?*

'I'm sorry, Mr Ordway, but who exactly are you?' Her counter-attack made her feel a whole lot better.

'Kara. Conditions are perfect in sector 2.' Tod, unaware of Ordway's pointed statement, was shouting from his workstation. 'We have a 9.2 window.'

'We're locked on.' Mario called over; his face still intent on the glow of his screen. Kara lifted her head in the direction of the team's only other female operative.

'Beany, what are the stats?'

'2 dot 9 8, 15 2, 7 dot 9 5.'

'Do it!' Kara commanded.

Each member of the team began calling out updates. Kara threw her arms into a tight fold, her right forearm extended to her mouth, her teeth gnawing at the skin above her thumbnail. 'Headsets and goggles on, everybody! Tod, give these to…him,' she ordered. She handed Tod a pair of ear defenders meant for the stranger that Kara had decided was a jumped-up dick. She also did not want Ordway to overhear what she was about to say.

Arthur Steel was now alongside Kara, who was leaning towards one of the computer screens. They had their backs turned to Ordway. The rain splattering on the canvas grew in intensity.

'Why the cloak and dagger stuff, Arthur? I could do without the third degree. Who the fuck is he?' Kara whispered above the deluge, her headset half on, hand cupping the mic.

'He's on our side, Kara. That's all I can say.'

'OK. We're ready.' Mario swung around with a big grin on his face.

'2 dot 9 9 5, 16 8, 8 dot 2 5.'

'Jesus, Arthur. At least tell me where he's from.'

'I believe he's CIA.'

'3 dot 0 2 and climbing fast. 16 9, 8 dot 39...'

'The CI...' she quickly checked her volume, 'The CIA? Oh, great. Thanks, Arthur. You sold us out to a bunch of spooks. What do they hope to achieve? I'm so confused.'

'Trust me, Kara. It's for all our good,' said Steel, putting on his headset and goggles.

Kara's attention was flicking from one screen to another. 'On my mark, Mario...Keep the numbers coming, Beany. Thank you.'

'3 0 7, 17 2, 8 57. 3 1, 17 5...'

'Engage!' Kara said.

Outside, the air around THEIS fizzled in anticipation of a gargantuan exchange of energy. A faint blue aura, gossamer thin, created a dancing curtain of light around the device. The air was ionised. Alive. Then, after a second or two, and for the briefest of moments, the charged air appeared to return to normal. To the initiated, however, this was the unmistakable precursor to a strike—a pulse, a shift in the balance of energy, as short as the gap between two heartbeats. At the very moment of realisation, it would be too late to react. The lightning would be upon you. And it was. In the camp, no one, apart from the out-of-place visitor, even flinched when the darkened scene outside the shelter exploded with the light of the enormous lightning strike and its deafening accompaniment. The bolt of lightning appeared to be sucked from the cumulonimbus that towered some forty miles into the upper atmosphere. The lightning's laddered path—imprinted on the retinas of the observers despite the eye protection—discharged into THEIS. The experimentation area was bathed in the lightning's blinding whiteness. There was an instant implosion of air and a short but deafening boom. Everyone then instinctively ducked with an accompanying 'Whoa!' except for Kara, who managed a flinch.

'YEH!' Tod shouted, typing furiously into his laptop. 'Never get tired of it.'

'Magnificent!' Ordway, having cowered briefly from the lightning assault, was quickly recovering his composure. Everyone was removing his and her ear and eye protection. The darkness, when it returned, seemed more intense. The terrific after-rumble rolled away in all directions. As it faded, Tod could be heard. '0 dot 3 and holding…Still holding.'

'That's 0.3 billion joules,' Steel clarified for the benefit of their guest.

'Shit,' Kara muttered and sighed.

The whole team went quiet, staring mostly at their respective screens. Arthur placed a friendly hand on her shoulder.

'What's the problem?' Ordway asked.

Steel could see Kara's disappointment and chose to answer. 'Well, over here you can see the energy we've managed to capture and retain from that strike. That's, I suppose, the good news. The bad news, if you can call it that, is that we missed about seventy per cent of it.'

'Maybe we shouldn't be messing with these God-like powers', Ordway called out.'

The team turned and watched Ordway walk out of the tent into the rain and disappear inside one of the nearby accommodation tents.

The following morning, Kara was standing near the edge of the bluff. The sun was out and the air was clear, making the view even more spectacular. The neighbouring plateaux, their rocky tops flanked by clouds, denied the observer any sense of scale but not a sense of awe.

'It's a beautiful day, ain't it, Dr Williams?' Ordway said, walking from his tent to join her.

'I trust you slept well.'

'I have no trouble sleeping, Doctor. Only sinners do.'

Kara turned to look at Ordway. *What an odd guy*, she thought.

'Tell me,' Ordway said as he looked out across the vast landscape, 'up here we seem to be above the clouds. I thought you'd need to be below them for your lightning experiments.'

Kara could not help but show her surprise at such an apposite question. 'Well, as you saw from our experiment yesterday evening, we can work fine up here. On this plateau, we're at an altitude of just under 2,000 metres. Whereas cumulonimbus, aka storm clouds can rise in height beyond 16,000 metres, giving us an unrestricted observational vantage point. Think of us like astronomers in our mountain-top observatories. Up here we're away from all the clutter of lower-level clouds.'

'I see,' Ordway said. He turned to face Kara and smiled. She could not help but find him attractive in an almost disturbing way. His eyes sparkled, but his smile seemed distant…insincere perhaps.

'We also have the means to generate or at least encourage the large electrical potentials needed to generate lightning,' Kara continued. She had looked away from Ordway and started gesticulating to emphasise her descriptions. 'Thanks to Professor Steel, we have what are called *seeders*. But rather than generate rain, Professor Steel's *seeders* help to build positive and negative charges. With them, we have been able to create lightning from quite normal cloud cover. So, yes, we have been running similar experiments at lower altitudes…' Kara's words faded. *You're being a total geek*, she thought. *Why can't you ever shut up?* She looked again at Ordway and found that he was still holding his smile. 'Sorry, I'm boring you,' she said apologetically.

'Not at all, Doctor.'

Kara smiled back awkwardly and returned her gaze to the distant plateaux. 'I always think of those old prog rock album sleeves every time I see this view. It's almost contrived,' she said, trying to lighten the conversation.

'"*For the Lord is the great God, the great King above all gods. In his hand are the depths of the earth, and the mountain peaks belong to him.*" D'you believe in God, doctor?'

'I, er, no, not really, I guess.' *There he goes again*, she thought.

'Let me tell you. I've worked for our government for twenty-eight years. I've sacrificed a lot in my life. For what? For freedom, for the American way, a Christian way, God's way. Doctor, I'm driven by a desire to rid this world of evil. I mean, take those Jihadi bombers. They've brought terror upon us for decades. Crazies! But I bet that all feels like a million miles away for you, stuck out here. You must feel lucky.'

'The world is smaller, Mr Ordway. So no, I don't think anyone can say they feel immune. Nor do I feel lucky or privileged in any way being out here. And I certainly don't feel safe if that's what you're implying. You saw how dangerous our work can be. This is my passion, Mr Ordway. We need sustainable energy like never before. If you think we're all out here having a bit of fun then you're wrong. I'd love to be at home, seeing friends, going out to decent restaurants, having a relationship…'

'Kara, may I call you Kara?' Kara sighed. *Whatever*, she thought. 'Kara, I fully get it, and I'm sorry if I come across as… abrupt. That's me. It's a by-product of what I do, or maybe the reason I do what I do. Professor Steel has told you, I know, but we require your services, your knowledge.

'Sorry, who's "we"? You arrive unannounced, do nothing but criticise.'

Ordway's smile returned. Kara then realised it was not an insincere smile but a creepy one. Scary even. 'We want you to succeed, Kara. I'm on your side. Believe me.'

'But what are you, Mr Ordway? I think I have a right to know. CIA, right?'

'Is that what the professor told you? It's not CIA.' Ordway could not keep his ego in check. 'It's above that. Just wish I could tell you more.'

'But you'd have to shoot me if you did, yeh, yeh. Wait a minute. Above the CIA?'

Arthur Steel was approaching them. 'Is she giving you a hard time again, Mr Ordway? I told you she would.'

Ordway snorted. His face had turned to stone. He said nothing and walked back to the camp. Kara mouthed an obscenity at his retreating back.

Steel gave Kara his winning smile and put his arm around her. She had missed Arthur. He was like a father to her. Seeing him out here after so long made her homesick and suddenly brought out her real emotions. She burst into tears. 'That guy. My god! Oh, and he's just told me he's not CIA. Oh no, of course, he isn't, he's too self-important for that shit. *No, I'm way above that, don't you know*,' she mimicked.

Steel laughed, reached into his pocket, and handed her a tissue. 'This is tiredness and frustration coming out. Nothing more. But you've come a long way in a short time. I'm delighted with the progress.'

'Why,' Kara blubbed, 'do men of a certain age always have a handkerchief to hand?' she asked looking at Arthur and smiling.

'With age comes wisdom. I also carry a small set of tools,' he said, taking the set out from his other pocket. 'You never know when you might need a screwdriver.'

They both laughed.

'I could do with a screwdriver of the liquid kind. Anyway, I call it chivalry, and I love it. Thank you,' she said and blew her nose, a bit too noisily, Steel thought.

'I was guessing with the CIA,' he said. 'He looked that type. But he *is* government. Besides, you should be honoured. If he is that high up and they send him all this way, it must be pretty darn important.'

'So, you don't know who he is or whom he represents.'

'Look, Kara. You just worry about the science. I'll take care of the politics. Don't forget, that's where the money comes from.'

Kara looked out across the landscape. 'Are we close to something huge here? I'm so wrapped up in detail it's hard to see the big picture.'

'Maybe. Perhaps the government has finally woken up to the worsening energy crisis and wants to fast-track the project. I just don't know.'

'Yeh, maybe. We've had enough climate summits to support that theory, and it's top of the latest G7 agenda again. I'm just worried that he didn't sound that impressed.'

'Don't worry. I think intimidation is his style.' Steel smiled, gave Kara an encouraging pat on the shoulder, and walked back to the camp. A few metres away he stopped and turned. 'You were right about one thing.'

Kara turned to face the professor. 'What?'

'He is an...' and the professor mouthed the words: *ass hole.*

Kara half laughed and wiped the last tears from her eyes.

Chapter 26
The Pursuit

Central London, 11.42 a.m.

DCI David Pearson was standing over Claire Yates' screen. Yates had pulled up six zoomed-in video feeds from the drone.

'They're under the trees still, sir, so I've switched to thermal. That's our target and that's the new guy. That's Rob and that's Phil, of course.' SO15's men on the ground were all flagged with numbers.

'OK, tag up our targets.' Pearson then reached for a microphone. 'Delta 2, I want you to cover exits to the east including Embankment tube. Delta 4, the south. Delta 3, Delta 5, and Delta 6, you're on. Stay sharp! And I want every bloody CCTV up now. I want more coverage than a Royal Wedding. Claire, run the drone video from about 11.24. Let's see where target number 2 came from.'

Yates opened a new window for the archived drone footage.

'OK. Is this target 2?'

'Er, yes, sir, it is.' Yates confirmed and tagged the image.

'Run it back.'

'Looks like Westminster tube, sir,' Yates commented. 'Zooming in.'

The image was crystal clear. Bakr disappeared back under the arches to the entrance of the tube station.

'Un-bloody-believable these guys are using the tube.' Pearson shook his head. 'OK, get the CCTV for the station and track his movements back.'

DI Sahay Prasad, one of the team's detectives, called out, 'Sir, we may have an ID on target number 1. Mohammed Faasil. Aged 20. UK resident since birth. Born and raised in Hounslow. Left school at 16. Has a flat in Wembley. Drives a Subaru Impreza. Clean licence. One older brother...'

'Good work. So, one home-grown terrorist. Who's the other?' Pearson turned to his team. 'OK, so let's assume that target number 1 thinks he's in the clear. And why not? It was only due to a bit of deduction on our part...'

'Nice one, Steve.' One of the team acknowledged Steven Jubb's detective work. Steve raised his hand.

'... and a bit of luck. However, it's still circumstantial.'

'Come on, sir. Really?' said Prasad.

There was a general murmur of agreement.

'Wait a minute,' Pearson said. 'We spot an Arabic-looking man near the scene some seventeen minutes before the attack and assume it's him?' Pearson let the rhetorical question hang in the air. The room fell silent. 'Anyway, it's all we have. He's thinking he hasn't been arrested, so he's meeting up with a) a member of his team or b) his boss. Either way, they're probably comparing notes.' Pearson walked over to the main operations display—a giant screen showing all the key event locations and times. 'So why are they meeting here of all places?'

The room erupted with suggestions.

'Planning another attack?'

'The London Eye?'

'Parliament?'

'Take your pick,' Pearson said. 'They're spoilt for choice.'

'So soon, though, sir?'

'Why not? They're probably on a high.'

'Perhaps they're planning to blow themselves up so we can all go home,' said Jubb.

'You joke, but, interestingly, that's not what they did,' Pearson said, 'which makes me think that these guys are on a mission. Delta teams will pursue. I want backup teams in place now in case they take taxis or buses.'

Rob Villiers was now walking alongside Westminster Pier, a good hundred metres past the bench where Bakr and Mohammed were still seated. His and Phil's roles were over. He was frustrated that neither of them would be involved when the action stepped up. He stopped at one of the boat hire kiosks and stole a glance back up the walkway. 'Just give me the word, sir, and we'll take 'em now.'

'That's a negative, Delta 7,' came Pearson's quick reply.

'Sir,' said Yates, 'They're on the move.'

'Right,' Pearson said, 'Delta 7, cross over the road and double back to your car and await further instructions. You may still be needed if they exit by road.'

'Roger that, sir.' Rob clenched his fist. 'Yes!'

Bakr and Mohammed had left the bench.

'It's scenario 2. They're looking for a taxi. Stand by, everyone!'

Moments later, a black cab pulled up to the kerb and the two terrorists entered. Phil and Rob ran the last forty or so metres to their car.

Pearson turned to one of the team. 'Jon. Track 'em!'

Jonathan Simmons was flicking between CCTV images of the street. He quickly isolated the cab. Got it.'

'Claire, we need that number,' Pearson said.

Yates deftly repositioned the drone and was soon zooming in on the taxi's licence plate. She punched it into her computer and a map on her screen updated to show the taxi's position. On the left of the screen, a list of the trips the taxi had made that day. 'He'll probably enter his destination at the next set of lights, or call through on his radio. Either way, we're covering both.'

The taxi headed towards Trafalgar Square and soon came to a stop in the heavy, late morning traffic. Sure enough, the cabbie updated his computer: St Pancras.

'Going anywhere nice, gents?' asked the cabbie.

'No.' Bakr replied. He looked at Mohammed. His companion was looking out of his window and biting his bottom lip. The cabbie looked in his rear mirror at his fare and decided against further conversation.

The Metropolitan Police's SO15 and Specialist Firearms Command, SCO19, leapt into action. Two helicopters sped over the city, landing in a building site adjacent to St Pancras Station. The foreman cautiously approached the first of the team to emerge from the choppers. The SO15 officer flashed an ID and hollered something into the foreman's ear. The foreman withdrew, ushering back the more curious of his workforce. Multiple specialist teams were being deployed in and around the area of St Pancras and Kings Cross stations. Regular officers were being radioed.

Commander Mike Boyd strode into the SO15 operations room. 'Good afternoon, everyone.'

'Afternoon, sir.' Everyone responded.

'Sir, advanced team now in place. Three more teams are arriving as we speak. There are about ten SCO19 in the main concourses of both stations. The suspects are currently in a cab on Southampton Row. About eight minutes out.'

'Good, thank you, David. Now, this is *not* an imminent threat, correct?'

'Correct, sir. Observation and possible arrest.'

'Are you *absolutely* sure?'

'I'm sure, sir.'

'Marksmen?'

'No sir, we want this as covert as possible.'

'Agreed. But we can't be too careful. What do you think they're up to, David?'

'Sir, I'm pretty sure they're oblivious to us. They met on Victoria Embankment. St Pancras would suggest they're taking Eurostar out of the country.'

Boyd scanned the information on the screen. 'This, um, UK resident, Mohammed Faasil. Has he made any advanced ticket purchases?'

'No, sir, he only has one credit card. Last purchase was a tyre last month. No ticket purchases from his current account. No notable cash withdrawals either.'

'So, his friend may have bought them. What do we have on him?'

'We're running his photo internationally. Nothing yet. We're retracing his steps. Might explain why they met where they did.'

Jurek Wójcik, steered his 32-tonne Scania dumper truck around the roundabout at Old Street and onto City Road. He was on his second run of the day returning to take more rubble from the building site next to St Pancras. Stopping at some lights, he started whistling, and reached for his tuna and sweetcorn sandwich.

'Delta 7 to Control. We have a visual. Suspects still in cab. Over.'

Rob and Phil were half a dozen cars behind the black cab edging slowly up Southampton Row.

'*Roger, Delta 7. Destination is St Pancras. Repeat, St Pancras. Over.*'

'Roger that.'

The cab pulled up outside the international terminal. Rob and Phil stopped on the opposite side of the road and surveyed the crowds. 'I don't see any of our lot,' Rob muttered, just as Bakr and Mohammed emerged. 'And there are a ton of people and shit going on. Control, do we have anyone near the entrance?'

'Delta 7, stand by.'

'Well, that was bloody helpful, not,' Phil said.

'Targets are at Pancras Road entrance. Do we have a visual from inside the terminal?' asked the radio operative in the control room.

'*Negative,*' came the various responses.

'Sir, only Delta 7 have visual.'

'Yates?' Pearson asked.

'Sorry sir, I'm repositioning the drone. The angle's wrong. The terminal building is obscuring the entrance.'

'Shit,' said Pearson.

'There!' Simmons said, 'We have them on CCTV.'

'I'm going in,' Rob said.

'No, Rob. You could blow the op.'

'Look, they'd have to be hypnotised to remember me. They hardly looked up.'

'Just sit tight. We have people in there.'

'Yeh, but how many? Ten, twenty? If they split up, we've halved our chances.' Rob was already half out the door and was soon jogging across the road. Bakr and Mohammed had entered the terminal.

'Bollocks, Rob,' Phil said to himself and decided to follow. 'Delta 7 to control. We're approaching the entrance. Have visual.'

'Delta 7. FALL BACK NOW!' Pearson barked. 'We've got people inside and have them on CCTV.'

Keeping a constant eye on the targets, Phil caught up with his colleague and tugged him around. 'Drop it, action man. We've got it covered. If they get on a train, we ain't gonna lose them.'

'Maybe. Let's just hope they don't blow the train up, too.'

Bakr looked up at the signs. When he lowered his head, his eyes met with those of an armed police officer. Two features made the SCO19 officer stand out: one was his blue baseball cap with its blue and white checked band; the other was the deadly-looking Sig Sauer automatic rifle slung across his body, its muzzle pointing at the ground immediately in front of him. It was the briefest of looks, but enough for Bakr. The officer was at least twenty metres away. Bakr scanned the hall. 'This way,' he said to Mohammed.

'Where are we going?'

'Change of plan.'

'But I thought we were going to Paris?'

'Stop talking.' Bakr was looking down as he spoke.

'What's wrong?'

'I said, stop talking. We separate now. I will contact you. Do *not* contact me!'

Bakr's sudden change of mood sent a chill through Mohammed. Earlier, Bakr was hinting at a new devastating target. He made Mohammed feel important and special. Now, he felt like a traitor. Mohammed stood gormlessly watching Bakr slip away through the crowd.

The SCO19 officer knew he had spooked one of the targets and had moved well away not daring to make further eye contact. 'Shit, shit, shit,' he kept muttering.

Simmons was switching between the CCTVs. 'There's target 1, but where the fuck has 2 gone?'

'Wake up all units and report for Christ's sake,' said Pearson.

'Delta 6, we have a visual on target one. No signs of two. Over.'

Bakr had reached the exit to the tunnel that divided the ground floor of the terminus. He crossed the underground road and entered the multi-story car park. He looked back as he swung around some railings. There was no one behind him. He turned forward and surveyed the scene. An elderly man was closing the boot of a silver Mercedes. Bakr started walking towards him and then began jogging. The car owner was alone. No one else was around.

The driver turned at the sound of footsteps, alarmed by the intent on Bakr's face. 'Is there something wrong?'

But the old man's words were cut short as Bakr, without slowing, raised a knee and buried it into the man's stomach. The man let out a dreadful groan and collapsed in a heap. His spleen had ruptured. Bakr bent down and prised the keys from the man's hand. He found the man's wallet and the car park exit ticket. With one more look around, he got behind the wheel and gunned the engine to life.

Mohammed stood staring, his head spinning. Something had spooked Bakr. That was the only explanation. He looked at the people around him. Most were going about their business. Some looked at him. *But that was natural*, he thought, *wasn't it? People exchanging looks.*

He glanced up and saw a CCTV camera; then another. They seemed to be pointing right at him. He immediately lowered his head and started walking. He bumped into several people, and nearly tripped over a pushchair.

Think! he said to himself.

He entered a shop and looked out across the station concourse and then into the shop. All looked normal. But his heart was pounding.

It was then that he saw Rob. Rob had stopped in the middle of the concourse to scan the crowd. Their eyes met. The man staring back just five metres away looked vaguely familiar to Mohammed. He did not know why.

The exchange of looks seemed to last for seconds. It was as though the world around Mohammed had slowed and blurred around him—the hubbub of the station now muffled.

Rob was quick. He knew that recognising one person from the hundreds anyone would encounter in London would be a miracle. So, he half smiled and began walking away.

Mohammed watched him. It was only when Phil raised his hand to his colleague beckoning him to hurry up that the penny dropped for Mohammed.

Rob was mouthing the words: 'Target 1. Behind me.'

Phil could not lip read, but got as much to recognise 'Target 1.' He looked past his colleague and saw Mohammed—staring right back at him.

Mohammed turned and ran. His original plan to head home was nowhere in his head. Suddenly, the people around him seemed to be moving chaotically and too fast; the sounds of the station were now loud and disorientating. He was running. Just running. Running towards some space, a gap in the crowds.

Jurek changed gear and the lorry stuttered then growled its way onto Pancras Road and past the terminal building. His foreman had warned him that some 'heavy police shit' was going on and that helicopters were sitting on the site. *This I have to see*, he thought. *Just round the next corner.*

When he bolted out the station exit, Mohammed was aware only of his inner self. Blood was pumping in his ears. Tunnel vision and his breathing were now the limits of his senses. The first moment that Jurek became aware of Mohammed was when he appeared in his peripheral vision. Half a second later, he heard and felt the sickening thud as Mohammed hit the corner of the truck and was crushed by the front left wheel. It was only after the lorry's rear wheel bumped over Mohammed's body did Jurek manage to hit the brakes. For a moment everything was quiet and still. Jurek, his arms outstretched, hands gripping the steering wheel, was looking straight ahead, trying to grasp what had happened. A woman's scream broke the spell. Jurek turned his head slowly towards the pavement. Passers-by had frozen, hands to their mouths, some already walking slowly away, not wanting to get involved. Jurek descended from his cab. He did not want to see. He wanted to walk away himself. Instead, he slowly looked under the truck. It was dark, thank God. He squinted, trying to make sense of what he saw. Someone was doing the same from the rear of the truck. They would have had a better view. When that person heaved and vomited, sick spattering around him, Jurek's initial fears rose. *Please, God*, he thought, as he walked slowly towards the rear of the truck. He took another look. Realising that the only thing recognisable was a pair of legs and two white trainers, Jurek promptly puked up his tuna and sweetcorn sandwich.

Chapter 27
Dark Days

MI6, SIS Building, Central London, UK

'Ah, Patrick. *Ça va?*'

'A little tired. But nothing an espresso cannot solve, thank you. And how are you, George?'

Sir George Bradbury ushered Lamotte into his office and closed the door. 'Could it be worse?' he replied. 'You know Evan, of course?' Bradbury's slurred question was more a statement of fact. Lamotte turned to locate the room's only other occupant and found Evan Samuels in a casual repose on a leather Chesterfield.

'Of course. Evan.'

'Patrick.'

Patrick Lamotte acknowledged the Director of the CIA, their American counterpart, with a handshake. Despite the pleasantries, neither man seemed particularly pleased to see the other.

Bradbury sensed that no one in the room was in the mood for small talk, even if it helped normalise an otherwise harrowing time.

Lamotte took a seat next to Samuels. Both men looked stony-faced at their host as he strolled towards the window and looked out.

'I love rivers,' Bradbury began. 'I love them for the same reason I love mountains and ancient trees.' His guests exchanged glances, both rolling their eyes. They knew his style well enough. Whatever point they knew he would eventually make, it was often preceded by a cerebral preamble. 'I love them for their longevity, their resilience, their...immutability. They have a kind of wisdom, don't you think? It's as though they look at the follies of man, as a parent would look at a child, and shake their heads saying: "one day you will learn." They provide a sense of history, proportion, and stability. They remind me that this city has seen it all before: pestilence, fire, and war. I'm sure that Londoners in a thousand years will look back at this dark episode as just one of many. And yet, our adversary this time is as old as this city.' Bradbury turned from the window, eyebrows raised, waiting for a response.

'You're referring to jihadists,' Samuels said.

'I think we're all in agreement about the source of this attack.'

'Christians and Arabs. Now there's a volatile mixture,' Lamotte said. 'Will we ever see reconciliation? Make your rivers and old trees smile for once.'

Bradbury huffed. 'You think?' His expression was dark.

'Noble sentiments, and, yes,' said Samuels, 'I like your sense of proportion, George. But come on, life would be a little dull if it was as predictable as a slowly flowing river. In the meantime, you've got a parliament that's gone ballistic, a public that's in a state of terminal shock, an economy in free fall, the press making wild speculations, and your right-wing extremists kicking the living crap out of anyone with a tan that won't fade or rub off.' He had no time for sentimental philosophising. And yet, he knew about the terror attack that had shattered Bradbury's life, an attack later attributed to the Somali-based militant group *al-Shabaab,* although never verified, and could not help but admire the man's outward calm.

'What's happened has happened,' Bradbury continued languidly.

'Christ! It's happened all right!' Samuels said.

Bradbury looked at the American and smiled. *Only a Brit can remain so fucking calm in a firestorm*, he thought.

'It's a shame we cannot divulge the details of the attacks we *have* stopped,' the French chief added.

Bradbury continued, 'Indeed. But if the public knew what keeps the security agencies busy most days, that would create a whole new level of terror. Look, it's no surprise that our governments are realising how impotent they really are. Ideology aside, they know their policies help to bring this kind of thing about, but now it's finally happened—The UK's had its very own 9/11. The politicians are spouting their usual bluster, but cowering in their beds like frightened lambs…if that doesn't sound too much like a mixed metaphor. They're being attacked on all sides. So, being the consummate politicians they are, they naturally start shifting responsibility, or, should I say, blame onto the experts. Us.' Bradbury raised his eyebrows and reached for a remote control. 'The one good thing about events like this,' he continued, 'is that the politicians stop squabbling over trivialities and unite in one desire: that we apprehend the perpetrators…' Bradbury's otherwise calm, some would say, rather irritatingly refined accent slipped into one that conveyed a true emotion, '…get the *bastards* who did this.'

Bradbury pivoted to his left. An image of a street in Central London, littered with corpses, burnt beyond recognition, appeared on one of the huge screens. The CIA Director and the DGSE chief both winced.

'Shit, they kept *those* images from the media,' Samuels said.

Bradbury punched the remote to reveal a new image of what could have been a woman, still standing but bent backwards over the railings outside Piccadilly Circus tube station. A second image revealed that her clothes had been vapourised and much of her skin fused into the metal fence. The hole where her mouth had been, was now frozen in a gaping yawl. It was like a scene from Dante's *Inferno* or *Hell* by Hieronymus Bosch. Except this was horror in high resolution. In London. Just days earlier. This was real.

'And it's none of your namby-pamby rhetoric, either,' the MI6 head continued in his normal tone. 'The Tories are desperate to send in the troops. But they're not quite sure where. And everyone knows that, after Iraq, it'd be political suicide. Naturally, the British public at large and most of the western world are incensed, in shock, and demanding retribution—somehow. No one does this on British soil and gets away with it, is the consensus. The sheer scale and audacity of the attack, right in the heart of our capital, means that fingers are pointing at the Middle East; there can be no one else.'

'We agree. And rest assured, George, this is our top priority.'

Bradbury continued. 'There's another COBR meeting tomorrow. The PM's under serious pressure, so it won't be an easy gathering. Obviously, all our security agencies are working overtime. But he'll want to know what you guys have if anything.'

'Early days from my side,' Evans said.

'DGSI are aware of new cell activity,' Lamotte added. 'But that's it. There is nothing to suggest there is a direct connection with the London attack. Naturally, we have raised our threat level to substantial.'

DGSI stood for *Direction Générale de la Sécurité Intérieure*, France's internal security agency—the equivalent of the UK's MI5. Lamotte headed up DGSE, the *extérieure* agency, the MI6 equivalent.

'Any hints at a direction?' Samuels asked.

'From our government? No, they're clueless,' Bradbury answered with a sigh. 'There's pure rage out there, and not just in Westminster Palace. I'm sure you've seen the reprisals on the Muslim communities.'

'Mindless and vicious,' Lamotte said.

Bradbury's mouth turned down briefly. 'I'd say an understandable reaction born from frustration. They know the PM's hands are tied as far as any approved retaliation is concerned. He did call me straight after the attack. It's never said during such calls, but the phrase *carte blanche* was implied. He wants a result at any cost. And I, gentlemen, am hell-bent on providing one. Of course, it depends on where the threat lies, which is why this is an inter-agency effort like no other, and an international one at that.'

'We get all the easy jobs,' Lamotte quipped.

George Bradbury was glaring at the screen. 'Oh yes. This one's a fucking beauty. The curse of the free world. It doesn't matter what precautions we take, they'll find a way of sneaking into our cities and towns, destroying property and innocent lives, then slipping silently back into the shadows, back into obscurity and anonymity.'

'Or oblivion,' said Samuels.

'You mean martyrdom and an eternity of joy,' Lamotte corrected.

'Not this time, though. Most of them slipped away like the slimy shits they are. Cowards one and all,' Samuels replied.

'*Cowards die many times before their death,*' Bradbury quoted.

'*...The valiant never taste of death but once,*' Lamotte completed.

Samuels raised his eyebrows. 'Don't tell me. Shakespeare?' he enquired.

'Abso-bloody-lutely. Julius Caesar to be precise,' Bradbury said.

'I have to admit,' Lamotte continued, 'Shakespeare, Churchill. They do— *comment on dit...?*'

'Stir the soul,' Bradbury replied.

'Hmm, I wonder how your Churchill would have dealt with this kind of enemy—the invisible, the suicidal, the fanatical?' Samuels drawled.

'In exactly the same way. Grit and determination. Never giving up. The battlefield may have changed, Evan, but the challenge is no different. Intelligence was key in World War 2. It's even more important now.' Bradbury looked at Samuels as if to say: *wasn't that obvious?*

Samuels picked up the thread. 'So, George, why the three of us? What's cooking?'

Bradbury sat down at his desk. In Lamotte and Samuels he was facing the embodiment of realism: real guns, real bombs, and cold, stark issues. The expression *it's written on their faces* could not be applied here, though; it—whatever darkness "it" represented—was evident only in their absence of expression; nothing seemed to faze them. They were utterly professional. Their job, like his, was to dig deep, provide direction, and steer policy. There was no room for emotion. They were immune to the cold hard facts because their own body temperature was already low. Like Bradbury, they also had that extra special gift: an ability to think left field. And they absolutely loathed failure.

Bradbury did have a solution in mind. Could it *actually* work? But that solution was not for this meeting. No way was it.

Anyway, Bradbury thought, *back to the here and now. Use whatever means you must—that was the phrase. What did it mean? Steam into some country SAS-style, take out a few known terrorists, blow up a few buildings or terrorist training camps, and claim a victory? Probably. When it's this close to home, the people want blood vengeance—even the pacifists were eating their words, or had suddenly fallen very quiet. Phrases like 'they will never win' seemed hollow. These terrorists had not only succeeded in their mission—with the exception of one, they had got away. The terrorists had struck and struck hard. The terrorists had certainly won, all right. Everyone was duly terrified.*

Bradbury had spent every waking hour pondering his options. Politically, it was clear that the PM would not entertain an Iraq War-like rerun. Besides, the US under Bush. and the UK under Blair, had had their fingers burnt when the rationale for war back-fired; Saddam Hussein had no weapons of mass destruction. And having paid little attention to the consequences, such a blunt approach had proven improvident. The UK would also need international approval, and no one believed that the UN would sanction another invasion. A full-blown military solution, therefore, had been ruled out from the start. Anyway, war with whom? A covert assassination or "over the horizon" retaliation were also the last thing this government wanted—it was instant martyrdom for the victims and too distant, too remote. No, the PM was expecting and needed a different response. *Easier said than done,* Bradbury thought.

No, the PM the perpetrators brought to justice in the UK.

The other solution, though, popped up again in his mind, but he brushed it aside. That had to be plan B.

And so, plan A it was. Bradbury continued. 'Our security services are at full tilt, pouring over everything from CCTV footage to social media. They're bugging, arresting, and interviewing POIs, as we speak. So, I'm sure we'll meet with *some* success. But I don't want a few token prizes. Otherwise, it's the same old shit, different circumstances. This time I want unmitigated success. Here's the challenge, gentlemen. These terrorists did not make the ultimate sacrifice. This wasn't a bunch of brainwashed kids with C4 strapped to their chests; these people took out half the London Underground, God knows how many people, several tens of buildings, and brought this capital to a grinding halt. And this was the clever bit: the underground trains acted as huge pistons, pumping the fuel vapour around a huge area of the tube system. One spark and boom! You have the world's biggest pipe bomb.'

Lamotte and Samuels nodded, as though in acknowledgement of the ingenuity and complete unpredictability of the attack.

Bradbury went on. 'Whoever's behind this attack is significant. The operatives are organised, well-resourced, sophisticated, and ruthless. But it's their leader I'm interested in. There's someone's money behind this. My guess is he's not a motivator of thousands, spouting inciteful rhetoric over the internet, more the leader of a close-knit gang of determined, dangerous, and now highly successful terrorists.' Bradbury paused for effect and poured himself a coffee. 'Whoever it is, he's slithering somewhere in the shadows, ready to strike again. We follow the money. We find the leader. We cut off the head of the serpent.'

'Christ, you sound more and more like Churchill each day,' Samuels said, smiling. 'But I agree. This attack has the air of something much bigger than some small opportunist cell. But this money thing? I'm not so sure. Let's face it, five hundred feet of piping, some false passports, and hi-jacking three tankers are hardly going to break the bank. I mean, they didn't even have to buy any explosives.'

Bradbury looked at Lamotte. 'Patrick?'

Lamotte wiped the corner of his lips with his thumb and forefinger. 'This does seem international. But maybe the Syrian who escaped is the leader. Perhaps he came over to mastermind the attack and used a UK cell for support.'

'He was smart enough to outsmart your best, George.'

Lamotte and Samuels had made good points, Bradbury thought. But it was the best he could come up with. For now at least. 'Alright,' he said, 'maybe money has less to do with it. Maybe it's more about coordination and deep motivation.'

'These fuckers don't need much motivation. You know that George,' Samuels muttered.

'Yes, but to do *this*?' Bradbury replied, pointing at the screen. 'A Syrian, a UK national, and go knows who else. That's unusual and new.' He was determined to win the argument.

'That's true. This was one hell of an attack.'

'No, maybe you're right: money, coordination, *and* deep motivation,' Lamotte said.

Bradbury studied the Frenchman's face. 'You have someone, don't you.'

'We all share the usual suspects. But someone with considerable wealth and the right nationality did come up on our radar recently. So, he fits the first two parts of the profile: money and coordination. It'll surprise you when I tell you.'

'Spill the beans, Patrick,' Samuels said.

'Prince Al-Musan.' Lamotte waited for a response. As expected, he got one almost immediately.

'What! Really?' Bradbury said.

'We all know *him*,' Samuels responded. 'One of the richest and most influential industrialists in the Middle East.'

'Friend of OPEC ministers, pop stars, world leaders, *and* our royal family,' Bradbury added.

'Wrong profile, surely,' Samuels suggested. 'He may be successful, but he comes across as an attention-seeking, libertine playboy. Someone who clearly enjoys the excesses of the West.'

'He's under surveillance, nevertheless,' Lamotte replied.

'He's certainly smart. You don't accumulate that kind of wealth without a brain. Can you tell us why?' Bradbury asked, looking at Lamotte.

'Let's just say a possible connection with some high-tech weapons destined for his home country.'

'That may be. But to me it sounds like arming his nation, not arming terrorists,' the CIA man said, shaking his head. 'Weapons from whom?'

'We suspect the Russians,' Lamotte lied.

'Even so,' Bradbury said, 'if he is behind clandestine arms deals, that puts him in a whole new category. We've all seen it before: the best place to hide is…?'

'In plain sight,' Samuels completed. He looked at Bradbury. 'You said that the one who got away was Syrian, right?'

'Yes. Bakr al-Ahdal. He evaded our passport checks. Slipped into the country on Eurostar from Paris using a false Moroccan ID.'

'My guess is that this Bakr character is now in Europe,' Lamotte said. '*En route* to who knows where.'

'I agree,' Bradbury said. 'This connection with Al-Musan; financial, I assume?'

Lamotte stuck out his bottom lip and shrugged his shoulders. 'Yes, but you know how long and complex an investigation that can be. Shell companies, tax havens, your very own ELPs.'

'If we can help with the English Limited Partnerships, you just let me know.' Bradbury was pondering. '…Yes, it would be a perfect cover, I suppose,' he mused. 'Overplay the playboy, as it were. Hide in plain sight. We just need to know why. We need to know Al-Musan's motivation.' He then got up from behind his desk. 'Well, gentlemen, thank you for making it over here, and so quickly. Your support, our *mutual* support is vital as always. Let's reconvene by video in two days. We need to see their ugly faces here, facing multiple life sentences.'

Ten minutes later, Sir George Bradbury was standing alone by his office window, watching the traffic on Lambeth Bridge. He looked up at the bright cloud cover. *Heathrow grey*, he liked to call it, as it almost always seemed to be overcast each time he flew in or out of the capital's main airport.

These past few days, the UK seemed a very grey, very dark place in more senses than one.

Throughout the meeting, that other solution had continued to float slightly submerged at the back of his mind. What resurfaced, though, was the recall of a dream: a great sailing ship on a dark ocean, its brilliant white sails emblazoned with large crimson crosses. He understood but could never divulge what was behind the imagery. To a select few others, yes. But to Lamotte and Samuels, never.

Did Al-Musan fit the profile? Maybe, maybe not. And what was his motivation?

No, Bradbury decided, the lead was too flimsy. Plan B was needed regardless. He picked up his mobile and made a call.

'*Bonjour*, Jean-Baptiste,' he began.

Chapter 28
Truck to France

London, UK

Bakr knew he had to dump the Mercedes. And fast. He had found what appeared to be a deserted road in a derelict commercial area of East London. He sat for a few minutes behind the wheel and surveyed his surroundings. Bakr was reminded of his village, his defenceless mother and sisters, and the war-torn streets across the Middle East, where cities had been reduced to rubble in a matter of days, and where residents were forced to remain indoors, unseen and in fear. Some had fled for their lives, abandoning everything they had ever known or possessed. Others, like him, planned for vengeance.

Here, though, the workers had left years ago, driven out not by tanks and missiles but by some unseen economic force. The old, faceless warehouses, caked in grime, had been left to suffer an entropic, and, it seemed, interminable decay.

The street was silent. More importantly, there were no CCTVs, and he had seen none since he left the A13 a few miles back. Bakr had plans for the car but could not take any chances. He began wiping down the steering wheel and all contact points. He then popped the boot. As he had hoped, the old man, whose car it had been, was a driver equipped for all eventualities. Inside was a medical kit, a blanket, a thermos, and a jerry can full of fuel. Bakr opened the thermos. Steam rose to his nostrils. *Tea*, he thought and took a swig. *Ugh, English tea with milk. Disgusting! The British have no idea…*

It was then that he heard an engine. Bakr swung around and saw a police car turn into the street. He cursed under his breath and grabbed the wheel brace, his hand out of sight inside the boot. The patrol car slowed to a stop.

'Everything all right, sir?'

Bakr lowered the wheel brace, turned, and smiled at the male officer. He leant forward and could see that the driver was a woman officer.

'Yes, fine, thank you. I run out of fuel,' he said and turned to the jerry can.

The officer nodded. Bakr thought that his story would at least look genuine. But he was acutely aware of his surroundings.

As if on cue, the male officer asked 'Are you lost?'

'No, I was er checking a property. For my business.' Bakr nodded up at a To Let sign.

'And what business are you in, sir?'

'Textiles. I need a cheap warehouse.' The irony of his quick response was not lost on Bakr.

Bakr noticed that the woman officer was busy with the computer. She was probably checking the vehicle registration, he thought.

'Bit of a dump around here if you ask me,' said the first officer. 'There are some new builds about half a mile from here. What's the name of that new industrial estate, Mel?'

'Er, Caxton something, I think.' Her colleague never looked up from the computer.

The two officers fell silent for a moment. Bakr saw them exchange glances. Both doors of the patrol car then opened and the officers began to step out.

'Could I see your driving licence, sir?' the first officer asked. His voice and demeanour had changed completely. Bakr heard radio static and a faint voice. His colleague, moving around from the far side of the patrol car, was talking into her lapel radio, but Bakr could not make out what she was saying.

Bakr had to move now. Even if the car had not yet been reported stolen, they probably had the registered owner's name, and it was clear that Bakr was no white Anglo-Saxon, aged seventy-plus.

The first officer was all but clear of his door when Bakr, in one fluid movement, grabbed the wheel brace from inside the boot and kicked out, slamming the car door hard against the officer's right leg and groin. The officer roared with pain and began falling backwards. Bakr followed through with a vicious blow to his head with the wheel brace. Blood erupted from his skull.

The woman officer was now reaching for her firearm. 'Fuck! Officer down! Officer down! Urgent assis...'

Before she could finish, Bakr had already leapt onto the bonnet, and heeled her square in the face. The officer's head jerked back, her face looked heavenwards, eyes wide with shock, her neck broken. She was dead before she hit the ground.

Bakr walked almost casually around to check the first officer. He was going nowhere fast or had chosen to play dead.

Bakr had minutes to get out.

He checked up and down the street, took the blanket from the boot, and dowsed it with the fuel from the jerry can. Unscrewing the petrol cap, he pushed a corner of the blanket into the filler pipe. He returned to the first officer, reached down, grabbed his arms, dragged him the few paces to the Mercedes, and hoisted his limp body face down across the driver's seat. He was unconscious or dead; Bakr had no time to find out which. To Bakr's surprise, the officer was also carrying a firearm. The officer began to moan. Bakr withdrew the gun and pointed it at the man's head.

A police siren whooped less than a mile away. *Destroy all evidence. Now!* Bakr thought as he lowered the weapon. He grabbed the jerry can, emptied the remaining fuel over the officer and back towards the blanket, and then took out a lighter. But it jammed. Bakr cursed. His eye then caught sight of a spray can in the boot. He grabbed it and thrust it along with his mobile into the folds of the blanket. A few paces from the car, Bakr turned and fired. The gun sounded like a harmless firecracker, echoing off the surrounding walls. The blanket twitched. He'd missed. The siren was much closer. He took two steps forward, held the gun in both hands, and fired again. The can exploded with a thump. The blanket caught and flames quickly engulfed the rear of the car. Satisfied, Bakr turned, picked up the thermos, and walked away. When he reached the next street, the Mercedes exploded. Bakr unscrewed the thermos and took another swig of tea.

***

Bakr approached the large service station shop, keeping his face lowered and away from any CCTV cameras. He quickly gathered the items he needed: two chicken wraps, a bottle of water, a torch, batteries, and some WD40. He spotted a camera behind the pay desk. Bakr scanned the shop and found one more item: a baseball cap, which he started to put on as he approached the pay desk.

'Next, please.' The man at the pay desk looked Arabic. He nodded at Bakr, who nodded back.

'I just need to be sure it fits,' Bakr laughed, keeping his face lowered and fiddling with the cap. The cashier was completely uninterested, as he scanned the items. 'Would you like a bag?'

'No…no, yes.'

The assistant looked up at Bakr, confused.

'I mean, yes.'

'£28.30.'

***

Bakr waited until dark before approaching the French container lorry he had spotted parked up with several others near the service station. News of migrants pouring into the UK was known all over the world. No one would suspect a lorry *leaving* the UK of harbouring a stowaway, Bakr had reasoned. This is how he would get to France.

The trucker was having his evening meal in the large cafe on the other side of the site. Bakr had already watched the driver secure the strapping around the lorry and open the rear doors as part of his check. The lorry's container was empty, and the rear doors had no lock.

Bakr reached up, raised the latch just enough to open the door then let it go. The latch slipped back slightly but not enough to lock it. He sprayed the hinge with the WD40 and checked the latch's movement again. It moved a little easier this time but still wouldn't close. Bakr grabbed the metalwork on the door and rattled. It was enough. The latch slipped into the lock position. Bakr repeated the process, adding more lubricant. Satisfied, he clambered up, reached around, raised the latch the required amount, and closed the door behind him. With a rattle, the latch fell into position. Bakr had locked himself in.

He turned on the torch and surveyed the empty interior. He knew he would have to stay alert. This container could be left for weeks in a storage area. If he fell asleep and missed the opportunity to get out, this could become a 40ft metal coffin. Bakr's coffin.

He guessed that about forty-five minutes had elapsed when he heard a door open and close. Bakr was unsure if it was his driver. An engine fired up and there was a shudder through to where Bakr sat. It was his truck. After the hiss of air brakes, the truck began its journey to Dover.

Two hours later the lorry had slowed and Bakr sensed they were close to the port. After a series of stop-starts, there was a hiss of brakes, and the truck juddered to a stop.

Bakr then heard nearby voices. He checked his gun and switched off the torch. He struggled to hear what was being said. He turned his head, following the sound, and pointed the gun at the door. If the doors were swung open to reveal port authority police, it was an easy decision, he thought: he would shoot his way out and if necessary die in the process.

The voices were trailing off. It was nothing. Bakr let out a long breath.

The truck jolted and was on its way again. As Bakr had expected and had prayed for, the port of Dover officials had simply waved the truck through. They had enough on their plate, checking the hundreds of inbound vehicles entering the country.

Bakr sat in the dark, imagining the Frenchman steering his way through the various lanes. He got his first whiff of sea air and heard the squawk of gulls and the general hubbub of port life. Then he felt the unmistakable rise of the trailer mounting the metal ramps, as the driver negotiated the truck into the bowels of the ferry.

***

It was quiet. Bakr woke with a start. He cursed the fact that he had no means of telling the time. The truck had stopped. He recalled the gentle movement of the boat and realised he must have fallen asleep during the crossing. He vaguely remembered the truck going at some speed. Autoroute speed. As he came to his senses, he knew that he may have just one chance of getting out. He took out the gun from his pocket and started banging on the door of the container.

'Hey! Hello! Hey!' Bakr yelled and repeated the banging. 'Hey!'

Bakr heard voices. *Thank, Allah*, he thought. There was movement outside. He pocketed the gun. The latch was being raised. The door swung open and bright sunlight flooded the interior. Bakr raised an arm to his eyes. '*Merci, merci*,' he said in his best French.

'*Ah, mon Dieu! Qu'est ce que tu fait là!*' The driver demanded. '*Poff! C'est un autre migrateur.*'

His driver had turned to a fellow driver and was raising his hands and gesturing at Bakr. The drivers were both about sixty years old. They were in another lorry park. Bakr determined that the men were no threat and jumped down, smiling.

'*Merci, monsieur. Vous êtres trés gentil.*'

'*Tu est fou! Imbécile!*' The drivers were both shaking their heads in disbelief.
'*Les Anglaises sont impossible. Je retours en Libye,*' Bakr continued.

The drivers continued their remonstrations, as Bakr quickly moved away. He soon saw signs indicating that he was in or very near Lille. *Perfect*, he thought.

Chapter 29
COBR

Cabinet Office Briefing Rooms, Central London, UK

The faces in the room were glum. The PM's special broadcast to the nation the previous evening was headline news across the globe. The message had been the usual mixture of outrage, sadness, resilience, and resolve. Number 10 were having to feed an army of international press, ever-hungry for updates and next steps.

Home Secretary, The Right Honourable Janet Carmichael MP, was taking her place at the head of the meeting table. 'Morning. The PM will be joining us shortly.' Behind her was a bank of displays, showing various images. After acknowledging Nadine Fuller, the Foreign Secretary, she looked down at the table. 'Mike, will you kick off, please.'

Commander Mike Boyd, head of Counter Terrorism Command, or CTC, also known as SO15, took the floor. 'Thank you, Home Secretary. The man on the screen is Bakr al-Ahdal, a Syrian national. He entered the country via Eurostar from Paris a few weeks ago in the name of Aaqib Jafari under a Moroccan passport.'

'A false passport?' the Home Secretary interjected.

'Yes, ma'am, it passed the scrutiny of our border control at the French end.' A new image had replaced the first, showing Bakr al-Ahdal at UK passport control, followed by another of him sitting on a bench on the Embankment. 'The Syrian government was quick in helping us to identify him.'

'Was he not known to us?' Carmichael asked.

'No. As you know, we have several thousand on our watch list. He's not one of them.'

'Which is probably why he was sent.'

'Yes, ma'am, we believe he was the cell leader.'

144

'And the one who escaped, killing two of our police officers in the process.'

Boyd pursed his lips. 'Yes, ma'am.'

'Look, I'm not going to ask how that happened and how one of the most advanced counter-terrorist services in the world, in a city bristling with CCTV, could completely lose him. Fortunately for you, this is not the time for incrimination. So, the other suspect. Tell me about him.'

'Mohammed Faasil.' Two new images appeared: one showed Faasil's passport photo, the other his mangled corpse outside St Pancras. '20 years of age, born and raised down the road in Hounslow. No known previous terrorist activities, not even a police record. He had a steady job at a mobile phone shop. Lives in a small flat and owns a car. He was doing OK.'

Carmichael shook her head. 'Why this? Such a waste. Muslim?'

'Yes, ma'am. We're interviewing the imam and other worshippers at his mosque as we speak.'

'Anyone else?'

'These are the other tankers that arrived in Down Street,' Boyd replied. A video ran showing CCTV footage of the tankers at various points in London. 'The bombers were smart. We trawled all the CCTV we had. No positive ID. We believe the tanker hijacking took place at around 4 a.m. near the depot, in a remote part of a large industrial area. No witnesses. Bodies in the burnt-out van near the depot are almost certainly theirs. Forensics are still working on that. The tankers were later dumped and burnt. The only image our team managed to capture was that of Faasil when he ran from the scene. He then led us to al-Ahdal.'

'Thank god for CCTV,' Fuller said.

'And what does all this tell you, Mike?' probed the Home Secretary, trying to ignore the Foreign Secretary's acerbic gibe.

Bradbury interjected, 'The attack was well-planned, well-executed, and need I say, shockingly devastating. And the passport appeared genuine, all of which would suggest that he is part of a very professional network. Well-funded, well-organised.'

Boyd did not disagree with the MI6 chief's assessment. Anything to let him and his team off the hook was welcome.

Prime Minister David Summers and his senior aide, Rory Daking, the Downing Street Chief of Staff, entered the room. 'Morning everybody,' Summers said. His face and tone of voice were grim.

Those present returned the welcome mutedly, 'Good morning, Prime Minister.'

The Home Secretary stood up, 'Good morning, Prime Minister,' she said, as she relinquished her seat, adding quietly, 'We've only just started.'

The prime minister took his seat at the head. His aide sat on one of the chairs behind him. 'Please continue.'

Carmichael looked across the table, 'Thank you, George. And is that network known to us? Are we talking international?'

Sir George Bradbury stuck out his bottom lip. 'I met with the CIA and DGSE chiefs yesterday. Early days. As Mike alluded to, it appears like a new cell or cells. The Americans have nothing. The French are aware of new cell activity. They're still looking, but there's no obvious link to the tube attack. Not yet, anyway.'

Bradbury purposely held back on Lamotte's tenuous lead.

'Except for the fact that this Bakr al-Ahdal arrived from Paris via Eurostar,' Carmichael said. She turned to the PM, 'Fake Moroccan ID.'

'So, are we saying the only lead we have is a possible cell in France?' Summers asked and looked at all the faces present.

With no immediate response from anyone, Bradbury cleared his throat, 'Well, as I said, er, just before you arrived, Prime Minister, we believe they're professional, well-trained, and well-funded.'

Summers spoke up. 'Oh, I heard that much. Look, I'm sorry, you all sound like a worn-out record. Well-trained, professional…Sounds like you're covering your collective arses for a complete fuckup.'

Bradbury was unfazed; he knew the PM well enough to know that he was reacting from some serious public pressure, let alone from the victims' families. 'To answer your question, Janet, I believe this *is* international. It has all the hallmarks.'

'International enough to include home-grown terrorists.' Carmichael clarified.

'Yes,' Boyd said, picking up from the MI6 chief. 'We've brought in Faasil's immediate family for questioning. But they seem genuinely shocked. My team are still dissecting the family home and everyone they know or have known.'

'Mobile data?' the PM asked.

'No. The mobile we found on him was crushed. And it looked like a burner. We found his mobile in his bedroom. Both phones and family laptops are with GCHQ.'

The room turned to Sir James Mace, the GCHQ chief. 'I should have a full report by tomorrow,' he said.

'OK, so we have *two* possible but very shaky leads, and not much in the way of evidence,' Carmichael stated. 'I assume we have nothing from Down Street.'

'There was a witness, er…' Boyd scanned his notes, 'a Mr Foster. He confirmed it was Faasil that he saw. Foster was the one who called the police.'

'Sadly, too late,' Fuller said.

'The officers on the scene did do their best to warn BTP, LUL, and TfL,' Nicholas Edgerton added. The MI5 chief was keen to have some positive minutes of the meeting recorded. The Metropolitan Police had indeed contacted the British Transport Police, the London Underground, and Transport for London. But the deadly act was just minutes away. 'In the meantime,' Edgerton continued, 'we have our hands full dealing with some pretty violent retaliations on Muslim communities across the country.'

'Indeed,' the PM responded. 'That is most regretful but not unexpected. I'll make another speech to the nation. Attacking innocent citizens is no answer.'

Carmichael continued to lead the meeting. 'Can we get more intel from the Syrians on this Bakr al-Ahdal, and his movements in France from the French?'

'Our French counterparts, Europol, and Interpol are already looking.' Bradbury answered. 'But I doubt they'll uncover much. This man knows how to avoid detection.'

'He also outsmarted SO15, SO19, and the Met.' The PM's aide said. 'God knows where he is now. Meanwhile, number 10 is having to deal with a total shitstorm like no other.'

'Yes, thank you, Rory,' Carmichael said. 'We are aware of that.'

Bradbury retained his cool, calm composure. 'We do have a motive for al-Ahdal,' he said. 'It seems he lost his mother and two sisters in a US drone strike about ten years ago.'

'OH, CHRIST ALMIGHTY!' the PM yelled. He turned to his Foreign Secretary, pointing a finger straight at her. 'Right, you tell the Americans they're to blame for all this with their armchair, so-called "over the horizon" tactics. And you, George, tell the CIA to pull their *fucking* finger out! And Rory's right,' Summers added. 'I really do wonder what you all do. This is our 9/11. And like

147

9/11, none of you have a *fucking* clue. God knows how many innocent lives have been lost. We have one dead terrorist—by pure chance. Another, possibly the ring leader, gets away. We need answers. We need arrests. We need *action*. AND WE NEED IT NOW!'

With that, the prime minister stormed from the room, followed by his aide.

Bradbury did not dare mention that the drone strike had been a joint US-UK operation with much of the intel on that occasion provided by MI6.

Chapter 30
Lille Cell

Northern France

Bakr was waiting patiently. He was now in the centre of Lille, strolling along *Boulevard de la Liberté* under a grey March sky. Every now and then, he would stop and peer into a store window, acting like a casual shopper. A cold wind made him hunch his shoulders and thrust his hands deeper into his jacket.

A police car swung onto the wide boulevard from the direction of a nearby park. Bakr timed his walk so that one of the bare trees that lined the street blocked their view of him, and then stopped and turned towards the nearest shop. The police car was driving slowly. France was also on high alert. Police presence had intensified in every city and major town; patrols on foot and in vehicles were a constant reminder. GIGN, the specialist tactical wing of the National Gendarmerie, was out in force.

Bakr glanced back down the road. The car was continuing at its steady rate and was now already fifty metres away. He turned back to the window. It fronted a small boutique. Female mannequins were backed by sheets of highly polished steel that distorted and multiplied Bakr's reflection. His mind suddenly jumped back to the day his world exploded like a mirror into a thousand shards, shredding his family's skin and his mind, and rocking his very soul. It was a memory that resurfaced with unexpected regularity. And with each flashback came a renewed clarity and sense of purpose.

Bakr closed his eyes briefly then continued his slow walk along the calm street—an angry man in a peaceful land. The faint sun low in the sky barely warmed his right cheek, as the bitter, northerly wind buffeted and chilled the rest of his body.

Thanks to their wealthy benefactor, Bakr and all those involved in their lethal quest had gone through rigorous training. Now experts in close combat, weapons, explosives, surveillance, subterfuge, and advanced driving skills, they were also up to speed with the types of advanced telecommunication monitoring and interception systems that were available to law enforcement agencies. He had received a message from one of the Lille cell's contacts. The app promised end-to-end encryption, but neither man trusted the veracity of that claim. It could be a ruse. For national security reasons, who knew what pressure intelligence agencies could impose to extract the data they needed? They also trusted no one except each other. Bakr and his men were therefore suitably circumspect in their communications.

Bakr looked at his phone. The message was from 'Didier.' But Bakr knew it was a man named Mansour.

Any luck? Mansour had written.

Bakr typed his reply: *Trying to find some new shoes. No luck.*

Mansour: *OK, I pick you up.*

Mansour had left his apartment and was sitting in his car. He was a second-generation Pakistani immigrant. His parents and elder brother had lived in Lahore, where his father had owned a successful clothing business. His exports led him to Europe and to the family's new and quite prosperous life.

Mansour had never been so driven, tending to drift from one job to another. It was when he was a courier driver that he met the man who inspired him to his new life—his *raison d'être*.

The man lived in a respectable neighbourhood. Mansour had made dozens of deliveries to the address over more than a year. One day, when Mansour delivered another package, the man had handed him two €50 notes.

'I can get you much more of that if you can be *my* courier.'

Mansour had stared at the notes, then up at his customer, not sure what to do. Little did Mansour know, but his entire background was known to the man standing on the doorstep. The man already knew Mansour's name from his name badge.

'Take the money, Mansour, and enjoy spending it,' he continued. 'You have my telephone number on your mandate. Call me if you're interested,' he said and closed the door.

After a quick look around Mansour looked at the notes again and slipped them into his pocket. His mandate showed the customer's name: M. Hasam.

That was two years ago. Now Mansour was approaching his 28th birthday and was a key player in the Lille cell. He had his own flat and car.

He wondered if his parents were suspicious. His father seemed pleased with his second son's independence and proudly told his friends how both his boys had made a success of themselves. His mother stayed quiet. She would simply look at Mansour with what seemed a pained smile.

'Be good, Mansour, and look after yourself,' she said on his last visit. Mansour could not face seeing them again.

The new, black Citroën pulled up outside the shoe shop. Bakr got in and nodded to his driver. Bakr's French was minimal and so was Mansour's English. They drove in silence for thirty minutes and finally turned into a quiet tree-lined street on the outskirts of the town. Mansour reversed into a driveway and killed the engine. Both men sat for a while surveying the street. There was no one around. Mansour nodded to Bakr and they both got out.

The house was chalet-styled, a few decades old, and set back from the road. The neighbouring houses were identical. The front door opened and Bakr was ushered in. There, waiting for him in the hallway was the leader of the Lille cell, Ahmed Hashim.

'My brother. *Ahlan bika*! Welcome!' Ahmed said, embracing Bakr once the door was shut.

'*Shukran.*'

'You had a difficult journey, I'm sure.'

'I need a shower and a change of clothes.'

'Of course. Mansour! Help our guest. *Des vêtements.*'

Mansour disappeared.

'Please. I have made us some tea.'

They entered the kitchen. Bakr sat at the table and lit a cigarette. He took a deep drag and released a long, slow stream of smoke.

'I must congratulate you for your success in London,' Ahmed said, as he busied himself with the tea making. 'It is truly inspiring.'

'What do the media say?'

Ahmed handed Bakr his tea and sat down opposite, smiling a mouthful of crooked teeth. 'Bakr. May I call you Bakr?' he said quietly. Bakr simply nodded. 'You are headline news around the world, of course.'

'Does that work?' Bakr asked nodding at the blank TV screen mounted on the wall.

'Of course.' Ahmed reached for the remote. It was already tuned to a news channel. A reporter was talking excitedly; a map of London showing the extent

151

of the attack was filling the screen. 'You see, Bakr. They talk of nothing but your heroic attack.'

The coverage then cut to the reporter standing on one of the temporary platforms constructed by the major TV stations. The world's media, it seemed, had been allowed into Green Park, where they had a view of Green Park tube station on Piccadilly. The walls of the white-grey Portland stone building above the station entrance were now black, and smoke could still be seen spiralling outwards and upwards. Police cordons had been set up along the wall that bounded the park and across every road leading into the area, from Harrods in the west, The Strand, and Chancery Lane in the east, the roads leading off Euston Road in the north, and all those south of Buckingham Palace. Most of central London was in lockdown and on high alert. It seemed like hundreds of blue lights were flashing behind the reporter. Fire engines, ambulances, and police vehicles were scattered across the road, and emergency personnel could be seen running this way and that.

'You can kill the sound,' Bakr said.

Ahmed hit the remote and the room fell silent. Bakr stared at the screen. 'We did this.'

Mansour joined them and looked at Ahmed then at the TV. '*Incroyable!*' he said.

'Yes, my friend,' said Ahmed. 'You did. You have struck where it hurts. They say this is the most devastating terrorist attack in the UK ever.'

'Wait. What is this?' Bakr sat forward. 'What are they saying?' On the TV was an inset image showing an aerial video of St Pancras railway station.

Ahmed fumbled with the remote. The coverage had returned to the news anchor in the studio. Ahmed listened and translated. 'She is saying that a man was pursued by the police. Er, St Pancras railway station…Oh, it seems he ran from the station and was hit by a truck…Sorry, run over by a truck.' Ahmed listened some more. '…They have not identified the body, as it was badly…badly crushed. I'm sorry, Bakr.' He looked at Bakr.

'Don't be. Mohammed should have been here with us. But he died a martyr.' Bakr said flatly and took another drag on his cigarette.

Bakr's face and name then appeared on the screen. It was then followed by an image of the burnt-out Mercedes, followed by the face of its elderly owner. Back in the studio, the anchor was talking with a colleague, shaking her head at the growing list of atrocities. The coverage continued with an earlier interview with the British PM, followed by the scene in the House of Commons.

'Enough!' Bakr said. The TV went dark.

After a long silence, Ahmed asked, 'What should we do?'

'We continue, of course.'

Mansour shuffled nervously. '*Il y a des vêtements à l'étage dans la salle de bain*,' he said to Ahmed.

'There's a change of clothes for you upstairs in the bathroom.'

Bakr stubbed out his cigarette and gulped down his tea. Before he left the room he stopped and turned. 'I need to lie low here. The next attack will be your mission, Ahmed. But I want to meet the others first.'

'I have arranged for them to be with us tomorrow night.'

'And I need to hear your plan.'

'Of course. Everything has been prepared.'

Chapter 31
Basilica of St Peter's

Vatican City

The heat was merciless. The sun seemed to press down on the ancient city, baking its tiled rooftops and bleaching its domes. With the drone of traffic, incessant car horns, and buzz of scooters—it was as though the city were a vast colony of insects, stirred up by the rise in temperature.

Cardinal Bianchi, oblivious, it seemed, of the stifling air and the agitated city sounds beyond the Vatican's walls, strode purposefully towards the great church of St. Peter's. His route took him along one of the paths of the private Vatican gardens, past the Grotto of Lourdes, along the very route His Holiness the Pope would often take on his frequent meditative walks. As the cardinal passed through the pools of shade and into the intense sunlight, his scarlet choir dress and white rochet seemed to light up; his cassock swishing from side to side and stirring up small eddies of dust from the path.

It was only after he had passed through a side door within the shadows of the basilica did the cardinal appreciate the cool relief of the interior.

It took a while for him to adjust to the gloom. He mopped his bald head with a handkerchief, and proceeded down a short corridor, at the end of which was another door, its latch echoing sharply as he raised it. He reached forward and flicked a light switch to reveal a narrow set of steps that seemed to disappear down into total darkness. The cardinal ducked under the low lintel, and clinging to a handrail, made his way down, his eyes adjusting to the gloom with each careful step.

For a moment, the cardinal stood at the base of the steps and closed his eyes, gently breathing in the stony mustiness of the ancient catacombs that lay before him. Soft lighting illuminated a long corridor beyond—the men he had arranged to meet were clearly already here. Just as they must have done, the cardinal flicked the lower light switch; total darkness now engulfed the steps above him. It was important that no one disturbed them, so every precaution had to be taken.

'Gabriele, we are here.'

A cardinal dressed in red stepped out from a side room a few metres from Cardinal Bianchi. The gold pectoral cross and chain that hung from his neck glinted in the dim light.

'Ah, Cardinal Dabrowski, you made it. Thank you. And Cardinal Romero?'

'I'm here, yes.' Cardinal Romero appeared from the same room, a faint smile on his heavily lined face. He wore a black cassock, a silver cross, and a scarlet *zucchetto*.

The three men were beneath the basilica in one of the city's many catacombs. All three entered the small room from which Cardinals Dabrowski and Romero had appeared and knelt in supplication, their heads bowed, murmuring their prayers in front of an aedicula.

Cardinal Bianchi was the first to rise, followed by the other two. 'It is appropriate,' he began but his voice trailed off. The words rang momentarily between the surfaces of the tiny room, the strange acoustics disorientating him and causing all three of them to look around at the cool earthy walls. He began again, this time barely above a whisper: 'It is appropriate that I brought you here in the presence of this holiest of relics—the spear that pierced Our Lord Jesus.' This time, the walls seemed to absorb his words, stultifying them, sucking them in forever, helping them die and join the many long-lost occupants of the necropolis. Cardinal Bianchi could think of no better location for his clandestine meeting. And yet, was it the profound silence of their surroundings, a respect for the dead, or perhaps the presence of what each of the men believed unequivocally was the spear that entered Christ's body that made anyone who entered here speak in hushed tones?

The cardinal reached out and touched the protective glass of the small shrine. A soft yellow light illuminated the relic: an incomplete spearhead. Cardinal Bianchi continued, 'We are privileged—if that is the right word—to know many dark secrets. But there is one I must discuss with you urgently. It concerns the Guild of God.' The cardinal paused and sighed as he gathered his thoughts. 'It seems that what we believed was a mere flight of fancy, a ludicrous but harmless fantasy, is, I fear, very much a reality and far from harmless. I have learned a stark and shocking truth behind this secret society.' The cardinal turned to face the other two princes of the Catholic Church. 'I'll get straight to the point. The Guild of God have a weapon. They call it the Spear of Destiny.'

The other two cardinals turned to look at the spear behind the glass.

'A weapon, you say?' the Spaniard asked.

'Please, allow me to finish.' Cardinal Bianchi began pacing slowly back and forth in the confined space. 'The Spear of Destiny is a fearsome weapon of unimaginable power—a power close to God's, no less. It is capable of harnessing the destructive force of Mother Nature herself and turning it to the…demonic advantage of those who wish to use it. The recent terror attack in London appears to have been the trigger; the Guild of God plan to use this weapon to strike at the heart of Islam. They want to finish the business that started nine hundred years ago.'

'The business that *we* started, you mean.' The Polish cardinal who spoke looked up as though to signify the great church that stood above them and the worldwide religion it represented.

'Indeed, my friend. The church must hang its head in shame for its history of violent bigotry and idealism. And now these fanatics want to revive that hatred, all in the name of Christianity.'

'Wait. Let me understand what you are saying, Gabriele.' Cardinal Romero was massaging his lower lip with a thumb and forefinger. 'We know of the Guild of God, of course. They are no more than a kind of benevolent, Masonic-like society. From what I know of them, they appear to have done a lot of good in promoting Christian values. Generous donations, civic projects, and helping the poor. Many good deeds for all of humanity, regardless of religion, and harmless, as you say. Now they have some kind of *doomsday* weapon? Is this really true?' Cardinal Romero almost laughed. 'It sounds so…implausible.'

'Don't you see, Juan?' Bianchi continued. 'The Guild of God see this *not* as an attack against the West, but an attack against Christianity. The Spear of Destiny is the response. A response in the defence of Christianity. They intend to unleash destruction on a truly massive scale.'

'What kind of destruction?' Cardinal Dabrowski asked.

'That's just it. I don't know.'

'Then how can you be sure of anything?'

'Marek, this is a secret weapon after all. Look, experiments in controlling the weather are nothing new. During the Vietnam War, it's said that the Americans seeded clouds in an attempt to induce torrential downpours to wash away the Ho

Chi Minh supply trail. There are also rumours that the US military can manipulate the upper atmosphere using a system called HAARP, which, commentators say, could disable enemy communications over a large area while allowing their own to continue to operate. Who knows what level of technology is out there now? It's advancing at an exponential rate.'

'So, this weapon. Where is it? Who has it?' asked Romero.

Cardinal Bianchi looked at his questioner. 'I don't know. But I do know that those behind this crusade hold some of the very highest political, religious, academic, and economic positions on earth. They have enormous power and influence. The Guild of God runs deeper and wider than we could have ever imagined. I fear there is nothing we can do.'

'Who here at the Vatican knows of these plans?' continued Romero.

'The three of us and my emissary, Father Brendon; possibly others. I can't be sure.'

'And His Holiness?' Cardinal Dabrowski enquired.

'No, I don't believe he knows. And I don't believe he should.'

'If this…organisation is so far-reaching and powerful, what can we do?' Cardinal Dabrowski raised his hands in desperation.

'From what little I know we should limit our association with the Guild of God. Our mere knowledge of its existence could implicate us,' Romero said.

'With respect, I disagree.' Cardinal Bianchi said. 'If we do nothing, they will succeed. If we are to do anything, we need information—proof, names, places, and that will mean involving more people—beyond the confines of the Vatican.'

'Is that wise?'   Romero asked.

Bianchi paused before replying. 'Juan, we cannot do this alone. We have a vast network of contacts—our own spheres of influence. We should use them. Speak with the people you trust, your closest friends and colleagues.'

'But how can we trust anyone?' Dabrowski asked. 'Who on earth could we approach to prevent this? If what you say is true, our spheres may overlap those of the Guild of God. The people behind this weapon may be the only people capable of actually stopping it.'

'I have considered this possibility, of course. But we are men of God. Choosing whom we trust and whom we do not is a luxury we do not have. We should have faith in all of God's children, otherwise, we deny the words of Our Saviour. We must trust in God. He will guide us. Indeed, our indiscriminate actions may be enough to draw out and expose those behind this weapon, who, I am sure, are a small minority within the Guild. It's our only option.' Cardinal Bianchi's voice was slowing and the last words trailed off.

Silence suddenly descended, as though the room was holding its breath. The three men were deep in thought. The Spanish cardinal broke the spell: 'How are you so certain about all this? You must have a primary source for this information. Who is it? Do you *trust* them? Indeed, I must ask this, and I must apologise to Cardinal Dabrowski in doing so, but how can you even trust us?'

Cardinal Bianchi did not reply. He swayed slightly, 'That is a wise question, Juan. Oh my god, what am I to do?' He suddenly slumped in despair. His colleagues instinctively reached forward, holding his arms to stop him from falling.

'Gabriele, what's the matter?' Cardinal Dabrowski was full of concern for his colleague.

'It's all right. I'm fine. Bless you.' The cardinal, the eldest of the three men, had regained some of his former composure. He massaged his brow, shaking his head slowly. 'My friends, I am certain about this. But where do I begin?' He looked at his colleagues, his eyes red and rheumy, his shoulders drooping. 'No one really knows when the Guild of God began. It may be centuries old. Many joined its ranks—all very carefully vetted. To be invited into its folds would be an acknowledgement of one's elite status. So, its numbers swelled thanks in some cases to a mix of ego, a desire for power, and a sense of purpose, but for many a desire to do good. Indeed, its main aim was to promote Christianity peacefully, benignly, and philanthropically through private donations, political decisions; even foreign policies. As you said, Juan, its intentions were for the good of all humanity—schools, hospitals, scientific institutes, museums; the list goes on. Its longevity was assured. But new forces are shaping it. So, yes, I am certain about this. I am also ashamed beyond words. You see...I...I am a Guildsman of God.'

The two cardinals could only stare at Cardinal Bianchi.

'Is it true that members carry a mark?' Romero asked.

Bianchi raised the hem of his cassock. Dabrowski leant down. A small tattoo was imprinted on the outside of Bianchi's leg just above the ankle.

Two intertwined letter G's, one mirrored, both encircled by the letter O. Guild of God.

Romero simply nodded, then said, 'But why are you ashamed if so much good has come from this new crusade?'

'True. Please believe me. I knew nothing of these plans. In fact, my activity in the organisation is negligible. And therein, I suspect, lies the problem. This crusade is being driven and distorted by men of real power.'

'But exactly how are you *so* sure? Of the weapon, I mean,' Cardinal Dabrowski pressed.

'What I am about to tell you breaks the code and sanctity of the Guild of God, of course, for which I bear no shame. My position within this…renegade society will also be revoked if they ever find out. I do not fear any retribution that may befall me. From this day forth I will do everything in my power to stop this madness, even if that means losing my cardinalship. I will even lay down my life. That's how much I believe.'

Romero looked again at the relic in its enclosure. Dubrowski followed suit and smiled. 'Well, Your Eminence, I didn't expect a confession. But I think I speak for Cardinal Romero, too, when I say thank you for your openness. If, as you say, the Guild of God has taken a new and treacherous direction, it is one that you plainly did not foresee or are party to. It is clear to me, and I am sure to my esteemed colleague that you speak truthfully and from the heart—not that I would ever doubt your sincerity. You have my undivided support.'

'And mine, of course,' Romero said.

'Thank you. God be with you both.'

As though on cue, Cardinal Romero took the old man's arm again. 'Please, sit down, Gabriele. Do you need air? Should we go from this lifeless place?'

'Thank you, thank you, my dear friends. Yes, we must all go. We need to find a way to stop this…Armageddon.' Cardinal Bianchi turned to the shrine and made the sign of the cross. '*In nomine Patris et Filii et Spiritus Sancti. Amen.*'

Cardinals Dubrowski and Romero crossed themselves, too, and murmured, 'Amen' in unison.

The three men left their small meeting place. Dubrowski led the way to the archway and turned on the lights to the stairs.

Romero was the last to leave. He paused for a moment, then switched off the lights to the catacomb, plunging it back into its deathly darkness.

Chapter 32
Steel Machine

Northern France

The well-lit autoroute from Paris was behind them, and the November morning fog was now reflecting the truck's headlights and obscuring the dark road ahead.

'Go faster! We cannot be late,' snapped Ahmed to Salim.

'But it's worse now,' replied Salim, struggling to keep their articulated vehicle on the road.

'Yes, but Bakr will not tolerate failure,' retorted Ahmed, before returning his attention to the GPS and his notes from months before.

'Look! There it is,' exclaimed Salim, as he drove past their dew-covered getaway car.

'Good. Our turning is very soon,' replied Ahmed, checking the GPS again.

Ahmed's previous Eurostar trip was now a distant memory, but the data he had gathered back then would prove invaluable. On that journey, he had surveyed the landscape rushing by, searching for a suitable spot. When he eventually pressed SAVE WAY-POINT on his GPS, Ahmed knew he had the perfect location for their mission.

As the 08.10 Eurostar slid out of the Gare du Nord, Lucy and Alex were still battling their way through the groups of passengers in the carriages. Finally, the young couple hoisted their bags into the overhead rack and slumped into their seats for their return to London. At the table opposite, a small French boy was bouncing up and down with excitement. His father grabbed his arm and admonished him with a loud whisper. Almost obscuring the view across the carriage, was a large woman of indeterminate age, huffing and puffing, as she searched for luggage space.

'Can I help you?' Alex volunteered.

The woman did not look down, responding instead with a complaint, 'It's always the same. Never enough space.' Alex raised his eyebrows and Lucy smirked. The lady squeezed herself in next to Lucy, before starting to rummage in her handbag. Only then did she look up. 'Thank you anyway,' she said.

Alex turned to Lucy, grinned, and gave her a wink. She smiled and leant towards him. 'Our walk around *Montmartre* was great, and dinner was lovely, too.'

Lucy and Alex's excited chatter was non-stop, only interrupted by the trolley waiter, asking for their order.

It was 09.00 and the train from Paris was now thundering blindly through the thickening fog. A seemingly unstoppable steel machine, hurtling relentlessly northbound.

'This is it. Turn off here!' exclaimed Ahmed.

As they passed a blue wayside chapel, not much bigger than a dog kennel, Salim swerved the hijacked fuel tanker off the main road. It made a surreal sight as the trailer smashed the small structure to pieces.

Salim was panicking. 'Where now?'

As they careered down the narrow lane, the truck straddled the tarmac, scraping on bushes and breaking the bare branches.

'There! Stop now!' commanded Ahmed, pointing through the fog. Under instructions from Ahmed, Salim drove the truck through a wire fence, stopping just at the top of an embankment.

'Let's go!' barked Ahmed.

Jumping from the cab, they quickly began to unload timber strapped to the trailer, and scrambled with it down the slope. Despite the cold, Ahmed and Salim were already sweating as they struggled to pack the heavy wood against the rails; the silence around them was only shattered by the whining truck engine. After completing several descents, clutching more timber, they were ready.

Time was running short. The northbound bound Eurostar was just six minutes away. And just eight minutes later, according to Ahmed's notes, another would be hurtling from the opposite direction.

Breathless, Salim climbed back up the slippery slope and jumped into the cab. Revving the engine, he rammed the truck into gear and it ripped down the embankment, fuel trailer in tow. With momentum gathering, he was able to bounce the truck across the timber and bring it to a halt, sprawled across the tracks.

As they ran and gasped for breath they did not look back, nor could they hear the approaching train.

Alex and Lucy were still happily chatting.

'You know, if we'd gone by plane, we'd have been delayed for sure. Look how dense that fog is!' Alex said. Lucy was nodding in agreement and watching the fields rush past when they felt a gut-wrenching deceleration and the sound of grinding steel.

The impact was disorientating. The small French boy along with his father and Alex were propelled into the air, their legs ripped from the floor and scraping the edge of the table. Lucy and the lady beside her were slightly more fortunate: the initial impact forced them back into their seats, protecting their necks but then they were catapulted forwards, smashing their faces on the table.

Only when the train crumpled with a massive screech of metal on metal did Ahmed and Salim look back. By then the sound had gone, replaced by the bright glow of burning fuel, diffusing in the fog.

Ahmed looked at his watch; more than ten minutes had passed in the eerie calm following the crash. Something was wrong: there was no sign of the other train.

Ahmed and Salim fell silent as they hurried back past the now-ruined roadside chapel and towards their getaway car. Only when they were back on the busy autoroute to Paris did they talk again.

'We will see Bakr tonight. He will know we are loyal,' stated Ahmed.

In the debris of the train, Alex gazed up from his position unable to move. Only the faint light of day filtering through the mangled carriage confirmed to him that he was still alive. Lucy could smell the acrid fumes of the fire but could see nothing. The blood from her head wound was pouring across her face and the taste of blood was on her lips.

By the time the fog had lifted the TV crews were already beaming images of the disaster across the world. The mangled wreck of the Eurostar was sprawled hundreds of metres along the track. From the wreckage, came the jumbled din of unanswered mobile phones; each one ringing persistently until its battery finally expired.

'No one knows how many casualties there are today,' exclaimed the news reporter into the camera. 'But by chance, a double disaster was averted. The train from London, which normally would have passed a few minutes later, broke down just ten miles north of here. Let me hand you over to St Pancras Station for some reactions there.'

A middle-aged lady was sobbing to the cameras. 'My son is on the train; I don't know if he's alive. Let us thank God for saving the second train.'

Chapter 33
Elysée Palace

8th Arrondissement, Paris, France

The sound of a France 2 news report was echoing around the *Salon Doré*, one of the many grand and opulent rooms of the Elysée Palace, the main residence of the President of France. The woman reporter was relaying the latest facts and theories behind the Eurostar terrorist attack. The widescreen TV looked incongruous flanked by the gilded stuccowork, in a room adorned with a Napoleon III crystal chandelier, candelabra, and the president's Louis XV-style desk.

'It is now confirmed that the intention behind this atrocity was to cause the crash of not one Eurostar train but two. It seems that the terrorists drove the hijacked fuel tanker down the slope behind me and onto the tracks. After this and the devastating attack in London, governments around the world are facing another enormous challenge. The fact that this latest terrorist attack could have been twice as bad will provide no solace for those that have lost loved ones in such a violent and horrific way. Questions are now being asked about the lack of security barriers. But what price do we need to pay for our freedom and security?'

'I'm watching the report now.' The man, sitting unseen in a high-backed chair, spoke softly in a French accent. 'After London and now this, it is imperative that we move forward. Now is the time.'

The man leant forward and picked up a remote. The TV went dark and silent. He rose slowly from the chair holding the phone to his ear. A slither of late afternoon sunlight revealed the fine dark cloth of a handmade suit. His shoulders were rounded with age. 'Was the experiment successful?' he continued. 'I see.

So, what happens now?' As he listened, he moved across the room towards the farthest wall, his head bent downwards nodding in time with his measured gait. 'Then you must double your effort.'

He stopped a few feet from the wall and raised his head. The sun caught the unmistakable profile of the President of France.

In front of him, the afternoon rays also illuminated several paintings, each mounted in an elaborate gilt frame. The president gazed at each of them, his eyes finally settling on the one he had personally commissioned. The artist had been chosen for his uncanny skill in producing works in the Baroque style. President Jean-Baptist Dumart contemplated the image with awe. The colours were sombre and rich. A heavenly light illuminated the subject, casting shadows across an anguished face. The painting depicted Jesus on the cross—his side being pierced by a spear. Threatening clouds, tinted with touches of red and deep browns, billowed dramatically to enhance the suffering of Man's saviour. The work of art was brilliant. It could have been by the great Caravaggio himself. 'We must succeed. You know that don't you,' the president stated. 'Good, I shall await further updates...No, I'm looking at my favourite painting...Yes, *The Spear of Destiny.*'

Washington DC, USA

Six thousand kilometres away, Richard Ordway was in his apartment. It was past midnight. He placed his mobile down and stood up. This was not his first such conversation. But the significance of those calls never faded. 'The President of France,' he said out loud to the empty room. 'Holy shit.'

He paced the room then picked up his mobile and made a call. The president's last words had been the signal. 'We have a go,' he said and hung up.

***

The following morning, the crowd of reporters and correspondents surged forward as President Thomas Palmer and his advisors filed into the White House press conference room. The US president stepped forward and gripped the podium firmly. Arrayed in front of him were the cameras of the world's media. As he gazed calmly about the room all fell quiet in an instant.

With a clear voice and a confident manner, he began his address. 'The attacks on London and in France were shocking. Our thoughts and prayers go out to all those affected by those atrocities. But these were not attacks on distant shores; these were attacks on people who share the same ideals as every decent human being on this small and fragile planet. None of us is safe. None of us is immune. Not while hatred and ignorance drive people to commit these monstrous acts. We must stand up for our security and for the permanent rights and the hopes of mankind. These appalling attacks mean the free world is facing an escalation in danger and instability. The threat of further attacks is substantial. Rest assured that the good men and women of our security services are on high alert, and doing all they can to seek out and stifle any attempt to harm the good citizens of the United States of America. We must choose between a world of terror and a world of justice and virtue. We cannot stand by while the storm clouds of fear gather. And I tell you, folks, now is the time for us to act and rid the world of this vile group of people. If you are one of these people watching this, let me tell you, we have the *patience*; we have the *capacity*; we have the *resolve* to bring you down. Thank you.'

Palmer ignored the clamour from the press, as he began to leave the room.

'*Mr President, are there any known imminent threats here?*'
'*Who was behind the attacks, Mr President?*'
'*Is it a new terror group, sir?*'
'*Mr President, are the attacks linked?*'
'*Sir, are we going to war again?*'

Chapter 34
The Prince's Palace

Syria

Prince Al-Musan was sitting at his hefty, antique desk when Hassan appeared at the far end of the room. He was soon followed by a cautious-looking man of around sixty years. The aide left. The visitor was dressed in a dark brown suit that had seen better days and carried a black, tatty briefcase. A thin wisp of black hair was swept across the dome of his tanned head. He stood motionless looking at the prince.

'I was intrigued by your message.' The prince's voice echoed off the plain, white tiled floor and marbled walls. 'Please,' the prince continued, pointing to a chair.

The visitor bowed and approached, not taking his eyes off his host. He placed the briefcase next to one of a pair of chairs in front of the desk and sat down awkwardly.

The prince looked up past the man and nodded. A servant had entered with a tray of tea, which he placed on a low table.

'*Shukran lakum*,' said the visitor to no one in particular.

The prince stood and walked around the desk. 'Allow me. You are a guest in my house,' he said, and poured the tea.

'*Shukran lakum*, Your Highness'

The guest seemed to relax a little. He looked at his surroundings. The room was large, indeed palatial, and yet it had a simple elegance. Two potted palm trees as high as the ceiling stood on either side of the shuttered French windows, which were open to let in the mid-morning air. Beyond, lay a verdant lawn split by a path that led some fifty metres to a garden wall. Sprinklers were showering the grass with a fine mist.

The prince had returned to his chair and was looking at the man in front of him. Feeling his gaze, the man apologised. 'I'm sorry, Your Highness,' he said, 'I was admiring your beautiful home.'

'It was my father's and his father's before him, and back further still.'

The man nodded. 'It is very fine, Your Highness.' His English was stilted but excellent.

The prince took a sip of his tea. 'You are Kadeem Salman?'

'Yes, Your Highness.'

'You are Syrian and yet choose to speak a mixture of Arabic and English. Why?'

'I, er…I can speak Arabic, of course. I…'

'It's fine. My background is known to many.'

Salman fidgeted in his chair. He was a slight man. Beads of sweat sat on his wrinkled brow, which he quickly mopped with a handkerchief.

'I am an international businessman,' the prince continued, 'so English is merely a lingua franca. It is no reflection of my politics, my allegiance, nor my beliefs.'

Salman nodded nervously. 'Of course. I simply do not wish to offend.'

'You do not offend. Now, to the matter at hand. Like I said, your message intrigued me.'

'Yes, Your Highness.' Salman placed the cup on its saucer, where it rattled briefly. 'If I may?'

The prince nodded and raised a hand in acceptance. Salman reached into his briefcase and took out a small roll of paper.

The prince beckoned him to the desk, where the man unfurled what was an old map.

'Please, hold,' Salman said holding the map flat. The prince placed a paperweight on one side of the map and a hand on the other. Salman again reached into his case and, like a magician pulling objects from a hat, took out a metallic disk around twenty centimetres in diameter, and handed it to the prince.

The disc comprised of an outer ring of brass, divided into sections, each containing an Arabic letter, and an inner circle of silver again with more letters. The prince turned the disk over and was surprised to see elaborate decorations etched into its surface. 'A cipher?' he asked, turning the disk back over to reveal its workings.

'Yes, Your Highness. A Caesar cipher, I believe it's called. Very old.' The prince had placed his index finger on the inner disk and was rotating it slowly. 'It is a beautiful instrument, no?' said Salman.

'Exquisite,' the prince almost whispered. He placed the cipher on the desk and looked over the map. 'You have my attention, Kadeem Salman.' The prince leant back in his chair.

Salman sensed he now had some power over his rich and successful host. The prince knew it, too. And yet, for the prince, here was a man he knew he could trust. There was a simple honesty about him, the prince thought.

'I have rehearsed our meeting many times,' Salman began, 'But now I am unsure where to start.' He paused. 'I, Kadeem Salman, am honoured to be the guardian of something special and mysterious. I am one in a long, *very* long line of guardians reaching back into antiquity. I have come to you, Your Highness, because I know you are a learned man, a scholar of history, a true Muslim, a man of purpose.' Again, Salman paused.

'Go on,' the prince pressed. 'What is it? You want to say something else. I can tell.'

Salman looked down. He was thinking hard. When he looked up, he knew there was no turning back. He just had to choose the right words if he could remember them. 'I am an admirer of your recent activities, Your Highness.' There, he had said it. If Prince Al-Musan was the man then the facts had to be faced.

'My recent activities,' the prince repeated slowly, squinting at his odd visitor.

Salman was no longer fearful of the man in front of him. Even if he was funding terrorism, the prince was also a man with blind faith; a man of destiny. Salman was sure of it. He had studied him for a long time. If anyone could be convinced of what he was about to reveal, it was Prince Al-Musan. Besides, the prince was courteous, welcoming even, and prepared to listen.

With growing confidence, Salman took out his phone and pressed the screen a few times. 'I am getting old and my responsibility needs to pass to someone new, someone younger. I have no sons. I have no heirs. I have no one to whom I can entrust this great responsibility. About two years ago, I awoke from a dream in which I saw the next guardian. I could not see his face, but I knew he was a believer. I then had an inspired thought. I asked myself the question, who could I be sure was the chosen one? And the answer was simple: the man who began searching for the objects in my guardianship.'

'The stones! You are the guardian of the stones! Please tell me I'm right.'

Salman had him. Rather than answer, he continued as best he could with his prepared speech. 'I installed a series of motion sensor cameras in a very remote place. To my surprise, and only weeks after they were set up, I saw this.' Salman pressed play on his phone. The prince stared at the screen. What he saw was unmistakable—it was he and his team outside the cave in the Mountains of Holy Light.

'So, it's all true. The stones exist.'

'They do. And in case you were wondering, the cameras were painted to blend into the rocks. Much like the cameras they use in wildlife documentaries.'

The prince jumped up from his chair and clasped his hands behind his head and smiled. 'Tell me!' he demanded. 'Tell me everything!'

'Then let me show you this.' Salman reached forward and spun the map on the desk. The prince leant over it eagerly. 'You were no doubt disappointed not to find the stones. Am I correct?'

'Disappointed? I had researched for years. I spent one hundred thousand pounds on a useless parchment. I was distraught, Mr. Salman.'

'But in your heart…?'

'In my heart, I knew the story was true. The stones existed. And I knew they had some special purpose.'

'And did you…sense that you were part of their destiny?'

'Yes. Yes, I did. And today…'

'And today, I arrive at your door.' Salman smiled. At that moment, the two men knew they shared something deep; almost divine. Salman now felt equal to the prince.

'And the map?'

'Ah yes, the map.' Salman picked up the brass cipher. 'You see, the cave in the Mountains of Holy Light was the first hiding place of the stones.'

'Yes, as described in the manuscript.' The prince's eyes were darting over the map, eager for clues.

'The place chosen by the sage not long after they had fallen from the sky. But they were moved later to another cave deep inside mountains in our country. And the knowledge of their new location, known only to those who became guardians. The secret was handed down, as it was to me, by word of mouth. Those guardians kept that secret safe for centuries, trusting no one else. However, around six hundred years ago, one of the guardians, upon learning about the art of encryption, decided to commit the stones' new location to this map. Look at the place names. Anyone finding this map would be none the wiser. The names are unrecognisable. Not without the cipher.' Salman rotated the inner sphere and lined up one of its letters with a letter on the outer disk. 'So, now *rā* becomes *mīm*, and so on. You see?'

The prince began walking back and forth. 'So, the whereabouts of the stones were never recorded elsewhere,' he ventured, 'and the map and cipher were guarded as closely by persons unknown, except to each other.'

'Precisely. The utter secrecy of the guardians and this map and cipher meant that your search reached a dead end.'

'And now you are here, sharing this with me.'

'Fate is a mysterious thing. But the story does not end there. This is a primitive cipher, simple to decrypt. It was good for a long time as extra insurance. Each guardian had to bequeath the cipher and map to a trusted confidante along with a cryptic message. If anything happened to a guardian before they could appoint a successor, the beneficiary of their will would be given these objects,' Salman explained, pointing to the cipher and map.

'But what if the beneficiary failed to understand the cryptic message or decode the map?'

'That would be the will of Allah.'

'But that would have been such a waste.'

'Indeed. And yet Allah has not failed us,' Salman said, smiling.

'Yes, that is true. Allah be praised.'

'But please allow me to continue. In the 19th century, the outgoing and incoming guardians agreed to move the stones to a more secure location. So, the map and cipher became *nearly* as worthless as the manuscript you acquired. Instead, they became symbolic tokens during each handover, helping to remind each guardian of the long history and the importance of that with which they were entrusted. That is why they are in my possession.'

'You said "nearly" as worthless as my manuscript.'

'The map has another use.'

'And this more secure location?'

Salman paused and looked at the prince. Yes, everything felt right, he thought. The man before him had spent time and money pursuing the stones, and not for financial reasons; he was wealthy enough. This was a deeper quest.

Perhaps, finally, this was the man to put the stones to their intended use and fulfil the will of God. 'The stones are in bank deposit boxes in Damascus.'

'All the stones are in one place?'

'Yes. They have always been kept together.'

The prince turned and closed the doors to the garden then faced Salman, now seated and drinking his tea. 'The stones. I have read much about them from the time of the Crusades. Then nothing. And now I know why. The guardians kept their word with utter devotion.'

Salman continued with enthusiasm. 'The sage who had the vision gave the stones a prophetic status. But he did not know why. It was only later that my predecessors discovered their…unique properties.' In the prince, he was sure he had found the next true successor. Perhaps more than that. A great weight was being lifted from his shoulders. 'The sage knew it was a sign from God and that patience was needed; that time would tell. And yet, here we are nearly one thousand years later. The stones have lain impotent, unused. As a guardian I know the power of the stones, but not how to use that power.'

'And what *do* you know of their…power?' the prince asked.

'It requires a specific demonstration in a special place. This is the one use to which the stones are put each time the guardianship is handed over.'

'You are choosing me as the new guardian?'

'I chose you some time ago, Your Highness.'

'But we have never met.'

'I hope that one day you will share the same intuition needed to choose your successor. I am convinced I have chosen wisely.'

The prince stared at his intriguing visitor—this familiar stranger. It was the most unusual encounter he had ever had, and yet it seemed inevitable. Fateful. 'When can this demonstration take place?'

'I would need a few days of preparation. Maybe you would like to see these stones first…in Damascus?'

'Yes, yes,' the prince replied a little too eagerly. 'We can take my helicopter now and be in Damascus by this afternoon. You can then make your demonstration.'

'Sir, it is not that simple,' Salman said slowly.

'Why?'

'The demonstration would need to be at the sight of the second cave.'

'Why there?'

'You will understand why. Besides, it's where it's always been done. I do not want to break that tradition. Please, I ask for your understanding, respect, and patience.'

Prince Al-Musan paced the room. Patience was not his strong point. He was used to things being done when he demanded. He had wanted to know the truth about these sacred stones for so long. 'Fine. But we can fly to Damascus now.'

'Of course,' Salman conceded. 'But I would need to call the bank.'

'Do it. I want the demonstration this evening.'

Salman was taken aback. He was unused to such swift decision-making and action. But perhaps this was a sign that he, too, would soon understand the true meaning of the stones. His belief that the prince was the rightful inheritor was reinforced.

'This cave. What is its location?'

'It's on the map.'

Salman rotated the cipher back and forth, stopping briefly and pointing at the letters and the map. The prince looked none the wiser.

'I have a feeling this will be the last time this location will be used,' Salman said. 'So let me show you. I'm sure you'd prefer precise coordinates.' He clicked on one of map apps on his phone and after a few seconds handed the phone over.

'Good,' said the prince. 'You will be my guest for lunch. We then fly to Damascus. First, make that call to the bank.'

'Yes, Your Highness.'

The prince punched a button on his internal phone. 'Hassan.' His aide quickly appeared at the far door. 'Lunch for our guest and get the chopper fuelled and ready.'

Salman made the call. 'It's arranged, Your Highness. The bank will expect us at 3 p.m.'

'Very good. Then let us eat.'

'Thank you, Your Highness. You are most gracious. First, please allow me to do what I must.' With this, he picked up the map and cipher and handed them over. 'I said that I had already chosen Your Highness as the next guardian. I am not sure you are the next guardian.' When he saw the prince's face darken, he quickly corrected himself. 'Perhaps I should have said I am not sure you are *just* the next guardian. No, more than a guardian. I believe that you may be the first *user* of the stones.'

The two men faced each other in silence. Both were bound by a deep sense of destiny and an inexplicable calling that neither man understood. Now, finally, both men felt that the veil of ignorance was slowly lifting.

'Allah will be our guide,' the prince said, breaking the short silence.

'*Allahu Akbar.*'

'*Allahu Akbar.* I accept these tokens and will honour you and the many guardians before you.'

Salman nodded.

A table under a brilliant white gazebo had been prepared in the garden.

'What did you mean by my "recent activities"?' the prince asked.

Salman slowed. A casual observer earlier would have interpreted the cave video footage and the prince's research into the stones as "the recent activities." But Salman's choice of words had meant to be ambiguous. He was a peaceful man and so could not condone the prince's alleged extremist involvement. But he accepted the fact that he, or was it Allah, had chosen the prince. Without turning to his host, he replied, 'May God be with you.'

The prince nodded to himself. '*Allah maeak.*'

Chapter 35
AI Search Engine

The Pentagon, Washington DC, USA

Richard Ordway was seated at his cluttered desk, his face illuminated only by three large computer displays. He rubbed his eyes and sighed.

His superiors were breathing down his neck. All eyes were on him to pull this off. His mission, his responsibility was to accelerate development of the project. The energy experiment in Venezuela was stalling and that was a crucial component. *Was he clutching at straws? Was this a waste of time?* he wondered.

He had been with the same thoughts every day and night for more than fifteen weeks, starting to wonder if the search program he had commissioned was working. 'So much for artificial intelligence,' he muttered.

Ordway had enlisted the help of one of the DOD's computer geeks. They had plucked him from one of the tech giants. He was only twenty-seven and could probably run the world if he really put his mind to it, such was his grasp of data manipulation. Luckily for Ordway—and the world—the programmer found satisfaction in writing awesome code and very little else.

The program was designed to infiltrate servers across the globe and to search and filter billions of documents and videos, from theories, theses, and experiments to reports, articles, blogs, and analyses, looking for keywords and phrases using more than one hundred and twenty of the world's languages. Ordway was staggered at the speed with which the geek had completed the core coding.

'It's quite a simple algorithm,' he had said. 'The machine learning bit will take a little longer.'

'But what about decrypting files, breaking through firewalls and all that stuff?' Ordway had asked him.

'Oh, we can already do that. I tagged that onto my code. No sweat.'

'Just like that.'

'Just like that.'

The problem, Ordway was starting to realise, was that there was simply too much information out there.

The idea of the program came to him almost immediately after the call from President Dumart. Back then, he was excited; motivated. But now? Now he felt he had embarked on a futile, truly Sisyphean task, one that may result in failure. His failure. He had summoned the programmer back in for a dressing down on several occasions. The cool response was always, 'Have patience. It's still learning. The more data and feedback it gets, the better it will get.'

The young man had seemed so confident. If the information Ordway wanted was out there, he said, his search engine would find it. If it did not exist…Well.

Sure enough, there was a glimmer of hope—the program had shown signs of improvement. AI was helping to refine the results. Over the weeks, it had whittled down the daily results from more than four thousand to forty. Still, Ordway had to sift through those final results manually. It was a hard slog but he was told it was part of the machine-learning process.

This evening, just two documents had appeared. He looked back at the centre screen. A box confirmed it: REFINED RESULTS: 2.

Ordway eagerly double-clicked the first document. The heading read: *Le Figaro*. It was an online news article. Ordway's French was not great, but he got the gist. The heading was: *INCROYABLE ROCHER DU CIEL*.

INCREDIBLE ROCK FROM THE SKY, or was a better translation: INCREDIBLE ROCK FROM HEAVEN?

But it was the first of the accompanying images that made Ordway lean forward even more. A spark clearly jumping from a Van der Graaf generator into a rock—or was it a gemstone? He realised the image had an embedded video link. He clicked it and watched the Van der Graaf experiment in amazement. He then scanned the rest of the document, picking out keywords and phrases. '*Météorite unique?*' and the sub heading: *Nouveau à la science?* Near the foot of the page were another image and a caption. Ordway assumed it was of the discoverer, a certain Dr Daniel Bayford.

Ordway clicked on the second document. This was a detailed article on the very same discovery in the esteemed science journal, *Nature*. Ordway's excitement grew. There were quotes from eminent scientists, each hypothesising about the amazing stone. Some suggested that it may have come from the mysterious Oort Cloud, a truly enormous cloud of icy objects that encircles the solar system. Others talked about the Kuiper Belt and comets. One dismissed these theories, believing the rock must have originated from something far more exotic, perhaps ejected from a massive supernova. Its origins were clearly debatable, but the article concluded with a consensus: that the stone had remarkable and inexplicable properties, new to science, and that it was a meteorite.

Ordway sat back. He looked at the date of the Nature article. It was January. Two months ago. He then clicked on the *Le Figaro* document—it was a year old.

He re-opened the French newspaper article, clicked on translate, and went through it line by line. He skipped through the first part of the article, which talked about climate change and the location of the discovery, and focussed on the conclusion:

Doctor Bayford told me: "Fires in this part of our country are nothing new, of course. But yes, we are seeing higher overall temperatures and more and more heat waves. I have been a fire watch for a number of years and there is a higher frequency of fires now than at any time before."

His comments would seem to support climate change. However, he went on to say: "I also noted an increase in lightning strikes. It's well known that lightning is a common cause of forest fires."

Thunderstorms and lightning are usually triggered after spells of high temperatures cause large amounts of warm, moist air to rise. But after Doctor Bayford stumbled across his remarkable stone and its extraordinary properties—properties which I have personally witnessed—he strongly believes that the stone along with, he asserts, "others yet to be found" are responsible for the localised increase in lightning strikes and therefore the increase in fires on the hills and valleys close to his home. He went on to say: "There are natural locations in the world known as lightning magnets; rocky hills that attract unusual levels of lightning. I believe this rock—this beautiful gemstone—is an extreme version of that. It may even be new to science."

I, for one, have never witnessed anything quite so astonishing! What I saw defies all common sense.

If scientific analysis confirms this meteorite's seemingly unique properties, then Dr. Bayford may have found not only a brand-new element but something that could alter the course of physics. It could also give credence to his theory that this stone may be a kind of "lightning super magnet." One thing is certain: this discovery could lead to some very new and exciting knowledge.

For Ordway, the last paragraph said it all. He also knew that the word 'magnet' had not been in the original search string. *Now that's scary*, he thought.

Chapter 36
The Bank Vault

Damascus, Syria

The bank official was the first to exit the elevator and led the way down the corridor. Following him were Prince Al-Musan and Kadeem Salman.

'I believe we are fifteen metres below ground,' Salman said.

The prince said nothing. He was filled with anticipation. After years of research and a failed search, he was finally about to see and hold one of the mythical stones.

'Please, gentlemen, if you would be good enough to stay here for a moment,' the official said.

The bank official approached a dark glass screen filling the corridor and placed his index finger on a keypad. A series of red lights illuminated. The official leant forward; his face close to the glass. The lights turned orange. He straightened and quickly entered a passcode. The lights turned green and a glass door, as if by magic, moved backwards and slid silently to one side. At the same time, the corridor beyond the glass screen was illuminated, revealing a large, steel security door.

Salman looked at the prince. 'Only the best security.'

'Thank you, gentlemen.'

The official stood patiently before the vault, his face reflecting in the steel. The door opened. Salman nodded upwards and mouthed 'Cameras?' and shrugged his shoulders.

The vault contained a wall of safety deposits. The official handed Salman a key. 'Please press this button when you are ready to leave.' The vault door closed.

The prince turned to see Salman opening one of the small deposit doors and starting to pull out a long container. 'I will need your help, Your Highness.'

'This is heavy!' the prince said, as the two men placed it on the vault's only table.

Without a word, Salman lifted the hinged lid to reveal five smaller metal boxes within. They looked pristine, but the style was clearly nineteenth-century.

'Except for moments like this, they have remained largely untouched for many years,' Salman said. 'Please, Your Highness.'

The prince gently turned the lever-like handle on the nearest box and raised the lid. He reached in and took out a red velvet drawstring bag. He looked up at Salman.

'Heavy, isn't it,' said Salman.

The prince prised open the bag and tipped its content into his hand. 'At last,' he said, smiling, as he raised the stone to his face. '…It's beautiful,' he finally whispered, after turning it over several times.

'That's what everyone says when they first lay eyes on one.'

'But I see only five boxes. The story tells of two hundred and sixty-three.'

Salman pointed to the wall. The rest are in there. There are fifty-three deposit boxes in total. Fifty-two with five stones, the last with three. Today, we only need one.' The prince placed the stone into Salman's open palm. 'It is safe inside here,' he said, placing it back into the bag and into its box.

As they waited for the vault door to open, Salman turned to the prince. 'Before we leave, I will sign over the responsibility of these deposit boxes to you.'

The prince looked at Salman. *What was that responsibility?* he thought. Would the demonstration that Salman had promised enlighten him, and satisfy the sense of destiny that he had held for so many years?

Chapter 37
Secret Military Base

North-East Alaska, USA

It was 11 a.m. The air temperature was -18 Celsius. The sun was shining low in a clear, deep blue sky, as a stream of the US army's latest Humvees tore from the remote, military airfield. More were exiting the two C-5 Galaxy aircraft that sat on the runway.

In the passenger seat of the lead Humvee, Colonel Mike "The Moose" Mason sat hunched in his thermal camouflage jacket, a black beret perched on his head, the rushing scenery reflecting in his sunglasses. His nickname suggested a man of considerable size. Mason, however, was relatively short. But what he lacked in height he made up with in bulk. He was a fearsome-looking soldier—muscular, lean, and no-nonsense. 'How far, soldier?' he asked.

'ETA 20 minutes, Colonel,' his driver hollered.

The line of Humvees only metres apart roared through the pine forest on the snow-sprinkled road. The new turbo hybrid models were maxing out at 120kph. *Fast enough*, the colonel thought.

The suggestion of a restricted area somewhere further up was marked by a single unmanned sentry post and a raised barrier. Mason shook his head as they roared past. After six or seven hundred metres, the trees on the left-hand side gave way to a large open area. The forest, flanked by a high, security fence, continued along the righthand side, eventually encircling the base off in the distance. The convoy passed through an open metal gate and lurched to a stop in the main compound.

A group of scientists in thick winter jackets and hats appeared from one of the five buildings, their collective breath rising like steam in the sub-zero air.

Mason had emerged from his vehicle and was marching straight towards them.

'Wow! These guys mean business,' said one of the reception committee.

'This must be Captain America,' another quipped. The others sniggered.

'Dr. Scott,' the still striding colonel called above the noise of more Humvees. It was an instruction, not an enquiry. The colonel never wasted time.

'He's down below. Are you Colonel Mason?' one of the group ventured.

'I am he.'

'Please, this way. May I ask what this is all about? We heard something, but, you know, we aren't supposed to know, right? It's serious, I guess? Pretty cool those Humvees. How fast do they go?' the scientist gabbled.

The colonel stopped, removed his sunglasses, and looked at his guide. 'All in good time. And fast enough, Miss...?'

'Emma,' replied the twenty-something.

'Doctor Emma Crusoe, I presume.' It was less a question and more a statement of fact. The colonel had done his homework. He always did.

'Yes, sir. Pleased to meet you, sir. Sorry. Yes, this way.' She pushed open a door and allowed the colonel to enter. 'We have to go through here. Then down the corridor to the elevator. Down and down about fifty metres, right guys?' The others were following behind.

'Yeh, forty-eight,' one said, and immediately realised how irrelevant that was.

Another of the group signalled discretely to the others that Emma could do this without them. They sloped off, leaving one male scientist and Crusoe as guides.

The colonel stopped abruptly. 'This door. Why is it open?' he demanded. They had reached the first of two huge blast doors, designed to withstand a nuclear shock wave. '*And* that one?' he continued pointing to the second door further along the corridor.

Emma blanched. 'We, er, opened them up for you, sir. They take a while to open.'

'LISTEN!' he boomed, 'This is a Category A facility. I don't care if the President of the United Fuckin' States comes down here. YOU FOLLOW PROTOCOL! GOT IT!'

Emma was shaking. 'I'm, er, so sorry...'

'You're sorry. Christ, you will be sorry if a foreign force or terrorists turned up! Whose idea was it?'

'Er, I, er…I'm not sure. The lieutenant's…?' She glanced at her companion, who simply shook his head and decided that he wanted to join the other scientists. He wanted to get well away from this snapping bulldog and began to edge away.

'Really. Lieutenant Armstrong, uh? Well, he'll be feeling the toes of my boot, that's for certain. Where the hell is he anyway?'

'I, er, don't know, sir. I'm just a scientist,' she replied with a faint smile.

The colonel huffed. 'No, I suppose you wouldn't. Lead on!'

Emma and the colonel reached the elevator alone.

'Sorry, er, Colonel. Your um pass, please.'

'Yes, very good,' he turned and handed her his ID. 'You got that part right. Let me tell you, Dr. Crusoe, I'll be cranking up the security here ten-fold. This is a goddamned joke.'

'Sure. I bet.' The young scientist looked awkwardly at the ID before handing it back. She stood for a while, smiling. 'Oh heck. Sorry.' She grabbed the ID hanging from her neck and swiped it through the reader by the elevator. 'It's coming now.'

The doors opened. Emma leant in, swiped a reader inside, and pressed the lowest button. The colonel stepped in, turned, and faced his guide, who was about to step in beside him. The colonel held up a hand. 'I'll be fine from here,' he said, smiling.

'Sure thing.' The elevator doors closed.

Emma blew a silent whistle. 'Intense or what?'

Chapter 38
First Class Ticket

La Gran Sabana, SE Venezuela

It was early morning high on the plateau. The canvas on the tents rippled in the warm, gentle breeze. A lone tepui wren was hopping amongst a clump of flowers.

Tod was running over to the tent the team jokingly called the *en suite*. 'Hey! Kara!'

Kara was taking a shower. A tank of water, heated by four gas burners, provided enough warm water for the entire team for two weeks.

'Ow!' came the response from within.

'Tod laughed. He guessed the water had suddenly got a bit too hot for comfort.

'You OK?'

'Yeh. Can someone sort this pump? I think I just got a third-degree burn. What is it?'

'The professor's here.'

Kara appeared, hair and shoulders wet, a towel wrapped tightly around her and another in her hand. She was smiling. 'Great. Tell him I'll be over in a minute.'

Tod returned to the jeep that had brought the professor up from the landing strip and was helping him with his bags.

'Hey, Arthur!' Kara called. She was in jeans and an off-the-shoulder top, rubbing her hair with a towel.

'Kara! I'm sorry. I didn't mean to interrupt your ablutions.'

'No worries. How are you and how was the journey?' she asked as they gave each other a little hug.

'It's certainly worth the trek. It's been months.'

'We're about to have breakfast. Have you eaten?' Kara asked, leading the way to an outside table.

'No. The plane ride from Caracas made me a little queasy. Maybe a black coffee to start.'

'Coming right up, Professor,' Tod said.

'So, Arthur. You told me that something's come up. Good, I hope?'

'Something important enough for me to make this trip, Kara. And I wanted you to hear it first-hand.'

'Thanks, Arthur. Sounds exciting. Tell me more.'

'Your government friend may have found something.'

'Oh god. Don't tell, a new level of arrogance?'

Steel laughed. 'No, something far more beneficial.'

'What? A blank cheque? No, wait, a mains cable that plugs straight into the clouds?'

'Not quite. But there's a plane ticket for you.'

'I'm intrigued. Don't tell me. I've been re-assigned to a project to turn rainwater into wine.'

Arthur Steel smiled. 'Forever the meteorologist.'

'Forever the lover of a good Claret, you mean.'

They both chuckled. Kara towelled her hair further.

'Well, that's good Kara, because you're off to the home of Claret.'

Kara slowly lowered her arm and her mouth dropped open. 'France? Whatever for, Arthur?'

'There was a very interesting discovery made there not so long ago. Something that could help you here. We want you to meet the man who discovered it.'

'We? You mean you and Ordway?'

'Yes, Kara. But I've seen enough to convince me that it's worth you going.'

'But why there? Can't I see it online? How long will I be gone? What about the experiment?'

'Slow down, Kara. Look, I'm pleased you're going. You could do with a break. They say a change is as good as a rest.'

'But we're making such good progress here.'

'You are. And everything is cool. Just take your foot off the gas. You'll be refreshed and reinvigorated. All the things that can help you finalise your work. You're close, Kara, I can feel it. And this discovery…'

Tod arrived. 'One black coffee. One skinny latte. Beany's sorting the food.'

'Thanks, Tod.'

'Can I stay?'

'Sure, Tod,' Steel said.

Kara had told Tod that something had come up and that the professor was making a special trip. He sat next to Kara and listened intently.

So, who's this French guy?' Kara asked the professor. 'What's he got to offer?'

'Well, he's a Brit for one thing. He moved to France. Early retirement, I believe. Anyway, that's for you to find out. Intelligence would suggest that he may have stumbled upon our lightning Holy Grail.'

Kara looked into her old friend and mentor's eyes. 'What intelligence? Other scientists?'

'Me for one.'

'OK.' Kara was nodding. She trusted Arthur implicitly, but her mind was turning over. 'So, why me and not you? You're the real expert.'

'We think you're better placed to get the necessary information.'

'What does that mean?'

'You're a scientist doing her bit to save the planet, sorry, doing a *great deal* to save the planet. Our Brit in France was a scientist for the British government and some kind of former activist, which would suggest he has strong morals and is certainly pro-sustainable energy. Although probably not a vegan—I can't imagine living in France would make that an easy life choice.'

'Funny. But you initiated this whole project, Arthur. You could also charm the…' Kara was struggling to find a suitably complimentary simile.

'The knickers off a nun?'

'Arthur!'

All three laughed.

'That came out a bit too easily,' he admitted. 'Anyway, I'm more the theorist, whereas you are the practical one, rolling up your sleeves and getting stuck in. I've never told you, Kara, but you are brilliant. You made it happen. It's time I showed you something.' Steel took out his phone and, after thumbing the screen, handed it to Kara.

A video ran. It was a TV interview with Daniel Bayford. Kara squinted. 'Sorry, I don't have my glasses.'

'Just listen.'

"…I stumbled upon it following a forest fire."

"And you believe it may be a meteorite."

"Yes, I do. But one with very strange properties."

"And that's why you think it could be the cause of the frequent lightning strikes in this area?"

"Yes, it would explain the many fires we have. It's a theory of mine. But I ran some tests. I have a small laboratory. I like to dabble, you know."

The video cut to the male reporter standing somewhere presumably near the place of the discovery. *"Strange properties indeed,"* the reporter stated. Another image appeared.

'Watch this, Kara,' the professor said excitedly.

Tod leant in for a closer look. Kara squinted even more. 'I'm guessing that's the stone or meteorite…,' she said.

WOW!' Kara and Tod exclaimed in stereo.

The spark from the Van der Graaf generator jumping across to the stone was clear enough. The reporter continued over the clip. *"The scientific community is abuzz with excitement. It's believed the meteorite if that's what it is, may contain elements new to science. This is Chris Mambwe in Southern France."*

Kara looked up at the professor. 'OK, I'm interested. *Very* interested!'

'That's amazing,' Tod almost whispered. 'May I?' Steel handed him the phone. Tod pressed play to rewatch the video. 'I've got to show this to the others. May I?'

Before Steel could answer, he was running towards the tents, hardly noticing Beany walking over with a tray of food. She gave him a quizzical look and continued towards the table. 'Grub's up, guys.'

'Why hadn't we known about this discovery, Arthur?' Kara asked.

'You're right. I'm surprised, too. *Le Figaro* reported it first about a year ago. The first TV coverage wasn't until this recent news story. It soon got picked up by other media channels. Now it's all over the internet. Science journals, too. Kara, you know as well as anyone about lightning hotspots. The Alberta foothills and Sable Island in Canada, the Congo Basin, and, of course, Lake Maracaibo, where we first experimented. A lot has to do with basic meteorology. But we also believe there are 'lightning magnets'—hills and mountains containing minerals that may attract lightning. This discovery could be a lot more than that. This may turn everything we know about energy on its head.'

188

'Right! We need to move fast then.'

'Exactly. And we need to thank Mr. Ordway for spotting it.'

'Yeh, well, don't tell him that.'

Later that morning, Kara was standing on the edge of the bluff. Hot air rose up the sheer sandstone cliff face from the valley below. She closed her eyes and breathed it in.

Arthur approached and stood by her side. She smiled when she smelt his cigar smoke.

'Do you know what Ordway said to me that day we stood here?' Kara asked.

Steel smiled. 'You certainly rattled his cage. He looked seriously pissed.'

'I don't mean all that *I'm above the CIA crap.* No, he got all spiritual and quoted the bible. Don't you think that's a bit weird?'

'For an ex-CIA man? I guess. But he's from the bible belt. So, I'm sure he went to Sunday School and church. He was probably trying to impress you. You know, show you he had a softer, more lyrical side.'

Kara huffed. 'Nah, it was just weird and creepy.'

Steel laughed out loud. 'Oh Kara, the man had the hots for you. Couldn't you tell? Anyway,' the professor continued, looking out over the scenery, 'with a view like this surely anyone would be overcome with God's work.'

Kara followed the professor's gaze and then looked at him with a slight frown. 'Yeh, I guess you're right. It is truly spectacular here. Shame Ordway is such a dick. I might have fallen for it otherwise.' Steel laughed again. 'Anyway, this trip. How long are we talking about?' Kara asked.

'Oh, a week. Two maybe. Beautiful place, France. Ever been there, Kara?'

'Er, no. Always wanted to. When do I go?'

'Today. You need to go today, Kara.'

'What?' Kara turned to him. 'You *are* joking. I know we said we'd need to move fast. But *really*? What about all this?'

'I'm staying while you're away. It's all taken care of. It's the main reason I came. Now go pack some things and try to enjoy yourself. You won't need to take much. Your trip is all expenses paid. I'd milk it if I were you. And you'll be flying first class all the way. So, think of me here, camping in a third-class tent.'

As though on cue the faint sound of a helicopter made them both look out across the dark green vegetation of *La Gran Sabana* far below. They stepped forward and peered downwards. There it was, some eight hundred metres beneath their vantage point, looking like a small, black dragonfly. They watched as it turned upwards, heading straight for them.

'For me, I assume,' Kara said.

'Yep. Compliments of Mr. Ordway. Red carpet all the way for you.'

Kara suspected it was Ordway's attempt to impress her. She was having none of it.

'I'm doing this because I believe in you, Arthur.'

'You're doing this because you have to. You'll be back safe and sound in no time.'

***

The pilot raised the Piasecki into the air. Kara peered out of her window and raised her hand. Her team and the professor had assembled to see her off and returned her wave. The helicopter banked gracefully, then, tilting forward, accelerated back across the plateau's precipice and away.

The group of scientists dispersed, returning to their work, leaving the professor standing alone, watching the chopper disappear. 'Godspeed, Kara,' he said to himself.

Chapter 39
Project: Spear of Destiny

Northeast Alaska, USA

The black SUV thundered its way along the forest track, spitting a mix of stones and dust from its fat low profiles. The early morning sunlight strobed as the car sped past the countless pine trees.

Ordway, behind the wheel, was secretly enjoying the drive. Surely, he had the best job in the world: working for the government of the greatest nation on earth on a mission straight out of a thriller. Still, he had hardly expected to *actually* get this top-of-the-range motor on such short notice but saw no harm in asking. The Venezuela trip had given him a real taste of what was possible and the strings his superiors could pull. He had requested first class to Caracas, and got it; a helicopter across the spectacular Guiana Highlands, and got it; a suite at the Caracas Intercontinental, and got it. He had even charged designer sunglasses to the room. At check-out, the hotel receptionist informed him that the room bill had already been settled, hoped he had had a pleasant stay, and looked forward to welcoming him again soon.

The missions he was being sent on were the main event. *Holy shit*, Ordway thought, *I'm their point man. The* main *man.* The realisation brought butterflies to his stomach and a slight loosening of his bowels. He shifted slightly in his seat and cleared his throat. *They clearly value me*, he thought, *so they'd damn well better look after me*. Ordway fiddled with buttons on the multi-function steering wheel. Country and western music filled the car.

'Whoa!' Ordway could not resist a small whoop of joy.

He had been driving just twenty minutes from the small military airfield along the road built for the single purpose of connecting the airfield to the base, and now he could see the checkpoint up ahead.

As the car slowed to a stop, two soldiers appeared from the small guard house. Ordway killed the music and passed his ID through the opening window.

While one of the guards scrutinised Ordway and the SUV's interior, the other was walking around the vehicle. 'Thank you, sir.' The soldier handed back Ordway's ID, drew back, and saluted. The second guard raised the barrier.

'Thank you, soldier. Good to see you boys are thorough.'

Ordway inwardly revelled. *Goddamn, they even saluted me.*

Soldiers and vehicles were everywhere. Ordway scanned his surroundings. *They weren't wrong*, he thought, *this place is a throwback to the 1950s.* It looked wholly unremarkable. An African-American lieutenant emerged from the largest of the buildings.

'Welcome to the base, Mr Ordway, sir. Lieutenant Armstrong.'

Ordway simply nodded and removed his sunglasses.

The colonel is through here,' the lieutenant said, leading the way into the building.

Inside was also a hive of activity. As they approached a door at the end of the corridor, a soldier stepped aside and saluted, screwdriver in hand. A brass plate inscribed COLONEL MIKE MASON needed one more screw. The lieutenant knocked.

'Come!' came the reply from within.

'Mr Ordway, sir.'

'Thank you, lieutenant. That's all. Please, take a seat, Mr Ordway. Coffee?'

'I'm fine, thanks.'

The colonel stood slowly from behind his desk, poured himself a coffee, and turned to take in Ordway—from his hair to his face, from his leather bomber jacket and expensive shoes to the outrageously priced designer shades.

'You certainly don't mess around,' Ordway said, looking through the colonel's window at the activity outside. 'Even time to put your name on the door. I hope you're good at prioritising, colonel.'

Colonel Mason bristled at Ordway's casualness and the underlying threat. He had not liked the man the moment he walked in. The colonel was pugnacious—one general even described him as congenitally belligerent—but he was no idiot. Ordway was reporting to those higher up the food chain, quite possibly to the Commander-in-Chief. 'Well, unlike many in this world, I don't piss around. Efficiency, proficiency, and expediency make for an effective fighting force.'

'Don't forget technology, Colonel. The reason you're here. I take it you read my report?'

The colonel picked up the report from his desk. 'Quite a read, Mr Ordway, although lacking in detail.'

'It's on a need-to-know basis, Colonel. And our scientific friends? Are they up to speed?'

The colonel looked at his watch. 'I've called the first general staff briefing for 0900 hours. Would you like to join us?' The colonel knew that Ordway would expect to attend, but this made it sound like a favour.

Ordway sensed the colonel's dislike of him and no doubt of ill-disciplined, political types in general. But the colonel may at least admire his sense of purpose and patriotism.

'We can't afford to have any more resistance to this project. You know that, don't you, Colonel.' Ordway did not need to remind the colonel that several of the scientists had been replaced due to their recalcitrance over the direction the project was heading. Ordway did not need to piss the colonel off. The colonel needed to succeed. It was just that Ordway could not resist the power-play. Both men were effectively seeing who had the biggest dicks.

'Ordway, let's get one thing clear. I've served this country for 31 years. I'll get my job done.' The colonel was sorely tempted to add that he did not need a prize jerk like Ordway to get in the way but knew better of it. 'Just make sure *your* scientists do their bit.'

There were fifty-four gathered in the large conference room. Thirty-two of the group were scientists, dressed in casual wear and lab coats and standing together to one side, the rest were uniformed soldiers. They were close to thirty metres below ground in a massive, nuclear bomb-proof facility, built in the 1950s. It had undergone a considerable upgrade since then, though: spotless floors, smoked glass, LED lighting, and huge displays. Room after room of hi-tech wizardry.

The colonel strode in; Ordway followed close behind. The soldiers stood to attention.

'At ease,' the colonel said, taking his position on a low stage. He wasted no time in making his point. Turning to the scientists, he announced: 'I'm Colonel Mason. I'm now in charge of this facility and everyone and everything in it. In the interest of national *and* international security, this base has been upgraded to what we call a Category A facility. That means one thing: we have one hell of a responsibility. My job, your job is to make sure we don't screw up. This project...' The colonel looked across the entire room, '...this project is of the topmost priority and will remain of the utmost secrecy. You are incommunicado for the duration of your tour. There are no means of communication other than our encrypted channels and they're reserved for military purposes only. When you do get home, keep the conversation clean. You talk to no one about what you do here. Not your wife, husband...' The colonel's eyes rested on one of the male scientists, continuing, '...partner, lover, your father, mother, grandmother, not even your dog. Talk instead about the lovely warm weather you're experiencing and the beautiful beaches.' A few, mainly military, laughed. The colonel did not smile. He waited for the room to settle. Faces were once again serious. After a long pause, he resumed, 'Anyone breaking this silence would be jeopardising the security of the United States of America and its allies. For that, the penalty will be severe, and you will be thrown in a *very* dark place for a *very* long time. Do I make myself clear?'

'SIR, YES, SIR!' the military personnel responded in unison. The scientists shuffled nervously.

'You're probably wondering why a colonel in the United States Army is the commanding officer of such a small unit. Well, that's because, one, I also oversee a much wider aspect of this project beyond these walls.' The colonel indicated their surroundings. 'Two, this is the most important and most sensitive part of the project, so personnel numbers are kept to the absolute minimum, and three, I'm the goddamn best there is to get this job done.'

The soldiers loved this. Keen to show their support, they whooped and hollered 'Yeh!' and 'Go, colonel!' There then arose a chant of 'MOOSE! MOOSE! MOOSE!' for the colonel's nickname and reputation were well known. They loved a ballsy leader. Made them feel secure. The room's other occupants were wondering if this was army humour, or if the colonel really was this arrogant.

The colonel raised a hand in acknowledgement and smiled as modestly as possible. Inwardly, he revelled in the adoration. Without an introduction, he stood aside and beckoned Ordway to the microphone. Had the colonel not done this, those in uniform would have been taken aback by his abruptness and lack of detail. Instead, all eyes turned to Ordway in his smart casual attire.

Ordway had not expected to make a speech, and it showed. The colonel folded his arms as if to say: *well, come on, big boy, impress us.* In truth, the colonel knew that he did not possess the information Ordway had. He had read the file, sure, but that was only two hours ago, not long after his unit had rolled in like a tidal wave into the remote and hitherto sleepy research facility. As much as he loathed the political class, they were his paymasters, and in Ordway, he recognised someone with the kind of power that could have a long-standing, highly decorated officer quietly removed from office. Ordway, though, could talk on his feet. It was one of his strengths. His southern drawl broke the short silence.

'Thank you, Colonel.' Ordway knew that his identity was as secret as the project. He addressed the military in the room, for whom the posting to Alaska was still a mystery. 'For decades, the military has been experimenting with the weather—not only trying to predict it, but control it, master it, and use it for strategic advantage. We call it environmental warfare. In Vietnam, the US ran a secret project called *Popeye*. Monsoon clouds were seeded to trigger torrential downpours. The British ran similar experiments in southwest England. Scientists have also tried to temper hurricanes. But all these experiments resulted in little more than minor changes in the weather. Imagine if we could *really* control it. More specifically, trigger powerful electrical storms. Then imagine what we could do if we had technology that was immune to that weather. The advantage we would have would be enormous. We could interfere with or take out altogether traditional means of communication then sneak in using our own advanced communications systems.'

The soldiers in the room seemed awestruck. To be working at this cold, remote base suddenly became the best thing in their lives. They were exchanging animated looks. Ordway sensed he had struck a chord. He wondered if the military contingent needed to know this kind of detail. Probably not. Unfortunately, his ego was taking over. He was on a roll. He also remembered that, technically, he was the highest-ranking man in the room.

'This base has been at the forefront of this research and has made a great many advances. The challenge, as our scientists know, has been energy. To influence what can be vast weather systems, we need vast amounts of energy and we don't get that by plugging into a mains socket.' Some of the audience smirked. 'But now we think we believe we've cracked that nut.' Ordway stole a glance at the scientists. *Bet you weren't expecting that*, he thought. 'We've been running related experiments around the globe and one of those has succeeded in harnessing the awesome power of Mother Nature herself.' Ordway let the words hang for a moment. He then turned to the scientists. 'Your mission is to combine that awesome power with the developments made here at his facility and finally create that dream weapon. Mega electrical storms with frightening intensity, on-demand, anywhere on the planet. Soon we will have the ability to strike the enemy with nothing less than *God*-like power.' Ordway did not need to pause here. The room was as electrified as the topic of his speech. He waited for silence and got it sooner than he had expected; his audience was eager for more. 'You people are in a unique and privileged position. Your work here will not only change the face of warfare but the very destiny of mankind. And this great country will reassert its place as the world's number one nation. Welcome, people, to the most exciting place on earth. Welcome to project *Spear of Destiny.*'

The room erupted with loud cheers. The soldiers were high-fiving or punching the air. Others stood, open-mouthed. The scientists looked around, clearly unnerved by the belligerent and nationalistic tone of Ordway's speech, but excited nonetheless.

'All yours, Colonel.' Ordway raised his eyebrows. *Eat that,* he thought, knowing he had outdone the colonel on the excitement scale.

Chapter 40
The Desert

Syria

The battered truck that had brought him to the remote spot was driving away, creating a plume of dust in its wake. The driver, an old man, never turned around. His job was done.

Bakr al-Ahdal turned and laid back against a solitary tree. He looked up amongst its ancient branches and thanked Allah for the shade of its lush, green leaves.

Around him, the earth was parched and strewn with rocks. Bakr marvelled at the tree's resilience. *How long had it survived here all alone?* he wondered *A thousand, two thousand years?*

He recalled a story of the young prophet Mohammed, resting with his uncle under such a tree. How a monk had recognised the boy as a prophet in waiting, advising the uncle to take good care of him. *Could this be the same tree?* Bakr marvelled. *Yes*, he remembered now, *The Blessed Tree*, they called it. Perhaps this was a sign, or perhaps the man who had summoned him here, the enigmatic Prince Al-Musan, had somehow pre-empted Bakr's thoughts.

A dried-up riverbed, a few feet below the flat expanse of the desert, carved an irregular route towards the mountains in the distance. The river was still alive, Bakr assumed, many feet under the sand and rocks, a trickle perhaps, but enough to sustain the tree.

A warm wind rustled the leaves; shadows danced over Bakr's upturned face. He lowered his gaze and squinted. In the distance, he could see a plume of dust and sand thrown up by a fast-approaching vehicle. It was tall and sure—a four-wheel drive. The sun flashed off its roof and bonnet causing it to almost disappear in an explosion of light. Bakr was reminded of his boyhood and the first time he saw a *haboob*—a frightening wall of sand thousands of feet high—

rolling towards his village. He remembered his father covering him with a robe, the tethered group of camels stamping and snorting restlessly, their hooves kicking up fine dust, and the once bright day darkening rapidly by the ominous cloud of sand. Bakr had covered his face with the robe, peering at the storm through a small slit. *'It will be upon us in no time, Bakr. Don't be hypnotised by its terrible beauty,'* his father had hollered. *'This is a big one.'*

'How fast is it moving, father?'

'At least 80 kph. Now cover your face! Don't be frightened by the noise! Stay close to the ground here with me!' Bakr's father had laid an arm across his son's shoulders, and the two of them huddled close. The camels had lain down but were calm. And then all was darkness and noise.

Bakr rose to his feet. Today it was the power of five hundred charging beasts that was drawing towards him.

The Range Rover lurched to a stop. Bakr shielded his eyes from the silver vehicle, which glinted like a mirror. The doors and tinted windows of the vehicle remained closed. Bakr waited. When the dust had settled, the rear window opened halfway. A hand emerged and beckoned him over, and the window closed. The driver's door lurched open and a suited man in sunglasses stepped out. He gestured for Bakr to raise his hands and proceeded to frisk the terrorist. Satisfied, the driver opened the rear door. Bakr looked at him, then peered into the car's dark interior.

'In! Before you let in the heat of a thousand suns,' came a voice from within.

Climbing in was like diving into a dark pool. From forty-five degrees to twenty-two in a second.

The car pulled away and powered its way effortlessly along the track. Bakr noticed a third person sitting up front. A young man, a boy even.

Prince Al-Musan turned and smiled at Bakr, 'Welcome, Bakr. I trust you had a pleasant journey back here to this, our beloved homeland.' The prince gestured with a raised palm at the bleak landscape.

Bakr frowned at the prince's impeccable English accent. 'Indeed, Your Highness. My flight was most comfortable. I thank you for your generosity.'

'It was not generosity but necessity. You are a wanted man across Europe. My private jet was the logical choice, not some frivolous extravagance.'

The prince's sudden change of tone unsettled Bakr. 'Yes, of course. Thank you.'

The prince looked out. 'The tree is truly remarkable, is it not?' he began. 'I like to think of the West as a tree. Outwardly, it looks healthy enough, although perhaps a little misshapen. It has strong, vigorous growth in its upper branches, where the leaves are rich shades of green, warmed by the sun. But in the shadows, deep down below in the gnarled branches, there is weakness and decay. Here the leaves are brown and wilting. And do you know why? Because the stream that feeds it with life-giving water is drying up.'

The prince had indeed chosen the pick-up point for a reason. 'And what does the stream represent, Your Highness?' Bakr asked.

'The stream, my friend, is their faith. It is but a trickle and disappearing fast into the earth, never to rise again. And why me, you must be asking? Lots of questions must be going through that troubled mind of yours. You do know who I am, I trust?'

'Of course, Your Highness.'

'You do? Then tell me what you know. I'm intrigued.' The prince rested his elbows on the armrests and arched his hands together over his mouth as if in Christian prayer. He wore a white silk thobe edged with blue embroidery and a matching *keffiyeh*; simple but elegant. 'But wait. What kind of host must you think I am? An Arab welcoming a brother into his abode and not offering a drink. Please.' A cooler box had been installed behind the centre console. Cans of iced coke and bottled mineral water were on offer. Bakr's hand hovered over a coke before settling on a water. The prince laughed. 'Don't feel guilty taking an American drink. It was canned here in Syria. Employment for our people.'

'Water is fine, thank you.'

'I own the drinks company and the canning factory.'

'I have never liked the taste.'

The prince laughed. 'I agree. Disgusting stuff. Then water it is. Now…' The prince's words hung in the air. It was a cue for Bakr to speak.

'You are Prince Al-Musan, you are…'

'Would you prefer that we speak in Arabic? I must apologise, my international business has made English my first tongue.' Bakr found the prince's politeness disquieting and irritating in equal measure.

'I am good with English.'

'You are *fine* with English', the prince corrected.

'I am fine with English,' Bakr muttered.

Bakr could see the mountains ahead of them rising from the desert floor. The sun was starting to cast harsh shadows over their crags and peaks.

Bakr continued, 'You are descended from Persian royalty, an only son of a successful father. You were educated in Damascus and Oxford. Your empire spans the globe. Fashion, hotels, publishing, pharmaceuticals. Your name means the high-life: big yachts, private planes, film premieres...'

'And don't forget beautiful women,' the prince added. 'All the trappings of a Western playboy and tycoon. You must despise me utterly.' The men stared at each other. 'But you were happy to accept my money; money to fund your personal jihad.'

'I only learned that it was your money many months later. And I do not ask you for money now, Your Highness. I accepted your invitation because I was told this...', Bakr gestured at the car's interior, 'was all a front. I have read articles in the Western press that suspect you of many things.'

'For many years, Bakr, I have run clean and successful businesses. That is the truth. But the Western powers have now decided that how I handle my money is, shall we say, less scrupulous.'

'Off-shore accounts. Tax avoidance?'

'Exactly. The very people and governments that had supported me, dealt with me, and lauded me, are now turning against me and those like me. We run the world, Bakr, we own the world, we create the wealth that keeps people off the streets. But now they say we should pay more tax. The very lawyers that create the loopholes are now creating nooses for our necks.'

'So, it's true, you are part of the corruption that is the West.'

'No! You must understand, Bakr. I joined that club to fund the jihad. Moving money through the BVI, the Caymans, or wherever, was acceptable. No questions asked. But now it's all blown wide open. My name is on the list.'

The prince looked out of his window and up at the sky. He then touched the video screen in front of him. What looked like a satellite image appeared. The prince turned it off and looked again out of the window.

'But today, Bakr, that will all change.'

'Can we still rely on your support?' he asked warily.

'I like you, Bakr. Your work has been impressive. In fact, brilliant.'

'Yes. I want them to taste the same horror that I tasted.'

The prince turned his face. 'I understand you, my brother. You want destructive revenge against the West. But terrorism does not work. They always say "terror will never win". They grow stronger with their defiance and self-righteousness. I've seen it. Worse still, it leads them to war, and war does no one any good. You know that better than most.'

'But if we don't...'

'LISTEN TO ME!' the prince boomed, holding up his hand. 'You are trying to break off branches, but they are only twigs, and new twigs grow in their place. Stronger than ever. I want you to use your imagination and meticulous planning for something I'm about to show you. Something that will shake that tree to its very roots by stopping the stream altogether. Now, sit back, relax, and drink your water.'

Bakr took a gulp of water and looked ahead. They were near the foot of the mountains.

The car had left the flat of the desert and began to climb a steep track strewn with rocks. The driver steered his way almost at a crawling pace. After ten minutes the car stopped and the prince stepped out into the blinding sunlight. The driver and front passenger did the same. Bakr's door opened. Outside the car, he turned to get a closer look at the young passenger. As he thought, he was a teenager. The boy was dressed in a pure white robe and holding a small metal case. He glanced at Bakr and then immediately looked at the prince.

A gentle breeze ruffled their hair. It seemed even hotter.

'Come!' said the prince and set off up a slope. Bakr and the boy followed.

After twenty minutes of climbing, Bakr could see that the trail split: one way down into a gorge, the other upwards. The prince took the latter. Bakr was hot and breathing heavily now, while the prince and boy, case in hand, hardly broke a sweat or their stride. Pausing for a moment, they looked down at the car now far below.

'May I ask, Your Highness, why have you brought me here?' Bakr panted.

'Patience is a virtue.' The prince then set off again. 'Do you know the origin of that saying? It's from a 14th-century poem. The narrator, the poet, is in search of faith. Not our faith I hasten to add, but Catholicism.'

'I have faith in Allah and the words of the great prophet, Muhammad. And I have patience if it is needed.'

'That's good, Bakr,' said the prince. 'It's not far now. And I promise it will be worth the effort.'

They reached a flatter area where the mountain cast its cool shadow. The prince and boy stopped and turned to Bakr, whose chest was rising and falling, his face in a grimace.

'You should exercise more, Bakr. I work out every morning,' the prince said.

The prince looked up. Some clouds were now billowing above them, casting shadows over the landscape.

'Come,' said the prince and disappeared behind a rock. The boy stood his ground as Bakr stepped past him to see the prince enter a cave.

'How is your Crusade history, Bakr?'

Bakr was taken aback by the question. 'Er, I know that Christians came to win back the Holy Land.'

The prince, now a few metres inside, laughed. 'You make it sound like a game of backgammon.' He swung round. His mood had switched as rapidly as the flick of a switch; there was now anger and hatred in the prince's eyes. 'The Crusaders were a marauding army of cut-throats, rapists, and plunderers!' he hissed. 'They killed and mutilated thousands upon thousands of our Muslim brothers and sisters. Accounts talk of streets knee-deep in blood. All were put to the sword, lance, or axe. All in the name of their god. They were on a divine mission. A merciless jihad.'

The prince turned and wiped a large stone with his hand, brushing fine grit and sand onto the cave floor, then sat down. 'Come inside, where I can see you better,' he said calmly.

Bakr stepped forward.

'Nearly one thousand years ago,' the prince almost whispered, 'the once great city of Antioch was besieged by the Crusaders. One night, a shower of meteorites rained down, falling mostly on the Turkish camp. At first, they assumed they were being bombarded by Crusader projectiles. But then they saw that these were small iridescent rocks, glowing blue with an inner light.'

Bakr was confused. He knew the prince was a doctor of history, but where on earth was this going? His mind began racing. Why were they here in this remote place and in a cave? Was it simply a dramatic history lesson? But this was also his paymaster; a man fighting the same cause, even if it was in the shadows. And yet Bakr wanted to hear more. His curiosity had been piqued.

The prince continued. 'This was in a time when natural events were seen as omens, both good and bad. And these meteorites were unusual. On this occasion, an old sage told the Turkish captain that he had had a vision of fire from heaven.

He didn't know why, but he saw the event as a good omen. The holy man was to hide the stones and knew of some caves like these in the Mountains of Holy Light near that ancient city. Bakr, after many years of research, I found those caves. But they were empty. I couldn't believe it. It seemed that the stones had been lost to history. Then, some months later, a stranger came to my palace. He produced two ancient objects: a cipher and a map. He told me he was the guardian of the stones, one in a long line of guardians over the centuries. I was right, Bakr! All my research had not been in vain. I was ecstatic.'

'And the map was their location?' Bakr suggested.

'Yes and no. The stranger explained that the stones had been moved from the Mountains of Holy Light to a new location. This location, Bakr. This very cave!'

Bakr turned and peered into the cave.

'The cipher and a map were used only as symbolic tokens of responsibility from one guardian to the next. The stranger handed *me* the cipher and map. He had decided that I, Prince Al-Musan, was the next guardian.' The prince could not contain his excitement. 'Don't you see, Bakr. This is fate. I was destined to be a guardian. Since reading about the stones as a student, I always knew they were special. I did not know why, but it has been my life's mission to find out. The sage saw the stones as divine providence, but he did not know why. Nor did the generations of guardians who followed. They knew the power of the stones but did not know how to use that power. I am the first to know.' The prince jumped up and headed out of the cave. 'Come Bakr.' He then turned to the boy, 'Now, Saadiq!'

The boy placed the case he had been carrying on a nearby rock, undid the clips, gently opened the lid, and stepped back.

Bakr moved forward for a better view. Lying in the case was a stone exactly as described by the prince. *What power*? he wondered.

The prince looked up at the sky. Bakr could just make out his face from the dimming light. 'The prince continued, 'Two centuries ago, the guardians decided to move the stones again. This time to the safety of a bank vault. I am today's custodian, Bakr. I hold the key to those stones. And you, my friend, are not the next guardian. That honour will fall upon my son, Saadiq. You, Bakr, will be one of the first to witness their God-like power! And I am the one who will help us unleash it. Unleash it on the infidels!'

Bakr had no idea where this was all leading. He had never met the prince before today; their relationship had been remote, clandestine, and anonymous. Indeed, he was still trying to reconcile the fact that this famous and often flamboyant prince had been funding a jihad. Now the man he was looking at seemed to be nothing short of crazy.

'You will see,' the prince said, knowing what was going through Bakr's mind. Again, the prince looked up. The clouds were denser and more ominous. Bakr followed his gaze. 'Look! There!' said the prince excitedly. He was now pointing at the stone.

Bakr could make out a faint shimmer within the stone. Some kind of white light was flitting within its blueness.

'Over here!' the prince called with some urgency.

The boy and Bakr stepped away to join the prince some twenty metres from the case and the stone within.

It was then that the air around them fizzed and crackled. Bakr looked around and at the sky. Static shot up his arms. His mouth opened in alarm.

'YES!' shouted the prince almost in a rapture.

And then, BOOM! The lightning bolt struck. All three raised their arms to their faces as the blinding flash flooded the entire mountainside. Bakr cried out. He and the boy fell backwards onto the ground.

'My God!' was all Bakr could say, panting and in shock, and trying to adjust his eyes. He sniffed the air, trying to work out the smell. It was like the odour of an electrical short mixed with the freshness of air following rainfall, he thought. It was the scent of ozone.

'You have witnessed the power of just one stone. I have two hundred and sixty-two more of them. For centuries the West has created war and wrought destruction and despair on our people. Now we will rise against them to exact our revenge by undermining their core belief.'

Still lying on the ground, Bakr stared at the prince. 'But how? I don't understand.'

'Imagine, Bakr, one of our brothers holding a stone, announcing the greatness of Allah and the desire to sacrifice his life for Him in front of thousands, no, millions of infidels, before being struck by what will seem the hand of God itself. They will see that God is on our side and we will change the world. Bakr, we will use these stones for martyrdoms!'

Chapter 41
The Scientists

Nice Airport, Southern France

'Doctor Bayford?'

After scanning the expectant throng of people in the arrivals hall, Kara's eyes quickly fell upon Dr Daniel Bayford. Although she had not needed to, she checked the image of him on her mobile. It was him all right. The description she had been given also matched: a distinguished gentleman, early fifties, and tanned, of course. His attire was not what she had expected, though. For some reason, she had imagined him to be a bit straight and stuffy. But the look seemed right for a semi-retired expat living by the Mediterranean: a fawn-coloured linen jacket, open white shirt, chinos, and deck shoes. Stylish and casual. *Not bad*, she thought. She liked the fact that he had not tried to disguise the emerging grey in his thick, dark, collar-length hair.

'Doctor Bayford? she called again, raising a hand.

'Daniel, please. And if you are the person on my sign, then we are doing well.'

Kara looked down and saw her name neatly written across the sign held in Daniel's hands. 'Oh, I'm sorry. Of course. Very pleased to meet you...Daniel.'

'And me you, Doctor Williams.' Daniel tried to be as cool as possible. It would have been so easy for him to just stand there and admire her looks. Instead, he focussed on her luggage.

'Hey, I'm Kara, OK?' she said smiling.

'Sure. Please, let me help you.' Daniel reached for her suitcase. 'My car's not far.'

As they walked out of the terminal and into the hot morning air, Daniel stole a glance at his American guest. She looked back and they both smiled. Upon learning of her arrival, he had Googled her and found several photographs of a rather serious yet attractive-looking scientist. The woman walking next to him, dressed in what Daniel believed was a shabby chic look—a pink, blue, green knee-length floral dress—now gave a spring in his step. She was drop-dead gorgeous. *Shame I'm not ten years younger*, he thought.

Kara stole several glances at Daniel and liked what she saw. An assured man with a certain sartorial elegance, and an effortless and genuine charm. *And that accent!*

'Your first time in France, I understand?'

'Yeh. I can't wait.'

'And your connection was in Paris?'

'Right. I only had to wait an hour or so. But I hope to spend a few days there before I return.'

'It is undeniably one of the world's most beautiful cities. The trouble is that it is also full of beautiful Parisians. Or so they like to think. That's an old joke, by the way.'

Kara laughed. She looked at the palm trees and the deep blue sky. *This trip's starting to feel like a holiday*, she thought.

In the car park, Daniel stopped. A frown furrowed his tanned forehead. 'Kara. I'm afraid now I have to shatter all your preconceptions of life here on the Cote d'Azur.' At this juncture, Daniel turned and inserted a key into the rear door of what Kara could only describe as a corrugated van. 'My automobile...I'm afraid.'

Kara sniggered, 'I'm sorry, I shouldn't.'

'No, you absolutely should. It should be a Ferrari. I call her Sadie, by the way,' Daniel said, as he hoisted the baggage into the back, 'Sadie because she's a sadistic son of a bitch.'

'Doesn't that make 'she' a 'he', then?'

They both laughed.

Daniel's villa, Tanneron, Southern France

Daniel threw the Citroën van into his drive. Hot early summer dust obscured the tyres for a few seconds as he brought it to an abrupt stop. Kara gratefully stepped out and looked up at Daniel's home—a generously sized villa.

'It's not the best time to come to work in the south of France. For one thing, it's very hot. Even now in May.' Daniel unwittingly made one of the very typical

French gestures: down-turned mouth, raised eyebrows and palms opened upward. 'Everything is dry and sad. But we make up for it here with some excellent wine! You like wine, I hope, Kara?'

'You bet. No problem there.' Kara, however, was feeling a little queasy after the tortuous trek up from the nearest town of Mandelieu.

Daniel carried her suitcase and led the way up some steps and onto the terrace. Kara stopped and surveyed the view. The villa was on the edge of a spur that jutted out from the hillside behind them. Squinting in the noonday sun, she raised a hand against some of the glare.

'On a clear day, you can see the Italian Alps. Eighty kilometres away. And that way, the island of Corsica,' Daniel said.

'Wow! It's an amazing place you have here.' Aware of the sound of cicadas below, Kara looked down into the surrounding valley and the dense, brittle vegetation. 'It certainly does look like it could spontaneously combust. I saw an interview of you by your cabin. Where is that?'

'My lookout tower, you mean? Over there. On my little hill. You see it?'

Kara turned and raised her hand again to take in the perfectly shaped hill that rose from the larger valley floor around a kilometre away.

'Forgive me, Kara. You must want a freshen-up. Let me show you to your room.'

'You know, I'm fine. They flew me here first class, so I had a shower during my stop-over.'

Kara followed Daniel into the cool gloom of the villa's kitchen and through into the spacious living room with its view across the valley. 'You have a lovely place, Daniel.'

'Thank you. It's probably a bit too big, but I'm glad I have the space. My sister-in-law and niece often stay here.'

'You live on your own the rest of the time?'

'Yeh, sad, isn't it.' Daniel replied laughing. 'I'm comfortable with my own company.'

Upstairs, Daniel swung a door open and stood aside. Kara stepped through.

'Oh, this is delightful. Thank you.'

Daniel was pleased he only had to wait ten minutes for Kara to reappear. She had changed into a dark blue linen dress. He did his best not to ogle by busying himself with the wine and some snacks. 'For someone who's just flown across the Atlantic, you look excellent.'

'Thanks. That's first-class for you. But really?'

'Really.' Daniel turned to look at her and smiled. 'Did I suggest you take a siesta? No, I didn't. Here.' Daniel handed her a glass of wine.

'Cheers,' she said, smiling. She took a sip and stepped out onto the veranda. 'I can see the lookout tower. Is that the hut?'

'Here, these will help.' Daniel handed Kara a pair of powerful binoculars. 'The hut is just there, to the right of that dark area. Can you see it?'

Daniel leant towards her so that she could follow his outstretched arm and his finger pointing towards the top of the small hill. In so doing he got a whiff of her perfume. He glanced at her auburn hair as it brushed his cheek, then straightened and quickly stepped to his right to give her space. *Christ, I've been up here on my own for too long*, he thought.

'Oh yes. I see it. How do you get there?'

'Er, well, we can walk. But why do that when one can enjoy the thrills of the local hairpin bends in Sadie? I can take you to view my little *laboratoire* after lunch.

'Great.' Kara tried to sound enthusiastic.

Chapter 42
Van Der Graaf Generator

Daniel's Hut, Tanneron, Southern France

For hours, only the chirp of cicadas, slivers of sunlight, and relentless August heat had penetrated Daniel's shack at the top of the hill. Now, outside movement and muffled voices were intruding on that natural immutability, as Daniel fumbled with the lock and opened the creaky door. Kara remained at the threshold and peered in; the brightness of the afternoon forming a glow around her silhouetted frame.

'One moment, please, Kara. I need...' Daniel strained to reach across and behind a flimsy cupboard, '...to find...the light. *Eh voila!*' He straightened up and looked around at Kara for a response, a smile across his face.

Kara took two steps forward and surveyed her new surroundings, her lips parting in amazement. 'It's...quite a place you have here, Daniel. I had no idea you had so much...?' Kara's voice trailed off, as she scanned the array of equipment and, over on a cluttered bench, the Van der Graaf generator she had seen in Daniel's TV interview. It was an apparatus, which, amongst the chaotic paraphernalia of Daniel's den, added, she thought, an element of the mad professor to his list of likeable traits.

'I've loved this kind of thing since I was 6 years old,' he said, wondering whether Kara was impressed or disappointed. 'I'm not going to stop, simply because I retire. Anyway, let me show you what I found. I'm sorry, this place was only designed for one. Let me clear this chair for you.' Daniel moved a stack of weather magazines from what appeared to be the only piece of luxury—a comfy-looking captain's chair. 'Now, where has it gone...ah, yes, here it is.' He dropped a faded cushion into the seat. Striding over to the bench, he reached underneath and produced a bar stool. Daniel waited for Kara to make herself comfortable. 'I, er...excuse me one moment, please.' Daniel began rifling around the bench. 'Hold out your hand.' Kara obliged. Daniel was looking into her eyes with schoolboy anticipation, as he placed something in her outstretched hand.

'Whoa! What the hell!'

'*C'est marant?* Weird, yes?'

They both stared at the object in Kara's hand—a small gem of exquisite blue.

'Excuse my French, but it's, it's so fricking heavy. No…dense!'

'That I can't explain. But let me show you what I do know.'

Daniel leapt up again.

Kara suddenly saw another Daniel—the scientist. *The man had an almost manic level of energy,* she thought, *an obsessive drive for… for what? Knowledge? An unquenchable enthusiasm from the age of 6 years. That's an obsession. Was she as driven as this? Yes, she most certainly was. Was that her problem? Did men find it a turn-off? Would Daniel? Christ! Shut up, Kara.*

Daniel turned and stared across the room. Kara followed his gaze to a shelf, stacked high and wide with books and publications, then watched him stride the short distance from the bench and pluck a sheaf of papers.

'My notes,' Daniel announced. 'OK. First thing. As you know, this may well be a brand-new discovery.'

'Oh yes, congratulations, Doctor. I'm sure you're right.'

Daniel welcomed Kara's use of his title. It seemed appropriate; as though she was acknowledging his academic background. 'Well, a discovery scientifically speaking at least. I hope to find a few more samples on the south side of the hill. If I do, I plan to send one to Cambridge University for analysis. I'm no geologist.' Kara handed the stone back to Daniel, who took it and held it up at eye level. 'The meteorite's density is indeed remarkable. Here are my measurements.'

'How did you find it?' Kara asked as she scanned his notes.

'Well, not so long ago. I was investigating one of the all too frequent forest fires. It was a hot day and a storm was in the air. I had my knife and had just…,' Daniel paused, '…been using it and threw it into the earth when I saw a spark. Naturally, I thought that the knife had hit a stone. But when I looked to the source of the spark…' Daniel's voice had become a whisper, '…there it was.'

They stared again at the gem in silence.

'It's quite beautiful.' *There,* Kara thought, *that was a perfectly normal, non-scientific, feminine statement.*

'YES, BUT WATCH THIS!' Daniel shouted, making Kara recoil with a gasp. He flicked off the light. Darkness engulfed the room.

'*Merd!* Sorry was that you?' Daniel stumbled back across the room, knocking unseen objects in his path. Kara could not help but giggle. A faint click was heard and almost instantaneously the two orbs of the Van der Graaf generator appeared in the blackness, as though suspended in space. *Just like two identical, silver planets*, Kara mused. The book, *Worlds in Collision* by Emmanuel Vilakovsky, which she had not read since her teenage years, had leapt, complete with the author's name, from the deepest part of Kara's memory. A small spotlight, angled up at the generator, was the source of the light. Daniel was standing at the bench, his back to Kara. Drawn by his activities and her growing curiosity, Kara slowly raised herself and joined him. Daniel had placed the gem in the jaws of a clamp.

'Observe and be amazed, Dr Williams.'

Kara also accepted the use of her title. They were scientists after all, even here.

She knew what he was about to do. But to see it first-hand…

Kara looked from the gem to Daniel and back, her lips were parted and she felt a tingle of excitement shiver through her.

A slow metallic whirring broke the silence: small cogs grinding against one another. Daniel was turning the handle of the Van der Graaf generator. The speed and the noise increased as the momentum built.

'There is only one gear, so it takes a little while to get going,' Daniel hollered to Kara over his shoulder. 'OK, I need your assistance, please, er, Kara.'

'Yeh right, of course.'

'Nice and slowly.'

Holding a lever on the contraption, Kara carefully applied pressure. One of the spheres slowly moved towards the other.

The whirring had now reached a regular, pulsing drone. A spark then suddenly cracked from the space between the orbs straight at the gem, then another and another, and then, finally, a streaming mass of blinding, twisted light simultaneously engulfed the apparatus and the gem.

She had seen the interviews with Daniel and the demonstration several times already. But seeing it live was something else. Like anyone familiar with the Van der Graaf generator, she still expected small sparks to jump across the void between the spheres. Instead, those sparks and the final large arc of electricity were drawn straight at the stone, like a star being sucked into a black hole. It defied all logic.

Daniel's cranking of the generator's handle slowed. The light show ended.

'That was remarkable,' Kara said, her mouth still open in amazement.

'But there's more. There, Kara! Look!'

The gemstone had become animated with a cloud of blue-white filaments that danced a fiery crackle around it.

Kara stared in awe. 'It's just like…'

'Miniature lightning?' Daniel prompted.

'I need to record this.' Kara pulled out her phone and started videoing. She looked up suddenly. 'Hey! Don't you go stopping that now!'

'Kara, we can always repeat the experiment. I just need to wind it up again. Wait, this will help.' Daniel produced a small tripod.

'Yes, perfect. Thanks.' Kara began fumbling with the tripod clamp.

'Here, let me help.' Daniel sat on the stool and leant towards her. She turned to face him and smiled. Daniel smiled back and they held their gaze for a second. 'There you are,' Daniel said, having quickly returned to the job in hand.

The two of them then fell effortlessly into experimental mode. Nothing was more important than empirical observations.

'Oh my god. I'm in macro mode. It looks incredible this close up.' Kara hit the record button again and then fired off a series of shots. 'How did you discover it had properties like this?'

'Well, in fact, I must thank my little niece for that. She loves to turn off all the lights and have me "make the sparks," as she likes to call it, oh, and for her amazing Electric Lady show.'

'That's cute.'

'I don't use the Van Der Graaf for anything else. It's become a toy. But can you imagine her reaction and mine when the gem, which I'd been looking at under the microscope came alive? Like this.'

Daniel wound up the generator once more.

Kara continued shooting. The crackling, the stream of intense sparks, the phone's camera clicks, and the grinding of the generator's cogs all built to a crescendo.

The arcing then stopped abruptly and the whirring slowed.

'Hey.' Kara looked up with disappointment across her face.

'Phew. I'm sorry. Too much excitement for an ageing scientist.' Daniel flicked on the light and opened the door. 'It's also pretty hot in here. We could do with some air.'

Kara joined him outside. 'So, what else?' she asked.

'What do you mean, what else?' Daniel looked hurt.

'What else do you know?'

Daniel gave his non-plussed look. 'That's it. It's an unnaturally heavy gemstone. It's blue. It creates its own lightning show. It's probably the first to be found anywhere in the world. It's beautiful. It's unique. It could be a…fricking major discovery. I found it. Jesus! What else do you want me to say?'

'Whoa, there! Peace. OK. Look, it's fantastic. No. Amazing! But, Daniel, don't get me wrong. You know, I love what I've seen of this country. I could probably do with the break and all that, and, hey, you've been the congenial host. But why on earth did I get flown all this way, when…'

'Oh my god. How could I forget?'

She followed Daniel back inside. He shut the door and turned off the main light. Darkness returned. And, out of the gloom, a faint, soft blue aura emanated from above the bench.

'The stone. It's…*still* alive.' Kara whispered.

'And will be for twenty minutes or more. I'm sorry, for a moment I'd forgotten you're working on some project.'

Kara brought her face close to the stone. Its candescence illuminated her features. She was nodding slowly. 'This is incredible. Not only does it draw energy in a way I'm struggling to believe, but it's also somehow retaining that energy. Understanding how could have profound implications.'

'So, tell me, Kara, what is this about?'

'I think, Daniel…,' Kara said, still gazing into the gem, 'I think you may have found what we've been looking for.'

Chapter 43
Lunch at the Villa

Daniel's Villa, Tanneron, Southern France

Kara was reclining on a lounger in the shade of a balcony, an open laptop resting on her thighs. But she was enjoying the view of the Mediterranean landscape.

She closed her eyes and breathed in the natural scents of lavender, thyme, and jasmine, as a light breeze rustled up from the valley below, through the olive trees shimmering in the hot, dry noonday air.

Her reverie was interrupted by the unmistakable sound of Daniel's van and his hallmark skid, as it lurched into the driveway. Daniel appeared at the kitchen door, clutching a long loaf, a bottle of wine, and a large brown, paper bag.

'*Voila! Pain restaurant, du fromage et du Bourgogne.* And a little French, just for you, Kara.'

'Hey.'

'Kara, you've been on that all morning. You Americans never stop.'

'I'm sorry, but it has been a productive morning. It's just that once I get onto something, I can't let go. I get butterflies in my stomach.'

Daniel set the bag on the large refectory table and started taking out the contents. 'Now, you must try some of this. It is, as they say, *bien fait.* Ripe!'

'Wow! Has this just died?' Kara joked, having sniffed the Camembert. She broke off a generous piece of bread, spread a little of the cheese onto it, and took a bite. 'Mmm, now that's what I call a cheese.'

'So come on. What have you found? You're being too polite to say, I know.'

'Well, you know a couple of nights ago…' Kara didn't wait to finish her first mouthful. '…after we were talking about the stone's uniqueness, that there may be other deposits somewhere? Right?'

'Right.'

'Given its extraordinary properties, its ability to attract electrical energy, I remembered what you said about experiencing a lot of lightning in this area, and your idea that the stone may be linked to that.'

'So, more than one stone.'

'Exactly. So, guess where I was this morning?'

'The hill? But…that means you walked?'

'Why not? You said one could. And I did. And I'm back.'

'So, you didn't encounter any *sangliers* down there? You were lucky.' Daniel's enquiry was purposefully casual. He knew it would induce the right response from Kara.

'Sangli what? Shit. What are you saying? Deadly snakes, scorpions, right?'

'You'd know when you met one.' Daniel was enjoying the tease but looked deadly serious.

'What? Come on, Daniel.'

'Well, I think you were brave, Kara. I certainly wouldn't venture down there. Alone. And especially at night.'

'OK, so what have these *sangliers* got? Fangs?'

'Not quite. They do have very sharp tusks, though.'

Kara exploded with a short laugh. 'Tusks? What are they? Mutant, pigmy elephants?'

'Wild boars.'

'Oh, boars. Ah, you're kidding? They're just little pigs.'

'Not around here. They can be very aggressive. Very territorial.' Daniel once again adopted a sinister tone. 'I have been chased on many an occasion by a large male.'

'Lucky old you.'

Daniel did his best to suppress a laugh. 'Imagine, Kara! There he is. Breathing fast and loud. You cannot move. You're transfixed. What will this beast do? What should you do? You have a knife. But then the unexpected happens. The adrenalin surges through your body as you become aware of a second and, my god, a third *sanglier* having appeared from nowhere. Your instinct for survival takes over. You run in blind terror, not daring to turn round, lest you trip and be savaged by…by the three little piggies.'

Kara, who had been transfixed by Daniel's story, burst into laughter again, just as Daniel let out a loud squeal, 'EEEEEE!'

They both laughed heartily.

'Anyway, just for that, I'm not going to tell you what I found.'

'Ah, now you're teasing me.'

Kara opened a small box and produced another gem almost twice the size of Daniel's specimen.

'My god!'

'I found it in a large depression. I looked for others for a good twenty minutes, but it was getting a bit too hot. I'm sure there are a lot more. I was so excited.'

'Was this depression on the south side?'

'Yes. Exactly where you said many fires started. So, then I had this brain wave. There may be other deposits elsewhere in the world if we look for unusually high instances of lightning.'

'So, you've been looking at data from OTD and other satellites.'

'Oh, that was the easy bit. I got my assistant Tod to do that for me. He was a little pissed I'd woken him up. But check this out.' Kara swung the laptop around on the table and punched a series of keys. On the screen appeared a darkened map of the northern hemisphere, the land masses outlined in faint, blue lines. Yellow, orange, and red splodges filled the image. 'Let me zoom in.'

Kara selected a magnifying glass tool and clicked twice on the Mediterranean. The map redrew, this time enlarging two prominent splodges of red. Daniel leant towards the screen. Kara waited for his response.

'That's here, Var. And this could be my hill,' he said, pointing at the smaller of the two splodges.

'And this...,' Kara clicked again, '...this is Southern Turkey. This is lightning activity from the last two years.'

'My god, the concentration. It must be ten times bigger! Has no one commented on this before?'

'No one has bothered to map lightning for longer than one year. I guess no one would suspect anomalies like this to occur. Anyway, like I said, that was the easy bit. I've spent the last hour on the internet. I wondered if anyone had found gems like this in Turkey. So, I checked the coordinates. The nearest city is called Antakya. I found nothing about Antakya but found that the city had a much older name: Antioch. So, I searched under that name. And blam! Loads of stuff. This is what I was looking at when you arrived back.'

Kara punched a couple more keys to reveal a website. 'Let me read this: "*It has long been considered that The Holy Wars, an illuminated book thought to have been written in the 14th century by monks in Northern Italy, is the definitive account of the events of the siege of Antioch, a city once part of Syria, now in Southern Turkey, besieged by the Crusaders in 1097. The accuracy of the account is attributed to the fact that descendants of one of the Christian soldiers present at Antioch lived in the same village as the monks.*" Bla, bla, bla. Ah, yes, listen to this: "*The book recounts how, on the fourth day of the siege, a star burned and fell from the sky causing fear and panic in Antioch and outside the city's walls in the Turkish army encampment. It is widely believed among historians and academics that this is a reference to a meteorite, a fireball, or meteor shower.*"

'Exactly! Meteorites. That explains their rarity and unusual characteristics,' Daniel said.

'But listen: *It is also mentioned that Count Raymond, one of the Crusader knights, saw the burning stones as a good omen and commanded that the largest be mounted in the Holy Lance. A curious reference to the stones being one hundred times bigger than their appearance is unclear and thought by scholars to be a misinterpretation of the Latin text. What is unambiguous in the book, however, is that the Turks located 263 of these stones. The whereabouts of the stones now are a complete mystery. Remarkably, The Holy Wars book has survived and is held at the Louvre in Paris.*'

'Ah, *la Musée du Louvre*. Fascinating stuff, Kara.'

'Yes, but don't you see, they talk about the stones being a hundred times bigger. I think the translation should have said a hundred times heavier. Like your stone. Like this one.' Kara continued, holding up her find.

'So, the same type of meteorite probably fell on the Crusaders as those that fell here.'

'Exactly, Daniel. Don't you think that's really cool?'

Chapter 44
The Report

Daniel's Villa, Tanneron, Southern France

'Hey, professor. Good to see you. Enjoying Venezuela?'

'Not as much as you are on the Cote d'Azur, I dare say.'

Kara tilted the screen of her laptop slightly. 'Oh, it's a tough assignment. You know, the weather, the food, the wine.' Arthur Steel laughed. 'How's the team?' she asked.

The professor's laugh turned to a smile. 'They miss you. I miss you. But all is good. Kara, I'm adding our friend, Mr Ordway to our chat. Give me a second...'

'Er, that would be *your* friend, not mine. I'm not a fan of that complete ass ...' Richard Ordway's face appeared in a new window in the video conference. 'Mr Ordway,' Kara said cheerily and trying not to laugh. 'As...I was saying to the professor, I've made good progress here.'

'I'm pleased to hear, Kara,' Ordway replied. He was leaning in towards his camera and smiling.

Kara bristled. *Calling me Kara again. God, does he think I may fancy him?* she thought. *He keeps giving me that look. What an utter jerk.*

'*Doctor* Williams,' Steel interjected, 'briefed me on her findings yesterday. I consider them to be significant. Thus, this conference call. Doctor?'

'Thank you, *professor*,' Kara said, echoing Steel with the slightest of stresses on *his* title. 'Significant and, I'd say, remarkable. First, I would concur that the stone found by Dr Bayford is of extra-terrestrial origin—a meteorite. However, my first analysis—and please bear in mind that meteoritics, is not my specialty— would indicate a brand-new category of meteorite. Its composition does not fit in with the three main types, namely siderites, aerolites, and siderolites —or, put simply, iron, stony, and stony-iron. But what this means is that of the many thousands of samples found and carefully analysed, this meteorite is in a class of its own.'

'With respect,' Ordway interrupted, 'you yourself said you were no expert in this field.'

'Yes, that's true. But this kind of find is not without precedent. In 2006, a pair of meteorites was discovered in Antarctica with a composition never before seen. Here's a link to one news article.'

Kara shared an online news report: ALIEN TO SCIENCE: UNIQUE METEORITES FOUND IN ANTARCTICA.

'We don't know everything, Mr Ordway,' Kara continued. 'Take the periodic table. For thousands of years, we only knew around ten or twelve elements like gold, silver, copper, lead, sulphur, and so on. There are now one hundred and eighteen. They added four to the table as recently as 2016.' Kara realised her temper was rising.

'Dr Williams is absolutely right,' Steel added, recognising his colleague's irritation and frustration. 'We certainly don't know everything. Maybe now's the time to show the video, Kara.'

'Yes, excellent idea. Thank you, professor. Mr Ordway, while there have been reports written about this discovery, what I'm about to show now has been witnessed by only a handful of people, and probably in the whole of history.'

Kara ran the video she had taken herself in Daniel's make-shift laboratory. She provided some live commentary: 'As you can see, it's translucent. Its mass is off the scale. I have full details in my written report. Gentlemen, I've never seen anything quite like it. It's baffling. It's exciting. It's scary. It's beautiful to behold in more ways than one.'

'Well, quite a spectacle, I must say, Doctor. And?' Ordway said.

'And what? Do you *actually* understand what you just saw, Mr Ordway?' Ordway acknowledged her question with a downturned mouth and a shrug of the shoulders. 'Clearly not.' Kara's blood was starting to boil, but she did her best to disguise her emotions with a forced smile. 'For *that* stone to draw *that* spark away from those orbs and across *three* metres is nothing short of unbelievable. Even *more* remarkable is that the meteorite appears to be retaining that energy. If we can understand the composition and the physics, harness it, perhaps synthesise it, the implications are profound.'

Steel then added, 'From our standpoint, it is early days, but I'm with Dr Williams. I can't stress this enough. This discovery may have far-reaching consequences. This is not just a curiosity. It could change our entire understanding of energy, sub-atomic physics, and the very nature of the universe.'

'Exactly,' Kara added, 'and therefore prove pivotal in the advancement and refinement of the atmospheric energy experiments in Venezuela.'

Ordway was nodding slowly. 'Well, that's great then.'

Chapter 45
The Martyrdoms

Cannes, Southern France, May

Daniel enjoyed Cannes during the film festival and would occasionally descend from the solitude of his villa to mingle amongst the throngs of people. Although he knew little of the world of film, Daniel was amused by the excitement, especially when a roving photographer spotted a celebrity. Within seconds others would appear from nowhere. Like ants finding a morsel of food, they would swarm around, creating a blur of stroboscopic light.

Kara had agreed to join Daniel for the evening, and although he saw no chance of romance, he was pleased to be out with an attractive young woman, so had made an effort to smarten himself up.

'Thanks for the invitation. I had no idea this was Cannes Film week. I have never been to anything like this before,' said Kara.

Daniel smiled back, 'We should walk up to the Carlton Hotel. We can experience the most expensive gin and tonic in France!'

Pausing for a few moments to watch the street artists creating clichéd charcoal drawings, Daniel felt a sudden chill. It was a puff of wind, a downdraft from the towering cumulonimbus just off the coast. It would not be long until the storm reached them, he thought.

'Let's go to the old town and find somewhere quiet to eat, Daniel proposed.'

They soon retraced their path back past the large concrete structure that was the *Palais de Festivals*.

'That storm is getting closer Kara, look at all the lightning strikes.'

Kara smiled. 'I can't seem to get away from storms. Hey, look how busy it is now. So many people!'

'Yes, everyone is hanging around, hoping to see a star. Brace yourself, Kara! We'll have to push our way through.'

Daniel was soon aggravated by the constant need to dodge people. '*Faites attention!*' Daniel snapped at a man who had just bumped into him. Although Daniel did not know it, the man was Bakr. In his typically intense manner, Bakr simply glared back. To Kara, it seemed a very long time before Daniel backed down and averted his gaze. Bakr pushed his way off through the crowd. This stern and mysterious man had unnerved Daniel. 'Come on Kara, let's get out of here,' he said.

'Hey, take it easy, Daniel!' Kara was surprised by Daniel's sudden change of mood.

Daniel ignored her and continued, angrily forcing a path for them. They soon emerged from the crowd and Daniel began to calm down.

'Are you OK? enquired Kara sympathetically.

'I'm sorry, I just needed to get clear.'

Bakr had made his way to a position to the side of the *Palais des Festivals,* from where he had a view all the way to the top of the red carpet.

He and most of the crowd then observed the curious sight of a young man with no shirt running up the steps, pushing astonished men in dinner jackets aside and tripping over one woman's long silk dress. A scabbard and sword were strapped to his belt.

As Daniel and Kara began to walk in the direction of the port, they sensed a change in the mood. Then a commotion behind them. As they looked back, a woman called out in English, 'He's going to kill someone!'

Daniel looked to the top of the stairs at the young man brandishing a sword. In a mixture of Arabic and French, the man was imploring Allah to take him from the earth.

Oh shit, Daniel thought.

As the crowd began to back off, Daniel found himself making a calm assessment of the situation. Following his years as a scientific advisor to the UK government he had given up his secure job and had become an activist. And it soon got serious. Military-like training became part of his life. And that training paid off many times; he had often found himself embroiled in tense situations.

This was one of them.

The man on the steps of the *Palais* was clearly unstable, if not deranged. His torso was naked apart from a necklace. Written in red on his body were the words: 'Allah is great.' It looked like blood, as though the words had been cut into his flesh. Two security guards approached the man but were quickly repelled as the man slashed at them with his sword.

'What's going on?' a nearby tourist asked.

'I think it's a film stunt,' someone in the crowd replied.

'Kara, there's something wrong here. This is no stunt.'

'What do you think it is?'

Instinctively, Daniel looked to the sky and the dark ominous clouds. He could feel his steel watch resonating. He knew this to be a sure sign of an imminent lightning strike. His time as a fire lookout had taught him that. Everything metal would begin to tingle; watches included. One had to do something quickly to avoid being burnt to a cinder.

'Quick, Kara! We should go. Now!'

Before they could move, a massive blinding flash shocked them, followed instantaneously by a deafening explosion, so loud it moved their stomachs.

A small group of people now lay slumped on the staircase; others sat cowering. Daniel then spotted the Arab man he had seen earlier moving amongst them. Daniel watched while Bakr leant over the body of the man and ripped something from his bare chest, before disappearing into the stunned crowd.

'Come on Kara, let's see what's happening!' Daniel was grabbing her hand. Something unusual was going on and his curiosity was aroused.

As he took her by the hand, they were already beaten to the bottom of the steps by a plucky news reporter. Sensing a great story, he was already ahead of them.

'This is George Simpson live in Cannes. An extraordinary event has just occurred. A few moments ago, a man was on these steps wielding a sword. There was a loud explosion and behind me. The attacker appears to be dead and many bystanders are seriously injured. I can't really tell at the moment... Ambulances are arriving, and the police are cordoning off the area.'

SUICIDE BOMBING AT CANNES FESTIVAL was quickly flashed on social media. In the TV studio, the presenter pressed for more information, 'George, can you tell us more?'

The reporter tried to gather his composure and breathlessly continued, 'Adam, we were here filming some of the celebrities. A bare-chested man ran up the steps and began waving a sword. Everyone thought it was a film-related stunt, but he started chanting. That's when people thought he may be a suicide bomber.'

'So, George, was it a large explosion?'

'This is the strange thing, Adam, there was a very large bang, but we do not think it was a bomb. People are now saying it was a lightning strike.'

'Thank you, George. We hope to bring you more on that breaking story…I'm now hearing that French police are saying it was a lightning strike. If correct, this would mean that the tragedy in Cannes was in fact…well, an act of God.'

Daniel and Kara stared at the incongruity of the scene before them. Only minutes earlier it had been one of happiness as the film industry elite posed for the admiring crowd. Now there was chaos. Many of those present seemed to be rooted to the spot, trying to take it all in. 'Wow! Did you see that!' one man said to no one in particular. Most were slowly moving away, leaving others to continue rubber-necking.

'*Attention!*' Two medics followed by armed police were pushing their way through and began to drive people back from the *Palais*. Daniel and Kara were amongst those being directed behind a hastily erected cordon.

'Daniel, I think we should go,' Kara said, looking pleadingly at her host.

'It's so strange…,' Daniel muttered, looking back at the steps. His reverie was then broken when a police officer grabbed his arm and pushed him back.

'Yes, we should go,' Daniel said, 'Are you OK?'

Kara didn't reply. She turned and began walking away, her head lowered.

Central London, UK

Heavy clouds hung over London's iconic Tower Bridge. That day in May, the murky waters that flowed past its piers and beneath its thousand-ton bascules, seemed even murkier.

No one had yet spotted the lone figure standing high on the west walkway of the bridge. Ten minutes later, when police sirens filled the air and flashing blue lights reflected off the twin towers, hundreds of phone cameras soon pointed at the strange spectacle.

'It's some kind of protestor,' said a young man to his friend. 'Look! He's got a banner.'

'Nah, mate. That's an Arab. He's wearing one of them long robes.'

More than forty-four metres above the river, the man in his white *jubbah* stood out clearly against the leaden sky. He began to attach a large, white sheet, securing one corner with tape to the roof of the glass walkway. Shuffling to one side he repeated the process, then let the homemade banner unfurl.

'What does it say?' a nearby elderly woman asked, raising an arm across her forehead and squinting.

Emblazoned in large black letters on the sheet, the bystanders saw the words:

ALLAH IS GREAT!
HE WILL WELCOME ME TO PARADISE

Four police officers were already ascending the north tower by lift. A member of staff was accompanying them.

'How did he get out there?' asked one of the officers.

'I've no idea,' said their guide. Whatever he's planning to do, he's got an audience all right. Thousands cross this bridge every day.'

The lo-fi sound of an urgent-sounding voice came over one of the officer's radios. '*Be advised that SO15 are en route. Do not engage.*'

'We're approaching the west glass walkway. There are people up here.'

'*Help in evac only. Over.*'

'Roger that.'

The lift doors opened and panicking tourists started pushing their way in.

'Is he a bomber?' a young Italian-sounding woman asked.

The guide was struggling to control the situation. 'We're full. No more!' he shouted. Two small children started screaming. 'You,' he said to their mother, 'take the stairs!'

Sergeant Trevor Reid was sitting up front in the blue and yellow police chopper, peering through his binoculars. He had two of his team on board in the rear. The helicopter was hovering over the Thames fifty metres west of the bridge level with the man on the walkway. 'Hold your position,' he ordered to the pilot.

High above the commotion, the man on the bridge was now standing stock still, arms by his side and head slightly raised. His white *jubbah* contrasted even more against the ever-darkening sky behind him.

Reid lowered his binoculars and spoke into his headset. 'Male. Mid to late twenties. I'm guessing you have a visual on the banner.'

The chopper's camera was relaying images back to base.

'*Roger that. This is Boyd. Potential suicide bomber. Stay alert. My team and a negotiator will be there. ETA eight minutes. See what you can do. Keep him calm.*' Commander Boyd ordered.

One of Reid's team was trying to get a better look. 'Is he a jumper?'

'God knows. Probably. He's prepared to die, that's for sure.' Reid took a deep breath and clicked on the chopper's megaphone. 'YOU DON'T NEED TO DO THIS. MAKE YOUR WAY CAREFULLY TO THE TOWER. WE WILL HELP YOU GET DOWN TO SAFETY.'

Reid clicked off the megaphone and waited for a reaction. When none came, he raised his binoculars again. 'Wait,' he said. 'There's a small box or something next to him. Get us closer.' The chopper edged forward and resumed its static position.

The bridge was now closed and Thames police boats had sealed off the river. Despite the potential threat, the swelling crowds were reluctant to move, transfixed with a morbid case of curiosity.

Reid had a bad feeling. 'Swing right.' The helicopter turned and was now side-on only metres from the walkway. The man lowered his face slowly. He was looking straight at Reid. 'What the fuck is he up to?'

As if knowing what Reid had asked, the man bent down and reached for the box by his left foot.

'Shit! That could be a bomb. PULL BACK!'

The chopper arced around in a circle away from the bridge and resumed its original, forward-facing position.

Reid raised his binoculars once more and peered straight ahead through the chopper's windscreen. 'He's putting on a necklace or something. What the hell...?'

The man was clutching something that hung from his neck. He turned, looked up at the sky, and slowly raised his hands high, his heels precariously close to the edge of the walkway's roof.

'He's gonna jump,' one of Reid's team said over the chopper's intercom.

'Let him, I'd say,' his colleague replied.

Loud static suddenly filled their headsets. Then a blinding flash. 'JESUS!' Reid yelled, dropping the binoculars. The pilot's reaction was worse. He let go of the controls and brought an arm across his face. The helicopter tilted violently forward and down. The pilot blinked and blindly grabbed the controls. But the intense flash had impaired his vision.

A lightning bolt had hit the man on the bridge, throwing him backwards and down towards the brown water below.

One of the team in the rear of the chopper tried to reach forward to help. 'LOOK OUT!' he screamed. His colleague opposite could only close his eyes and mutter a silent prayer.

The pilot desperately tried to clear his eyes of the pulsing flash. 'I CAN'T SEE!' he yelled. He pulled on the stick, but the chopper hurtled towards the bridge, the main rotor clattering against the blue and white metalwork. Their last ever image was a spattering of blood across the windscreen, as the falling man's body was sliced by the chopper's blades.

Times Square, Manhattan, New York City, USA

The crowd below the huge advertising hoarding on 7th Avenue was swelling by the second. Many were pointing; yet more were filming with their phones. Young children were being led away quickly by their parents. Those that remained were staring up at a man standing precariously eight floors up on one of the girders that supported an advertisement hoarding. He was dressed in a white *thawb* and matching *gahfiya* cap, making him stand out against the dark of his surroundings.

'Oh, man. He's a jumper,' someone said.

It was late afternoon and the last of the sunlight illuminated the upper levels of the buildings, but the sky above was dark with clouds. A rumble of thunder momentarily drowned out the cacophony of man-made noises.

The man on the girder was looking up. He was young, no older than twenty-five, with a well-groomed beard.

'He's crazy, man. Look, he's talking to God or something,' another bystander suggested.

A police car whooped its siren close by. It lurched to a stop and two officers ran towards the building. Realising the man was on the roof they stopped. After a brief discussion, one entered the building; the other remained and stepped back to view the situation. He then ran back to the car and returned with a loud hailer. 'SIR, CAN YOU HEAR ME? SIR?'

The man on the girder continued to look skyward. Another rumble of thunder, this one louder.

The officer lowered the loud hailer. 'Oh shit,' he mumbled before trying again. 'SIR, PLEASE CLIMB DOWN. WE'RE HERE TO HELP YOU.'

Still no response.

A loud gasp went up from the crowd. The man on the girder had reached down to something by his left foot. The girder was only inches wide, so his action was like watching a tightrope walker wobble.

'He's got a box,' someone called.

'Cool. Girder man's gonna have a late lunch,' someone joked. Those around him laughed.

Girder man, as he became known, stood erect, and raised his hands level to his head. He was placing something around his neck.

'Is that a necklace?' someone suggested.

More police arrived, some heading into the building. One officer had a zoomed-in image of girder man on his phone. 'Looks like a rock on a string,' his partner said, peering over his shoulder.

One of the officers on the roof called up, 'Sir, please come down. We're here to help. Nice and easy now.'

Girder man looked down over his shoulder. 'NO! Stay BACK!' he shouted. He then resumed his stance with his face upwards and eyes shut.

After a brief pause, he called out, 'ALLAH IS THE ONE TRUE GOD! ALLAHU AKBAR!'

'Oh, crap,' the officer with the loud hailer said under his breath. He brought it to his mouth and bellowed, 'EVERYONE, GET BACK NOW!'

He did not need to repeat himself. Everyone had heard what girder man had said. More importantly, everyone knew what it meant. People began shouting.

'HE'S GOT A BOMB!'

'SHOOT THE FUCK!'

New Yorkers knew about terrorism all too well. Not all, but most of the crowd were now running. A deafening crack of thunder stopped them in their tracks. They all cowered instinctively, frozen in fear, their brains fooling them into thinking it was a bomb. Those that stayed raised themselves and stood defiantly, staring up.

'DO US ALL A FAVOUR AND JUMP!' a woman almost screamed.

The police also held their ground. All of them had drawn their weapons and were pointing them at the terrorist.

People then began pointing at one of the large displays in Times Square. Realising it was broadcasting a live feed from the scene, they began tuning in on their phones. Many more across the nation were already glued to their TVs.

'We are taking you live to our reporter in Times Square,' announced the TV news anchor. 'David, please tell us more.'

The reporter raised his microphone. 'From where I'm standing, this is now beginning to look like a repeat of the bizarre events in London and France. Events that many are calling martyrdoms. I don't know if you can see, but a man is standing on girders high above me.'

A police lieutenant arrived on the scene. As he ran to the officer with the loud hailer Times Square exploded with light and the loudest bang those present had ever heard. The pressure wave caused windows to shatter and eardrums to pop. People cowered and screamed, but not before most of them had witnessed what had happened. The terrorist had not blown himself up. He had been hit by a bolt of lightning, its impact propelling him backwards violently. As he fell he smashed against one of the angled girders below, cracking his skull open and spattering blood across the roof.

The officers on the roof recoiled, falling against the back wall.

'Holy shit,' one of them managed to say.

Still shaken, they stood up slowly, the ringing in their ears masking the commotion below.

The body, lying just a few feet from them, was charred from the chest to the forehead. Remarkably, the *gahfiya* cap was not only unscathed but still on his head. The officers could not help but look at what remained of the blackened face. One of them leant down. Something was glowing. Whatever it was, it was partly obscured under the dead man's arm. He flinched slightly from the acrid smell, screwing up his face, but pinched the terrorist's sleeve between finger and thumb and raised the lifeless limb. He leant in closer still. His fellow officer, a hand over his mouth and nose, did the same.

'What the hell?' said the first officer.

The officers could only stare. The stone around the man's charred neck seemed alive. Filaments of white light danced about deep within its lustrous, blue interior.

Chapter 46
The Raid

Tanneron, Southern France

The sun was a rich orange orb, low in the western sky, as the pool maintenance van eased past Daniel's villa and pulled up a few metres past the gates.

The doors opened in unison and three men dressed in matching overalls stepped out. Each of them looked up and down the dusty road, now deserted save for a black cat stretched out under a tree.

The driver and passenger walked through the gate and headed straight for the villa's rear entrance, while the third man, having taken a metal toolbox from the rear of the van, disappeared up a track. None of them said a word.

The driver produced a small device, which he pointed at the alarm box located just below the roof overhang. There was a short zapping sound. Three seconds later they were inside the villa. He was quickly followed by his passenger, who set down another toolbox, from which he took out a small scanner and two headsets. He passed one set to the driver and wrapped the other behind his head. Finally, he took out two 9mm Heckler & Koch MP5 machine pistols, handing one to his accomplice. The man with the scanner set off, holding the device in front of him and reading its screen.

The first man activated the mic on his headset. 'Gamma One to Gamma Three, come in. Over.' he said in a low American voice.

'Gamma Three in position. All quiet. Over.'

Gamma One walked through the villa to join Gamma Two, who was standing in the middle of Daniel's study, sweeping the room with the scanner, and shaking his head.

'Not a squeak, sir.'

'Keep trying. Check every room, the roof space, outside. Everywhere,' Gamma One commanded.

After several minutes, Gamma Two joined Gamma One back in the kitchen. Gamma One produced a mobile and punched a quick dial. 'The pool's empty.' After listening for a few seconds, he ended the call and pocketed the phone. 'Look for a box or container, somewhere the stone could be stored safely. This thing can attract lightning out of blue sky, so it won't be in a paper bag.'

The men renewed their search.

Outside, Gamma Three was squatting amongst some shrubs, his binoculars raised. 'Car,' he said into his mic. With his spare hand, he reached down and picked up his MP5. The car, however, turned off some fifty metres short of the villa. 'Clear.' Gamma Three placed the gun back on the ground.

Gamma One returned to the study and started to rifle through some of Daniel's papers. Looking up at a board on the wall, he studied the photos, various magazine articles, and notes pinned there. One photo showed a young girl sitting on a bench, scientific equipment behind her. Another showed Daniel standing in front of a hut. The hut door was open. Gamma One could see some of the same equipment inside. Beyond the hut, a hill could be seen. Alpha grabbed the photo, went to the window, took out his binoculars, and scanned the landscape, finally settling on Daniel's hill. He looked again at the photo and then back at the hill. 'Gamma Two, Gamma Three, rendezvous at the van in 5.'

'Go ahead,' Gamma Three responded.

'It ain't here. We scoped the entire pad. But I think I know where it is.'

Back in the van, Gamma One pulled out his phone and selected a map app. Their location was quickly revealed. With his thumb and index finger, Gamma One zoomed in and then pointed at the screen. 'Right here.' Handing the phone to Gamma Two, he gunned the engine to life. 'We can get closer by taking the road round that hill over there. But we'll go in at nightfall.'

***

In Cannes, the shops, cafés, and restaurants along *Promenade de la Pantiero* were all but empty. Everyone—citizens, tourists, waiters, shopkeepers, and film fans—was either leaving the area or was rubbernecking at the police cordon set up around the Palais des Festivals. Blue lights were still flashing everywhere, with the largest concentration up by the *Palais*. The film industry finest had already been whisked away in a convoy of limousines and police outriders, and most of them were now back in their luxury hotel rooms packing their bags.

Daniel and Kara were among the majority, fighting their way through the busy traffic. There was a common desire amongst everyone to put as much distance between themselves and the site of the day's shocking yet bizarre event.

'We could be here a long time, Kara. Cannes can be very busy even at the best of times.' Daniel glanced over at her. They had hardly spoken. She was biting her lip. 'You OK?'

'Mm? Yeh. I guess.' She turned to Daniel and smiled faintly.

'We should get back. It's a shame. I had so wanted you to sample the delights of my favourite restaurant, too,' he said, desperate to cheer up his guest.

Kara snorted a half laugh. 'Food first. You must be naturalising into a Frenchman. No, you're right. We should go.'

***

Dusk was rapidly descending into darkness as the three SEALs made their way up the hill to Daniel's hut. Gamma Two and Gamma Three stayed back among the shrubs while Gamma One approached the hut, bolt cutters in hand. With a small torch, he checked for an alarm. Satisfied he sheared the padlock and entered the hut. Gamma Two emerged and followed him in, re-activating the scanner.

'You can forget that. It won't pick anything up. The stone will be heavily concealed. It needs to be.'

The two SEALs then began a systematic search.

'Just what is this place?' Gamma Two was touching one of the smooth globes of the Van der Graaf generator. 'Is this guy some kinda mad professor? Man, this has to be the weirdest mission I...'

'Hey, zip it will you! Just find the damn rock! The Frenchies would have a field day if they knew we were here.'

Gamma One had paused. He had spotted a small, heavy-duty metal case on a shelf. As he began sliding it off the shelf, he was taken by surprise at its weight and could do nothing to stop it from dropping. He jumped back as the case thudded on the wooden floor. 'Shit! That's heavy.' He picked it up and with some effort placed it on the bench. There was no lock, so he carefully raised the lid.

As he did so, Gamma Two's scanner went ballistic. He raised it and showed the meter reading to his leader. 'Jesus! I think we find the son of a bitch, sir.'

The two men stared at the blue stone. Small traces of static leapt across its surface.

'Whoa! Guess we'd better put this baby back to bed.' With that, Gamma One closed the lid and reached for his mobile. 'We've successfully cleaned the pool and are now heading back to the office.'

Chapter 47
Private Rendezvous

Elysée Palace, Paris, Late Evening

While not the longest street in the French capital, *Rue du Faubourg Saint-Honoré* is perhaps one of its most famous. With its origins dating back to medieval times, it was also one of the oldest. Today, it boasted high-end antique and haute couture stores, art galleries, embassies, and the *Elysée Palace*, the official residence of the President of France.

The palace gates opened wide and motorcycle outriders surrounding four identical black Mercedes limousines swept through and into the floodlit courtyard.

Inside, palace officials stood waiting as half a dozen secret service men and women disgorged from the cars. The front passenger of the third car emerged and opened the rear door. Thomas Palmer, President of the United States of America, stepped out.

'Thank you, Bob,' he said to his security chief, as he gazed up at the palace windows.

'Sir,' Bob Doyle acknowledged.

One of the palace officials stepped forward. 'Monsieur Le President, good evening and welcome. I am George Clairmont, the president's private secretary. Please follow me.'

'Thank you, George.'

The US security chief nodded to his colleagues and watched as the president and his guide climbed the steps alone and disappear into the grand building. This was normal protocol for the president on these 'personal' visits.

'President Dumart is in his private quarters.' The guide seemed to over pronounce each word.

President Palmer took in his surroundings. *Such an opulent residence for a republic*, he thought. The guide paused at some double doors and knocked. There was a muffled '*Entré*!' from within. Palmer half expected the doors of the salon to open to reveal King Louis XIV himself, resplendent upon his throne, surrounded by his doting and flamboyant courtiers. Instead, he knew, he would be greeted by a slightly hunched, bespectacled man in his early seventies.

'Jean-Baptist, how are you, my friend?' The US president was genuinely pleased to see his old acquaintance.

The two men had known each other for over thirty years. Separated by twenty-four years of age and a vast ocean, they had shared a similar and steady rise to power: two boys with a privileged upbringing and a happy family life, who built a following that went from loyal to fervent; from thousands to millions of devoted supporters. Each would win the hearts and minds of a nation in turmoil, a nation desperate to reassert its power and identity in a world of fear and uncertainty. Almost to the day, each would ascend to the highest office in their respective and much-loved land.

The two presidents soon recognised in each other a common and passionate desire for a particular world order. In more recent years that goal had drawn them together in a way that neither of them could have ever imagined. Not when they were junior politicians. Certainly not when Dumart, aged nine, had tasted his first champagne at his family's chateau in the region made famous by that drink; nor when Palmer, nearly two decades later, sat in the rear of his father's pickup as he drove them across their vast cotton ranch. But both men were destined for power. Wheels were set in motion by unseen hands. Blessed as they believed they were, the two men took it all in their stride, oblivious of the invisible greasing of those wheels—the first-class degrees, the parties with the rich and famous, and, later, the heady rise to political greatness.

It had been Dumart who had made the first contact. Palmer was in his early thirties and a rising star in the Republican Party. Dumart had been Minister of Foreign Affairs and International Development. He had taken Palmer to one side during a small gathering at Camp David. Four years later, Palmer had become governor of his state. Four years after that, he was Secretary of State; five more and he was running for president.

'Not as youthful looking as you, but considerably more handsome, nevertheless.' President Dumart smiled and the two leaders embraced.

'*Les hommes françaises sont insupportables*!' said President Palmer.

'Insufferable, indeed, but so likeable, don't you think?'

'There you go again,' Palmer laughed.

'Now, does your daily 5k running regime allow you to partake of some of France's finest champagne?'

'If it's as perfect as your command of English then how can I refuse?'

'And how do you think this year's G7 went?' Dumart asked.

'I wonder if holding it in that grand chateau sent out the wrong message. It makes the whole thing seem elitist. Politicians are accused of being disconnected from the real world.' Palmer's brow was furrowed.

'Are you all right, Tom?'

'I'm joking,' Palmer said laughing. 'Best G7 to date. And yes, I think we achieved a lot.'

Dumart smiled and shook his head at being caught out by his old friend. 'I hope you don't mind our secret rendezvous. I didn't want to make our meeting too obvious. With G7 done and dusted, I thought that a meeting here this evening was perfect.'

'I was intrigued, of course. But I'm sure my motorcade sweeping into the Elysée Palace didn't go unnoticed.'

'Private meetings are not unusual. Anyway, let the newshounds speculate.'

'Well, they know we are friends, Jean-Baptist. Can't friends be allowed to enjoy one another's company? I think they forget we are human.'

'Please, Tom,' Dumart said, handing Palmer his drink and offering him a seat. Palmer took a sip and sat back. He knew the pleasantries were over. Dumart lit a cigar and handed over a small scrap of paper. It read: '*This conversation must remain inside these four walls.*' Palmer nodded and handed back the paper, which Dumart burnt in the ashtray. 'Tom, I want to share a secret with you.' Palmer raised his eyebrows but remained silent. 'Did you know much about your father?' Palmer raised his eyebrows again. This was a curveball. 'Or indeed, your father's father? You see, there's a connection between you and me that goes back a long way. A very long way indeed.'

'What the hell, Jean?'

'I'm sorry, it's not like me to be unprepared. I thought I knew how to tell you everything, but it's difficult to know where to start.'

'The beginning?' Palmer suggested, leaning forward.

'Ah, the beginning. By the way, this is not some skeleton-in-the-closet scandal or anything like that. I didn't screw your mother if that's what you're thinking,' Dumart said.

'Or my grandma, I hope!'

Dumart chuckled and puffed on his cigar. 'Look, you trust me, yes?'

'Of course, I do, Jean, even if you are a politician.'

'I'm serious, Tom. Do you regard me as an intelligent human being? Because some of what I must tell you may seem incredible.' Dumart took a swig of champagne and continued. 'Your father knew several US presidents. One of them—it doesn't matter which—helped to instigate the secret I'm about to tell you. You see, your father, along with a small number of select people on this planet, was a member of an important and secret…interest group.'

'I hope you're not going to say the words Illuminati or the Masons.'

'This is deadly serious, Tom. They're the same people that helped you and me along the way. Think about it. All those convenient moments in your life that led you to who you are now. You're talented and charismatic. Of that, there is no doubt. It's why *you*, not your father nor any other person within this sphere of influence, hold the most powerful office in the world. But your parents were rich and influential. So were mine. Everyone involved in this group also shared a common belief. That's the connection.'

'So why didn't my father mention any of this to me?'

'Well, that common belief was founded on a simple modesty amongst its patrons. These people were essentially philanthropists. Their benefaction helped promote what they believed in: a stable world based on Christian values.'

'So, this interest group, as you call it, was made up of good people. I'm relieved to hear that,' said Palmer.

'Exactly. But there are aspects of this group that go much deeper. On the surface, that common belief was preserving a good Christian ethos. It was the background to what had been for centuries no more than a group of rich and influential people. But that simple belief has been constantly under threat. Now more than ever.'

'You're damn right there.'

'I want to read you something, Tom.' From the table in front of them, Dumart opened an envelope and took out a letter. 'It's in Spanish, but I'll do my best to translate it. It reads: *Your Excellency, I have witnessed much good bestowed upon people throughout the world by the generosity and charity of our members:*

schools, medical aid, care for the elderly, and donations to the church and the arts. For centuries, it has been a cause for good, bringing support and hope to countless millions, and long may it continue. But I know that you and I both fear that all this good is being threatened. Recent events have heightened my concern. Your speech last week echoed my thoughts and, I know, the concerns of millions. We cannot have the work of generations undone. We must act before all is lost. There are those amongst us who would resist such actions. But I believe it is our destiny. I remain your devoted brother and servant to the one true God. Yours faithfully, Cardinal J. Romero, Vatican City.'

Dumart handed the letter over and leant back as Palmer gazed at it. 'So let me clarify,' Dumart said. 'First, Cardinal Juan Romero holds a long-standing position in the College of Cardinals and is therefore one of its most senior and most respected. The cardinal is cautious in his use of words. Second, the members he refers to are the Guild of God—the very same people who helped you and me. The Guild of God has been in existence for centuries. Its sole purpose has been to promote Christian values through generous donations.'

Palmer stood up. 'Wait just one goddamned minute, Jean.'

'I did say this would seem incredible.'

'You are talking about a secret society. This is a joke, right?' Dumart remained silent. 'I feel like a stooge, a fake, Jean. A puppet for Christ's sake.'

'You're still the most powerful man on the planet, Tom. That doesn't change. Look, the recent events the cardinal talks about, we all know what he's referring to. It's gone from terrorism to a fundamental shift in belief. People are saying, there is a god, but it's not ours. Our people have taken to the streets. They want to believe that they're right. It's why they look to you and me. They want an answer.'

'These martyrdoms are some kind of trick, that's all. Once revealed, the whole thing will be over.'

'You're right. It is a trick. Or, should I say, there is a rational, scientific explanation.'

Palmer sat down. 'Is there more?'

'Yes. The cardinal's mention of destiny is a reference to the secret I referred to earlier.' Dumart was relishing the moment. *Knowledge is power*, he thought. Right now, he had more power than the President of the United States of America.

'So, what the hell is it?'

'A weapon.'

Palmer stared at Dumart.

'I'm sorry, Tom. If this seems like I'm playing games. I'm not. As I said, it is difficult to explain this without...how do you say, without causing incredulity.' There was truth in what Dumart was saying, and Palmer sensed this. But he also knew that Dumart was enjoying the moment. Palmer was not to be drawn into the little game and simply nodded slowly. 'It is, or should I say, *was* a weapon,' Dumart continued, 'masterminded and funded by your country but shelved after a series of technical problems.'

'Jean, I'm aware of hundreds of such projects,' Palmer said. 'So, it's probably no secret to me.'

'Maybe. But I'd be surprised. Yes, I'm sure that hundreds of dead projects lie in the vaults of the Pentagon. Why should anyone bother you with this one?' Dumart had a point. Both men knew it. Palmer had failed to gain back a point in their little game of one-upmanship. 'The weapon was designed to destabilise the troposphere and thus cause major disruption above specific parts of the earth.'

'A weather weapon?'

'Precisely.'

'Like the cloud seeding experiments in World War 2?'

'More sophisticated than that. Tom, please allow me to introduce you to someone.' Dumart reached forward and pressed an intercom button on the coffee table. '*Envoie-le dans.*'

A few moments later, the door to the sitting room was opened by the private secretary. A suited, red-haired man strode in.

'Tom, this is Richard Ordway. He's one of yours.'

'Sir, it's a great honour.' Ordway nodded and shook Palmer's hand.

'One of ours?' Palmer asked.

'DOD, sir.'

Palmer raised his eyebrows expecting more. When it was not forthcoming, he nodded slowly. *One of those political men that worked in the shadows. Secretive, effective, and usually ultra-patriotic*, he thought.

Dumart leant back in his chair and puffed on his cigar.

Ordway looked to Dumart, then addressed Palmer. 'Sir, the original aim of the project was to cause blackouts in traditional forms of communication, while simultaneously developing a communication system that could work in the area affected. That meant screwing with the atmosphere in the same way solar rays do. Imagine the advantage that would give in a military operation. The new communication system of the project was the difficult part. But the equipment developed to disrupt the atmosphere showed far more potential. As part of the project, scientists had been researching lightning to find ways of protecting military equipment and personnel, even to the point of discharging electrical storms. In parallel to the military research, several civil projects were looking at ways of harnessing the electrical power in the atmosphere. There's a hell of a lotta electrical activity going on up there. Fast forward a few years and we're now in a very interesting position.'

'But you said it was shelved, Jean,' Palmer said.

'It was,' the French president replied.

'Yes, sir,' Ordway continued, 'the military communication experiment was. But the various experiments on atmospheric electricity proved far more fruitful.'

'You mean another crazy weather weapon.' Palmer said, looking somewhat annoyed. 'This is ridiculous. And the name of this project?'

Ordway handed Palmer a file. Palmer looked at the file's title and quickly thumbed its contents, shaking his head. 'Come on Jean, this has to be a joke. "The Spear of Destiny"? Wasn't that something Hitler owned?'

Dumart leant forward to reply. 'The spear that pierced Christ on the cross. Thought to bring untold power to whoever possessed it. But *that* Spear of Destiny is a little more than a superstitious relic, very possibly a fake. Nevertheless, it currently resides in the Vatican. *Our* Spear of Destiny is no fake and is, you could say, also part-owned by the church. So, the name of the project has a certain irony, *n'est ce pas?*'

Palmer was looking at Dumart, but pointing a finger at Ordway. 'Does *he* know about what you just told me?'

'Yes, Tom. He's coordinating the entire project on our behalf.'

Palmer turned to Ordway. 'So how long have *you* been a member?'

Ordway looked to Dumart for guidance. Dumart simply nodded. 'I was recruited when I was a student at MIT, sir.'

Palmer began pacing the room. 'Let me get this right, Jean, my father was in this Guild of God. The president you referred to earlier was also a member, and it was he who developed this weapon thanks to private donations from my father and others including, it would seem, the Pope, no less!'

240

Dumart smiled, 'The Pope, no. But a handful of senior ecclesiastics, yes. Cardinal Romero being one. The majority of funds come from large corporations and billionaires.'

Palmer looked again at the letter. 'So, a weapon,' he began slowly, 'developed by the American government, which I know nothing about, but about which the president of a foreign country, with all due respect, Jean, is going to tell me everything.'

'Mr President, if I may?' Ordway interjected.

'Please, Mr Ordway, I am all ears,' Palmer said, sitting back down and trying to suppress his anger.

Ordway paused, realising that what he was about to impart was like a sales pitch like no other. 'In the 1930s, following the disastrous dust storms that decimated crops across the US and Canadian prairies…'

'The Dust Bowl,' Palmer said as if to demonstrate some knowledge.

'…yes, sir, US scientists were working on ways of controlling the weather. This led to some interesting developments. In January 1942, a month after the attack on Pearl Harbor, the government set up a military base in Alaska and moved scientists there. Activity at that base never stopped, nor did the development. It is still active today.' Ordway opened the file and showed Palmer an aerial image of the base.

'STOP RIGHT THERE, MR ORDWAY!' Palmer bellowed and stood up again. 'I'm sorry, Jean. We may all be friends, members of NATO, part of the free world, and all that bullshit, but these are state secrets, goddammit!'

'Tom, Tom,' the French president smiled. 'Come on.' He gave Palmer a look of *let's not be naïve.* 'If it pleases you, let's conclude this meeting.' He leant forward and held up the file. 'This is real, Tom. Look at the facts. As a friend, I beg you.'

Palmer took the file. His anger subsided. *Dumart had won his little power game*, he thought. *And perhaps he will win one back if this Spear of Destiny is true. And who the hell is this Richard Ordway?* he wondered. He turned to Ordway, 'I need a word with the president. In private.'

'Of course, Mr President. Thank you for your time.'

Palmer waited for the door to close then turned to Dumart. 'So, Jean, why am I not a member of this Guild of God, whereas you, this Ordway fella, and god knows who else, are?'

Dumart took one last puff of his cigar and stubbed it out. 'I was waiting for that question. It's quite simple to answer really. You see, it made more sense to allow you to work the political system. Think of the Guild of God as your guardian angels during that process. Your knowledge of the Guild or direct membership would have served no purpose. An unnecessary distraction, you could say. And it worked. Like I said, Tom, you now hold the highest office in the world.'

Palmer shook his head. 'And like I said, Jean, I feel like a goddamned puppet.'

'Well, if it appeases you, you are now most certainly an honorary member. And this,' Dumart said raising the Spear of Destiny file again, 'could be the one reason why I, or should I say, the Guild of God wanted you here tonight. We need your support now more than ever.'

Five minutes later, Palmer descended the steps to the illuminated courtyard and the waiting cars. Ordway and Clairmont were on the lower step.

'Goodnight, Mr President,' they both said.

Palmer was stony-faced. 'You'll be hearing from me, Mr Ordway,' he replied, and the presidential motorcade, flanked by the motorcycle outriders, swept out from the palace courtyard and into the city streets.

George Clairmont watched them leave and turned to Ordway. 'Your car will be here shortly, Mr Ordway.'

A few minutes later, Ordway was turning onto *Rue du Faubourg Saint-Honoré.*

Me with two presidents in one night, he thought, and could not help but smile to himself, as the richly illuminated boutiques and designer stores flashed past.

Chapter 48
Investigation

Tanneron, Southern France

The peloton of cyclists was crawling its way around another tight bend on the narrow road up to the villa. Daniel did not want to share his hatred of cyclists with his guest, but found himself muttering in his adopted language, '*Pour l'amour! Plus vite!*' as he followed in his rather hot and noisy van.

Kara smiled and looked out at the sun-baked Mediterranean flora. She was enjoying her time in France. 'They really like their bikes here.'

'You could say that,' Daniel replied with a forced smile.

'I mean, this is a serious climb.'

'Yep, any normal person would use some form of motorised assistance. You know, I wouldn't mind, but they take up more space than a juggernaut. No consideration whatsoever.'

Well, I'm enjoying the view,' Kara said, looking forward as one of the male cyclists raised himself off his saddle to pump his legs harder.

They both laughed.

The road straightened and Daniel spotted a chance to overtake, only to be thwarted by the appearance of a dark grey van coming down the hill. Daniel cursed and repositioned the van behind the peloton. He glanced at the driver and then the side of the van as it passed. 'Swimming pool maintenance,' he said to himself.

Daniel brought the van to its habitual dust-raising stop on the villa's driveway.

'I'm desperate for a beer. How about you?' Daniel asked as he began entering the alarm code by the front door.'

'Water and wine, I think.'

That's weird...'

'What?

'The alarm seems to be unresponsive. Perhaps we've had a power cut.'

'Is that normal?'

'Not really, but it's not impossible.'

Daniel entered the hallway and flicked on a light. 'Great, so the alarm is out. Anyway, drinks and some lunch…'

'Daniel, tomorrow I'd like to take some measurements on the hillside.'

'Happy to help. What kind of measurements?'

Kara began following Daniel through the villa and into his study.

'Residual electrical energy, rock samples, magnetism, fulgurites for a start.'

'Magnetism and fulgurites…remind me.'

'Fulgurites are where lightning has quite simply melted rock. The temperature of lightning is more than two and half thousand degrees C. If we find a fulgurite, its volume could help us establish how powerful the lightning strike that formed it was. Fulgurites are like lightning fossils. But we may only find sand fused into glass rather than anything more substantial. It depends on the geology in these parts.'

'Right. And magnetism?'

'Well, rock like basalt has a lot of magnetic material. When it formed millions of years ago, the direction of the earth's magnetism was effectively imprinted into it. As the rock moves and shifts through the aeons, its magnetism remains locked. Locked, that is unless struck by lightning. When that happens, the rock's magnetism suddenly shifts in line with today's magnetic north. So, if you find one rock with a different direction of magnetism than those around it, it's almost certainly been struck by lightning. There are places on earth with an unusually high frequency of lightning. The Alberta foothills in Canada, for instance. Lightning magnets are what they're called, although that's somewhat of a misnomer. Your hillside may be one.'

'And your plateau in Venezuela?'

'Not so much. But we needed somewhere remote. We initially started experiments on Lake Maracaibo, which has one of the highest lightning strike rates in the world—up to forty strikes a minute each night for nearly half the year.'

'Wow!'

'You can say that again. It was intense *and* spectacular. It's quite the attraction. There's even a Catatumbo Lightning Tour.'

'Catatumbo?'

'That's the river that feeds into the lake.'

'But surely that's the perfect location for lightning research.'

'It was up to a point. But working on boats proved impractical. We were also more interested in experimenting in those 'lightning magnet' areas. You see, lightning can do things like split rock apart. And you won't see things like that bobbing about on a boat...Daniel?'

Daniel appeared distracted. He was looking at the wall. 'Someone's been here.'

'What?'

'That photo of me. It was slightly underneath the one of Sophie.'

'You sure? Has anything been taken?'

'I'm sure. And no. At least I don't think so. That's what's weird. My camera's here. And everything else seems to be untouched.'

'Why the photo?'

'I have no idea...Unless...' Daniel was striding back through the villa.

'Where are you going?'

'The hut. I think you should come, too. I don't want to leave you on your own. The alarm was clearly tampered with. Whoever did this could still be around. We'll take Sadie most of the way, but we'll need to walk the rest; she's too noisy.'

Daniel parked the van off the track half a kilometre from the hut and turned to Kara, 'OK, let's investigate.'

'What are you thinking?' Kara asked as they began the climb towards the hut.

'I'm not sure. It's probably nothing. Maybe it's just a nutty meteorite collector. Either way, I don't want anyone snooping around my possessions. By the way, watch out for snakes.'

'Great. Welcome viewers to a day in the life of Dr Daniel Bayford: glamour, death, burglary, snakes...' Kara stopped her mocking when Daniel came to an abrupt stop. He raised a hand and looked from side to side. The hut and tower were about fifteen metres ahead of them near the hill's summit.

'The padlock's gone.'

'It's there on the ground.'

Daniel was annoyed. He ran the last few metres and kicked in the door. If anyone had been in there, *God help them!* he thought. But the hut was empty.

Daniel stood at the threshold, catching his breath, hands on his hips, looking into his favourite hideaway.

Kara peered over his shoulder. 'It looks OK, doesn't it?'

Daniel simply nodded up towards one of the shelves. 'It's gone. The box with the stone has gone.'

Chapter 49
Harvest

Tennessee, USA

Ordway stepped from the government chopper, removed his D&G sunglasses, and looked up the slope that rose ahead of him. He was deep in the Great Smoky Mountains National Park. The scenery was breath-taking, but he was not here to admire the views.

It was a hot day. Ordway removed his leather bomber jacket and slung it over his shoulder.

Clutching a tablet PC, an army captain approached him from a large, open-sided, tarpaulin shelter—the nerve centre of the operation—inside which were laptops and radio equipment on a series of tables manned by soldiers.

Ordway replaced his shades and turned to him. 'Where are they?'

'Sir, we have two teams. One in sector 7 further up the valley.' The soldier pointed to a map marked out with grids on the tablet PC. The other should be entering sector 4, about halfway up...that way,' the officer continued, now pointing up the mountainside.

Ordway followed his gaze to a patch of forest that had seen a recent fire. 'How big is the exclusion zone?'

'Sir, we've closed off this entire area. Around 40 square miles. All routes in, including rivers. Anyone we come across—campers, hikers—we ferry them out. State police are also helping.'

'Under what excuse?'

'We're telling folk there's a dangerous black bear up there.'

Ordway smirked. He turned and spotted some army vehicles. 'Can you get me up there?'

'Sure thing, sir.'

Up amongst the part-burnt trees, around fifteen soldiers were making their way slowly up the mountainside. Each was holding a scanner.

The captain steered the open-topped Land Rover up the winding, narrow track through a still lush part of the forest. The special operations vehicle was perfect: the track was more of a trail for hikers, but the 4x4 weaved its way amongst the trees with ease.

When the edge of the greenery gave way to the more open, fire-ravaged side of the mountain, the captain brought the vehicle to a halt. The smell of nearby burnt timber and leaves was subtle but acrid. 'Up there, sir.'

The line of soldiers was clear to see.

Ordway leapt out and followed the captain across ground that was dry and grey with ash, and past the first of many blackened tree trunks. They soon reached the lefthand flank of soldiers. The captain called over to the nearest of them, 'Soldier!' and beckoned him over. The soldier turned and jogged towards them.

'Sir?'

Ordway held a hand out and the soldier handed him the scanner. 'Any luck?' he asked, handing it back and looking at the young private.

'Sir, yes, sir. We came across a cluster about twenty minutes ago in, er, sector 3, sir.'

'Who has them?' the captain enquired.

'Sir, the Sarge. He's...' the private turned and scanned the charred forest ahead of them, '...up there, sir.'

'Good man. Carry on,' the captain commanded.

'Sir,' the private replied, and re-joined the ascending line of soldiers.

Ordway and the captain marched up and across towards the sergeant and more of the soldiers.

'Sergeant!' the captain called out.

'Sir?'

'Success in sector 3, I hear.'

'Yes sir,' the sergeant replied, reaching around, and patting the pack on his back.

'Anything in this sector?' Ordway asked.

'We think so. We're getting strong signals over on the right.'

As though on cue, a soldier behind the sergeant raised an arm and called out, 'Got one, Sarge!'

Ordway, the captain, and the sergeant headed over. Ordway, though, hung back slightly. In front of the soldier's grey, dusty boots, half buried in ash, the unmistakable blue of another of the remarkable meteorites glimmered in the mid-morning sunlight.

'Secure it, quickly, Sergeant.' Ordway instructed from a distance. 'You really don't want to know what these pretty stones are capable of.'

All three soldiers gave Ordway a quizzical look. None of them had any idea what this was about. Some soldiers had dismissed it as a bizarre team-building exercise, and that the gemstones had been planted. After all, when was the last time the US army did anything like this?

The sergeant returned to the task at hand. He removed his backpack, took out a small black container, and placed it on the ground. The soldier and the captain stood back as the sergeant placed the meteorite into the container and quickly sealed it shut.

'Can we ask what this is all about?' the soldier asked, looking at Ordway.

Ordway realised he had made a faux pas, and chose to ignore the question. This was the first of many surveys and possible collections of the meteorite he had initiated. He was eager to have success. But, more importantly, it had to be kept under wraps. He ignored the question and instead asked his own, 'How many is that, Sergeant?'

'Fourteen in total, sir.'

'And eight more sectors to go. We've only just started,' the captain said.

'Excellent. Keep looking!' Ordway said and strolled off towards the Land Rover.

The sergeant looked up at the captain, who simply shrugged his shoulders and muttered, 'He's DOD.'

Catalonia, Northeast Spain

A hundred kilometres inland from the relative cool of the Mediterranean coast, it was a blistering 44C in the foothills of the Pyrenees.

A line of more than fifty soldiers of the Spanish Army was spread across the hillside. Progress was slow. They were struggling in the heat and kept stopping to rehydrate. All the troops kept their field caps on but wished they had sombreros.

The low vegetation under their boots and around them had been burnt to a crisp—not by the sun, although it certainly felt like it could scorch the very life from every living thing—but by another devastating lightning storm.

The complaints were relentless. *Why were they here, in this heat, looking for gemstones, for god's sake?* But orders were orders, and they pressed on.

Like the sweat on their collective bodies, the monotony of the task suddenly evaporated. A female voice rang out. It was the first such call after two hours.

'*AQUI!*'

Curious to see an example of what they had been ordered to look for, several of the soldiers gathered around her and the blue stone at her feet.

She bent down to pick it up. '*Ay! La piedra es muy pesada!* As if to emphasise its weight, she bobbed her hand up and down. Some of the other soldiers tentatively touched the stone.

'*¡VOLVER!*' The commanding officer pushed his way through and struck the stone out of the soldier's hand. 'ES PELIGROSO!' he shouted.

The soldiers all stepped back. They looked utterly confused. *Dangerous? A stone?* The female soldier looked at her hands with concern.

The officer then looked up. His sergeant was running towards him, removing his backpack as he did so. The officer stepped back to give him room. They all watched as the sergeant placed and sealed the stone inside a small black container.

'*Est radiactivo?*' the female soldier asked now with fear across her face.

'*No, pero no toques!*' the officer replied and smiled.

After her superior's response, she certainly had no intention of touching one again.

'*¿BIEN?*' the officer roared, looking at them all.

The soldiers walked back to their positions and resumed the long, hot search.

Democratic Republic of the Congo, Central Africa

The Congolese troops, sitting in the open truck as it sped down the sandy road, were in a good mood. This was a welcome break from fighting militias. Four more trucks followed behind.

'*Si je trouve un bijou, je le vends et j'achète une nouvelle voiture!*' one of them joked. The others smiled.

250

'*Moi, je le donnerai â ma femme pour le meilleur sexe de tous les temps!*' another countered. This brought about raucous laughter.

Several miles down the road, the lead truck pulled over and the troops jumped down. Several of them lit up cigarettes. Their officer climbed out from the truck's cab and began handing out maps, which the soldiers studied.

They were a long way from the nearest habitation. To one side of the road was dense rainforest; on the other, hilly, open grassland, dotted with shrubs and trees.

This was the direction the officer and his sergeant headed. Only they had scanners. They split up; the soldiers, rifles slung over their shoulders, followed, spreading out in wide lines behind them, and studying the ground around them as they progressed slowly forward.

When the troops reached a small hill after half an hour of searching, the first of many of the blue meteorites was discovered.

'PAR ICI!' the soldier called out triumphantly.

Chapter 50
Accusation

Daniel's Villa, Tanneron, Southern France

'Here, you look like you need it.' Kara handed Daniel a glass of white wine. He was seated on the low stone wall by his pool, looking out towards his hill.

It was late morning the day after the break-in, and already blisteringly hot. The cicadas were in full chorus and a woodpecker's communication efforts could be heard echoing across the valley. Daniel gave Kara a half smile and took a swig of the chilled Chablis.

'Hey, so what's got you in such a mood, Mr Grumpy?'

Daniel put his glass down on the wall. 'Someone disabled my alarm, I'm not sure how, broke into my home, found a photo that led them to my hut, where they broke in using bolt cutters, and took nothing except that stone.'

Kara could sense that Daniel's mood had changed dramatically since the incident—changed for the worst.

'Something's bugging you. I can tell.'

Daniel pursed his lips before replying. 'Kara, I'm just concerned that all this happened very soon after you reported your findings.'

'What, you mean my video conference with Professor Stone and Ordway? What are you saying?'

'I don't know.'

Kara glared at Daniel. He looked away and took another swig of wine.

'No, no. That won't do, Daniel. Are you accusing me of something here?' Her voice was level, but there was hurt within it.

'Like I said, I don't know. You work for the US government. Maybe they know something I don't...'

'Oh what, so organised a raid on your villa? Come on!'

'Maybe.'

'Maybe you have an overactive imagination.'

'I'm sorry. But something doesn't feel right. That's all. And I'm sorry if I offended you.'

'Apology accepted.'

They fell silent. Kara took a gulp of wine. Daniel glanced at her. She was breathing heavily through her nose. Her breasts swelling under her t-shirt. She took another gulp. *God, I love wine*, she thought. She looked out into the valley before taking a seat on the wall close to Daniel. 'The measurements we took this morning were interesting,' she said, trying to diffuse the tension.

'Yeh.'

'I was going to share the findings with a geology colleague at my old university. But maybe not. We don't want more thieves running amok across your hillside.'

'What do you mean?'

'Well… meteorites are extremely valuable. And I mean *valuable*. And let's face it, the one you found is pretty darn unique and heavy. So, your theory about an avid collector making off with your stone makes sense.'

'Shit. I hadn't even considered its value. How much are we talking about?'

'Well, let's take a look.' Kara removed the phone from her shorts and began thumbing rapidly. She then held the screen towards Daniel, her eyebrows raised.

'You're kidding! €300,000!'

'Oh, that's the entry price for the best. Here, let me scroll down.'

'My God! That's nearly €2m!'

'Yep. And your beautiful stone was a worldwide sensation.'

Daniel stood up and faced Kara. 'You're right,' he said rather sheepishly. 'I'm being stupid. But now I don't know if I'm angrier about the break-in or about the fact that I could have been rich. I could do with some extra funds.'

'You've clearly forgotten about the one I found.'

'Of course! You've still got it, right?'

'I'm a scientist. I look after my samples.'

'But where? Whoever came here surely searched the villa from top to bottom.'

'The villa maybe.' Kara smiled and nodded towards the pool.

Daniel squinted, smiled, stepped to the edge of the pool, and scanned its floor. 'I don't see it.'

'The far side, on the ledge just under the water line.'

'But why there? It's in one of your special flight cases.'

'Good question. Maybe I have a funny feeling about all this, too. Or at least…'

'At least what?'

'A funny feeling about Ordway.'

'Oh, you mentioned him. The guy who ordered you here.'

'Yeh, a prize jerk of the first order.'

'Maybe we're both right. The press article, my TV interviews, and all the coverage happened weeks ago. Anyone planning to steal the meteorite for money would have done so before now, surely.'

'Unless it took them this long to track your location down.'

'No way. The media showed and published maps of the area as part of their coverage, for heaven's sake.

'And yet within hours of my video conference…But hang on Daniel, what are you saying?'

'Who knows, Kara? I, we may have stumbled upon something significant. You tell me. You could be the unwitting link in all this.'

'Well, yeh. Whoever harnesses the energy stored in the atmosphere could solve the world's energy crisis.'

'And you reported that this extra-terrestrial rock,' Daniel said nodding towards the pool, 'could help in that quest.'

'I did.'

'Kara, forget the value of these meteorites at an auction. These rocks could be worth trillions.'

'In which case, your idea of a government-backed raid doesn't seem that farfetched after all.'

'Kara, these things happen, believe me. I've seen all sorts of shit done in the name of power and sovereignty.'

'Ah yes. You worked for the British government.'

'Huh, so you read up about me.'

'Sounded exciting.'

'It wasn't. But what I did afterwards was.'

Kara cocked her head to one side. 'Man of mystery,' she said playfully. 'So, what *did* you do afterwards?'

'All in good time. Right now, I think we should find out more about this Ordway chap.'

'Right now, I think we should eat.'

'Hey, that's my line.'

'Well, you know. When in Rome.'

When she smiled and gave him a wink, Daniel melted inside, and butterflies fluttered in his stomach.

Chapter 51
Marid

Cannes, Southern France

Even anchored half a mile off the coast, the lights festooning the mega yacht were spectacular. Had there been any night-time strollers on the *Boulevard de la Croisette*—and there were none tonight, the authorities had closed down the entire area—they would have been treated to a tantalising glimpse of how the super-rich could party. The vessel's entire outline and every deck were bejewelled in hundreds of white lights. Searchlights criss-crossed from the superstructure, while a green laser drew palm trees and cocktails images against the inky backdrop of the night sky. The muted thump of dance music from somewhere inside the vessel drifted across the water.

A Sikorsky S-76 sped low over the shoreline just beyond the palm trees that lined the boulevard. It turned seaward, pitching forward just metres above the water, its main light rippling over the gentle waves. It was heading straight for the mega yacht, named after the mythological jinn of Arabic folklore.

A temporary pontoon was positioned aft of *Marid*. Several smaller boats were moored against it, some discharging more party-goers, who watched the helicopter—part of the standard equipment of the mega craft—as it settled on the helideck above them. A man alighted the chopper and was met by two men in dark suits.

From his position in the centre of the yacht's ballroom, Prince Al-Musan was looking towards the top of the sweeping stairs. The talk in the room was of the incident at the *Palais des Festivals* three days earlier. The guest in front of him, the mayor of Cannes, an obsequious small-time politician, was sensing he was losing the prince's attention. 'It was as though the man knew he would be struck by lightning, don't you think, Your Highness?'

'That would be a power to envy, don't you think?' the prince replied, smiling. 'I'm sorry, please excuse me.' He nodded politely to the mayor and other guests around him. 'Enjoy yourselves, I beg you. My boat is your home tonight.' The congenial host strode off, smiling and acknowledging his other guests.

'If only,' one of the guests muttered, looking up at the opulent surroundings.

Bakr was approaching the top of the stairs, two security men behind him. Nodding almost imperceptibly to Bakr, the prince did not break his stride as he disappeared through a side door. Bakr and the two men exited the way they had come.

Leading the way along the central corridor, one of the security men stopped and knocked at a door. A muffled 'Enter!' came from within. The first security man followed Bakr into the prince's boardroom and took up position by the door. His colleague had remained on guard outside. The prince was taking a cigarette from a box on a Louis XV Boulle inlay writing desk.

'Allah be praised! Prince Al-Musan, it is a great honour to be with you again. I am filled with—' Bakr began.

'Bakr.' The prince silenced Bakr with a raised hand, 'I have to return to the party, so listen to me.' He lit his cigarette and continued, 'Allah is indeed great, as he has led me to this place. Find this man.' The prince handed over a photo. 'His name is Dr Daniel Bayford. He has a villa in this area. He has one of the sacred stones. Find it. Then silence him.'

Bakr had noticed the scientific journal on the prince's desk and the headline: *Lightning Stone from Space*?

'He has a sacred stone, Your Highness?'

The prince saw Bakr glance again at the journal. 'Bakr, you are an intelligent man. You know that these stones are not *sacred*.' Bakr looked anxious, unsure how to respond. Reading his face, the prince laughed, 'No, they're not, my friend. But they are inexplicable, immensely powerful and until now they had been in our sole possession.' The prince picked up the journal. 'This man has clearly discovered a stone of similar if not the same properties here in France. They believe it was a meteorite. So far, this is the only one of a handful of reports of the finding. Right now, it is a scientific curiosity, a mere side-line in a world awash with news and information. But if we allow these scientists to test it and reveal what it truly is then these martyrdoms will be seen as nothing more than an elaborate hoax, a cheap trick; not the will of Allah. Someone somewhere will make the connection. Without the evidence, they cannot.'

Bakr nodded with growing comprehension.

The prince sat down behind the desk and drew on the cigarette. 'I assume you *did* retrieve our brother's stone?'

'Of course, Your Highness. There was much confusion at the scene. People were more interested in getting away. It was easy.' As he spoke, Bakr produced a small, heavy-duty container no bigger than two packs of cards. He pushed one side with his thumb to reveal a concealed drawer. Inside lay the necklace and its stone. 'And what of the other martyrdoms, Your Highness? Were our brothers as glorious as Mohamed was here?'

'Let me show you the effect of that great day.' The prince leant forward and picked up a remote. Bakr turned. Six widescreen televisions came to life, each tuned to a global news channel. All but one was covering the wave of martyrdoms that had swept the world. '24-hour news. It's like feeding time at the zoo. Look at them, greedily digesting and spewing out every morsel of information. It'll be the same on the internet.' The prince punched the remote. One of the screens updated to reveal various social media feeds. 'You see, Bakr, instant free advertising for the great Islamic cause. Except this time, they will stop and watch not in revulsion, but in awe. They will believe that we hold the hand of God in ours.'

'Allah is great.' Bakr stared at the silent screens; his mouth stuck in a toothy smile.

The prince did not reply. Instead, he brought up the sound of one report. They were interviewing a large and animated, middle-aged man. The top of the screen announced that it was: LIVE FROM MISSISSIPPI.

'He just stood there, bold as anythin' and shoutin' about All-ah saying that he was a chosen one and all that. Next thing, boom! This flash of lighnin' just came from nowhere.'

Another voice interjected and the camera swung to bring the face of a young man into view, *'Yes ma'm, mighty weird. Lightnin' with no storm an' all.'*

'But was there no doubt it was lightning?' the reporter probed.

'Hell yeh!' the first man came back. *'It struck the freak down right there. Fried to a crisp he was.'*

The screen abruptly cut to the reporter, her back to a wall of police cars and security forces.

'*Authorities and scientists here in Jackson are at a loss as to how this man came to be struck by lightning. Eyewitnesses say he was shouting repeatedly...*' Here the reporter looked down at her notes, '"*The hour is coming, Al-Bahith. Allah is great!*" *Moments later he was struck dead by what people here are saying was quite literally a bolt out of the blue. This is Carolyn Anderson in Jackson, Mississippi.*'

The prince flicked to a UK channel. One of the anchors was in mid-flow: '*...at least twenty-three similar events throughout the world. Martyrdom and Act of God are the words being used more and more to describe these shocking but bizarre incidents. We have on the line from Florida, Professor Charles Blackwell an expert on meteorology. 'Professor, thank you for joining us. Now you and your team have carried out extensive research into lightning and storm activity.*'

'*Yes, you could say we're the leading light in this branch of science.*'

'*Very good. But joking aside, what is going on here? Twenty-three almost identical incidents. Lightning strikes on men, all of whom calling upon Allah. This is uncanny if not a little scary, isn't it?*'

'*Well, we've only seen footage from two or three of the incidents so far...*'

'*But reports from hundreds of eye-witnesses at the others.*'

'*Yes, true. But without more video material it's difficult for us to draw any real conclusions.*'

'*Are you saying that what seems to be a series of lightning strikes could be something else?*'

'*No, not from what we saw from the footage or what we hear from the eye-witness reports. We do know there was a storm in the Cannes area at the time. I'm sure the same will be true in the other locations.*'

'*But s*everal of those eye-witness reports describe how the lightning was, to coin the phrase, a bolt from the blue. Presumably, that saying has some scientific basis.*'

'*Right. It's possible for lightning to strike many miles from the heart of a storm often in clear skies. That's where the saying comes from.*'

'*But a bolt from the blue refers to a completely unexpected event, so lightning of this type must be rare.*'

'*Yes, the most common form of lightning is what we call intra-cloud lightning. There's also a lot of inter-cloud lightning. Cloud-to-ground lightning, which is what is happening here, is the next most common.*'

'*Is it possible, Professor Blackwell, that these men somehow invoked the lightning?*'

The prince sat up, 'Ah, this will be interesting…'

The professor smiled. '*I very much doubt that. You would need some kind of rocket, a powerful laser, or some other device to trigger lightning, and you'd have to be right in the line of fire if you really wanted to be struck by the lightning. I haven't heard of one report of anything being fired into the air before these incidents took place.*'

'*So do you think this is a series of bizarre coincidences?*'

'*No, there'll be a rational explanation, I'm sure.*'

'*But at the moment you can't offer one.*'

'*Not without more data, no.*'

'*Thank you, Professor. If you wouldn't mind staying on the line as we go now over to our correspondent in Rome, John Wetherby. John, what's the latest there?*'

'*Theories abounding here are that this is a very elaborate Islamic suicide campaign, except that the victim is giving the impression that he is calling upon God to strike him down in some kind of martyrdom.*'

'*That's interesting John. Putting aside for the moment how they're actually doing this, the multiple worldwide events that we're seeing do seem to suggest some kind of co-ordinated plan, which would give that theory some credence, I suppose.*'

'*That's absolutely right. But the big question among many here—and elsewhere, I'm sure—remains the same: is this some kind of very clever but lethal trick, or is it, as many here believe, an act of God?*'

The prince powered off the bank of televisions, and the panel began its slow, silent slide back across the screens.

'The stones *were* sent by God. After centuries of safe-keeping, I was the one destined to unleash their power on the infidels. So, yes, Mr TV man, you could say that these are acts of God,' the prince said. 'Something the blood-stained Christians would never understand.'

Chapter 52
Silence

Daniel's Villa, Tanneron, Southern France

'Daniel?' Kara whispered.

It was dark. Kara had woken to find that Daniel had left their bed. She lay there listening. Faint noises were coming from somewhere in the villa. Kara clicked on her phone. It was 2:45 a.m. More noises, this time louder. Then a light went on.

'I WOULDN'T DO THAT IF I WERE YOU!'

It was Daniel's voice, loud and commanding. Kara's heart began racing. 'Daniel?' she called anxiously. *What was happening*? she thought. She threw back the covers and ran towards the stairs. 'Daniel?' she kept calling.

'Stay there, Kara!' Daniel called up.

Kara descended the stairs slowly and stopped. Below, in the lounge was Daniel, his back to her. He was holding a shotgun at waist level and pointing it at someone she could not see. She bent down to peer under the living room ceiling. Her hand went straight to her mouth in shock, her eyes wide.

Fifty minutes earlier, Bakr had been seated in his cabin on board the *Marid*. It had not taken him long to find Daniel Bayford's home address. His laptop had been open in front of him showing a Google Map satellite image of Bayford's villa. Bakr had scanned the area, zooming in and out. He had then switched to Street View and had spent a good ten minutes viewing the property from various angles, then the approach road. Satisfied, he had closed the computer, and retrieved a knife from a nearby drawer.

Now, he was standing, knife in hand, facing Daniel.

'Who are you and what do you want?' Daniel's words were slow and assured.

Bakr looked up at Kara. She backed up the stairs, ran into the bedroom, and grabbed her phone. 'Shit, what's the emergency number here?' she said. 'DANIEL! WHAT'S THE EMERGENCY NUMBER FOR THE POLICE?'

'112, Kara.'

Daniel sounded in control, but Kara's hands were shaking. She dialled. 'Police!' was all she could say when a female operator answered. She ran back to the top of the stairs. 'Daniel, what do I say?'

'Put it on hands-free, Kara, and come next to me,' Daniel continued in his measured tone, not moving one inch, his gaze and gun fixed on the intruder.

A male voice on the phone could then be heard. 'Police. Madam…?'

'Er, *attend*! Don't go. *Un moment,*' Kara replied as she slowly descended the stairs, her heavy breathing now the only noise in the room.

'Stay behind me, Kara.' Daniel said. Kara held the phone up. Her hand was shaking, so she grabbed the phone with both hands. Daniel began, '*Je m'appelle, Docteur Daniel Bayford, Villa Marmosa, chemin de la colline, Tanneron. Il y a un intrus avec un couteau. Je le garde avec mon arme. Je suis avec Docteur Kara Williams.*'

'*Alors, restez calme, Docteur. Nous serons trés bientôt chez vous. Je resterai au telephone jusqu'à leur arrive. Ou êtes-vous exactement?*'

'What are they saying,' Kara asked.

'It's OK, the police will be here shortly.'

'*Nous sommes dans le salon. La lumière est allumée.*'

Bakr stood motionless, his eyes darting this way and that. He had miscalculated this Bayford.

'*Connaissez-vous l'intrus?*'

Daniel paused before replying. '*Non,*' he began slowly, '*Mais je pense que je l'ai vu au Palais de Festivals.*'

'What's he asking?' Kara asked.

'Do we know the intruder,' Daniel replied.

'*Pouvez-vous décrire l'intrus?*'

'*Arabe, svelte, un metre soixante dix-huit—quatre-vingts. Les cheveux courts et noirs.*'

Kara slowly began moving her thumbs across the screen of the phone. She clicked on the photo app and tilted the phone ever so slightly for a better angle. Bakr was in full view. Kara clicked on the x2 zoom button and took a photo. It was a silent action. Kara always put her phone on silent when she went to bed.

'Nice one,' Daniel muttered.

'*Un moment, Docteur.*'

A good thirty seconds passed when a new voice came on the phone. 'Hello, Doctor. My name is Chief Inspector Beaussant. I've been patched through to this call. Rest assured that my men will be with you shortly. Doctor Bayford. Are you or...*qui est la?...?*'

'*Docteur Williams,*' someone else on the line said.

'...Doctor Williams hurt?'

'No, we're fine.'

'Good. Please describe your situation.'

'The intruder is by the main window. About eight metres from us. He's holding a large knife. I am standing near the foot of the stairs. Dr Williams is behind me.'

Bakr was thinking fast.

'And what kind of gun are you holding?'

'A shotgun. A *loaded* shotgun,' Daniel enjoyed the emphasis. 'I have a licence.'

'That's fine, Doctor. We're not concerned about the legality or otherwise of your weapon.'

'Dr Williams? Can you hear me?'

'Yes, I'm here.'

'I suggest you leave the property. Is there a car?'

'But I'm holding the phone.'

'It's OK. Dr Bayford seems to have control. Can you place the phone somewhere? And how is the battery?'

Kara scanned the room. There was a chair by a small table to her left. With her eyes on Bakr all the time, she walked over, dragged it back to the side of Daniel, and placed the phone down. 'Can you still hear us? Kara asked.

'Yes, loud and clear.'

'And yes, the battery is fine,' she added, checking the phone's display.

'Good. Take the car and drive to Mand...' He was interrupted.

'Have you ever killed a human being?' It was Bakr. Daniel raised his gun slightly higher.

'As a matter of fact, yes, I have.' Daniel replied coolly.

Kara looked at Daniel. Was he bluffing, or was this another fact she did not know about her man of mystery? His confidence made her think that maybe he had.

'*Daniel, stay calm,*' Beaussant said after a moment.

'I *am* calm, Chief Inspector.'

Bakr looked around the room again. He needed an exit strategy. And fast. This Bayford meant business.

Beaussant spoke. 'I am addressing the intruder. You understand English. Can you hear me?'

Bakr remained silent.

'He can hear you fine,' Daniel said.

Beaussant continued. 'You are in a hopeless situation. Put down the knife. The police will be at the property in minutes.'

Kara heard it first. Bakr's head then moved slightly, as if to confirm what she thought she had heard. There it was again. It was barely discernible. But it was the unmistakable sound of a helicopter, the faint thumping of its blades fading in and out. *Please God let this be the police*, she thought. When the sound came again, it was either triggering an echo off the hills, or a second or even third helicopter had joined it. Either way, it was clear enough to hear.

The villa overlooked the valley, the land sweeping away in two directions, west towards Grasse and south towards the coast, with Daniel's fire lookout hill at the intersection. These helicopters were coming up from the direction of the coast. Daniel could almost pinpoint their location in his head. They were heading their way.

Bakr had no choice but to make a move. To his left was an opening to the kitchen and the door to the outside. Once in the kitchen, he would be shielded by the living room wall. It was his only option. He knew that throwing his knife or trying any other attempt at distraction could cause Bayford to shoot. Even if he ran and was fired upon, there was a chance at this distance that the buckshot would miss him. There was also the possibility that the gun was not loaded. *Why had Bayford made the point of saying that it was?* He then decided that some form of distraction may help.

264

He kicked hard at a large, ornate lamp on a coffee table to his right and ran low to his left. The lamp skidded across the tiled floor. It was enough. He was in the kitchen and through the partly open door in seconds. *No gunfire*, he thought. He ran downhill. Although the light from the living room helped, he knew which way he was going. He vaulted over the low stone wall and into the heavily wooded valley below.

The first of the three helicopters shot overhead, a good eighty metres to his left, its searchlight fixed forward. Bakr prayed that they were not equipped with thermal imaging cameras. It was dark, but Bakr's eyes were adjusting. He moved quickly, dodging the trees. The other two helicopters passed further away to his right. He paid no more attention to them. He was focussing hard on his progress. Twigs and pine needles cracked and crunched under his pounding feet as he ran, leapt, and jumped his way towards his pre-planned destination.

He emerged from the trees almost falling onto the dirt track. He could hear the helicopters and now the sound of sirens. Police cars would be coming up the only main road from the nearest coastal towns. The track ahead of him bent to the left. And there it was. The rental car. There had been little chance of it being discovered when he parked it almost one hour earlier.

Bakr threw his knife onto the passenger seat, cursing his stupidity for not taking a gun. He released the handbrake, and the car rolled forward slowly. Once on the track proper, he straightened up and let gravity do the rest. The car gradually picked up speed. He opened his window and listened. The tyres crunched the grit and gravel. Otherwise, his progress was almost silent. After several hundred metres, the car began to accelerate down a steeper part of the track. He knew he would now be well out of view of the villa. It was safe enough to flick on the headlights. The car was now coasting at about 30kph. Bakr was pleased with this part of his planning, but not the rest.

The track levelled. Up ahead was the small back road that led deeper into the wooded countryside. He started the engine, swung right onto the tarmac, and pressed down hard on the accelerator.

Bakr's thoughts then turned back to his failed mission. How would the prince react? Not only had he failed to get the stone, but he had failed to silence the scientist and the female—*his wife, presumably*, he thought.

All the lights were on in the villa. Daniel was talking in the kitchen. Two police officers were taking notes. Other officers were checking the property inside and out. Two of the helicopters could be heard somewhere over the valley.

In the living room, Kara sat hunched on the sofa, her knees up to her face, a woollen throw over her shoulders.

After two hours, most of the police had left. Two officers had remained as protection. Chief Inspector Beaussant followed Daniel into the living room.

'Hey, why don't you get some sleep,' Daniel said walking towards Kara. He placed a hand on her knees.

'What the fuck, Daniel?'

'Yeh, that was a dumb suggestion. You OK?'

Kara stared ahead. 'Er, *no.*'

'You were both very brave. I commend you for your actions,' Beaussant said. 'But you will be in a state of shock.'

'What did he want?' Kara asked. She had hardly said a word until now, leaving Daniel to field the police questioning.

Beaussant sighed. 'I am as confused as you, Doctor. The incident is most unusual. But thanks to your quick thinking with the photo, and the detail provided by Doctor Bayford, we have much to go on. Rest is a good idea— Doctor Bayford is right. You are perfectly safe now.'

'Well, that depends,' Kara said, now more animated. 'I mean, we don't know who he is or what he wanted. He had a knife. Maybe he came here to kill us.'

'I'm not so sure,' Beaussant said. 'My suspicion is that he was an opportunistic burglar. Perhaps from Marseille or Toulon. Unfortunately, knives are the standard weapon of choice amongst this type of criminal. I'm just glad that you are both not hurt.'

'Unhurt.' Kara corrected.

'Thank you, yes, unhurt.'

'I'm sorry. I shouldn't…Your English is really excellent. I'm sorry, Chief Inspector.'

'It's no problem. You are tired and in shock.'

Kara looked up at Daniel. 'Why didn't you shoot him?'

Daniel looked at Beaussant, raised his eyebrows, and disappeared into the kitchen. Beaussant replied on his behalf, 'Doctor Bayford's gun was not loaded.'

'H-o-l-y shit,' was all Kara could say.

Daniel reappeared holding two large glasses of red wine. 'The sun's not over the yard arm, but it is up. And I think we deserve it. Are you sure I can't tempt you, Chief Inspector?'

'I'm afraid not. This is going to be a long day for me. Good day.'

'Thank you, Chief Inspector,' Kara said.

'Yes, thank you for your prompt action, Chief Inspector,' Daniel added.

Daniel sat down next to Kara. They supped their wine in silence. Daniel finally spoke. 'It's all connected, Kara.'

'I'm sorry?'

'The man in Cannes. Our stone.'

'What are you saying?'

'Our stone attracts lightning. That man was struck by lightning. And our night intruder was in Cannes, I'm sure of it. He brushed right past me.'

'And…if he came here to take your stone, he wouldn't be the first.'

'Exactly.'

They sat in silence once again; both now wide awake and thinking hard.

Chapter 53
The Oval Office

Washington DC, USA

President Palmer sat perched on the front of his desk holding the Spear of Destiny file.

'Well, I've read it. But I may as well have read Shakespeare. I'm none the wiser, which is why you're here, Mr Ordway,' Palmer said.

Richard Ordway, the only other occupant in the world's most famous office, was sitting forward on one of the sofas. 'It's ultra-secret, sir. So, we…I could not risk a detailed written report.'

Palmer found Ordway more than irritating. He was also remembering the humiliation of being in the same proverbial dark during the meeting with President Dumart—*the pumped-up shit*, Palmer thought. And now Ordway was clearly revelling in the same way. Time to make him squirm. 'WELL, GODDAM TELL ME THEN!' Palmer boomed.

'Yes, sir,' Ordway suddenly looked unsettled. 'Um, well, at the *Elysée Palace*, I mentioned that there was a military communications project that was shelved, but that there were other projects looking at harnessing atmospheric electrical energy. Well, we began funding the most promising of these.'

'The one in Venezuela.'

'Yes, sir.'

'By "we" you mean the Department of Defence.'

'Yes, sir, that's correct, sir. The project's run by civilians, who still believe the project is for renewable energy purposes.'

'And these…,' the president opened the file, '…scientists are ignorant of the specifics regarding these funds?'

Ordway hesitated. 'Er, yes. The team based in Venezuela believes the government is funding the project directly to accelerate its switch to renewables. They're just grateful for the recognition.'

'And the extra cash, I dare say.'

'You bet, sir. They had successfully managed to retain huge amounts of atmospheric energy but were struggling to draw the power effectively. There was always a lot more up there they failed to capture.' Ordway nodded upwards as though to indicate the sky. 'From their standpoint, they need to draw the maximum amount of energy possible to make it economically viable.'

'I'm with you so far.'

'When I was given the go-ahead to ramp up the…er…project I needed data—other experiments and papers on the same topic. Of course, there are millions of documents online. So, I had one of my team develop a search algorithm using artificial intelligence and machine learning. The algorithm eventually worked. I saw a report about a strange anomaly. A retired British ex-pat living in France had discovered what turned out to be a potentially unique rock—a meteorite in fact. The story caused quite a sensation.'

'I recall the news reports. Didn't give it much thought, I have to admit.'

'You wouldn't be alone in thinking that, sir. More the kind of thing you'd see on one of those strange-but-true channels. It seemed that this meteorite could, bizarrely, not only attract electricity but retain it, too. The man who discovered it reported that the meteorite must be the cause of an unusually high frequency of lightning strikes, lightning strikes that led to multiple forest fires. He's a fire lookout in the south of France.'

Ordway had expected the president to cut him short, but Palmer was now walking to the chair behind his desk, where he sat down.

Ordway continued. 'After the meteorite's unusual properties were confirmed by a series of geologists and meteoriticists…'

'Meteor what?'

'Experts in meteorites, sir, as opposed to meteorologists. I decided to investigate further. Anyway, there's been a lot more coverage: TV interviews, major newspapers, science journals, you name it. So, I sent the lead scientist from the Venezuelan project to visit France to see this meteorite first-hand. To be frank, I had expected the whole business to be a waste of time. But her report was, how should I say, more than enthusiastic. It seems the rock is comprised of elements new to Man. It may lead to an enlargement of the periodic table yet again. Theories by astrophysicists, planetary geologists, and other specialists are being proposed about how this mineral could have formed and where it came from, but they remain theories. One irrefutable fact remains: this stone, this meteorite attracts and retains electricity in an extraordinary way.'

'But are we talking about a single, unique, solitary rock?'

'No, others were found, presumably from the same meteor shower.'

'In France.'

'Yes, but we rightly assumed that others fell elsewhere on earth sometime in the past. Fast forward several months, and the good news is that we have now harvested more than enough of the mineral. It wasn't easy. We had to send teams across the globe. We knew this was impractical, expensive, and very hit-and-miss. So, in parallel, we began experimenting to see if we could synthesise the rock. Early results are extremely positive.

'OK, so our scientists in Venezuela can already retain energy from clouds and, thanks to this celestial rock, may now be able to attract that energy with more certainty and possibly retain it using the same rock. Is that what I think I'm hearing?'

'Absolutely, sir. Strange but true. This is like killing two birds with one stone if you'll excuse the pun.'

For several seconds, Palmer looked silently and intently at Ordway. He then said, 'Surely, this is more important than any weapon? My god if we can eradicate our reliance on fossil fuels…'

'Indeed. There is that, too.'

Palmer jumped up from his chair. 'We're filing patents on all this, I hope, Ordway? I'm serious about the renewable energy aspect of this. Every day, this nation is slipping from greatness. We're losing ground to China and a bunch of other countries. This discovery could be…my god, world-changing. We could not only secure the United States of America as the number one nation but raise it to become an economic powerhouse like never before. *And,* Mr Ordway, save the fucking planet in the process!'

Palmer walked over to Ordway, who immediately stood up. 'Well done, Mr Ordway. Get this right and you're on the fast track to some serious kudos.'

And a whole lot more! Ordway thought.

Palmer was beaming and slapped Ordway on the back.

'Thank you, Mr President. It's been a hard but fascinating ride so far. But, sir…'

'But what?' Palmer hated to hear negative words.

'The rest of what I'm about to tell you is, how should I put it?…*equally significant.*'

Chapter 54
Rebel

Daniel's Villa, Tanneron, Southern France

After another sultry night, the fresh pre-dawn air seeping through the shutters and open windows had been a welcome relief. The sheet that had covered Kara and Daniel was now an untidy pile at the foot of the bed. They lay asleep; the cool air bathing their nakedness like an exquisite balm, their bodies and semi-conscious minds enjoying a blissful, near-sublime state of equilibrium.

Daniel opened his eyes. Someone had opened the shutters; the early morning sun made him squint. He then remembered the night before. He turned over and smiled at Kara, who was sitting upright next to him, a pillow behind her head, her laptop opened on her lap.

'Hey, good morning,' she said and smiled.

'Good morning. Wow! That was the best night's sleep I've had in a long while.'

'Yeh, me, too. Must have been all that late-night exercise,' Kara replied, smirking.

Daniel could not suppress a broad, boyish grin. 'How long have you been awake?' He reached over and kissed her on the cheek.

'Oh, not long. My body clock is slowly adjusting.'

Daniel propped himself on one elbow and looked at Kara as she clicked away on the computer. *Did I really make love with this vision?* he thought. *Does she really like me, or was it some weird reaction to all the recent excitement?* He had no intention of reminding her of those shocking events. It would break this beautiful spell. 'Breakfast?' he asked suddenly.

Kara looked up from the laptop, 'Is that a command or an invitation?'

Daniel smiled. 'Er well, in these days of equality, I thought we could make it together.'

'*Touché,*' she replied and turned her attention back to the screen.

'Ah ha! You're picking up the lingo…Are you working already?' Kara swung the laptop around. Daniel scanned the page she had found and recognised it immediately. 'Oh, I see. Checking me out, are you? I think I'll make breakfast after all,' he said, sliding from the bed.

'Not so fast, man of mystery. You were quite the rebel.'

'Don't believe everything you read,' he said, walking out of the bedroom.

'It's not what I'm *reading*, it's the photographic evidence.'

'Photoshopped,' he called back from the stairs.

Kara put the laptop down and followed him downstairs. 'Spill the beans, Bayford. I want to hear it in your words.'

Daniel started his coffee ritual, then perched himself on the kitchen table. 'Those stories always make it sound more glamorous and daredevil than the reality. I was just one of a crew on the boat.'

'You were the captain, Daniel.'

'Not quite,' he laughed. 'I was the leader of the group. To captain a vessel that size requires qualifications and training.'

'The leader and therefore the brains behind the, what would you call them, raids? I mean, they sounded pretty dangerous to me.'

'The one that got most of the publicity was the one in the Persian Gulf.'

'Oh yes, the one where you managed to set fire to an oil rig.'

'Yeh, that one. Anyway, we didn't burn it down or blow it up. It was verging on the spectacular, though. It certainly got our hearts racing,' he said laughing.

'But isn't that verging on terrorism?'

'That's a moot point. When is violence justifiable? I'd say when all other avenues have been explored. You know the back story, right? That company had single-handedly devastated the marine life and eco-system for years.'

'So, what happened?'

'Amazingly, no charges were brought against us. The oil corporation wanted to quash the whole incident. The general opinion was that we were heroes, so any action against us would make them look even worse. We had the moral high ground. We were also in international waters, so no country or government had the power to do anything. Besides, after the sinking of Greenpeace's *Rainbow Warrior* back in the eighties, no government would dare get involved. That incident was a PR disaster for the French government.'

'But how come you went from being a government scientist to an eco-warrior on the high seas?'

'My government was backing companies like that oil company, who make out they have green credentials by pumping millions into renewables. It's good up to a point but fossil fuels drive economies, steer government policies, and fund our pension pots. So, governments turn a blind eye to ecological catastrophes. They shrug their shoulders as if to say, well, what can we do? What they don't do is come down hard on this level of negligence.'

'Too big to fail, and all that.'

'Exactly. Look, I get it that our economies are still reliant on fossil fuels. I just didn't want to be part of that old, hypocritical establishment.'

'But you weren't to blame. Surely, you weren't doing anything wrong when you worked for the government.'

'No, I wasn't. My role was purely research-based and analytical. But many people didn't see it that way. We all got tarred with the same brush. Talking of which, some activists dumped a load of old sump oil over my lawn.'

'That must have pissed you right off.'

'You could say that. They'd vanished by the time I discovered it, so I had a rant on social media instead. And that's how it all started. Eggs?'

Daniel jumped down and grabbed a pan from the collection suspended above the table.

'Yeh, sure. But how could you go from a secure job to that? What about your income?'

'It wasn't overnight, I can tell you. I was surprised to learn that there were people out there prepared to donate quite large sums to support our cause and others like it. So, although I took a hit money-wise, I was comfortable enough. There were three of us who finally met up and took things to the next level. It was exciting, Kara. I never felt so alive.'

'Wow. And now this,' she said, pointing outside.

'From the sublime to the ridiculous.'

'Do you miss it?'

Daniel turned to face her. 'I'm not sure. It can get pretty hairy here when we get a major fire.'

Kara approached Daniel and gave him a hug. 'Well, I think you're a hero, too.'

'Thank God for that. Not mad, then?' Daniel said laughing.

'Are you lonely up here, Daniel?'

'There are moments, yes. But I always keep myself busy.' He fell silent for a moment. 'And my sister-in-law and niece visit me often.'

'You've not met anyone?'

Daniel laughed. 'Here and there. Tried some online dating, too.'

'And?'

'It was fun. What about you?'

'Oh, I er…' Kara kicked herself for broaching the subject of relationships. 'Well, you know…busy life, travelling here, there, and everywhere.'

'And you're passionate about your work, right?'

'Yep. I'm a fricking geek, Daniel. Who'd be interested in a geek?' she replied laughing.

'Well, I am.'

Tears had welled in Kara's eyes. 'I'm sorry. I…'

'Come here, you.'

She walked up to Daniel and welcomed his embrace.

'And to answer your question,' he continued, 'yes, I really am quite a bit more than just interested in you, Kara.'

They held each other in silence for some time, wondering what the other was thinking. He imagined that Kara would head back to the States and that their time together would be looked back upon like a holiday romance. *Stay cool*, he thought. *She's way out of your league anyway. And she probably thinks you're a nut job.*

Many more thoughts, though, flashed through Kara's mind. She could only marvel at Daniel's truly radical changes of direction. *Such a brave thing to do— to drop everything to try to right the wrongs of the world in some way. And now this? A fire watch in Southern France!* She liked the romantic sound of it all. Here was a man free from convention. *But does that make him too impulsive, too impetuous, reckless even? No*, she concluded, *don't be such a bore. It makes him different, exciting; alive. Better still—he's not dating!*

'I feel better already,' she sniffled, looking up at him.

'Good. And you'll feel even better filled with wonderful free-range eggs, infused with ground pepper, cream, and fresh Mediterranean herbs.'

Kara laughed and they kissed.

Just like every moment that he had spent with Kara so far; Daniel savoured that kiss. *Oh god, please say you'll stay with me for the rest of our lives*, he thought.

Chapter 55
Fishing Trip

On Board Marine One, Alaska, USA

The president's helicopter, Marine One, was flying fast and low over the Alaskan wilds, escorted by three military choppers. Weather conditions were calm, and the mid-summer sunshine was unbroken.

Rosemary Turner, the US Secretary of Defence, was sharing the screen of her mobile with President Thomas Palmer. They and the small presidential team were listening to a TV news anchor in full flow.

'...a well-earned break, is what one White House official told us. President Palmer—an avid angler—will spend a few, private days fishing in Alaska. We hope you catch a big one, Mr President. In other news, more signs of climate change...'

'Well, looks like they bought it,' Turner said, closing the app on the phone.

'Hook, line *and* sinker,' Palmer said, winking, prompting groans from his team. 'This had better be worthwhile otherwise you *will* see me in my waders in an icy river casting my rod.'

Michael Springborn, the president's personal secretary, sitting across the aisle, looked up from some papers. 'Actually, I have arranged for some river poses. Jane thought it'd be a good idea.'

'She's right, of course,' said Palmer, 'Press secretaries usually are. So, you did bring my waders and rod.'

'The full tackle, sir,' Springborn replied.

'*"Thy rod and thy staff they comfort me",*' the president quipped again.

'Ouch, don't give up the day job, Tom,' Turner said, feigning a pained expression.

'I thought it was very good,' Springborn said, laughing. 'With respect, sir, I wouldn't have put you down as a man of the Bible.'

Secret military base, Alaska, USA

Colonel Mason stood at the podium inside the large auditorium, now packed with soldiers and scientists. Three US flags hung behind him. The colonel leant towards the microphone. 'Well, I promised you a surprise,' he began, his opening words prompting a few cheers and some amusing suggestions from the soldiers. The one that got the biggest cheers, laughs, and a shake of heads from the women, was "Strippers!" The colonel was inwardly pleased that he had a room full of upbeat soldiers. Since Ordway's speech to those present, the colonel had ramped up the morale of his troops. The scientists, on the other hand, remained less demonstrative. Mason accepted this fact; they had a job to do and were under more pressure. Protecting them, and a base that very few knew existed, was relatively simple. He raised a hand and continued, 'And I do *not* disappoint,' he said with increased volume. More whoops and cheers. 'Ladies and gentlemen...THE PRESIDENT OF THE UNITED STATES OF AMERICA!'

The presidential anthem, *Hail to the Chief,* suddenly boomed out of the PA system, and the room exploded with cheers, fist-pumping, and loud applause.

Palmer was all smiles. He was used to the adulation and just wanted to get on with it. But he did not become president without milking that adulation first. 'Thank you, thank you,' he mouthed, pointing out random members of the audience and doing a thumbs up. The music faded away and the room went quiet. Palmer suddenly looked deadly serious, 'I'm sorry to disappoint some of you. But...I won't be taking off my clothes.' The room erupted in laughter.

'Oh, go on, Mr President!' one brave female corporal called out, raising even more laughter.

'No. It's way too cold up here even in summer. And you know what happens to us guys in the cold.' The laughs and cheers were deafening. The soldiers were loving it. Palmer was like one of them. Palmer then turned to the base commander. 'Thank you, Colonel. Well, it looks like you have a GREAT set of people here!' The colonel tried to look modest. 'I'm excited to be here,' Palmer continued. 'What our amazing scientists are doing...where are you? Come forward, let me see you.' Some of the scientists tentatively moved forward. 'Great job, guys. What you are doing is ground-breaking, revolutionary, incredible, and one of *the* most important missions for this country in generations. You should be proud. The United States of America certainly *would* be, if only we could tell them,' Palmer said, smiling and raising his hands in mock disappointment. Some laughter rippled through his audience. 'But, as I'm sure Colonel Mason has continuously reminded you, your work here, that's every last one of you, is not just top secret, *it—is—ultra-secret.*' Palmer almost whispered the last words in the microphone, his face suddenly stern. It had its effect. There was seriousness written across every face in front of him. All stood completely still, eyes on the president. He held them for a good twenty to thirty seconds, as though memorising the faces of each and every one of them. 'So, no leaks!—except...' he paused, ...for bodily ones in the restroom.'

Smiles returned. Palmer walked off the stage to a crescendo of cheers, applause, and more *Hail to the Chief.*

Backstage, the colonel was joined by Richard Ordway, Lieutenant Armstrong, and Dr Jeffrey Scott. Together they led the president and his entourage to an open elevator. Two of the secret service contingent took position on either side of the door. The president, Secretary of Defence Turner, the two military officers, the head scientist, and the president's head of security, Bob Doyle, entered. The lieutenant selected the lowest button and the elevator began its rapid forty-eight-metre descent.

'Mr President, may I introduce Dr Jeffrey Scott,' Mason volunteered.

'Great to meet you, Doctor,' the president said, crushing the doctor's hand with a handshake that the lead scientist would never forget.

'My honour, Mr President.' Scott was a lean, self-assured-looking man with little sign of the responsibility on his shoulders.

The doors opened. Doyle exited first, followed by Palmer and the rest of the group.

They had entered what could only be described as an underground hangar. The room was vast.

Scott began walking and talking. 'This is the main experimental area,' he began. He spoke quickly in a soft, New England accent. 'It's divided into various zones, but having everything in one space makes it more efficient. There are other floors above us, but the most important labs are up there on the mezzanine floor,' he said pointing up to a high, metal walkway that ran back along the entire lefthand side of the room, '...for specialist development, data analytics—that kind of thing. Ah, here's the rest of the team.'

Two additional elevators to their left were discharging project scientists, who dispersed in different directions. Three of them headed towards the presidential party.

'So, here we have Dr Emma Crusoe, Dr David Dimitriou, and Dr Jayden Joseph,' Scott said. All three of the scientists shook Palmer's hand with a polite 'Mr President.' Each was still dumb-struck at his presence.

The group approached the centre of the complex. Dominating it was a round, dark, metallic structure, around thirty metres in height and around fifteen metres across. The visitors looked up at the industrial-looking tower of metal. Close to its top, they could just make out a large window.

Emma Crusoe followed their gaze. 'That's the observation window of the control room. We'll show you that shortly.' She pressed a button, and a thick, metal door at the base of the chamber hissed open. She stood aside to allow the group to enter.

'Er, I'm sorry, only those with red passes can enter,' Scott said, looking first at Bob Doyle and then to the president. Palmer held up a hand in understanding and nodded to his secret service chief to hang back. The remaining group made their way in.

'Wow!' said Palmer, looking up.

Above them appeared to be thousands of stars suspended in the black void of space. Ahead, on the floor, was a scale model of a small city, complete with roads and skyscrapers, lit faintly by the myriad small lights above.

'Mr President, I'm sure you're aware of nanotechnology. Above, are around one…?' Scott looked to Dimitriou, who nodded, '…one thousand nano drones. Or more precisely, ADND's, Autonomous Discriminatory Nano Drones, each smaller than the average house fly. But we've illuminated them with miniature LEDs for the purposes of this demonstration. Jayden, if you would be so kind.'

Dr Jayden Joseph was holding a tablet PC. He looked up and with his index finger punched the screen. The lights in the artificial sky above them shot down, showering the small city. What made it all the more spectacular was that the ADND's not only plummeted at an amazing velocity, their individual trajectories appeared completely random; some moving at shallow angles, others more obliquely, and the remainder more vertically. All at the same speed, and without one colliding with another.

'We've enhanced the same technology you often see for light shows by making the drone autonomy even more accurate and therefore faster,' Scott continued. 'Each drone has been pre-programmed with a designated destination coordinate, down to the nearest one square centimetre. Once programmed, the drones do the rest, without hitting each other. David?'

David Dimitriou stepped forward. 'As you can see, the ADND's have only covered specific buildings in our miniature city. We now need to retire to our observation gallery and control room.'

The group was guided back through the door and around the rear of the structure, where a flight of steel stairs led up to the mezzanine level.

'Apologies for the lack of an elevator, Mr President,' Emma Crusoe felt obliged to say. 'Dr Scott said we would all benefit from the exercise.'

'Fine by me,' Palmer said. 'Lead the way.'

Chapter 56
Suspicion

Mougins, Southern France

'This is so lovely, Daniel.'

Kara and Daniel were seated outside a café in the old, hilltop village just north of Cannes. A handful of tourists were strolling across the square in the mid-morning sunshine. This was a slow and peaceful haven that seemed centuries behind the rest of the world.

'It's a pretty famous place,' Daniel said. 'Napoleon passed through here. Artists like Picasso and Man Ray lived here, as did the writer Jean Cocteau. Film stars often come up here to eat.'

'Ooh, maybe we'll see someone famous.'

'You know people are giving you a second look.'

Kara blushed. 'Oh, come on.' Secretly, she was revelling in his compliments.

Kara's attention had turned to her phone. 'Well, I can see that Ordway studied at MIT, then spent eighteen years in the CIA. Counter-terrorism. But that was ten years ago. And that's it. So, we're none the wiser.'

'What is it you don't trust about him?'

'I'm not sure. And I'm not sure if it's a matter of trust. He clearly has an ego the size of a small planet.'

'What was it he said again?'

'That he wasn't with the CIA. He was above that. Or something like that.'

'He was flirting with you. I wouldn't blame him.'

'Why, thank you. Yeh, he was struggling to contain his little secret, that's for sure.'

'Assuming he has one. He could have just been trying to big himself up.'

'No, my gut tells me he's involved in something shady.'

'What about Professor Steel? Could he help?'

'Arthur's great. But, you know, I hardly see him. He's always supportive. He's like a bridge between what I'm doing and Ordway, and whomever Ordway represents.'

'Your professor's smart. Political.'

'Right. But look, he's just a professor. What would he know really? He's just keen to see the project succeed, get the funding we need; keep everyone happy. He's probably as much in the dark as we are.'

'But you sensed a change in gear since Ordway's involvement.'

'I did. I do. Ordway flew thousands of miles from Washington to Venezuela when a video conference could have worked almost as well. He seemed sceptical back then. But now, suddenly, we seem to be under time pressure. I called Tod yesterday to see how things were going. He told me that some equipment we asked for months ago, and got nowhere, simply turned up. Gear worth more than 250k.'

'A quarter of a million dollars?'

'Yeh. Just like that. Even Arthur was surprised, according to Tod. Have you found anything?'

'Well, I was trying a different tack. I was looking into weather-related projects run by various governments. There have been several attempts at harnessing electrical energy, as I'm sure you know. But the vast majority of projects were, if you hadn't guessed, started during wartime. Communications and...'

'Weapons,' Kara interjected. 'Yes, I've read a lot about those. It was all part of my research at university. But I'm not sure if that kind of thing is still beyond us.'

They looked at each other.

'It's plausible, though, yes?' Daniel suggested.

'Maybe. I don't know. We've come a long way since those crazy experiments decades ago. I've not given it much thought. I mean, why should I?'

'OK, but let's say I asked you to make such a weapon. Where would you start? And I'm talking about a weapon based on your work.'

'Well, we now have the means of retaining a ton of power.'

'Thanks to you.'

'Thanks to me and my amazing team. We don't yet have the means to capture all the energy available. And that for me is the big hurdle.'

'And no doubt the reason you were sent here.'

'Right…I suppose that if we analysed the meteorite's properties…'

'…Yes?'

Kara was deep in thought. 'There's no reason,' she continued, 'why we couldn't reverse engineer the stone's properties and replicate it.'

'Meaning?'

'Well, if we understood how the stone attracts energy the way it does and how it seems to hold that energy, we could artificially manufacture a material that replicated that process. The problem is that it may involve a level of subatomic physics beyond our current understanding. Things like quantum electrodynamics—stuff way above my head…No, wait. That would be impossible. What am I thinking? Whatever the meteorite is composed of, it has properties that probably came into existence deep inside, I don't know, a white dwarf star or some other exotic heavenly body, and somehow blasted its way here. We could never replicate those conditions.'

'But our knowledge is expanding exponentially. It only takes someone like you who specialises in that stuff…'

'No. We're not at that stage. Unless…'

'Unless what?'

'Well, you've heard of synthetic diamonds, right? The ones they create for industrial purposes. They have the same chemical properties as natural diamonds. Pure carbon. Maybe using a similar process, they could synthesise this meteorite.' Daniel smiled. 'What?' she asked.

'I love hearing you think.'

'That's the geek in me coming out. Attractive. *Not*.'

'Alright, so let's assume the technology is there to capture, retain and deploy that power in a controlled way. What next?'

'The energy would need to be beamed very precisely. Perhaps into the ionosphere to disrupt enemy communications.'

'Like the famous HAARP experiment?'

'That's right. Mess with the atmosphere…' Kara cut herself short when the waitress arrived with coffee and patisseries.

'*Et voilá! Ma'm'selle. Monsieur.*'

'*Merci,*' Kara replied before continuing, '…Mess with the atmosphere in the same way that a thermonuclear explosion triggers an electromagnetic pulse, and thus take out the enemy's ability to communicate, but use the same technology to improve our communications. Or…' She picked up her coffee cup and brought it to her mouth, but paused and placed it back down. 'There was this other experiment,' she continued. 'The CIA was behind it. The idea was an early version of how we attract lightning in my project. OK, you know why lightning follows a certain path, right?' she asked, smiling.

Kara was onto something. Daniel studied her. *What a beautiful face. What a beautiful mind*, he thought.

'I do,' Daniel replied. 'It follows paths of ionised air.'

'Ten out of ten. It was a rhetorical question, Daniel. But yes, step leaders— random paths of ionised air. Random being the operative word here. So, the CIA planned to use *artificial* leaders made of very long, thin wire, guided down onto the target by a drogue chute.'

'A parachute designed for deceleration.'

'Yes.'

'Thus, directing the lightning where they wanted.'

Kara was on a roll. 'Exactly. But that seems a bit low-tech, right? Today, we have drones. Now, if those drones were made of our new wonder material, you wouldn't need to drop wires from planes. A drone could be placed precisely.' Kara was nodding to herself. 'Yeh, that would work.'

'So, this is less to do with retaining energy and more to do with the stone's ability to attract lightning.'

'Absolutely. We've already seen what one or two relatively small ones can do on your hillside. And, if your theory is right, what one can do around someone's neck.'

'The question we need to ask, Kara, is what *really* motivates a government more: energy or defence?'

'Right now, I'd say it was even-stevens. But it depends on the government in power and the geo-political situation.'

'Well, that's never stable. And I'd say the current White House incumbents are the nationalistic, protectionist, screw-the-rest types.'

'That still doesn't mean they're developing a weapon,' Kara said. 'We're on the brink of a momentous breakthrough in sustainable energy. That would provide the USA with a staggering advantage. I believe that carries more weight than some form of weather weapon. Like you said, this kind of green energy could be worth trillions.'

'You're talking as a rational human being, Kara. Not a power-crazy, paranoid politician. Without wishing to repeat myself, I've seen too much shit to know that not everyone thinks about doing good in the world. Although they'll do their best to say that it's in our best interest by fuelling the fear propaganda.'

'Now you're sounding like a conspiracy theorist,' Kara said laughing.

'Come on, it's true. We're all plebians at the end of the day, kept in our place for a reason.'

'You Brits really are pessimistic,' she said, taking a bite of a *Macarón*. Daniel smirked and swigged his coffee. He then picked up his phone and began typing.

'What?' Kara asked, sensing he was eager to find something out.

'Just a hunch. A van passed us near the villa. I'm looking up swimming pool companies in Cannes and…let me try *maintenance*…Well, either that van is from a company without an online presence—unlikely, me thinks—or they were the guys that burgled me. Rather elaborate, don't you think?'

'Assuming it was them.'

'I noticed the swimming pool logo and made a mental note of the name on the van. I have a pool after all. But the company doesn't exist.'

'So, what now?'

'We need more intel on this Ordway character.'

'Good luck with that!'

'You forget. I used to work with the British government. I still have contacts.'

Kara was chewing on her *Macarón* and had to cover her mouth when she laughed. 'Are you flirting with me, Dr Bayford?'

Chapter 57
Lightning Chamber

Secret Military Base, Alaska, USA

The control room was surprisingly spacious. On the nearest wall was an observation window, but the view beyond was dark. In front of that in the main area of the room was a series of large computer surfaces and desks.

As though following a rehearsal, Emma Crusoe took over as guide. 'The main experimental area we were standing in is in fact a complete 500:1 scale representation of an imaginary four hundred square mile area on earth and the atmosphere above it. Up here, we are level with what would be an altitude of approximately fifty thousand feet.'

She leant forward, touched a large, angled computer interface, which lit up, then pressed one of the icons on the screen. Beyond the control area, one of three wide displays came to life. 'This shows the entire chamber,' she went on. 'Floor to ceiling, it stands thirty-four metres high.' The display was showing the experimental structure in cross-section. 'The chamber is hermetically sealed. These conduits,' she continued, pointing with a laser pen at various points on the diagram, 'provide the necessary air pressure and moisture needed.'

It was now Dr Jayden Joseph's turn. 'We are particularly pleased with this next part.' Dr Joseph pressed another icon and the diagram disappeared. In its place was a live video stream of the chamber's interior. 'It should have taken years, but thanks to atmospheric modelling using the most advanced quantum computers on the planet, we did it in months.' He pressed a series of icons on the glass interface. 'First,' he continued, 'let there be light.' An intense light illuminated the chamber, and a cloud appeared almost immediately above the model city. 'The vertical scale shows the altitude in feet from zero to fifty thousand near the top. You're now seeing cloud forming at the equivalent of around six thousand feet.'

The scientists looked to their audience for a reaction. Without averting her eyes from the spectacle, Turner obliged. 'It's so realistic,' was as much as she could say.

'Indeed, everything is to scale, except for the electrical energy being created. We needed to scale that back. The accuracy of the cloud formation was a surprise, I must admit,' Dr Scott added.

'We're slightly better than Mother Nature here,' said Dr Joseph. 'As you can see, the cloud is already climbing. In a few short moments, we will have our very own cumulonimbus.'

They all watched the cloud billow and climb with as much detail as the real thing. The cloud's fine, clumpy edges were highlighted by the artificial sunlight; within its countless folds, dark areas were forming. It was like witnessing the birth of a real storm in time-lapse.

'That's incredible. A miniature storm cloud,' Palmer mumbled.

'The energy in a *real* cumulonimbus cloud of this size would be equivalent to ten Hiroshima atomic bombs.' Jayden Joseph said rather matter of fact.

'Don't worry,' Scott interjected, smiling, 'As I said, we've scaled back the energy here *considerably*. If we hadn't, our little demonstration here would be like blowing up, er, well, three hundred tons of TNT!'

Keen to contribute something, Ordway said, 'That's about six hundred Tomahawk missiles.'

Joseph touched the console to kill the main chamber light.

The cloud could now be seen pulsing with internal light.

'Is that lightning?' Palmer asked incredulously.

'Yes, Mr President,' Scott replied.

'My god,' said Turner. 'Let me get this straight. Are you saying that weaponizing the energy of a real storm would be like letting off three hundred thousand Tomahawk missiles?'

'Yes, ma'am. Your math is correct,' said Ordway, smiling.

Turner turned to Ordway with real concern on her face. 'We are safe here, right? This is the President of the United States.'

Ordway's smile was replaced by a sudden blanching of his face. He looked around the room for support.

Mason stepped forward, 'Absolutely, ma'am. The explosive force being generated is no more than a handful of grenades spread across the targets. We're also protected up here by walls two metres thick. I've witnessed the experiment many times. We're perfectly safe.'

'Sir, would you like the honours?' Crusoe was indicating an icon marked ACTIVATE on the interface.

'No more big red buttons,' Palmer joked. 'Well, I'm not sure what to expect, but here goes.'

In the space of one second, multiple, blinding, miniature, near-vertical lightning forks flashed, filling most of the large display, each producing a shockwave and a resulting loud, sustained, thunderous crack—the sound blasting out of the loudspeakers in the control room.

'WHOA!' cried Palmer and Turner. The rest had seen and heard it all before but grinned at the reaction and the spectacle in equal measure. This was the first time anyone from 'outside' had witnessed their work. It was show-time and show-off time.

While the visitors recovered from the intensity of the lightning flashes and the unexpected sound, Dr Jeffrey Scott pressed another icon. The main display showed the model city.

Colonel Mason stepped forward to speak. 'As you can see, Mr President, total discriminatory destruction.'

'What's that in plain English?' the president asked.

Scott clarified, 'Only the ADND-marked buildings were destroyed.'

'Hmm,' Palmer mused. 'And all caused by what would appear to be "an act of God".'

The room fell silent, as everyone pondered the implication of such a weapon.

'The Spear of Destiny, sir,' Ordway added.

Turner turned to the head scientist, 'Impressive. So, how does it work exactly, Dr Scott?'

Before Scott could answer, Ordway stepped forward. This was his time to shine. 'Madam Secretary, I have been driving this project for a long time. I spotted an article on a discovery made in France. It seemed remarkable; unbelievable in fact, but it turned out to revolutionise our understanding of energy.' Ordway turned to the scientists. 'Run the video.'

Crusoe knew what he meant. She reached forward and opened a video file using the computer interface. A freeze-frame of the meteorite filled most of the screen. It was held in position by a clamp. Beyond, held aloft by wide pillars, were two spheres glowing like two dull, red-orange planets. It was as though

Mars had a conjoined twin. Hardly visible to the side and below one of the main spheres was a tiny sphere atop a thin, vertical pole.

Ordway continued in his southern drawl. He was on a roll. 'This remarkable lump of rock is a meteorite. Once I realised its potential, I ordered…managed to secure one.' Ordway thought it best not to mention the SEAL team mission in France. 'What you can see takes place here in one of our largest laboratories. A spark is generated by the equipment you can see in the background.'

'Like a Van der Graaf generator,' the president ventured.

'Exactly, sir,' Ordway said. 'Although this one is somewhat more advanced and more powerful than those we all remember from our school physic lessons. Millions of volts more powerful, in fact. I should point out that those spheres are thirty metres from the meteorite.'

'They must be enormous,' Turner said.

'They each have a diameter of six metres,' Scott said.

'I think what you're about to see from this video will not only be self-explanatory but truly amazing.' Ordway nodded and Crusoe hit play.

The video ran. The light emanating from the spheres could be seen pulsing slowly. It was like a scene from Fritz Lang's 1927 science fiction film, *Metropolis*.

A deep hum filled the control room. There was an overriding sense of power as the generator built up energy. After ten seconds the video went into super-slow motion. A brilliant flash signalled the moment: a huge pure white bolt instantly bridged the space between one of the spheres and the rock. The flash and the accompanying low-pitched cracking lasted a second at the new frame rate. It was an unearthly sound. The massive spark and its sound stopped abruptly; the energy had been discharged. The video returned to normal speed and then zoomed slowly in on the meteorite. The translucent blue rock seemed alive with energy. The president and Turner stared in awe at the image.

'That's incredible,' Palmer said eventually. 'Are you telling me that all that energy has been…,' he looked for a word. '…captured by that rock?'

'Yes, Mr President,' Dr Scott said.

Turner turned to Scott. 'Quite remarkable. So, this rock—this meteorite, is it new to us?'

Scott was quick to reply. 'Yes, Madame Secretary. We've never seen anything like it. It seems we'll be extending the periodic table yet again.'

'A new element?' Palmer asked.

'Yes, sir. We analysed the rock using an array of techniques: X-ray crystallography, petrographic analysis, electron, and atomic force microscopes. We are still trying to understand what's happening. It may even upset our current understanding of sub-atomic physics. We knew we'd need more meteorites to develop the weapon. So, we despatched several teams across the globe. We focussed on areas that received higher than normal lightning.'

Palmer turned to Ordway and nodded as though to acknowledge what Ordway had told him in the Oval Office.

Scott continued. 'But what we have been able to do, using super-high temperatures and pressure, is effectively synthesise its properties to create a new variant. We call it *Donarium*.'

'*Donarium*,' Turner repeated. 'As in Donar, the Teutonic god of thunder?'

'Yes, ma'am.' Dimitriou looked impressed with the Defence Secretary's knowledge. 'It had to be *Donarium* because thorium is an existing element. Thor was the Norse…'

'Yes, we get the god of thunder references,' Turner interrupted. Dimitriou looked a little embarrassed.

Scott went on. 'Modifying the developments achieved by our lightning research team in Venezuela, we added the ability to switch those properties on and off. Using nano-technology, we developed a brand-new class of miniature drone, onto which we can plant a requisite quantity of *Donarium*. The *Donarium* acts like a lightning magnet.'

Scott then looked at Mason. The Commander-In-Chief prompted the base commander to speak. 'Colonel?'

Mason was ready. 'In a live scenario, each target would be carpeted with ADNDs…'

'Autonomous Discriminatory Nano Drones,' Turner clarified.

'Yes, ma'am. One every five metres or so depending on the structure's build material. The ADNDs would be practically invisible. They are activated remotely; with the resulting destruction, you have just seen. The ADNDs are of course completely destroyed in the process, leaving no trace.'

'No evidence whatsoever?' Palmer asked.

'Witnesses would simply say they saw a devastating lightning storm. No one could possibly imagine it was man-made.'

'And you mentioned earlier that these drones can be programmed with a target destination?' the Defence Secretary queried.

'Indeed, ma'am. Anywhere in the world.'

'But how are they deployed?' she pressed.

'Excellent question, ma'am.' The colonel approached the smart console, cleared a section of its screen with a swipe of his finger, dragged another icon downwards, and pressed several icons in quick succession. Above them, the left-hand display showed a 3D rendering of a missile-shaped object and "D3" written next to it. 'This,' he continued, 'is another state-of-the-art drone. The D3 or Discreet Deployment Drone. We developed it some time ago, but its full potential has only been properly realised with this project.' Dimensions and specifications flashed up in panels to its side. 'It has a range of twenty-five hundred miles. It's equipped with ultra-high-resolution, stereo cameras, including ultra-low-light image sensors for night-time vision. With these, we have better eyes than an owl with binoculars.' Mason pressed the smart screen again. An image appeared on the control room's right-hand display. After a few seconds, it was apparent that it was a video taken in mid-air with clouds racing by and occasional patches of blue sky.

'I don't see anything,' Palmer said, frowning.

'Exactly, sir.' Mason smiled. He paused the video and turned to the politicians, who were now squinting at the screen. The colonel held out a hand to Crusoe, who handed him the laser pen. He clicked it on and drew a circle with its red dot in the middle of the screen.

'Impressive!' Palmer said. He and Turner both shook their heads in disbelief. With the video frozen, a faint outline could be discerned. 'A D3, I assume.'

'Yes, sir. We've had this cloaking technology for some years. It's simply undetectable on radar. And a sparrow has a greater infrared signature than a D3. It's the most advanced low-observable technology ever developed. For all intents and purposes, they're invisible. They can release their payload—in this case as many as two thousand ADNDs per D3—up to five miles from the target. The ADNDs drop in free-fall then power up to negotiate their final approach.'

Scott then added, 'Activation of the ADNDs is achieved with a single pulse at an Extremely Low Frequency or ELF. Similar to the method we use to communicate with submarines. The pulse is triggered from this base. If anyone had monitored it, they would assume it had emanated from the storm.'

'Yes,' said Dr Joseph. His enthusiasm and excitement were unrestrained. 'You see, storms generate extremely low frequencies, too.'

'Making the whole process undetectable,' said Scott.

'But you need a storm for all this to happen, right?' Turner asked.

She was sharp, Scott thought. 'Dr Joseph can answer that best. Jayden?'

'Great question, ma'am. Well, the answer is yes and no. You see, we've been able to manipulate weather for decades. So, we can in fact generate clouds. Clouds are great for creating electricity because within them there's a lot of ice and graupel, sorry, that's like a soft hail. Releasing similar particles artificially would have the same effect. The D3s release these along with the ADNDs. We call them *seeders*.

'Like the old cloud seeding experiments,' Palmer suggested.

'Not so old, sir. They actively cloud seed in the Middle East today. Cloud seeding is more about enhancing the rain droplet process using hygroscopic particles.'

'To stimulate rainfall,' Turner said.

'Yes, ma'am. Our particles, though, are used to build up a charge. They collide with each other and become negatively or positively charged. The lighter particles are positive and stay at higher altitudes. Whereas the heavier particles are negatively charged and drop to lower altitudes, resulting in electrical potential and eventually an electrostatic discharge. Exactly like a storm cloud.'

'I'm not sure our guests need a science lesson, Doctor,' Ordway said, sensing that the scientists were getting too technical.

'Not at all, Mr Ordway,' said Turner sharply. 'I like to know. I'm sure the president does, too.' Ordway nodded apologetically. 'So, Doctor Joseph,' Turner continued, 'do your, what did you call them, *seeders* generate the required energy for this weapon to be effective full-scale?'

'We asked ourselves the exact same question, ma'am. We knew that many of our targets may be in arid locations with little to no moisture. So, we ran experiments in New Mexico. The results were, well, pretty amazing. You see, our *seeders* contain a special combination of metals, which attract even the smallest amounts of moisture to create a kind of supercharged triboelectric effect. We ran experiments here, too. We also knew that a storm doesn't need to be over the target. We know that lightning bolts have been known to travel a very long way indeed. In 2020, one was recorded measuring four hundred and seventy-seven miles across three states.'

'My god,' Palmer said. 'A bolt from the blue.'

'Absolutely, sir. Lightning has often been seen across clear skies.'

Scott interjected. 'The seeding particles together with the *Donarium* created a kind of link between large clouds and storm activity many miles distant. We can draw enormous energy from those distant clouds and from the atmosphere in the vicinity of the drop.'

'That's right,' Jayden Joseph said. 'There's an atmospheric electrical circuit across the globe. Most of the energy is in the lower altitudes. Thunderstorms are a way of discharging that energy. But we can do that with or without a storm.'

'So, a storm or heavy clouds over a target would help, but not essential?' Turner asked.

'Exactly, ma'am.' Joseph replied.

Ordway, sensing that the colonel and the scientists were getting all the glory, was eager to win more recognition for his contribution to the project and the president's respect. 'Mr President, this takes remote warfare to a new level. This weaponry is not just mind-blowingly effective, it is cost-effective. In fact, dare I say, by harnessing the power of Mother Nature like never before, it is positively cheap. Billions can be saved on our defence budget. Better still, we have plausible deniability. We can strike our enemy wherever they are with impunity—and strike them hard. This is the twenty-first century Spear of Destiny, Mr President.'

'And it's ours,' Palmer said.

'Indeed, sir,' Ordway said with a broad smile.

Chapter 58
Revelation

Daniel's Villa, Tanneron, Southern France

It was early morning two days after the night-time incident. Kara and Daniel were seated at his kitchen table, laptops open. One of Beaussant's patrolling officers could be seen walking slowly past the open door and window and along the terrace.

'This is incredible,' Daniel said, looking at his screen. 'More than twenty similar events. Rome, London, New York, Berlin, Jackson, Toronto, Sydney. All within twenty-fours.'

'The headlines are all so similar: GLOBAL MARTYRDOMS! BIZARRE SUICIDES; UNEXPLAINED; TERROR STRIKES AGAIN AND AGAIN; BOLTS FROM THE BLUE?; ACTS OF GOD? and ACTS OF ALLAH?'

'My favourites are SHOCKING! and SHOCK HORROR! Our tabloids really are the best for bad taste'

'Funny but wow, Daniel! So weird,' Kara said shaking her head.

'Well, we were there, Kara. We saw the first. And, yes, weird is not the word.'

'Anyway, you said you had a reply from your contact. What does he say?' Kara asked.

'A lot.' Daniel swung his laptop around.

'OK, so Ordway was CIA for more than two decades,' she said. 'At least I was right about that. Seoul, Hong Kong, Minsk, Lahore…He's been around.'

'Read this paragraph.'

Kara scanned the screen. 'Department of Defence!' she said, looking up. 'I fuckin' knew it!'

'Seems our suspicions about some kind of weapon are holding up.'

'But hang on. What was all that the other night? What's that Arab guy got anything to do with this?' Kara looked perplexed.

'Well, you remember I said this was all connected?'

'Yeh. And?'

'I had a revelation in the shower this morning. Hey, don't laugh.'

Kara was sniggering. 'Just as well I didn't join you this time.'

'All the events that led to that incident in Cannes. I remember them. I closed my eyes and recalled nearly every detail. Our Arab friend was definitely there. During the commotion, I remember him leaning over the dead man and ripping something from him. He was wearing some kind of necklace. That's what our Arab intruder took. It didn't make sense at the time, but now it does.'

'Oh. My. God.' Kara said slowly.

Daniel was nodding. He knew Kara was already on the same page. He continued, 'He had one of our lightning stones.'

Kara threw her hands in the air. 'Of course, he did! It makes total sense. How did we not see that before?'

'The scene was chaotic. No one could be sure what had happened. And we certainly weren't aware of the scale of this…stunt.'

Kara stood up and paced the room, thinking hard. 'One of our stones, or one of his own?' she asked, turning to Daniel.

Daniel sat, digesting what she had said. 'That's a good question. Maybe he'd found one nearby, but couldn't find any more, so came here after seeing me plastered over the world's media.'

'No, no, no.' Kara sat down suddenly, leaning towards Daniel. 'Don't you see? They must have multiple stones and are using them for these martyrdom stunts, as you call them. They must have. Loads of similar events happening across the globe. It's the only explanation. Whereas *your* stone and the publicity it caused is already the subject of intense scientific scrutiny.'

'I'm not with you,' Daniel said slowly.

'These martyrs are using the stones for some kind of religious declaration. You saw the headlines. ACTS OF ALLAH is the one that hits home for me.

'I get it! Whereas a rational, scientific explanation of our stone's properties would completely undermine the martyrdoms. Brilliant, Kara!'

'Which would explain why our Arab friend, as you like to call him, paid us a rude house call.'

'To find and take our stone.'

'Which someone else had already taken.'

'That person or persons probably working for Ordway.'

They both fell silent. Daniel got up and poured himself a coffee then held up the jug to Kara.

'No thanks,' she said. 'I'm wired enough. She looked up at Daniel, 'We need to tell the government, the media.'

'No! If Ordway did have someone take our stone, then we may be facing an altogether more dangerous situation running in parallel to this…quasi-religious stunt. Besides, we don't exactly understand how this stone does what it does. We may be seen as crackpot as this lot', he said pointing to the laptops.

'We may not understand the science—yet—but we have empirical proof of the stone's properties.'

'Maybe. But not on this scale. I haven't actually seen lightning strike the stone. My forest fire theory is just a theory. Talking of which, I have two hours of fire watch duty this afternoon.'

'But the presence of these meteorites on your hill would explain the unusually high frequency of lightning strikes and therefore fires.'

'Again, supposition, Kara. You're a scientist. You know that. We need proof.'

'Well, with so many of these crazy events, the proof must be there. Let's check the footage.'

Daniel started searching the news websites, running one video after another. Not one showed lightning.'

'Nothing. They're all after the events.' Daniel said.

'Try YouTube. There must be loads of private footage.'

Daniel typed.

'There,' Kara said, 'try the one in New York.'

The two of them watched intently.

'Can you see anything round his neck?' Daniel asked, screwing his eyes to focus better.

'He's too far away, and whoever's filming this is all over the place. Stop! Rewind that bit.'

Daniel clicked on the play bar a few millimetres back.

'There! Did you hear that?' Kara asked.

'Sounded like a thunderclap.'

'It's a shame we can't see any higher. It's all building.'

'Wait, what's he doing?' Daniel said, leaning forward.

'He's got a box next to him.' Kara said. She and Daniel exchanged quick looks then returned to the unfolding drama. 'There! He's putting something around his neck! Now he's shouting at someone behind him…Oh my God, he's looking up. Looking to Allah, no doubt.'

'Or the storm,' Daniel suggested.

The New York martyr could then be heard over the constant noises of the crowd and city. "ALLAH IS THE ONE TRUE GOD! ALLAHU AKBAR!"

'Ooh shit, this is intense.' Kara could hardly breathe. They watched and listened as the video quickly panned down to reveal one of the police officers coming into view. He was ordering the crowd to move back. Shouts went up, one very close to the person videoing, "HE'S GOT A BOMB!" Another, further away, "SHOOT THE ARAB FUCK!" People were running this way and that; others remained transfixed. The video panned up again.

'WHOA!'

The same exclamation came from Kara and Daniel simultaneously. An intense flash had suddenly obscured the scene. The next part of the video was chaotic: images of the sidewalk, people's legs, and feet. Whoever was holding the phone was now running.

'*That* was a lightning bolt,' Kara stated.

Daniel had returned to the list of videos. There were hundreds. 'We need a better angle. I want to be sure. Ah, this one has millions of views.' An ad for life assurance appeared on the screen. 'Unbelievable!' Capitalism and algorithms at their best.' The video then started.

'This clip is from 7th Avenue,' Kara said.

Daniel dragged the play button to the right. The small preview images raced by. Kara knew what he was looking for, and there it was. And it was better than they had hoped. A freezeframe of a clear lightning streak directly to where the martyr was standing. Daniel clicked slightly to the left and they watched in silence as the video rolled by. Daniel then paused the playback and scrubbed on either side of the frame. One of the images showed the afterglow. But the main image was perfect. It was the incontrovertible proof they needed.

'Well, that was easy,' Daniel said.

Kara was dumbfounded. 'It's unbelievable.' Kara stared at the frozen image. 'It's such a pure lightning bolt.'

'What do you mean?'

'Well, no smaller forks are coming off it whatsoever. Just bang! One intense beam of jagged light.'

'Here's the one in Rome.'

'Don't. I've seen enough.' Kara stood up and walked to look out the window. 'You know, for some reason, don't ask me why, but I feel sorry for those guys.'

Daniel scoffed. 'Sorry for them?'

'They're little more than kids, Daniel. Misguided kids.'

'At least they're blowing *themselves* up and not innocent members of the public. Those terror attacks in London and Paris weren't that long ago.'

'I guess. It certainly is a new and radical strategy.'

'Wait a minute. I doubt this is a new direction. You can bet your Yankee bottom dollar we haven't seen the last of that kind of terror.'

Kara was looking out over the valley. 'Slight change of subject,' she said, 'but don't you fire watch all day?'

Daniel joined her. 'No, there are three of us. It's too hot up there for one person all day.'

'Of course. Do they have access to your hut?'

'Well, it's not strictly *my* hut. But I made it mine if you get my drift. And I trust them implicitly. In fact, they've been standing in for me since your arrival.'

'That's sweet of them. Will I meet them?'

'You can join me later if you like. It's as boring and hot as hell, though. You'll see Luc first then Pierre later.'

'No, I'd like that. I guess we should tell our guards.'

'Oh yeh. One of them may have to tag along.' Daniel said, suddenly looking disappointed.

'So, what do we do? And what about our Arab friend? He looked like a nasty piece of work. I'm worried for our safety.'

'We're safe here. Beaussant said he'd provide protection until they catch him. Even if we go into town.' Daniel's mobile then rang. 'Hello?' Daniel cupped the phone, 'Talk of the devil, he whispered. '…That *is* interesting…Yes, we will. Thank you, Chief Inspector.'

'What was the "interesting" bit?' Kara asked, making speech marks with her fingers.

Daniel took a swig of coffee. 'It seems our Arab friend was seen leaving the yacht belonging to the famous Prince Al-Musan.'

'What! Really? That mega yacht lit up like a Christmas tree?'

'What else did Beaussant say?'

'That was it, really. After I'd told them I'd seen our intruder at the Palais des Festivals, the police have been back-tracking, working out his possible movements.'

'I saw that prince-what's-his-name on a US chat show. He seemed OK.'

'He probably is. But what on earth is his connection with a knife-wielding thug?'

'This is *so* weird.'

'Do you want to know what I think? I think these so-called martyrdoms are a side-show compared to what Ordway and his cronies could be up to. Ever since you hypothesised that weapon idea, I've thought of little else.'

'Yeh, and I keep thinking about how Ordway and his cronies may be exploiting me, Arthur, and the entire team.'

'He hasn't been honest with you, that's for sure.'

'Ordway's a lying shit.'

'Yeh, but a powerful one. I mean, if he is involved in some next-level weapon, it's gonna be as secret and secure as the president's launch codes. We've absolutely zero chance of finding out about it.'

'Not even you, with all your activist exploits?' Kara teased.

Daniel smiled and wrapped his arms around her. 'I meant to say,' he said, 'how brave I thought you were the other night. I'm so glad you weren't hurt.'

'Yeh, if I'd known your gun was empty, I may not have been so brave. I'll say one thing. You have balls, Doctor Daniel Bayford.' He lowered one of his hands and squeezed her bum. 'Oh, I shouldn't have mentioned them,' she said laughing and pulled away, nodding towards the window where the police officer had reappeared. 'And you didn't answer my other question.'

Daniel frowned. 'What do we do now?'

'Yeh.'

'How long can you stay?'

'I should really get back next week. Although Arthur seemed cool with the idea of me taking a short vacation. He said I worked too much.'

'Then stay. You know you're more than welcome.'

'Thank you. But I was thinking of a plan B.'

'Oh? And plan B being?'

'You come with me to Venezuela.'

Daniel's eyes widened in surprise. 'Wasn't expecting that. But I'd be in your way.'

'No, you wouldn't.'

'Anyway, why?'

'Because you and I will work together. Find out what Ordway is up to.'

Daniel studied Kara's face. 'You're serious.'

'Never more so. Ordway has clearly used me. Duped my entire team. And, without sounding like I'm using you, I could do with your know-how and moral support.'

'Happy to provide it. Are you sure I'd be allowed?'

'It's my experiment. I'm team leader. You'll have to pay your way there, but I can organise the paperwork to get you to our test site. The Venezuelan government will demand it. Should be a piece of cake, what with your doctoral status'

'Well, I guess I could take a break. Pierre and Luc will be happy to get the overtime.'

'Great. Then it's a deal. You know, what the hell. I'll pay for your flight. If Ordway questions it, I'll tell him where to stick it. Hope you like First Class.'

Daniel laughed. 'I like your style. You've got balls, too.'

'Ordway owes me big time.'

'Well, you have your very own stone. It may be the key to your experiment's success.'

'Yeh, true, but I bet he has yours. And I'm pissed about that.' Kara looked towards the window. There was no sign of the police officer. 'Of course, coming all this way has had some *other* benefits,' she said, pouting her lips. 'When are you on fire watch duty?'

Daniel grinned and looked at his watch. 'Ooh, now let me see.'

Chapter 59
Warnings

Vatican City

Cardinal Romero was standing at the window of his office with a mobile phone to his ear.

'The secret is out,' he said. He waited for a reply. 'Hello?… Oh, you are there…No, you are the first person I've called…No, I don't think they know that much. But Señor Morales, please listen, I'm worried. I don't think this is a good idea…Yes, I *am* having second thoughts…No, I want you to pass on my concerns…What development?… I see. So, are you saying it works?… Oh my God…But what good will it be if people know?' Romero listened then suddenly lost his temper. 'You're wrong, Señor! This is a big mistake.'

The cardinal hung up. He was shaking badly and had to steady himself against the window frame. He picked up a bible and dropped onto his couch with a deep sigh, his lips moving in silent prayer.

Steel Company Headquarters, Mexico City

The underground carpark of the corporate headquarters was all but empty. It was 06:10. Santiago Morales, as owner and CEO, liked an early start. He sat alone in the driver's seat of his steel-coloured Mercedes. He touched the screen of his infotainment system. 'Call Ordway cell,' he said. The fast dial tones and ringing sound filled the car.

Ordway answered, '*Santiago, my friend.*'

'Richard, it seems that certain non-members know about the project.'

'*Really? Now* that *is interesting,*' Ordway drawled. '*Is it a problem?*'

'I don't know,' said Morales, his deep voice enriched by his strong Mexican accent. 'You tell me. I mean, what can they do?'

301

There was a pause in the conversation. Ordway was thinking. '*What* can *they do?*' he said, repeating Morales' words more to himself. '*Nothing, I would suspect. The technology is too advanced. The project is ultra-secret and predicated on plausible deniability.*'

'But if others know…'

'*It's fine. Believe me.*'

'You say we can blame it on climate change, right?'

'*Right! There's nothing to worry about. Anyway, it all depends on who else knows. So, who told you about the leak?*'

'Romero.'

'*Romero…Do I know him?*'

'Cardinal Romero.'

'*Oh yeh, our man in the Vatican. Will he talk?*'

'No! He's a cardinal for Christ's sake. But he thinks we are making a big mistake. He sounded pretty upset.'

'*A mistake? Does he think getting our revenge on non-believers is a mistake? Of all our members, I really thought we could rely on those who preach the Lord's word. Do you think he's talked already? Maybe he was the one who spilled the beans, and called you as a cover-up.*'

'Cardinal Romero is a good friend of mine. He is devoted to the cause.'

'*Truly devoted? I wonder.*'

'He's upset. You're talking about massacring thousands.'

'*All in the name of God, Santiago. We have to act. Don't forget, plausible deniability is our advantage.*'

There was silence.

'Yes. I suppose you're right.'

'*Of course, I'm right. Now don't get like Romero and start having second thoughts. Don't forget you helped pay for this.*'

'Is that a threat?'

'*No, no, no, my friend. I just want you to benefit from your investment.*'

Morales felt unnerved. Perhaps he had overstepped the mark with his last comment, he thought. The Guild of God had taken a new and sinister direction. Who knows how far they would go in this deadly mission—this 21st-century crusade? 'So, the project—it's going well since the discovery of the stone?' he asked, keen to show his support.

'*Oh, it's going great. Don't you worry. All systems are go.*'

'OK. That's good. You know best, of course.'

'*Trust me, Santiago. I do. This will happen. Hey, you should come and see it. You're one of our most esteemed and biggest donators, after all.*'

'I would like that very much. Thank you, Richard.'

'*No sweat. I'll let you know when and where. You can jump on your private jet and be there in half a day. In fact, you know what? I may organise a big opening party for all our important benefactors. How does that sound?*'

'It sounds like a vote of confidence on your part. Sign me up!' Morales said with a forced laugh.

'*I appreciate your call, Santiago. You have a great day.*'

They hung up.

'What a dick,' Morales said. But secretly, the Mexican wanted the project to succeed as much as anyone.

Chapter 60
Dropped

Daniel's Villa, Tanneron, Southern France

Kara was on her mobile. 'I don't understand,' she said. Daniel walked out onto the terrace with their evening meal. Kara was looking out over the valley, but Daniel could sense the call she was on was serious. He quietly lowered the plates on the outside table and gave her a concerned look.

Kara turned to face him. She was listening to her caller and shaking her head. 'So, that's it. Do the others know? …Yes, please. They need to hear it from you, Arthur… I don't know. I guess I may stay over here for a while.' Kara pursed her lips tight. Daniel only had an inkling as to what the call may have been about but nodded his assent. 'Yeh, I'll be alright… Sure, thanks, Arthur.' Kara hung up. 'That was Professor Steel. He tells me they've pulled the plug on my experiment.'

'Oh shit, Kara. Did they say why?'

'Nope.'

'Which makes it all the more suspicious, right?'

Kara looked down at the table. 'That looks nice.' To Daniel's surprise, she sat down and tucked into the grilled fish, rice, and salad.

Daniel disappeared into the kitchen and returned with a chilled white wine and two glasses. 'Are you OK?' he said reaching forward from his seat and placing a hand on hers.

'Yeh, I'm fine,' she lied. 'Looks like our Venezuela trip is off. You would have loved it, too.'

They ate in silence. Daniel was unsure what to say. He took away their empty plates and returned with another bottle raised high. 'We *could* get rat-arsed.'

Kara laughed. 'Rat-arsed! I've never heard that before. You Brits are the funniest. Yeh, why not.'

'Look,' said Daniel, 'tell me to shut up if you want, but it's clear to me that Ordway has what he needs. Like you said, he used you all along. They hijacked your research for their own ends. Anyway, there's *every* chance you could get new funding. If not through the government, then privately. What you've helped develop is verging on revolutionary and unique. That spells money. Big money! You said yourself that the stone could be the key. My guess is that it is.'

'I just feel sorry for my team. They're such a great bunch of people.'

'They can be part of your new team.'

Kara looked at her wine. 'I guess.' She welcomed Daniel's optimism but felt utterly deflated and powerless. She was so close. A new, renewable form of energy was within her grasp.

'No, let's go there. I've never been, and seeing your photos it looks amazing.'

Kara looked up. 'You want to go to Venezuela?'

'Why not?'

'I thought you wanted us to dig into this Ordway business.'

'I do. Look, let's take a week off. We can still do some digging.'

Kara thought hard. 'OK,' she said. 'I do have some business to conclude there, and I would like to see my team before we go our separate ways.'

'Great!'

'And after?'

'Back here, of course. You know you can stay here for as long as you like...Forever would be better.'

'You're not just saying that, are you?'

'Kara, you make me feel...alive.'

'And you me.' Happy tears welled in her eyes.

'Well, let's DRINK TO THAT THEN!' Daniel boomed.

Kara laughed. 'Yeh, LET'S GET RAT-ARSED!' she yelled.

And they clinked glasses.

Chapter 61
The Emissary

Nice, Southern France

Kara and Daniel had left the old quarter of Nice and emerged from a passageway onto the bustling seafront. Ahead of them, beyond the constant stream of vehicles, palm trees quivered in the warm breeze.

'I thought we could walk off our lunch along the *Promenade des Anglais*. The locals call it, *La Prom*. They probably don't like the fact that the English came up with the idea of its construction.'

They were soon amongst the strolling pleasure-seekers and weaving in-line skaters on the famous promenade. Kara looked out at the Mediterranean and the bathers in its blue, sparkling waters. She felt a sense of calm immutability about the place.

'I feel like a celebrity,' she said.

Daniel glanced back over his shoulder. The police officer assigned to protect them was following some ten metres behind.

'What, having a personal bodyguard?' Daniel said, nodding to indicate the policeman.

She laughed, 'No, walking along here.'

He looked at her in her sleeveless, white top and sunglasses. *She certainly looks like a celebrity*, he thought but resisted making the compliment out loud. *Too cheesy*, he realised. *Or was it?* He was distracted from his dilemma when he spotted a kiosk.

'Ice cream?' Daniel asked, reaching for the wallet inside his linen jacket. 'Let me know if you need anything translated,' Daniel said.

'Doctor Bayford? Doctor Williams?'

The voice behind them made them turn sharply. To their surprise, a young priest dressed in a black cassock stood before them. His hands folded in front of him. His face was pale and beads of sweat sat on his brow.

'I'm sorry,' said Daniel, 'who are you?'

'Please forgive my intrusion,' the priest said, raising a hand and removing his steel-framed spectacles. 'I am Father Brendan.' He reached out his other hand to shake theirs. Daniel and Kara both accepted his greeting tentatively. 'If I may?' The priest indicated he had something to give them from within his cassock. Daniel nodded. Their police escort was walking over. Daniel held up a hand. The police officer stopped. The priest looked over his shoulder, then looked back at Daniel with a quizzical expression.

'Don't worry,' Daniel reassured him.

The priest then produced a small card and gave it to Daniel, who read it, raised his eyebrows, and showed it to Kara, who mirrored Daniel's expression.

'The Vatican?' Daniel questioned.

'Yes,' the priest said calmly. 'I am, I suppose, an emissary, here on behalf of Cardinal Romero.'

'Cardinal Romero,' Daniel repeated. 'Am I supposed to know who that is?'

The priest smiled politely. 'No, of course not.' He fell silent and glanced back at the police officer. 'May we talk somewhere more private?'

Daniel turned to Kara, tilting his head as if to say, what the hell is this about? He looked back across the road. 'There's a hotel. Will that do?'

'Yes, of course,' said the priest. His voice had a subtle lilt to it that Daniel was trying to place.

Inside the hotel, Daniel strode confidently through the lobby. He seemed to know where he was going. The hotel receptionists and some of the guests looked on somewhat bemused; the sight of a priest following closely behind an attractive young woman did have a rather comic air about it. The sight of the serious-looking police officer following soon after, though, changed the mood very quickly.

Daniel stepped out into the garden beyond and led them to an isolated table.

'Please,' he said to the priest, holding out his open palm, before leaning back in his chair to listen. Kara leant forward in anticipation.

The police officer looked around and decided to sit on a nearby bench out of earshot. An elderly couple were already walking back towards the hotel. Another guest, a young, dark-skinned man, exited the same door and took a seat close to

307

the hotel's rear windows. What appeared to be the hotel manager then approached the officer. They exchanged some words, but not without looking over at Daniel, Kara, and the priest.

'This may all seem pretty dramatic,' Father Brendan began. Daniel now recognised a hint of southern Irish in the priest's accent and rapid speech. 'And, to be frank, I'm not quite sure where to start, even though I rehearsed my lines, so to speak. Please forgive me.' The priest realised he was gabbling and stopped talking. He looked down at his lap, trying to compose his thoughts, rubbing his hands together slowly. Daniel smiled at Kara, who looked away, seeing a funny side to the delicate and nervous young priest sitting opposite. She could never understand how someone could devote themself to faith so completely. It was an admirable yet strange life choice, she thought. But then realised she was no different; her faith lay in scientific discovery. Nonetheless, both she and Daniel remained intrigued. *An emissary from the Vatican. What the heck!* Father Brendon looked up. 'I believe I mentioned that I was here on behalf of Cardinal Romero.'

'You did,' Daniel said, encouragingly. 'But first, how did you find us?'

'Ah yes. Well now, I had to play detective there,' the priest replied, laughing nervously. 'I have to admit that once I knew where you lived, Doctor Bayf...'

'Please, call me Daniel.'

'Yes, Daniel, I will. Thank you. Once I knew the whereabouts of your residence, I...um...well, I simply followed you. I also took the liberty of finding out the identity of your friend here. To be frank, I'm now surprised that the police did not pull me over.' The priest looked at the nearby police officer warily.

'You don't look a threat, Father,' Kara said, smiling.

Father Brendon shot her a look and blushed. 'God bless you. I'm sure that dressed like this also helps.' Feeling a little more confident, he continued. 'So, Cardinal Romero instructed me to tell you that he has grave concerns. You see, apart from holding one of the highest offices in the church, or maybe because of that fact, he is also a member of a group. This group has been in existence for centuries. Its members are modest and generous. They do not look for recognition or praise for their work. They simply want to spread goodness and charity. And they help those that have the same belief. Christian belief.' Daniel and Kara looked at each other. *Where was this going?* they wondered. 'Many influential people *are doing* much good in the service of this group. However, some within its ranks have less desirable and more extreme intentions.'

Daniel leant forward. 'Sorry,' he said, 'are you talking about a secret society like the Masons?'

'Er no, the cardinal is not a Freemason.'

'Please don't say Illuminati,' Kara said, now starting to wonder if they were wasting their time.

'Hardly. They were anti-religious and their existence is questionable, to say the least. No, the group I speak of is real enough. You have to believe me.'

'And what has this got to do with us?' Daniel said with equal irritation in his tone.

The priest again began rubbing his hands slowly. 'The cardinal has been following the recent events, as we all have.'

'The terror attacks and martyrdoms,' Kara ventured.

'No, I meant only the martyrdoms.' Daniel and Kara exchanged looks. 'You see, Cardinal Romero, is concerned that belief in God and Christianity itself is being destabilised, damaged, possibly beyond repair by these events. People across the globe are claiming they witnessed acts of God but acts not of *their* God. They say they were acts of Allah. Thousands are converting to Islam. Our church has already seen a worrying and rapid decline in popularity over the decades. These events are like a tipping point.'

'That's why we need to go to the press, Daniel. I told you. There are too many gullible people out there. They need to know the facts.'

Daniel held up a hand, his gaze still on the priest. 'But why us? Why has this Cardinal Romero sent you to find us?'

Father Brendon took a deep breath. 'Please allow me to explain. His Eminence wrote a letter to a very prominent person, in which he effectively approved the use of something...' He took another deep breath. '...something called...The Spear of Destiny.' The priest paused. He waited for a reaction.

'The what?' Kara asked eventually.

'The Spear of Destiny. Cardinal Romero saw it as the means to fight back, figuratively speaking,' the priest replied.

'Where've I heard that?' Daniel said more to himself.

'The Spear of Destiny is quite famous.' To their surprise, Father Brendon pulled out a large smartphone. 'This is the true Spear of Destiny. Also known as the Holy Lance.' An image of a spearhead filled the screen.

'Yes, of course,' Daniel said. 'The spear that pierced Christ on the cross.'

'That's right. There are many in existence. The true one is believed to bring power to whoever possessed it. During the First Crusade, a French soldier had a vision in which he saw the Spear of Destiny's location buried in a church in Antioch. When the Crusaders found it, they saw it as a sign, a talisman. It was enough for them to break the siege of Antioch and lead them to victory. Hitler famously took the one currently held in the Hofburg Palace in Vienna. But the real one is held deep within the Vatican. I've seen it. The cardinal showed me.'

'Power to take over the world,' said Daniel. 'Now I get it.' Kara looked at him. 'The mystical power of the relic. Whoever possessed it had the power to take over the world. That's right, isn't it, Father?'

'Yes, that's right.'

'Well, it didn't do Hitler much good,' Kara said as if to back up her faith in science.

'You say that,' said the priest, 'But when the Americans took possession of the Spear, Hitler committed suicide the very next day.'

Kara was shaking her head. She had to interrupt. 'Wait, are you telling us that the church is resorting to the use of some ancient religious relic? A relic with, I'm sorry to say, questionable authenticity.'

Father Brendon smiled at Kara but with a look of pain in his eyes. 'I understand your scepticism, Doctor. You are a scientist. Faith is not for everyone. But please allow me to continue. His Eminence had heard mention of the Spear, but never really paid much attention. Why would he? The group was peaceful, caring, and benevolent. Trust amongst the members of this group is implicit. He thought that the real relic would be used somehow to convince the world of the truth of Jesus. He later learned that it was not what he had thought.'

'What do you mean?' Kara asked.

The priest was struggling to find the words. 'These people are powerful. Some hold the highest offices in the world. As a member of this group, His Eminence is privy to most of its activities. Like I said, most of these have been for the good. But he became aware of other darker activities—clandestine developments. As a trusted member of the group, he soon learned the truth. Doctor Bayford, Doctor Williams, The Spear of Destiny of which I speak is not this relic. It is a weapon.'

'Oh my God, Daniel. We were right.'

The priest was surprised at their reaction. 'You knew? Really? How?' he asked incredulously.

'It's complicated,' said Daniel. 'But I think we're both beginning to understand why the cardinal sent you to us.' Kara was nodding but sensed that Daniel wanted them to hold their cards close. Besides, Father Brendon may look and dress like a priest, but the theft of Daniel's stone and the need for police protection had put them both on guard.

'The meteorite. It's the key, right?' the priest asked in a loud whisper. For the first time, he seemed to display a youthful enthusiasm for the mysterious.

'We believe so,' Daniel replied. 'But carry on. I feel you have more you can tell us.'

'Wait!' Something was troubling Kara. 'Are you saying that the cardinal had full knowledge of this weapon and that he sanctioned its use in this letter? And I'm guessing the recipient of this letter was a fellow member of this group in government somewhere. Why on earth would a man of God do that?'

Daniel could not resist interjecting. 'It's not the first time the Church has used violence.'

'I'm ashamed to admit that you are right.' Father Brendon said. The young priest was clearly in turmoil.

Kara felt sorry for him. 'It's alright, Father. We're not here to shoot the messenger. I'm sorry.'

'No, it is I who should apologise. But, please, allow me to continue,' the priest pleaded. 'His Eminence is a passionate man. That passion got the better of him. But now he is wracked with guilt. He has anguished over the words he wrote, so much so that I fear for his health.'

'But surely he could simply write another letter,' Kara suggested, 'denouncing what he said before.'

'I'm afraid it's gone beyond that. The powers behind the Spear of Destiny are far greater than those of a cardinal, and knowledge of the Spear has become more widespread. He tried to make amends by calling another member he knew was close to the people behind the weapon. It was during that call that he heard about how the stone you found helped to accelerate the development of the weapon.'

Kara brought a hand over her mouth, her eyes wide.

'And now,' the priest continued, 'he has learned of the true power of the weapon, he is a broken man.'

'And His Eminence thinks that we can help somehow,' Daniel said flatly.

'Like I said, I had to play detective. Part of that detective work involved looking into your careers and past. Don't you see? This group is everywhere. We had to find someone we could trust.'

'You keep talking about this group. What is this group called?' Kara's question seemed to hit the priest in the face.

'They go under the name of The Guild...,' Father Brendon hesitated, 'The Guild of God.'

'Oh my God, that explains everything,' she said.

'Wow!' said Daniel. 'Now that's an arrogant name. Don't tell me, they're conducting some kind of crusade.'

'No,' the priest said, desperate to reclaim some lost ground for the church. 'It was a crusade for goodness, and has been for centuries.'

'Until now,' Kara said, cutting him short.

'Look, when His Eminence told me all this ...' The priest had suddenly and unexpectedly raised his voice. When he noticed that the police officer had looked up, he quickly tempered his tone. 'When His Eminence told me all this, he broke the Guild of God's strict vow of silence.'

'So, you're not a member of this Guild of God, Father?' Kara asked.

'Me, no! I've no power and certainly no money,' he said almost laughing.

'Well, I wouldn't lose any sleep, Father,' said Daniel. 'It sounds to me like this Guild of God is now being run by a bunch of religious zealots. And you should tell His Eminence that he has done the right thing.'

Father Brendon looked at Daniel for several seconds, taking in what he'd said. 'Yes...yes, of course. You're right. This has to be stopped.' He seemed much calmer, but looked down at his lap once again and resumed his hand rubbing.

Daniel continued, 'But I'm at a loss as to how *we* can be of any help. Did Cardinal Romero say anything else, I mean, about us?'

The priest looked up. 'Just that Doctor Williams here is the most qualified to understand the technology and be a respected voice, and that you, Daniel, have experience in government and, well, His Eminence also said he had a deep admiration for your activism. Besides, your joint involvement already makes you the natural choice. As Dr Williams suggested, you could make this public.'

'Maybe,' Daniel said. 'But like you said, these Guild of God people are everywhere. So, whom can *we* trust?'

'Quality press, Daniel,' Kara said. 'The quicker we get this out there the better. That's all *we* can do.'

'I have a better idea.' Daniel said and turned to the priest. 'You said that the cardinal learned of "the true power of the weapon." Can you expand on that?'

'Only what His Eminence told me. That the weapon has God-like power.'

'It's what you said, Kara.'

Kara suddenly looked very concerned. 'It sounds a whole lot worse.'

Chapter 62
Contact

Whitehall, Central London, UK

The black cab pulled over on Parliament Street. After the strange meeting they had had with Father Brendan, Daniel had convinced Kara that they should make a detour on their way to Venezuela via London.

'This is it,' Daniel said, nodding towards one of the side streets, its entrance, blocked by automatic security bollards, was dominated by three archways, topped by an ornate entablature. 'And by the way, his name's Sebastian.'

An armed police officer appeared. Daniel handed him a document, which the officer scrutinised and handed back. He looked at Kara.

'Your bag, miss?'

'Er sure.' Kara opened her small clutch bag for the officer to peer inside. Satisfied, the officer nodded.

After they had passed through, Daniel turned and said, 'Welcome to the heart of the UK government. Security is always tight here.'

'This is pretty cool,' she replied, looking up at the grand buildings. 'But I'm worried. I sense you have a plan and you're not sharing it with me.'

Daniel did not reply. They had arrived at the entrance to the Foreign Office, and a more thorough security check.

'You'll like where we're meeting Sebastian, Kara. By the way, he's what we call old school. And he's not a secret agent, so don't get your hopes up. But very good at what he does,' Daniel said as he led the way into the building. Soon, they arrived at the magnificent, marble-floored Durbar Court. Sunlight flooded down through the enormous glass roof.

'Wow!' was all Kara could say.

'This used to be the India Office—when we had an empire.'

'But why here? I thought this Sebastian was MI6.'

'He is. I guess he has business here today. Ah, there he is.'

Standing at the foot of a short flight of stairs, was a bald, willowy man in his early fifties, dressed in a dark suit. He spotted Daniel and raised a hand. Kara thought him rather dull-looking. But when he spoke, the man transformed into someone altogether more amenable. 'Daniel! How the devil are you? Or should I say, *comment allez-vous*?'

Daniel smirked. 'Sebastian. I see your schoolboy French hasn't deserted you.'

The two men shook hands warmly and hugged. Sebastian turned immediately to Kara with a broad smile.

'May I introduce you to Doctor Kara Williams.'

'*Enchanté, Mademoiselle,*' Sebastian gave a short nod of his head and shook her hand.

'Kara, this is my good friend Sebastian Sadler-Smith,' Daniel said.

'A meteorologist, ay?'

'That's right. Pretty dull stuff really,' Kara said then gave Daniel a questioning look.

'Quite a wonderful place, don't you think?' Sadler-Smith said, panning his arm around in a gesture as grand as the surroundings.

Daniel patted him on the back. 'And you look the part, Sebastian. I'd mistake you for a diplomat any day.'

Sadler-Smith leant forward as though about to impart a state secret. 'Met with the FS. Thus, the posh attire,' he said in a whisper loud enough to be heard by anyone within ten metres.

'You'll have to excuse Sebastian,' Daniel said to Kara. 'He means the Foreign Secretary. Too many TLA's as always.'

Sadler-Smith laughed heartily. 'Not quite. I thought a TLA was a three-letter acronym. Mine was only two. Oh, hang on, that still works. Anyway, guilty as charged, sir.'

Daniel shook his head. He liked Sebastian but sensed he was now showing off in front of his lady. Nevertheless, Daniel hoped this would not be a wasted trip. 'Seriously, Seb. I appreciate you taking the time. Where can we talk?'

'Well, it's a glorious day. Why don't we take a stroll in the park?'

'Sure.'

The other end of King Charles Street led to St James' Park. It was a very warm day. Daniel, Kara, and Sadler-Smith followed one of the paths around the nearby lake and past pockets of people sitting in the shade of the trees.

'So, Daniel. I thought you'd retired. What's all the mystery? I hope you're not craving that rebellious life again.' Sadler-Smith suddenly seemed like a different person, Kara thought. His face looked drawn and deadly serious. 'And I hope it has nothing to do with the recent terror attacks.'

'No, of course not.' Daniel replied quickly. He wasn't lying either, Kara thought.

'I'm guessing you want more intel on that Ordway character.'

Daniel took several more steps before replying. 'We've discovered something. Something shocking.'

'I'm listening.'

'And yes, we believe Ordway is behind it.'

'I see. Are you going to enlighten me as to the nature of this shocking something?'

'Well, that's why we're here. We want to be sure. Gather more facts.'

'Not even a little teaser? A political scandal? Terror threat?'

'The less you know right now, the better. Look, it could be nothing.' Daniel was purposely playing it down.

Kara was walking a step behind the two men and now sped up to draw level with them. 'Sebastian...' Sadler-Smith turned and smiled. 'Daniel's right,' she said. 'We want to be sure before wasting your time.'

'OK. I can buy that. I'm up to neck in stuff anyway. But always happy to help an old friend, and you, of course.' The Sebastian Sadler-Smith she had first met was now back. Daniel gave Kara a sneaky wink. She had applied some feminine charm. And who could resist her? Sadler-Smith went on, 'I just worry about Daniel, you see. Did he tell you we tried to recruit him?'

'Seb, no. Please.' Daniel sighed.

'After his rebellious exploits, one of our recruiters approached me and asked about our Daniel here.'

'Why am I not surprised?' Kara said.

'You see, Daniel. Even your good lady friend can see the sense. But no, instead he chose semi-retirement as a bloody fire lookout. You could have been good, Daniel.'

'Well, I'm too old for all that now.'

'No, you're not. I bet you're aching for some action. Anyway, come on. I need to head back. What is it you want?'

'It's a big ask, Seb.'

'Oh God, I knew it.'

'We need to track Ordway. Know where he goes.'

'Bug him, too?'

'Well sure, if…'

'I was joking,' Sadler-Smith said but without humour. 'He works for the US DOD for God's sake.'

'All I'm talking about is for you to discretely find out if he jumps on a plane and where that plane is heading. That's all. I know you can access that.'

Sadler-Smith stopped. 'Let's head back.' They retraced their steps.

'Well?' Daniel pressed. He knew Sebastian would help. He was just showing off again; bigging up his position.

'It's not easy. If this Ordway is up to something shocking, as you put it, he may have ways of circumventing the plane's manifest. Military plane or any other.'

'The thought had crossed my mind. But it's all we have, Seb. We need to know what he's up to, and we can only know that if we know where he is.'

'OK, let me see what I can muster up… I'm curious, though. You will share your findings with me. Quid pro quo and all that.'

'Seb, if we're right, I guarantee you will be the first to know.'

'Shocking, you say. What *are* you up to, Daniel?'

Back in their hotel room, Kara sat on the bed as Daniel unbuttoned his shirt.

'So, that was your plan.'

Daniel turned. He looked animated. 'Yes, don't you see? Ordway could lead us to this weapon.'

'Of course, I see. But what are the chances?'

'I reckon better than eighty per cent. Seb is a bit of a wizard. And he has a list of contacts as long as both his arms.'

Kara looked sceptical. 'Is it *really* that simple? Ask a spook to spy on a close ally?'

'Don't be naïve, Kara. You don't think the CIA isn't tracking UK citizens as we speak? The only difference is that we share intel with friendly countries. Anyway, what are old university friends for?'

Daniel looked into the bathroom mirror, wondering if he could be bothered to shave.

'Well, it's clear you trust your buddy. Enough to tell him all about me. *A meteorologist, ay?*' she mimicked.'

'Whoa! Actually, no I didn't. I swear. He's a spook, Kara. And he *loves* showing off.'

'Oh. You disappoint me. So, I'm not worth mentioning,' she teased.

Daniel laughed and walked back into the bedroom. 'Kara, believe me, I want more than anything to stand on the highest mountain and shout to the world: "I LOVE DOCTOR KARA WILLIAMS!" Kara looked at Daniel. 'Why are you crying?'

'That was lovely, Daniel.' She jumped up and threw her arms around him.

Chapter 63
Paladin

Palace of the Grand Master, Rhodes, Greece

'Welcome everyone. Welcome all. And good evening.'

The speaker was seated at a large table in the main hall of the fourteenth-century *Kastello—The Palace of the Grand Master of the Knights of Rhodes*—more a fortress than a palace. The imposing fortification, located on the Street of the Knights in the medieval town of Rhodes, stands at the northernmost tip of the island.

That evening, the incongruous presence of luxury cars filled its floodlit courtyard. The hall was softly lit by a single chandelier that highlighted the lighter tones of the geometric brickwork. The speaker, known simply and appropriately as Paladin, was addressing a room of one hundred and thirty-two smartly-dressed men and women, seated in rows between columns. Those present were the Guild of God council; the elite, chosen to vote on significant proposals. Only a handful outranked them; too well-known to be seen at such conclaves, clandestine though they were. The council had convened from across the globe for a rare, plenary meeting. The fact that the castle had been closed for them came as no surprise; their influence was considerable.

'Thank you for attending. I hope you like the choice of venue,' the speaker continued, smiling. He was tall and lean with deep lines on his cheeks and brow. His dark suit was adorned with a handkerchief tucked neatly in the breast pocket. Paladin ran a hand through his hair before continuing in his rich sonorous tone. 'As many of you know, in medieval times this was an important site for Christians and our former brothers, the Knights Hospitaller. Those must have been dark times. Christianity was under threat. Thousands gave up everything to defend the Holy Land. It was a long fight against the heathens, but a fight they eventually lost. During the First Crusade, the Knights Hospitaller devoted themselves to caring for the sick, elderly, and injured pilgrims to the Holy Land. But the threat of Muslim invasion forced them to turn benevolence into one of protection. The medical order became a military order. When the Arabs took Jerusalem in 1291, the Knights Hospitaller were forced to move first to Cyprus and then here, where they remained for more than two hundred years. We, the Guild of God, continued the Hospitaller tradition of care and benefaction.' Paladin rose from his chair slowly. 'But today, *this day*, is different. Today, we must follow in the footsteps of our predecessors. Today, we must arm ourselves against those that defy our God. We must turn patronage into armed resistance. Not since the Crusades all those years ago has the threat against Christianity been so great. So, I repeat the call to arms uttered by Pope Urban II on the fields of Clermont: God wills it, GOD WILLS IT!'

His audience rose from their seats and the room erupted with: 'GOD WILLS IT!'

Paladin sat down and nodded to a man standing on one side of the hall. He was holding a tray loaded with small black, cotton bags and a pile of tiny, slim, silver objects. He nodded back and began handing out one bag and one object to each of those present. A woman in the front row studied the object, turning it over. It was a miniature spear. The assistant approached Paladin's table, where he set down the tray. Two bags and two spears remained, which they each picked up.

Paladin stood again. 'You are all aware of the project. I am delighted to say that it has been a great success. Everything *and* everyone is in place. It only remains for you to decide. You have each been given a bag and a silver spear. If you agree that we proceed then place the spear in the bag. If you disagree then please keep the spear as a token of our thanks for your support of our great cause. Either way, place your bag on the tray when my assistant returns.'

The assistant began the collection and returned to the table. Paladin added his and his assistant's bags to the pile and shuffled them all briefly.

'And now, ladies and gentlemen the count begins.'

Paladin took the first bag and tipped it over the table. A spear dropped out. He repeated the process with the second bag. A spear dropped out. Then the third, the fourth… His assistant had picked up a pad and was recording the numbers. After a few minutes, the count was complete. Only one bag was empty. The pad was handed to Paladin, who held it aloft. 'One hundred and thirty-one, if any of you had any doubts.' He reached over and picked up his and his assistant's bags and tipped them onto the table. 'And that makes an *almost* unanimous one hundred and thirty-three.'

Paladin looked at the faces before him and wondered who the sole dissenter was.

'Ladies and gentlemen, that concludes the proceedings,' he announced. 'Thank you and may God be with you.'

Cardinal Romero was seated near the rear of the hall. He looked at those rising from their seats to his right and left, hoping that no one had spotted the silver spear he was clutching tightly in his right hand. When his row had cleared, he opened his hand slightly and peered at the small spear. He then clenched his hand, stood up, and made his way to the door.

'Cardinal!'

Romero looked up. He recognised the voice. It was Morales. The Mexican businessman was holding out a hand. Romero brought his own hands together as though in prayer and deftly passed the spear into his left hand, which he slipped under his cassock.

'*Señor* Morales. How are you?'

'Please, I am Santiago to my friends.'

The men shook hands. Morales put an arm over the cardinal's shoulder as they strolled through the hall. Romero was regretting his outburst during their last phone conversation.

'It's a shame the vote wasn't unanimous, don't you think?' Morales said.

'Yes, I suppose. But that's the nature of a democratic system.'

'Very true. But you know, I wonder why anyone would want to prevent such an important mission.'

The cardinal caused them both to stop. The last of the council had now exited the hall. They stood alone facing one another. '*Señor* Morales…Santiago,' he said in barely more than a whisper. 'We were voting on the use of a weapon. A weapon of unimaginable power and destruction. I can understand why someone would have doubts about such a strategy.'

'Someone like you, Cardinal?'

'You know I don't have to answer that.'

Morales stared hard at the heavy lines across the Spaniard's face. He then laughed heartily. 'Come, you must join me on my boat. We can celebrate the success together. You're allowed a little wine, yes?'

The men continued walking.

'You came from Mexico by boat?'

'Wait 'til you see my boat!'

The Mexican put his arm around the cardinal again and laughed.

Chapter 64
Dawn

An Airfield, Essex, UK

'Here it comes.' SO15 officer, Rob Villiers was looking down at the radar app on his phone. He watched as the small red plane icon made a turn for its final approach to the airfield, its flight path trailing back to the South East. He zoomed out and scrolled. The flight path had started in northern France around sixty kilometres northeast of Paris. '*Compiègne?*' Villiers asked.

'Yeh, that's the one,' Phil Evans replied. He was at the wheel of their van. He had parked it up alongside a series of grey containers, from where they had a good view of the landing strip and any vehicles entering the airfield.

The radio crackled. '*This is Delta 1. Comms check.*' It was David Pearson, the SO15 team leader.

'*Delta 3 in position.*'
'*Delta 4 in position.*'

Villiers pressed the talk button on his radio, 'Delta 2 in position.'

David Pearson spoke again, '*Everyone hold position and await instructions.*'

It was 05:25. The weather was calm. A thin layer of clouds white-washed the sky.

'Nice day for flying terrorists,' Evans quipped. He raised his binoculars and picked out Pearson in his car with the Delta 1 team, and two other SO15 cars parked up nearer the airfield entrance. He swung the binoculars around and focussed on the incoming Piper Archer.

Slumped by the door in the passenger seat, Villiers popped open a Tupperware box and took out a sandwich. 'Want one?' he asked, before filling his mouth with bread, egg, and cress.

Pearson lowered the binoculars and looked at his colleague. 'What the fuck, Rob?'

'I'm starving. All right? Been up since 3 fuckin' 30.'

Pearson peered into the open box. 'Go on then.'

'So, what d'ya reckon?' Villiers asked.

'I reckon we'll soon be bagging another victory and slamming two more Jihadi bastards in the clink.'

'No, I meant the pilot. The plane's registered here.'

'Yeh, that's a mystery. Mike said the Delta 4 boys will deal with them.'

The Piper Archer's wheels touched down. Delta 2 watched as it slowed and turned towards a group of small hangers to their left.

'This is it.' Evans said, wiping his mouth and starting up the engine.

Villiers took the binoculars and focussed on the plane. The door nearest to them opened and three men clambered out. Villiers could just make out the pilot. One of the men—blond hair, sunglasses, and flying jacket—had a mobile to his ear, looking towards the edge of the airfield. Villiers lowered the binoculars and followed the direction the blond man was looking. He then raised them again when he saw a distant car and someone with a mobile to his ear. 'Hello,' Villiers said, more to himself, 'Who do we have here?' With one hand holding the binoculars up, he pressed his radio button. 'Potential suspect on the eastern perimeter road.' Villers scanned to the left and right. 'Approximately two hundred metres north of us. Black Ford saloon.'

Delta 3 responded. 'Yeh got 'im. Leave it with us.'

Mick Crambrook looked around nervously. 'Come on, Pete!'

Peter Reeves was still at the controls of the Piper Archer. 'Coming. Keep your hair on.'

Mick could wait no longer and started walking towards the car park. Their two passengers followed. They were Bakr al-Ahdal and Ahmed Hashim. Mick turned, 'You're on your own, so I hope for your sake your man is here.'

Mick clicked the key remote to his Porsche, placed his overnight bag behind the seat, and closed the door. As he walked round the driver's side he looked back towards the plane. Peter was placing chocks behind the wheels. Mick jumped in. The Porsche engine roared to life and he spun off towards the plane. *This is getting too nerve-wracking*, he thought. He had no intention of being this involved. *Next time, Pete will do it on his own*. He then thought about the money and started spending it in his head. This always made him feel better. *I'll take Cathy and the kids to Hawaii*, he thought.

Bakr and Ahmed had already spotted their ride—a grey Audi saloon. It was parked fifty metres or so nearer to the car park exit. Ten minutes later, they were already well on their way to London but oblivious to three facts.

One…

That the moment they had entered the slip road to the motorway, Delta 4 had raced across the airfield towards the plane. Mick had been sitting behind the wheel cleaning his sunglasses when the black SUV suddenly appeared and lurched to a stop in front of him.

It was fast. All too fast.

The two nearest doors of the SUV swung open and two armed police officers jumped out, one with a Glock 17 self-loading pistol raised, the other a Sig Sauer SG516 semi-automatic rifle, both pointing directly at Mick through his windscreen.

'ARMED POLICE. PUT YOUR HANDS ON THE TOP OF THE STEERING WHEEL!'

Mick froze. But his bowels did otherwise. His sunglasses fell in his lap. He shot his hands onto the steering wheel, and gripped it hard, his mouth and eyes wide open, staring at the barrels of the guns.

Two more officers had exited the vehicle on the far side. They were pointing their weapons at Peter Reeves.

'ARMED POLICE! ON THE GROUND! NOW! DOWN! GET DOWN! NOW!' They shouted in unison.

Peter cowered instantly and collapsed to the floor, hands covering his head.

Two…

The Delta 3 team were questioning the man on the perimeter road.

'I'm just a plane spotter.' The young man was no more than twenty-five years old and cocky.

'At 5:30 in the morning? You're coming with us.'

'Under what charge?'

'You don't want to know. And I'll take that,' the officer instructed, holding out his hand.

The man reluctantly handed over his mobile. 'What about my car?'

The Delta 3 team had had enough. One of them stepped forward. 'Why don't you shut the fuck up. There's a good lad,' he said, as he grabbed the man and bundled him into their car.

Three…

And crucially—that their dawn flight into the UK had been far from unnoticed. SO15 had been tracking it.

Evans looked away from the road briefly. The main display in the van showed a map. 'How far are they?'

Villiers looked at the screen. 'One eighty, two hundred metres. We're fine.'

'Delta 2, let's rotate in 5 miles.'

'Roger that, Delta 1.' Evans made a note of the milometer. In just a few minutes he would be taking Delta 1's place as the lead vehicle, driving ahead of the target vehicle.

Both teams were feeling relaxed; they were also tracking the target vehicle on their in-car displays. Earlier that morning, the SO15 team had spotted the lone driver sitting in the grey Audi. One of the team had crept up and placed a tracker under the rear of the car. As a precaution, a helicopter had also been patrolling the area, making a note of any other vehicle movements in and around the airfield, its cameras picking out the registration plates with ease. It was now following the convoy at a discrete distance.

Evans spotted Delta 1's car. It had slowed right down. He looked at his milometer. The grey Audi was overtaking it in the middle lane. *Time to rotate*, Evans thought. He accelerated, indicated, and moved into the fast lane. They were closing in on the Audi. Villiers leant his arm on the door and raised his left hand to cover his face. As they overtook the Audi, Villiers sneaked a peek through his fingers. 'Don't recognise the driver,' he said.

Delta 1 took up its new position a hundred and fifty metres behind the Audi. Evans passed several cars, pulled in then looked in his rear-view mirror and eased off to match the speed of the Audi, now some one hundred metres to his rear.

'Are we cool?' Villiers asked over the radio.

'We're cool,' Pearson responded. *'If we spook them, we'll all drop back and let the chopper take over. Anyway, the traffic's building in our favour.'*

They passed an overhead gantry sign. The right two lanes were for central London. The Audi moved into the middle lane. Central London it was.

Chapter 65
Act of God

Central Iran

The D3 Discreet Deployment Drone sped high over the mountains. Its path was being monitored by just one person on the planet: an operations specialist aboard the US warship, several hundred kilometres to the southeast in the Gulf of Oman.

'*Seeder* deployment in 5, 4, 3, 2, 1. *Seeders* released.' The Navy specialist said calmly into his headset.

The D3 arced a wide circle as the *seeders* fell. The build-up of electrical potential they created was rapid. Several minutes later and seven kilometres from the city, two thousand Autonomous Discriminatory Nano Drones were then jettisoned from the D3 and began their freefall.

The ship's operations room fell silent. Richard Ordway was sitting near the back. In front of him stood the captain, arms folded. Six personnel were stationed around the room, all wearing headsets, eyes fixed on their displays.

The drone specialist watched the data update on his screen. 'Activate ELF in 3, 2, 1. Now!'

Nearly ten thousand kilometres away, an extremely low-frequency pulse radiated out from the base in Alaska, unseen, unheard. It was the trigger: all two thousand of the ADNDs powered up. Now, like a swarm of killer bees, each hurtled towards its designated target.

Ten kilometres from the swarm, Yasmin's elderly grandmother was seated in her usual chair by the open door. Beyond was the roof terrace shared by six other families.

'Yasmin! Yasmin! The washing. When are you getting it in?' she cried out.

'Yes, grandma. I'll be there in a minute. I'm just texting the boys.'

Her grandmother enjoyed her view, especially at this time of day, an hour or two before sundown. She could make out the planes as they took off and landed at the main airport, their engines often audible over the constant beeping of car horns. Her favourite view was of the mountains. Today they seemed to glow in the rays of the sun, but the sky above was dark and brooding.

The *salat al-'asr* call to prayer then filled the air. The loudest emanated from the cluster of horn loudspeakers high on the minaret towers of the nearby Grand Mosque, where her great-grandsons would be joining their father in prayer.

'Yasmin!'

'Yes, I'm here, Grandma. Do you want me to help you inside? It'll get chilly soon.'

'No, no. Don't worry about me. You have all that to bring in,' her grandmother said, pointing at the mix of clothing and bedding strung out over the terrace. 'Your husband and the boys will be back from prayer soon and they'll be hungry.'

Yasmin began with the large bed sheets. As she folded the first, she looked up and out across the rooftops. A dark cloud seemed to be hanging like a large disc above the entire city. Beyond it, the last of the sun's rays cast an eerie light on the buildings. Yasmin frowned. 'I don't think it'll rain,' she said.

Her grandmother had not heard her but was also looking up. 'There's a storm coming. I can feel it,' she called out.

Like an irrepressible infestation, the first cluster of ADNDs landed silently on the roof of the Grand Mosque. Others settled on various rooftops across the city—targets provided by the CIA.

The D3 was now circling some ten kilometres distant. An onboard camera began transmitting a video feed to the warship's operations room. The ship's captain turned to Ordway. But Ordway said nothing. Instead, he stared at the main screen. *This is it*, he thought. *Finally, a real test.* The captain turned back to view the unfolding spectacle. This was his first experience with the new weapon. He had been briefed, of course, but had no real idea of what to expect.

The drone's vantage point provided a perfect view. The low city was spread across the bottom of the screen. Above that, was the base of an enormous cumulonimbus that towered upwards, finally stopping with a characteristic anvil-shaped top. It was like, Ordway marvelled, the mushroom cloud from a nuclear explosion. He was struggling to contain his excitement. This was the culmination of years of research and his coordination. The recent laboratory and small-scale field tests in Alaska had been flawless. Everything was going to plan. It was working. Ordway's confidence was at an all-time high.

The nano drones now sat poised, like myiasis in an open wound, awaiting to inflict their deadly purpose. Above them, the electrical forces were mounting.

The clouds above Yasmin were now inky black interwoven with folds of browns, greys, and traces of purples. Her laundry basket was almost full. As she folded the last shirt, she suddenly stopped. The shirt fell onto the rooftop tiles. Her hands went up as a tingling sensation made the fine hairs on her arms stand up. Hairs on her head, too, had suddenly shot outwards. Her brain had just received these sensory messages when the intense flash blinded her vision, followed almost instantly by the loudest bang Yasmin had ever experienced.

She fell to the floor. The bang had developed into a series of ear-splitting cracks. Then another bang. And another. Yasmin cowered in absolute terror. *WHAT WAS HAPPENING?* her inner voice screamed. She feared the worst. They were under attack. Missiles. Deadly missiles. She looked back towards the door of her apartment. Her grandmother was sitting rigidly. Another flash lit the old woman's face. 'GRANDMA!' But her voice was drowned by the ensuing booms. Yasmin looked to her right. A bolt of lightning imprinted itself over the nearby rooftops and on her retinas. *OH MY GOD!* she thought. *A LIGHTNING STORM AND I'M ON A ROOF!* She got to her feet and scrambled across the terrace towards the door, keeping as low as she could.

Ordway had stood up. 'Holy mother of God!' he said.

Everyone in the operations room had stopped to look at the silent images, mouths open.

'My god,' was all the captain could say.

The space between the city and the base of the cloud was ablaze with light, pulsing like a stroboscope. It was hard to distinguish the individual lightning strikes, so numerous and frequent were they.

'When will it stop?' the captain finally asked and looked at Ordway.

Ordway simply shrugged. *This is frickin' awesome*, he thought. 'Zoom in!'

One of the operatives hesitated before clicking on his screen. Repeated lightning bolts could clearly be seen concentrated heavily in eight districts. Nowhere else. Individual buildings could now be made out. Those targeted were being pounded by successive, brutal-looking strikes. It was as though a divine being was unleashing an unimaginable fury.

The drone operations specialist, his role already completed, had removed his headset. He was now staring at the screen, his fingertips resting on his temples, as though about to block his ears, even though there was no sound. The images seemed surreal, and yet he knew he was now part of this man-made apocalypse.

Yasmin had reached the relative safety of her kitchen. But the lightning was incessant; the continuous deafening thunderclaps were disorientating. She stood for a moment then without a word grabbed her grandmother and helped her away from the door. They were now as deep as they could get into the apartment and were huddled together against a wall.

The onslaught then stopped with an abruptness that was almost as terrifying as the storm itself. For a moment, an eerie, deathlike quiescence seemed to smother the city, before the sounds of humanity slowly returned, dominated by screams and alarm bells.

Yasmin and her grandmother looked at one another. Yasmin began to get up.

'Stay here, Yasmin!' the old woman pleaded.

'It's OK. I think the storm is over.' Yasmin approached the open doorway and tentatively peered out and up. The cloud was still there, but it seemed lighter and more benign. It was as though the energy of the entire cloud had been discharged in just two terrifying minutes.

A large plume of smoke caught her attention. *The lightning has started a fire,* she thought. She ran to the edge of the terrace with a horrible feeling in the pit of her stomach. With the city spread out in front of her, what she saw seemed inconceivable. The beautiful Grand Mosque had been reduced to an unrecognisable, smouldering ruin.

Then the realisation hit her.

As she fell to her knees, her scream then added to the many others that day.

'NO! MY BOYS!'

Chapter 66
Threat

Central London, UK

Commander Mike Boyd entered the busy Counter Terrorism Command room and stood looking at the wall of screens. Things may move fast and he needed to know who and what they may be dealing with.

'They're on the move, sir. New Bond Street.' Claire Yates said.

'Anyone else with them?' Boyd asked the room.

Sahay Prasad answered, 'No, sir. Just the two of them.'

'Christ, I can't believe this Bakr al-Ahdal. He's either got balls of steel or just plain stupid coming back into this country. Have we IDed this other guy?'

Jonathon Simmons pulled up details onto the largest of the screens. 'You won't like this, sir.'

'Blacklisted, ay?' Boyd then read out loud more. 'Ahmed Hashim. 31 years of age. Born in Luton. Muslim. Lived there all his life. No siblings. Parents studied at Cambridge. Smart family, then. Then left to fight in Syria.' Boyd shook his head. 'Another with balls of steel. Hang on, weren't his parents the ones on tele pleading for the government to reinstate him?'

'I think you're right, sir.' Prasad said.

Simmons pulled up more data. 'Sir, NCNRLT, Europol, and Interpol all confirm he's now living in France. They have records of him leaving France on a number of occasions over the last few years.'

'Where?'

'Um…Morocco, Syria, Lebanon. It's quite a list. And get this, he's a POI to them.'

'Is he now.'

'Well, sir, he is a UK Muslim.'

'Oy!' Prasad said. 'So am I.'

'I don't make the rules, mate. Anyway, I meant a blacklisted UK Muslim. Sorry,' Simmons said with an awkward smile.

'Yes,' Boyd added. 'If he's a POI then that's why they've not arrested him. This is beginning to sound like a France-based cell. When was the TGV attack?' Boyd asked.

'November, sir,' Yates replied.

Everyone turned and looked at Boyd. 'Thinking what I'm thinking? Jon, see if you can get more from the French. See if he was in France at the time. I'm sure our French counterparts will appreciate any help we can give them.'

'Can I tell them about this, sir?' Simmons asked pointing up at the live video feeds.

'No need for the moment. Let's see how it pans out. I suspect they're on a recon.'

'You don't want us to bring them in, sir?' Yates asked. 'We can get Hashim for illegal entry.'

'Oh, believe me, I'd love to. But the powers that be want us to cast a bigger net. There's someone with money and resources behind all this, and we need to know who that is.'

'But we know Bakr and no doubt this Ahmed killed hundreds of innocent people, sir,' Prasad said.

'And two of our own,' another of the team added.

'Sorry, no can do. Orders from high,' Boyd said. 'So, how did they get in?'

'Sir, these guys flew them in under the radar, so to speak,' said Cummings, as passport images of Crambrook and Reeves were flashed onto the main display.

'Where are *they* now?'

'Down below, sir. Pearson, Jacobs, and Taylor are questioning them.'

'What's your gut, Jon?'

'No previous records, no transgressions except for Crambrook. Speeding in his Porsche. Nine points.'

Boyd looked over at Simmons. 'What is it about Porsche drivers.'

'Inverted hedgehogs, sir. Pricks are on the inside,' Yates said. Everyone laughed, even if it was an old joke.

Simmons carried on. 'Reeves has been a pilot for fourteen years. Member of a flying club. We think they're opportunists making a quick buck.'

'And probably not for the first time,' Boyd suggested.

'Right. They may have been bringing all sorts over for years. Illegals, criminals, terrorists. Checks at these small airfields are pretty lax by all accounts. NCA are looking into their bank accounts and lifestyles for us.'

'Bloody people smugglers. They're just as bad. I wonder if this Hashim character has ever used them to sneak in before. He may be one of the tube attackers we've been looking for.'

'Yeh, well, there's certainly no way al-Ahdal could enter this country any other way,' said Yates.

'I'm beginning to think this Bakr al-Ahdal is the main man,' Boyd continued. 'He was smart enough to outfox us. I think he's coordinating a cell here *and* in France. He's taking a big risk coming back, which means that whatever they're up to, it must be bloody important.'

'Or bloody big again.' The room fell silent at Simmons' stark suggestion.

Boyd walked in front of the bank of displays to address the room. 'Alright, team, we need to watch these guys like hawks. We already know what Bakr al-Ahdal is capable of. He got away, so probably thinks he can do it again. And now he has a new accomplice. I want 24-hour surveillance. I want to know where they go, who they meet, what they eat, and what time they shit. Got it?' His team all nodded. 'Call me in the middle of the night if needed. Just keep me up to date. The Home Secretary is on my back.'

'Yes, sir.' Came the unified response.

'Not staying now, sir? Simmons looked surprised.

'No Jon.' He held up a file. 'Another bloody COBR meeting. Give me a copy of that, will you,' he said nodding at the Ahmed Hashim profile.

New Bond Street, Central London

Evans and Villiers were in plain clothes. Both were walking southwards on the fashionable street; Evans on the east side, Villiers on the west.

Villiers pressed the talk button on his earphones. 'You still got them, Phil?'

'Yeh, yeh. They're about thirty metres in front of you.'

'Got 'em. What the fuck are they doing here?'

Back at CTC, Claire Yates was typing rapidly into her computer. 'Brook Street. I'm getting up the CCTV.'

Both Villiers and Evans had now lost sight of their marks. Evans started jogging. Villiers did the same.

Claire had an image on her screen. She watched and looked at the map on her other screen. 'Lancashire Court. Repeat. They've gone into Lancashire Court. Turn right onto Brook Street and cross over. It'll be right in front of you.'

Evans and Villiers reached the intersection between New Bond Street and Brook Street at the same time. Evans nodded to Villiers to go first. He then crossed over and followed a few paces behind.

'Keep talking, Claire. We don't want to lose them.' Evans said, before crossing the road.

'Sorry, guys. Blindspot.'

'Shit!' Evans muttered. Villiers had crossed the road and was standing to the side of the entrance to the narrow passageway. Evans joined him.

Villiers edged to the corner of the building and peered around the corner. Their targets were not in sight.

'OK,' Claire said. 'Lancashire Court splits after about fifteen metres. To the right, it arcs back round to Brook Street. After another forty metres, it splits again: right to Avery Row; left, back on to New Bond Street.'

'Great, three options and only two of us,' Evans said, as they both walked slowly down the passageway.

'We're getting CCTV at all those exits, guys,' Claire said.

Evans put out a hand across Villiers to slow him, although there was no need. Villiers, too, had spotted Ahmed and Bakr. They had stopped just past some café tables and were looking back at something out of sight. Evans and Villiers knew they needed to act as naturally as possible and continued to walk, pretending to chat. To their left, they could now see the gaudy colours of a lingerie shop, where a man and woman were gazing into the window. Villiers and Evans tried to weigh up the situation. Their targets had not moved, and nor had the couple. Villiers pointed to the café table in a way that could have meant it was their planned destination or an impromptu decision. Evans sat facing Bakr and Ahmed, Villiers the couple.

Villiers leant forward and mumbled quietly, 'Any movement? And what are they looking at?'

Evans continued their charade by picking up a menu. 'No, movement, but they seem to be watching that couple.'

'Or thinking about buying some kinky lingerie.'

'What if they split up? We need more guys on the ground,' Evans said, hardly moving his lips.

'Good point, Phil. We need to stick together.'

'Yeh, but fuck protocol. We may need to split.' Evans was thinking ahead. 'Let base know.'

Facing away from Bakr and Ahmed, Villiers was in the best position to use his comms. He looked intently at Evans as he spoke. Missing any sign of trouble in his colleague's eyes could be a difference between life and death. 'Have eyes on targets. What do we do if they split? Advise.'

There was a pause. Villiers made a face that told Evans he was waiting for a response. He then heard Mike Boyd's voice in his earpiece. Boyd spoke quietly. 'Both of you stay on the targets. Split up if necessary. We're getting up CCTV on all possible exits.'

Villiers looked up. A waiter had appeared next to Evans ready to take their order. It was at that moment that Villiers watched Evans simultaneously stand up and reach under his jacket. He knew instantly what was happening. Evans was drawing out his gun.

'DOWN!' Evans shouted. Villiers ducked and reached for his own gun. The couple swung around. Villiers, too. Bakr al-Ahdal was pacing towards the shop with an arm straight out, clutching a gun. The woman cried out. It was Kara. 'DANIEL! IT'S HIM!'

But Bakr had turned his head sharply on hearing Evans. He redirected the gun and fired. The waiter, who was frozen to the spot, mouth open in shock, got the bullet in the chest and was thrown backwards, crashing into the table behind. Evans had ducked but had lost balance and had fallen to the ground. Bakr turned again towards the shop. He was aware of Villiers. *Damn*! he thought, *the police are on to us.* Villiers' presence threw him; Bakr knew he would have a gun. He fired blindly at the couple. They were cowering below the window. The bullets smashed the window above them triggering an alarm and screams from the shop. Bakr turned back towards the café. Villiers was taking aim at him. Bakr ducked and ran, firing off two shots. Villiers threw himself to the ground facing the fleeing terrorist. He could see Ahmed was hovering, not sure what to do. Bakr ran past him, shouting 'RUN!' Villiers pulled the trigger three times, but his body angle was all wrong. He missed. Bakr had fled down through a short and was now out of sight.

Evans was getting to his feet. 'GET HIM!' he shouted. Villiers could see that Evan's fall had hurt him, but knew what his priority had to be. Bakr had escaped, but Ahmed was still standing metres away and probably armed. Villiers looked to his right. Ahmed Hashim was motionless. A movement to the left then made Villiers turn back. The man at the shop had got to his feet and was now running full pelt towards Ahmed. Ahmed thought about running but was too slow. Daniel was almost on top of him. Ahmed managed to pull out his knife, but Daniel grabbed his forearm and in one slick movement twisted Ahmed's body to the left then brought his knee up sharply into his right kidney. Ahmed groaned loudly. Daniel had not finished though. He was now behind Ahmed. He wrapped his free arm around his neck and yanked hard while driving his knee into the back of Ahmed's knees. As Ahmed collapsed, Daniel drove the knife into his neck. Blood spouted violently over the paving. A short, faint gurgling sound left Ahmed's lips. Daniel need not have bothered with the final blow. Ahmed was already dead. Daniel had broken his neck. He let go and stepped to the side. The body crumpled to the ground, the face splashing into the bloodied paving.

Villiers was already running. He stared in amazement at Daniel as he passed him.

Evans winced as he straightened up, then turned to the lady by the shop. She was now crouched in a tight ball, shaking.

'You OK?' he asked her. The woman's wide eyes darted to Evans. 'It's alright. We're police. You're safe now.'

But Doctor Kara Williams felt far from safe.

Bakr had emerged running from the short tunnel. Ahead was a narrow walkway lined with chairs and round tables. He pulled at them as he ran. People were already backed up against the walls. Others were running into the nearest doorway.

He had minutes, he thought, possibly only seconds.

He ran hard, soon entering Avery Row. More people, this time staring at him and then at his gun.

Villiers was picking his way through the tangle of chairs and tables. 'POLICE! MOVE!' he yelled. No one helped; they were all rooted to the spot. A woman had her back to the wall at the end of the passageway. 'WHICH WAY?' he shouted as he ran towards her. 'WHICH WAY?' he repeated. A waiter pointed to Villiers' left. 'I'm in pursuit of Bakr,' he panted. 'Ahmed is down. Evans still at the scene.'

Villiers emerged onto Avery Row. 'POLICE! WHICH WAY DID HE GO?'

The bystanders just stared at him. They were wary and certainly did not want to get involved. And understandably. He reached down inside his sweatshirt and pulled out the ID on the end of a lanyard and held it up. 'COME ON!' It worked. Several people pointed south.

Bakr felt he was in a maze. This was as foreign to him as the Tangiers Kasbah would be to an Englishman. He looked back. No sign of the police. He pocketed his gun and slowed to a walk. He was surprised that no one was looking at him. *Busy in their own pathetic little worlds*, he thought. He looked calm but his mind was racing and his heart was thumping hard. Yet again, carjacking may be his only option. To the side of the building nearest to Bakr, there was a wall of construction site hoarding with a partially open doorway. Without bothering to look around, Bakr kicked the door gently. The site ahead of him was open ground being made ready for new development. The site seemed devoid of workers. Several bags of cement were piled up near the wall. He dragged one of them up against the door.

Villiers had slowed. He started approaching pedestrians, holding up his ID and his phone with an image of Bakr on the screen. Everyone was shaking their head. 'Control, talk to me! I'm on Avery Row,' he panted.

'Avery Row southbound. He turned south.'

Villiers shook his head and swore under his breath. 'Where the fuck are you?'

Bakr heard the unmistakable sound of a helicopter. He looked around for some kind of cover and ran to a doorway, but it was locked. The tone of the helicopter's engine changed. Bakr looked up and stepped onto the narrow porch. He felt trapped and exposed.

Two police cars and more SO15 officers had joined and were in consultation with Villiers.

Bakr realised the police would soon start to cordon off the streets—no one in or out. He would have to move now. But where? The scaffolding on the adjacent building extended across its entire structure. It was also covered in opaque sheeting to keep out the elements. He spotted a ladder and began climbing.

Halfway up he saw a walkway that appeared to give him access to the road at the front of the building—covered access at that. Bakr stopped and called up a map on his phone. He quickly formulated a plan. As he made his way forwards, he spotted a hi-vis jacket, and better still, two hard hats. Bakr could not believe his luck.

Suddenly, the helicopter sound was amplified. Bakr looked up. The chopper was hovering directly over the street at the far end of the site.

He quickly continued forward along the walkway towards the front of the building, descended another set of ladders, pulled back some plastic sheeting, and scanned the street. No one was nearby. And no sign of the police. He emerged and set off west towards Hyde Park.

What was the expression? he thought. Then it came to him: *hiding in plain sight.*

Chapter 67
Interview

Central London, UK

Daniel looked across at Kara. She had not said a word since the attempt on their lives, nor would she return his look. Instead, she stared out of the SO15 SUV as it sped through the streets of London, the vehicle's bright blue lights flashing from its grill and bumpers.

Evans was in the front passenger seat. He had his own rear mirror and was looking intently at Daniel.

'I need to make a call,' Daniel suddenly announced.

Evans turned to face him. 'You'll have plenty of time for that.' He turned to Kara. 'Are you alright, Miss?'

Kara simply nodded but continued to look at the countless pedestrians going about their normal lives. Her mind was swimming. The excitement of her experiment in Venezuela all seemed like a lifetime ago. She longed to return to that life and her fellow scientists. The feeling of betrayal was also there; her own government using her for ulterior and deadly purposes. And that snake, Ordway. And the weapon, the conspiracy behind it. Should she come clean and reveal what is undoubtedly a highly secret development? *Stay quiet,* she told herself. *Deny any connection. Don't mention the fact that the one who tried to kill them had been in Daniel's villa.* Then her thoughts turned to Daniel. *Do I love him? Yes, of course, I do.* She had finally met a man who understood her. But now this. *Who was he?* She realised he was a dark horse. But this! And yet, he had done what he did to save them. He had saved *her* life. She stole him a glance, but Daniel was holding his phone typing a message.

The SUV swung into a compound of vehicles surrounded by a high wall. Evans and the driver got out and opened the rear doors. Daniel looked up at their destination—a drab, multi-story building.

When they entered the windowless meeting room with its single long table, they were surprised to see it full of police officers. Neither of them realised those present were in SO15, the Metropolitan Police unit specialising in counter-terrorism. None of the officers wore IDs. On the wall at one end was a single large, blank computer display. Daniel and Kara took their places. Two cups of tea had been placed in front of them.

'I understand that you are both unharmed and fit to be questioned,' said Commander Boyd. Daniel acknowledged him with a nod then cast a look at the others present. Kara did not. She just reached forward and took a sip of the tea.

Unnamed photographs of Bakr al-Ahdal and Ahmed Hashim appeared on the screen. Boyd directed his first question at Daniel. 'What is your connection with these men?'

Daniel looked at the screen. He was quick with his reply. 'We have never seen them before,' he said and looked back at Boyd. Kara remained focussed on her cup of tea. She knew that Daniel would handle it better.

Boyd was not satisfied. He wanted to hear Kara's reply. 'Dr Williams?'

'No, I've never seen them before,' she replied shaking her head. *Thank goodness they weren't being interviewed separately*, she thought. She could not be certain she could lie like Daniel seemed to do so easily. *Keep it simple*, she thought.

Boyd continued with Kara. 'I see you're a meteorologist.'

'Yes.'

'Why are you in the UK with Dr Bayford?'

Daniel replied for her, 'We're on our way to South America. I'm joining Dr Williams to help with her experiment.'

'The question was clearly for Dr Williams.' Boyd was irritated. He already had background on Daniel and, of course, intel on his latest actions. He recognised in him a man capable of fending off awkward questions. Daniel held up an apologetic hand.

Kara finally looked up. Daniel's strategy was the same as hers. Time to build their story. They were amongst police officers dealing with a gun attack. There was no reason why they would have joined the dots between the meteorite discovery, and the recent martyrdoms, let alone the Spear of Destiny. 'That's right,' she replied. 'Meteorology was also Daniel's specialty. His expertise has proven to be invaluable in advancing my research. He's joining me in...' Kara hesitated before continuing, 'to help complete my project. He wanted to come via London. I fancied doing some shopping.'

Some of the officers in the room smirked. The draft report they had seen described how the interviewees were standing outside a lingerie shop.

Boyd looked down at his notes. 'But you worked for the British government, Dr Bayford, decades ago.'

'True. But that doesn't mean my expertise goes away.'

'It was a chance discovery,' said Kara. 'These things happen in science.'

One of the officers swung his laptop around in front of Boyd. Boyd nodded. The screen then displayed a news article with an inset picture of Daniel. 'Is this the chance discovery?' Boyd asked.

Daniel smiled. 'Yeh, my fifteen minutes of fame.'

'And this is related to your research, Dr Williams?'

'Yes,' she said.

'Research into…?'

'I'm not at liberty to divulge any details. Sorry.'

Boyd looked at his two interviewees for several seconds. He did not like Kara's last answer. What was a scientist doing that she could not divulge? He conferred quietly with two of the officers next to him. The images of Bakr al-Ahdal and Ahmed Hashim reappeared on the screen.

'Let me tell you something about the two men that attacked you, Dr Williams. The one on the left is a known terrorist. He was involved in last year's tube attack; the other, by association, *was* a suspected terrorist.'

Kara's mouth dropped open. This was news to her and Daniel. They may have previously encountered the one that escaped, and the same man may have been involved in the Cannes martyrdom. But they had no idea of his involvement with the tube attack.

Boyd saw her reaction. It was genuine. But he wanted clarification in order to draw a line under his current line of enquiry. 'So, Doctor, what can't you divulge about your work? And I would remind you to keep quiet, Dr Bayford.'

Kara had already considered her answer and spoke calmly. 'All of my team have signed NDAs. We're working on something from which a multitude of patent-pending products and technologies may arise.'

'I see. So, you don't want to be sued.'

'Or lose my job.' Although knowing her experiment had been pulled, the renewed anger and frustration within her were helping.

Boyd seemed satisfied—with Kara at least.

Boyd, having returned his attention to Daniel, began again. 'My officer here has described how you not only overpowered the assailant but broke his neck and stabbed him with the assailant's own knife. You used methods, my officer said, that indicated signs of professional combat training.'

Daniel smiled. 'No, I was trained in karate,' Daniel stated bluntly.

Boyd was unconvinced. 'When was that?'

'After I left the government department.'

'Ah yes, that would be the time you became…' Boyd referred to his notes again, '…an eco-warrior.'

The other officers in the room looked at Daniel mostly with a sense of admiration. As far as they were concerned, he was a bloody hero.

'Yeh, around that time. I'd received a number of threats when I was working as a scientist. Some misinformed nutters thought I was responsible for the actions I later felt compelled to fight against. Self-defence lessons made sense.'

It was a good answer.

Boyd nodded 'Well, you clearly got your money's worth.'

The reaction around the room indicated strong agreement.

Was this officer buying all this? Kara thought. A new image appeared on the screen. Daniel recognised it immediately; Kara, too. It was one of the pictures she had found at the villa when researching Daniel's past.

'Quite a rebel, weren't you, Dr Bayford,' Boyd said. The screen showed an oil rig with huge flames engulfing one half of it. Daniel looked back at Boyd and wondered if it was sarcasm, or this police officer's way of saying he suspected him of more than a story about meteorology.

'I have no regrets. Our actions were justified and widely applauded.'

The meeting room door then opened and an officer stepped in. She whispered in Boyd's ear. Boyd stood up and made a signal for the other officers to carry on in his absence.

Evans was sitting directly opposite Daniel. He asked, 'As you know. I was one of the officers at the scene today.' Daniel nodded. 'Why do you think these men attacked you?'

It was a question Daniel had been expecting. Like Kara, he had already decided to plead ignorance. 'I have no idea. It must have been a random attack.'

'Come on Doctor. This doesn't fit the profile of people like this. Central London, a gun attack? To me, it looked more like an assassination attempt.'

'Would you say that the tube attack or the TGV attack followed the profile of your average terrorist?' Daniel asked.

'True. But doesn't that then support my assassination theory?' Evans asked, pleased that he may have outsmarted a doctor on a point of logic.

'But what's their motive?'

'That's precisely what we'd like to know.'

'Assuming they had targeted us in the first place.' Daniel countered. '*My* theory is that they saw you and your colleague and perhaps assumed we were also officers.'

Evans knew that scenario was very plausible. After all, it was he and Villiers that had first encountered Bakr up close on the Embankment. It was quite possible they had been recognised. He decided to press on. 'Your reaction time and combative skills were very impressive.'

Daniel looked at Evans as if to say, *And, what's your point?* 'Look,' he said, now raising his voice a notch, 'I reacted. I was afraid, yes, but also angry. I've just met a woman I love,' he turned to Kara and put an arm around her. 'I would truly die for her. My training just kicked in along with a ton of adrenalin. OK?'

A mixture of relief, delayed shock, and love for Daniel flooded Kara. She burst into tears. 'I'm sorry,' she said and fumbled with her teacup.

The SO15 officers looked at each other awkwardly. One of them felt sorry for her. 'Would you like more tea?'

'No, thank you. I'll be fine.'

Evans had not expected the love connection. It threw him. 'I'm sorry, Dr Williams, Dr Bayford. Please understand where we're coming from. We lost one of the assailants after the tube attack. We may have lost him again. He's a lethal individual. We need to be sure we're covering every angle. You have to admit that given the attacks these terrorists have committed, today's incident is very unusual.'

'I understand,' Daniel said calmly. 'But again, your analysis assumes we were *not* seen as police officers, and we *cannot* think of any reason why they would want to attack us, let alone kill us. I'm sorry we couldn't be more help.'

'Between us, and off the record, you helped a great deal, Doctor. We now have one less terrorist to worry about.'

'For the record,' Daniel said, 'I had no idea they were terrorists. I acted on impulse.'

'Noted.' Evans said and stood up. The other officers followed suit. Evans saw that Kara was upset. A break would help. 'We will need you to remain in the country until further notice,' he added.

'Really?' Kara asked.

'Are you charging me?' Daniel suddenly lost his earlier composure.

'No. But we have to follow procedure.'

'Are we being held here?' Kara asked.

'For a short while, yes. We'll then drive you to your hotel.'

After the room emptied of officers, Kara turned to Daniel and put her arms around him. 'Thank you,' she said quietly.

'For what?'

'For saving my life…I love you.'

'I'm so happy you're OK, Kara. But I'm sorry I got you into all this.'

Down the corridor in the main operations room, Boyd was perched on the edge of a desk. The team had assembled around him, including Pearson, Jacobs, and Taylor. 'I've just had a message from 6,' Boyd announced. 'They want us to let them go.'

'What?' Evans was lost for words.

'What the hell have MI6 got to do with this?' Jacobs asked.

'It's Bayford. There's something about him.' Evans said.

'I agree,' said Boyd. 'But they're not terrorists and we, if I need to remind you, are counter-terrorism. So let it go and go find a terrorist. Find that fuckin' Bakr!'

The meeting room door opened. Boyd leant in. 'We'll take you to your hotel now.' Kara and Daniel stood up. 'Seems you have friends in high places, Dr Bayford.'

Daniel feigned confusion. 'I'm sorry?'

'You can both carry on with your plans. Fly to South America or whatever you need to do.'

In the rear of the SO15 car, Kara and Daniel stayed quiet. It was approaching 7 p.m. After a few minutes, Daniel held his phone for Kara to see. It showed a text conversation:

Re Lancashire Court. Need your help, urgently! 16:38

On it. 16:42

Kara looked at the top of the screen where she saw the name of Daniel's MI6 contact: Seb.

Chapter 68
The Block

M1 Motorway, England, UK

Bakr knew he would have to lie low. A contact he had in Birmingham suggested he stay there.

It was four days after the failed assassination, and now well over a year since the tube attack. He had evaded capture not once but twice. The police had failed again. At least so far. And they had also failed in tracking down the surviving members of his team. Bakr was pleased with that fact; his careful planning had paid off. But he bitterly regretted Mohammed's stupidity in using the Underground. Of all his team, he should have known to avoid the plethora of cameras around stations. Still, one loss out of five was good.

He had managed to reach Abdul and Bekkali in more recent months. Miraculously, they had returned to their home countries of Morocco and Lebanon. Jamal, a fellow Syrian, however, had been convinced by Bakr to stay in the UK. But he was desperate to leave. Months alone in a grimy North London flat was getting too much for him. Jamal did not have to work. Enough money arrived in his bank account each month for him to afford essentials, a car, and to take a driving test. But he was bored and frustrated. When the offer to drive Bakr to Birmingham came, he jumped at the opportunity.

Bakr was fiddling with the car's air vents. He was surprised by how warm England could get in September. Jamal was at the wheel. The grey Kia was crawling northbound along yet another average speed check section of the M1 motorway.

'Here, 'Jamal said, 'let me turn on the AC.'

Cool air wafted across Bakr's face. He closed his eyes and leant his head back. 'Are you still getting the money transfers?' he asked.

'Yes, Bakr. Thank you.'

'Don't thank me. Thank our great benefactor and guide.'

Jamal turned quickly to look at Bakr. 'Bakr, I want to return home. I'm doing nothing here. Why am I being kept here?'

Bakr sat up and opened his eyes again. 'Jamal, you helped us bring this decadent country to its knees. Be patient. There will be more opportunities.'

'Why can't I have one of the martyr stones? I want to die a martyr like our brothers.'

'No.' But Bakr could not give a reason why.

Jamal fell silent.

The cars ahead suddenly thinned. They had left the average speed check zone. *How can so many cars seem to disappear so quickly?* Jamal thought as he indicated to overtake a black BMW.

'Don't speed,' Bakr said.

Jamal looked at the speedometer. '68 mph. That's OK,' he said.

The BMW passenger watched the Kia pass and clicked on his radio. 'Hotel Sierra Zero One.'

'*Sierra Zero One, go ahead,*' came the response.

'Can I have a vehicle check, please? Grey Kia. Reg plate LP4...' the police officer began.

'The martyrdoms have shaken the world, yes?' Jamal said smiling.

'They have. It is a great thing our leader has brought about.'

'You met him, correct? What's he like?'

'I cannot tell you. Anything I say, any small detail may reveal his identity. I have sworn to remain silent.'

'I understand.'

'Can you ask him for me? About a stone, I mean.'

Bakr looked at Jamal. As he did so he noticed that a black car had pulled level with them in the second lane. Bakr looked at the passenger. It was a police officer in an unmarked car. He was indicating for them to pull over.

'Jamal! It's the police!'

Jamal turned to look. 'Shit! Does he want us to stop?'

'I don't know. I think so.'

The police car accelerated and pulled in front of them. The blue lights lit up.

'Shit. I'll have to stop.'

They were approaching an exit. The police car stayed in front and indicated, slowing all the time. Jamal slowed with it. On the exit ramp, the police car pulled onto the hard shoulder; Jamal followed. The cars came to a stop.

'We weren't speeding, were we?' Bakr asked, watching an officer exit from the driver's side. His colleague had remained in the vehicle.

'No, definitely not.'

'Lights?'

'What?'

'Do all your lights work?'

Before Jamal could answer, the officer had reached his window.

'Good afternoon, sir,' said the officer.

'Hello.'

'Switch the engine off, please.'

'Yes, sure.'

The officer took a look along the length of the car and through the rear window. He returned to address Jamal. 'Is this your vehicle, sir?'

'Yes, it is.'

'May I see your driver's licence?'

'Yes, of course.' Jamal fumbled in the centre console for his wallet and passed his licence over.

'It's a lovely day today,' the officer said.

'I'm sorry?'

'I said, it's a lovely day today.'

'Ah yes. Very warm.'

'A nice day for a drive,' the officer carried on. 'Where are you heading?'

'Heading?'

'Where—are—you—going? The officer asked again, spacing out the words and speaking a little louder.

'Oh, sorry. The noise of cars. I couldn't hear. We go to Birmingham.'

'We *are going* to Birmingham, are we,' the officer corrected, mockingly. 'A new driver, I see.'

'Yes. Is there something wrong?'

'I'm afraid there is. I can see that the car is registered in your name. But you don't seem to be insured Mr...Ibrahim. That's a very serious offence.' The officer bent down to look at Bakr. Bakr looked straight ahead then out of his window. He did not want the officer to get a full view of his face. The officer handed Jamal's licence back to him. 'Wait there.' The officer was returning to the unmarked BMW.

'Go!' Bakr said suddenly.

Jamal looked over at him. 'Go? Are you crazy?'

'GO! NOW!'

But Jamal hesitated. The officer was leaning into his window, clearly talking to his colleague. Then the other officer's door opened and both were now heading towards them.

'Shit!' Jamal said and gunned the engine to life. He selected first gear and floored it, swerving violently past the first officer. A car horn blasted. Jamal had nearly crashed into a car coming up the slip road. 'Shit!' They reached the top of the exit road. There was a small roundabout. No left exit, only one back onto the motorway and a second across the motorway bridge.

'Take the motorway!' Bakr ordered.

Jamal swung the car around the island and took the first exit. It was downhill. The car accelerated. 'They will catch us!' Jamal's breathing was fast and loud. Bakr remained calm and turned to see where the police car was. Just as they merged back onto the motorway the police car appeared at the top of the slip road, lights ablaze; siren whooping. Jamal pressed his foot down harder. He was in the fast lane. The road was relatively clear. *Thank Allah*, he thought. He switched on his main beam. A car upfront had started to pull onto the fast lane in front of him, but quickly swerved back when he saw Jamal's lights bearing down.

'Keep going!' Bakr instructed calmly.

Jamal was sweating badly. He was gripping the steering wheel with both hands. He glanced at the speedometer. 95, 98, 105.

The police were still there.

The highways traffic officer passenger in the pursuit car was doing the talking. 'Hotel Sierra Zero One in pursuit. Vehicle now exceeding one hundred miles per hour. Approaching M6 interchange. Repeat M6 interchange. Stand by.'

The control operator came back, *'Roger that Sierra Zero One.'*

Jamal took the M6 turning. He almost laughed at himself for following his planned route. But when checking the traffic situation on his phone app earlier, he also remembered that this part of the motorway was relatively quiet.

The police comms continued. 'Yeh, now exiting onto the M6. How we doing for more uniform? Over.'

'Sierra Zero One be advised that we have two crime vehicles six miles in front of you. We're coordinating with them now for an enforced stop. Over.'

Traffic was sparse, thankfully. But the driver of the pursuit vehicle was fully focussed. 'Any luck with that mugshot, Dan?' he asked his colleague.

'Hello, boys. This is Echo Bravo One Four. We're in the next patrol area. What's your speed?'

'Still over a ton.'

The road was straight. Dan had brought up an image. It was of Bakr. The pursuit driver glanced at the display. 'Is that the best we have?'

'Yeh, taken from a CCTV.'

The driver looked again. 'I don't know, Dan. I didn't see him front-on. But it could be him.'

'Good enough for me. Jesus! Mate, if it *is* him! This is Hotel Sierra Zero One, possible ID match on Bakr al-Ahdal. Repeat Bakr al-Ahdal.'

'Er, roger that Sierra Zero One. Standby.'

'Keep it steady, Ryan.'

'Yeh, yeh. I'm cool,' the driver said.

Jamal glanced at his petrol gauge. *Plenty*, he thought. 'Why aren't they trying to stop us?'

Bakr turned to look through the rear window. He then reached into the back and pulled a holdall onto his lap.

Jamal looked over quickly. 'What are you doing?'

Bakr remained silent. He had unzipped the bag and was now pulling out a handgun. He checked its chamber, then returned it to the bag, which he placed at his feet.

'Bakr, no!' Jamal said. Bakr remained silent and looked straight ahead. His cheek muscles were pulsing.

The police response was building rapidly. *'All units. Be advised, we're putting the block on. ARVs are en route.'*

ARVs were armed response vehicles. The UK police had decades of experience. With terrorists, it was a whole other level of intensity.

'This is getting pretty serious,' Ryan said. 'You must have a sixth sense.'

'Call me Columbo,' Dan quipped.

'There's one of ours,' Ryan said.

A dark grey Jaguar was moving across towards the outside lane. '*Echo Bravo One Four to Hotel Sierra Zero One, we'll come up behind you. Over.*'

'*Roger that Echo Bravo One Four.*'

The pursuit driver glanced in his rear mirror. Sure enough, the Jaguar had joined the high-speed chase in the fast lane.

'Do we have a sterile area?' Dan asked over the radio. The cars were fast approaching junction 2. 'Stay alert, mate,' he said calmly to Ryan.

'I got this,' his driver replied. 'Whoa!' He slowed rapidly. A car had pulled out in front of him to overtake a high-sided truck.

'I've lost visual,' Dan said, craning his neck. 'Come on, move, there's a good fella. And…thank you. My god, some drivers. Blind and deaf.'

The car in front had completed its manoeuvre and had cleared the way. Ryan floored it.

'There! Three cars ahead,' Dan said.

'Yeh got him.'

The cars flashed by the exit.

'Hotel Sierra Zero One. We've passed junction 2. Target car speed ninety-eight.'

'*All units. Three TPACs are four miles ahead. Enforced stop before junction 3A. Repeat, RVP will be before 3A. Traffic is light. We're locking down east and westbound carriageways on either side. Pursuit is authorised. Tactics authorised.*'

'OK, there'll be five of us. How long do we have?' Ryan asked.

'Two, two and half minutes, tops.'

Jamal looked in his rear mirror. 'There's another one behind. What should I do?'

Just a few miles ahead the police were now positioning cars up ahead ready to block the target car. The two cars following Bakr and Jamal would block from behind, essentially boxing them in. Vehicles approaching the motorway at the next junctions were being prevented from entering the motorway in either direction. A helicopter had also been deployed and was now tracking the target car.

'Let's hope he stays in the fast lane,' Ryan said, knowing that boxing in the target car would be easier, although very dangerous.

'Here we go,' said Dan.

Up ahead he had spotted two of the three marked police cars, all blue lights ablaze. They were already motoring, but holding back, waiting for the target car to reach them. One was in the slow lane, the other in the third. They then accelerated to match the speed of the target car.

Jamal could not fail to notice them. He then saw the third of the new cars in the fast lane. 'They're going to block us in!'

Bakr was transfixed. The blue lights ahead were almost hypnotic. And it was hard to think travelling at this speed and so close to the concrete barrier that split the two carriageways.

Jamal began to move across to the third lane. The car head then moved to straddle lanes three and four. The car behind Ryan and Dan moved across and forward. There were now five crime cars creating a semi-circle.

It was working. The lead car was slowing. Jamal was now travelling at 92 mph. The rear of the police car up front only feet from his bonnet.

'RAM HIM!' Bakr shouted.

Jamal was now terrified. The brake lights on the police car in front went on. Jamal's natural reaction was to brake, and he did. Once, twice…and again.

Their speed dropped rapidly. 85, 77…

The controlled slowdown continued. At 38 mph, the lead car braked hard. Jamal crunched into it. 32…24… The action was repeated, several times in quick succession. It was enough. They had stopped and were penned in.

Three ARVs appeared from nowhere, one on the opposite carriageway. A dozen Authorised Firearms Officers were surrounding the vehicle, assault rifles aimed from all directions at its occupants.

Jamal had raised his hands. He was shit scared. Bakr was looking down. The bag was between his legs.

'OPEN THE DOOR, GET OUT SLOWLY WITH YOUR HANDS ON YOUR HEAD!' The officer outside Bakr's window shouted.

Jamal looked at the armed police officer to his right.

'PUT YOUR HANDS ON THE STEERING WHEEL WHERE I CAN SEE THEM!'

The AFO officer was standing on the other carriageway, his gun pointing directly at Jamal's head. The officer could see that Jamal's door was jammed up against the concrete barrier.

Again, Jamal obliged. 'PLEASE, DON'T SHOOT!'

Bakr looked up and straight ahead. This was it. He could die a martyr, or he could fight again. *Somehow*, he thought.

The officer reached forward, pulled Bakr's door open, and quickly resumed his grip on the assault rifle. He then spotted the bag. Instinctively, he took a step back. He desperately tried to see if Bakr was holding a trigger. He was not. One of his colleagues had spotted it, too. They both shouted at Bakr.

'GET OUT SLOWLY WITH YOUR HANDS ON YOUR HEAD!'
'HANDS ON YOUR HEAD! SLOWLY!'

Bakr climbed out. The two officers continued with their loud, intimidating commands, designed to disorientate:

'ON THE GROUND! GET ON YOUR KNEES! KEEP YOUR HANDS ON YOUR HEAD!'

The officer overlooking the motorway barrier remained with his gun angled down at Jamal's head. A fourth AFO was now leaning in through the passenger door, his gun held firmly in both hands and pointing at Jamal. He released his left hand quickly and carefully prised the unzipped bag open. The gun was lying on top of what looked like clothing. 'THERE'S A FIREARM IN THE BAG.'

The officers with Bakr had already tied his hands. Bakr's identity had been confirmed. He was forcibly pushed to the ground face down and frisked. No gentle policing was necessary here.

'CLEAN,' the officer called out.

'Requesting Expos,' his colleague said over the radio.

There was a high chance the bag contained explosives. There could be more in the boot. Explosive officers, nicknamed Expos, would be needed for sure.

The officer facing Jamal could see that he was cooperating. But how would he get him out across over the passenger seat? The bag and the gun were still there. Moving the bag was out of the question.

'PLEASE DON'T SHOOT, I'M JUST A DRIVER.' Jamal had to shout. His window was shut.

'LISTEN TO ME,' the officer shouted as calmly as possible, 'I WANT YOU TO STAY EXACTLY WHERE YOU ARE. KEEP YOUR HANDS ON THE WHEEL. DO YOU UNDERSTAND?' Jama nodded. 'WHAT IS IN THE BAG?'

'I... I DON'T KNOW. IT'S HIS.' Jamal lied nodding towards Bakr. He then turned to his right. The officer's gun was still pointing at his face inches from the window.

The officer withdrew himself from the car. Knowing that Jamal was covered, he began discussing tactics with his fellow officers. Radio chatter was continuous.

'*Expo ETA 8 minutes.*'

'Passenger now decamped and restrained. Driver still on board,' an officer reported over the radio.

Bakr was being led to one of the ARVs. Jamal felt very alone. He tried to think rationally. Did they have anything on him? Bakr was known to them. He knew that much. *I can deny everything*, he thought. *They would have arrested me before now. I can say I'm a hired driver...But how would Bakr have contacted me? I'm not a licensed taxi driver. They will ask so many questions...* Jamal's heading was spinning. He would need to build a credible story.

Two new thoughts—stronger than the rest—then entered his mind...*Why have I been ignored for so long? Why was I not chosen for the Tower Bridge martyrdom?*

Suddenly, it all became clear. Jamal looked down at the bag. *I could die a martyr here. And I can kill one maybe two first. Yes!*

He looked to his left. The officer who had just spoken to him had his back turned. The one to his right still had his gun angled down at him. *If I move quickly...*

Jamal rehearsed his next move in his head just once: *Shoot the officer to the right, turn, and shoot the others.* It was now or never. He dived to his left and plunged his hand into the bag. He had the gun. The AFO at his window responded instantly. Jamal did not feel much except the briefest of sensations, as though his head had been struck by a hammer. There was no pain, no sound. Just black. Eternal blackness.

354

Bakr had stopped and turned at the sound of the gunshot and a dull crunch of breaking glass. He could see their car, but could not see Jamal. He did not need to.

Chapter 69
The Restaurant

Central London, UK

'It's Michelin starred. French cuisine,' Daniel whispered, as he and Kara were led to their table.

With its exposed roof beams and arched windows high above their heads it was like being in a church—but one filled with excitable chatter, and the gentle clatter of cutlery on china. Huge potted palm trees helped further dispel the ecclesiastical illusion. Daniel smiled; men and women were turning their heads to take in Kara in her red, figure-hugging halter dress.

'Wow!' she whispered, oblivious of her admirers.

Daniel leant towards her ear. 'Not as wow as you. You look stunning.'

Sebastian Sadler-Smith had stood up as they approached the table. 'Kara, you look ravishing,' he said kissing her on the hand. 'Daniel, you look…like a lucky bastard.'

'I hope this is on you, Seb,' Daniel said, looking around.

'Relax, Daniel. These people are paying,' Sadler-Smith said in his trademark loud whisper, casting an arm around at the fellow diners. They took their seats.

'Witness, Kara,' Daniel announced, 'an unashamed public servant, happy to revel in a free Michelin-star meal paid by the proletariat.'

Sadler-Smith shook his head and turned to Kara, 'Are you sure you want to be associating yourself with this lefty, my dear?'

'Are you going to ask if Kara is alright?' Daniel was already finding his friend's breezy chatter inappropriate and somewhat irritating.

'I'm sorry. How *are* you, Kara?'

Kara looked up at him and then at Daniel. So much had occurred. Sitting here in these lavish and vaguely foreign surroundings made the recent events seem like a dream. Daniel had seemed so perfect, she thought. *But such a dark horse and lethal!* Should she forget all this and go home? Her head was in turmoil with conflicting emotions. 'Er, well, I'm OK, I guess,' was all she could muster. She suddenly wanted to burst into tears. 'Please excuse me. I just need to powder my nose.'

The two men rose to their feet.

'The ladies are through there,' Sadler-Smith said.

Sadler-Smith reached for the bottle from the wine chiller bucket and poured a glass for Daniel then hovered the bottle over Kara's. Daniel nodded. 'It was a nasty business, Daniel. I saw the reports. And you, the hero of the hour. Jesus, Daniel! A knife in the fuckin' throat?'

'Yeh. But don't bring it up in front of Kara. She's badly shaken. I think you can tell. So, any luck?'

Sadler-Smith gave Daniel a look as if to say, *what, you doubted me?* 'Of course.' He reached inside his jacket and handed Daniel a folded piece of paper.

Daniel unfolded it and read. 'That's quite a list. How on earth...'

'Dark web,' he said under his breath. 'It has its uses.' Daniel looked up. 'Don't look so surprised.' Sadler-Smith leant forward. 'There are thoroughly venal people out there willing to sell their very souls for a more comfortable financial situation. Anyway, asking them to sell their country's secrets is piss easy. We just found a particular military individual in a tight situation. The rest...well, you know.'

'No, I don't think I *do* know.'

'There are people, hackers, you know. We just ask them to ply their trade, delve here, delve there. Anyway, it's not that hot,' he said, pointing at the paper. 'It's a series of flight manifests; not how to build a WMD.'

Daniel studied his old friend. *If only you knew what this was about*, he thought. 'There's more, right?'

'Well...' Sadler-Smith rocked his head back and forth as though weighing something up in his mind. 'May I?' he asked, reaching for the paper. He scanned the list and pointed to one of the entries. 'This,' he continued, 'is a secret installation in Alaska. He visits it again the following month...here.' Sadler-Smith pointed to another entry. 'Fast forward to this month and he's on a warship in the Gulf of Oman. He certainly gets around does this Ordway fella.'

Kara returned to the table and a waiter helped with her chair. 'Are you ready to order, madam, gentlemen?'

Daniel reached over and put a hand on Kara's arm. 'Are you OK?' he asked. She nodded and smiled back.

The men both waited for Kara. 'I think something light for me. And just a main, please.'

'Madam,' said the waiter, 'may I suggest the grilled fillets of red mullet with shellfish Provençal, saffron potatoes, and bouillabaisse sauce?'

'Yes, that sounds perfect. Thank you.' Kara took a large gulp of wine.

'You were saying, Seb,' Daniel prompted and handed Sadler-Smith's list to Kara.

'Ah yes, the Gulf of Oman.' He took out his phone and made a series of taps with his index finger. 'You saw this, no doubt?' He slid the phone across the white damask tablecloth. 'Happened two days ago.'

'No,' said Daniel, glancing at the screen. 'What happened? We've seen zero news these last few days.'

'That's true. You were bloody making it.' Sadler-Smith laughed. But the laugh soon faded when he saw Daniel's look. 'This is a city in central Iran. Local reports describe it as the worst electrical storm in living memory.'

Kara and Daniel exchanged looks—an exchange that did not go unnoticed by their host. They then studied the still image in more detail. Half of a domed roof lay at an angle, surrounded by blackened rubble, from which thin columns of smoke were spiralling straight up. A group of people, their backs to the camera, were staring at the devastation. Behind them, a minaret, damaged but still standing.

'What! You're saying an electrical storm did this to a complete building?' Daniel asked.

'A mosque,' Kara corrected.

Sadler-Smith turned to Kara. 'Exactly, Kara. A mosque. One tabloid had the insensitivity to use the phrase "Act of God." Talk about incitement to riot.'

'Maybe it was. Maybe it was a freak of nature, combined with structural weakness,' Daniel said as earnestly as possible but fearing the worst.

Sadler-Smith snorted. 'Come on guys,' he said in hushed tones, turning to check that the nearest table was well out of earshot. 'You ask me to track this Defence Department guy. He goes from a secret military base in Alaska god knows how many thousands of miles to a warship operating a relative stone's throw from this.'

'What, you suspect this was some kind of strike?' Daniel asked. Kara realised he was trying to extract as much information from his friend as possible before volunteering what they knew. If, indeed, Daniel considered it a good idea to do so. She would leave that decision to him.

'Well, my friend, from what we can tell, at least five other buildings suffered the same consequences. It all looks very much like a targeted strike. And to be fair, I wouldn't have given this a second look had it not been for your suspicion about Ordway and his rather convenient and suspicious itinerary.'

'If it was a strike, as you call it,' Kara began, 'then surely your satellite surveillance, or whatever you use, would show a missile launch from this warship.'

'Excellent point, Kara,' Sadler-Smith said. 'We don't have any data to support that. But that's not to say it didn't happen. We may have just missed it. Unless we're talking about something…new. Below the radar, so to speak. And I strongly suspect that's where you two come in. So, Daniel, Kara, I think it's fair that you share your intel with me. All of it. You owe me now. Big time.'

'We do,' Kara said. 'Thank you for helping us. Daniel showed me his message to you after our release.'

Sadler-Smith pursed his lips in a half smile and held out the open palms of his hands. *Pulling rank over the Met Police was the easy bit*, he thought. *I want to know more about Ordway and what the Land of the Free is up to.*

Daniel had his elbows on the table and was resting his chin on his hands, his gaze firmly on Kara. It made sense for her to do the talking.

'As you know, Seb, I'm involved in…' Kara stopped. 'I can't do this,' she stuttered. 'I'm sorry.'

'Do you need a moment?' Sadler-Smith asked as gently as possible. 'Actually, I could do with visiting the little boys' room anyway. All this bloody wine at my age. Goes right through me.

Daniel watched him disappear. 'What's wrong?'

'I don't know what I was thinking. Our countries may have a "special relationship",' Kara said, making quote signs with her fingers. 'But I'm a US citizen about to share god knows what information with a British spy.'

'Hey, to be fair to Seb, he's done the same in reverse. And, as I said, he's not technically a spy.'

'That may be. But he…' Kara had to check herself after realising her voice was a little loud. 'He does this shit for a living.'

'Fair enough. You're right. Why don't I tell him alone?'

'Tell him what, though? That we *think* Ordway had your stone taken. We *think* they somehow replicated it. We *think* they may have developed a drone-based stealth weapon. That was just a quick theory I had.'

'We saw the evidence with that New York martyr.'

'Yes, but not a direct connection with this unknown weapon.'

'No, Kara, you're forgetting the priest. What did he say again? God-like power. Kara, this incident Seb has just shown us—it looks like a perfect fit.'

Kara massaged her brow. Even stressed she looked gorgeous, Daniel thought. 'OK, so these Guild of God zealots have fashioned a doomsday weapon capable of this. What would a British spy do other than share the intel with his own government? Wait, you feel bad, cos he got us out of a tricky situation.'

'You can say that again. I *killed* that guy,' Daniel said, hardly moving his lips. Kara fell silent. The memory of those moments flooded back. She looked around the restaurant and wondered if anyone was watching them. 'And don't forget what you told me about Ordway taking you and your team for a ride,' he added. 'Hang on, he's on his way back. What do you want to do?'

'If this Guild of God thing is true then I guess we have an obligation to share what we know. But can you do it, please?'

'Of course.'

Kara leant towards Daniel to mutter her next words: 'Let's just hope your friend isn't one of its crusading knights.'

The thought had not even entered Daniel's head. He frowned and looked into Kara's eyes. Then shook his head.

'So,' said Sadler-Smith, arriving back at the table.

'Kara's still upset after, you know…Can you and I meet somewhere tomorrow?'

Sadler-Smith puffed his cheeks. 'Sure. It'll have to be at SIS, though.' He was referring to the famous Secret Intelligence Service building, the headquarters of MI6, overlooking the Thames.

'Hey, nothing heavy, Seb.'

Sadler-Smith crossed his heart with his hand. Daniel smiled. *God, I haven't seen anyone do that since primary school*, he thought.

Two waiters arrived and presented their dishes with a smooth flourish before one provided a detailed explanation of what was in front of them.

'*Bon Appetit*!' their host said in his usual bombastic way.

Chapter 70
SIS

'Here we are.' Sadler-Smith opened the meeting room door deep inside the iconic Secret Intelligence Service headquarters, otherwise known as the MI6 Building, a blend of 1930s industrial modernist meets Aztec temple. Inside its walls, and beyond the heaviest security Kara and Daniel had ever encountered, it felt disappointingly corporate.

Kara had insisted on attending. She and Daniel followed Sadler-Smith into the windowless room.

'Sir, Dr Kara Williams, and Dr Daniel Bayford,' Sadler-Smith announced.

George Bradbury stood up from the head of the table. 'I'm George. How do you do? Very good to meet you,' he said walking up to the couple and shaking their hands.

Daniel gave Seb a look, but his friend appeared to be ignoring him and was taking his seat. Daniel knew who Bradbury was. He had been the main man for years, including the time when Seb had encouraged him to join their ranks. Two other MI6 staff, laptops opened in front of them, were sitting at the table. Faced with a room full of suits, Kara felt a little underdressed in her jeans and dark blue blazer. Daniel was undeterred. In fact, he was slightly annoyed.

'I thought this was going to be a low-key chat, Seb,' he said.

Sadler-Smith gave an awkward smile but remained silent.

'Please,' Bradbury said, indicating their seats. 'Dr Williams, as a US citizen you are not required to contribute to this discussion. Indeed, I would strongly advise that you don't. My colleague here can accompany you to our reception area.'

'If it's alright with you, I'll stay.' Kara sounded slightly nervous, but there was determination in what she said.

'You do realise the consequences of sharing state intelligence with another sovereign nation, even a friendly one?'

'I have my reasons. Besides, I've not signed anything to say I wouldn't.' Kara had been pondering their discoveries and the recent events long and hard. 'And I'm assuming you want me to stay since you wouldn't have shown me to my seat.'

Bradbury smiled. 'You have me there, Doctor. Yes, I am most intrigued.'

'Is this meeting being recorded?' Daniel asked brusquely, looking around the room for cameras.

'No,' Bradbury replied. 'Just good old pen and paper.' As if to verify the fact, he held up his pen. 'My colleagues will be taking notes, too. Let's just call this an initial interview.' He cleared his throat and smiled at both interviewees. 'Now, I have the facts since your arrival in London last month,' he said, looking down at his pad of paper. He then looked up at Kara. 'I trust you are both well?'

Kara and Daniel were surprised by Bradbury's concern.

'Yes, thank you,' Kara replied. She glanced at Daniel next to her. He simply nodded.

Bradbury then looked at Daniel. 'What is your connection with the assailants?'

Daniel looked from Bradbury to the two MI6 officers sitting opposite. There was no point in bending the truth. It was likely that the British secret service had information from the French police on the one that had raided his villa. 'We recognised one of them.'

'The one who threatened you in your villa?' Bradbury quickly interjected.

Daniel snorted. He was right about not deviating from the truth. 'Yes.'

'Right,' Bradbury continued. 'This is where I'd like you to help me join the dots. You see, the one who threatened you with a gun in...' He looked at his notes. '...Lancashire Court was arrested recently. His name is Bakr al-Ahdal.' Bradbury nodded to his female colleague, who clicked on her laptop. A mugshot of Bakr appeared on a screen behind Bradbury. 'Can you confirm that this was the same man?'

'That's him. Thank God.' Kara said. Her relief was palpable.

'Yes, that's him,' Daniel confirmed. 'So, what will happen to him?'

'He'll be put away for the rest of his life. You see, Bakr al-Ahdal was also one of the terrorists behind the London Underground attack in March last year.'

'So we heard,' Daniel said.

'Wait!' Kara said leaning forward. 'Are you suggesting that we're somehow involved in that?'

Bradbury looked genuinely surprised. 'No, not at all. Please, you're not under any suspicion. I'm just trying to understand why a terrorist would risk returning to this country to assassinate you. Do you know *this* man?'

A new image appeared on the screen. It was of Jamal Ibrahim.

Kara and Daniel were both shaking their heads.

'No. we've never seen him,' Daniel said.

'Doctor Williams?'

'No, definitely not.'

The bearded agent typed something briefly and looked at Bradbury, who continued. 'Now, according to French police reports, you found Bakr al-Ahdal in your villa in the middle of the night, but managed to chase him off.'

'Yes, I confronted him with my shotgun,' said Daniel. 'He only had a knife.'

'Do you think he was there to kill you?'

'Well, in hindsight, almost certainly, yes.'

'But we also think he was there to take something,' Kara added. She looked at Daniel before continuing. 'Let me explain what we think is happening. It's complicated.' She gathered herself. 'Some of this may also sound…far-fetched, but please bear me out.' Kara took a deep breath. 'I'm a scientist. Until recently I was conducting a series of experiments in Venezuela. The aim of my team *was* to harness the electrical power in our atmosphere and create a new source of renewable energy.' Bradbury remained impassive. 'It was an American project, sanctioned by the Venezuelan government. In return, we had to employ some Venezuelan students.'

Bradbury frowned and scribbled a few notes on his pad. 'An interesting arrangement. Dr Williams, are you *absolutely* sure you wish to continue?'

'Yes. You will understand why. Anyway, last year, Professor Steel, my close friend and the man who initiated the project, arrived with a visitor. The professor told me he was from the government.'

'The US government?'

'Yes. Given the ever-growing world energy crisis, we assumed they were fast-tracking our project. Fast forward to this year and I'm, well, pretty much ordered to drop everything and fly to France to meet Daniel, here.'

Daniel took his cue. 'As Kara said, this is complicated. It's also bizarre.' Bradbury remained silent. The two officers sitting opposite were now both typing. Daniel looked across at Sadler-Smith, who merely raised his eyebrows at him. Daniel realised that he would need to make his narrative sound as plausible as possible. Any mention of meteorites and Bradbury would almost certainly call a stop to the meeting. 'Two years ago, I made a rather interesting discovery on a hill near to my home. The following spring, a journalist interviewed me. My discovery made the news. A year later, this spring, in fact, I'm contacted and told to expect a visit from Dr Williams.'

'I'm sorry, a discovery?' Bradbury asked.

'One that could assist Kara, Dr Williams, in her research.' Daniel stopped. The screen behind Bradbury refreshed. One of his officers had found one of the news articles. Bradbury swung around to look. WONDER STONE FROM SPACE was the headline. A colour image showed the stone up close and glowing with its miraculous internal light show.

Damn it, Daniel thought.

'Before you jump to any conclusions,' Kara said, 'or write this off as some kind of sensationalist trash, this meteorite has properties new to science. I and a host of leading scientists can personally attest to that.'

'That's right. It was important enough for Dr Williams to find me, run tests, and verify what we now know is true.'

'There's an article in a leading journal if you want a more scientific viewpoint,' Kara added.

'And the original article in *Le Figaro*,' Daniel said.

'Listen,' Bradbury said. 'I've been in this business long enough to know that fact can be stranger than fiction. Without facts, without intelligence, we would be remiss in our duty. So, please continue, Dr Bayford.'

'Thank you. OK, so the next events are even stranger. It was Dr Williams' first visit to France, so one evening we drove to Cannes. The film festival was on...' Daniel paused and looked around the room. 'We witnessed the first, what has widely been called, martyrdom.'

Bradbury was super-fast. The dots were beginning to join. 'They used the same stone,' he stated.

Daniel and Kara looked at him in amazement.

'Yes, that's right.' Kara said. 'We later studied video clips of the New York martyrdom. Daniel saw the man put something round his neck.'

'I then remembered seeing a necklace of some sort around the man in Cannes. How did you work that out...?' Daniel said, looking at Bradbury, his voice fading to nothing.

'Let me put you out of your misery,' Bradbury replied. 'We gathered this after the Tower Bridge incident. It's not a pretty sight, I'm afraid,' Bradbury said and nodded to the woman officer. On the screen appeared the half-charred remains of what was left of the martyr after being diced by the helicopter. Kara winced. The upper half of his body had been propelled onto the Tower Bridge roadway. The lightning had struck him in the chest. Remarkably, the necklace was still around his neck; the stone was plain to see. 'Apologies for the gory detail,' Bradbury said.

Daniel was nodding. 'Good,' he said, 'you're with us so far. So, a few days later, we arrived back at the villa. I could see that someone had broken in. The alarm had been disabled. Nothing of value had been taken. I then spotted that a photo had been replaced differently. We then went to my hut on the hill. Sure enough, the stone I had discovered had gone.'

'I thought it could have been someone who knew the enormous value that meteorites can sometimes fetch,' Kara said.

Daniel continued. 'But I ruled that out because it was a long time after all the news stories. Plus, it would have been easy to find where I live. So, I reasoned that such a theft would have already been attempted. A week or so later, I recalled seeing a van on a road near my villa the same day of the break-in. It was a swimming pool maintenance van. Sure, not unusual, but having remembered the company name I later looked it up. Nothing. That made us suspicious. It seemed like a professional job.

'This was the same day that we made the connection between the stone and the martyrdoms,' Kara added.

'We thought that another martyr had stolen it,' said Daniel.

'But I reasoned that with so many martyrdoms taking place around the world, these people must have had their own stones. Many of them.'

'Wait,' the bearded officer said, 'when was the theft?'

'In May, shortly after the Cannes martyrdom.'

The officer looked at his screen. 'Was this before the Bakr al-Ahdal incident?'

'Yes,' said Daniel. 'Sorry, I told you this was complicated. This Bakr guy arrived just a few nights later. When we got hold of the local police, I told them that I recognised him. He'd knocked into me at the *Palais des Festivals* in Cannes.'

'So, he was at that martyrdom incident?' Bradbury asked.

'Yes. After he got away from us at the villa, the police gave us protection.'

'Oh yes,' Kara said, 'the police mentioned that he'd been spotted leaving one of the mega yachts belonging to that playboy Arab prince. Prince Al someone.'

'Prince Al-Musan?' Bradbury suggested, not disguising his surprise.

'Yes, that's him.'

Bradbury beckoned the woman officer over and whispered in her ear. She picked up her laptop, made a slight nod to Daniel and Kara, and left the room. 'Why and when did you decide to contact Mr Sadler-Smith?' Bradbury continued.

'That would have been in June. Dr Williams had a bad feeling about Ordway.'

'Your government visitor in Venezuela,' Bradbury stated, turning to Kara.

'Yes,' she said, 'what he said didn't add up. His ego almost gave him away.'

'I mentioned to Dr Williams that I had a friend who may be able to help.'

Bradbury consulted his notes again. 'You had suspicions about the government visitor who visited your experiment in Venezuela and found out that he was from the US Department of Defence.'

'Yes,' said Kara. 'When we saw that, the pieces started falling into place. You see, we'd been hypothesising about these stones. As soon as we knew Ordway was DOD my suspicions made sense.'

'Your suspicions about what, Dr Williams?'

Kara suddenly felt nervous. And yet she had reasoned with herself so many times. Only yesterday evening Seb had shown them what looked like the aftermath of what she imagined a weapon could do. *What had the priest called it?* she thought. *The Spear of Destiny.* 'A weapon,' she announced. 'A deadly, new weapon capable of untold destruction.'

Bradbury and Sadler-Smith exchanged looks.

Kara suddenly panicked. She hoped that Daniel would not expand on her answer; that he would not mention the name of the weapon nor the Guild of God. She was ready to prod him if she thought he was about to.

Bradbury then stood up. 'Interesting. We'll certainly look into that. Well, thank you both. We appreciate your time and your candour. You can relax now, knowing that Bakr al-Ahdal will soon be behind bars.'

'Yes, that it is mighty relief. Thank you,' Kara said.

'So, what are your plans?' Bradbury asked, looking at Kara.

'We're planning to have a break. I think we need it!'

'I think you most certainly do. Anywhere nice?'

'I want to show Daniel where I was working. It's a magnificent place. Then a week on a beach somewhere. Not sure yet.'

'Well, I wish you a pleasant vacation, Dr Williams.'

'Thank you, Sir Bradbury,' Daniel added and shook his hand. 'May I ask how you caught him?'

'Can you believe following a routine registration plate check? The car was uninsured.'

'Lucky then.'

'I suppose. But you'd be surprised what routine police work can unearth.' Sadler-Smith and the bearded officer were exiting the room when Bradbury placed a hand on Daniel's arm. 'Still don't want to be involved in all this fun, Daniel?' he asked quietly.

'I already am, Sir George.'

Bradbury watched them walk down the corridor then took out his mobile.

Chapter 71
Spear Unleashed

Eastern Mediterranean, Greece

For thirty years, the Panama-registered reefer, *Deep Odyssey*, had sailed the world's oceans transporting perishable cargo—fruits from Brazil and the USA, plant oils and wine from Europe, fresh vegetables, tea, and spices from China.

Today, it lay alone and motionless in the Sea of Crete. The nearest shipping lanes to and from the main ports of *Piraeus* in Greece and Istanbul's *Ambarli* were to the west. Few cruise ships passed *Deep Odyssey's* chosen location, even those heading for nearby Thera, the famous volcanic island known also as Santorini.

From the outside, *Deep Odyssey* looked like any other cargo ship. Except that the vessel was under new ownership with a hidden payload that did not bring health and sustenance, but death and devastation.

The *Deep Odyssey* was now a US naval asset.

This had been no clear requisition for war, at least not in the traditional sense. Its original owners had been made an offer they could not refuse. They had no idea who the new owners were. Nor did they care.

The navy had quickly set to work on modifying the ship's interior. The three forward holds were now a single fifty by fifteen metre space, freshly painted white. The aft hold had been converted into a state-of-the-art operations room. The derricks on deck remained. So, too, had the original exterior paintwork and the ship's name, all to maintain the outward illusion of an active, commercial freighter.

Richard Ordway stood on deck. He was looking down through one of the large hatches at the activity below: eight men were inspecting the cargo—thirty D3 drones were spaced out in a grid and pre-loaded with more than fifty thousand ADNDs.

Ordway reached into his black leather bomber jacket and took out his phone. 'Weather conditions are perfect. Cargo is good. We're on schedule.'

Military Base, Alaska, USA

Deep below ground in the Category 'A' facility, Colonel Mike "The Moose" Mason's team were stationed at their computers in the command centre. Dr Jeffrey Scott, the lead scientist, was the only one on the development team present. He stood alongside Mason. They were on a raised section of the room overlooking the military personnel and four huge displays that spanned the wall.

Lieutenant Armstrong entered the room and approached the base commander. 'Sir,' he said, acknowledging his superior.

Mason simply nodded. He was viewing one of the main displays. 'I thought we had a feed from *Deep Odyssey*,' he barked across the room.

'Yes, sir,' replied one of the operatives. 'It's coming up now.'

A video feed from within the forward hold of the ship filled one of the main screens.

Mason turned to Scott. 'You must be proud, Doctor.'

Scott hesitated before responding. He looked at Mason and gave him a half smile. 'I now know how Oppenheimer must have felt.'

Mason snorted, '*Now I am become Death, the destroyer of worlds,*' he quoted. 'But Oppenheimer was wrong, Doctor. The atomic bomb stopped a war in its tracks and almost certainly saved lives as a result. Nuclear weapons are the best deterrent we have.'

'Oppenheimer was quoting the *Bhagavad Gita*,' the doctor said, a sacred Hindu text. Hindus believe in Karma. Do you believe in Karma, Colonel?'

The colonel turned to the lead scientist. 'What do you think?'

Scott knew that the colonel's question was rhetorical. Here was an experienced, high-ranking soldier, a man who lived in a very real world, whose decisions were based on fact, strategy, and the endgame. When a satellite image appeared on one of the main screens, Scott decided to leave the room.

For years, Scott had woken excited at the thought of a new day of tests and research. The focus had been on the technology, never the consequences. He turned and took one last look. A new image showed the Mediterranean, most of north Africa as far south as Sudan, the whole of the Middle East, and across to Pakistan.

'D3s one through ten are programmed,' one of the team reported.

Ten bright red dots lit up across the screen. A single green dot north of Crete showed the location of the *Deep Odyssey*.

As Scott looked at the first of the Spear of Destiny targets, his only hope was that what he and his team helped develop—the ADNDs, the D3 stealth and tracking technology, and of course *Donarium*—would one day be used for the good of mankind. He tried not to think of the destruction and pain his developments would wield today, nor the consequences. He turned and left the room.

'Sir, we'll be ready in approximately three minutes,' Armstrong said.

D3s eleven through eighteen are programmed.'

Eight more red dots flashed up on the map.

'This is it, Lieutenant. Time to reverse the tide. This will be another Hiroshima moment. The Spear of Destiny will be unleashed and we will stop the war against Christianity in *its* tracks.'

Nine more red dots. Twenty-seven in total now glowed across the screen like fairy lights. Each was a major city. Each was a target.

'Sir, all D3s now programmed and ready,' said the operative, having turned to face the colonel.

'And ELF?' the lieutenant asked.

'Online, sir.'

Mason picked up the desk phone. 'Sir, authorisation request...' Mason listened for a second or two. 'Thank you, Mr President.' He placed the phone back in its cradle. 'Light 'em up!' he ordered.

'Going for staggered launch,' came the response from another operative.

Deep Odyssey

The first of the D3s rose silently from the hold. Ordway shook his head in amazement. He had been told about the D3's incredible technology and knew all the specifications. But this was his first close-up experience of one. This was something else. The radar-absorbing shell surrounding the drone was coated with the military's latest development: an 'intelligent' nano paint—a super thin, hyper-durable layer containing nanotubes. These nanotubes were effectively frequency-conscious, light-sensitive paint cells. Sensors on the top, bottom, and sides of the drone picked up the light frequencies around them. These data were sent to the nano paint on the opposite side of the craft. The nanotubes altered their frequency to match the data. The result would have been similar to the chameleon paint often seen on cars—a smooth transition from one tone to another—except that this paint was dynamic, adjusting in colour and intensity across the surface of the drone, mirroring the tones of its surroundings. This was a true chameleon paint. The drone was near invisible.

The craft hovered level with Ordway. If it were making any sound, he could not hear it. The craft then turned and shot up and away. He put on his D&G sunglasses and looked up. But the drone, for all intents and purposes, had already disappeared.

Ordway headed aft and descended the steps to the control room.

He pondered the overriding objective of the project: plausible deniability. There could be no room for failure. To minimise the possibility of anyone discovering an ADND, unlikely though that was, or the equally remote possibility of a D3 being detected, Colonel Mason had devised a simple yet devasting plan. The drones had been programmed with their respective targets and were now being launched in order; the one with the furthest to travel first. The aim was for all fifty-four thousand ADNDs to be released and activated at the same time.

In terms of explosive power and geographic extent, the strike would be the biggest in history. In destroying their pre-defined targets, the ADNDs would be drawing energy from the atmosphere equivalent to two hundred and seventy Hiroshima bombs.

As Ordway entered the ship's control room and viewed the main displays, butterflies took flight in his stomach. He was filled with a sense of achievement, nerves, and excitement.

Chapter 72
La Gran Sabana

Southeast Venezuela

The twin-engine Piper emerged from the dense white cloud and into the late morning sunshine. Daniel peered out of the window. Below was an undulating and seemingly endless carpet of lush green vegetation. He turned to face his pilot. Kara smiled back and pulled the headset mic over her mouth.

'Enjoying the flight, sir?'

'This is amazing.'

Kara looked down at the chart. 'It gets really cool soon.'

'I still can't get over the fact that you didn't mention you could fly.'

'It's nice to have a few surprises, no? I mean, you didn't think of mentioning that you could kick the crap out of people.'

'*Touché.*' Daniel said. He was relieved to see that Kara appeared to be back to her normal self, even if she was now effectively out of work.

'So, how long have you had a licence?'

'I was lucky. My dad flies. He took me up one day when I was sixteen, and I was hooked. I got flying lessons from my parents for my twenty-first. I was lucky. My parents supported me all the way. Whatever I wanted to do. Whether it was back-packing in the Rockies or taking up meteorology.'

'That's great.'

'Yeh. I was pretty insecure back then. Giving me that autonomy helped me push through with my education. You know that, of course, right?' she asked turning to him.

'You bet. Knowing what we wanted to do from an early age makes us the lucky ones.'

Kara nodded her head forward. 'Check it out.'

The flat plains of the savanna were giving way to highlands. Hills and mountains rose ahead of them from one horizon to the other.

'We're over *La Parque Nacional Canaima*. We're not far from the border with Guyana and Brazil.' Kara announced. 'They call those table mountains *tepui*. Not far now.'

Daniel viewed the approaching mountains with awe. The vegetation swept up their slopes but stopped abruptly at the base of the vertical cliff faces, against which the sun was casting deep shadows.

'Down there!' Kara said and tilted the plane to allow Daniel a better look. Two thin waterfalls cascaded uninterrupted from the roof of one of the tepui, disappearing into a bank of white clouds.

'It's breath-taking, Kara.'

She reached out a hand and squeezed Daniel's.

'OK, we're about twenty kilometres out. She banked the plane gently and began a gradual descent. 'Our landing strip is straight ahead.' The wide valley floor opened up in front of them. 'Wonken approach, this is November Three Six Five Zulu. Piper Twin, 8 miles to your northwest, inbound, request joining instructions.'

'Three Six Five Zulu cleared to enter our zone for straight in approach Runway 24. Wind five knots, 175 degrees. QFE 998. Hola Kara.'

'Hola Ramon. *Cómo estás?'*

'Extremadamente bien. And you?'

'I'm extremely well, too, thanks.'

Kara made a final adjustment to their course.

'I see it now,' Daniel said.

Kara was back on the radio. 'Three Six Five Zulu, one mile final for runway 24. See you in a minute.'

'Three Six Five Zulu. Clear to land. Safe landing.'

Kara turned to Daniel, 'It's a landing strip that serves the nearby village. So don't expect much. The landing will be a bit bumpy.'

Kara brought the plane down perfectly onto the grass airfield and taxied to a stop. 'Not quite Heathrow,' she said.

'What, no duty-free?' Daniel joked.

Not long after, Kara was doing her post-flight checks. She had stooped under the wing and was placing chocks behind the wheels. The sound of an engine made Daniel turn. Kara looked up. 'Here's our lift,' she said.

The 4x4 pulled up and Tod jumped out. 'Hey, Kara! Long time.'

'Hey, Tod!'

The two gave each other a quick hug.

'You must be Daniel. Great to meet you.'

As he loaded the luggage in the rear, Daniel whispered to Kara. 'You didn't tell me he was a bit of a hunk.'

Kara suppressed a laugh and shook her head, giving Daniel an *are-you-serious?* look.

They set off. Kara and Daniel sat in the back. 'How was your trip? You guys must be whacked.'

'Yeh,' Kara said. 'Ordinarily, I'd be looking forward to scalding myself under that shower.'

'Funny, we actually fixed the pump soon after you left. Then we got the news that we were closing down.'

'Yeh, I was telling Daniel. I'm so sorry, Tod,' Kara said.

'I'm gonna miss the team,' Tod said. His upbeat demeanour suddenly faded. 'Already do.'

'You'll find your feet soon, Tod. You're young. Speak to the professor. I'm sure he'll fix you up on another project.'

'How come you're still here, Tod?' Daniel asked.

'We couldn't get the gear back to the States until early last month. The government here was going through another crisis, so paperwork got delayed. I then decided to hang out for a month.'

The track they were on ended. Ahead lay a narrow river. 'OK, this is where we go *off-piste*, guys,' Tod announced, as he manoeuvred the 4x4 amongst the rocks and through the shallow water. 'So, tell me all about it,' Tod said enthusiastically. 'The professor told us you were attacked in London! What the hell was *that* about?'

'Later, Tod,' Kara said. 'It's been an eventful few weeks.' She suddenly felt exhausted and leant her head on Daniel's shoulder.

An hour or so later, Tod was parking up. They had reached the site of the old camp. 'Welcome to the Lost World, Daniel.'

Daniel stepped out and looked in all directions. 'This is some place.' He turned to see that Kara had walked away. She was strolling along the edge of the bluff, looking out across the magnificent landscape. It was clear she needed some time on her own.

Tod could not hold back. 'So, what happened in London, Daniel? Are you OK? Is Kara OK?'

'We're fine. Kara's still a bit shaken up. So, please don't bring it up in front of her.'

'Gotcha. But what happened?'

'It's complicated. God, I keep saying that. And it's not for me to talk about what happened. You don't need to know. In fact, it's probably best that you don't. But I'll leave that to Kara,' Daniel said. He was watching her. 'She's an amazing woman, Tod.'

Tod looked from Kara back to Daniel. 'Are you guys…you know?'

Daniel turned to the student. 'That obvious, huh?'

'Yay! That is so cool.'

Daniel laughed. 'I'm a lucky guy for sure.'

'Hey, just remembered. I brought us some food.' Tod headed around the 4x4. 'Homemade chilli and some ice-cold beer,' he called.

After the meal, the three of them sat side by side near the edge of the bluff supping their beers.

'I love this view,' Kara said. 'We all did.'

'It was a blast, Kara,' Tod said. 'Best time of my life.'

'He wants to know what happened, Kara,' said Daniel.

Kara was looking back out at the mountains. Daniel knew she was thinking hard—the pouting of her lips was a sure giveaway. 'Why not. You tell him, Daniel.'

So, here he was again, this time with a young student, recounting the strange and dangerous events that had taken place since meeting Kara. Tod did not say a word. He was spellbound; hanging on Daniel's every word.

Half an hour later, Kara stood up. 'Come on. It's time we went.'

'I'm so glad you wanted to share this place with me, Kara,' Daniel said, as Tod loaded up the 4x4.

'We both needed it. And it's helped me.'

Daniel was reaching for the rear door handle, but stopped and turned to face her. 'That's good to know.'

'No, I mean it's helped me make a decision. We need to stop it.'

'Stop what?' Daniel looked concerned. Was she talking about their relationship?

'The weapon. It has to be us. Don't you see? There's no one we can trust.'

'Kara, that's madness. How can we…'

'I don't know. But we need to do something.'

'No, Kara. It's out of our hands. No way!'

'She's right, Daniel.' Tod had moved around from the back of the vehicle. 'From what you told me…Oh, man! And, Kara, you can count me in.'

'Whoa! No way, Tod,' Kara said. 'This is *not* your problem. God, I wish we hadn't told you.'

Daniel put a hand on Tod's shoulder. 'Tod, listen. Kara's still angry about her research being hijacked. Don't worry, I'll talk sense into her.'

'I'm still here, you know,' Kara said.

Daniel could see the determination on her face. 'Alright. We can talk about it.'

Two hours later, Kara and Daniel were once again airborne. They had hardly spoken a word. Kara consulted her chart.

'I'm sorry,' she said, looking straight ahead. 'Perhaps I am mad.'

'No, you're not. In fact, I had reached the same decision.'

Kara turned to face him. 'Really?'

'Yes, really. I just didn't want to say so in front of Tod. He's at a loose end and I was worried you would have asked him to help in some way.'

'Come on! There was no chance of that. He's a good kid, but a kid all the same.' Kara looked at the chart again and then at the instrument panel. 'We'll need to refuel before we carry on to Caracas. I've planned a stopover at an airport by the Orinoco. Here.' She pointed at the chart.

As though in an act of defiance, the plane's starboard engine then suddenly spluttered. Kara looked past Daniel. The engine resumed its normal tone but spluttered again. She looked down at the instrument panel.

'What's wrong?' Daniel asked.

'I don't know.' When the engine wound down to a stop, Kara looked again at the panel. 'We have plenty of fuel.' She looked to her left at the other engine. It seemed to be OK. 'I'm gonna try the boost pumps and the fuel mix.' She reached forward and toggled two switches then pulled on a red knob. She tried to restart the starboard engine. 'Come on, come on.' But the propeller remained still. 'Daniel, I'm gonna need your help. Take the controls. Just keep it level.'

'Got it.'

After setting the transponder to squawk 7700, Kara picked up the chart and made calculations. 'OK, we should have…' But the port engine began to falter. Kara looked out. 'Shit,' she muttered.

'That doesn't sound good.'

'No. This is definitely not good. Daniel, we may need to do an emergency landing. The good news is that we're flying over fairly flat land. The bad news is that if the port engine fails, it could get a little hairy.'

'I trust you, Kara.'

'Thanks. Don't worry, I've glided down before.' She clicked on the radio. 'Mayday, mayday. This is November Three Six Five Zulu. Mayday, mayday, squawking 7700.'

'November Three Six Five Zulu, this is Caicara del Orinoco. We hear you. What is your status and position? Over.'

'Um, we have lost power in one engine. We are…' The port engine then stopped. Kara nodded at Daniel and retook control. 'Correction, both engines have failed. Repeat, both engines have failed. Heading three-three-zero. One niner zero knots. Southeast Caicara. Twenty-eight hundred feet and descending. Over.'

'November Three Six Five Zulu, we have you on radar. Maintain heading. Descend to twelve hundred feet. Then turn zero one five on my mark. Repeat zero-one-five on my mark. Over.'

'Roger, descending to twelve hundred. Turning one-five-zero on your mark.' Kara turned to Daniel. 'We won't make the airfield.'

'Mark. Turn zero-one-five,' came the instruction from Caicara tower.

'Turning zero one five. What am I looking for? Over.'

'There is a river heading due north. The land immediately to its east is flat. You should see it soon. Over.'

Kara leant forward. 'Yes, I can see the river.'

'Roger that November Three Six Five Zulu. Be advised that we have scrambled a rescue chopper. Good luck. Over.'

'Homing beacon now on. Thank you, Caicara.'

'OK, this is it. Daniel. We're on our own now. It's down to me. Don't worry, we'll be OK. But if for any reason I'm knocked out or whatever, get yourself out. Get well away from the aircraft. According to the gauge we still have half a tank of fuel.'

'Kara. I won't be leaving you…I love you.'

She turned to Daniel, but tears had welled in her eyes. 'I love you, too, Daniel. I'm sorry. I did the pre-flight checks and—'

'Kara. You're doing great. Now go for it, girl! You are the most amazing woman I've ever known.'

'Oh shit, Daniel. *Now* you tell me!' she said and half laughed.

There was the river. She looked ahead and spotted their best bet. There was a strip of land that seemed flat enough. *It will have to do*, she thought. She gently banked the plane onto a smooth glide descent. 'Shit, landing gear!' She yanked down the lever and the wheels clunked into position. There was no second chance. She glanced at the instruments and lowered the flaps but the airspeed dropped a bit too quickly. She made a correction. The ground was rushing up. Daniel braced himself and held his breath. Kara did her best to hold up the nose but the wheels smashed down and the plane slewed violently to the right. Kara pushed the left rudder pedal just as they hit a huge bump. The impact snapped the front wheel strut and the nose ploughed into the earth. Then, the starboard wheel strut gave way, causing the plane to pivot hard right, jerking them violently in their harnesses and back against their seats.

There was silence inside the cockpit. It was over. They were safe. For now.

Kara was the first to react. 'OUT! DANIEL! OUT! THIS SIDE!'

He winced as he straightened his head. His neck hurt like hell. The wing on his side was half off, his door only inches from the soil. Kara threw open her door. But the precarious angle of the plane caused it to slam shut. Kara turned the handle and together they pushed hard. This time the door banged open. They clambered out, falling on their knees. As they picked themselves up, she pushed Daniel forward and they ran across the rough terrain, before collapsing.

They looked back at the plane, trying to take it all in. Kara rubbed her shoulder; Daniel rotated his neck and let out a long breath.

He then heard giggling. Kara had her phone in both hands. She could hardly utter the words as she began filming. 'So, did you enjoy the flight with us today, sir?' Her giggling turned to uncontrollable laughter and she toppled sideways, clutching her stomach.

Daniel's confusion soon dissolved. He wiped the smile that was broadening across his face. 'Well,' he began in a deadly serious voice. Kara quickly pulled herself up, giggling once again, and resumed filming. 'The crew was lovely. …Oh yes, and the in-flight entertainment was excellent.' This sent Kara into new paroxysms of belly laughter, this time falling flat on her back. '…Yes, a most memorable flight,' he concluded. Daniel then succumbed and lay down beside her laughing out loud.

After a few dying chuckles, lying on their backs and gazing up at the sky, Daniel rolled onto his side and placed a hand on her cheek. Looking deep into her eyes he smiled. 'Like I said, you are the most amazing woman I've ever known.' Kara turned and cupped his face in her hands and shook her head. Their foreheads came together and she laughed, smiled, and then laughed again.

Chapter 73
Bellum Sanctum

Military Base, Alaska, USA

Colonel Mason stood, arms folded, overlooking the command centre's main displays. Across three of them, twenty-seven D3 video feeds were arranged in 3 by 3 grids. He leant forward and selected one on his computer. An enlarged image mostly of waves rushing past filled a fourth main display, as the drone sped across the Mediterranean. Rapidly changing data in the bottom right of the screen showed the selected D3's position, altitude, heading, energy status, and target distance. In larger text was the name of the target: ALGIERS. The Algerian coastline appeared on the left. A promontory rushed past. Then another. Soon, it would be flying inland over the coastal towns of Tigzirt and Zemmouri with only fifty kilometres to go.

Mason chose another image at random. He looked up again. This D3 was racing low over a range of dry, sandy-coloured mountains. Target distance: 176...175...174 km. It was closing in fast on its destination: ASHGABAT—capital of Turkmenistan. 'Do we have synchronisation?' the colonel bellowed across the room.

One of the main displays then updated to show an inset graphic of twenty-seven identically-sized green bars extending slowly across the screen, representing the squadron of D3s. A large numerical display below showed a countdown: 10 MIN 22 SEC. An operator turned to face the colonel. 'One hundred per cent synchronisation, sir.'

'Excellent.' The colonel resumed his stance with his arms now behind his back.

'*Seeders* and ADNDs released,' one of the operators reported.

Thousands of *seeders* were now helping to generate enormous electrical potential in the atmosphere, while thousands of Autonomous Discriminatory Nano Drones began their freefall towards their designated targets.

The colonel puffed out his chest and turned to his second in command. 'ELF in ten minutes, Lieutenant.'

'Yes, sir.'

Armstrong stole Mason a glance and sensed that his commander was perhaps finally showing excitement or nerves—or both. All those present knew that the communication pulse to activate the ADNDs would be triggered automatically at zero hour. The colonel's powerful, squat body swelled with each deep breath he took. All twenty-seven drones with their enormously destructive payloads were on track.

The clock showed 1 MIN 00 SEC.

'Which one shall we watch in close-up, Lieutenant?'

'Sir?'

'Choose a location.'

Armstrong hesitated then reached forward to touch the computer screen. His finger wavered over the images, then pressed on one. The video feed showed countless buildings, shops, apartments, and roads rushing past.

'Cairo. Good choice, Lieutenant.'

0 MIN 0 SEC.

'ELF pulse activated,' another operator announced.

'ADNDs activated,' another called out.

Just as if a new and malefic species of four-winged insect had simultaneously completed its metamorphosis, multiple swarms of nano-drones powered up and began homing in.

Khartoum, Sudan

The late afternoon heat was an intense 42C. Across the northern part of the city, the competing calls to prayer sounded from the loudspeakers positioned high on minarets.

Across the road from the Grand Mosque, Farid was concluding a sale in his jewellery store. He needed to finish and close the shop. It would soon be time for prayer. But the customer seemed uncertain. He had placed the gold bangle back on the glass counter and was shaking his head.

'OK. Today, I can give you a very special deal. But if my father returns, please don't tell him,' Farid said, smiling his perfect white teeth. The customer mopped his jet-black brow and looked at the bangle once more. Farid picked it up and almost forced it into the man's hand. 'For your wife? She will love it. Look how good it looks against the skin.'

Farid sensed a sale was imminent. But a new sensation entered his consciousness. He looked at his arms. The hairs on them had sprung up. Then a brilliant flash and almost instantaneous boom made them both wince. Farid and the customer turned and looked out at the street. Their first thought was a bomb. With the second dazzling flash and thunder crack, it was clear it was lightning.

To Farid it made no sense. There was hardly a cloud in the sky. A third bolt almost identical to the last then seemed to explode the very air. To Farid's horror, he realised the lightning was striking the same place. The storm was centred on the Grand Mosque only metres away! The lightning kept coming, each time into the heart of the beautiful building.

Then, two angled lightning bolts, one a half second after the other, struck the nearest minaret. Worshippers and pedestrians were running everywhere. A van smashed into a car, sending it into a row of parked vehicles. Parts of the mosque's walls were crashing to the ground. When the minaret started to topple, Farid threw himself to the ground and began praying. '*SAEADNA ALLAH*!'

Help us, Allah!

Cairo, Egypt

Like most of Africa's most populated and ever-expanding city, the streets around Zahur's school were filled with chatter and shouting and the incessant hooting of vehicle horns. The air was dry and choking with fumes.

A few hundred metres above the human chaos, two thousand ADNDs had fired up and were homing in on their pre-assigned targets. Like the eighth of the ten ancient plagues of biblical Egypt, they descended like locusts, settling on the pre-determined rooftops.

Zahur was ten years old. He said goodbye to his school friend and turned off the main street. He was ambling along when he spotted a stone on the dusty paving and began kicking it in front of him. Sensing a change in weather, he looked up. Roseate clouds were rapidly swelling and darkening. He clutched his books under his arm and started running. Up ahead was the mosque. His home was in the street beyond. He dodged the other pedestrians, half running, half skipping, pretending to be a footballer dribbling his way to a goal and a glorious victory for his team. *Not far now*, he thought. He kicked an empty can of coke and shouted, 'GOooooAL!'

The first lightning strike was enormous. For the briefest of moments, Zahur thought he had caused it when the coke tin clattered against a parked moped. When another flash and deafening clap of thunder exploded over the roof of the mosque, those in the street ran for cover. But Zahur had remained; transfixed and alone in the middle of the street. A series of six lightning bolts smashed into the mosque in quick succession. The noise was ear-splitting and terrifying. Zahur began to scream. And yet the onslaught did not stop. It got worse. A lot worse.

'*HUNA!*' shouted a man. He was at the doorway of his vehicle repair shop. He was beckoning the small boy. But Zahur could not hear above the thunderous attack. His books tumbled to the ground as he pressed his hands against his ears. When the dome of the mosque collapsed, the man ran out and grabbed the boy. The man said nothing but steered Zahur past a car raised high on a hydraulic lift, as rumble crashed into the street. The lightning lit up the workshop in a series of rapid and never-ending pulses. They reached the back wall, turned, and blocked their ears.

It's the end of the world! Zahur thought and looked up at his rescuer. He had never seen anyone look so terrified.

Eastern Mediterranean, Greece

The captain of *Deep Odyssey* and his crew simply stared at the screens. Their job was done. They had the same feeds as those in the Alaskan base and were now witnessing the unbelievable and catastrophic power of the Spear of Destiny.

The D3 camera feeds were faultless; the screens were ablaze with hundreds of lightning flashes.

Ordway was smiling. He was sitting on a swivel chair in the middle of the operations room, his left foot resting on his right knee. He swung the chair around to face the captain. 'Wow! Fuckin' wow!' He then swung back around. He did not want to miss any of it.

The main display was switching from one city to another. Every single target was being pulverised. The captain looked at the back of Ordway, who was shaking his head slowly from side to side. If it had been anyone else, the head shaking would have been interpreted as an act of disbelief and horror. For Ordway, the captain knew, it was a sign of awe and unashamed delight.

The main display then showed an unmistakable city view. The angle was such that in the far distance, to the side of the nearest mosque, now being showered under a blaze of lightning, were the tops of the Giza pyramids, peeping through the smoggy haze over countless rooftops. The main text on the display confirmed it was Cairo. Ordway laughed, reached down then raised his arms as though to embrace the multiple images. He was holding a copy of the bible in one hand and almost shouted: *'SO THE LORD RAINED HAIL ON THE LAND OF EGYPT; HAIL FELL AND LIGHTNING FLASHED BACK AND FORTH.'*

The rest of the crew all turned and stared at him.

'Exodus 9:23 and 9:24. No?' Ordway said, looking around the room, smiling. There was no response. Ordway shrugged. 'Hey, shame there's no sound. I bet it's biblical.' He laughed again.

One of the officers muttered to the captain, 'What the sound of people dying?' The captain said nothing.

The coordinated attack had lasted three minutes when, little by little, the flashes began to diminish. The last to show any activity was brought up on the main screen. It was Kabul. The image showed a massive thundercloud over the city. Ordway stood up and walked to the rear of the room. 'Nothing like good ol' Mother Nature to give us a hand,' he said, pointing back at the screen. 'Still, how impressive was that! Most of those locations had very little air-born moisture.' He turned to watch the final few moments. All the screens then went dark. 'And strike! All pins are down. Well, thank you, gentlemen. A job well done.'

Ordway turned and left the room and several raised eyebrows. He entered his cabin, threw the bible on the bunk, and took out his phone. 'Juan, how are you?'

Vatican City

Cardinal Juan Romero was alone in his office, standing once again by the window. The autumn sun was sparkling through the branches of the parasol-shaped pine trees. 'I'm listening,' he replied, bristling. *No respect,* he thought.

'It was incredible, Juan. A one hundred percent success. No failures. It worked like a dream. You should have seen it!'

Romero sighed a deep sigh. 'I'm sure we'll *all* see it. And I fear many will also see *through* it.'

'No, they won't. They can't. It's fool-proof. Plausible deniability. Remember?'

384

'But twenty-seven similar events? All mosques?'

'Well, not all mosques. We did include a few Islamic universities and known terrorist hideouts. Anyway, that's the whole point. People will start to question that faith, just as *they* made many Christians doubt theirs after those martyrdoms.'

The cardinal shook his head. He turned and looked at the crucifix hanging behind his desk.

'*Bellum Sanctum,* Mr Ordway.'

'*Say again?*'

'*Bellum Sanctum.* It means Holy War, Mr Ordway. You have started another Holy War!'

Ordway laughed. '*You are joking? We didn't start anything. What about those countless acts of terrorism against our way of life? The Christian way of life. What about those martyrdoms? Crude attempts to convince any doubters that Allah is the true god. And what about the Arabs taking the Holy Land from our ancient Crusader brothers? No, we're finishing what we should have finished nine hundred years ago.*'

'What about forgiveness? That's the Christian way.' Romero waited for a response.

'*Forgiveness, eh? That's a great question. Hmm...should I forgive you, Juan?*'

'What does that mean?'

'*Should I forgive you for your betrayal?*'

The cardinal blanched. He needed to sit down. He knew exactly what Ordway meant.

'*Your silence says a lot, Cardinal. But just in case you're in any doubt, let me simply say the names, Santiago Morales and, oh yes, Father Brendon. You see, I'm so confused. One minute you're writing to the President of France, giving your approval for the weapon. The next you're calling Santiago. He told me all about your call to him and your doubts.*'

'But I didn't know what the Spear of Destiny really was!' Romero hissed. 'I genuinely thought it was a plan to show the world the true Spear that pierced

Christ. A sacred relic that would inspire millions. NOT SOME DIABOLICAL DOOMSDAY WEAPON!'

'So, you decide to despatch Father Brendon to meet with the scientist that helped us refine the weapon and the man who discovered the very thing that helped her. You thought they may be able to stop us.'

'You listen to me!'

'NO, YOU LISTEN TO ME! Through Father Brendon, you betrayed the Guild of God by sharing names of its members and, worst of all, the secret of the Spear of Destiny!'

'YOU BETRAYED THE GUILD OF GOD LONG BEFORE THAT, MR ORDWAY, WHEN YOU STARTED BUILDING THAT INFERNAL WEAPON! YOU HAVE BETRAYED GOD AND THE VERY SPIRIT OF CHRISTIANITY. YOU ARE MAD AND EVIL; DO YOU HEAR ME? YOU HAVE SLAUGHTERED INNOCENT, PEACE-LOVING PEOPLE. MAY GOD DAMN YOU TO HELL, ORDWAY!'

Romero stabbed his phone with his index finger and terminated the call.

Chapter 74
The Rescue

Southeast of the Orinoco, Venezuela

The rescue chopper was a welcome sight. Kara and Daniel stood up and waved. The man by the open side door waved back.

'I need to check something,' Kara said.

She began walking back to the wrecked plane.

'Are you sure it's safe?' Daniel called and began following, wondering what had suddenly entered her mind after their three-hour wait.

'I have a feeling it's *more* than safe,' she called back over her shoulder.

The chopper had settled further up by the river. With the rotors still turning, two men dressed in jumpsuits and carrying medical bags, began jogging over.

Kara reached the Piper's port wing and started removing the fuel filler cap. She sniffed the air, then peered in and tapped the wing. Although she detected the smell of fuel, she could only hear a hollow echo. She looked at Daniel.

'What?' he asked.

Kara did not reply. *Oh my god, I never made a visual check,* she thought. With her heart pounding, she ran over to check the other tank. Kara somehow knew it would be the same story. The same hollow sound rang out. 'God how stupid!' She uttered to herself in dismay.

'*HOLA!*'

Daniel turned. '*Hola*! Do you speak English?'

'Of course. Are you OK?'

'Yes, we're fine. And thank you.'

'What is she doing?'

Kara had stood up, and was simply staring down at the wing. The men looked at each other.

'What are you looking for? Can I help?' the second medic asked.

'There's no fuel!' she snapped.

'What?' Daniel exclaimed.

Kara turned. 'We ran out of fucking fuel. The gauges showed plenty but…' She stopped herself. She had failed to check the tanks. Admitting that in front of potential witnesses could be deeply damning. There would be an investigation for sure.

The same rescuer stared at Kara, '*Señorita*, the tanks are empty?'

She did not like his tone. Guilt and anger over her negligence coursed through her. 'YES! YES, THEY ARE!'

'*Señorita*, so how were the tanks when you left?'

Kara then realised that the medic may have also been a pilot. And all pilots know they should *always* make a manual check of the tanks. 'The gauges must be faulty,' she replied. 'Oh, God! I'm sorry, Daniel. I've done this trip so many times. I don't understand.'

'The crash will be investigated,' the first medic said. 'They will find what went wrong. Is this your plane?'

'No. It belongs to the US government. I have papers.'

'No problem. First, we must get you to hospital.'

'No! Not yet!' Kara almost shouted. 'I don't need a fucking hospital, just some answers.'

'You are in shock, *Señorita*. We should go,' the medic said. He then looked at Daniel for some assistance.

Their rescuers' equanimity and patience surprised Daniel, but sensed it would not last.

'Kara,' he said softly, 'it's OK. That can wait. These men are here to help us.'

She straightened and stared back. Daniel knew his words were futile. She had that look again. Without saying anything, she strode purposefully past the buckled starboard propeller, jumped onto the port wing, and leant into the cockpit.

When the first medic raised his eyebrows, Daniel responded with an apologetic shrug of the shoulders and a raised finger. 'One minute, please,' he pleaded.

'*Bien. Vamos ahora!* Let's go now!' The medic had lost patience.

As they headed for the chopper, Kara turned to Daniel. 'I'm telling you, the gauges showed full when we left. I know the guys at that airfield. I've done the trip so many times,' she said and fell silent. Daniel simply placed a hand on her shoulder. He knew she needed some head space. She would be thinking, assessing; analysing. 'No,' she continued, 'the gauges or the fuel sensors *must* have been tampered with.' They stopped and exchanged looks. 'The plane was sabotaged, Daniel. I know it… Someone was trying to kill us.'

The medics said nothing. They simply stared at Kara and Daniel.

Chapter 75
A Small White Church

Caracas, Venezuela

Having sustained only minor injuries, Kara and Daniel were discharged from hospital within hours. The next day they were in the Venezuelan capital, determined to enjoy the rest of their holiday. Kara was happy simply to stroll the streets and absorb the sights, sounds, and aromas. She was enjoying being amongst people in a city that felt less threatening than London. And yet anxiety washed over her in waves.

'Who's the statue of?' she asked, trying to shake off the memories of the plane crash.

'Simón Bolívar—*El Libertador.* The man who led much of South America to independence from the Spanish.'

They had arrived in the eponymous and leafy *Plaza Bolivar.* It was full of families. Kara smiled as two youngsters ran past them. She stopped and looked up at the grand and heroic statue. 'It's funny how some people in power do good, while others do so much that is wrong,' she said.

'Yeh, I know what you mean. Well, this guy was certainly the former. Imagine having the currency named after you.'

'A proper hero.'

A group of people had stood up from a nearby bench. Kara nodded towards it.

They sat and Kara clutched Daniel's hand. 'What are we going to do? We don't have wealth, power, or influence. We don't even know whom we can trust.'

Daniel did not know how to reply. He was disappointed in himself. What she had said in front of Tod—the idea of going up against the mightiest army on earth—was inconceivable. Maybe it *was* beyond them. Perversely, the idea of doing so appealed to his rebellious nature. *Damn, I miss that excitement,* he thought. But that was then; this was now. He had met Kara. Things were different. But the desire to do something would not leave him, and there was more he needed to understand. 'Can we talk about what happened yesterday?' he asked.

Kara responded quickly, 'The plane was tampered with. I know it. The plane was never refuelled. They simply messed with the electrics somehow to indicate full tanks.'

'I believe you. But tampered by whom? Who knew we'd be there?'

'Well, apart from you, Tod, and air traffic control, no one else. And we can rule out you and Tod. Fact.'

'Shit, didn't we also mention Venezuela during that police interview?'

'I nearly did but managed to check myself. I'm pretty sure you only said South America. Whoever did it, knew precisely where we were in Venezuela. They then chose to do it when they did, because it increased the chances of us coming down far from civilisation.'

'That makes sense. So, who?'

Kara thought long and hard. Then she turned to Daniel. 'Oh shit, I did mention it during the MI6 meeting. Your friend's boss.'

'Bradbury?'

'Yes. It was when we were leaving the meeting.'

'You're right. I remember now. Jesus!'

'"Anywhere nice?" he asked. It seemed such a causal question. And I'd stupidly said I'd show you where I was working. Do you think he could be involved?'

'Remember what Father Brendon told us? Powerful people. Some with the highest offices in the world.'

The ping of the key remote echoed in the underground car park.

Daniel looked over his shoulder. He had spotted two men in the lobby. They had been there when they arrived back at the hotel, and were still there when he and Kara had descended from their room some two hours later. The men looked like locals, but there was something not quite right about them. When he caught their eyes, one looked away; the other stared back. They were also heading in their direction. But theirs was the only car in this part of the car park. *Muggers*, Daniel immediately thought.

Daniel opened the passenger door of their hire car. 'Madam.'

'Why, thank you, sir.' Unaware of the threat, Kara hitched her long white dress and climbed in.

'Come on, Daniel, where are you taking us?'

'Out of town,' he replied.

Kara looked at Daniel and frowned. His face said it all. Hearing the approaching footsteps, she turned and saw the two men pacing towards them.

Daniel had moved to the driver's side. He opened the door and looked over the roof. One of the men was drawing out a knife. Daniel reached under his jacket and held his hand there. With the other, he banged hard on the roof. The sound, amplified by the low concrete ceiling, was as loud as a gunshot. Kara jumped. 'STOP RIGHT THERE OR I'LL BLOW YOUR FUCKIN' BRAINS OUT!' Daniel yelled.

The bluff worked. The men stopped in their tracks—whoever they were, the chances of their victim owning a gun were clearly plausible. But Daniel knew the pretence would only buy him a few seconds. He jumped in, gunned the car's engine to life and pressed down hard on the accelerator, turning hard right towards the two men. The tyres skidded and squealed. There was one thing on Daniel's mind: *run them over. Kill them if necessary*. With his foot hard down, he headed straight for the two figures. One dived to his right. The other was not as fast. The car smashed into him. The man folded in two, before his body disappeared under the car. Daniel swerved, and the rear of the car bounced as one of the wheels crushed the man's head. Daniel slammed the car into second gear. *Where was the exit*? he thought.

As though reading his mind, Kara pointed. 'THERE!' she shouted. She looked back through the rear window. The other man was running after them but stopped.

Daniel did not stop as he turned onto the back street and accelerated away.

After several blocks and turns, he slowed and looked at Kara. She was breathing hard, facing straight forward.

'Do you have your passport?'

Kara turned to face him. 'What?'

'Do you have your passport?'

'Er, yes, I always carry it with me.' She reached down for her bag and pulled it out.

Daniel looked. 'Good.'

'We need to go to the police.'

'No. No police.'

'But…'

'They were going to kill us, Kara.'

'Exactly! Trying to kill us! And don't tell me, you don't have a gun. What if they had? You're unbelievable!'

'Look, it was all I could do. OK? And it worked.'

'You probably killed one of them!'

'He had a fucking knife, Kara. I really don't give a shit. He asked for it!' Kara stared hard at Daniel. 'I'm sorry. I wanted to protect you,' he said more calmly.

'Oh god! This could get bad, Daniel. What do we do?'

'Look, there were no witnesses. No one saw us. But we can't risk staying here.'

'Then what now?'

'We'll go to the restaurant I was planning on. It's in the mountains. Well away from here.'

'Restaurant? I don't have much of an appetite, Daniel. In fact, stop the car!'

'What? Now?'

'Yes, NOW! I'm going to puke.'

He pulled over. Kara leant out, and threw up in the gutter. Daniel reached over and rubbed her back.

They merged onto a wide *avenida*. The traffic was heavy. Daniel looked in his rear mirror, then at Kara. 'You OK?'

She gave a long sigh, 'No. I need some water.'

'Of course. I'll pull in somewhere.'

After twenty minutes of stop-start, the traffic thinned out. Daniel flicked on the headlights. Kara looked out at the blur of buildings, lights, and people, and suddenly felt very far from home.

Daniel spotted a small convenience store and pulled up.

'Thanks,' she said and swished a mouthful of water around before spitting it through her open door. 'They're onto us, Daniel. That's two attempts.' Kara dampened a handful of tissues, mopped her face, then leant back.

'We don't know that. They may have been muggers targeting tourists. It's not so unusual.'

'If that was meant to make me feel better, it didn't.'

'Anyway, I wasn't going to take any chances. But it does mean we need to get away. And fast. So, get your thinking cap on.'

'Wait! What about our stuff? We need to get our bags. It'll look suspicious if we don't.'

'You're right. Damn it!'

As they set off, Kara reached into her bag, took out a small bottle of perfume, and sprayed a little on her neck. Daniel looked over to give her encouragement, but her eyes were closed. *I've blown my chances with her, that's for sure*, he thought.

Not long after, Daniel turned off the main highway. They began climbing into the hills along a narrow, twisty, tree-lined road. A small white church, lit by spotlights somewhere on its grounds, appeared ahead of them.

'Stop here,' Kara said.

Daniel pulled in front of the church and turned off the engine. He turned to her. 'Are you feeling sick?'

'I just need a few moments. On my own,' she said.

Daniel sat and watched as she disappeared into the shadows of the porch and stepped inside.

The church was empty. A few candles were flickering by the altar. Kara stood for a while then walked slowly down the aisle and breathed in the mix of mustiness and incense. A calmness seemed to infuse her with every step. She was not Catholic, but Protestant, although certainly no churchgoer. Not anymore.

She stood before the altar and closed her eyes. It felt familiar. She recalled the late-night Christmas Eve services in Vermont. The folk in her small, picturesque town would converge onto the road leading up to the church, wrapped in their winter coats and hats, holding lanterns to light the way. It was magical. And she wanted to be back there.

She opened her eyes, moist with tears. No one could hurt her here. Not in a house of God.

As she returned to the car, she could see Daniel's face glowing from the light of his phone.

'Don't worry about this evening,' Daniel said, as she climbed in. 'I've messaged Seb. He'll arrange for one of the British Embassy staff here to have our clothes collected from the hotel. They'll forward them.'

'Forward them where?'

'Martinique. I booked us a room the other morning. You'll love it. You did want to get away from it all, right?'

'Why there?'

'I wanted it to be a surprise. But after, you know…'

Concern swept across Kara's face. 'What about the police here? Do you think…'

'Kara, it's fine. Don't worry.' Her face said otherwise. Daniel looked down at his phone. 'Er…I know we said we'd avoid the news,' he continued, 'but this you have to see.' He passed the phone over.

Kara stared at the simple headline: DEVASTATION!

There was a series of accompanying images. A sub-heading stated: FREAK OF NATURE WREAKS HAVOC. Kara scrolled and scrolled. 'Oh—my—God.'

'We have to stop them, Kara.'

'But Daniel. This is my fault. I helped do this!' She dropped the phone and threw a hand across her mouth, her eyes wide.

'No! No, you didn't. It was that bastard, Ordway. He used you. You know that.'

Daniel put his arm across her and pulled her to him. She was shaking.

'I felt so calm in that church.'

'I'm sorry. But our worst fears have come true. It's real, Kara. The bloody Spear of Destiny is real.'

Being held by Daniel seemed to calm her. She then slowly pulled away from his embrace. 'You don't have to be sorry. But I tell you who does, and you're right: that bastard, Ordway! We need to expose him and everyone involved.' The regret and sadness within Kara had been swept away by renewed anger and determination. 'What about the journalist who interviewed you?'

Daniel shook his head. 'I don't know. I've thought about that. But who's to say the story won't get suppressed? You can bet your bottom dollar they have people in the media. Look at that sub-heading, "freak of nature". I think they're already at it. In fact, they're probably concocting an elaborate cover-up right now.'

'Then what?'

Daniel had had one word in his head since Kara's suspicions about the plane.

'Sabotage. When you mentioned the word yesterday, it suddenly became clear to me.'

Kara stared into his eyes. 'You mean sabotage the military base?'

'Yeh, why not?'

'But how? If Seb's intel is correct, the base is in Alaska for heaven's sake.'

'Exactly. Very, very remote, and very, very secret. That's all to our advantage.'

Kara began nodding slowly. 'So, you think military personnel may be minimal…Wait a minute! What am I saying?' she said, grasping the top of her head.

'It can be done. We'll need help, of course.'

'Help? Whose help?'

'I'm working on it.'

'Don't tell me, your old oil rig saboteur buddies. Come on, Daniel. Get real.'

Daniel fell silent. It did seem like a lost cause. But he could not share his doubts. 'I'm telling you, with the right planning and, you know, resources, anything is possible. That oil rig attack was no walk in the park.'

'I'm sorry. I'm just not used to this kind of talk.'

'You yourself just said it, Kara: security at the base may be very low-key. They wouldn't want to attract any more attention than necessary. Especially now! Don't forget that bases are being spied on all the time,' he said pointing upwards.

'Well, for our sake, I hope you're right.'

'You mean, for *my* sake. There's no way *you're* getting involved.'

'Whoa! Wait one goddamned minute, Dr Bayford. Or should I call you *Señor* Daniel Bolivar? You may be the militant all-action hero, but I'm more qualified than you when it comes to the technology.'

Daniel laughed. Kara did not.

'You're serious,' he said.

'Hell yeh! There are people coming after us. I want to turn the tables.'

Daniel studied her face hard. 'OK then. We do this. Somehow.'

'*We* do this,' Kara repeated. 'Besides, what did you say to me in France about terrorism and justifiable violence? When all other avenues have been explored.'

'Kara, we don't need to justify anything. We're not the terrorists. Your government and the Guild of God are.'

Chapter 76
Cover-Up

Caracas, Venezuela

The overweight, taxi driver seemed happy enough. Having collected Daniel and Kara from the rental car company, his meter had started clicking over more than thirty minutes ago, ten of those outside the hotel. He was absorbed with the football results on radio and would respond with short exclamations of irascible disgust or undiluted delight, each time turning to Kara. Her disinterest, though, was evident. But it was a good excuse for the cabbie to take another look at her legs.

Kara was oblivious to his leering. She was looking out nervously through the rear window at the steady stream of hotel guests passing in and out. *Come on, Daniel! Where are you?* she thought.

Seb had given Daniel the name of the embassy contact, and, to her amazement, Daniel had agreed to meet at their hotel. Kara took some comfort in the fact that there was no sign of any police activity but breathed a sigh of relief when Daniel finally appeared.

'*Aeropuerto, por favor,*' he said.

The taxi pulled off and merged into the morning traffic.

'Well?' Kara asked. Daniel simply nodded. 'Why on earth did you agree to meet at the hotel?'

Daniel leant over and whispered, 'I wanted to be sure we were in the clear.'

'By coming here?'

'It's OK. Everything seemed completely normal. My guess is that the other guy cleaned up, so to speak.'

Kara shook her head and looked out the window. 'And our stuff?' she asked without turning back.

'All taken care of. Hey, you're angry. Please don't be.'

Kara remained quiet. She *was* angry. She hoped she would feel a whole better once they were far away.

'Oh, I grabbed your carry-on bag and put a few clothes and basics in there. It's in the boot. Looks better travelling with something than nothing at all.' This did little to appease Kara.

'So, why Martinique?' she asked abruptly.

'I went there once. Many years ago. It's relatively close and the only place I know near here. We'll be safer there.'

The sports reporter on the radio had reached a crescendo of excitement. Whatever he had reported caused the taxi driver to bang his steering wheel and curse. Daniel looked at Kara, half smiling and nodding towards their driver. Kara raised her eyebrows but did not return his smile.

East of the Lesser Antilles

In an almost playful way, Dolphins and flying fish were weaving and leaping ahead of the *Marid's* bow, as the mega yacht ploughed its way across the deep blue waters of the southern Caribbean.

Prince Al-Musan was alone in the relative quiet of his study. The deep thrum emanating from the engine room indicated that they were under full power. He sat motionless, a deep frown across his brow as he watched another news report.

A drone shot was showing what was left of a mosque in Casablanca. The coverage cut to a young female reporter on the ground, taking amongst the rubble, as she rounded off her report. '*Witnesses say that the storm was relentless. No one had ever seen anything like it. The death toll is likely to rise. This is Amani Kalpar in Casablanca, Morocco…*'

The prince selected another channel. Four faces were superimposed on the main display behind the anchor in a heated video debate.

'*No, you can't say that!*' one of the interviewees said, shaking her head.

'*Ma'am, look at the facts!*' a bearded young man responded.

'*Facts? What facts are you actually referring to?*'

'*Largely Muslim cities. That's all I'm sayin'.*'

'*Your words are not only hateful but inciteful.*'

'*OK, ok,*' the anchor interjected. '*I'd like to hear from Pastor Jennings. Pastor, you believe this to be the wrath of God?*'

A large, bespectacled African American smiled. '*This is retribution, the retribution of God Almighty.*'

The bearded man was nodding vigorously. *'Yeh! Amen to that!'*

The anchor held up a hand. *'Carry on, Pastor.'*

'"For the wrath of God is revealed from heaven against all ungodliness and unrighteousness of men, who hold the truth in unrighteousness." Romans 1:18.'

The woman interviewee could not hold back. *'You quote the bible, Pastor. But you quote a jealous God, not your so-called God of forgiveness. And what did these poor people do to deserve this? They were innocent!'*

The fourth interviewee, a twenty-something student, tried to interrupt. *'You are all talking trash. How—'*

The bearded man was incensed. *'This ain't trash! The pastor is right. This is retribution for all the hurt those Muslims have done to us.'*

'How...' the student continued as calmly as possible, *'how can you talk about the wrath of God when this was clearly an act of nature? This is science, not thunderbolts from heaven!'*

'And how can you, whatever your name is, you, the man with the beard...'

'Craig,' the bearded man replied smiling. He was enjoying the shouting match. So, too, were the news anchor and the production team in the gallery. The channel's ratings were on fire.

'How can you talk about my Muslim brothers and sisters as though we're all evil? True Muslims deplore any act of violence.'

Al-Musan was far from happy. Another channel was covering the same story. A map showed the reported storms across the affected region. The female news anchor was in full flow.

'But were these storms forecast?'

An inset video image showed an elderly man and the caption DR FRANCOIS SAUVAGEON, WMO. *'Possibly. I would need to see the forecasts for each location. But localised, rapidly-developing storms are not unusual.'*

'Even in some of the most arid regions on earth?'

'It's rare, but not impossible.'

'But we have reports of more than twenty all within minutes of each other. Are we seeing another worrying effect of climate change?'

'People are becoming obsessed with climate change. There are more than three million lightning strikes across our planet every day. We also have another obsession: twenty-four-hour news coverage. Our reporting of events has never been so intense. No, this, in my opinion, is a freak event.'

'A freak event of nature?'

'Well, yes. What else? Look, storms, floods, and forest fires are nothing new. We just get to hear about them a lot more these days.'

'Can you explain why so many mosques were struck? It does seem bizarre, don't you think?'

'I believe other buildings were also struck.'

'I'm sorry to interrupt, but the vast majority of buildings were mosques.'

'Well, these storms were coincidently in Islamic countries and mosques have minarets. We all know that tall structures attract lightning. The lack of electrical storms in those regions may have meant a lack of lightning conductors. That's my initial thought.'

'Well, I'm sure we'll know more soon. Thank you, Dr Sauvageon. That was Dr Francois Sauvageon of the World Meteorological Organisation. We can now go over to Mark Young, US Climate Envoy. Thank you for joining us, Mr Young.'

'My pleasure.'

'You may have heard the comments of Dr Sauvageon just now, I hope?'

'I did.'

'Do you agree? Do you believe these to be a freak of nature?'

'Yes, I do.'

'Let me clarify. Do you think they were as a result of climate change?'

'I think that one thing is certain and that is, we don't know how climate change can affect us.'

'So, you disagree. You believe climate change is responsible.'

'Well, not quite. What I'm saying is that we just don't know if climate change has played a part. The world's climate is extremely complex. We struggle to provide reliable forecasts even with our latest supercomputers.'

'Hang on! Your position regarding climate change is described by many as being blinkered and unscientific. You are on record for blaming nearly every natural disaster on climate change. Now, you're saying that our climate is complex. Surely that contradicts your opinion.'

'No, not at all. Unusual events have happened for millennia. I believe that these...'

'I'm sorry to interrupt. We don't have much time. Let me ask you this, and to your last point: one eyewitness we interviewed used the word biblical in their description. That's quite a scary adjective, don't you think?'

'Well, I think the word biblical supports the very thing that Dr Sauvageon and I just said, that this is nothing new.'

'I see. Some are suggesting that there is a more sinister reason behind these storms. That this could be the result of some kind of weather weapon.'

The politician half laughed. *'Absolutely not. Unsubstantiated speculation. Mumbo jumbo. Conspiracy theorists love to stir things up. Look, I think most people accept the fact that forecasting weather is hard enough. The idea of controlling it to that extent is, quite frankly, ludicrous.'*

'It does seem strange, though. Twenty-seven very similar storms all within minutes of each other.'

'Mother Nature is full of surprises. I think it goes to show how much we should take heed.'

'What about the recent martyrdoms? They were lightning related. What do you say about that? You have to admit, equally strange.'

'I wish you people would stop calling them martyrdoms.'

'But, Mr Young, we have video evidence that these men were calling on Allah. Surely you saw the words on the banner the man unfurled on Tower Bridge here in London...er, "Allah is great. He will welcome me to paradise".'

'Unrelated. It's all coincidence. There will be a rational and natural explanation for those men being struck and these storms. Look, you should be reporting facts. Not wild and unfounded speculations.'

'It's our duty to explore and discuss all possibilities.'

'I'm sure we'll know more about those so-called martyrdoms. It was no doubt an elaborate trick. As for the storms, it's very likely that our influence on climate has played its part. And that's why it's my job, my mission to push for less reliance on fossil fuels. The effects of rising sea levels, failing crops, extinctions, and the loss of biodiversity—the list goes on—could lead to mass migrations and the loss of life to countless millions. That is what I would describe as biblical.'

The prince powered off the TV and stared out the window. He had spent the morning watching news reports and poring over images and videos.

Chapter 77
Trail

Martinique, Lesser Antilles

Daniel had booked them a room in a resort on the south coast. The drive from the airport would take no more than an hour through the heart of the island.

Kara looked out of her window as Daniel wound the all-electric Citroën around the countless twists and turns. As they ascended, there were glimpses of the densely wooded valleys. Tidy, well-maintained houses, and gardens planted with exotic flowers and palms, dotted the route.

'We could be in France,' Kara declared.

'I know. That's exactly what I thought when I came here. Martinique *is* in fact a department of France. Even the road signs are the same.'

Half an hour later, the trees thinned to reveal their first view of the sea.

'The resort's over there on that headland. You'll love it.' Daniel said, pointing.

'Any ideas about, you know?'

'Alaska? Yes. I contacted Seb again. We need the exact location of the base.'

'But if Bradbury is involved and knows Seb is your friend, won't they be watching him like a hawk?'

'Seb's smart. He'll find a way.'

Two days later, Daniel awoke to find Kara was already up. 'Kara?' Kara was paddling in the sea just metres away. 'Good morning!' he called.

She turned and smiled. 'It's beautiful. Look at this beach and look how clear the water is.'

Daniel walked over the white sand and waded in. He sensed her mood had shifted for the better. 'Ever been on a jet ski?'

'No. Oh god, you really are a man of action,' she said laughing.

They kissed. 'Well, you know what a man of action must always do, don't you?'

Kara could sense mischief was afoot and tried to get away. 'No, don't you dare!' But Daniel had grabbed her, lifted her, and ran further into the sea, where he plunged them both into the warm, shallow water. Kara squealed with delight. They both knelt on the soft sand, laughing, and hugging each other tightly.

***

Anchored in the bay five hundred metres behind the resort's headland, the *Marid* dwarfed the flotilla of other boats gently bobbing about.

On the upper sun deck, Prince Al-Musan had finished his fifty, morning press-ups. He lay on his back, hands behind his head, and began as many sit-ups.

Hassan approached, casting a shadow over the prince.

'You're blocking my sun!'

'I'm sorry, Your Highness.' His aide stepped quickly to the side.

The prince stopped his routine and sprang to his feet. 'What?'

'They are in the resort.'

Al-Musan pointed to the nearby lounger and clicked his fingers. Hassan went to pick up the towel. 'No,' the prince shouted, 'the phone!'

The prince dialled. 'Tell me!' He listened then hung up. He looked over the railing onto the deck below. 'You two! Follow me!' The prince descended to the deck below and entered the bar area. The two men followed and waited for their instructions. 'You know what to do,' he said. 'But use your brains. I don't want another failure. And I especially don't want a scene. Do you understand? They're hiring a jet ski. Take two of mine. Now go!'

***

'OK, here we go. Hang on tight now!' Daniel said as he eased the jet ski away from the beach. With that, he opened the throttle.

'Whoo-hoo!' Kara yelled, laughing. The jet ski skidded across the smooth water, bouncing gently, and throwing refreshing spray over them both. Daniel was enjoying the feeling of Kara's breasts against his back and her bare legs tucked up tight against his thighs.

Not far from where they launched, in the shade of a palm tree, an Arab man stood up and pocketed his phone.

Daniel was in the mood to explore. He made a sharp turn to the right. A plume of water shot up and crashed behind them as he sped forward towards a headland. 'Let's check out the next bay,' he hollered.

Unbeknown to them, two jet skis had left the *Marid* and were now hugging the coastline and heading towards the resort. They then swung right and began to close in on Daniel and Kara.

Kara heard the other motors first. She turned her head. Two black jet skis were twenty metres behind them. When they started weaving and arcing up sheets of water, she smiled and waved. 'Looks like we may have a race,' she shouted into Daniel's ear.

Daniel turned to look. As he did so, one of the jet skiers shot across their wake. After everything they had been through recently, he was now hypersensitive. The positioning and behaviour of the two jet skis felt threatening.

'Go on! Race them!' Kara hollered.

But Daniel did not reply. He turned to the right, slowing slightly. *Let's see if they follow us*, he thought. They did, keeping their formation and matching Daniel's speed. Daniel looked at the jet skier on his right rear flank. The man looked powerful and very tanned. More to the point, he was not smiling or waving like a friendly holidaymaker having fun.

The three jet skis were at least three hundred metres out from shore, and the beach Daniel and Kara had left was already a good kilometre away.

'Hang on!' Daniel shouted. He accelerated and looked back. They were still there—and closer. Daniel started to weave. Then, without warning, there was a collision. The man to their left had rammed them.

'WHAT THE HELL!' Kara shouted and squeezed Daniel tighter. She turned to look. The man had pulled away. She turned the other way. The other jet ski was heading straight for them. 'DANIEL!' The second jet ski hit them, its driver kicked out with a foot, and the craft glanced off Daniel and Kara's. It was enough to destabilise them.

This was no game. This was now getting dangerous.

Daniel reasoned to himself that if they had wanted to hurt them—or worse— they would have done so by now. He slowed to a crawl. The black jet skis followed suit, then began circling them. When Daniel sat upright, bringing their jet ski to a stop, one of the men brought his craft alongside. 'Come with us and we won't hurt you,' he shouted. A handgun was tucked into his shorts.

'Where?' Daniel shouted.

The man was pointing. The realisation hit Kara and Daniel at the same time. It was the same mega yacht they had seen in Cannes.

'Daniel, the London Underground terrorist, the man who attacked us, he was seen leaving that boat!'

'I know. It's OK, Kara. If that's Prince what's his name, he won't want any trouble. They would have killed us by now.'

The man with the gun set off. Daniel followed. The other jet skier brought up the rear.

Up close, the yacht was even bigger than Kara had first thought. They passed slowly beneath its bow shimmering with watery reflections. She looked up at its name, inscribed in gold on the pure white hull. The lead jet skier led them to a floating pontoon deck. He brought his craft into one of two landing bays and directed Daniel to moor up in the other.

Daniel steadied the jet ski as Kara was helped off. Ahead of her on the rear deck of the yacht sat Prince Al-Musan in a squat purple chair, shaped like a cupped hand. He was bare-footed and wearing a sky-blue t-shirt, white shorts, and sunglasses. 'Welcome aboard *Marid*,' he said, standing up. 'Please,' he continued, beckoning them both forward. He took both Kara's hands and brought them together, kissing one of them. 'Please accept my sincere apologies for the unconventional and rather uncivilised invitation.'

'Your men could have killed us,' Kara said blankly, pulling her hands away sharply. She was clearly in no mood for any feigned courtesies.

The prince laughed. 'A woman with spirit. I like that.'

'Oh god, a chauvinist,' Kara muttered. The prince continued to smile.

'I'm sorry if I offended you. You probably think I'm a rich but backward Arab from some oppressive state.'

'The thought had crossed my mind,' Kara continued.

Removing his sunglasses, the prince looked at Daniel and raised his eyebrows. 'May I get you a drink?'

'No thanks,' Kara said flatly. 'Just tell us why you have effectively kidnapped us.'

'First, I have no intention of hurting you. So, please relax.'

The prince clicked his fingers and Hassan appeared with two towels. Dressed in a scanty bikini, Kara suddenly felt very under-dressed. Her body, wet with sea spray, glistened under the morning sun. After rubbing her shoulders and arms, she wrapped the towel around her.

Daniel was in no mood for pleasantries either. He cocked his head to one side. 'Bakr al-Ahdal. Did you know he's been put away for a very long time?'

'Who?' the prince asked, holding his arms out, palms up.

'He was seen leaving your boat in Cannes.'

'Ah, that was probably during the party I held. I had so many guests. I hardly knew any of them. Film stars, local politicians, the mayor...'

'Terrorists,' Kara added.

The prince turned to Kara, but before he could respond, Daniel continued, 'He then broke into my villa.'

'That's terrible. I would have let you review my CCTV. But if you say he has been arrested then that's good. One less criminal on the streets.'

'He's a lot more than a street criminal. He blew up half of London and God knows what else,' Kara said. She seemed calm, but inwardly she was seething.

The prince turned to his two jet skiers and waved them away.

'So, you don't know Bakr al-Ahdal,' Daniel said. 'Then how about Ahmed Hashim?' The prince frowned and shook his head. 'Well, in that case, you won't care if I told you I killed him. Oh, and the Met Police think I'm a hero for doing so. You see, he and that Bakr chap tried to kill us.'

Kara sensed that Daniel was telling the prince, in no uncertain terms, not to mess with them.

The prince lowered himself back into the purple chair, put on his sunglasses, and crossed his legs. 'That's an interesting story, Doctor Bayford. Quite the adventure. But I'm not sure why you're telling me. Aren't you curious to know why I brought you here? ...No? OK, I'll tell you. Three words: Spear of Destiny.'

Kara responded a little too quickly. 'The what?'

Prince Al-Musan smiled and stood up. 'Follow me, please. I have something to show you.'

They followed the prince into an air-conditioned lounge bar encircled with sumptuous white sofas. The floor was made of toughened glass. Small white LED lights shone through from below, highlighting subtle Arabesque patterns inscribed in the glass.

The prince approached an immaculate curved bar, shaped, like a reptile. Gold and silver scales across its sides and the bar top added to the effect. It reminded Kara of the head of a cobra. 'Are you sure I can't tempt you to a drink?' As much as they both wanted a real taste of this wealth and opulence, they shook their heads. The prince turned away and poured himself an exotic-looking fruit juice. He then reached for a remote and pointed it at one of four wide screens. An image of an Arabic city filled the screen. 'I'm sure you saw this shocking news. This is one you may not have seen. It's of a city ignored by the West. Algiers.' He turned to his reluctant guests. 'Ever been there? ...No, I thought as much.'

Unlike the news reports that widely circulated the world, this one had been videoed in its entirety by an eyewitness a few hundred metres from the onslaught. Countless lightning bolts were already striking a mosque. The camera panned to the right and left. A man's voice could be heard expressing disbelief, edged with excitement. No other buildings were being touched. The witness then panned up. Low, grey clouds hung in the sky, from where lightning was emanating across a wide area. Some of the lightning forks were angled; others were channelling straight down. All of them focussing on the confines of the house of worship. It was intense. Daniel and Kara watched with a mixture of shock, awe, and perverse fascination, as the building began to succumb to the bombardment. The man videoing started raising his voice. Holes appeared in the dome. The image suddenly became chaotic—the man was now clearly running for his life.

'Stop it. We've seen enough,' Kara suddenly said.

The prince punched the remote and the screen went dark. He looked at Kara. Then took out his phone and touched its screen. 'Doctor Kara Williams. Graduate of Brown University, Rhode Island, awarded a DSc from Harvard for ground-breaking work on atmospheric energy. Now researching renewable energy for the US government. Impressive.'

Was he quoting one of her bios? she thought.

'And Doctor Daniel Bayford, privately educated, a first from Durham and a DPhil in Atmospheric, Oceanic and Planetary Physics from Oxford. Worked for the British government. You are a clever couple. You make my DPhil in History seem trivial. You should have children and enhance the gene pool! After all, they say world intelligence is on the decline. Allah preserve us! Oh, and you, Daniel— you don't mind me calling you Daniel, do you?—I read that you helped attack an oil rig. Now that is impressive! I'm beginning to really like you both.'

'Are you interviewing us or something?' Kara asked as sarcastically as possible.

The prince laughed. 'I especially like you, Doctor Williams.'

'Well, the feeling is *not* mutual.'

The smile left his face. 'As clever people, you know exactly why you're here. As a graduate of history, I'm used to doing a lot of research. I've been researching you. In fact, more than that. I've been trailing you.'

'Well, there's a surprise,' Daniel said. 'And, pray, what triggered your interest in us? I'm sure it wasn't academic.'

The prince finished his fruit juice and sighed. 'I'm sorry, I'm playing with you. I like doing that. Daniel, you came to my attention with your little discovery.'

'Cut all the crap,' Kara interrupted. 'Of course, we know. We know everything, everything about you for starters.'

'Go on, please. I'm all ears.' His smile returned.

'We know you're behind the so-called martyrdoms. The fact that you were in Cannes was no coincidence. You have stones like the one Daniel found. I don't how many, or where you got them, but you saw Daniel's discovery as a threat. Science would undermine your crazy martyrdom plan. So, you sent your man Bakr al-Ahdal to do your dirty work. He failed, so he tried again in London. He failed again. Big time!'

The prince was nodding throughout. 'Very good. But, Doctor Williams, you have to admit that my plan was impressive and worthwhile. It only failed after the stupid copycat attempts. Fools that believed they could be struck down by the hand of Allah without a stone. But I did manage to convert thousands to Islam.'

'Hopefully, the true Islam and not your distorted, perverse version, you mean,' Daniel said.

'Oh, well, of course, Christianity is so much better, isn't it? Countless thousands were slaughtered, tortured, burnt at the stake, and persecuted in the name of *your* religion.'

'Most of that was a long, long time ago,' Kara argued. 'And I completely agree with you. But those were times of ignorance and fear. And we certainly weren't alone in that mindless slaughter and persecution. But this is now!'

Daniel stepped forward to expand on Kara's last point. 'Today, there's no excuse for religious bigotry and violence. And yet your people turn to terrorism.'

'Pure retaliation,' the prince countered calmly. 'Terrorism is the only weapon against the most powerful military forces on the planet. And it's not all about religion. It's about the invasion of our lands by that hegemonic and sanctimonious nation, America, and its ingratiating Western allies, led by self-righteous, corrupt politicians with agendas steered by multinationals. You try to impose your way of life on us at any cost.'

'That's rich coming from you!' Kara said with a mocking laugh and cast her eyes around their surroundings.

'Let me explain, Kara. I employ thousands of people in the West. I make plenty of money doing so, yes, but I'm also helping the economies of the US, the UK, Germany, France—the list goes on. And what do those countries do in return? No, I use my wealth to fight their injustice, their hypocrisy.'

'Oh, so you fund terrorism. That's interesting,' Kara said.

The prince smiled and shook his head.

Daniel continued. 'We then learn that Bakr al-Ahdal was one of the London tube bombers. So, why the sudden change from good old-fashioned terrorism to martyrdoms?'

The prince had spent years protecting his reputation. Deflecting accusations came naturally. 'I recruited him *after* that attack,' he lied.

'You must have an interesting circle of friends,' Kara said with disdain.

'The martyrdoms were my answer. I do not agree with violence,' the prince continued. 'It only makes Western governments more resolute and bellicose. But all they do is end up creating the very terrorists that attack their cities. It's an endless cycle. You see, Bakr was a victim of that Western aggression. He lost his family when a US drone struck his village. He had every reason to exact his revenge. You would have done the same if you had guts,' the prince said, turning to Daniel.

Kara moved forward and pointed a finger at the prince. 'He's got a damn sight more guts than you! You just sit here on your fancy boat dishing out money and orders. If *you* had guts, you would have been the first martyr. But no, you enjoy all the decadence and hedonism you can buy. You're a coward and a god damned hypocrite.'

They were unsure if they had hit a nerve. The prince fell silent. He sat down on one of the long, white sofas. 'OK, I think our slanging match should end. And please desist from your accusations. My lawyers aren't cheap because they're very, very good in cases of slander.'

They all fell silent.

The prince stretched an arm across the back of the sofa. 'Now, let me tell you what *I* know. When Bakr told me about you, Doctor Williams, I became curious. I knew that Doctor Bayford had family. Let me see…' The prince looked at his phone. 'Ah yes, Sophie and Brigitte Penaud. Sister-in-law and niece.' At this, Daniel clenched his fists. Kara sensed him tensing and subtly tapped his arm. 'And yet the description Bakr gave me was of someone else. I thought I need to know who this mysterious and beautiful woman is.'

'Did your Bakr happen to tell you that I *scared* him off?' Daniel said snidely.

'No. But now, I don't care. You see, I managed to find out who the beautiful and mysterious woman was. I didn't even have a photograph. Aren't you impressed?' Kara and Daniel simply stared back at him. They weren't going to rise to the bait. 'Like I said, research is one of my specialities. So, it wasn't long before I found out that you were an eminent scientist from the US of A. But then I asked myself why would she visit—let's face it, Daniel—an unknown fire watch? But then it hit me.' The prince was being sardonic. 'Daniel had just discovered a remarkable meteorite, the kind that attracts lightning and causes fires. So, I thought, she'd want to know more because *she* was researching atmospheric energy.' The prince stopped and looked at them both. 'But I was so, so disappointed to find out that her work was a front. No, she wanted the stone to help build a *weapon*.'

'Nice try, Einstein,' Kara said. 'Your research skills aren't as good as you thought. You smug bastard. I *am* a scientist researching, or should I say, *was* researching an incredible new form of energy. One that would see you and your rich oil friends return to poverty. Oh, and perhaps save the fuckin' planet in the process. But, no, the government hijacked my work, then killed my project. If you really want to know, we actually want to *stop* this madness!'

For the first time, Prince Al-Musan looked genuinely thrown.

'Surprise!' Kara added, again mockingly.

'Well, thank you for that insight, Doctor Williams, you've now confirmed that it's true. That the weapon exists. I mean, it did seem pretty obvious, given what I know about those wonderful meteorites. I'm assuming you also know it's called the Spear of Destiny. The name has—how can I put it?—a certain majesty and determination about it. And I wasn't disappointed. It's the name of the spear that pierced Christ on the cross. That's a nice touch. Oh, and I bet you're wondering how I could possibly find that out. No? Well, following your little trail across the globe, I learned that you met a priest. Anyway, the priest was very helpful.'

'What did you do to him, you bastard?' Kara hissed.

'Oh, please. My men were gentle. Well, he may have been a little shaken. But he's alive if that's what you're worried about. Like I said, I'm not a man who likes violence.'

Daniel was shaking his head. 'You really are a prick. Bakr al-Ahdal murdered thousands, and he and Ahmed Hashim tried to kill us in London. They were working for you.'

'I genuinely did not know about that. I can only assume he had his own agenda.'

'Bullshit! You sent him to silence us in France. He failed, so you sent him out again with help from Hashim.'

'I don't know who Hashim is.'

'Was, you mean. Who he *was*. I killed him, don't forget. I broke his neck and stabbed him for good measure.'

The prince jumped up from the sofa. 'Look, this is getting us nowhere. You say you want to stop this weapon. Why?' He studied their faces, waiting for an answer. He then smiled and began pacing the room. 'I know…You want to stop it because you were betrayed. Weren't you, Doctor Williams?' At this, he stopped and turned to her. 'Betrayed by your own people. You've even lost your job. You're pissed, as you Americans like to say.'

'Yes. Yes, I do want to stop it,' she said. 'I want to stop the madness.'

'And yet you're down here on a tropical island, enjoying yourselves.'

'Funny,' Kara said coldly. 'The enjoyment somehow stopped when *you* came along. And I will have a drink now. I don't suppose you have alcohol in your bar, or is that forbidden?'

'Of course. I don't partake, but what is your tipple?'

'Whiskey. Straight up.'

The prince poured the drink and handed her the glass. Kara swigged it in one go and handed it back.

'And how *do* you plan to stop the madness, Doctor Williams?'

'We have a plan,' Daniel said.

'You have a plan. I'm guessing it'll be along the lines of your oil tanker adventure. You and a bunch of amateur but well-meaning saboteurs will take on the might of the US army. Well, good luck with that.'

411

'So, what would *you* do?' Kara asked, her face like thunder.

'Ooh, now that's a great question, Doctor Williams. What *would* I do?' He folded his arms and began pacing the room again. 'I would do it properly for starters.'

'I can believe that,' Kara said, 'the tube and Eurostar attacks were pretty impressive.'

'You really won't let that go, will you? Look, let me tell you again, I recruited a terrorist to help coordinate a far more impactful campaign. One not built on death and destruction, but on something far more troubling. Millions began questioning their faith.'

'You're totally mad,' Daniel said. 'Millions saw those martyrdoms as unnecessary deaths of young, misguided men. It was a freak show. Nothing more. Everyone knew there would be a rational explanation. Those men's sacrifices were for nothing.'

'We will expose the truth. The truth about your so-called acts of Allah, *and* the weapon.' Kara declared defiantly.

'You may be able to stop me, but can you stop the Spear of Destiny in the same way? I suspect you want to stop it more dramatically than that. I suspect Daniel here wants a bit of action. Right, Daniel? Not some lame press release. I can see it now. Your claims will be dismissed as the ramblings of yet more loony conspiracy theorists.'

They knew he was right. They did not possess the details of the weapon technology. If not ridiculed, their claims would be regarded as wild speculation.

'I could help you,' the prince suddenly announced. 'Assuming you are happy about becoming a traitor to your own country, Doctor Williams.'

'They're the traitors. Traitors to mankind.'

'Well said! Wow! Magnanimous in fact,' the prince said.

'And thanks, but no thanks. We don't need your help.'

'She's right. It's also time for us to go.' Daniel grabbed her arm.

'Of course. You are free to go.'

Daniel led Kara out of the cool interior onto the now sweltering deck and to their jet ski. The prince shook his head and called out, 'Watch your backs now! You don't want to get burnt.' He laughed and sat down. Daniel fired up the engine. Kara climbed on and they sped off.

Chapter 78
In Deep

West London, UK

'And now, an in-depth look at this week's news with Joanne Summers.'

The short, punchy title sequence for the programme ran and the camera zoomed in on the fifty-something presenter. An image of one of the damaged mosques was spread across three screens behind her.

'Hello and good evening. Tonight, on In Deep, we discuss the electrical storms that ravaged much of the Middle East and North Africa this week. Were they a freak of nature, another consequence of climate change, or something more sinister? Whatever caused them, most would agree that they were not only bizarre but terrifying.'

The screens updated to show three interviewees.

In his small Kensington flat, Sebastian Sadler-Smith slurped his wine and reclined on his sofa, his feet resting on his coffee table. This he had to see.

'To discuss this, I have Professor Charles Blackwell of Florida State University, General Sir Gordon Henderson-Moore, former head of the British Army, and Ryan Mortimer of Question Everything, which he describes as an alternative think tank. Thank you for joining us, gentlemen. Let me start with you, Professor. Since your last interview with us, have you come to any conclusions? Were these storms natural or man-made?'

'So, my team and I have now looked at video footage from seven of these events. We also studied the prevailing weather conditions in each of those

locations. With the exception of Cairo, there were no storms present in the other locations. But, as I mentioned before, lightning can be unpredictable.'

'Hang on! Are you suggesting that six of the seven events you've looked into were all bolts from the blue?'

'To call them bolts from the blue, in this instance, is misleading. The other locations did have varying degrees of cloud cover. A number of the cities are also close to the sea. Combine that with high temperatures, and you have warm, moist air rising, changes in pressure, and the build-up of enormous electrical potential; all the components for lightning without the obvious sign of a thundercloud.'

'You mention high temperatures. Many argue that this is yet another sign of global warming; climate change running out of control.'

'Well, you asked if this was natural or man-made. I would have to concede that at this point the jury is out. I must admit that lightning in the more arid regions is unusual. But the atmosphere is complex.'

'So, you think climate change could be responsible?'

'It can't be ruled out.'

'I see. And what do you say to the growing number of voices who claim that these storms were caused by some kind of weapon?'

The professor laughed. 'We have neither the technology nor the sheer power to control weather in that way...'

Summers interrupted the professor. 'That's not the opinion of many of your peers, eminent scientists like you.'

'They're entitled to their opinions. But to control weather on such a scale is, in my opinion, beyond our capability. Cloud seeding, yes, but not this.'

Summers continued, 'We have heard from climate experts over the recent years to expect more and more extreme weather events. So, is your conclusion that this was a natural set of events that could fall into that category?'

'In short, yes.'

'But you have to admit that the sheer repetition, similarity, timing, and location of these events is strange, to say the least.'

'It's quite plausible that we are witnessing a new and alarming result of climate change. To put this into context, my colleagues in Fairbanks, Alaska, recently reported a significant increase in thunderstorms in Siberia and Alaska. So, if thunderstorms are now cropping up in some of the coldest parts of the world, the prospect of more in hotter climes is almost inevitable.'

'*Thank you, Professor. Sir Gordon, if I could come to you, social media has been awash with theories about a deadly, new weather weapon developed in the West. It's not an unreasonable theory, is it not, especially in light of the fact that some of the countries that experienced these electrical storms like Iran could be regarded as not particularly close, even hostile?*'

'*I think the professor has answered the question for me. We struggle to predict the weather, especially on these islands! So, the notion of some kind of weather weapon is, quite frankly, ludicrous. I'm surprised that a respectable broadcasting company like yours is falling for that ridiculous theory.*'

'*But it does seem curious,*' Summers pressed, '*that twenty-seven reported incidents occurred a) within minutes of each other, b) all in cities that are predominantly Muslim, and c) soon after the so-called martyrdoms.*' Ryan Mortimer on the third screen started to nod vigorously.

'*I think it's natural for people to make that connection.*'

'*You mean the martyrdoms?*'

'*Yes. Even if we were capable of constructing such a weapon, and I'm afraid that just sounds utterly fanciful, why would anyone…*'

'*Do you mean, why would any Western government?*' Summer clarified.

'*…Well, anyone in power…Why would they want to sow further division and hatred in countries that do not pose a threat and in many cases are friendly allies and economic partners? With so many other global threats beyond our control, it's in our mutual interest to work with one another. Look, the idea of a weapon is ridiculous.*'

Summers had been looking at the screens. '*I can see that Ryan Mortimer is keen to have a word.*'

'*Thank you, Joanne.*' Mortimer said. He was the youngest of the three interviewees. The caption at the top of the screen indicated that he was speaking from San Francisco. '*I'm afraid your experts are missing one key element in this debate: religion. Those were martyrdoms. There is no doubt. We have all seen and heard the proclamations made by many of those young men. They were calling on Allah to take them to paradise. We are all too aware of the rise in radical thinking in Islam over the decades. But more recently, there has been a similar rise in Christian fundamentalism.*'

The other two guests had been muted but were shaking their heads. Summers stepped in. '*If I may, Mr Mortimer, I'd like to explain to our viewers that your organisation, Question Everything, does indeed question everything, but seems to come up with rather—to use Sir Gordon's word—fanciful explanations.'*

'That's an unfair appraisal. I don't pretend to have all the answers. But by asking the questions, we encourage thinking and debates like this one. Too many people are fooled by their governments and those in power. We are too accepting, too compliant, too gullible.'

'You're a conspiracy theorist,' Summers said.

'I prefer plain theorist. The word "conspiracy" is divisive and the phrase "conspiracy theorist" has become synonymous with crazies and geeks.' The other two guests could not suppress a brief smile.

'One US senator described you as anti-government, anti-establishment.'

'I know whom you're referring to. She would say that. I helped to expose a pharmaceutical company in her state. Look, I ask this question: if you were a very strong believer in the Christian faith and you saw a continued decline in your congregation and then conversion to an alternative faith, and you had the means to fight back, would you?'

'So, you believe this could be a weapon? That doesn't sound like a religious solution.'

'Try telling that to the people slaughtered by the Crusaders.'

'Surely, you're not suggesting some kind of twenty-first-century crusade?'

'All I'm saying is that if you could go back in time and meet your very own Sir Isaac Newton and you told him that we could split certain atoms to release unimaginable power, do you think he'd dismiss it as crazy? We also know that lasers can be used to attract lightning. Who really knows what is possible?'

'That's a fair point, Sir Gordon. Technology is advancing faster than at any time in history. Perhaps someone somewhere does have the means to manipulate our atmosphere for belligerent means.'

The venerable, retired general smiled. 'Well, I'd be very surprised. First, your guest assumes that religion is the motivator. Second, a weapon of this magnitude would have to be funded at a government level. Now, I can't think of a government or country with that kind of technology combined with that kind of religious zeal. I also think we have to remember one very important fact: there are absolutely no reports of any missiles during these storms. Nor was there any weaponry evidence amongst the ruins. And for that reason, I say there has to be another explanation.'

'Professor?'

'*If I could just say one thing?*' Mortimer interjected.

'*Quickly. I want to hear from the professor.*'

'*The general says it would have to be funded by a government. What about the recent advances in space technology? They were all developed by private firms.*'

'*Another fair point. But it would seem the consensus is that a weapon is implausible. Professor?*'

'*I can only agree with Sir Gordon and reiterate my earlier point: the energy required to control weather with this kind of accuracy is, I'm sorry to say, absolutely impossible.*'

'*I will be looking into this further,*' Ryan Mortimer began, '*and one more thing, don't you think it's strange that lightning was the common factor with these events and the martyrdoms...*'

'*I'm sorry, we've run out of time. I'm sure we haven't heard the end of this intriguing and disturbing story. Thank you, all. Now, has the economy again hit the buffers...?*'

Sebastian-Smith sat up. 'What?' he said to himself. 'It was just getting interesting!'

He took another gulp of wine and began typing a message:

Daniel, Happy Birthday you ol' git. I've sent you a bottle of that wine you raved about when we met. It was very, very expensive! But I guess you're worth it. Cheers, Seb.

Chapter 79
Message and a Bottle

Martinique, Lesser Antilles

The resort lobby—pleasantly cool and stylish—was deserted but for Daniel and the smart young receptionist. In the early morning light, the lush palms and plants cast long shadows across the white marble floor—all the way to the desk.

Daniel waited patiently as the receptionist ducked underneath the counter. Finally, she looked up and presented him with a soft, round package.

'Here you are. Have a good, sir.'

'Thanks, you, too.'

Daniel strolled through the gardens towards their room. The package was from Seb and included a message. Daniel read it and frowned. He then pulled at the wrapping and could see the top of a bottle.

The moment he was back in the room, Kara's question came. 'So, what is it, Daniel?'

'It's from Seb.' Daniel removed the rest of the packaging to reveal an expensive bottle of red wine. 'He's backed down.'

'What d'you mean?'

Daniel handed her the document. Kara could see the personal message and began reading.

'I don't get it,' she said.

'I do.' Daniel held out a hand and Kara handed back the paperwork. Daniel read it out loud: "*A little something for my dear friend. It was great seeing you and the lovely Kara. I envy you! I love Americans, don't you? You made me think about my retirement. Maybe I'll sell up and become your neighbour. One bit of advice: give up trying to put out fires. That's a crazy job. I don't want you to get hurt. BR, Seb x (PS: the kiss is for Kara!)*" He's pulled out because he doesn't want to risk losing his pension. That's the bit about his retirement. He mentions

Americans because he's referring to the "special relationship." And he's not referring to my part-time job when he talks about putting out fires. Damn it!'

'So, no hidden message elsewhere?'

'That *was* the hidden message. And no, there's no microfilm or encrypted message on the wine label. This is not James Bond.'

'Sorry I asked,' Kara said, looking hurt. 'I just thought…'

'No, I'm sorry. I'm also disappointed.'

'He cares for you. It shows.'

'He's also caring about his own future.'

'Or perhaps he's just a good patriot.'

'But he could have just as easily sent me what we needed with a similarly clever message. Damn and blast! I just wish I'd taken more notice of those flight manifests he showed us. Finding that base may be like finding the proverbial needle.'

'You're not giving up on me, are you, Doctor?' Kara teased, raising her eyebrows. Her look made Daniel melt. He cupped her face in his hands. 'I am so glad I met you. Without you, yes, I probably would have given up. So, what next, Doctor?'

She pulled away. 'I faced a shit load of dead-ends and disappointments during my project. But, as team leader, I had to rally the troops and try, try again.'

'Like Robert the Bruce.'

'Who?'

'The Scottish king and the spider…? Never mind.'

Kara gave him a bemused look. 'Whatever.' Daniel had picked up the bottle. She studied him and her face turned to one of concern. 'A penny for your thoughts?'

'It's what Seb said: *a crazy job.* He thinks we're crazy to even think about taking this on.'

'You know, one of my weaknesses is my stubbornness. I hate to give up, even when everyone around me says I should.'

Daniel looked at her and shook his head slowly. 'I'll never understand women.'

'So, come on. Let's put our thinking caps back on.'

'Well, you've certainly changed your tune.'

'Wait a minute! What did you say? Finding that base may be like finding the proverbial needle. What if we looked for something else a bit like a needle?'

Daniel stayed quiet. Here she was again with her exceptional intellect. He tried to anticipate where she was going, for he was sure she had the route already mapped out in her head. Kara swung around, flipped open her laptop, and sat down with it on the bed. 'Needles are silvery and bright. A bit like?'

'Er…lightning?' Daniel answered cautiously, suddenly catching her drift. He also felt like he was back at school, the smart teacher having picked him out to answer a question in front of the entire class.

'Exactly. Full marks.' It was as though Kara had read his mind. She was now typing rapidly on the keyboard. Several browser windows popped up. She flicked from one to another. 'These are satellite-based reports…Here we go, Alaska. What's the betting that they tested the weapon up there? Now, Alaska is not somewhere you see much lightning. Too damn cold.' She opened another window and started a search. A news report filled the screen. 'That's interesting. Look at this! I was about to show you how little lightning activity takes place in colder climes.'

Daniel read the headline: FREAK RISE IN ARCTIC LIGHTNING STORMS NORTH OF ALASKA BAFFLES SCIENTISTS

They both read further.

'Lightning in the region,' Daniel said, 'has tripled in the last year. But they're saying it's the result of climate change.'

'The perfect smokescreen?'

Kara called up one of the previous pages and began typing again. A list appeared. More data flashed up, but Kara was already on another page. Daniel was finding it hard to keep up. 'What are you looking for?' he asked.

Kara simply held up a hand and typed again. When a satellite image appeared on the screen, she removed her hands from the keyboard and leant back. A white outline showed the extent of the state of Alaska. Blotches of colour were dotted over the map ranging from yellows and oranges to reds and purples.

'I can see what you're doing. But heavy lightning activity may not necessarily centre on the base we're looking for. They may have done tests miles away.'

Kara wiggled her head. 'Maybe. Maybe not. But it's all we have,' she said. She began opening more windows. She was on a roll, and they both knew it. 'OK, we need to find some likely candidates for our base. Any ideas?'

'A map app?'

Kara gave him a look, but then said, 'Why not?' She opened an app and typed. A series of red locators popped up. 'No, these are all too public.'

'Go back to that lightning image…What about that one?' Daniel pointed at a deep red smudge towards the northeast of the state. Kara clicked on the screen. A map coordinate appeared in a box. She copied it and pasted it into the app.

'Hmm, let's take a closer look.' She switched to satellite view and zoomed in. 'Damn, it's blurred.'

'That's it then.'

'You mean that could be it, or simply somewhere that had a lot of lightning activity for more natural reasons.'

Daniel leant forward and clicked to zoom out.

'What?' Kara asked.

'Seb's list. For some reason that name there rings a bell.' He zoomed in and scanned the area. After a minute or so of going backwards and forwards in an ever-wider area, he stopped. 'Hang on, what's that?' He zoomed in. 'Well, if that's not a landing strip.'

'An unmarked landing strip at that.' Kara returned to the lightning map. 'Well, there are no other obvious locations. I think we've found our needle.'

Chapter 80
The 49th State

Alaska, USA, Three Weeks Later

Daniel was behind the wheel of the large 4x4 SUV, as it cruised along the road from Fairbanks, now a good hundred and twenty kilometres behind them. It was very cold. The car heater was on high and the radio was playing an old Joe Walsh rock classic. Light snow was hitting the windscreen from a uniform-grey sky. Close to the sides of the highway, dense coniferous trees obscured the countryside beyond. Occasionally, gaps would appear to reveal gentle hills and mile upon mile of forest.

'I have a confession,' Daniel said, turning down the radio.

Kara, almost hypnotised by the oncoming snowflakes, snapped out of her reverie. 'I'm listening.'

'A few of my friends will be joining us.'

'Ha! I knew it! Your oil rig saboteur buddies, right?'

Daniel glanced at her. 'You're not angry, are you?'

'No. But you could have told me earlier. When did you arrange all that?'

'In Martinique.'

'When?'

'I made a call when you were having a siesta one afternoon.'

'And they agreed?'

'Yeh. Actually, I didn't think they would. That's why I didn't mention it to you. The one call I made was to a guy called Stu. He said he'd call the others.'

'How many are you talking about?'

'That I don't know. Stu wouldn't say. But we'll find out soon enough.'

'So, what else haven't you told me?'

'Nothing. That's it! Listen, I'm not purposely keeping things from you. But you have to admit, it's going to take more than you and me.'

Kara looked out of her window. 'No, you're right. But…'

Daniel gave her another look. 'But what?'

'But this all sounds like it's gonna get a bit scarily real.'

'Kara, I did say before that I didn't want you to get this involved. In fact, the more I think about it, the more I'm sticking to that idea. And don't think it's because I'm some old stick-in-the-mud chauvinist. It's more about experience or, in your case, lack of it.'

Kara turned to face him. 'What are you and your buddies likely to do?'

'That's what we plan to discuss. But I can guarantee one thing, we won't be messing about.' Daniel looked at the Sat Nav. 'We're meeting them here,' he said, pointing to the northeast. 'On the banks of the famous Yukon.'

'So, what would you have done if they'd said no?'

The thought had not entered Daniel's mind. 'Maybe what we're doing now. You know, just trying to get close. Play it by ear. Who knows? Anyway, that's academic.' He toggled the volume control. The Beatles' *Drive My Car* chorus line: "*Yes, I'm gonna be a star*" blasted out. Daniel secretly hoped the lyric was a prescient description of him and his half-baked plan.

Nearly an hour later, Daniel swung the car up a single track. The snow had stopped; sunrays flashed through the branches of the countless pine trees. After ten minutes, Daniel slowed and consulted the Sat Nav, then accelerated and took a turn to the left. This track was narrower and led them into the dark of the forest. The Sat Nav displayed 2.3km to their destination. The SUV's headlights were now more useful than the barely discernible sun.

They emerged into an opening, surrounded by tall trees. Ahead was a large cabin. Three men and a woman were emerging from its door. To one side of the cabin stood two vehicles: the first, another 4x4, a bit meatier than Daniel and Kara's; the second, an ATV, or All-Terrain Vehicle, the size of a tank, and almost built like one, with a bank of floodlights and eight massive wheels. Daniel pulled up and killed the engine.

Kara zipped up her thermal jacket and stepped out. *God, it was cold*, was her first thought. Daniel had reached his four buddies and was hugging each of them in turn.

'Nice tan, Dan. Shame you can't show it off,' the last in the line joked.

'Chris. Good to see you,' Daniel said, acknowledging the only woman in the welcoming party. He turned and held out his arm for Kara. She smiled at the group. Daniel put his arm over her shoulder as they all entered the cabin.

Kara took in the open plan room. It felt warm. A large log-burning stove dominated its centre. Beyond was a split-level dining area. The smell of something cooking wafted through. *It's actually quite cosy*, she thought.

'OK, introductions,' Daniel said. 'Kara, this is Jack.' She shook his enormous hand. Jack was bald with a thick bushy beard. He was at least six foot four and powerful with it. 'This is Stu.'

Kara took in Stu's steely blue eyes, short fair hair, and stubble. *Jack is as tall as a beanstalk. Stu for stubble*, she thought—it was her way of memorising names. 'Hey,' she said.

'Next, we have Chris.'

'Hello,' Kara said smiling. Kara had not expected a woman to be part of Daniel's buddy group. Christine's short-cropped hair and iron-grip handshake soon dispelled any doubts Kara had about her potential.

'And last but not least, Dante.'

'Dante. That's a great name,' Kara said. She took in the final member of Daniel's team. His name was the easiest to remember and suited his exotic good looks. For some reason, seeing a black man was not what she had imagined. He also seemed younger than the others but with a certain calmness and assuredness in his eyes.

Dante smirked, 'Yeh, but I'm no poet.'

'He certainly isn't,' Daniel said, laughing. 'He's not so much creative as destructive. He likes blowing things up.'

'Er, excuse me, I create in the kitchen,' Dante added, smiling; keen to sell a more positive side. 'I'm the designated cook, Kara, because the culinary skills of this lot are non-existent.'

'Cooking. Is that what you call it,' Jack teased.

Kara guessed that Jack was the comedian among them. He was certainly the biggest.

'Yeh, something smells good,' Kara said, turning towards the dining area.

'Hope you're not a veggie. It's, er, beef stew and rice,' Dante announced.

'I could eat a horse, I'm so hungry,' Kara replied.

Daniel started making his way to the table. 'Me, too. I'm starved,' he said. 'And we need to talk.'

Kara took them all in again, as they settled around the table. *These guys look darn serious and very professional*, she thought. And Daniel looked and sounded like their team leader. She was not sure if her assessment was reassuring or frightening. She turned to Stu. His eyes said it all. Kara knew what he must be thinking: *Why bring a civilian scientist to the mission? She could be a liability.* She half-smiled and decided not to say anything in her defence.

Minutes later, the plates were empty and beer bottles were slid across the table.

Chris was the first to start talking business. She opened up one of the laptops. On the screen was an aerial image. 'I did some initial surveillance with the drone as soon as we arrived yesterday.' She clicked the play button. The drone shot was some distance from the perimeter of the base. The images were partly obscured by the tops of nearby trees, but most of the base was in view. The drone then rose slightly to take in the remaining areas of the base.

'Don't worry,' Stu said, 'we did some ground-based surveillance before deploying the drone. The base seems pretty quiet. You were right, Dan, they're opting for a low-profile approach.' He then leant forward and opened up a satellite image. 'There are just two sentries at the SPE—here,' he said with just a hint of a Scottish accent. 'They rotate every six hours.'

Daniel turned to Kara to clarify. 'Single point of entry,' he whispered. Kara nodded. 'Good. So, what about patrols, helicopters, dogs?'

'We've monitored the base for only thirty hours,' Jack said. 'But it's as quiet as a graveyard.'

'No external activity? Experiments?' Kara asked.

They all looked at her.

Daniel was quick. 'Kara helped us find the base using lightning activity images. It would seem they ran some initial weapon tests here.'

'This weapon,' Stu said looking at Daniel and Kara. 'What did you say it was called?'

'The Spear of Destiny,' Daniel replied.

'The Spear of Destiny,' Dante repeated slowly. 'That certainly has a ring of determination about it.'

'The people behind it are not only determined. They're fanatical,' Daniel declared. 'If you don't already know, the Spear of Destiny is the name of the spear that pierced Jesus on the cross. They've adopted it, because, yes, it's a cool name for a weapon. Except, this time, it's not killing off Christ, but killing off Muslims. These people are Christian zealots on a whole new level. As determined as any Jihadist.'

'And with the backing of the most powerful military force on the planet,' Kara added.

'Man, we saw those images on the news. That was pretty awesome stuff. Like, weird.' Jack put in.

Stu was shaking his head and frowning. 'I just don't get it, though. The world saw those lightning storms…'

'Attacks, you mean,' Daniel corrected.

'…OK, attacks. My point is surely everyone must see through it. It was clearly a coordinated assault.'

'The people behind this aren't just military,' Kara said. 'They're people in high places. Who knows what news is being suppressed by them? We're dealing with a seriously messed-up situation here.'

Jack leant forward. 'Dan, when Stu called me about this mission, he mentioned something about that meteorite you discovered.'

'It's how I met Kara,' Daniel said turning to Kara by his side and smiling. Chris smirked. 'Let me explain. Kara has been running experiments on atmospheric electrical energy. She's on the verge of something momentous: a new form of renewable energy. They were lacking the ability to draw that energy with reliability. And that's where this amazing meteorite comes in. You read the stories and saw the TV coverage, right?'

'Your fifteen minutes of fame, Dan. How could we not miss that?' Dante said. They all smiled.

'Well,' Daniel continued. 'That stone turned out to be Kara's Holy Grail. But her project was not what it seemed.'

'The military had their eyes on it,' Stu suggested.

'Exactly,' Kara said. 'Seems they were funding it all along. Not, as I thought, the Department of Energy.'

'You were royally shafted,' Chris declared.

'That's one way of putting it,' Kara said, raising her eyebrows.

'It's a British expression,' Daniel said.

'More Anglo-American, I'd say,' Jack observed.

'Alright, how about royally fucked?' Chris said.

'Anyway,' Daniel announced, keen to bring the meeting to order. 'We need to develop a POA. Like you said, Chris, you've only done an initial surveillance. I propose that tomorrow we get in close. Find out what we're dealing with as far as the perimeter fence is concerned, make doubly sure there are no patrols,

426

cameras, etcetera.' Daniel pulled the laptop towards him and studied the satellite image of the base. 'Where did you get this? The image we saw was blurred.'

'Christ, Dan, you weren't using an app, were you?' Jack said. 'Chris, got this courtesy of the best HD satellite imagery out there. Down to 15cm resolution. No hacking required, right Chris?'

'Yep. Easy-peasy.'

'Well, great,' Daniel continued and turned the laptop back around. 'OK, so where are *we*?'

Chris touched the screen, 'Right there.'

'OK. So, here looks like a good point.' Daniel pointed at a dense area of trees. Stu?' Stu studied the screen and nodded. 'OK, three of us will go by foot before sunrise. That'll be me, Stu, and Jack. The rest of you remain here and find out what you can about the base. Chris, can you get a live satellite feed?'

'Yeh, already on it.'

'Good. Kara, see if you can find any data on the base. Old, new, anything you can find. We need all the intel we can get. Dante, see if you can get an idea of the types of buildings here.'

'Sure.'

Daniel started to stand up but sat back down. 'If you get any unexpected visitors, you know the story. We're conservationists, working for The World Land Trust. It's a UK-based charity, so you'll be seen as harmless do-gooders.'

Stu handed out fake IDs to everyone. Kara looked at hers. *Impressive*, she thought.

Chris had been fidgeting with a small device throughout and now held it up. 'I'll set up our own perimeter with a bunch of these.'

'Perfect,' Daniel said.

'What are they?' Kara asked. But after seeing Chris' look, she wished she had not asked.

'Motion sensor cameras. They'll stream images back here if anything triggers them off.'

'Right, of course,' Kara said. She was feeling out of her depth. 'I guess they'll help with the cover story, right? I mean, we can say we're recording wildlife.'

Daniel smiled. 'That's a good point. Nice thinking. We may even catch ourselves a bear.'

Chris snorted and began fiddling again with the camera.

'Do you want me to set up some little surprises?' Dante asked, grinning.

Daniel knew exactly what Dante was referring to. He had a penchant for IEDs. 'Very funny. Thanks, but no thanks.'

'Only kidding.'

Daniel looked at his watch. 'OK, we have an early start, which means, brush your teeth and get-to-bed time. Oh, and two things: one, neither I nor Kara can be seen by anyone outside this group—we have connections with all this and the people behind it. Two...' Daniel opened an image on his phone and showed the group. It was of Richard Ordway. 'If this guy should turn up, kill him.'

Chapter 81
Reconnaissance

It was dark and a bone-chilling -22 Celsius. Daniel, Stu and Jack were moving forward in a line, ten metres apart, treading carefully over the forest floor. Each of them was wearing night-vision goggles and thermal, *snow camo* combat gear. Semi-automatic assault rifles were slung across their chests.

Daniel had briefed Stu three weeks ahead of his and Kara's arrival. In that time, Stu and the team had secured enough equipment and weapons for a small war.

Daniel had not needed to advise them of specifics; he knew each of them well enough to know that they would focus on their specialities: Jack Chaffry had spent fifteen years in the British Army. He was their weapons specialist; Dante Morgan was also ex-army with twelve years in the Royal Logistic Corps. What he did not know about explosives was not worth mentioning; Christine Packmore was their tech expert and total gadget freak. Drones, spyware, satellite hacking, imaging devices, and comms were her bag. And then there was Stewart 'Stu' Gibson; a surprisingly quiet man, but when he spoke, everyone listened. Out of all of them, Daniel had the most respect for Stu. The man had some seriously heavy special ops missions on his CV, from the Middle East and Africa to Central America and South East Asia. Stu was ex-SAS. He never divulged details of those operations. He did not have to. Daniel had witnessed what he was capable of. The one thing Daniel knew about his assembled team, was that they were some of the most resourceful and reliable people he knew. How they had managed to acquire so much equipment in so short a time was impressive but no surprise.

They had been walking now for twenty minutes. Up ahead, the trees were thinning. Daniel checked his GPS. They were fifty metres from the perimeter fence. He raised an arm and they all stopped.

It was quiet. Stu removed his goggles. Dawn was still an hour away, but through the last few trees, the vaguest sense of a lightening sky could now be made out. Daniel indicated to Stu to take the lead. Daniel and Jack followed a few metres behind and still wide apart.

When they reached the forest edge, Stu squatted for a few moments then removed his gun and lay belly down. He replaced his goggles. The eerie green image provided by the night vision image intensifiers showed the fence a few metres ahead. The built-in display of the goggles indicated that the main building complex of the base was five hundred metres ahead.

Stu had advised against any form of radio comms. Hand signals only, he said. It made sense. It was very likely that the base had sensitive monitoring equipment. The army may be adopting a low-key strategy, but this was a top-secret base after all. Stu clicked a button on the goggles. The image zoomed. After scanning the area, he stood up and joined Daniel just inside the tree boundary. Stu squatted next to him and signalled to Jack to keep a lookout. Jack acknowledged. Stu then spoke quietly, 'The fence is electrified. But that won't be a problem. Now, what *may* be a problem is the open ground. It's half a click to the buildings.'

'Shit,' Daniel muttered. If Stu said it may be a problem, then it may indeed be a problem.

'Ay, this tree cover is good for this reconnaissance, but not for the ATV's entry point. I'll know better once we have a live satellite feed. We may have been looking at old images. I just wanted to make sure.'

'So, what are you thinking?'

'We'll split into two teams. See over there,' Stu said pointing to their left. 'That's where the ATV team will emerge and cross this open ground. The other team goes in via the service road. There's less cover, but it's a shorter way in.'

'Yeh, but what about the sentry post?'

'We take them out on the way in. My guess is that they just sit there, bored shitless. We're in the middle of fuckin' nowhere. They won't be checking in every five minutes. So, we strike sixty minutes after the sentry rotation. That'll be 02 hundred hours. The retiring guards will be fast asleep by them, so that'll be two less bodies to worry about. We need to maximise our chances.'

'OK. Are we done here?'

'Ay, we're done.'

Chapter 82
POA

Kara woke with a start. She clicked on her phone to check the time. It was 5:48 a.m. and Daniel was not beside her. She sighed and laid back, face up, and listened. There were low voices downstairs. A good night's sleep had eluded her ever since the gun attack in London. And then she realised that it was that very event that had caused the nightmare from which she had just awoken, except the dream was not in the streets of London but outside Daniel's villa, in the snow, and she was not the target; she was firing the gun. And with each shot, there was a flash, not from the muzzle of a gun, but from the sky in the form of lightning. These early hours before most of the world had arisen were her least favourite time. The only solution, as always, was to get up and face the day.

A shiver ran through her body as she reached for her hoodie and tracksuit bottoms.

Down below, Daniel and his team were gathered around the table.

'Morning,' Daniel said.

'Is it?' Kara said with a half-smile, running a hand through her hair. *Maybe I could have done with an extra hour or two*, she thought.

Daniel, Stu, and Jack had returned from their sortie.

'There's coffee on the stove,' Dante said without looking up. He and the others were focussed on a piece of paper in front of the ex-SAS man. On it was a sketch of the entire base and immediate environs, the approach road, the compound, and military vehicles. The main complex had been marked C; the remaining four smaller buildings, B1 to B4.

Stu, pencil in hand, was recapping his plan of attack. 'OK, one more time. There are eight phases to this operation, so listen up. Phase 1. There can be no traces of our presence here, so Dante will place explosives for remote detonation. Phase 2. The ATV needs to be in position here no later than 01:55. That'll be Jack, Dante, and Chris. You're Team Bravo. 'Oh, and Chris, this morning, work

431

out your route and the hold position. Dan, we're Team Alpha. I'll drive your SUV here. You follow in the large SUV and pick me up. Phase 3. Alpha neutralise the sentries. Both teams move in. Based on our limited intel, I'm still banking on the fact that this sleepy little base has been around for decades without incident. They'll all be tucked up in their cosy little beds. Either way, we'll be hitting them hard and fast.'

'Do we have any idea of numbers?' Jack asked.

'No. But based on the size of the base and its secrecy, I'd say around thirty tops, probably a lot less. Any more than that and it may raise suspicion amongst the locals.'

Kara was standing near the stove for warmth with a coffee mug in both hands. 'Sorry,' she said, 'Are you talking about thirty soldiers?'

'Ay,' Stu replied flatly.

'But...'

'But there's only five of us?' Stu asked rhetorically, anticipating her concern.

'Yeh,' was all Kara could say.

Daniel got up. 'Sorry, Stu. Carry on,' he said and led Kara away to the lounge. 'You're right in thinking this sounds like madness,' he said under his breath. 'But Stu wouldn't even be thinking about it if he had any serious doubts. He's a man who plays the odds. Dangerous odds, I grant you. But he *is* ex-SAS. Kara, they've planned every last detail: exact times, locations, vehicles, and weaponry.'

'I don't like it, Daniel. He's talking about you driving one of the vehicles,' she whispered loudly.

'Of course, he is. I'm not planning on sitting here. Look, I'm not going to tell you what they brought along, but it's...'

'You're talking about weapons, aren't you,' she stated.

'Well, yeh.'

Kara massaged her forehead. 'Jesus, I was just about to ask you how a bunch of Brits managed to get weapons here. But this *is* America.'

He grabbed her upper arms, 'Kara, this is me. I have to do this.'

'But you're not military. Experienced soldiers are defending that place. Surely, you're not trained to that level?' Daniel didn't reply. She looked at him. 'Oh god, you are, aren't you.' It was more a statement than a question. 'Another Doctor Bayford secret.'

She pulled away.

432

'If it makes you feel any better. Yes, Stu was the one who taught me the hand-to-hand combat stuff. Stu and Jack gave me six weeks of weapons training. OK, I'm not SAS material. But I know enough.'

'Enough to get yourself killed.' Daniel looked hurt by her comment. 'I'm sorry,' she said, conceding slightly. 'Yeh, OK, what you did in London was impressive. I'm just...I'm just still not used to *this* other Doctor Bayford.'

Daniel kept glancing back at the table. 'I can't deal with this now. I knew you should have stayed away.'

'Don't you care? Don't you care about yourself? About us?'

'What do you want me to do? I can't call this off. Not now!'

'Because you'll be seen as a pussy. Oh, I get it. You're back amongst your...your gung-ho gun buddies...'

'Kara, think about what we've witnessed. Think about what the Guild of God is doing. It must be stopped. We are the only ones who can do that. *You* know that. We talked about it. *Christ*, did *we* talk about it.'

Kara could not look him in the eye. She stood silently, breathing heavily. 'In that case,' she said defiantly, 'I'm coming with you.'

Daniel's mouth opened. 'NO WAY!'

She looked up into his eyes. 'Yes, way,' she replied calmly. 'If you think I'm gonna stay here, not knowing if you're OK, then you're crazier than I thought. I *am* coming with you.'

Daniel had seen that look of hers before and her tone was emphatic. He looked towards the table. His team had stopped talking on hearing the raised voices and were looking at them.

'You guys OK?' Dante asked.

'We're fine,' Daniel said. 'Let's eat.'

As the team made their breakfast requests, Kara returned to the table. Daniel nodded to Stu, who stepped away from the noise and joined him. 'Kara insists on joining us,' Daniel declared.

They both turned to look at her. She seemed to have perked up and was smiling at the other team members as they called out their specific orders.

Stu looked back at Daniel. 'And? Are you happy with that?'

'More to the point, are *you* happy with that?'

'Not really. It could get very messy out there. Can she handle a weapon?'

Daniel puffed his cheeks. 'I don't know. No, is my guess. We're not gonna expect her to...Are we?'

433

Stu pondered for a moment. 'She could drive the large SUV, stay in it out of sight and be ready for a quick evac. That would free you up and keep her relatively safe.'

Daniel nodded his head slowly. 'Yeh, she'd probably buy that.'

'Great. Well fuckin' ask her then.' As they walked back to the table, Stu laid a hand on Daniel's shoulder. Daniel stopped and faced him. 'Knowing how to shoot a gun in a gunfight sounds like sensible advice to me. Have a word with her, will you?'

Daniel took his seat next to Kara.

'Talking about me behind my back?' Kara asked quietly. 'It's fine, I get it. You don't want me to compromise the mission.'

'Well, no, we don't. But Stu said...' Daniel paused.

'Stu said what?'

'...he said you can drive the large SUV.'

'Oh!...Really?'

'What Stu says is one thing. I'm still...well, unhappy about it. We're talking radio comms, we're talking about...'

'I can use a radio. We used them all the time in Venezuela.'

'OK, so you can use a radio. What about a gun? You may need it.'

'Listen, I'm not planning to shoot *anyone*, especially a US soldier!'

'Even to save your own skin or one of ours?' Daniel waited for her to answer. 'You really don't have to do this, you know. But we need to know, and know now.'

'My dad let me have a go with his hunting rifle.'

'Well, that's certainly better than nothing. But we're talking about a handgun.'

Kara shook her head.

'It's OK. We'll practice this morning. It's mainly for your own protection. That's all. You'll stay in the vehicle all the time, listen out for any instructions and be ready to get us out sharpish.'

Kara stared at the table in front of her. 'Oh, shit...OK. I'll do it.'

Stu wanted to wrap up the briefing. There was much still to do. 'Right. Phase 4. We know there are scientists on site. So, until it becomes clear which are army barracks, don't go blowing up any of the smaller compound buildings.'

'Does it really matter if scientists get snuffed? They designed the fuckin' weapon,' Jack pointed out.

'I say we wipe the fucking place off the earth,' Dante added.

'NO!' Stu shouted. 'I don't kill civilians. OK? Never have. Don't intend to. Even dodgy boffins. Just use your discretion. Now shut the eff up!'

Jack and Dante conceded.

Stu continued, 'For the benefit of Dan…and Kara, we've managed to get enough intel on this base to know it was upgraded during the Cold War. So, think nuclear bunker, which is no doubt where all the development takes place. Our main target, then, is the main complex block. Here.' Stu circled the largest of the buildings marked C with his pencil.

'Wait,' Daniel said. 'Kara, you remember you theorised about this weapon. How much space would they need to develop it?'

'That's a question and a half. Well, I guess it depends on how much of the total development is done here, right? Who's to say that other developments weren't done elsewhere? Why do you ask?'

Daniel turned to Chris. 'Can you get that satellite image up?' Daniel grabbed the laptop. 'OK, if these are barracks and stores, we assume Building C is the main complex. But 25 by 30 metres doesn't sound particularly big.'

'So, you're thinking there's more underground?' Jack suggested.

'Of course, there is,' Stu said. 'You don't build a fucking nuclear bunker above ground.'

Daniel continued, 'Right, but my point is, will that cause a problem? Multiple levels, elevators, multiple doors.'

'In short, no. But let's discuss that. First, let me finish with Phase 4. There are six Humvees here, and two trucks and two SUVs here and here. Use the AT4 on the Humvees, Jack. Chris, you take out the SUVs, then the trucks in that order. Slowest vehicles last.'

'Do I get an AT4?' Chris asked enthusiastically.

'No, an M320 is more than fine,' he replied smiling and shaking his head. 'Dante, you focus on popping off any unwanted faces. Dan and I will be doing the same. Once those vehicles go up in flames, there'll be plenty of action. I've got us a load of SA80-A3s. When we all get in close, switch to the Sigs. If it gets really hot, use the AT4 and M320 on those smaller buildings. Got it?'

Jack and Chris nodded.

One thing that Stu had taught the team was the SAS strategy: if a plan goes wrong, improvise.

Stu rolled off the weapon designations like old friends. Jack, the big guy, had the big boy weapon. The AT4 was an 84mm rocket launcher with a range of 300 metres, designed to take out tanks. The M320 was a 40mm, single-shot, and very mobile grenade launcher. As for guns, Stu stuck to his two favourites: the SA80-A3 assault rifle—one of the most lethal weapons on the planet—and the Swiss, German Sig Sauer P228 pistol.

'Grenades?' Dante asked.

'Plenty. Smoke grenades, stun grenades, and flares, too. But don't use the flares unless absolutely necessary. Stick to NVGs.'

Kara was fascinated by the lingo but correctly assumed that Stu was referring to night vision goggles.

'I'll familiarise Kara with the NVGs.' Daniel said.

Chris dropped her knife and raised her hand. 'Whoa! What was that? Did I miss something here? Miss Pretty is coming?'

'Her name is Doctor Kara Williams,' Stu said, quick to defend. 'And ay, she *is* coming. She'll be Alpha 3 and driving our SUV.'

Chris shot a glance at Daniel for confirmation. He looked straight back at her without a word. 'OK, fair dos,' Chris said and carried on eating. Kara smiled awkwardly.

Stu carried on. 'Phase 4's objective is to a) disorientate, b) neutralise any resistance, and c) disable their vehicles. Timescale doesn't matter. The fireworks will have begun. Any questions? Good. Phase 5. At this point, we open up comms. But this is where improvisation may need to kick in. So, I'll leave you to review the rest. I need a coffee!'

The team studied Stu's notes.

'All clear?' Stu asked. 'Good.'

'Phase 6. Assuming we have secured inside the complex, Dante will place explosives. We extract any scientists. But that is not a priority. We save ourselves first. This is not a hostage situation. Everyone else we can burn.'

Kara was still agitated by Chris' reaction to her involvement. She asked, 'Have any of you considered how you plan to breach what will be a series of nuclear bomb-proof doors?'

Just thought I'd throw that one out there, she thought and did her best to continue eating, even though her appetite had vanished.

Stu was quick to respond. 'I visited a similar site in the UK. Facilities like this usually have an outer door, less secure and breach-able, electronically, or destructively. The main blast-proof doors would be very heavy, and strong enough to withstand the shockwave from a nuclear explosion. There is a simple, fail-safe, manual method of opening them. Near the door, there'll be a hand pump with hoses attached. Connect those hoses and simply pump the door open.'

'That simple?' Daniel asked.

'Ay, that simple,' Stu replied. 'Now, one thing to note: you can't go through a subsequent blast-proof door until the other one has been closed.

'Makes sense,' Dante said. 'But won't that delay us? I mean, my job is to place explosives in the heart of this place, then for us to get the hell out ASAP.'

'Right. So, here's the good news. The facility I visited was a missile silo. When they load or unload propellent, there's always a high risk of a pretty catastrophic fire. So, people would need a fast exit. For that reason, *all* the doors can be opened at the same time. Beyond the first blast door, there'll be a hydraulic mechanism. Simply manually pressing down on the valves will open all the doors.'

'All the manual overrides described make sense,' Kara said. 'You wouldn't rely purely on electronic entry.' She was keen to show Chris that she had her uses. 'A nuclear explosion generates an NEMP. That would take out any electrical circuits. If I was building a bunker, I'd definitely have a manual override if the worst were to happen.'

'Kara is exactly right,' Stu continued. 'I'm pretty confident we'll get in and get out.'

Kara looked at Daniel and gestured that she wanted to use the laptop.

Jack posed the next question with his mouth half full of fried egg. 'What if we nabbed one of the officers or scientists? You know, in case we did need a code or something.'

'One, we'll be creating one hell of a shit storm in the dark,' Stu replied quickly. 'Two, if we can breach the blast doors, the rest will be easy. And three, we don't have time to …pressure anyone. But, as always, if the situation presents itself, we embrace it. It's called improvisation, guys.'

Kara nudged Daniel and pointed at the laptop screen. Daniel frowned and then raised his eyebrows.

Stu carried on. 'Phase 7. We begin our exit. Phase 8. Team Alpha will drive to this location, where Dan and Kara will switch vehicles into their SUV. They'll be on their own from then on. I'll drive the large SUV and join Team Bravo at these coordinates where we'll lay low for a few days. It's another remote cabin.

'When do I blow this place?' Dante asked.

'*En route* from the base.' Everyone clear?'

There were nods all around.

'Good work, Stu. Sounds good,' Daniel declared.

'Hang on,' Kara said, swinging the laptop around. 'There's another type of door you may need to consider. To open it manually requires a special key.'

'That doesn't sound good,' Jack mumbled.

Dante reached for the laptop, 'Let me see that. Yeh, I've seen something like this before. It's pretty low-tech. There are two locks, no more complex than your standard front door, except deeply recessed.'

'And where do we get this key?' Chris asked.

'There's a very good chance, that the key will be right by the door,' Stu said.

'And if not?' Chris pressed.

'We make one,' Daniel announced. 'Look,' he said, reaching for the laptop and zooming in on the image. 'It's just a long simple key.'

'Could you make one, Dan?' Stu asked.

'Leave it with me,' Dante said. 'I have all sorts of stuff in my kit, and I'm used to making improvised tools.'

'Great,' Daniel said. 'Then let's eat up. We all have plenty to do, including some shut-eye later.'

Chapter 83
Day Minus 1

Jack was standing by the door of the cabin. 'Ready?' he asked. 'IDs?'

Kara and Daniel nodded. Kara held up the fake World Land Trust ID hanging around her neck. All three were dressed in civilian winter wear.

'Remember,' Daniel said, addressing both of them. 'It's not unusual to see rangers and even the police on patrol out here. Gunshots are a bit of a giveaway and you need a hunting licence, which we don't have. So, we're simply practicing self-defence. Got it?'

It was 07:50 as they stepped outside. The cold hit their exposed faces instantly. Kara exhaled sharply.

They followed Jack over a light snow covering past the Russian-built 8x8 all-terrain vehicle towards a shabby, disused-looking outbuilding. Jack removed some branches then unlocked a padlock on the door.

Inside it was dark, but the outside light was sufficient to reveal the interior. Kara could make out piles of logs to one side, chainsaws, various tools, and a large mound covered in tarpaulin. She watched as Jack lifted the sheet off and away.

'My God,' Kara exclaimed.

Under the tarp, there were at least eight similarly sized metal cases and a stack of heavy-duty black plastic containers. He slid one of the metal cases around and removed a package. Kara had seen enough movies to recognise the waxy material used to store guns. Jack handed Daniel one of the team's P228 pistols, then popped open another case, and withdrew a couple of magazines. After closing the cases, he reached for one of the black plastic containers. Inside was an assortment of equipment: binoculars, NVGs, black woollen hats, scopes, small medical kits, light sticks, flashlights, and battery packs. 'Here, you'll need these, too.' He pulled out two ear defenders and handed them over. 'I'll leave you guys to it. I need to check all this,' Jack said.

'This won't take long,' Daniel said to Kara. 'I just want you to get a feel for it, know the basics, and fire off a few rounds.'

Kara followed Daniel out and towards the edge of the clearing.

'OK, we'll use that tree over there as our target,' he said. 'Let me see your gloves.' Kara held up her hands. Daniel held one and turned it around. 'They're fine. You'll need them in this weather! Put your ear defenders half on. OK, this is the safety. This is off. This is on. And this is a magazine. Stu tells me these are limited to ten rounds. You load it this way round, like this. Here, you try.'

Kara slotted the magazine clip into place.

'Good,' Daniel continued and took hold of the pistol again. 'OK, when you're ready, slide this back firmly. Use all four fingers. It's called racking the slide. Make sure you hold the gun in your hand firmly with your trigger finger outside the trigger guard. Like this.' Daniel then pointed the gun at the tree. 'Hold it like this and with this stance.'

Kara had watched intently. She repeated the operation exactly and adopted a good stance, lining up the sights.

'Excellent. Now, take a deep breath and hold it, then squeeze the trigger. Go for it!'

Kara pulled her ear defenders on completely and fired off the first shot. She hit the tree.

'That's quite a kick,' she said.

'You're a natural. And again.'

She took more time, her eyes narrowing, and fired again.

'That was more central,' Daniel remarked. 'I think we can move to stage two. This is a semi-automatic. So, this time pull the trigger repeatedly and try to hit the same area. Don't forget to adjust after the recoil. And grip firmly!'

Kara steadied herself. To Daniel's surprise, she unloaded six shots. The bark on the tree exploded with every shot.

'WHOA! That was intense,' she gasped.

'It was also damn impressive.'

'Beginners luck?'

'Well, let's see. Empty the magazine.'

Kara fired off the two remaining shots. The first hit the tree, but the second missed. She slid her ear defenders down around her neck and turned to her gun tutor. 'How come you're in charge of this lot? I would have thought Stu would be the natural choice. Don't get me wrong. They all seem to respect you.'

440

'It's a fair question. I've not really thought about it. For some reason, they all look to me to bring things together. You know, keep things in perspective. Maybe none of them wants the overall responsibility. Besides, they operate better when they can focus on their specialities. It's why Stu is so good at those details. He's done it before; many times. He knows what to look out for.'

'Some people are born to lead, right?'

'I guess. I was the one who came up with the plans. In fact, thinking about it, all this lot joined me. Not the other way round.'

'The oil rig?'

'Yeh. All of them except Chris. She joined a year or two later.'

'She's pretty feisty.'

Daniel laughed. 'I've heard worse.'

'Where did she come from?'

'Believe it or not, she had a respectable job as a communications engineer. Outside broadcast, huge sporting events. That kind of stuff. She just craved more excitement. I mean, look at her.'

'She's chosen well. And the others?'

'Well, as you know, Stu is ex-SAS. Without him, we'd be half as effective. Need I say more? Dante and Jack are both ex-army, too. Dante, as you know, is our resident explosives expert. He served eleven years in the Royal Logistic Corps. They specialise in ordnance search and disposal. And yes, he likes blowing things up. That's why he left. He got frustrated defusing bombs and only got his kicks when they did controlled explosions. Neither of them is trained to Stu's elite standards, but my god, they're good. Jack knows everything there is to know about weapons. He's had plenty of combat experience and is also a crack shot.'

'I'm still amazed they turned up after so long.'

'They're adrenalin-fuelled junkies. I thought that was obvious. I only had to call Stu. He arranged the entire gig.'

'They certainly seem professional.'

'They are. They have to be. May I?' Daniel said, holding out his hand. Kara flicked on the safety and handed the weapon over. 'This is how you remove the magazine.' He caught it in his other hand and pushed it back in. 'Your turn.'

Kara repeated the action. Daniel then reached into his pocket, took out a second magazine, and handed it and the gun back to Kara. 'You're on your own now. No guidance.'

441

Again, to his surprise, Kara was almost too slick. She loaded the magazine confidently, flicked off the safety, racked the slide, aimed, and fired off four shots. Pointing the gun up slightly she released the empty magazine, caught it, flicked on the safety, and laid the gun into Daniel's open hand.

'Marks out of ten?' she said, smirking.

'For a first lesson, a firm ten. Are you sure you've not handled a pistol before?'

Kara tilted her head and raised her eyebrows. 'Nope. Come on, I need a coffee. It's cold enough to freeze a penguin out here.' With that, she strode off towards the warmth of the cabin. Daniel watched her with his mouth agape. Was it his imagination, or had she grown in confidence every day he had known her? Sure, she was shaken by the threats on their lives. Who wouldn't be? But something had changed in her. He hoped he was the reason for her rapid transformation.

Eight kilometres from the cabin, Chris, wrapped up in *snow camo* combat gear, had negotiated a path through the forest in the Russian 8x8. She had now turned off the engine and was sitting in the single captain's seat, studying a GPS logger app on her phone. It showed the precise route she had taken. Satisfied, she opened the door and jumped down onto the forest floor, the twigs and pine needles crunching gently under her boots. She gave the area a 360 sweep. She then consulted the app again and headed towards the base perimeter. As she moved, she constantly checked the width of her route. It needed to be wide enough for the ATV.

Before walking towards the base perimeter, she looked back and re-checked her GPS. Every step she had taken was duly recorded.

As she approached the tree edge, she could make out the perimeter fence and the base beyond. She squatted down and listened. A light breeze was rustling the branches of the pine trees above her. Other than that, and her light breathing, nothing. She checked her GPS location, then scanned her surroundings.

Spotting a potential hold position for the ATV to her right, she headed towards it. It was at that moment that she heard a vehicle engine. She dived to the ground and lay flat. The vehicle was ahead and to the right. It was behind the fence, inside the grounds of the base. Chris reached forward slowly and pulled fallen tree debris into a pile in front of her face. She then tilted to one side and removed her Sig pistol.

It was a Humvee, no more than twenty metres away, moving slowly.

'What the hell are you doing here, uh?' she muttered to herself.

The Humvee came to a stop almost directly opposite her.

'Oh shit,' she whispered and almost buried her face into the woody detritus. She could make out a male voice. Very slowly she tilted her face up and peered through the branches and twigs.

A soldier had climbed out of the vehicle.

Chris held her breath. A torch beam was flashing this way and that. She watched as the soldier walked straight towards her position. The light beam briefly flashed across her face. He then stopped. Chris could see he was also holding a small box with cables dangling from it. He tucked the torch under his armpit, raised the first cable, and clipped it to the fence with its crocodile clip. Chris let out a breath and lowered her face again. They were checking the electric fence. There must be a fault. She stayed motionless for a good thirty seconds. Only when she heard a door open did she look up. 'The break must be somewhere further up,' she could hear him holler. The Humvee revved up and rolled off in the same direction as before.

Chris let out a sigh. *All clear*, she thought. She got to her feet cautiously and reviewed her immediate surroundings. *Perfect*, she thought. The Humvee was far enough away. She reached down and pulled up a large branch dense with foliage, and angled it on a nearby tree. She then looked around for similar branches, dragging them over to the same area. After ten minutes, she stood back and admired her handiwork. 'I should have been girl guide,' she muttered.

Just one more job to do. Resting against a trunk, she took out her mobile, and a handheld RF spectrum analyser. The display showed a graph with spikes plotted against radio frequencies. She opened the device's app on her phone and took a screenshot. She was done.

Back in the cabin, Daniel was at the dining table with Dante, watching him fashion a key under a desk lamp. 'There,' Dante announced, leaning back, 'That should do.'

'Aren't you going to file it?' Daniel asked.

'Mate, we may be dealing with a completely different lock to the one in this video. What I've made here is a key blank. I'll use it to make an impression. Lengthwise, it's fine. On site, I'll take this,' Dante said picking up a small power file. 'And this.' He then held up a lighter. 'I wiggle the blank inside the lock, get my impressions, and then file away. It's made of brass, so nice and soft.'

'What's the lighter for?'

'Ah, that's a little backup technique. Smoking the blank sometimes helps you see the marks made by the lock better.'

'How the hell did you know all that?'

'I didn't. I *YouTubed* it half an hour ago.'

Kara joined them.

'Here,' Daniel said. 'You forgot these.' He handed her the P228 pistol and a magazine. 'Keep practicing. The magazine's empty.'

'Sure. I could do with the distraction.'

'Nervous?' Dante asked, looking up from his metalworking. 'You should be. I am. Keeps us on our toes.'

'Well, I've managed to keep my breakfast down.'

It was now 10.10 p.m. Daniel and his team had somehow managed to rest and eat. Kara had tried doing both, but nibbling on some bread was all she could manage. She now felt sick with worry but did her best to conceal it.

'Listen up,' Daniel said. 'Final briefing.' He was standing in the middle of the cabin by the log burner. 'Dante?'

'I've wired the cabin, checked and double-checked. All set for some serious pyrotechnics. I've also made a key blank in case we need it. And I've got enough bang material to take out the entire base.'

Jack did not wait for his name, 'Checked the weaponry and kits. All good.'

'Good. Chris?'

'Yeh, had a bit of a scare. There was a Humvee patrol only feet from me. They'd obviously found a problem with the fence.'

'Well, they'll have a bigger problem soon,' Jack quipped. The team all smirked.

Chris held up her GPS logger. 'Here's our hold location. I made a double camouflage screen just in case. But it was pretty gloomy in those woods even this morning.'

'You did the right thing,' Stu said. 'If there's another patrol at night with headlights, that monster truck would stick out like a horse's cock. Sorry, Kara.'

'Hey, what about me, you shit. I'm a lady, too, you know?' Chris joked. They all laughed. She was a woman, and a very useful one at that, but no lady. 'Here's the RF scan,' Chris said, passing her spectrum analyser over to Stu, who studied it for a moment, then said:

'Dial this frequency into your radios.'

Stu pushed a fresh piece of paper forward for all to see. Once the radios had been set, he threw the paper into the log burner.

Daniel then continued, 'Wipe that data, Chris. Remember, clear any mention of this operation. The only stuff on laptops needs to look like World Land Trust save-the-planet-shit. Right, before we clean this place and load up, let's synchronise watches. 22:12 on my mark…Mark!'

Chapter 84
Phases 2 and 3

The ATV and the SUVs were parked, headlights off, outside the log cabin.

Chris glanced at her watch and then at the GPS. Her tortuous route was clear to see. She was sitting up front in the vehicle's unique driving position behind the centrally positioned steering wheel; the 8x8's diesel engine already throbbing in readiness. It was 01:22. The headlights went on, and she pressed down on the accelerator. Team Bravo was a go.

Daniel and Kara were behind in the team's larger SUV. They watched the ATV disappear into the forest. Kara was looking straight ahead, trying to control her breathing. Stu was behind them at the wheel of their SUV. The lights and engines of both vehicles were off.

The wait seemed interminable.

After a few minutes, Kara turned to Daniel. She was about to reach out for his hand. But Daniel's left arm was raised. He was counting down. It was almost a relief when he calmly said, 'OK, let's go.'

Kara swallowed hard and started the engine. Team Alpha was on the move.

Team Bravo in the ATV was progressing well. Chris kept up a steady speed through the pine trees, the headlights bouncing up and down. Jack was seated on one of the rear captain's seats. He looked like he was going on a picnic trip, were it not for the semi-automatic between his legs. Dante was beside him, his weapon resting across his lap. No one was speaking. Chris glanced at her watch, then back at the GPS.

They were halfway.

She slowed slightly. Then, without a word, she killed the headlights, pulled down her NVGs, and switched them on. The forest in all its detail lit up in front of her. Chris accelerated slightly. Twelve minutes to go.

'It's about five hundred metres,' Daniel said, looking down at the GPS locator.

'I know.' Kara said a bit too curtly. She realised she sounded stressed. She was.

The track was smooth. There were low shrubs on either side and the blackness of more forest loomed up ahead of them.

'I'm using the NVGs,' she said. 'I can't see much.' She had them perched on her head.

'Sure.'

She pulled the goggles down over her eyes and fumbled for the switch. Daniel quickly leant across and killed the headlights. 'You good?' he asked.

'Yeh, thanks.'

Daniel switched on his goggles. *That was a smart move*, he thought. They could see everything, right down to the smallest twig and pine cone.

Kara spotted the clearing off to the side of the track. She pulled in and did a one-eighty.

Stu had followed her lead with the NVGs, and parked up.

The rear door behind Daniel opened and Stu climbed in. 'Here, you might need these,' he said, reaching forward and handing Daniel the keys.

Kara set off again. 'How are we doing for time?'

'We're good,' Stu replied. 'Just you focus on the driving.'

Chris slowed right down to a crawl and opened her window to listen.

'Christ, this engine could wake the dead,' Dante muttered. 'We should have gone electric.'

'Yeh, but you tell me an electric all-terrain vehicle that can do what I'm about to do.'

She stopped the ATV and selected a new drive mode then pressed the accelerator gently. The vehicle started to crab sideways to the left. It was its party piece.

'Nice,' Jack said.

'It's necessary,' Chris said. 'There's no way through up there. Not unless you want to power up a chainsaw and fell about twenty trees.'

After fifteen metres of lateral driving, Chris stopped, re-selected off-road mode, and set off through the trees at a crawl.

'This is it,' she said and manoeuvred the 8x8 between her foliage screens and quickly killed the engine. 'Bang on time.'

Up ahead through her NVGs, glowing bright against the backdrop of trees, Kara could see part of the service road that led to the base. As planned, she removed her goggles and handed them to Daniel, then flicked on the headlights. It was a straight run to the sentry point, which could be seen on the left-hand side thanks to a powerful floodlight.

Stu leant forward. All three hardly blinked as they approached the small building and the lowered barrier. There was no sign of any soldiers. And yet they now were less than thirty metres away. Still nothing. Kara glanced at Daniel. But he remained fixed on the building, tight-lipped.

They had reached the barrier. Stu had opened the door behind Daniel and slipped out.

The sentry building door opened and a young regular stepped out. Kara buzzed the window down.

'Hey,' she said and gave the soldier her best, toothy smile.

He smiled in return. 'Good morning, ma'am. Are you expected? You scientists do turn up at all sorts of times.'

For a moment, she had planned to improvise. But she stuck instead to the rehearsed story. 'Scientist?' Kara questioned.

'Oh, I'm sorry, ma'am. I assumed you…' He looked flustered. He had clearly made a *faux pas* and a serious breach of security protocol. He looked nervously back at the sentry building.

'No, my husband and I are lost,' she said, turning to Daniel, who leant across and raised a friendly hand. We booked an Airbnb cabin near here and the Sat Nav has been sending us here, there, and everywhere.'

'No problem. Well, there's no way through in this direction. As you can see, this is a military base.'

'Oh really? Out here?'

A second soldier emerged and walked to the front of the SUV.

Kara turned again to face the soldier at her window.

'I'm afraid I'm not at liberty to help you, ma'am,' he said. 'I'm sorry. You need to turn around and keep trying. If you get totally lost, there is a small town about twenty miles west.'

The other soldier was holding a clipboard. Kara and Daniel could see he was taking down their number.

'OK, thanks. And I'm sorry to have bothered you at such a late hour.'

'No problem, ma'am. You take care now. And good lu…'

His words were cut short. A hand had suddenly appeared over his mouth, then a knife sliced his neck open. Blood gushed out and splattered Kara's face.

As the young man fell, gargling to the ground, she was aware of another fast movement and a whooshing sound. Stu had thrown the knife at the second soldier. She looked forward. The soldier had dropped the clipboard and was standing, mouth open, looking at and clutching the handle of the knife buried deep in the middle of his chest. He looked up towards his attacker then fell to his knees. As he pitched forward, his face hit the SUV's bumper with a sickening thud.

Daniel quickly got out and ran to the building. Stu extracted his knife, ran to the side of the building window, and quickly looked inside. Daniel kicked the door open and threw himself to one side, while Stu ran in, a pistol gripped in both hands.

Kara watched; mouth open. The men emerged seconds later. Stu dragged the dead soldier away from the front of the SUV and got back in.

Daniel handed Kara her goggles. She put them on and killed the headlights.

'Go!' Stu ordered.

Kara floored it and smashed through the barrier. The cold air through her open window made her aware of something wet on her face. She wiped her cheek and inspected her hand. The floodlight behind them was enough to confirm what it was, and she suddenly felt nauseous. She buzzed the window back up. Her heart was beating loud in her ears. She took a deep breath then another. *This was it*, she thought. *There's no going back now. We've crossed the Rubicon.* Kara stole a glance at Daniel, hoping for one of his reassuring smiles. Daniel, though, his face ghostly white through her goggles, was busy inspecting his weaponry. She looked forward at the onrushing road. The young soldier's face, alive only moments ago by her window, flashed before her. And then the shock on the other soldier's face; the knife protruding from his chest. American soldiers. Men who protected *her* nation. She imagined their devastated families and friends. *Oh, God! What are we doing? What am I doing?* The justification was far from her thoughts.

She jumped when she suddenly felt a hand on her arm. Daniel knew what was going through her mind. He did not say anything. But he did give Kara a smile. It was far from reassuring. If anything, the NVGs made it look horrifying.

Chris switched on her NVGs, powered up the ATV, and the vehicle launched itself from the forest, crossed the short clearing, and smashed through the high, electric fence. Sparks flashed across the bodywork and windscreen, as the vehicle dragged part of the fence with it before the ATV's eight massive wheels churned up the tangle of metal and wire and spat it out as though with disdain. Chris accelerated. The ground was clear and flat and the ATV thundered across it; the base buildings getting larger in her enhanced night vision view.

Chapter 85
The Assault

The distance from the sentry point to the main compound was several hundred metres. Kara wanted to get this part of her job done as quickly as possible. She was going as fast as she dared; headlights off and NVGs back on. A break on the left of the tree-lined road was where they would stop. She slowed to a crawl and steered the SUV off the road and in amongst the last few trees.

She turned to Daniel and raised her NGVs. 'Be careful,' she said.

'You, too. Hide the car back there.'

Kara nodded.

Stu was already making his way forward, walking slowly close to the trees, assault rifle raised to his face. He turned and waited for Daniel.

Kara had replaced her goggles. Seeing a suitable gap in the trees, she edged forward, then reversed several car lengths into the forest.

Stu indicated for Daniel to hold. He was listening. The unmistakable sound of the ATV's engine could be heard on the far side of the buildings. Stu checked his watch. It read 02:02. Exactly as planned. He pointed forward and they both ran towards B1, the nearest building.

The area lit up to their left. The first of the lined-up Humvees had just blown up. Jack had let loose the first of the projectiles from his rocket launcher. The glow of the flames lit up Jack, who was lining up to fire again. The second rocket left the 84mm muzzle; its sharp crack only to be masked immediately by the ensuing explosion, as the anti-tank projectile ripped two more Humvees apart.

More explosions. Chris was taking out the SUVs out of sight on the far side of the compound.

Stu and Daniel reached Building 1. Daniel edged along its righthand wall, while Stu headed left through the gap with its neighbour, Building 2, from where he heard muffled shouts.

Stu retreated and flashed his torch twice towards Jack.

Jack had already wiped out another two Humvees. He saw Stu's light and flashed his back twice to confirm that Building 2 was the target.

Stu rejoined Daniel. Ahead of them stood the two trucks. One of them exploded in a ball of flame. Chris had already destroyed the two SUVs near Building 4 and had just fired another thermobaric grenade. The second truck went up soon after. They then heard and felt Building 2 explode. Daniel gave Stu a confused look. Stu mouthed 'Barracks,' and pointed forward.

Moving slowly across the compound—Stu walking backwards; Daniel forwards—Stu aimed his assault rifle quickly between the door of Building 1 and what was left of Building 2. There was no movement from Building 1, but the door of Building 2 burst open, and a soldier staggered out. Stu took him out with a single shot to the head. They continued walking and scanning the entire area.

Stu looked for Dante across the compound and spotted him easily enough. Dante raised an arm. He was squatting between Buildings 3 and 4. Daniel then spotted Chris and raised a hand briefly to acknowledge her.

Stu was now close to the side of Building 2's open door. Smoke was billowing out. The roof had collapsed and a fire was raging within. Daniel and Chris headed for the main complex and took up position in the recessed doorway. They watched as Stu took out two grenades and threw them through the doorway. After the muffled explosions, he disappeared into the building. Three rapid shots rang out then a fourth. Eight agonising seconds later, Stu reappeared and gave a thumbs-up. Daniel and Chris sighed with relief.

Another gunshot. Daniel looked right. Dante had taken out a soldier and was now pointing repeatedly to Building 3 to his right. He then ran towards the main complex, where he joined Daniel and Chris.

It was time for comms. He held up his radio. 'Bravo 1 take out B3.'

Jack did not bother to reply. He had appeared at the far end of Building 2, now engulfed in flames, and was loading up the AT4 rocket launcher. He turned to face Building 3, hoisted the launcher up onto his shoulder, steadied himself, and fired. The projectile ripped across the compound and through one of the building's windows. The front and side walls exploded out, sending debris and shrapnel as far as the rest of the team, who took cover.

Stu came over the radio 'Bravo 2, check out B4. Bravo 3, B1 with me. Go!'

Chris got up and ran towards Building 1, where Stu joined her. They crouched to the side of two of the front windows, Chris by one, Stu by the other. Stu took out a grenade and held it up. She nodded and did the same. Stu nodded again and they both stood up, smashed the windows with the butts of their rifles, and threw in two stun grenades. Chris ran to the door, kicked it in, and stepped aside. Stu walked in, gun raised high, and scanned the interior. 'Clear,' he shouted. Chris followed him in.

They split up, Stu taking a corridor to the left; Chris another door towards the rear, which she kicked open. 'GET DOWN! SHOW ME YOUR HANDS!' she shouted. Inside the room were at least a dozen terrified-looking scientists, dressed mostly in night attire, although some had somehow managed to throw on joggers and hoodies. They duly raised their hands high. The scientists had retreated into the back room and were cowering in one corner with the lights off. Chris could see them well enough. They were no threat. She removed her NVGs and flicked on the light. 'I'm not going to hurt you. But I will if you make a single move.'

'I've got more,' Stu called out. Chris turned quickly to see at least ten more scientists walking ahead of him. 'In there,' he instructed them. Chris stood aside as they joined their colleagues. 'ON THE FLOOR! HANDS ON HEAD!' Stu shouted. He then walked around the room taking in its contents. There was a sink, a fridge, and several tables. He opened the fridge. There was an assortment of drinks cans, milk, butter, sauces, and fruit. He slammed it shut. Then turned the tap on and off. 'How many of you are there?'

The scientists looked at each other. 'Just us. These are our quarters,' one of the women scientists replied.

Chris did a head count. 'Twenty-three,' she said.

'Are there more of you? Be careful what you say,' Stu demanded.

After looking at her colleagues, Dr Emma Crusoe replied, 'No. We're all the scientists. But there are military personnel…Actually, there may be one more scientist. He sleeps in a building across there,' she said pointing.

'Which building?'

'I, er, don't know. Sorry.'

'Are you *English*?' one of the men scientists asked.

'No, I'm fuckin' Scottish,' Stu snarled. 'Right, listen up. You *will* all stay here. Stay here and stay safe. Got it?' There was no response. 'GOT IT?' They all nodded. 'You've got water. You! Stand up!' One of the men stood up. Chris frisked him. Stu then took out a batch of large zip ties. 'Hands behind your back.' Stu tied the man's hands tight. 'Now you!'

The next scientist gave Chris a defiant look but knew there was nothing he could do. Chris pulled a mobile from his jeans and placed it on one of the tables. Chris and Stu operated quickly. Three minutes later, there were twenty-three scientists sitting on the floor, zip-tied. On the table were fourteen mobile phones. Chris raised her rifle and smashed its butt down into every one of them. 'That'll be your head if you give us any trouble,' she said.

'What if we need the bathroom?' one of the female scientists asked.

Stu looked at his watch, 'It's 2:25 a.m.; your body clock says you piss at dawn. So shut the fuck up and do *not* move! One of my men will be on guard.'

With that, Stu and Chris left. Chris slammed the door shut behind her.

'I'll go get the ATV,' Chris said, as they left the building.

Stu held his radio to his ear. 'Talk to me Bravo 2.'

Dante responded. 'B4 seems clear. Some kind of storage facility. Thicker walls, reinforced door.'

'Probably basic ordnance like small arms. It won't contain heavy munitions. Not that close to the barracks. Alright, forget it. We need to move into the main complex.'

'Roger that.'

Stu ran the short distance across the compound from Building 1 to join Daniel and Dante.

'Looks like we'll have to blow the first door,' Daniel said to Stu.

'No worries,' Dante said. He walked into the middle of the compound, swinging the grenade launcher from behind his shoulder as he did so. Stu retreated to one side. Daniel, as planned, ran towards Kara's position. Dante stopped and turned around to face the complex entrance, popped in a grenade, aimed, and pulled the trigger. The M320 made a disappointing-sounding click as it propelled the grenade at the door, but the explosion took the door clean off its hinges. 'Oh yeh, baby!' Dante said, grinning. 'In we go!'

Chapter 86
The Descent

Colonel Mason emerged from behind a pile of cases and approached a window. He was in the dark in Building 4. Lieutenant Armstrong and two regulars joined him. All four were fortunate. Having heard the first explosions, the officers had exited the main complex by a side door. The regulars had staggered from Building 3, the secondary barracks, the only survivors following Jack's rocket assault.

The colonel peered through the window. Minutes earlier, Dante had kicked in the front door, made an all too cursory sweep, and had left, satisfied that the building was unoccupied. The colonel had held up his hand. He had needed to assess the situation before killing the intruder, which they could have easily done.

'We should have taken him out,' the lieutenant said, fuming.

'And risk getting a rocket up our asses.'

'It's a handful of them.'

'We don't know that,' the colonel countered. 'Now, shut the fuck up and listen!'

They watched Chris approach the ATV, parked to their right. She climbed in, started it up, and drove it towards the main building entrance.

Daniel had reached the tree line and flashed his torch towards Kara. She flicked on her radio, leant her head back, and let out a long breath. Daniel was OK. But she felt afraid, sitting alone in the quiet of the SUV. She reached for her NVGs and put them on. Seeing her surroundings in the spooky green glow of the goggles was small comfort.

Daniel headed back to the complex. Dante was already inside. Stu had remained on watch by the exit. Stu then led the way down a corridor into the heart of the complex. As anticipated, they reached the first blast door. Daniel and Stu took up crouched defensive positions, their assault rifles pointing back up the corridor. Dante passed through to a wider area covered in pipes, and metal boxes. Beyond this, the corridor narrowed, blocked by the closed, grey blast door.

'Phew!' he whistled. 'Quite a beast.' He returned to Stu and Daniel's position and studied the mechanisms set to one side. Sure enough, there looked to be some kind of pump secured to the floor. Dante could see two hoses curled up behind it. He reached for one of them and attached it to one of the pump's outlets. He reasoned that the hose would the perfect length to reach a tap. But he could not see any. There were a number of possible candidate boxes mounted on the walls nearby. He then spotted one with two narrow pipes attached, leading upwards. *They look like high-pressure pipes*, he thought. He looked at the box and found a simple locking device. He turned it and the front of the box flipped down to reveal two taps. 'Gotcha!'

'How we doing?' Stu asked, looking back at Dante.

'Give me a second.' After wiggling the two hoses against the taps to ensure he had a solid connection, he went back to the pump and lifted the lever. 'OK, time for a workout. Let's hope I haven't missed anything.' He pushed down on the pump lever. There was some resistance, but it went down as easily as it had gone up. He repeated the process and looked towards the door. It was opening.

Daniel turned to look. 'Doesn't need to be fully opened,' he said.

'Right,' Dante said, as he pumped away.

Lieutenant Armstrong was by the same window on the opposite side to Mason. They both stepped back and into the shadows.

'They're inside,' Armstrong said. 'We have all the hardware we need here. I say we go in now.'

'Yeh, but I don't like it. We don't know who else is out there. We need eyes,' Mason said and looked out the window again. He then retreated into the room and peered into the gloom of the storage facility. 'Can we get a D3 up in the air?'

Armstrong raised his eyebrows. 'Well, yeah, I guess. But we need an open space out of sight to set her off.'

'Sir, there's a fire door in the rear,' one of the regulars said to Armstrong. 'It leads out onto open ground.'

'What about ADNDs and *seeders*?' Mason asked.

'Yes sir, it's all here,' the same soldier replied, pointing at the numerous metal crates. 'This is our test equipment.'

'And tablet PCs?' Armstrong asked. Without one, there would be no control and no point.

'Sure,' the regular replied. 'They're in the cases over there.'

'Then get that bird out there and flyin'!' Mason ordered. 'And load her up!'

The soldiers set off towards the centre of the building followed by Armstrong. Mason resumed his position by the window and peeked out.

Stu, Daniel, and Dante had passed through the first door and were approaching a second. It was a double door.

'Shit!' Daniel muttered.

'What?' Stu asked, but then saw Dante pointing at the door mechanism. It was the type that required the key to manually open. There were two large wheels at chest level on both doors. To the side of the righthand wheel was a keypad, and above that, a small ring-like latch, flanked by two keyholes.

Dante went up to the first keyhole and carefully inserted his handmade, rod-like key blank. 'We can thank your good lady for this,' he said, as Daniel watched him twist the rod gently a few times. He then withdrew it and studied the end. There were some faint impressions. He reached into his bag and took out the lighter. Holding it under his uncut key, he waved the flame back and forth. A black soot appeared over the brass. He re-inserted the key and twisted it again.

'How long is this gonna take?' Stu asked. For the first time in the operation, he was looking agitated.

Dante did not reply. He was rummaging in his bag for the electric file.

Daniel had other ideas. He entered the corridor between the two blast doors and studied the signage around more mechanisms. *What had Stu said during the briefing? A hydraulic override,* he thought. Daniel scanned the pipes and controls. *This had to be it.* There was no signage, but there were two valves. He looked around the area. No buttons. *Perhaps...*He pressed down hard on the tops of the two valves. There was a short sound, like someone letting out air from a car tyre. The first door beside him started opening wider. He looked towards the second door. It, too, was opening.

'Nice one,' Stu said. 'Let's go!'

Up ahead, as expected, was an elevator.

Dante spotted a key protruding from a panel. He turned it and the panel opened up. Without waiting, he slammed his hand onto a large red button. An alarm blasted out, but the elevator door slid open. As they entered, Dante turned and shot the nearby loudspeaker into silence. Stu hit the button for the deepest level. The doors closed and they began their descent.

From Building 4, Mason watched Chris leave the ATV and take up a position in the recessed door of the main building.

His men had positioned a D3 across a large case. Armstrong and one of the soldiers were loading the drone with a payload of ADNDs and *seeders*. Armstrong then secured the D3's hatch. The two regulars raised the D3 and headed towards the rear door. Armstrong followed and eased the door open, beckoning the soldiers through.

'Right here is fine,' Armstrong whispered.

The men placed the D3 on the dirt. Armstrong clicked on his tablet PC and began typing. His first command signal switched on the D3 and its nanotubes. Half a second later the D3 seemed to disappear. It was ready to be deployed.

Chapter 87
Charges Set

Stu was pressed against one side of the elevator as it rapidly descended the forty-eight metres; Dante was up against the other, with Daniel crouched behind him.

The door opened. For a moment, whatever lay ahead was in darkness, but automatic lighting came on to reveal an enormous hall.

Stu exited and turned left, gun held high, aiming this way and that. Dante did the same to the right. Daniel was aiming straight forward.

Stu and Dante then set off silently in opposite directions, continuing their sweep of the area. Daniel stopped to take in the vast space they had entered. It was like an aircraft hangar.

Ahead, dominating the cavernous room stood a tall round structure. *Looks like an enormous boiler*, Daniel thought. This was clearly the main experimental area. He took out his phone and took several photos. He was keen to know what the silo-like structure was for. He headed for it, continuously checking the area around him. There were only three of them and this was a big space to cover.

Stu clicked his fingers; the sharp snap echoing as though they were in a cathedral. Stu was pointing at two more elevator doors. Daniel nodded and continued towards the metal tower.

Dante had done a circuit of the area to the right. The place was devoid of life. He and Daniel converged on the central structure.

'This looks important,' Dante said sarcastically. He set down his backpack and began taking out explosives and timers.

'Yeh, give me a second, will you?' Daniel could see green and red buttons by the side of the door. 'Guess no one here suffers from colour blindness,' he quipped and pressed the green button. The metal door slid open and Daniel stepped inside.

Dante snorted and attached the first of the plastic explosives against the base of the structure. He plunged in a timed detonator and primed it for 09:00 minutes.

Stu had found a metal staircase that led up to a high walkway with rooms leading off it.

Dante placed more of the explosives. He now had a ring of them around the base of the chamber.

A flash across the road in front of her made Kara remove her goggles. And then she heard it.

'Oh shit,' she breathed.

It was more than one vehicle. At first, it had not been obvious through the night vision goggles. But now she realised it was a headlight that had first caught her attention.

And now those approaching headlights were flashing past the trees at high speed to her right. They were just metres away. Kara lowered herself in the seat and checked her gun.

Four powerful-looking SUVs thundered past her and towards the base. They had not spotted her. But she was shaking. She grabbed the mobile and dialled Daniel.

No ring.

She tried again.

'Come on!' she said between her teeth. The phone showed she had a signal. She decided to call Jack. Her phone had been set up with quick dials from Alpha 1 to Bravo 3. She scrolled down. 'Damn it!' She just could not think straight. 'Chris is Bravo 3, Dante is 2, Jack is 1.' She hit the call button.

Jack was still positioned by the complex entrance with Chris. He felt and heard his phone vibrate. Chris heard it, too.

'*We've got company*,' Kara blurted. '*4 SUVs have just gone past. They'll be on you. I tried calling Daniel, but can't get through.*'

'Slow down. You should have used the radio.'

'*Fuck. Yes, I'm sorry.*'

'Stay there. I'll call them. Out.' Jack hung up. He and Chris could now hear the approaching engines.

Jack hit talk on the radio earpiece. 'Alpha 1. Do you copy?'

Kara threw the mobile onto the passenger seat. 'Shit, shit, shit!'

Stu heard his radio crackle, *Alph... you co...?*

His voice was calm, 'Alpha 1. Go ahead.' But all he could hear was static. 'Damn it,' he muttered. 'Alpha 1. Repeat. Over.'

Nothing.

They were too far below for any signal.

Jack shook his head. 'I'm not getting through…Alpha 2 do you copy…? Alpha 2 come in.' There was no response. 'I need to warn the others,' he whispered, pocketing his radio, and lowering his NVGs.

Jack and Chris looked up across the compound. The four SUVs were tearing in. Chris removed her grenade launcher. She then nodded at the rocket launcher.

'Negative,' Jack murmured. 'Too confined a space.' He checked the clip in his assault rifle, then raised it.

Daniel's torch was flashing up across the inside walls of the lightning chamber. As he walked towards its centre, he felt a crunch under his foot. He pointed the torch down. It was a scale model of a city. Daniel nodded to himself, reeled off some more photos then pointed his torch upwards. There was little to make out except for some pipes, the top of a ladder, and a door. He lowered the torch, following the route of the ladder down to the floor. His radio crackled. He looked at the radio display. The signal was barely present. 'This is Alpha 2. Go ahead…I repeat this is Alpha 2…'

Stu then appeared at the chamber doorway. 'Psst! Someone up top is trying to get through.'

'Yeah,' Daniel said, holding up his radio. 'Something must be wrong.' He raised his radio again, 'This is Alpha 2. Do you copy?'

'There's no signal. Too much metal and we're God knows how far down. We carry on. We're going up to the next level.' Stu said and disappeared.

In the compound, the SUV doors were flung open. Eighteen men, armed with submachine guns and wearing balaclavas, poured out. All of them had single-eye night vision goggles. They split up into groups and spread out across the compound. Six were heading straight towards the main building. Chris and Jack fell back into the recessed doorway.

'Shit! They must know we're here. But who the hell are these guys?' Chris whispered.

'SEALs?' Jack whispered back.

'I'm not waiting to find out,' Chris replied. She stepped forward, knelt on one knee, and popped off a grenade. Three of the approaching men were blown off their feet. Jack stepped forward and began firing his automatic rifle. Two more men crumpled to the ground. Bullets began streaming in, whistling over Chris and Jack's heads, smashing the masonry around them.

'FUCK! THEY HAVE SMGs!' Jack shouted.

They withdrew a step back and behind the wall. The last of the first six men had retreated. Chris loaded up another grenade and repeated her previous action. The grenade exploded near one of the SUVs but failed to take out any of the remaining men.

'We're too exposed. They could take out this doorway if they have any heavy weapons,' Jack shouted, as the bullets continued to rain in.

The new arrivals were now shouting to each other.

'You hear that?' Jack said. 'What are they saying?'

'Fuck knows. But we need to join the others. We have a better chance together,' Chris said. 'I'll call the elevator. You hold them off then get your ass back there with me.'

Jack glanced into the building behind them. 'No sweat.'

She gave him a wink and ran towards the elevator. Jack carried on firing. Chris slammed the call button.

Daniel had left the chamber and was looking up. He saw Stu and Dante approaching the top of the open stairway. The main elevator off to Daniel's left then closed. Daniel hoped it was one of their team that had called it. He ran over to the stairway.

More headlights. This time, Kara quickly reached for the radio. It was another SUV, travelling more slowly. 'Alpha 1 come in…Alpha 1?' Kara looked at the radio. *Was it working*? she thought. 'Alpha 2 come in…Anyone? Over.'

The SUV came to a stop thirty metres in front and to the right of Kara. She held her breath.

Dante was now in the far most room on the mezzanine level. It was a laboratory-cum-production line. Down the centre was a long table. Dante walked over and peered into a deep plastic tray. 'What the hell?' he muttered, as he picked up a tiny dark object.

Daniel reached the top and advanced along the mezzanine walkway. He spotted Dante.

'What do you make of this?' Dante said holding up the object between his thumb and forefinger.

Daniel entered the room and looked at the object Dante was holding, then saw the tray, picked up one of the objects, and scrutinised it closely. 'My God, Kara was right,' he muttered and thrust a handful of the objects into his pocket.

Dante shrugged. 'Sorry I asked. I'll just carry on then,' he said and began placing explosives.

'Yeh, you do that,' Daniel mumbled. He scanned the rest of the room, then went out onto the walkway. Stu was at a doorway at the far end. He beckoned Daniel over.

Colonel Mason, Lieutenant Armstrong, and the two regulars were back inside Building 4, watching the events unfold on the tablet PC. The D3 drone had been successfully deployed and was now hovering silently over the compound; its ultra-low-light image sensors switched on.

'Who the hell are *they*?' the colonel said between gritted teeth.

'Are they ours?' Armstrong suggested. 'Maybe an attack on the base triggers an automatic response.'

The colonel gave him a withering look. 'You don't think I would have known about something like that? They're not ours. Just look at them! They're a goddamned rabble. And they certainly don't like that first lot. What the fuck is going on?'

'What should we do?' Armstrong asked tentatively.

The colonel shook his head. 'We take them out with the ADNDs, you dumb fuck. And those,' he ordered, pointing at the four SUVs in the compound.

'Yes sir. I er...' Armstrong clicked on the screen and typed briefly.

The colonel was losing patience. 'I er, what?'

'I need to ready the ELF. And raise the D3 for the *seeders*.'

'You *can* do this, can't you, Lieutenant?' The colonel's voice was deep and minacious.

'I believe so, sir. I'm familiar with the procedure. I've just not done it all myself.'

'I don't wanna hear some lame, pussy excuses. Just do it!'

The colonel began pacing the darkened room. He so wanted to get out there and blow the attackers of his base into kingdom come.

Kara let out a long, slow breath. The SUV had set off slowly and drove past her towards the base. She checked the time. 'Come on, guys,' she muttered.

The elevator door opened. Chris turned and whistled to Jack. But he was way too busy and the gunfire was too intense. He was now sitting a few feet from the

463

door with his back against the wall, loading a fresh magazine. Chris whistled again, but Jack had raised himself up and was letting rip with his weapon; firing a stream of bullets in all directions across the compound.

Chris began running down the corridor towards him. The impact took her by surprise. It spun her sideways. She fell against the wall and slumped to the floor.

Then the pain came. Chris groaned and looked down at her side. She looked towards Jack. He was in his zone, picking out targets; using his ammunition wisely. 'I'm hit,' she cried out as loud as possible.

Jack swung round. 'Shit! Hang on!' He fired off more rounds then turned and ran up the corridor, stooping as he did so. Bullets were ricocheting off both walls.

He reached Chris, laid down his rifle, and pulled out his pistol. 'Come on, let's get outta here.' He grabbed her by the scruff of the neck with one hand and dragged her towards the elevator, his other hand pointing the pistol towards the entrance. It felt like the longest five metres he had ever walked, but they made it. He let go of Chris and she slumped down on the elevator floor with a groan. Jack punched the lowest button and the doors closed just as a figure arrived at the first blast door. Jack took aim and fired through the last few inches of the closing door. The distant figure collapsed in a heap. Jack raised his NVGs, crouched down next to Chris, and tried to find the wound.

The fifth SUV rolled slowly into the edge of the compound and stopped. It was a good fifty metres from the other vehicles. In the rear, a man had just lowered his balaclava over his face. He placed a single-eye night vision goggle over his head, positioned the eyepiece over his eye, switched it on, and exited the car.

The gunfire had ceased.

The new arrival walked across the compound, raising a radio to his mouth. 'Team 1, report.'

'*They got into the elevator. I think they're all inside.*'

He reached some of his men and looked around. Then raised his radio again. 'Team 1, follow them. Team 2, search all the other buildings. The rest of you stay here.'

With that, he removed the NVG and lifted his balaclava.

'How can anyone live in this climate?' Prince Al-Musan said, more to himself, and shuddered in the bitter cold of the Alaskan winter night.

Chapter 88
Countdown

Kara was unsure what to do. *Should she get out and head for the base?* she thought. *No. Stick to the plan. For the moment at least.* She opted to try the radio again.

'Anyone receiving this? Come in Alpha 1...Alpha 2...Anyone?'

She threw it down in frustration, grabbed the mobile, and short-dialled each of the team in turn. Nothing.

The horror of what may have befallen Daniel and the team then hit her. And hit her hard. Kara closed her eyes and tried to control her breathing. After one deep breath, she opened her eyes. Her pistol was on the seat beside her. She checked the magazine and stepped quietly into the night, her pockets brimming with ammunition.

The elevator plunged to the lowest floor. The door opened and Jack scanned the area beyond and above. There was no sign of the other guys. He whistled loudly. The echo reflections amplified the sound.

'HEY!' It was Dante. Jack looked up. Dante had emerged from the last of the mezzanine rooms.

Jack held up a hand. 'CHRIS HAS TAKEN A HIT,' he shouted back.

'IS SHE OK?'

Jack looked back at his partner. She looked pale. 'YEH, SHE'LL BE FINE.'

Chris tried to laugh, but winced in pain and clutched her side.

Stu shot out of a door near Dante. 'Use the fucking radio! It'll work down here,' he hissed, pointing at his own backpack.

'Sorry, chief,' Dante said.

Down below, Jack set about heaving Chris out of the elevator. 'Come on,' he said to her, 'let's get you out of there.'

She seemed heavier this time. Jack sensed she was losing strength; she was like a dead weight. He propped her against the wall next to the elevator and undid

465

her jacket. Her side was soaked in blood. Jack dipped a hand into one of his pockets and pulled out a first-aid pack. He placed a swab against the wound. 'Hold this.' Chris looked down with dazed eyes and raised her arm slowly. Jack helped her. He then unravelled some bandage, and began to wrap it tightly around her body.

'That's a waste of time,' Chris muttered.

Jack ignored her and finished off the dressing. There was a sound to his right. He looked up. The elevator door had begun to close. 'Shit!' He leapt up and tried to stop it. But he was too late. He returned to Chris.

Her eyelids were heavy. 'They'll be down here in seconds,' she said. 'Leave me. Get some cover.'

Jack looked around desperately. There was no cover, except for the round structure. *Could he drag her there in time?* he thought. The elevator had taken seconds to descend. Double that time and add a bit for the doors. *No way*, he realised. He needed to take cover and take cover now!

'You're right. Hang in there, girl.'

He spotted the open door at the base of the tower structure and sprinted for it. As he ran, he looked up towards the high walkway. He whistled loudly, but there was no response from Stu, Daniel, and Dante.

With her free hand, Chris groped for her pistol and managed to get hold of it. She turned it over. It was loaded.

In the ordnance building, Armstrong was almost ready. The targets had been acquired. On the tablet's screen, a series of red dots could be seen over the compound. A cluster of them covered the various vehicles. And there were single dots, too. But unlike those on the SUVs, these were moving; they were tracking the men as they moved about. These latest intruders were moving targets.

Armstrong now just needed to access the extremely low-frequency pulse generator. He typed furiously. The ELF was vital, as it activated the Autonomous Discriminatory Nano Drones.

'Well?' The colonel's impatience was not helping.

'The D3 needs to be higher. Much higher,' Armstrong replied. 'The *seeders* are ineffective at low altitudes.' He was sweating profusely. He wiped his brow. This operation was normally handled by a team of people, not just one man.

Fifty metres over the compound, the D3 started to rise. Armstrong watched the ultra-low-light video feed on screen as the compound started getting smaller and smaller.

Daniel followed Stu into what was clearly a control room. Beyond the array of computers and screens, was a large window, a fire exit, and another door.

Stu had finished a quick circuit of the room. 'So, what's that thing out there?'

Daniel knew that Stu was referring to the cylindrical structure. 'It's some kind of test chamber. There's a model city in there. My guess is that they've developed some kind of scaled-down version of the real thing. And these,' he added, taking out a handful of the small objects, 'look like the weapon itself.'

Stu reached out and scrutinised one of them closely. 'That's a tiny drone!' He handed it back and suddenly looked impatient. 'Anyway, we need to speed up. Dante! Get in here!'

The main elevator had reached ground level. Eight of the prince's balaclava'd men entered. The doors closed and they began their descent. The elevator stopped before the bottom floor. The door opened and four of them stepped out into a corridor. The elevator door closed and the remaining four continued down. Three seconds later, the elevator reached the test area floor and the door began to open.

It was eerily quiet. There was no wind in the trees to help disguise her footsteps, as Kara trod carefully over the cold and brittle forest floor, mightily grateful for the NGVs. But realised they were adding a surreal aspect to her situation.

Her route was far from straight; the trees were numerous, and so were the large fallen branches, which she had to negotiate with care. A few more trees and she would be at the fence surrounding the base. She raised a leg over another branch and brought it down.

CRACK. She had snapped a thick branch—the sound reflected and amplified by the countless tree trunks.

Kara paused and held her breath. She raised her foot, held it mid-air, looked down, then lowered it gingerly into a patch of pine needles. She slowly lowered herself into a crouching position and cursed inwardly. Then turned her head to check the area.

Jack was now half concealed behind the door of the chamber. *The radio!* He suddenly thought. *It'll work here. Stu was carrying a repeater in his backpack.* He reached for the talk button on his earpiece cable. But he was too late. The elevator door was opening. He raised the assault rifle and took aim.

Chris, still slumped up against the wall only feet from the elevator, had been fading fast, but a rush of adrenalin coursed through her veins. She raised her pistol and aimed it towards the elevator.

The barrel of a gun, a hand gripped on its front handle slowly appeared. Despite her fuzzy brain, Chris recognised the weapon immediately: a B&T submachine gun. In fact, she realised, the variant with an integrated suppressor: the APC9-SD—a short, very compact, and lethal weapon. She raised her pistol higher. But a loud shot cracked the air of the subterranean hall and the man fell forward and crashed to the ground. Jack had taken him out.

A short burst of rapid *phut phut phuts* from the elevator told Chris to expect more. Jack countered with an almost equal number of shots. Chris could no longer hold the weight of the pistol and her arm dropped. She looked towards Jack. He was reloading. Chris raised her weapon again. The next man's gun muzzle appeared then the unmistakable 175mm-long barrel of another APC9-SD. He began firing at Jack. The man then emerged fully and Chris pulled the trigger four times. The man's body convulsed with each shot. He never even saw who had shot at him and was dead before he hit the floor. Jack was raising his gun again. He could see two more crouching within the elevator.

Daniel was picking up a pad full of notes when he heard the gunfire. The sound seemed to be coming simultaneously from down below and nearby. Instinctively, he and Stu ducked, before realising there were loudspeakers in the control room. Daniel ran and pressed his face up against the window, raising a hand over his eyes to shield the glare from the control room lighting. Ahead of him was the top of the curved chamber. More gunfire. Daniel then spotted one of the sources: two men were in the elevator, both firing submachine guns; two more lay motionless on the floor in front of them. Worse still, he saw Chris slumped against a nearby wall. *Where was Jack?* he thought.

Stu joined Daniel at the window. 'There,' Stu said pointing downwards—he was thinking the same.

Jack was firing from a position just inside the chamber.

Dante suddenly rushed in, 'Jack and Chris are downstairs,' he blurted. 'Chris is hit.'

'We know,' Stu said.

'Who are these guys? Dante murmured. 'I thought we'd sterilised the place.'

'They ain't US military,' Stu said.

'Whoever they are, they're a threat,' Daniel said. 'And there could be a lot more on the way. It's time we got out.'

'But the timers,' Dante said.

'You do the ones up here,' Daniel ordered. 'I'll do the ones down there.'

'They're all set for 9 minutes. Just click the small red button,' Dante called back, as he ran from the room onto the walkway and into the first of the four laboratories.

Kara was crouching low as she edged forward. The perimeter fence was just in front of her. She stopped and got down onto her belly. She could make out armed men walking between the nearest buildings. She started counting them. Eight, nine, possibly more.

She lay there and thought hard. *What can I do? Where are Daniel and the others? I can't reach them.*

She then tried to apply her logic. It was a horrible thought, but saving herself may be the only option. At least she could go to the press, even though they had ruled that out. But what else was there to do?

Kara made up her mind. She would return to the SUV, hope she would remain unnoticed, wait for these new intruders to leave, and then go in and look for the others. She did not want to think about what she may find.

Raising herself up, she turned.

Her stomach then dropped. The outline of a man with a submachine pointing straight at her was dead centre in her night vision. She dropped her gun. 'DON'T SHOOT!' she yelled.

Chapter 89
Nine Minutes

Two floors above the mezzanine level, the first four balaclava'd men were going methodically from room to room. They had one more floor to sweep before they would descend to the chamber level.

Jack felt exposed. Each time he took a shot, the two remaining gunmen strafed his doorway. He thanked God that the chamber was built like a tank. He turned and studied its interior and quickly flicked on his torch. Pinned to the far side was a ladder leading to a door at least twenty metres above. *Higher ground. That's always good*, he thought. He peeped out but spotted only one of the two men. They had split up. He fired off five rounds and then bolted for the ladder. He did not care to look down when his boots crunched and shattered something with every step. Slinging the rifle over his shoulder, he climbed as fast as he could.

High above the compound, the D3 had almost reached the minimum height for a release of its payload.

Mason had joined Armstrong. They both watched the altitude readout increase. The drone was only two hundred metres short of the requisite height.

The four balaclava'd men had completed their sweep of the other floors. One of the two service elevators opened and they entered. The elevator interior was silent. Nothing penetrated its walls, not even the noise of the whirring motors high above. Moments later, the elevator stopped and the doors opened to the sound of gunfire. They held their position, machine guns raised, while the lead man peered out.

Stu was outside the control room, looking down through the meshed walkway. He spotted one of the two men that had been exchanging fire with Jack. The gunman was now by the chamber. Stu fired two rounds, but his target moved back at the last second; one bullet punctured the floor, the other, the chamber wall.

Daniel knew the mezzanine staircase was an unwise option. But he needed to get to the base of the chamber and arm the explosives. He looked around the control room. *The door past the observation window—it must lead to the chamber,'* he reckoned and ran towards it. It was unlocked. He threw it open. Sure enough, there was a short gangway to a door on the outside of the chamber. He looked down at the floor a good thirty metres below and drew out his Sig Sauer pistol. Bullets suddenly ricocheted and sparked off the metalwork around him accompanied by the *phut phut phut* of a submachine gun. Daniel raised his pistol as he ran and fired off three shots. The gunman below quickly retreated.

The barrel of the submachine gun prodded Kara hard in the back, causing her to wince and stagger forward. The gunman had removed her NVGs and was directing her towards a man standing in the centre of the compound. He turned to face her. Still adjusting to the gloom, Kara had to squint.

'Kara! What a nice surprise.'

The voice confirmed it. Kara tried to hide her shock, but failed; her mouth had already opened. It was a gormless look that did her looks no credit.

'I spotted you when we drove in,' Al-Musan said calmly. 'I just thought I'd play along a bit. See what happened. You don't think I stopped trailing you and your friend, did you?' He walked closer and nodded to the gunman to lower his weapon. 'So, Daniel and…now, let me guess, some of his former revolutionaries are inside. Probably dead, I'd say.' He looked down at the ground and shook his head with a feigned expression of sadness.

'I wouldn't bank on it.' Kara snapped.

'Ah ha! There she goes again,' he said, referring to her in the third person. How Kara hated that use of language and she showed her disdain. 'How I love your tenacity and heroism,' he continued.

'You *know* why we're here.'

'Of course, I do, Kara. You want to stop the Spear of Destiny.'

'Then you should be grateful.' Kara snarled.

'Oh, I am. Believe me.' The prince looked around the compound. What was left of Building 2 was now an inferno. 'And it looks like your friends *were* doing so well. Thank you. Makes my job so much easier and far less bloody.'

Kara followed his gaze and was shocked to see a dead US soldier in front of the burning building and another at the far end of the compound.

'There are a lot more inside there,' he said, pointing at the fire. 'All dead— How sad. I *do* dislike violence.'

471

'You are *so* full of bullshit; I'm surprised you're not choking on it.'

'Such colourful language, and from a lady, too.' Some of his men laughed. The prince turned towards them. 'SHUT UP!' he roared. 'You see, Kara. After the US slaughtered my brothers and sisters, I thought, maybe the true destiny of the Spear is mine.'

'Oh, so blowing up London and Eurostar didn't work, nor your next hair-brained martyrdom idea. Let me see, that just killed your own people. Now you want to hijack this weapon. You really are quite mad.' The prince took two paces forward and slapped Kara hard across the face. It stung like crazy, made worse by the icy-cold air. But Kara straightened up and stared back. 'I thought you disliked violence, you fucking hypocrite.'

'YOU...YOU...YOU'LL SEE DOCTOR WILLIAMS!' he almost screamed. The prince's attention suddenly turned towards Building 1. His men were leading out the scientists. 'Oh look, the architects of death and destruction,' he said.

Daniel reached the end of the gangway, flung open the access door to the chamber, and looked down. Jack was halfway up the ladder.

'Psst!' Daniel called.

Jack looked up and accelerated his ascent.

There was movement near the lower door. Daniel raised his gun. One of the gunmen was edging into the chamber but had failed to look up. Daniel fired two shots and the man collapsed. The sound was deafening. Jack stopped and pressed himself tight against the ladder.

'Move it, soldier!' Daniel said in a loud whisper.

Jack reached the top and took up position by the doorway. *Where was the other gunman?* he thought, as he looked down through the gangway.

Daniel was thinking the same, watching the bottom of the chamber intently. He withdrew a grenade in readiness.

Armstrong pressed a button on the tablet PC.

High above the compound, the hatch under the D3 drone slid open and the metallic *seeders* were released. Once they had done their work, they would be followed by the ADNDs.

The *seeders* dispersed quickly in all directions. They spread quickly, attracting moisture, and freezing in the already dense cloud. The lighter *seeders* were rising to the top of the cloud, crystalising and becoming positively charged;

the heavier ones, designed to attract more moisture, were falling as hail and graupel, colliding and becoming negatively charged.

The result was rapid: an enormous electrical potential was building above the base.

When the shooting ceased, the four new gunmen exited the service elevator. They saw two of their own, dead by the main elevator, and Chris slumped nearby, eyes shut. Two of them split off in her direction. The other two headed towards their associate by the chamber, guns occasionally pointing up towards the mezzanine walkway. The man already by the chamber pointed to the explosives and the timer locked on 09:00. The lead gunmen shook his head. They had no time for that. The priority was to take out whoever was there, and then secure data and samples. He pointed for one to enter the chamber, and the other to go around its base.

Back by the main elevator, Chris opened her eyes, raised her pistol, and fired. The man approaching her roared with pain and surprise. As he fell, he pulled his trigger. But his grip was already loose and the bullets flew wildly in all directions. Chris' effort had been lethal. But the other gunman pivoted and opened fire, walking towards her as he did so. Chris had no chance. She had taken eight or nine hits. Her body had already given up. Her arms lay limp as she looked into the eyes of the man who would end her life. 'Fuck you,' she managed to mumble, before closing her eyes one last time.

Stu and Dante appeared at the control room end of the gangway.

'Hey! We need to go now!' Stu whispered loudly.

Jack turned. 'What about the charges below?'

'I'll do those,' Daniel said, without dropping his gaze from the bottom of the chamber. 'I can take the ladder. Just give me two minutes.'

'You don't have two minutes,' Stu responded. 'Dante's set the ones on this floor.' He turned to Dante, who looked at his watch.

'Seven minutes, forty seconds,' Dante said.

Stu set his watch to countdown 'OK,' he conceded. 'Make it snappy. I'll get Chris.'

The gunman allotted to enter the chamber had heard their voices and looked up. Daniel had already stepped back out of view. He pulled the pin on the grenade and threw it into the chamber. The explosion was eardrum-shattering. Daniel peered down. The gunman was down and was staying down.

A burst of a machine gun from below the gangway forced Jack and Daniel back inside the chamber.

'I make it three of them,' Jack said.

The two gunmen by the chamber had now been joined by the one who had killed Chris. They had spotted Daniel and Jack above them but not Stu, who had quickly taken up his assault rifle. He had a good view from the control room doorway when one of the men suddenly appeared—his gun pointing straight at Stu. But Stu had the measure of him. One shot was enough. The man was thrown backwards, jerking violently, as the bullet passed right through his head, turning his black balaclava red.

Jack peeped down from the chamber doorway. 'Make that two,' he said, giving the thumbs-up to Stu, who stepped back into the control room.

Jack realised that his vantage point was limited. He decided to join Stu and Dante. Speed was of the essence. With one quick check below, he bolted across the gangway and into the control room. 'It's me!' he called out, as his buddies swung their weapons towards him.

Stu held up two fingers and pointed down. Jack nodded.

Daniel grabbed the opportunity. It was time to set the other charges at the base of the chamber. Once he had positioned himself on the ladder, he began a swift descent.

Stu pointed to the fire exit. Dante and Jack both nodded and ran towards it.

Stu stayed. Daniel needed help first. He removed a glove and gently tapped the glass on the observation window. He then took out a small mirror on the end of a stick and stuck it out over the walkway. The observation window had one-way glass: one could see out, but not in. He retracted the mirror and positioned himself slap bang in the middle of the window. He had a clear view of the chamber, the upper half of the stairway, the mezzanine floor, and a good portion of the floor below. He checked his watch. His countdown display showed 06:48. 'Come on you bastards. Show yourselves,' he mumbled and raised his assault rifle.

Unseen by Stu, one of the two remaining gunmen had already made it to the lowest flight of steps on the stairway and was creeping up. He could see his associate just outside the lower door of the chamber.

Daniel had reached the floor of the chamber and was following the curve of the wall towards the door. He paused, then peeped out quickly. He spotted the boots of the gunman on the stairway to the mezzanine level.

Stu had still not seen the man on the stairs. His focus and his gun were on the base of the chamber. Just as well. One of the gunmen made an appearance. The first of Stu's three rapid rounds shattered the window, but he maintained the same stance and the following two bullets followed the same path. All three hit the gunman in the chest. Stu stepped away from the window and began reloading. He then looked at his watch: 05:14, 05:13, 05:12…

One gunman left, Daniel thought. Seeing that gunman near the top of the stairs, Daniel crept out of the chamber and approached the timer. He was surprised to see the cabling was still intact. *Maybe these gunmen have no experience of explosives. Maybe they saw the timer fixed at 09:00. Who cares*, he thought. He was about to start the timer, but his finger hovered over the red button. There was a small dial to one side. How long ago had Dante set the other timers? He made a quick calculation in his head and turned the dial slowly until 05:30 was displayed. He then pressed the button. 05:29, 05:28…

Stu ran past the shattered window, through onto the gangway, and stepped across quietly into the chamber. There was no sign of Daniel below. *He must be outside setting the timer*, he thought. Stu slung the rifle over his shoulder and began climbing down the ladder.

Above Daniel, the last of the prince's men had reached the mezzanine walkway. The gunman looked back along its length before stepping inside the first laboratory. Daniel, seeing him disappear, sprinted for the main elevator. As he ran, he glanced at the two service elevators under the mezzanine floor. One of them was open and, unlike the main elevator, it was clear. He could also see Chris up ahead. Stu said he would get her. But even from that distance, he knew there was nothing they could do. Still, he had to be sure. He ran towards her. 'Chris!' he whispered loudly. Her body had been riddled. Daniel crouched down and held two fingers against her neck. 'Ah shit,' he muttered. He glanced back— still no sign of the gunman—and then at the bodies blocking the door of the main elevator.

Dante and Jack were making good progress up the multiple flights of the emergency stairs. Dante looked at his watch. 02:32, 02:31…

Stu had reached the bottom of the chamber. Unlike Daniel, he jogged straight for the door, crushing more of the scale city with his boots. He peered out. Daniel was by the main lift, but Daniel had not seen him. Stu, not knowing that the last gunman was up on the mezzanine floor, was about to risk using the radio just as

Daniel spotted him. Stu jabbed a finger at him and then pointed up. It was time to exit. Daniel knew his best chance was the service elevator. He ran for it.

In the first laboratory, the gunman darted sideways to look down behind the long workbenches. No one was there. He was about to check the next room when he spotted the red digits of a display. He knew it was a timer. It was taped to explosives near the base of one of the benches. Leaning down for a better look, his eyes widened in horror. 00:21, 0:20…

Chapter 90
Storm Force

The smallest of slithers in the thick cloud allowed the moon to illuminate the military base and surrounding forest with a soft, blue-white wash of light. But the skies were far from tranquil. Electrical forces were building amongst the roiling folds of what was fast becoming a massive storm cloud. No sooner had it appeared, did the moon vanish, plunging the landscape back into darkness.

The gunman on the mezzanine floor was transfixed by the countdown. 00:16, 00:15.

At 00:14 he made a run for it. He bolted out of the room and clattered down the stairway three steps at a time.

Stu was still inside the chamber when he heard the metal stairway rattle with the sound of heavy boots. Was it Daniel running up, or a gunman running down? he thought. He peered out, gun raised. He was about to fire when something told him not to. He glanced at his watch and then the chamber timer nearest to him. His watch read 00:09; the timer 00:08. 'OH SHIT!' Stu bolted towards the main elevator.

The gunman spotted Stu, but self-preservation was also foremost on his mind. He had almost reached the last flight of stairs when the chamber structure to his left erupted in a fireball.

The blast threw the gunman sidelong into the stairway railings. A huge chunk of the chamber wall then smashed into the stairs, sending them crashing and screeching across the main floor, before coming to a rest in a mangled heap. The rest of the lower part of the chamber was blasted in all directions, bringing its top half along with the gangway crashing down and disintegrating. The man groaned. He was under the distorted stairway, across which, only inches from his face, was the mass of chamber wall that had blown away. The stairway was protecting him. *Thank Allah! I'm alive*! he thought. His ears were still ringing when the control room exploded. The gunman lay there. The explosion was far enough away. A broad smile developed across his face. But a series of thunderous booms somewhere directly above him wiped that smile instantly. He could not move, nor could he see beyond the slab of wall above his head. Desperately trying to wriggle free, a new sound made him stop. He recognised it as the sound of metal slowly buckling. Then silence, as four tons of mezzanine floor fell noiselessly nearly thirty metres, before hitting the chamber wall, crumpling the stairs like tin foil, and crushing the life out of him.

'We're good to go,' Armstrong reported.

'And ELF?' Mason asked.

'One more button push, sir.'

'Then do it!' Mason retorted.

Armstrong was inwardly pleased with his mastery of the weapon's systems. This had been a crash course like no other. Remote control of the D3 had been flawless. The *seeders* had helped to generate a storm cloud. There was more than enough energy up there. It was time to release the ADNDs. The onboard, ultra-low-light image sensors showed the miniature drones disappear away from the D3 and into their freefall. At an altitude of eighty metres, they would automatically power up and home in on their designated targets. One more button push to activate the extremely low-frequency pulse and they would be armed.

Kara knew that she must buy time. There was no sign of Daniel and the others. She now feared the worst. 'You are mad,' she repeated defiantly.

Prince Al-Musan ignored her. He was watching his team line up the scientists in front of him.

The tiny motors that powered the ADNDs registered just 15 decibels; quieter than rustling leaves and barely above the level of human breathing. They silently peppered the prince's SUVs and all those now in the compound. Kara and the scientists included.

Dante and Jack had reached the ground floor. Jack slowly opened the emergency stairwell door and quickly exited, his assault rifle pointing down a short corridor. It was clear. Dante followed and the two men soon turned onto the main corridor. It, too, was empty, and the blast doors lay open. When they reached what was left of the main door, now hanging precariously, Jack raised a hand. They stopped and Jack peered out through his NVGs then immediately pulled his head back in.

The building then rocked. There was the slightest of muffled booms somewhere deep below them. Loud alarms then rang out.

'The explosions must have set them off,' Dante said.

'Well, that's good,' Jack responded over the din. 'But bad news; we have company.'

Dante peered out. 'They're not army.'

'No, that's what I thought,' Jack said.

In the compound, the prince was shouting orders. Three of his men were running towards the main complex.

Dante saw them coming but a series of brilliant white flashes nearly blinded him.

'JESUS!' he cried out and drew back inside. He threw off his NVGs and rubbed his eyes.

The compound ahead of them was ablaze with intense light as though rock concert strobes had reached a climactic encore. Jack raised his NVGs and looked out. *LIGHTNING? THE WEAPON?* he thought. To say that he and Dante were thunderstruck by the rapidly developing spectacle was perfectly apt. The bolts were targeting the vehicles one by one; two exploded in a ball of flame. More amazingly, the lightning was striking down the fleeing men. And the instantaneous thunder was relentless and utterly deafening. Jack and Dante retreated into the shadows of the corridor and watched with mouths agape. Neither of them had experienced anything like it during their army years, even in the most intense firefight or airstrike. A lone balaclava'd man ran full pelt off to the right only to be hit and burnt to a crisp. The three men coming towards the complex building were then struck by two massive bolts; the thunder cracks amplified by the walls of the corridor.

Daniel had no idea where the service elevator would lead him. Like the main elevator, its ascent was rapid. He had adopted a crouched position and had also opted for his assault rifle. The door opened. There was a wall a few feet in front of him. It was dark, but he could hear *and* feel the low and sub-frequencies of countless thunderclaps. *Surely not*, he thought. He pulled down his NVGs and quickly peeped out. It was a long corridor, and it was empty. At the far end, the wall was flashing in time with…*Oh my god,* he muttered. He raised his NVGs. There was his exit.

To their horror, the scientists knew exactly what was happening.

GET YOUR JACKETS OFF!' one of them shouted.

Kara was the quickest to respond. She unzipped her jacket and threw it with all her might. Seconds later, a single bolt almost vaporised it. She then threw herself flat on the ground.

Those that had not heeded the warning, notably those wearing little more than a sweatshirt, were fleeing in sheer terror. The lightning bolts picked them off one by one. Those who had shed their tops, but ran too close to those that had not, were thrown clear across the ground by the deadly shafts of light, only to be combusted by the super-heated air.

Prince Al-Musan had reached cover under the porch of Building 1. But he certainly did not feel safe. He watched as his vehicles and his fleeing men were taken out one by one. *HIS MEN WERE BEING TRACKED*! he realised. He saw some of the scientists desperately discarding their tops. He looked down at his own jacket and ran a hand over one sleeve. There were small bumps. Quickly, he pulled it off and flung it out into the compound. It was still in mid-air when it disappeared in a blinding flash. The prince fell backwards into the building wall and watched his jacket hit the ground and burst into flames.

Kara was lying face down flat on the compound ground, her arms wrapped over her head. She could feel the heat; each bolt would be around twenty thousand degrees Celsius, and they were striking every half second, concentrated in an area barely larger than two or three tennis courts. She could also hear the screams and the ear-splitting thundercracks all around her. But look? She did not dare.

Chapter 91
Stand-Off

Mason, Armstrong, and the two regulars had exited the rear of the ordnance building and had taken up position along a side wall, locked and loaded. They watched in awe at the scene before them.

'My God!' Mason muttered.

'It's quite something seeing it up close and personal,' Armstrong shouted.

Mason looked at his watch. Based on their Spear of Destiny attack across North Africa and the Middle East, he knew it would be over soon.

Sure enough, after more than two minutes of unrelenting lightning, and as though someone had flicked a gigantic switch, the manmade storm suddenly abated, then stopped altogether. The storm cloud swiftly broke apart, and like a symbol of peace, the lucent moon reappeared, casting a cool, feeble glow over the compound.

Mason turned to his men. 'Listen up. We finish this now. Anyone still alive out there, you take them out.'

His men nodded, and all four of them pulled down their NVGs and raised their weapons.

Mason led them forward.

Daniel had reached the end of the corridor and a door with a small window. The flashes and thundercracks, though, suddenly stopped. He switched on his goggles and peered out. Beyond, was the forest and the burnt-out army trucks. He knew exactly where he was. To his right would be the compound, with the scientists' quarters beyond.

Those in the compound were either dead, dazed, or screaming in pain. Jack and Dante wasted no time. They ran out in two directions, assault rifles raised; their focus was on those wearing balaclavas. Dante saw one of them, curled up but moving, and unloaded two rounds into his head. Jack found another, face down. He kicked a boot under the gunman's stomach and flipped him over. Even battle-hardened Jack recoiled slightly at the sight: the balaclava and the man's charred face seemed to be fused together.

Daniel had reached the corner of the main complex. He heard the shots and saw Jack and Dante walking amongst the bodies and wounded. Ahead of him were burning vehicles that he knew must belong to the gunmen. It was then that he spotted Kara lying close to one of them.

New gunfire then came from the far end of the compound. Dante responded immediately, diving down, and taking cover behind a body; Jack ran behind one of the prince's SUVs.

Daniel saw the new threat: more soldiers. Shit! *Where had they come from?* he thought. He looked back towards Kara. She had spotted him and was raising herself off the ground.

'DANIEL!'

'GET DOWN, KARA!' he shouted.

She squinted in the gloom. Her relief in hearing him alive was enough for her to smile. But Daniel was making a frantic hand movement for her to get down. She did and quickly.

Daniel scanned the area. *Where was Stu?* he thought.

Jack and Dante were returning fire at the advancing soldiers.

Daniel assessed the situation. The soldiers were now no more than forty metres away; one of them had taken up position behind their now disabled ATV. Daniel turned and sprinted away along the side of the main complex—he would outflank them by running round the back and up the far side of the building.

Jack had peered over the bonnet of the SUV when bullets whistled past close to his head. He ducked down as more punctured the engine bay and far wing. He had seen enough to know the almost exact source of these latest shots. He threw himself to the ground, rolled sideways, and let off six rounds. One of the regular soldiers pivoted from the bullet impacts before crumpling to the ground like a rag doll.

Armstrong and the other regular had joined Mason by the ATV. 'There's one by the righthand SUV and another between the scientist quarters and the barracks,' the lieutenant reported.

Mason quickly looked. 'He's exposed. He's using a body as cover. Give me that,' he said holding out a hand for the grenade launcher. The colonel mounted it on his shoulder, aimed, and pulled the trigger. Dante, though, had been ready. The colonel's stance was unmistakable, and Dante moved quickly. The grenade exploded where he had been just moments earlier, blowing apart the body he had used as cover. It was young Dr Emma Crusoe's. Dante skidded to the ground alongside his buddy.

'Fuck me, that was close,' Dante said, panting.

Jack simply prodded Dante and made direction gestures. They both ran in opposite directions. It was a timely move; the SUV took a direct grenade hit.

Al-Musan had sneaked into the scientist's quarters and was leaning back against a wall well inside. He closed his eyes and took long slow breaths.

Armstrong stepped out and began firing his M16 assault rifle towards Jack and Dante's new positions. There was no return fire. Armstrong stood his ground and began reloading. It was his last mistake. A burst of machine gun fire pummelled his legs and he collapsed onto his knees. He looked down through his NVGs. Then the pain came and he screamed. Another burst of machine gun silenced him as it punctured his torso, forcing his body backwards into a bizarre kneeling posture, his head lolling, mouth open.

Mason and the regular stared at the now motionless Armstrong.

'Shit! Where the hell was that from?' Mason said.

'Sir,' said the regular, 'I think we're facing two opposing groups.'

Another burst of gunfire showered and perforated the ATV's metalwork. Mason took a peek. 'I see him. Balaclava. Two o'clock. The regular nodded and checked his M16 then leant out. Half a second later, he let off six rapid shots and took cover again. Mason did a quick recce. 'He's down. Good shooting, soldier. Now let's get the oth…'

'DROP 'EM! NOW!'

Daniel stood five metres from them, his gunsight darting between the colonel and the regular. 'DO IT!' Daniel shouted.

There were running footsteps. Daniel flashed a glance towards them. It was Jack.

Jack pulled out his pistol. 'Do as the man says because I just love using my P228.'

The regular dropped his rifle and raised his hands. The colonel was livid. But he, too, lowered the grenade launcher and raised his hands. 'Who the FUCK are you coming on to *my* base?' he hissed.

'We're the good guys,' Jack replied, nonchalantly.

'Are you a fuckin' Brit?' the colonel asked with disbelief.

'Shut it!' Daniel said. 'Get over there! Now, on your knees, hands on head!' The soldiers complied.

The colonel swelled his barrel-like chest. He was steaming. 'Let me tell you boys, you have made a *big* mistake. No one messes with the United States Army and gets away with it.'

Jack walked up to the colonel and placed his Sig against his head and whipped off the colonel's NVGs. 'Oh, I'm not so sure about that, colonel.' Jack then frisked him. He found a pistol, ammunition, grenades, and a knife, all of which he pocketed. He then moved on to the regular, removed his NVGs, a knife, some M16 magazines, and grenades. Taking out some zip ties and walking behind the colonel, Jack did not need to say anything; the colonel placed his hands behind his back. Jack zipped them tight. The regular followed his commander's lead.

'Get Bravo 2 over here,' Daniel said.

Jack raised his radio. 'Bravo 1 to Bravo 2, come in. Over.'

'*Bravo 2. Over,*' Dante replied.

'Head for the ATV. We've secured the compound. Proceed with caution. There may be some more balaclavas out there. Over and out.'

'*Roger that. Over and out.*'

The colonel's eyes squinted in the gloom. He needed to know what the hell was going on. 'The men in balaclavas, who *are* they?'

Jack looked at the colonel. 'I thought that would have been obvious to an officer in the United States Army of Fuckwits. *They* are the baddies.'

Daniel could not help but smile at Jack's unrelenting wit.

Prince Al-Musan opened his eyes. The only sound he could make out was a pitiful cry from someone nearby in the compound. He headed for the window and peered out. He could just make out some figures at the far end of the compound. The nearby moaning resumed. A scientist was writhing on the ground; small wisps of smoke were rising from whatever he had been wearing. A movement immediately outside the window made the prince retreat quickly. It was Dante making his way across the compound.

The prince considered his options. He had lost all his men. He looked back inside and set off down the corridor. A feeling of panic was slowly building in him. *There must be an emergency exit somewhere*, he thought. The corridor ended with a T-junction and he looked left.

'SHIT!' he shouted.

But his shoulders dropped with relief. It was two of his own men that faced him. They quickly lowered their guns. 'What are you doing in here?' he whispered loudly, anger in his eyes.

'Your Highness, the storm!'

The prince's fury subsided. They were right. And he was glad he was not alone. He looked the other way down the short corridor. Finally, a fire exit. 'Ammunition?' he asked. The two men nodded. 'Good. Follow me!'

Behind the building, the prince surveyed the line of wrecked and smouldering Humvees. The nearest vehicle seemed to be intact.

Daniel looked across the compound. He could see Dante moving carefully amongst the nearest bodies, prodding those with balaclavas hard with his rifle.

'The balaclavas are all dead. There are some scientists still alive,' Dante called out, as he ran the last few feet to join Daniel and Jack.

'Keep a 360 lookout,' Daniel instructed. 'I don't want any more surprises.' Dante nodded. 'I'm going to get Kara.'

Prince Al-Musan, followed closely by his two men, had reached the corner of the scientists' quarters and looked back across the compound. Ahead were his SUVs—now useless—and an armed figure was walking towards them. The prince pressed his body back up against the wall and looked out again. Someone was getting up from behind the nearest vehicle.

'DANIEL!' Kara's voice was as clear as the cold night air.

The prince smiled. 'Stay here,' he told his men. 'If I shoot, *you* shoot!' The prince looked again at the approaching figure and made his move.

The bright green running man in Daniel's NVGs stood out like pixels on a 1980s video game. But Daniel was too slow. The prince grabbed Kara and thrust his pistol into her back. She cried out with a mixture of pain and surprise but offered no resistance when she felt the gun barrel jar painfully against her spine. 'Hello again, Kara,' he whispered calmly in her ear. 'Tell your hero to drop his weapon, or I swear I'll finish you here.'

Daniel had sprinted the last few meters. It took only a moment for him to recognise Kara's assailant. *Of course, it's him*, he thought, before shouting, 'DROP IT!'

'Oh, I don't think so, Daniel,' the prince retorted and waved his gun briefly, before thrusting it again into Kara's back. Kara winced. Having shed her jacket, there was little to soften the barrel's impact.

'It's alright, Daniel,' Kara said. 'He won't shoot me. He detests violence. Isn't that right, Your Highness?'

Daniel continued to aim his rifle at the prince. 'Look at the situation, Al-Musan,' Daniel reasoned. 'Your men are all dead. You're on your own.'

'Are you *sure* about that, Daniel?' the prince taunted.

Daniel scanned the area. Seeing that the prince had escaped, it was possible some of his men had, too. With his gun still aimed at Al-Musan's face, Daniel moved behind the bonnet of one of the disabled SUVs. 'There are no more vehicles,' he continued. 'How are you going to get away?'

'No one is going anywhere.'

It was a new voice, and the compound was then flooded with light.

Daniel ducked down, quickly raised his NVGs, and swung around. Kara's mouth dropped open. From the direction of the main complex, Professor Arthur Steel was walking towards them. Behind him were Doctors Jeffrey Scott and Jayden Joseph. All three were armed with pistols and they were pointing at Daniel, Kara, and the prince.

'Arthur?' Kara could hardly speak.

'Drop it!' Scott said.

'No!' Kara cried, 'he's with me.'

Making sure he was beyond the prince's line of vision, Daniel reluctantly lowered his rifle. Dr Joseph retrieved it.

'I'm sorry, Kara. I hope you don't think bad of me. This,' the professor said, momentarily waving his gun around, 'was my true mission. And I'll be damned if I see it fail or fall into the wrong hands.'

'I *can't* believe this, Arthur. Why?' Kara implored.

'To be frank, Kara, I'm as surprised to see you here as you are me. But then again, I can understand your motivation. Having your research hijacked and then closed down must have hurt.'

'You can say that again! I was on the brink of something that could save the world, not destroy it, and enflame religious hatred. Someone had to stop it,' Kara said, anger growing inside her. 'And there's me thinking that shit, Ordway, was the crazy one.'

'You're wrong, Kara. What needed to be stopped was the rise of forces against two thousand years of Christianity. Did you know that Christian persecution is almost at the level of genocide? Then there's wave after wave of terror attacks. We are losing, Kara, and we are not prepared to stand by and do nothing. This is a crusade like no other, and you can't stop it.'

'Oh God, help me. So, even you joined that sect of deluded zealots,' she said, shaking her head.

The professor looked from the prince to Kara and sighed. 'So, you know about us. I'm impressed. In case you're interested, one does not join; one is invited. Oh, Kara. Why did you ever come here?'

'I told you. This is madness. You're mad. Creating this…this weapon. It had to be stopped.'

'No, the Spear of Destiny is perfect,' Steel continued calmly. 'The world is obsessed with climate change. These storms are seen as another unpredictable consequence. We have the perfect cover: plausible deniability.'

'Not unless we tell the world what's really going on,' Daniel countered. 'They already know about the meteorite and the martyrdoms. The link to your weapon will be incontrovertible.'

'Ah, Dr Daniel Bayford. The meteorite man. Under other circumstances, I would have said it's nice to meet the man who unwittingly helped in all this. I'm also impressed with your efforts to try to stop it. I underestimated you, and Kara, of course. But I don't think either of you is in any position to tell anyone anything.'

'Is that a threat? Are you going to kill us?' Daniel said scowling.

'I never imagined I'd have to hurt you or Kara. But, I'm sorry, your efforts will end here.'

'Well, sabotaging our plane didn't work.' Kara said with pain in her eyes.

Steel looked genuinely surprised. 'I know nothing of any sabotage.'

'Really? Your life is obviously one big lie. Why should I believe you now?'

'I swear, Kara….But…'

'But what?'

'We are many.'

'We being the Guild of God. It's OK, we do *know* about your band of maniacs.'

'I'm sorry to break up your little reunion here,' the prince announced, sarcastically. 'But who are you?'

Steel turned to the prince. 'My name is Arthur Steel. Professor Arthur Steel.'

'The man who masterminded all this. Maybe I should shoot you right now.'

'Arthur, he's got a gun in my back.'

'You could. But I know who you are, Prince Al-Musan. Although not a real prince, or so I read. More a self-proclaimed royal, who claims he's the descendant of a Persian emperor and calls his home his palace. A man who funds the very terror we plan to end.'

'SHUT UP! I am a successful industrialist. And my forefathers were great…'

'Huh!' Kara snarled. 'So, you're a fake as well as a failure, Al-Musan. 'I'm surrounded by liars and maniacs!'

'Don't push it, Kara,' the prince whispered loudly, his mouth close to her ear.

Arthur Steel smiled. 'Well, let's not make this too personal,' he said, turning to Al-Musan. 'So, I know why Kara and Daniel are here. I also learned about the threats on them in France and London. Now, you wouldn't come all the way to freezing-cold Alaska on a new assassination mission. So, let me guess your real reason for being here. You want the Spear of Destiny for your own ends.'

'Oh, you're so smart, professor. Top of the class. I knew damn well that the US had developed a weapon. Your prodigy, Dr Williams, and her boyfriend, Daniel, confirmed it and led me straight here.'

Steel was curious. 'How did you know?' he asked, cocking his head to one side.

Kara spoke up, 'Daniel's discovery would make science undermine his crazy martyrdom plan. So, he tried to silence us twice and failed. But in pursuing us, he saw us talking to one entrusted by your lot, who spilled the beans about the Spear.'

'Ah yes,' Steel said. 'I had heard about some dissension amongst our ranks.'

Al-Musan laughed. 'This is so entertaining. Scientists always love to have answers.'

Kara ignored him. 'We made the connection between Daniel's stone and the martyrdoms,' she added. 'And thanks to my suspicions about that freak Ordway, along with some detective work, here we are.'

'I had my suspicions about those martyrdoms,' Steel said, nodding and smiling. 'Now it all makes sense. Two parallel uses of the same stone but for different ends. Fascinating. So, you have your own little collection, do you?'

'I am the current guardian of stones handed down over centuries. I was the first of many to realise their true power. But now, with the help of *your* Spear of Destiny, I will use them again against the infidels that slaughtered my people. It is my destiny,' Al-Musan declared grandiosely.

'Yeh,' Daniel said. 'Your martyrdom was *such* a great idea.'

'I did convert many from your flagging faith.'

'As well as kill naïve, misguided young men. It was others that realised the true power of those stones. Not you.'

'Yes, thank you for that,' Al-Musan said, trading sarcasm. I never thought I'd be thanking the US government, or what was it? The Guild of God. Let me guess. Hmm, Kara called them deluded zealots and a band of maniacs. Right, Kara? So, clearly a group of puritanical, Christian extremists. Which makes them…what's the word…? Oh yes, TERRORISTS! And I'll bet they're the ones who drove and funded the entire project. And you, Kara, have the *audacity* to accuse me of funding terrorism. Who's the hypocrite now? And yes, Professor, you're right, I plan to and *will* take your doomsday weapon—very impressive it is, I must say. And I will unleash it on, ooh, where shall I begin? Washington and New York for starters. Then, Chicago, LA, Frisco, and that abomination of excess, Las Vegas. Then London, Berlin, Paris… Gosh, so many cities to choose from. I can't wait. And I simply won't stop. Not until I've killed A THOUSAND TIMES MORE PEOPLE THAN YOU DID!' he screamed.

At the far end of the compound, Dante was scoping the area around the ordnance building and the other burnt-out barracks. Only Jack had seen the floodlights go on and heard the raised voices. He looked up. 'Shit!' He looked down at Mason and the regular. Mason returned his look with anger and contempt written across his face. *They weren't going anywhere fast*, Jack thought. Using the ATV as cover, Jack ran to find Dante.

Steel continued, 'Which is why killing me would be a bad idea.'

'And why's that?' Al-Musan asked.

'Well, do you have the Spear of Destiny? No. Do you know how it works? No. Could we override it from anywhere in the world? Yes.'

'Oh, you'd be surprised at the extent of my resources, Professor. I'll be using your weapon. You can mark my words.'

'And how do you plan all that on your own?' Daniel called out from behind the SUV.

The prince pretended to look doubtful. 'Hmm, you've got me there, Daniel. Why didn't I think this through? Oh, wait a minute.' With that he swung his gun and shot Dr Joseph in the forehead.

Kara brought a hand to her mouth, her eyes wide with fear.

Machine-gun fire then erupted from the scientists' quarters and Dr Scott was cut down. He fell onto his back and clutched his stomach with a bare hand. The warmth of his blood felt almost pleasant in the icy air. He looked up, confusion now on his face, then back at his bloodied hand. 'I guess this is what they call Karma.' He grimaced and his body fell still.

Steel dropped to the ground; his gun fell from his hand. Daniel leapt forward, retrieved his rifle, and took aim at the prince from behind the SUV.

'As you can see *and* hear, I'm not so alone,' Al-Musan said quite calmly. 'Now drop it, Daniel!'

Daniel hesitated then lowered his weapon. Where the hell are Jack and Dante? And Stu? he thought.

'Out where I can see you!'

Daniel stepped out into the open. 'You hurt one hair on her head and I'll...'

Al-Musan cocked his head. 'You'll what, Daniel?' He then turned to the professor. 'Get up!' Steel struggled to his feet slowly. The prince shuffled himself and Kara towards Steel's gun and kicked it away. 'You,' he said to one of his men, 'get all the weapons and his goggles.'

The prince then pushed Kara away. She ran into Daniel's arms and looked at Steel with disdain. 'Now look what you've done!' she hissed.

'He followed *you*!' Steel said almost spitting the words. *You* led them here. Not me.'

Daniel held Kara tight. She started shivering badly. Daniel removed his jacket. 'Put it on.'

Watching Kara, the prince realised that adrenalin would not keep him warm. He beckoned one of his men over. 'Give me your jacket!' His gunman reluctantly handed it over. 'Keep them covered while I put it on.' The prince then whispered in the gunman's ear. The man set off. Daniel watched him head towards the gap between the scientists' quarters and the barracks.

'KILL THAT FUCKING LIGHT!' the prince ordered the other gunman, who raised his B&T and fired. The compound was plunged into darkness. He then pointed the weapon at Daniel and Kara.

Jack had not needed to catch Dante's attention; the recent gunfire had already done that.

'Sounds like more balaclavas,' Dante said.

'You got it. Come on! Daniel and Kara are in trouble.'

Chapter 92
Sweet Shop

Dante, now in night-vision mode, had reached the rear of the main complex. He turned the corner and began making his way forward, keeping close to the wall. The army trucks that Chris had taken out during their initial assault were ahead to his left.

Jack had gone in the opposite direction, around the back of the buildings opposite. He had reached the nearest wall of the burning barracks, now partially collapsed, when he heard the unmistakable sound of a 6.5 litre V8 fire up. He ran to his right and looked at the line of wrecked Humvees and cursed under his breath; his 84mm rocket assault had failed to disable the farthest one, which suddenly pulled forward.

The gunman swung the Humvee through the gap in the buildings and towards the compound.

Mason and the regular, kneeling and tied near the ATV, heard it, too, and watched as it shot past them.

Jack looked back across the compound and saw it reappear and come to a stop outside the ordnance building.

'Come on, professor, you're going to show me your sweet shop.' Al-Musan lowered his NVG and raised the gun against the back of Steel's head. 'MOVE IT!' he shouted and ushered the professor towards the waiting Humvee.

The professor half-tripped over a body. 'I can't see so well,' he said. The prince simply jabbed him in the back of the head with the barrel of the gun.

Still kneeling and zip-tied, the base commander and his subordinate then heard the approaching footsteps. 'What's your name, soldier,' Mason whispered.

'Marino, sir' the private whispered in reply.

'Well, Marino, you're now a corporal, and I want you to get down—slowly and quietly.'

Mason knew they were quite literally sitting targets. He also knew that one of his soldiers had been right: two separate groups had attacked his base. The Brits had been reasonable. *Brits, God damn it! I thought they were on our side!* The colonel was seething at the thought of it. But the other group was unknown and deadly.

The two soldiers lowered themselves slowly and quietly onto their sides. They could just make out the professor now walking in the middle of the compound from their left, followed closely by a gunman.

Mason knew exactly where they were heading. He had to stop them. At all cost. He looked around. Marino nodded towards one of the fallen gunmen only a few feet from the colonel. It was dark, but Mason could just make out a knife strapped to the gunman's leg. Mason began to shuffle. But the noise of his combat jacket against the cold ground was too much. It was like sandpaper across rough timber. He stopped, deciding to roll longways instead. He was alongside the body. Now he needed to shuffle feet-first. It was a difficult action and as noisy.

The prince had not taken his eyes off the back of the professor's head. But the faint scraping sound off to his right made him stop. 'Hold it!' And prodded Steel in the back.

Mason stopped, too.

The prince scanned the area. Then nodded slowly. Even in the monochromatic green light of the night vision goggles, the soldiers' shade of uniforms was sufficiently different from the clothing on the other bodies. He took four quick paces towards the prostrate figures and fired three times at the first. It was Marino. He died without making a sound.

Dante had now reached the front corner of the main complex when gunshots filled the compound. But ahead was the main threat. He could see the lone gunman guarding Daniel and Kara. He raised his rifle and adjusted its sights. But quickly lowered the weapon. His angle was wrong. Kara and Daniel were immediately behind the gunman. 'Damn it!' he mouthed.

The colonel could do nothing but continue his ridiculous shuffle. He looked like a short, fat caterpillar. 'I'll get you, you fuckin' piece of shit,' he said.

'Or maybe you won't,' the prince said under his breath, then fired. The bullet cut the colonel's spinal cord in two, severing any sense of pain immediately. The colonel let out a long *oof,* as though he'd been punched in the back, and fell still.

Al-Musan turned the gun back on Steel. They continued their way forward, past the Humvee, where Al-Musan's man was now propping open the vehicle's rear hatch. Al-Musan pushed the professor into the ordnance building.

Jack had watched the events unfold from his position by the barracks. Stu had said to take out anyone and everyone. He could easily take out the two gunmen. If the scientist died, too, no problem. But he could not risk it; not with Daniel and Kara being held at gunpoint. Jack decided to bide his time.

Mason was still alive. Just. He saw movement in the doorway and tried to raise himself. *My legs!* He looked down. He could feel nothing below his waist. His resulting anger was volcanic. He looked again towards the ordnance building. The prince's gunman was loading up the rear of the Humvee with assorted cases. He re-entered and a minute later re-emerged, this time sharing the load of a long case with the professor, Al-Musan directing them with his pistol. They heaved the case onto the vehicle and the gunman closed the hatch.

Mason knew the final case was a D3. He hurled himself backwards against the leg of the dead gunman. His hands then groped for the clip holding in the knife. He popped it and withdrew the blade a few inches, then began a sawing motion with his tied hands. The blade cut through the zip tie in two strokes. The colonel shook his hands, rubbed his wrists then pulled the B&T submachine gun from under the corpse. 'I'll take that, too,' he mumbled and yanked the NVG off the dead gunman's head.

Al-Musan heard the gun being loaded. '*ADKHAL!*' he shouted. His gunman climbed into the passenger seat and lay down low.

At the other end of the compound, Dante needed a clear shot. He had two options: one, head right towards the middle of the compound—*too exposed*, he thought. Two, head left around the back of the other four SUVs. He decided on option two.

The colonel flung the gun down in front of him and then rolled himself behind it. Lying on his stomach, he raised the B&T and began firing.

Bullets sparked off the Humvee and blistered the wall beyond. Steel threw himself inside the building. Al-Musan, having retreated behind the vehicle, simply waited. He knew that the colonel was badly wounded and that his gun would soon empty.

The gunfire was not particularly loud, but in the dead of the night and with the cold, dense air, it was loud enough. *Perfect—a distraction*, Dante thought and ran behind the farthest SUV and peered around. He had the line of fire he needed, and he required less than a second. He raised his assault rifle. The gunman had turned towards the sound of the gunfire at the far end of the compound. The back of his head filled Dante's sight.

The colonel ejected the magazine and was rifling through the pockets of the dead gunman when the realisation dawned that his adversary was standing over him. He looked up into Al-Musan's face. 'Who *are* you? Let me know that at least.'

'I'm the man who is, quite literally, stealing your thunder,' the prince replied and laughed at his spontaneous wit.

The colonel scowled. 'Fuck you, you piece of camel shit.'

'This is for my brothers and sisters,' the prince said, before pulling the trigger three more times.

Al-Musan then leapt into the driver's side of the Humvee. He had what he needed.

The professor, hearing the Humvee accelerate away, peered out of the doorway. This was his chance. He slipped out of the building and ran off into the night.

The Humvee shot across the compound.

'There goes my pension,' Mason muttered. Blood burst from his mouth and he fell forward, never to rise again.

Dante, momentarily distracted by the sound of more gunfire, again raised his rifle.

Al-Musan leant forward. He could see what was happening. Instinctively, he pressed down on the horn. It was a futile action. Two 45mm shells left the muzzle of Dante's SA80-A3 at 950 metres per second. The gunman guarding Daniel and Kara had only half turned his head when the shells burst through and shattered his skull less than two-hundredths of a second later.

'FUUUUUCK!' the prince screamed in anger.

Bullets then spattered the rear of the Humvee. Jack was now standing mid-compound, trying to take out its tyres.

'SHOOT THEM!' the prince screamed and accelerated. The gunman in the passenger seat threw open his door, propped himself precariously, half-hanging out against the door frame, and began firing his B&T.

Daniel scrambled for one of the guns. Bullets whistled and ricocheted all around him.

Kara had already taken cover. 'DANIEL!' she screamed.

The Humvee was heading straight for him. He dived out of the way. The Humvee lurched to a stop. 'GET HER!' the prince shouted. The gunman sprang out, grabbed Kara, and bundled her into the vehicle. The Humvee sped off towards the base exit.

Daniel got to his feet, raised the machine gun, and joined Dante and Jack firing low, trying to stop the fast-retreating monster vehicle. But without his NVGs, Daniel's attempts were ineffective. The Humvee soon disappeared behind the scientists' quarters, and was away, accelerating along the service road.

Daniel turned. 'THE SUV! COME ON!'

Daniel spotted his NVGs and grabbed them. Jack had sprinted across the compound. The three of them ran towards where Kara had hidden the SUV.

Chapter 93
Silhouette

The Humvee was thundering along the access road, its headlights off, its wheels spitting out the gritty snow covering. The gunman to Kara's right had a pistol buried into her jacket. Her mind was racing as fast as the Humvee: *she may be able to reason with the prince. But what frame of mind was he in? He had lost all but one of his men. If only she had stayed in her vehicle. If only she had listened to Daniel and not come. She had so much more she could do in her life. And Daniel...* She feared she would never see him again. She feared the worst.

The floodlit checkpoint was up ahead. The prince flicked the NVG away from his right eye, checked the rear mirror, and began to slow. Kara saw the two dead sentries. *Oh god*, she thought, *they'll kill me using one of the sentry's guns. It'll look like I killed them.*

The Humvee came to a stop. Kara closed her eyes. This is not how she had imagined she would die.

When the passenger door opened, she opened her eyes. Al-Musan turned to her. 'Go, Kara,' he said calmly.

'You're letting me go?' she asked, immediately wishing the words had not left her mouth.

'Yes! Get out! I told you. I don't like violence. And I like you, Kara. I like your resolve and your mettle. Besides, it doesn't end here. I want you to be a witness. You deserve to see more fruits of your labour. A second, but much bigger harvest.'

The gunman stepped out. Kara wasted no time. She shuffled across the seat and jumped down. The gunman, stood facing her and smirked, then raised his pistol to her face. 'Phoof!' he uttered, and pretended to shoot.

Urine ran down her legs and her knees buckled.

The gunman climbed back in, laughing.

'So long, Kara!' the prince said. And the Humvee was off.

Deep down inside the main complex, the last of the dead gunmen blocking the main elevator was being dragged slowly away. Stu, stood upright, clutched his side, and winced. He almost fell into the elevator but managed to prop himself up against the wall with a bloodied hand. He took a deep breath, and punched the top button, then checked his weapons.

Daniel prayed that Kara had left the keys under the seat. She had.

'Buckle up!' Daniel pressed down hard on the throttle and the SUV bounced its way through the trees and onto the road.

Kara was still kneeling. Her hands pressed down onto the tops of her thighs, thumbs and elbows pointing outwards. She began to sob.

Stu had reached the ground floor. The elevator door opened. But he was too weak and collapsed as the door closed again.

To Daniel, her profile, silhouetted by the checkpoint floodlight, was unmistakable. His heart pounded. *Oh God, please, please, please, let her be ok,* he thought.

'Is that…?' Dante began.

When she raised her head, turned her face towards them, and slowly began to rise, Daniel slammed a hand on the steering wheel. 'YES!… Oh, thank God!'

He could not get out of the car quickly enough. He ran to her and hugged her close. She raised her arms and was soon squeezing him as tight.

Chapter 94
Phase 8

Sunrise was still hours away when the SUV turned onto a track and into the gloom of the forest. Daniel was using his NVGs. Beside him, Jack was looking straight ahead. He had had enough of night vision for one night. No one had said a word.

Kara was tending Stu, mopping his brow with a damp cloth. He was clearly in pain.

Dante was next to them with an open laptop wedged on his knees. A night vision image showed the clearing in front of the cabin and the cabin itself.

In the back, under some tarpaulin, Chris' body gently rolled with each bump and turn.

'And now tonight's explosive new movie,' Dante muttered. He picked up a remote, flicked its switch, and pressed the button. The cabin on the screen disappeared behind a series of white flashes. Seven kilometres away, six explosions went off one after the other, blowing the cabin into a thousand pieces.

Under the first glimmer of dawn light, Daniel brought the vehicle to a stop. The track had opened out onto a large clearing. Ahead, the ground dropped away for an uninterrupted view of the rolling, forested landscape. Set back against trees and overlooking the drop was another cabin—now the hideaway for all of them for the next few days.

Jack and Dante helped Stu from the vehicle. Kara joined Daniel, who had walked to the edge of the clearing and was looking out across the valley. Kara pulled the jacket collar closer to her face.

'Damn it!' he said. He looked down at her face and threw an arm around her. 'We failed, Kara…And Chris…' His words faded away.

'Come on. Let's get inside with the others. It's cold and you don't have a jacket.'

'So much for our plan of attack,' he said. 'You must think we're fools. And we were on track until Al-Musan turned up.'

'We underestimated him.'

Daniel suddenly remembered something. He reached into his pocket and withdrew a clenched hand. 'We did find these.'

Kara looked from Daniel's face to his upturned hand as he opened it. She squinted in the gloomy light and picked up one of the tiny objects then looked at Daniel.

'You were right,' he said. 'These are drones.'

Kara stared again at the device. 'But they're so small.'

'We found a box of them. They must have made thousands of them.'

Kara turned towards the valley and held up the device in front of her. 'Of course. Spread across a target, they'd have the same effect as one single stone around someone's neck. That also means they must have synthesised the meteorite.'

'Exactly like you said. The lightning they induce must also destroy them. What did the professor say? Plausible deniability.'

'And they must get them to the target using some kind of stealth vehicle.'

'Another drone.'

'Right. They've brought together multiple developments, including my research. Remember what Seb said about that Iranian city? They couldn't detect any strike.'

'They've created the perfect weapon.'

Kara let out a long sigh. Her breath was visible in the chill. She shuddered. 'Come on, I need a hot drink.'

'So, now what?' Daniel asked as they headed towards the cabin. Kara had been spot-on with her predictions and analysis.

'Well, I've been thinking. Do you remember what Arth... ...what the professor said? That they could override the weapon from anywhere in the world.'

'That could have been a bluff. He's a clever liar, Kara. He kept the biggest lie from you.'

'I don't think so. Look, I may not have known who he really was, but I know he's a man who likes facts. The way he said it...it sounded genuine.'

They walked a few steps in silence.

'D'you think he got away?' Daniel asked.

'Well, you guys checked the base after finding Stu…and … and Chris. Oh god, I said all those bad words about her.'

'Hey.' Daniel stopped and pulled her towards him, hugging her tight.

'Are you really going to bury her here? No headstone? Nothing?'

'We have to, Kara.'

Inside, Stu was laid out on a sofa being tended by Dante. Daniel and Kara joined Jack in the kitchen.

'How is he?' Daniel asked in low voice. They could hear Stu moaning and letting out a string of expletives.

'He'll be fine. Dante's removing some shrapnel.'

'Thank god.' Daniel sighed and turned to Kara. 'To answer your question, the professor and those other scientists materialised from somewhere we missed. Maybe he's gone back there. I mean, he'd be mad to head off in this wilderness this far from civilisation.'

'If it meant getting away from almost certain death, I'd have taken the same chance.'

Daniel pondered for a moment. 'If you're right about the override then we need to find the professor.'

Chapter 95
Death and Denial

Washington DC, USA

It was a warm spring afternoon nineteen months later when the young female tour guide stopped by the railings of the White House and waited for the Chinese tourists to gather around her.

'1600 Pennsylvania Avenue. The official residence of the President of the United States of America,' she announced and waited for her colleague to translate her words before continuing. 'Following trade and shipping conflicts involving the USA, Britain, and France, Anglo-American relations deteriorated, eventually leading to the War of 1812, in which many government buildings in Washington including the White House, known then as the Executive Mansion, were set ablaze by the British.'

The tourists listened to the Chinese translation and made ooh and ahh noises, some pointing at the building through the railings.

'The White House has been extended many times. The famous West Wing, where the even more famous Oval Office…' Her words were cut short by a loud rumble of thunder. The guide and the tourists all looked up. The clouds, a mixture of black, darkest greys, yellow and purple, were churning with menace. Some of the tourists opened umbrellas. 'OK, I think maybe we should move on to the National Gallery of Art,' the guide said.

The first bolt of lightning exploded one hundred metres from where they stood. The guide and her group along with pockets of other sightseers all cowered and turned towards the president's residence. The lightning had hit the roof dead centre. The flag pole that proudly flew the Stars and Stripes had been vaporized by the intense heat of the strike. Six more bolts then pounded the building. There were screams and the tourists scattered in all directions; others simply stood and stared.

It seemed the entire city was alight—the flashes made even more intense in the growing gloom. The Washington Monument and the Lincoln Memorial were blasted into crumbling ruins. Worse still was the United States Capitol—the seat of the United States government. Its dome and façade disintegrated under a relentless barrage of lightning bolts; the roof collapsed, crushing its denizens like ants.

A TV helicopter returning from a recent traffic report hovered over the Potomac River.

'Tell me you're getting this,' the reporter said, not taking her eyes off the apocalyptic scene.

Her cameraman was already filming. What he and the reporter were witnessing seemed unreal and otherworldly. The pilot had seen enough. Without a word he began to descend, looking for somewhere to land.

Realising what the pilot was doing, the reporter snapped out of her reverie. 'STAY UP!' she shouted into her mic. 'WE NEED TO GET THIS!'

A series of flashes to their right made them turn. The cameraman swung his camera around and pointed it towards the Pentagon.

'Oh my God! We're under attack!' the reporter said.

The chopper's electrics suddenly cut out. Then the motor.

The pilot frowned, jiggled the cyclic stick, and looked desperately at the controls. 'What the fuck?'

Unbeknown to the pilot, an electromagnetic pulse used to activate more ADNDs had just disabled the chopper. 'MAYDAY, MAYDAY. THIS IS NBC CHOPPER 2. I'VE LOST CONTROL. GOING DOWN.'

The pilot attempted autorotation, trying, as they fell, to gain some control by using the air to rotate the now almost static main rotor. It was a futile attempt. The chopper spun slowly but plummeted fast, hitting the side of the Arlington Memorial Bridge, and exploding, before dropping into the river.

California, USA

Nearly four thousand kilometres to the west, Silicon Valley was ablaze with lightning. Cars and trucks were piling into each other, as drivers looked away at the unfolding spectacle all around them.

New York City, New York, USA

High above the skyscrapers, a D3 hovered over Manhattan Island. Its hatch door opened and thousands of *seeders*, glistening in the late afternoon sunshine, poured out.

London, UK

It was night-time in London when the sky lit up like the biggest New Year's firework display. Except this display was not confined to the banks of the Thames. This was across central London and deadlier than the Blitz. The Houses of Parliament, Downing Street, the London Eye, the MI6 Building, the Foreign Office …building after building. The death toll rose every second. Citizens and workers in the great city ran in all directions, a mixture of fear and determination on their faces, unsure whether to stay in the open or take cover in a building. Mayhem and panic on the streets then ensued. The sound of multiple emergency service sirens only added to the terror. Queues at the tube station entrances began to back up with the pressing hoards, as they pushed and jostled their way underground—memories of the tube attack now far from their minds. Politeness and calm—the normal British way—had been replaced by a brutal, uncaring survival instinct.

Paris, France

Simultaneously, in the French capital, the Elysée Palace, Notre Dame cathedral, the Eifel Tower, the Arc de Triomphe, and even the Louvres, were under attack. Those who had been enjoying the panoramic views of Paris at night from the foot of the Sacré-Coeur steps now watched and recorded the lightning show from afar. But their excited chatter was cut short when the famous Montmartre Basilica behind them was struck repeatedly. The central dome shattered on one side; a large hole appeared, and the rest of the dome toppled and fell into one of the two smaller domes below. Half of the famous Catholic church then imploded under the weight sending white dust onto the fleeing crowd. A group of three young nuns ran from the collapsing church, one making the sign of the cross, her other hand covering the top of her black veil. They turned the wrong way. All three disappeared under a shower of deadly masonry as one complete side of the church gave way.

Washington DC, USA

The following day, President Palmer stepped through the door and into the temporary but packed press conference room. The gathered reporters all stood and the room erupted with questions. Palmer took his position at the podium and raised a hand for calm. He tried his best vote-winning smile, but the questions kept coming loud and fast. Palmer stayed silent and waited. One by one, the reporters sat down, arms raised high.

Palmer looked around for a more friendly face. He spotted one and pointed at him.

'Thank you, Mr President.' Zak Sullivan.' Sullivan bristled with his small victory, making sure his fellow journalists and the audience of millions knew who he was.

'Yes, Zak,' Palmer prompted, hoping for a gentle start.

'Will you now admit that the devastation we have witnessed is the result of a *weapon* designed by the United States and which has fallen into enemy hands?'

The room erupted again: *Is it Iran, Mr President? Is this retaliation by an Islamic country? How many dead, sir?*

Palmer seemed to wait patiently. In truth, he was rehearsing his lines. 'There is a lot of fake news out there,' he began in a raised voice. 'Social Media is to blame for the confusion and hysteria.'

'But the devastation was real, Mr President,' one reporter managed to shout above the din.

'Yes,' Palmer responded. 'And our hearts go out to all those poor souls and the many more injured. We…' Palmer struggled to be heard but pressed on. 'We will offer our support in any way we can. Naturally, our citizens will take priority. But I can tell the world that the United States of America will lead the way in helping less fortunate countries. This very morning, I have pushed through an emergency package to provide immediate medical support across the globe. The army and the National Guard have been deployed to every US city affected.'

The room had fallen silent. Palmer's voice and charisma were enough to quell the barrage of voices.

'As everyone has now seen, climate change has brought about a new threat…'

But the noise of voices quickly grew to a new crescendo. As it subsided, one loan voice could be heard: 'Who can we trust, Mr President?'

'That's the best question so far, Miss…?'

'Deboeuf, sir. Isabelle Deboeuf, Le Figaro.'

'I can tell you whom we should trust. The voice of reason. The voice of this government and the voices of our esteemed scientists. Not the ramblings…' Palmer had to raise his voice over the rising clamour. 'Not the ramblings of misinformed conspiracy theorists and doomsayers. As I've said many times before, what we are seeing is the result of climate change. Scientists across the globe…'

'Sir,' Deboeuf had stood up. Maybe it was her rich, French accent and looks, but she now had the floor. Palmer smiled. 'Sir, I was the journalist who broke the story about the meteorite discovery in France. We saw those martyrdoms, and now this. Are you saying there is no connection?'

Palmer laughed. 'Meteorite? Next question. Er… Felicity?'

Unlike all those around her, Felicity Brackman, a middle-aged woman reporter was still seated. She was a battle-hardened political journalist. She smiled and stood up. Deboeuf looked across, annoyed at the president's dismissal and unspoken rebuttal. Brackman was well-respected amongst the journalist community; an icon no less. The room fell silent.

For Palmer, her question came as a body blow: 'Are you a member of the Guild of God, Mr President?'

Palmer had had enough. 'Felicity, I've no idea what you're talking about. That's all. Thank you.' He held up a hand and started to leave the room.

'Did the Guild of God sanction this weapon, Mr President?' Brackman continued, as Palmer turned his back on a cacophony of more questions. 'Are you involved with an ultra-right-wing Christian sect bent on revenge against Muslims, Mr President?'

'Another conspiracy, Felicity. More fake news,' Palmer shouted back.

Deboeuf watched Palmer disappear through the door. She then sat down, raised her phone, and rapidly typed in the words: *Guild of God?*

Chapter 96
The Ceremony

A Subterranean Auditorium, Somewhere in USA

The buzz of excitement and anticipation amongst the five thousand men and women was palpable. They had travelled from far and wide to attend. Hundreds of thousands more were watching online.

The auditorium was dark but for a low light over a large, central, circular stage. A single, deep, sustained synthesiser bass was building in volume from the array of massive subwoofers. The nearest of the audience, their faces just discernible, were watching on with growing expectation.

The bass drone stopped abruptly. The audience was hushed into silence and held its collective breath. For three seconds the room was still. A loud fanfare then burst from the loudspeakers hanging above the stage, accompanied by a fan of intense white lights that swept across the audience. The full, rich blast of brass instruments held a long, sustained chord. The lights went out and the chord stopped, but its presence reverberated in a long decay through the auditorium. The effect was stunning. The audience laughed in relief from the shock of the audio-visual impact. At the next repeat of the massive chord, the stage was flooded in a powerful white light. And the audience went wild.

A group of performers, dressed in black, had materialised from nowhere. They stood stock-still in a tight circle, facing out, hands raised high.

A pulsing thrum began building into a powerful drum beat, and the performers slowly lowered their arms. From their centre, a figure, dressed in a white suit, rose slowly several feet above the stage. The performers had lowered themselves into a kneeling position. The main lights then dimmed and a single spotlight fell on the central figure, and a new major chord of brass filled the hall. The figure raised his arms. The audience whooped and cheered, raising their arms in response.

Richard Ordway smiled back. He felt like a god.

He waited for his audience to settle.

'Welcome. Welcome, all. Welcome to the Guild of God,' he began. More lights flashed Guild of God logos randomly across the stage:

The auditorium house lights then came on. Ordway looked at the thousands of expectant faces. In the space of fourteen months, his online sermons had helped swell the Guild's numbers close to six hundred thousand, and the ranks were growing at an increasing rate. And there had been no resistance from the Guild's council, not even Paladin. The Guild of God had emerged from the shadows.

Ordway's expression then turned dark. 'One hundred thousand, eight hundred and twenty-nine. That, my friends, is the number of people who died in those storms across our great cities.' A murmur arose, many of the audience shaking their heads. 'There are rumours. You've all heard them, I'm sure. Rumours that these storms were the result of a weapon. Let me dispel that myth right now. There is no weapon. No. That's right, there is no weapon. I used to work for the Department of Defence. For many years I was there. You can look it up if you like. Let me tell you right now. *There…is…no…weapon.*' Ordway emphasised each word. 'The storms that ravaged our nation this month were the unrelenting and worrying result of climate change. Yes, it's true. I have spoken with our top scientists: meteorologists and climatologists. They all agree. I then asked if we could manipulate weather in this way. Do you know what they all said…? They all said no. No way. So, I spoke with weapons experts and professors of physics. They all agree. There is no way such a weapon could exist.

'So, I hear you ask, what about those lightning storms in the Middle East and North Africa? Are they the result of climate change? It seems possible, right? But think again. Those same scientists, those people of learning, reminded me of some obvious facts: storms require clouds. Clouds require moisture. Lots of it.

And, you guessed it, the Middle East and North Africa are the driest places on God's good earth.'

The audience were exchanging looks and nodding.

Ordway continued, 'So what could have caused *those* terrifying storms if it wasn't a weapon—if it wasn't normal; if it wasn't climate change?'

'The wrath of God,' an audience member called out.

'YES!' Ordway declared and pointed in the direction of the voice. 'Yes indeed. Who said that? Show yourself to the audience.'

A spotlight danced around the front rows, eventually falling on a middle-aged woman, who was standing with her hand raised.

'What's your name?' Ordway asked gently.

'Rosemary.'

'Come and join me, Rosemary.'

Rosemary smiled and looked at those around her for encouragement, which they duly gave. She shuffled along the row of seats, excusing herself as she went, and mounted the stage. Ordway positioned her in front of him and placed his hands on her shoulders. 'At least Rosemary has been listening to my sermons. Right, Rosemary?' Rosemary nodded coyly, almost giggling with excitement. The audience laughed. 'Rosemary is right,' Ordway said, squeezing her shoulders. 'That was the wrath of God! We all witnessed His power. "*The adversaries of the Lord shall be broken to pieces; out of heaven shall he thunder upon them.*" Do you know your bible, Rosemary?'

Rosemary nodded as she turned to face Ordway and whispered her answer.

'Rosemary says Samuel chapter 2 verse 10. Is she right?'

'YES!' the audience replied in loud unison.

'YES, SHE IS! Now she feels like she's on a game show.' Ordway joked and waited for more laughter to subside. '"*Clouds and darkness are round about him: righteousness and judgment are the habitation of his throne. A fire goeth before him, and burneth up his enemies round about. His lightnings enlightened the world: the earth saw, and…?*"'

Rosemary was less sure this time, but replied quietly.

'Speak into my microphone, Rosemary,' Ordway said encouragingly.

Rosemary leant towards Ordway's headset mic. 'Trembled?' she said.

'Yes. "*His lightnings enlightened the world: the earth saw, and trembled.*" Psalms, chapter 97. And so, we should tremble. For this is the power of the one true God.'

'HALLELUJA! PRAISE THE LORD!' the audience cried out.

'A round of applause for Rosemary, please.'

Stagehands appeared and guided her off the stage. Her family and friends hugged and patted her on her back.

'Oh, your prize, Rosemary...' Ordway said smiling. He was relishing his starring role and spontaneity. 'A place in the Kingdom of God. That's for sure.'

'AMEN!' the crowd responded. There were smiles all around.

The lights suddenly dimmed, the stage went dark, a dense orchestral score began to build, and the audience went silent, eager for more. They would not be disappointed.

High above them, six giant widescreen displays began to descend, forming a hexagon over the stage.

The music stopped and a deep male voice boomed out over the PA system. *'Nine hundred years ago, our brave Christian brothers fought for the Holy Lands. Many of them lost their lives.'*

The screens all came on. The audience gazed up. They all knew what they were seeing. Crusaders were storming a city. Swords were swishing. Blood was spraying. Citizens of the city were being slain. The musical score had restarted, underpinning the powerful images. Little did the audience know, but the scene had been directed by one of Hollywood's best. It was a masterclass in cinematography and realism. Many of the audience recognised the rich tones of the actor providing the commentary.

The famous voiceover continued, *'After many months of battles, sieges, and hardship, the heroic Crusaders had finally reached their goal: the city of Jerusalem.'*

The scene lasted for several gory minutes, before fading into another in which the victorious Crusaders were mounting their gonfalons high on the towers and walls. A new scene then unfolded. The crusading knights were celebrating with song and laughter.

The audience was then transported high above the city. A new day was dawning. The sun, low in the sky, was rich and golden. As though through the eyes of a bird swooping down on its prey, the viewer zoomed towards the city, skimming low over the rooftops, down through the bloody streets, over the countless dead bodies, then rising high over its domes, finally coming to rest where the Crusader leader was standing proud, blood still across his face and tunic. He watched as his men raised a large wooden crucifix. When the task was complete, they stood back. The leader then cried out, 'God wills it!' The other men raised their swords and repeated the words in unison, 'GOD WILLS IT!'

Again, like a bird taking flight and rising high into the sky, the viewer watched as the scene got farther and farther below. The camera then turned towards the horizon and the rising sun.

As the scene and the music faded, the voiceover concluded the short narrative, '*They had destroyed the unbelievers. The city was theirs. Christianity had won!*'

The film finished and the auditorium was now dark and quiet as night.

An intense downlight then suddenly illuminated the centre of the stage. Standing there, dressed like a crusading knight, was Ordway, a large red cross emblazoned on his dazzlingly white tunic. He was holding a lance in front of his splayed legs.

The audience's mouths opened. It was as though Ordway had materialised from the film.

Soft, angelic music filled the air at the same moment, and the performers reappeared, this time dressed in white. A young female performer then walked slowly forward, stopped, and raised her arms. In her hands was a small box. Ordway reached forward, opened the lid, and withdrew something.

The audience was desperate to know what it was. Many were craning their necks for a better view or asking those around them. But this was all part of the act.

Ordway, clutching the object, raised his hand and placed it at the top of the lance. He stepped forward and placed the lance into a hole then stepped back.

'Like our Christian brothers of old,' he said with gravity, '*this* will be our talisman. *This* is the time we Christians will rise again.'

The light over Ordway went out. The music faded to silence.

What happened next, many of the audience later agreed, was almost divine. A laser light beamed into the top of the lance, hitting the object, and splitting into a thousand rays of blue light. Choral voices filled the auditorium. The audience stared at the light with awe and rapture.

On the other side of the world, five of the Guild of God council viewed the final scenes of the ceremony on a large display. Paladin closed the laptop and the screen went dark.

Only the council members and Ordway knew the significance of the blue stone.

Chapter 97
Conversion

Daniel's Villa, Tanneron, Southern France

The lamps on the terrace table flickered as a warm gust of air blew from the valley below, now veiled in darkness.

Daniel stood up. 'Guys, I'd like you to meet Isabelle Deboeuf.' With a smile, Deboeuf acknowledged the hellos from Stu Gibson, Dante Morgan, Jack Chaffry, and Sebastian Sadler-Smith. 'Isabelle interviewed me...when was it, Isabelle?'

'Three years ago,' Deboeuf replied.

'Wow! Who'd have guessed?' Daniel said, letting the words hang, as everyone contemplated the intervening events. 'Isabelle, this is Stu...Dante...Jack ...my even older friend, Seb...'

'Watch it,' Seb joked.

'...and Kara, my wife.'

'Yes, congratulations to you both,' Deboeuf said.

'I'll drink to that,' Seb said, standing up and raising his glass. 'To the luckiest man in France and his most beautiful and most amazing lady. To the happy couple!'

'TO THE HAPPY COUPLE!' they all repeated. Jack winked at Deboeuf.

'Thank you, Seb; everyone,' Daniel said. 'I would also like to make a toast.' He stood up and raised his glass. Everyone waited for him to speak. But Daniel looked up into the night sky.

Kara knew he was struggling. Ever since Alaska, she had noticed a change in his mood. She knew he was wracked with guilt. One day, several months back, he had broken down in front of her. She had held him tight and loved his sudden vulnerability. That was when she knew she wanted to spend the rest of her life with him.

With a half-formed smile, Daniel lowered his gaze and looked at his friends' faces. 'To our brave friend, Christine,' he said, his voice cracking slightly. 'Her contribution was huge. Her attitude and skills were exemplary. She is sorely missed. To Chris!'

'TO CHRIS!' they all repeated.

Kara and Daniel exchanged looks. Tears sparkled in her eyes. Daniel was trying to hold his back. This time he managed. They were the same tears he had once shed in front of his wife; tears not just for Chris, but for nearly losing Kara.

There was a moment of silence as the assault team remembered their fallen colleague. Daniel cleared his throat and continued. 'Isabelle was working for Le Figaro back then. She's now an independent investigative journalist. Isabelle?'

Deboeuf looked around the table. Daniel nodded, and she stood up. 'First, I apologise for my bad English.'

'It's not as bad as Stu's,' Jack joked.

'Shut it, you oversized Sassenach!' Stu responded. Everyone laughed. Laughter was always the best medicine. Deboeuf smiled but missed the joke.

'Ignore my childish friends, Isabelle,' Daniel said. 'Tell the others what you told me.'

'*Oui*, during President Palmer's press conference last month, one of the journalists, accused 'im of being a member of the Guild of God. I was, er...*intrigué*...'

'Intrigued,' Daniel said smiling.

'...*Oui*, intrigued. There were many talks about the meteorite. The martyrs and attacks. *Alors*, I contacted Daniel again. I knew there must be a connection. He told me about the Spear of Destiny and what you all did. *Incroyable!*'

'Isabelle is being modest,' Daniel interjected. 'She has already unearthed some shocking facts about the Guild of God. The people behind it reach the very highest echelons of society. And I mean the highest.'

'Like who?' Dante asked.

'Sir George Bradbury, head of MI6 for one,' Seb said.

'Professor Steel, my old professor. The man behind the Spear project itself, and the co-ordinator, Richard Ordway, formerly of the US Department of Defence,' Kara added.

'And Palmer?' Stu asked.

Daniel looked at Deboeuf for an answer.

'I don't think so,' she said. 'But President Dumart, yes.'

'Christ!' Jack muttered. 'That's already quite a list.'

'I think this just scratches the surface,' Daniel continued. 'Kara and I already knew that a cardinal of Rome was also a member.'

'Ay, and I bet that base commander knew all about it, too,' Stu said.

'We can only imagine who else is part of it and how far it extends. The Guild of God is a dangerous cabal with enormous power and influence. It's the one reason why we did what we did, and not go to the press,' Daniel added.

Kara looked at Deboeuf and asked, 'Isabelle, how did you find this out so quickly?'

'Palmer and Dumart have been very close for many years,' Deboeuf explained. 'This is well known. I…er…well, we journalists have many contacts, you know…I have one. He works at the Elysée Palace. Two years ago, after a G7 meeting, he told me that Palmer met Dumart for a private meeting. Another man was also present. At the time, I did not think this was important. Like I said, Palmer and Dumart are good friends. But Dumart is, how you say, a passionate politician. He talks sometimes like a preacher. When the journalist at the press conference accused Palmer of being a member of this Guild of God, I wondered if Dumart was involved, too.'

Daniel picked up the narrative. 'Isabelle's instincts were correct. When she mentioned this secret rendezvous to me, I asked if she had the name of the other man. She had to consult her notes. But when she came back with the answer, the connection was made. The man was Richard Ordway.'

'The man, along with Professor Steel, who hijacked my research,' Kara said.

'Four months later,' Seb added, 'we saw the first of the Spear of Destiny attacks.'

The group fell silent. Kara then stood up. 'I'll get some more wine,' she said and headed off to the kitchen.

'So, what now, Dan?' Stu asked.

Daniel looked down and shook his head. 'This is too big now. The Spear is back and all over the US military, possibly other allied forces.'

'What! You think they'll continue to use it?' Dante exclaimed.

'Absolutely they will, especially now. They'll be out for revenge,' Daniel replied.

'But everyone will see that these are weaponised storms—it's plain as day,' Jack said.

'Maybe they will,' Seb said. 'But the government, aka the Guild of God, will continue to deny involvement. They'll continue to claim that the rumours are the wild imaginings of conspiracy theorists. They'll continue to thrust their own paid experts in front of the cameras. Add to that, the fact that the weapon was designed to give them plausible deniability, and they'll be sitting pretty.'

Kara returned holding two bottles of wine. 'So,' she said, 'we gather all the proof needed. We already have some of the drones. I believe they used the meteorite samples they had to synthesise a compound to coat the drones. We find out how they are deployed, and we get samples of whatever they are using to generate the enormous electrical potential. It must be some kind of super-fast seeding technology.'

'You've converted your wife into a full-blown activist, Dan,' Dante said.

'He converted me, too,' Seb said.

'And there's me thinking you were just jealous of my lifestyle down here,' Daniel quipped, smiling at his old mate.

'Well, I must say, that was the icing on the cake. Like you, Daniel, I was disillusioned with all the bullshit.'

'And I'm simply following in all your footsteps,' Kara said, as she placed the bottles on the table. 'We have something in common. In my case, it was a betrayal by the country I once loved. Can you imagine how I feel, knowing my research is now an integral part of a WMD that's slaughtered countless innocent people? A WMD that is now being used against my own people!'

'Yeh, and that was our fault,' Jack said.

'No!' Daniel argued, 'It was *my* fault. It's my fault that Chris lost her life. *I* suggested we attack the base, and *I* created the trail for Al-Musan. The forces behind all this are unstoppable. I was stupid even thinking we could stop them.'

'Ay, but *I* should have planned for something like that. Reinforcements arriving...' Stu countered.

'Shit happens. We were just unlucky,' Dante said. 'We did blow the fuckin' place apart, though.'

'OK, let's drop the blame game,' Daniel said, holding up a hand. 'We screwed up. And I'm sorry.'

Kara began topping up everyone's glasses, as they sat in silent contemplation.

'So, what do we do?' Stu then pressed.

'What about this Al-Musan character?' Seb asked Daniel.

'Al-Musan is our target. That's where we'll get the proof Kara was referring to. He'll be a softer target than the US army, for sure.'

'And we need to find Professor Steel,' Kara reminded Daniel.

'Yes, thank you, Kara. Now that the Spear has fallen into the wrong hands, we believe Steel will be on our side. And even if we can't stop the Guild of God, we may at least be able to stop Al-Musan. If what we heard the professor say about disabling the weapon remotely is true, we may be able to pull his plug, so to speak.'

Kara frowned. 'I wonder why that hasn't already happened...'

The talking stopped once more. The group supped their wine and listened to the night-time cicadas.

Deboeuf looked around at the faces and settled on her host. 'Daniel,' she said. 'I would like to help. Let me be your researcher. Your eyes and ears.'

He looked at her for several seconds before replying. 'Er, well, sure. But it could get dangerous, Isabelle,' he said.

'I know,' she replied, taking a sip of wine. 'But what a story.'

Chapter 98
A Perfect Summer's Day

Three months had passed since the devastating lightning attack on the West and President Palmer's heated press conference.

Brackman's leading question had sparked an avalanche of new theories, debates, and documentaries. What and who were the Guild of God? Information about a secret and extreme Christian sect, and clandestine sermons were beginning to surface.

Palmer had been on the defensive for weeks and felt isolated. His advisors were baffled and confused. Fortunately for Palmer, enquiries regarding his involvement, made by some of the most skilled and persistent of investigative journalists, had hit a proverbial brick wall. But rumours and doubts still abounded and were clouding his presidency and administration. And yet his popularity seemed to be holding up.

A day after the infamous press conference, President Dumart had tried to reach him by phone.

'Tell him, I'm unavailable,' Palmer told Springborn.

'But he's the President of France.'

'I don't care if he's the president of the fucking universe. I'm unavailable!'

Palmer had realised he needed to distance himself from the Guild of God. The United States…No, *he* had let them down. Let them down big time. The Spear of Destiny had backfired. Using it again was out of the question. Suspicion would only mount. No, he needed to think about number one. It was time for some political deflection.

It, therefore, came as some surprise to his closest allies, and his party, when, unlike many of his predecessors, President Palmer announced a new and aggressive net zero emissions target commitment.

The strategy worked. He understood the fickle nature of the press at large. News coverage, as it always did, had almost forgotten the momentous events only a month or two before, and was now focussed back on the broader issues of climate change. With momentum on his side, Palmer had pushed through new legislation that foreshortened the USA's net zero target by ten years. With no further lightning storms of any note, and no further uses of the Spear of Destiny against them, nor any significant weather events since, his policy seemed to buy him time, if not a legion of new supporters. He had even won over most of the press. With the USA now leading the way in combatting climate change, the pressure was mounting on other major economies to follow suit.

Palmer's deft political skill had not only saved his presidency, he was now seen as saving the world. His deflection had worked.

The motivation and inspiration for Palmer's new tack had come following a product demonstration a month earlier. The president had been given a tour of the hi-tech plant and was now on the main factory floor facing the company boss, whose staff was standing behind him.

'Are you telling me this equipment can suck electricity from the very air?' Palmer asked incredulously.

'That's right, Mr President,' Professor Steel replied, smiling.

'Free electricity, right?'

'Green electricity would be more accurate, sir.'

Palmer laughed. 'Right, you boys need to make your profit. And don't worry, I'll make sure we tax you accordingly.'

Everyone on the factory floor laughed. Their president was on form.

Palmer knew damn well the source of this new technology, but could never let on. Of course, he would have to keep up the pretence if he were to distance himself from the weapon and those associated with it. Ever since his meeting with Ordway in the Oval Office, he had recognised the truly enormous potential of the technology. Not only could it save the world, but it would transform the US quite literally into an undisputed and unchallenged economic powerhouse.

His anger over the terror attacks had been the tipping point. That and learning that his life had been controlled and steered by people unknown. The weapon was a way of showing *his* power. But he rued the day he gave the go-ahead for its deployment. *Why didn't I follow my gut and push for this incredible energy solution instead?* he thought.

What Palmer did not know was that the man in front of him, Professor Steel, was a member of the Guild. For that reason, Steel had not been listed as one of the project scientists on Ordway's report. The Guild of God protected their own.

Ordway, though, was potentially exposing Palmer's involvement, but Palmer dismissed those concerns. The money and power being afforded Ordway were worth the risk.

Fortunately for Palmer, Steel was unaware of the president's knowledge and eventual sanctioning of the weapon. Nor did he know that Palmer had been for decades an unwitting puppet whose strings had been pulled by the Guild. Likewise, the president had been ignorant of the fact that Steel and Ordway had filed the patents soon after the first successful weapon tests, and were about to become the richest men in history, although Ordway, having found his true vocation, seemed more interested in inflating his super-sized ego even further.

'Now tell me,' Palmer continued, 'you have patents on all this, right?'

'Absolutely we do, Mr President. And lots and lots of orders.'

'I bet you do. My God, I love this country. Shame I can't buy any of your shares. People would accuse me of insider trading.'

'You'll just have to settle on the billions we'll be paying in tax.'

Palmer laughed again. 'Oh, I think I could live with that, and the massive boost to our balance of trade,' he said looking around at his White House team. 'In all seriousness, this new green energy will put the US in an unassailable lead. The rest of the world won't know what hit them. How did you say it worked?'

'I didn't, sir. Trade secret.' Steel said with his broadest smile yet.

Kentucky, USA

One month later, the president was in an even greater frame of mind as he stood on the fourteenth tee of the Kentucky golf course. It was a perfect summer's day if perhaps a little hot and sticky. The sky above was blue, the *cheer-cheer-cheer* birdsong of northern cardinals rang out, and the trees lining the course were lush and vibrant.

Nearby, and dotted across the course, were the president's secret service team. Clustered around the tee, were TV crews, journalists, and photographers. The president's personal secretary, Michael Springborn, stood on his own, busy on his mobile. Palmer's playing partners were Santiago Morales and Evan Samuels, Director of the CIA.

'What's the score, Mr President?' a journalist called out.

'I think I'll need five holes-in-one if I'm to beat these two.' His audience all laughed, then fell silent as Morales began some practice swings with his driver before addressing his ball. It was a confident strike. Morales' ball sailed off down the fairway. Palmer showed his appreciation with a pat on the Mexican tycoon's back. 'Good shot, Santiago. I'm guessing your clubs are made from steel forged in your factory.'

'Of course, Tom. Only the best,' Morales joked back.

Palmer took his shot and jumped back into his golf buggy. At the wheel was his head of security, Bob Doyle.

'Bob, let me drive. I need to speak with Evan.'

'Of course, sir,' Doyle said and stepped out. The CIA head climbed in, and they set off down the fairway.

'So, Evan, what's up?' Palmer asked.

'Tom, it's about Morales.'

'What about him?'

'We have a number of recordings and transcripts of him speaking with a cardinal in Rome.'

Palmer turned to Evans. 'So, perhaps he's repenting his sins. He's committed plenty.'

'Sir, the cardinal in question, Cardinal Romero, has been linked to this clandestine group everyone's talking about. In fact, it's more than that. This cardinal has just gone public about it.'

'What are you talking about, Evan?'

'The group called the Guild of God. He's done a tell-all on Spanish TV. He says they're responsible for something called the Spear of Destiny. He says it's the weapon that caused the lightning storms.'

They had reached the president's ball and Palmer brought the buggy to a stop. 'And you believe that?' Palmer stepped from the buggy and grabbed the 7-iron from his bag. 'As the Director of the Central Intelligence Agency, start showing some real intelligence. I don't want to hear another word of this crap.'

'Your shot, Tom,' Morales called out. Palmer was flustered but tried to settle for his shot. He lined up and viewed his target. The green was one hundred and forty yards away. 'I'd use a 5-iron from here, Tom.'

Palmer stopped and looked at Morales. 'You're right. And thanks for the advice, Santiago. Us oldens can't hit 'em like we used to.'

The blinding white flash and ear-splitting crack were simultaneous. Evan Samuels and Santiago Morales instinctively ducked and threw their arms across their faces.

Bob Doyle and the pursuing entourage had witnessed it all. The image of the lightning was still seared on their retinas. Everyone stopped in their tracks and looked up. The sky was a deep blue. The deep thunder boom rumbled away across the undulating fairways.

Doyle blinked repeatedly and rubbed his eyes. *The president!*

Palmer was lying face down and motionless, his golf club still in his outstretched arm. A whiff of ozone and burning reached Doyle's nostrils as he ran towards the president. The secret service agents were sprinting from the nearby trees and fairways towards the scene. One of the journalists whispered to her cameraman. 'Tell me you got that.'

Doyle knelt and gently turned Palmer over onto his back. Palmer's face and arm were charred, his shirt and shorts smouldering. 'MR PRESIDENT? TOM?' There was no response. Nothing. 'WE NEED A MEDIC. NOW!' Doyle looked up. 'GET THAT LOT OUT OF HERE!' he ordered, pointing at the press. His men began forcibly pushing the men and women away. 'AND GET THOSE CAMERAS AWAY! ALL OF THEM!'

'HEY, YOU CAN'T DO THAT,' one of them protested.

'YES, WE FUCKIN' CAN!' one of the agents replied and pushed the journalist hard to make his point.

Palmer's eyes and mouth were wide open. To say it was an expression of surprise would be an understatement. The flesh on his face looked gruesome. Doyle only hesitated a moment. He was professional. He lowered and tilted his head to one side and listened for any breathing. There was none. He began chest compressions. 'One, two, three, four, five…' After thirty he stopped, held the president's nose, blew into his mouth, and listened. More chest compressions. 'One, two, three…'

The paramedic truck rolled into view and shot down the fairway. Doyle carried on with the CPR until he was pushed away by one of the paramedics. 'How long has he been like this?' the medic asked.

'Two, three minutes.' Doyle answered.

Springborn stepped forward slowly. 'Is he…?'

Doyle did not reply. He stood up and watched the paramedics in silence. Doyle then noticed that the president's watch had slipped off, exposing a small tattoo. *Strange* he thought. *I guess we all do dumb things when we are young.*

The press remonstrated loudly as the secret service forced them back up the fairway. The journalists craned their necks, desperate to catch a glimpse. Others were excitedly reporting the news live, their cameramen struggling to keep balance as they tried to point their lenses back towards the scene. They could see very little except for the paramedic vehicle, its flashing light, and more secret service agents forming an outward-facing circle around the fallen president.

'Oh my God! President Palmer has been struck by lightning!' one animated American reporter announced. 'And yet the weather…,' she said, looking up briefly, '…the weather here is perfect; not a cloud in the sky. Can this be…,' the reporter had to stop talking after nearly tumbling backwards. After recovering, she continued, 'As you can see, we are being forced away from the scene. But it was *definitely* lightning. We all saw it. It's not clear if the president is OK. Oh my God! Maybe he raised his club, I can't be sure. Maybe…I just don't know!' The reporter turned forward to check her progress over the undulating grass, before facing the camera once again. 'So, was this a bolt from the blue? A freak of nature? Or, was this the weapon that many believe was used against our cities? Was this the so-called Spear of Destiny?'

Twenty-seven minutes later, television stations across the globe jumped to the breaking news, and billions of mobile phones pinged with the news:

THOMAS PALMER, PRESIDENT OF THE UNITED STATES OF AMERICA, WAS STRUCK BY A FREAK BOLT OF LIGHTNING TODAY DURING A GAME OF GOLF IN KENTUCKY. ATTEMPTS TO RESUSCITATE HIM AT THE SCENE SADLY FAILED. HE WAS PRONOUNCED DEAD AT 2:26 P.M. LOCAL TIME. OUR IMMEDIATE THOUGHTS AND PRAYERS GO OUT TO HIS BELOVED FAMILY AND MANY FRIENDS ACROSS THE WORLD.

Somewhere in the Middle East

Prince Al-Musan stood, arms outstretched and gripping a handrail. Below him, the factory floor production lines were in full flow. A foreman approached him and handed over a tablet PC. 'Your Highness, I estimate we can manufacture twenty-four thousand ADNDs before we run out of the mineral.'

The prince studied it before handing it back. 'Don't worry. I have already arranged for more to arrive.' The foreman looked surprised. Al-Musan turned to face him. 'I have two hundred and forty more stones. In my bank vault,' he said.

The prince's mobile then pinged. He raised the screen to his face, and a smile slowly formed on his lips.

Author's Note

Imagination is an intangible and mysterious thing, born from a lifetime of sensory stimuli.

The small hill in Southern France described in the opening pages of this novel was the initial inspiration for the entire story. You see, that hill exists; so, too, does the hut upon it.

Researching the science behind the story revealed the strange account of a meteor shower falling on a Turkish army encampment during the First Crusade, as recorded by the contemporary chronicler, Raymond D'Aguilers.

As for the other science behind the plot, experiments on weather manipulation are well known—Project Popeye and HAARP, for instance. The idiom, "a bolt from the blue", is often attributed to the rare phenomenon of a bolt of lightning from a cloudless sky. Attempts at weaponizing weather are also true.

There is so much yet undiscovered. So many possibilities. And so many shifts in our understanding...

While quantum leaps in technology and knowledge of the natural world are transforming our lives, human nature, intolerance and religious misinterpretation sadly remain unchanged.